APPLE TREE LEAN DOWN

Apple Tree
Lean Down

Mary E. Pearce

BALLANTINE BOOKS • NEW YORK

Library of Congress Catalog Card Number: 75-40802

ISBN 0-345-25655-7

This edition published by arrangement with
St. Martin's Press, Inc.

Manufactured in the United States of America

First Ballantine Books Edition: August 1977

Contents

Within the woodlands, flow'ry gladed,
By the oak tree's mossy root,
The sheenén grass-blades, timber-shaded,
Now do quiver underfoot;
An' birds do whissle auver head,
An' water's bubbblén in its bed,
An' there for me the apple tree
Do lean down low in Linden Lea.

William Barnes

BOOK ONE

1886

To Beth, for the first eleven years of her life, Grandfather Tewke was merely a strange old man who sometimes passed through the village, driving a smart little pony and trap. He never came to call at the cottage, nor even glanced towards it, but drove past with his gaze fixed on the road, his head held back, and his billycock tilted over his eyes.

"There goes your grandpa, cross as two sticks and twice as snappy," Kate would say. "Somebody's in for a sharp bit of business this morning, I shouldn't wonder." And John Tewke, coming home from Capleton or Chepsworth, would sometimes say he had passed the old man on the road. "He gave me a nod and I did the same for him and that was all that was said between us!"

Once, when Beth was sitting on the front doorstep, shelling peas, Grandfather Tewke went by on foot, across the green and up to the church. He passed so close that Beth could hear the squeak of his boots and the jingle of coins on his watch-chain, and could see the silver hairs that sprouted from his long fine nose. But even then, passing so close that his shadow fell across her, he took care not to glance her way. Beth was seven or eight by then, and beginning to ask questions.

"Seems like Grandfather Tewke don't know who I am," she said when she went indoors. "He don't never nod nor nothing when he goes by."

3

"He knows who you are well enough," Kate said. "He couldn't well fail to, seeing that you're the spitten image of your dad. But he's queer with us. He likes to pretend we don't exist."

"Why does he?"

"You ask your father," Kate said. "He's the one for telling stories, sitting there with nothing to do. Here, give me them peas!"

Kate was always too busy to stop and talk, but John Tewke would always make time, and now, having put aside his paper, he drew Beth onto his knees.

"Let's have a look at you," he said. "Your mother says you're the spitten image of me, but I dunno about that, I'm sure. You've got a corn-thatch of fair hair like mine, it's true, but you ent got a beard, have you? Eh? You ent got a fine set of gingery whiskers like mine?"

"Such nonsense you talk!" Kate said. "Such nonsense you talk, instead of telling the child what she wants to know."

"All right. Anything for a quiet life." He leant back in his chair, leaving Beth to balance as best she could on his knees. "Your grandpa and me fell out," he said. "Years ago, before you was born, and all on account of my leaving the carpenter's shop."

"Where is the carpenter's shop?" Beth asked. "Is it far from here?"

"Laws, no! It's only the other end of Huntlip, out by the Middening turn. There's a house there called Cobbs and there's ten acres of land, too, left over from the days when the Tewkes was farmers. Your grandpa turned the old stables into a workshop and over the years he's built up a tidy business there. That's why he took it so hard when I cut loose like I did."

"Why did you cut loose?"

"Because I didn't want to be a carpenter all my life, that's why. I wasn't happy, whittling away at old bits of wood all day. That went against the grain with me somehow."

He looked at her with a little smile, but she remained perfectly solemn, ignoring his joke and waiting for him to go on with his story.

"Mind you, I served my time," he said proudly. "I could turn my hand to any carpentry job you care to mention. Ah, and make a better showing than most, I dare say."

Kate was rattling spoons and forks on the table.

"Hark at you!" she said. "I've got a washboard there that's all worn to splinters, and I've got a chair with its arms broke off. In fact, there's a score of jobs just crying out for you to show your famous skill, John Tewke."

"I know! I know! And I'll tackle the lot together one day, when the spirit moves me." He winked at Beth. "Your mother don't understand," he said. "But that's murder to me, taking a tool in my hands after all them years in the workshop. It gives me the creeps just to think about it."

"It's a pity for you!" Kate said. "It's a crying shame, it is, really!"

"Now horses is something different," he said. "There's something about an untrained horse that makes me just itch to work him. I dunno why it is, but I've got a feeling for horses that I never had for timber, and hardly a day goes by that I don't thank my lucky stars I'm out of that workshop. But I'm sorry the old man's as sore as he is."

"The old man is silly," Beth declared.

"Oh, I dunno. He likes his own way, that's all. I'm the same, only I get my way with the horses, you see, and that's enough to keep me happy. Which is just as well, cos I don't get much of a say at home, do I? Your mother's the gaffer here and no mistake!"

And he nodded and winked, making faces and wagging his beard until Beth had to laugh even though she knew that his nonsense vexed her mother. He liked to pretend that Kate ruled him, that he was under her thumb, but the truth was, that although she nagged and grumbled, Kate very rarely had her own way. He was the one who made the decisions, and she obeyed his slightest wish.

There were often quarrels between them because she, according to him, had no sense of fun, and he, according to her, had far more than his proper share. There were quarrels, too, because he was foolish with money.

"Kate, you look as though all the woes of the world've sat theirselves down on your shoulders."

"So I might, with a husband who comes home market-merry, stinking of beer and refusing good food."

"Dammit! A man's entitled to a little celebration, surely? Specially after a day's successful business. How much d'you think I got for that mare and her foal?"

"I've no notion, but I hope it was more than you paid out on feed, that's all."

"More! Of course it was more! Here, take these two sovereigns and put them away in your purse. I rely on you to make them last."

"And where's the rest gone to, I wonder?"

"Ploughed back into the business, that's where. I bought a couple of cobs from a Welshman. And here, Kate, you'll never guess who I saw at Ross!"

"Who?" Kate asked.

"Everybody I looked at!" he said.

"Oh, get away, you great tipsy fool!"

"Beth! Your mother's as grave as a churchyard today. How did I come to marry a woman like her?"

"Nobody else wouldn't have you, I don't suppose."

"Hah! So now my daughter's turning against me and all! Well, that's a pity, that is, for it means she won't want the present I've bought her."

"What present?" Beth said.

"Oh, just a little work-basket with needles and coloured threads and a little tambour, that's all. It's nothing much. I reckon I'll give it to Hetty Minchin."

"No!" Beth said. "You must give it to me."

"Well, what do I get in exchange, then, eh? Don't I get a kiss? And what do I get from my wife for this nice plaid shawl I bought her? Oh, that's smiles all around now, ent it? It's a wonderful thing, the way the women know how to get round a man. They're nearly human, the way they know!"

"That's all very fine," Kate said. "But you ought to save your money, seeing we never know where the next lot is coming from, nor when. Shawls indeed! No wonder I'm grey."

Always, after the horse-market or horse-fair, the scene was the same. Kate knew she would never change him and yet she continued to scold. But Beth, although she began, as a small child will, by echoing all her mother's complaints, soon learnt instead to accept him as he was. He was her father, and that was enough. He brought warmth and colour into her life, and comforted her when she was sad.

"Where's the sun today, then? Gone behind the clouds? Ah, I'll soon make you laugh, you see if I don't! How much do you bet? A shilling on the nose or a penny for every nail in a shoe? There, that's better! That's the face I like to see!"

Sometimes, in the evenings, she sat on his lap, mending the rents in his clothes or sewing on his buttons. She went through his pockets, removing the contents, blowing them clean of dust and fluff, sorting and making them tidy, and then restoring them one by one.

"That's my tobacco-pouch, and a bit thin in tobacco, too," he would say. "And that's my twitch. I was looking in Niggerboy's mouth this morning. Ah, and that there is a knob of coal I found in the road this evening. Put it back. It might bring me luck."

When the weather was bad, he stayed at home and was lazy. He sat in his chair, with his feet on the hob, his hands tucked in the waist of his breeches, letting Kate struggle in with pails of water or bundles of wood. But out on the common, working his horses, he often drove himself until he was numb with exhaustion, and at these times, it was Beth's duty to fetch him home and stop him from falling asleep in a ditch on the way. Often, he walked twenty miles to a sale, and coming home, leading a couple of raw new colts, perhaps, his arms would be bruised black and blue all the way to the shoulders. "The beggars led me a dance," he would say, "but I'll do the same for them in the morning."

Farmers all around Huntlip respected him for his honesty and for his judgment. They entrusted their money to him, to buy good horses for work in the fields, and they often asked him to doctor their cows. Beth, if she could, went with him on these errands about the farms, and once, when they were taking a cart-horse to Middening, he pointed out the place where Grandfather Tewke lived and carried on his business.

"There you are. That's Cobbs, where I was born, and there's the carpenter's shop I told you about that time."

He preferred to avoid meeting the old man, and so he stood well past the gateway, in a place where the hedge grew high. But Beth, sitting up on the horse, could see right over. She could see the house, with its black timbers and its panels of warm red brick and its twisty chimneys, half in sunshine, half in the shade of surrounding oaks and elms. She could see the big workship yard, with its stacks of planking all around, and the sawyers at work in a cloud of dust in the sawpit. And she could see the carpenters moving about within the long, low workshop. The sound of their hammering came through the open doors and echoed all around the enclosure, and the sound of the saw was like the voice of some great tireless chiff-chaff.

"Laws, what a din!" her father said. "Specially your grandpa. There's nothing he likes better than that old ding-dong all day long. Here, Beth, can you see him anywhere about?"

"No, but I reckon he's there somewhere, the way the men are shifting theirselves in the workshop."

"I'm glad it's them and not me!"

"I can see Sam Lovage," Beth said. "And Bobby Green. They're hopping about like crumbs on a griddle."

"Can you see the big oak growing there in the yard?"

"I should think I just can! The size it is, I couldn't hardly miss it, could I?"

"That's been there since domesday, that old oak tree. It's been there ever since the house was built and that's going back a year or two."

"Grandfather Tewke's come out of the door," Beth said. "He's looking this way with a bit of a squint. I suppose he thinks I'm walking on hopstilts, up in the air like this."

"Time we moved on, then," her father said, and pulled at the bridle. "We don't want him to think we're snooping, do we, eh? Even if we are."

"Does he live all alone in that big house?"

"Yes, he does, and he must be lonely sometimes."

"That's his own fault," Beth said.

"Maybe it is, but I'm sorry for him all the same. And I'm sorry for you, too, cos I've gone and done you out of a grandpa."

"I don't care," Beth said.

When she was not at school, she spent her days up on the common, watching her father at work. But she had to be good, and keep away from the horses. She had to be quiet, and not make a fuss when he used his whip. She must sit like a little mouse, he told her, and then, when they ate their dinner together, she should have a share of his beer.

In spring, the upper slopes of the common were yellow with flowering gorse. The colour leapt and danced in the sun. The scent was rich on the changing air. Beth would be out day after day, from the first blink of light to the last, till her father came and swept her up in his arms and carried her home in a trance to bed. She swam to sleep with the singing of larks in her ears, and the taste of the day still sweet on her tongue, and the yellow flare of the gorse blossom would go with her into her dreams.

In summer, she had to be careful to wear a hat. Her mother was very strict about it. But her fair skin always burnt just the same, and the freckles would smother her cheeks and nose. She never cared, however much her mother scolded, for she liked to feel the heat of the sunshine stored in her skin.

As she grew older, her father began to give her a few little duties to perform. He let her reward the horses with bits of oil-cake. He allowed her to mix their feed. But he never allowed her to ride them, even when they were broken in to the saddle.

"No, not Paddy. No, nor Tessa, neither. They're too full of fire. Look at that Paddy! Just look at the way he rolls his eyes. Why, if you was to get on his back, he'd pitch you into that there pond in no time at all."

"Why would he?"

"Well, he's bigger than you for a start, and he's got his pride, too, you see. He'd think you had a sauce, getting up on his back, an oddity bit of a girl like you."

"But he's bigger than you, too."

"Ah, and a lot better looking, I dare say?"

"He lets you ride him," Beth said.

"Only just! It's touch and go oftentimes. But he's getting to know that I mean to be master, and he knows I've got the answer to all his tricks. Here! I'll tell you what! One of these days," he'd say, "I'll fix you up with a nice polite little pony of your own, and teach you to ride like a proper lady, side-sitting saddle and crop and all. How's that?"

"When?"

"One of these days! You'll see."

Later the pony was duly bought at Capleton Mop. His name was Silas, and he was a four-year-old gelding, sooty brown about the body, sooty black in mane and tail. He was mild as milk and already schooled. Beth learnt to ride in a saddle, specially made for her by James Bluff, and to carry her crop with a certain air. But what she liked best was to mount the pony just whenever the impulse moved her, and to sway along, letting him carry her slowly about as he pleased. She liked the feel of the rough mane between her fingers, and she liked to feel the shape and strength of his body surging beneath her.

"Oh, you'll break my heart," her father said.

"You've got no style. You've got no seat. Don't you want to ride like a lady?"

"No," Beth said. "I just want to be what I am."

"You're two of a kind, you and that pony. You don't care a cuss what anybody thinks of you."

"Why should anyone think at all?"

"Don't ask me! I'm damned if I know. So long as you're happy, that's all the odds, I suppose. But don't look to me to take your part when your mother flies out at you for getting dirt and grease on your clothes."

Silas always came to her, nodding and blinking, the very moment she passed through the common gate. He nuzzled her pockets, searching for crusts, and he plodded behind her, nudging her gently in the back or pulling her pinafore strings undone. If she turned to reprove him, he looked away with dreamy, innocent eyes, dipping his head as though deep in sober thought. He followed her round when she gathered blackberries in the autumn. And when she just sat, with nothing to do but listen to the larks overhead, he grazed as close to her as he could, or nibbled the gorse that gave her shade.

She liked to see him nibbling the gorse. It astonished her that a tongue so large could lick so daintily round the prickles, that such great teeth could winkle out the newest, tenderest shoots from among the old hard spines. She liked, too, to see him start when the stonechats clacked in the bushes or flew out with a whirring of wings, and to see the fuss he made if a feather happened to light on his nose.

"He's a proper molly-coddle, that's what he is," her father said. "He follows you round like a lamb with its mother."

That winter, Kate was ill with a cold on her chest, and Beth stayed away from school to manage the house. The weather was bad. There was deep snow.

"Don't go traipsing about in this," her father said. "I don't want you catching cold like your mother. You stop at home and keep in the warm."

"But I want to see Silas," Beth said.

"He's all right. You leave him to me. I'll look after him, don't you worry."

When at last she went to the common, however, the pony was not there.

"Where's he gone?" she demanded; confronting her father at the sheds.

"Eh? What, Silas? Oh, I sent him away to a sheltered place on a farm. It was getting cold for him up here."

"What farm?" Beth asked.

"A place further south, down Teazle House way, where it's sheltered and warm."

"When did he go?"

"A couple of weeks ago. Maybe three. I don't recall the day exactly."

"He's gone, hasn't he?" Beth said. "He's gone for good. You've sold him away."

Her father was scattering hay for his horses, making a fuss of puffing and blowing and pitching the hay about in the snow. Beth stood, stubbornly waiting, and eventually he turned towards her and leant on his fork.

"I had to," he said. "I needed to buy special things for your mother. I had a wonderful offer for Silas. He's gone to a capital good home. A gentleman farmer wanted him for his son."

"You should've told me," Beth said.

"I was banking on luck. I hoped I could get you another pony to take his place by the time you came up here. And I will get another, too, one of these days, you mark my words."

"No!" she said. "I don't want another pony! We can't afford it. Only gentleman farmers can afford ponies."

"There wasn't no choice, Beth. You do understand that, don't you, eh?"

"I understand," she said, and turned and went home.

At first she was angry, for she knew that no extra things had been bought for her mother, but in the time that followed, her father's dejection drove all

her anger clean away. It was wrong that a grown
man should have to answer to her for his actions.
She hated to see him so ashamed, and she hated
the way he made himself small, trying to win back
her favour.

"Here, Beth! How about going with me to the
Whitsun Fair next Friday? I'll buy you some ginger-
bread men. I'll buy a kerchief. No, I won't, I'll
buy you some beads."

"You don't need to buy me things at all."

"I don't see why not. I reckon I owe you a shilling or two, selling Silas the way I did."

"No, you don't. I'm all right. I'm not crying."

"Ah, you're a good little hob, sure enough. You
don't never cry when you get a knock. But supposing I take you to Henry Mapp's for a ride on his
Boxer? You'd like that. You and Boxer is old
friends."

"No," Beth said. "I'm getting too old to sit on a
cart-horse, showing my legs. I'm all right. Don't
worry about me. I'm quite happy as I am."

Every morning, before school, Beth went out to the
green to fetch the day's water. On this particular
day in October, while she was waiting her turn at
the pump, Grandfather Tewke drove by in his trap,
and Freddie Lovage, whose father was one of the
carpenters in the workshop, stopped pumping and
gave the old man a smart salute.

"There's your grandpa," he said. "Ent you going
to bob him a curtsey?"

"Hah!" said Beth. "I'd sooner bob to that there
pail or that there goose of Mrs. Merry's."

"I reckon your dad's a fool, cutting hisself off
like he done," said Freddie. "Old Mr. Tewke's got
a tip-top business down there at Cobbs."

"Right so. And my father's got a tip-top business of his own up here."

"Horses!" said Freddie. "There ent no money in
that gipsy game."

"My father's his own master. That's more than you can say for yours, Freddie Lovage."

"My dad's got a proper trade," said Freddie.

"Then tell him to mind it and not to be so free in yapping about other folkses'!" Beth said. "Now get a move on with that there pump. I ent got all day to wait for you."

When she went indoors, her father was brushing his boots on the doorstep.

"I heard you giving young Fred what-for," he said. "You did right, sticking up for your dad." He took the pails and carried them for her into the kitchen. "I shan't always be working my horses on commoner's rights. Oh dear me no! One of these days I shall have a bit of land of my own and build a stables and then I shall start a proper stud."

"And what'll you use to buy the land?" Kate asked. "Shirt buttons or bottle tops?"

"Money'd be better," he said. "All I need is a bit of good luck to start me off."

"You won't find luck on Chepsworth race-course,"

"Race-course? Who said anything about the race-course? It's the fair I'm going to, woman, I'll have you know."

"You don't need to tell me where you're going, sprucing yourself up so fine like that."

"As a matter of fact, there is a couple of runners I fancy this afternoon, so which shall it be, Rufus or Penny-Come-Quick?"

"Safe-in-the-pocket, that's what I'd choose."

"Beth!" he said. "Tell me which horse you fancy."

"Rufus," said Beth. "A name like that other is asking for trouble, it seems to me."

"Rufus it is, then. And we're in for a fair return if he comes in nicely." He took a crown from his pocket and held it up for Beth to kiss. "A bit of luck and we could be fifteen pound the richer by two o'clock. And one of these days I'll be breeding horses that's famous throughout the three counties. Ah, one of these days! You'll see!"

That afternoon, he was killed by a stallion he had bought in Chepsworth. His body was found on Hunt-lip common and carried down by the haywarden's men. They said he must have died in an instant, caught unawares, hammering a hobbling-iron into the ground. His eyes were wide open and he had one big black wound in the back of his skull.

Beth heard the news while she was at school and ran home at once through a heavy rain-storm. Kate sat in the darkened kitchen, rocking backwards and forwards, arms crossed over her chest, hands clutching her hunched shoulders. She seemed not to notice when Beth came in. She was locked inside herself, like a stranger. But when at last, putting out a hand, she found that Beth's clothes were sodden, she came to life again sharply. She stirred and got up and began to scold.

"You'd better strip! You're like a drowned rat. Why didn't you shelter instead of coming through all that rain?"

Standing naked on the hearth, Beth had a violent fit of shivering. Her flesh would not be still however hard she clenched her muscles. She rubbed herself with a rough towel and scrambled into warm clean clothes. The warmth and comfort made her feel guilty, for she had thought, running home through the storm, that nothing could ever matter again. But her body, it seemed, had a will of its own: she could still feel glad to be at home; to be warm; to be safe; to be alive.

Kate lit the lamp and her face as she stooped to blow on the flame looked suddenly old. The lines that puckered her mouth were deeper. She moved about, drawing the curtains, setting the kettle to boil again, warming the teapot and making tea. But now and then she would stand quite still, staring before her with hurt, angry eyes. And then, coming to, she would say: "I'm glad he was found before that storm. I'd hate to think of him lying out there, all smothered in mud."

Later, she said: "Parson Wisdom was very kind. He took your father into the vicarage."

"What became of the horse?" Beth asked.

"They catched him and put him in the pound. I suppose he'll be sold . . . if anyone's mad enough to buy him."

"There's a mare, too, up there somewhere. And saddles and bridles . . . things like that."

"Yes, well, I must see the haywarden. Maybe he'll fix a sale for us. God knows we shall need the money."

"Queenie Lovage called in. She asked if your dad's coffin was to be made at Cobbs. I said no.—I'd sooner deal with the man in Chepsworth."

"That don't seem right," Beth said. "Grandfather Tewke makes coffins for all Huntlip. He should surely do the same for his own son?"

"I don't want dealings with *him,*" Kate said. "Though nobody's stopping him coming to the funeral, of course."

But Grandfather Tewke was not at the funeral, and they heard that work had gone on as usual in the carpenter's shop that day.

"It's what I'd expect," Kate said. "An unforgiving man, your grandpa."

The horses and gear were sold by auction, and the undertaker was paid on the nail. Then accounts were settled with the Chepsworth corn-chandler and the smith at Collow Ford.

"Leaving precious little!" Kate said. "But we're shut of debts, finally, and I aim to keep it that way."

"I could go into service," Beth said.

"There's no need. I'm taking up the gloving again. I've still got my old wooden donkey and I hope I've still got my skill too. I can surely do as well as the other women hereabouts, anyway."

The gloving materials were brought, and the finished gloves collected, by a man who came every week in the carrier's cart from Chepsworth. His name was Arthur Roberts, but because of his lisp and his smart clothes and the scented handkerchief he held to his nose when entering a cottage kitchen, he was known in Huntlip as Lily-Milly-Bobs. Beth disliked him because, although her mother's work was good, he always found excuses for reducing the payment.

"This quirk's rather clumsy, don't you think, Mrs Tewke?"

"I don't cut the patterns, Mr Roberts."

"Even the stitching is not what it might be."

"There was no complaints when I worked in the factory. Mr Ganty called me his best glover."

"One-and-nine the dozen pairs. That's the best I can offer today, Mrs Tewke."

"It's not enough!" Beth said, before her mother had time to accept. "Leave the gloves and we'll take them in to Mr Ganty ourselves."

The young man looked down his nose.

"Shouldn't you be at school?" he asked.

"I came home early on purpose to see you."

"Indeed! Little meddlers are ripening early these days. But you'll get no change from Mr Ganty."

"We'll see about that."

"One-and-eleven," he said, wearily. "A special concession, you being so poor."

When he had gone, Beth took a duster and fanned the air.

"What sort of man is that, I wonder, going about, smelling of violets?"

"You were very sharp," Kate said. "I don't hold with a scrap of a girl speaking up like that. Supposing he'd took a huff against us?"

"How can he?" Beth said. "When he pockets the coppers he knocks off folk's earnings? All Huntlip knows he does it. You have to stand out like old Mrs Topson."

Kate worked hard, but poor sight made her slow, and although Beth helped, the weekly earnings were never more than seven shillings. Often, indeed, they were a good deal less.

One day in January, when Beth came home, her mother was lying on the settle, grey-faced and in pain. A neighbour, Mrs Wilkes, was with her, and the kitchen smelt of burnt feathers.

"Your mother's sick," Mrs Wilkes declared. "And it's not to be wondered at, seeing she don't eat enough for a sparrow! Yes, you can stare, miss, but I'd be ashamed if I was you.—A great girl of eleven, going to school when you should be out earning."

"Annie, be quiet!" Kate said. "It was only giddiness, that's all."

"What did you eat for your dinner?" asked Beth.

"I ate what I wanted," Kate said.

"You ate a cup of tea!" Mrs Wilkes exclaimed. "I know what dinners you have!" Fiercely, she rounded again on Beth. "There's two eggs and half a loaf in that cupboard. But it ent to be touched! Oh, no! It's for *your* tea and *your* breakfast."

"Rubbish!" said Kate, struggling to sit erect on the settle. "I just ent had time to get to the shop. Besides, it's none of your business, Annie Wilkes, and I'll thank you to keep out of my cupboards."

"Then I'll be off!" Mrs Wilkes retorted. "That's what I get for being a good neighbour!"

As the door rattled shut, Beth went to look in the jug on the dresser. She found it empty.

"A man came," he mother said. "A stranger to me, but he said your father owed him a debt. Thirty shillings, he said it was."

"And you gave it to him, without question? A man you'd never seen before?"

"Seemed to me he was speaking the truth. And I don't want debts hanging over me."

"No, you'd sooner go hungry and make yourself ill."

Beth brought in sticks and made up the fire. She boiled an egg, cut thin slices of bread and lard, and persuaded her mother to sit up and eat.

"All this fuss!" Kate said. "Just because of a giddy turn!"

"How d'you feel now?"

"Fit as a flea. Never fitter."

"Then you won't mind if I go out for a little while?"

"Why, where you off to all of a sudden?"

"I told Hetty Minchin I'd help her with her sums. I shan't be gone long. You take things easy till I come back."

"Here! It's a sight too early for lighting that lamp."

"It's a nasty dark evening, that's all I know. And it's cold and damp, so see you keep a good fire."

"See this! See that!" Kate exclaimed. "You're getting too bossy by half, my girl."

"Somebody's got to keep you in order," Beth said.

With the dusk, a mist had risen from the Derrent brook and was creeping, cold and grey, all along the village. Always in winter the mist came up from the Derrent like this, and the villagers called it the Huntsman's Breath. According to old tales, Huntlip had once been a place of evil, for the Devil's Hunt had ridden there. The hounds had savaged little children, and sparks from the horses' hooves had blinded anyone that stood in the way. According to some, the riders were heard even now on certain nights in winter, leaping the brook at Collow Ford. The smith, it was said, had heard the crack of the Huntsman's whip and the baying of the hounds outside his forge.

Beth wore a coat of her father's, its upturned hem thick and heavy, sweeping her heels at every step. She had to thrust her hands in the pockets to keep the folds wrapped close around her. The collar stood up high at her throat, and when she snuggled down inside it, the warmth of her body rose in comforting waves to her face.

Huntlip was deserted. Her footsteps echoed along the Straight. She passed the Minchins' and kept on, over the bridge and along the other side of the Derrent. At the Middening turn, having left the last light far behind her, she had nothing at all to guide her on the way. Night was fully come, the mist surged against her face, and she felt she walked at the edge of the world, about to fall into everlasting darkness. But she kept on, groping her way along the hedge, and came at last to the gates of her grandfather's workshop yard.

The workshop was lit from end to end, every window casting its shape on the squirming mist. The twin doors stood open, and Beth looked in, the warmth and lamp-smoke stinging her eyes.

Four men worked at a bench beneath the windows, backs bent, ankles deep in shavings. Another two worked on the centre floor, driving home the slats of a sheep-crib. One was Sam Lovage, a born gossip, and as he whispered in his neighbour's ear, Grandfather Tewke, who stood with his back to the stove nearby, making notes in a notebook, turned around and saw Beth. He hesitated; then came across.

"Who might you be?" he asked with a frown.

"I reckon you know who I am," she said.

"Maybe. Maybe not."

"I want to talk to you," she said.

"Talk away! I'm all ears."

"So's the rest of the party here."

"All right. We'll step outside."

Outside in the yard, against the mist, he seemed enormous. His shoulders, although rounded because of his trade, were thick and broad and his bearing stiff. In the light from the doorway, his face, under the peak of a tight-fitting cap, had the sharp edges and smooth planes of a statue carved in clean pink wood. His mouth had a strong curve downward. His nose was very straight and fine.

"Well? What d'you want with me, miss?"

"My mother's sick," Beth said. "She ent getting enough to eat."

"Whose fault is that? It surely ent mine! But maybe your mother thinks it is?"

"She didn't send me. She'd sooner starve."

"Kate's got her pride. I know that. But what about you? D'you know the meaning of that little word?"

"Pride won't feed us," Beth said.

"You don't look all that hungry to me."

"My mother's the one that's been going without. I only discovered that today."

"And you came straight to me?"

"There's nobody else to go to."

"Ent you heard of the row I had with your father? And how I turned him out of my house? Well, then! —What makes you think I'd be willing to help you?"

"I just thought you would, that's all."

"You've got definite notions for a girl your age. You have, that's a fact! Here, hang on a minute. I'll come with you and see your mother."

He went to the door and called to the men.

"I shan't be here at knocking-off time, so see you turn out the lamps and lock the door, will you? And don't go jumping the clock, neither.—I shall soon know if you've skimped your work!"

He came back, buttoning his jacket to the neck, and set off with Beth. The mist and the darkness seemed nothing to him. She was the one who tripped and stumbled.

"Here, take hold of my hand, before you go tumbling into the brook," he said. "You want to eat carrots. Then you'd be able to see in the dark."

In the cottage kitchen, Kate was busy stitching gloves, and her eyes, sliding up, blind at first from the close work, sparked into sharp little points of light as she saw the old man standing before her.

"What's all this? I wasn't expecting company that I know of."

"It'd be more civil if you asked me to sit."

"Since when have we been civil together?"

"Damnation! It's *your* daughter that's fetched me here, Kate Tewke!"

Kate turned and glared at Beth, who was bringing a chair for the old man to sit.

"My daughter's a sly little toad! She'd no right, sneaking away behind my back."

"The girl's got sense. She says pride is a poor provider."

"I'll have something to say, too, when her and me is by ourselves."

"Listen," he said, sitting stiff and upright in his chair. "You ent thriving on a feed of pride, so why pretend you are? A good puff of wind would send you floating up that chimney! Well, I ent prepared to see my son's widow going on the parish, so let's get down to brass tacks."

"A lot you cared for your son! Cutting him off the way you did!"

"That's ancient history. I'm concerned with here and now. The best thing for you is to come and live at Cobbs. I ent short of a shilling or two. I can provide for you and the girl."

Kate sat perfectly still, her lips pressed together, her eyes set in a hard stare. Beth moved quietly about the room, taking off her coat and scarf and hanging them on the hook on the door. Then she went and stood at the table, within the circle of yellow light, and the old man glanced from her to Kate.

"Well?" he demanded, making them jump. "I'm still waiting for some sort of answer!"

"Charity," Kate said. "I'm not stuck on charity, whether it comes from you or the parish."

"If you come to me, you'll earn your keep by running the house, taking over from Goody Izzard. That ent charity, surely, is it?"

Kate looked at Beth. She was no longer angry. She seemed resigned.

"Ah, you think of the girl!" the old man urged. "She's the one you've got to consider."

"All right," Kate said. "All right. I'll come."

"Good! Good! That's settled, then. That's all in the book!" He got up and moved to the door. "I'll send Izzard down with the cart on Friday. Ten o'clock in the morning, sharp."

"Here!" Kate said. "You're rushing me, ent you? I must get sorted out and see Mr Bates about quitting the cottage."

"Well, you've got three days, and Izzard will help

with your bits and pieces. As for Bates, you leave him to me."

The old man went. Kate sat and stared at the door.

"I suppose it's all for the best," she said. "But I dunno! I'm all of a heap!"

"At least you can stop straining your eyes with the gloving," Beth said. "Now! This minute! Mrs Topson'll take this lot."

"Living at Cobbs!" Kate said. "The ways things change! All in a twinkling! Out of the blue! I dunno what your father'd say, I'm sure."

"He'd be pleased. You know that."

"Seems you started something, girl, going behind my back like that."

"Seems I did," Beth agreed.

Promptly at ten o'clock on Friday, Walter Izzard knocked on the door. The pony and cart stood outside, the cart covered because of the rain.

"I'm glad of that rain," Kate said. "It'll keep the neighbours indoors where they belong, instead of poking about among my belongings."

"Yes, they're a neighbourly lot in Huntlip," said Walter. "I'm always glad I live away out at the Pikehouse."

He was a thin streak of a man with a narrow face, all nose and cheekbones, and frizzled grey hair cut close to his skull. Beth had seen him often, tramping the lanes with his bag of tools over his shoulder, and she knew his son Jesse, a boy of nine, always in disgrace at school for failing to learn his lessons.

Walter loaded the furniture onto the cart, and, with Kate and Beth sitting up beside him, drove round the green and into the Straight. Some neighbours came out to wave them off, and Kate nodded, sitting sedately, dressed in her best black hat and coat, with the clock, swathed in sacking, on her lap. As they went through the village, the clock chimed, and a few people, hurrying past in the rain, turned to stare.

"That's a nice clock," Walter said. "I like a clock with a nice chime. Did you see Peggy Marvel gawping as we went past? She'll be full of tales when she gets home. She'll say she actually heard the time passing!"

They drove past the workshop, turned down a track, and rattled into a cobbled fold at the back of the house. Goody Izzard came out to help them. She humped their belongings up the stairs, showed them their rooms, and helped Beth to set up the beds. Kate was listless, moving about as though in a dream, and Goody had to make the decisions. When they were finished, she herded them down into the kitchen and gave them hot cocoa.

"You must be shravelled, riding that cart in this freezing rain. Come to the stove and steam yourselves dry."

"We're pushing you out of a job," Kate said. "I'm sorry for that, Mrs Izzard. I am truly."

"It's only right," Goody said, "that old Tewke should have his family to live with him."

"Don't worry about Goody," Walter said. "She's never liked traipsing in from the Pikehouse every day. She'd just as soon work in the fields."

When Walter had gone, Goody took a last look round the kitchen, and put on her coat.

"There's a stew of sheep's corsets on the stove and baked apples in the oven. The old man'll be in at twelve. Oh, yes! Just one thing more. That's the cows."

"Cows?" Kate said.

"Two of them. Out in the pasture. The old man milks them hisself in the mornings and he leaves it to me in the afternoons. That's your job now so beware of that Cherry. She'll lean on you if she gets the chance."

"Cows!" Kate said, left alone with Beth. "I never milked a cow in all my life!"

"I have," Beth said. "Oftentimes, at Henry Mapp's. I'll manage all right."

At twelve o'clock, Grandfather Tewke came in for his dinner. He went straight to his chair at the table, still with his cap on his head, and sat waiting for Kate

to serve him. While he ate, he kept eyeing the helping
on her plate.

"You should eat more'n that. You need to put some
flesh on your bones."

"I've lost my appetite," Kate said. "It's all this
upheaval. I'm upside down."

"You'll buck up in time, I suppose. You better had,
'cos I don't hold with pecking at food." He looked
across the table at Beth. "You're playing hookey from
school, I see. I don't hold with that neither."

"I'm not going to school in future. I'm staying at
home to help my mother. There's too much work for
her in this big house."

"Dammit! Goody Izzard always managed!"

"My mother's not as strong as Goody Izzard."

"You stop at school and be a proper scholard. I've
got ideas about you. I want you to help me in the
business, keeping the books and things like that."

"I'm scholard enough," Beth said. "I'm top
standard in reading, writing, and reckoning."

The old man glared.

"Top standard, eh? Well, we'll see what sort of
scholard you are!"

At the end of the meal, he got up and went to the
dresser. He brought paper, pen, and ink to the table,
and set them out in front of Beth. He returned to his
chair and opened a newspaper.

"Now, then!" he said. "You write what I read and
we'll see what janders you make of it. Are you ready?
Right so! 'Mr Thomas Lissimore, Esquire, of Clay
Hall Farm, near Kitchinghampton, noted for his
foresight in matters pertaining to the weather, the
yield of crops, etc., having made certain predictions
for this, the year 1886, has asked us to publish the
said predictions in the hope that they may prove
useful to fellow farmers throughout the western
midland region.' "

"Is that all?" Beth asked.

"All and enough," the old man said.

He took the paper and blew on the ink. Beth

waited, biting her pen. But when he had finished, he seemed pleased enough.

"You've made a pickle of some of the words—there's no x in predictions for a start—but you write a clear hand, that's the main thing, and you don't skitter blots all over the place. So now let's see what your reckoning is like."

He leant back in his chair.

"I buy a chisel at tenpence, a hammer at one-and-six, a saw at a florin, a gimlet at fourpence, and eight pounds of brads at twopence a pound. How much change shall I get from a crown?"

"Nothing," Beth said. "You owe a shilling."

"I build a shed for Arthur Kyte, costing me eighteen pounds in labour and materials. I aim to make a profit of fifteen per cent. But Arthur pays cash so I give a discount of one and a quarter. How much do I charge in all?"

"I'll need a pen and paper to do that."

"That's all right," the old man said. "I needed pen and paper myself when Kyte called and paid this morning."

Beth wrote for a few minutes, then looked up.

"Twenty pounds, eight shillings, and tenpence."

"Who got the best of that split farthing?"

"You did. It seemed only fair, seeing you was giving the discount."

"Are you being pert, miss?"

"I'm waiting to see if there's any more problems."

"Just one and that's the lot! Which is the heaviest—a pound of feathers or a pound of flour?"

"You don't catch me with that old trick," Beth said. "A pound's a pound whatever its compound."

The old man rose and pushed his chair in under the table.

"You're as cocky as a dog's hind leg," he said. "You're certainly top standard in sauce."

"Then I can stop school?"

"Suits me," he said, with a shrug. "But mark this! I'm the master in this house and I'm the one to make the decisions. Is that clear?"

"Clear as glass," Beth said.

"You should've been a boy," he said. "It vexes me to have nobody following in the business. Still! It can't be helped now. And I've got plans about that too!"

Kate, at first dismayed by the big house, was soon enjoying the importance it gave her. She dealt with tradesmen at the door now, instead of shopping in the village. She took pride in her cooking and make great batches of puddings and pies. And she kept Beth busy all the time, scrubbing the floors in kitchen and dairy, cleaning the rugs in the hall and parlour, burning lavender to sweeten the air in the disused rooms; dusting, polishing; hunting for moths and mice and ants.

Later, she took to inviting old friends from the green, giving them afternoon tea in the parlour, with the best Worcester china, the silver spoons, the pearl-handled knives, and the dainty napkins edged with lace.

"Your Grannie Tewke must've been a lady, judging by some of the things in this house. It'd be a pity not to use them. It gives pleasure, you know, to simple people like Annie Wilkes and Mrs Topson."

"And simple people like us," Beth said, slyly.

Beth had a bedroom at the back of the house,

looking down on the buildings surrounding the fold, and out over the fields beyond. She woke every morning at half past five, when her grandfather clomped across the cobbles, on his way to milk the cows. The rattle of pails, the lowing of the cows, the answering whicker of the pony in his stall: these sounds were the start of her day; and, winter or summer, she sprang from bed in a single bound.

Every morning, while washing, she looked out of her window and guessed the weather. Dew on the cowshed roof meant sunshine. Martins flying in low from the fields meant change. Excitement among the pigs at Anster, the farm adjoining Cobbs, meant wind on the way. And a clear view of Houndshill meant a soak of rain.

But whatever the weather, the weathercock on the workshop roof was always pointing northward. The workshop had once been stables and had a clock in a little turret on the roof. Every morning, going downstairs, Beth looked out of the landing window to check the time: the clock was in order, but the weathercock was stuck fast, and she often wished she could reach out and set it spinning true to the wind.

Every morning, she and Kate were in the kitchen, with the stove alight and bacon frying in the pan, when Grandfather Tewke came in to breakfast. His temper was always bad in the morning, and if they dared to speak together, he silenced them with a sour look. Just before seven he went to the workshop and soon afterwards, when the men arrived, the hammering and sawing would begin, filling the whole house with noise.

For Beth, the workshop yard had a deep fascination now that it was part of her life. The butts of oak and elm and ash waiting to go to the sawpit, and the planks and beams stacked up to season, all chalked with their dates, gave her a sense of provision and richness. And she shared the carpenters' pride in their work; their satisfaction when a new gate or door or ladder went to stand in the store-place.

Often, when Beth went to gather the chips and

shavings for use as kindling in the house, she stayed in the yard to watch the men. Her grandfather disapproved at first: if he found her there, he would drive her out.

"But I want to know what's going on," she said. "I want to understand what I write in your ledger."

"There's sense in that, I suppose," he said. "Yes! Yes! There's sense in that."

By the end of her first year at Cobbs, he had ceased to grumble. Within two years, he was leaving her to cast up accounts without his supervision. He never praised her but little by little he gave her freedom to come and go as she pleased.

One of her duties was to collect the notes of work done away from the workshop, but some of the men were unable to write and had to give her the details directly, and this caused some resentment at first, because she was only a half-pint girl. After a while, however, they came to accept her, though a kind of sly warfare continued for years. They liked to tease her and were always trying to catch her out.

"Three days at Norton mill," said Steve Hewish. "Forty feet of elm planking. Five pounds of tenpenny nails. That was repairs to the granstead luccomb."

"Luccomb?" said Beth. "How d'you spell it?"

"That's your problem, not mine. We're only the wooden knows."

"Poor old numbskulls, that's what we are," said Timothy Rolls. "We ent much use except to labour."

"The hardest work you do is with your tongues," Beth said.

"Here, Beth," said Sam Lovage. "You must get young Kit to show the misericord he's making for the church. That'll make you open your eyes! He's carved old Adam and Eve and the apple, all as naked as can be."

"So what?—I've seen a naked apple before!" said Beth. "And I certainly ent running round after Kit Maddox, telling him what a clever boy he is. I've got better things to do with my time."

"Lumme!" said Sam. "D'you hear that, Kit?"

"Ah, I heard," said Kit, working.

Kit was the youngest carpenter in the workshop. He was at this time about eighteen. His father had been killed by a fall of rock in the quarry at Springs. His mother had thrown herself under a train. Kit had been raised in an institution, but now lived with his widowed grannie at Collow Ford. He was dark-haired and dark-skinned, with the sharp good looks of a gipsy. He liked to be different from everyone else, and he always dressed in a showy way. Even at work he wore a crimson velvet waistcoat.

At times he was merry, playing tricks on the older men, and telling them stories picked up at the barracks in Capleton Wick. At other times he would be silent, absorbed in his work, and in this mood, if anyone teased him, he would turn on them with savage contempt, dark eyes alight with temper, fists ready to hit out. His work was good, which made him a favourite with Grandfather Tewke.

"Kit's a tip-top craftsman," the old man was always saying. "He'll go far, so long as he keeps his mind on his work."

"He's wild," Kate said, "and a sore trial to his poor old grannie."

"Who says so?"

"All Huntlip says the same.—Too free with the girls and too free with the little brown jug."

"Tittle-tattle!" the old man said. "I'm deaf to that."

Between Kit and Beth there was constant conflict, and her battles with him were different from those she had with the other men: the conflict was sharper, more tinged with spite.

Once, when she went to the yard as usual to collect the chips and shavings, she found them burning in a heap, and Kit standing by with a rake, watching.

"What d'you think you're doing?" she demanded.

"I'm tidying up. Making everything smart and dandy." He leant on his rake-shaft, smiling at her, enjoying her rage. "I reckon I could get work as a charcoal burner if I was ever at a loose end, don't you?"

"You've got work already. You should stick to that and not waste time annoying me."

"You should stick indoors, then, instead of poking about out here."

"The chips is mine. Just leave them alone in future!"

"You should get out of ribbons before you start giving me orders!"

Grandfather Tewke came out of the workshop to see what all the noise was about.

"Who lit that fire? You, Maddox? You ought to know better'n that.—The chips've always gone to the kitchen."

Kit went red in the face. Then he laughed. He pushed the rake into Beth's hands and walked away.

"Seems you like provoking that boy," the old man said. "You're like all the girls!—Can't keep away from a handsome chap."

"Handsome!" Beth said. "I'd sooner look at Timothy Rolls!"

But Grandfather Tewke would not believe her, and made a great show of searching the sky.

"I fancy I heard a cuckoo!" he said.

Whenever the old man was driving out on business, Beth would hang about the fold on the chance of an outing. She polished the trap. She beat the cushions. She fetched the harness and backed the pony between the shafts. But the old man, though he must have known what she wanted, would never invite her. And so, since she could be obstinate, too, she dressed herself up one afternoon and arrived as he was mounting the trap.

"Where are you off to, then, so smart?" he asked.

"I'm going with you," Beth replied.

"Hah! Is that so! Very well, you can nip and fetch young Maddox as well. Say I'm looking at a stand of timber on Lodberrow farm."

"Why take him? He'll only spoil things."

"You nip along and do as I say!"

Beth went to Kit, who was splitting stakes in the yard.

"Suits me," he said. "I'd sooner be out larking than splitting these damned stakes."

It was mid June, and a hot day. They drove down rough lanes, raising a dust that whitened their clothes, the trap, the pony, and the hedgebanks on either side. The pony, Jakes, would not be hurried that day, but jogged along steadily, blowing through his nose because of the heat and the flies and the dust.

On every farm, the hay had been cut early, and its scent was with them all the way. In some fields, men were already carting. In others, men and women were turning the swaths. The hay looked yellow, spread on the aftermath of live green grass. The women's pinafores were patches of dazzling whiteness, and the kerchiefs on their heads were blobs of red or blue.

Beth sat back, looking from left to right all the time. She liked to see what went on in the fields. Kit, beside her, was peeling the bark from a twig of hazel. Today his mood happened to be friendly and he wanted to talk: he dropped bits of twig into her lap to attract her attention; he hummed a tune; he sneezed loudly.

"Bless me!" he said. "It's all this dust. I'm like a miller, except that I'm honest."

Beth was silent, removing the bits of twig from her lap and throwing them out into the road.

"Nice bit of sun, ent it?" he said.

Beth still refused to be drawn, and after another little silence, her grandfather spoke over his shoulder.

"You seem to be talking to yourself, boy. If Beth fell off in the road back there, you should've told me."

"No such luck!" Kit answered. "She's here all right. But the cat's got her tongue."

"You're making her shy, then, for her tongue is busy enough at home."

When they drove into the farmyard at Lodberrow, the farmer, a red-faced man named Charley Blinker, came from the stackyard to meet them and led them to

a hillock on high ground. They crossed a stretch
of pasture and skirted great sloping fields full of corn.
In the pasture, the cattle moved as though enchanted,
or stood in the brook in the shade of the willows. In
the cornfields, the corn stood motionless in the heat.
The ears of wheat stood erect, out of the fountains of
grey-green blades, and the barley bowed its awns to
the sun. Beth pulled a fern from the hedge to wave
away the flies that buzzed round her head. With
her other hand, she kept her skirts from sweeping the
corn.

The neat round hillock was crowned with oaks, the
trees growing wide apart, spreading their boughs and
making a green twilight below. Blinker led the way to
the foot of the mound, and they all stood in the outer
shade.

"There's your timber, Mr. Tewke. You can make
me a bid."

"You never said it growed on a hill," the old man
said. He went to a tree and kicked it with the toe of
his boot. He opened his knife and stabbed the bark.
"They're sound enough if this is a sample, but hill-
grown timber ent all that useful. It's too twisty. Still,
I'll pay fifty pounds for this little lot."

"Get away!" Blinker said. "You'll make that on the
bark alone."

"That's my bid—take it or leave it," the old man
said.

"All right. When d'you pay?"

"When I fell the trees. Next winter or next spring."

Going back, Charley Blinker walked with Beth, while
Kit and her grandfather went ahead.

"I remember your father. The best man with
horses I ever knew. I liked him a lot."

"I liked him myself," Beth said.

"You wouldn't happen to have his touch?"

"What, with horses? Good gracious, no!"

"I wondered, that's all. Your dad had a sort of
magic about him. I thought it might've got handed
down."

"He always said it was just common sense."

"Whatever it was, I wish I had it," Blinker said. "I've got a mare that's slinked two foals and I'm blessed if I can fathom why 'cos she's healthy as beans."

"That's nothing," Beth said. "Mares is often awkward that way."

"But she gave me a foal the first time, easy as falling off a log. Here, come and see her, just on the chance. You never know! She'll be coming in season again directly and you might work a charm."

Beth smiled.

"All right. No harm in looking."

In the farmyard, Kit and the old man sat on a bench, and Emily Blinker brought them beer. Blinker took Beth through to the stackyard, where a load of hay was being transferred to the stack. The hay was low down in the waggon, and the carter was sweating, pitching high to the man on the stack. Both men stared as Beth approached the mare in the shafts. Then they went on working again. But the carter kept a watchful eye.

The mare was as black and as sleek as treacle, gleaming sweatily in the sun. She was big but docile, standing at ease between the shafts, one rear hoof tilted on edge on the ground, one great haunch relaxed sideways.

Beth offered a knob of cowcake, and the velvety lips tickled her palm. She moved to the mare's side and ran her hand down the hot, moist flank. The sweat dripped from her fingers, and she put her hand to her nose and sniffed.

The carter stopped pitching and came to the off side of the waggon.

"What d'you think you're doing?"

"I was admiring your mare's shiny coat."

"Oh, ah!" the man said.

"She's nice and quiet, too, ent she?"

"Hah! She wasn't always. She was nervy as a bird when I first had her. But I soon cured that!"

"Why, what d'you give her?" Beth said.

"Give her! I never said I gave her nothing."

"But you *do* give her something," Beth said. "I can smell it in her sweat."

"I dunno what you mean," the man said, and half turned away.

"I've heard mistletoe's good for nerviness," Beth said. "I remember my father telling me that. But he said he never used it hisself 'cos that'd make a mare abort."

"What!" said Blinker. "God almighty, I'll have his guts!" He went to the waggon and shook his fist at the carter. "Great flaming fool! Risking my mare with muck in her feed! Wasting two lots of stud fees! I've half a mind to heave you in the horse-pond!"

The carter was sullen. The man on the stack stood gaping down. And the mare looked round, her ears twitching as Blinker bawled at the top of his voice.

"I've got to go," Beth said. "My grandpa's waiting."

"Hang on!" said Blinker, following her. "I owe you something for helping me. What'll it be?—A flask of cider? A few eggs?"

"You owe me nothing," Beth said.

"You got hens of your own at Cobbs? No? Then I'll give you some pullets to start you off."

He lumbered about the stackyard, chasing the pullets into the barn. He caught two and thrust them, flapping and squawking, into a basket with a lid. He caught a third and then a fourth.

"There! How's that? They've been with the cock so let them go broody and you're all set up!"

In the farmyard, Grandfather Tewke was sitting alone, his beer-mug on the bench beside him.

"Chickens?" he said. "Who said you could keep chickens?"

"Why shouldn't I?" Beth said. "We've got the ground."

"All right. If you do the work."

"Where's Emily?" Blinker asked.

"Gone off with Kit," the old man said.

"What? I ent having that! I've heard a few things about your young mitcher. Which way did they go?"

"Search me! I ent their keeper."

"Hell's bells! This is my day!" Blinker said. "I'll smash that boy if he's trying it on with my daughter. I'm just in the mood!" And he lumbered off.

Grandfather Tewke sat at ease, looking at Beth in a thoughtful way, as though he were guessing the weight of a pig.

"Kit seemed struck with Emily Blinker. You'll have to get a move on, growing up, if you want to catch him your own self."

"I'd sooner catch cold," Beth said.

"How old are you now? Nearly fourteen? Ah, well, you're coming on in your own way. You've got a bit of a shape now, and you ent too bad to look at, neither."

"Thank you, I'm sure."

"The trouble is, that tongue of yours. The chaps don't like the taste of sorrel."

"They must look elsewhere, then," Beth said.

Kit came sauntering into the yard, his hands in his pockets, his velveteen cap on the back of his head. Emily Blinker came behind him, looking tearful and flushed, and at that same moment, her father returned from the other direction.

"What d'you mean by running around with my daughter? Eh? She's a lot too young to be pestered by you, so just keep away or I'll tan your backside for you, big as you are!"

Kit said nothing, but looked away, bored and superior.

"Well?" Blinker shouted. "D'you hear what I said?"

"No," Kit said. "I heard nothing."

Blinker turned to his daughter and took her arm.

"Did he lay hands on you? Eh? Did he? Answer me, girl, or I'll shake you apart!"

The girl looked up with frightened eyes.

"No," she whispered. "We went to see the kittens, that's all."

"Very well! I'll believe you! Now get back to your mother in the dairy."

Blinker subsided, mopping his brow; Emily hurried

into the house; and Grandfather Tewke stood up to go.

"If the entertainments is come to an end, we'll get along home! Mr Blinker, I'll bid you good day. Kit, give Beth a hand with this basket of poultry."

Now, as they drove along the lanes, the sun was aslant in the open sky, and the workers in the fields had long shadows. Now, in the pastures, the cows were moving with more purpose, eager for relief at the hands of the milkers, who were calling them home.

Kit sat wedged in his corner, resting an arm on the side of the trap. He was looking at Beth in a way she hated, with a dark bright stare like that of a lizard watching a fly. Suddenly, he thrust a hand before her face, showing a deep scratch on his knuckles.

"That's what I got, looking at kittens. One little cat had sharp claws."

"Good," Beth said. "Emily Blinker's got some sense."

His hand dropped like a stone to her lap, and he squeezed her thigh with vicious fingers. Her foot shot out, kicking the basket containing the pullets, and it skidded across the floor of the trap, the pullets squawking and fluttering inside.

"Keep your hands off me," she said, through clenched teeth, "or you'll get worse than a little scratch!"

From Grandfather Tewke came a loud snort of laughter.

"If I was you, boy, I'd wait till the girl's grown up full size. She'll have more nous than to grouse then!"

In the morning, she asked if one of the men could make her a hen-hut, and her grandfather promised to send Walter Izzard.

"The one man I can spare and not know the difference!"

Walter came and worked in the orchard. He built a hut from old bits of timber, up off the ground on

stone blocks, with a ramp at the door. Beth soon perceived the truth of her grandfather's sneer. Walter
was clumsy. He handled his tools in a haphazard way
and ruined a great many nails and staples. But he had
a peaceful, easy-going temper, and Beth liked him.

"I reckon you're laughing at me," he said. "I reckon
you knowed I was splitting that fillet. You saw it coming a mile off!"

"I thought you wanted to split it," she said.

"Glory, no! I'm club-handed and that's all-about-it.
Just look at that hut! Did you ever see such a tarnal
botch-up?"

"It looks all right to me."

"Why, that rocks like a see-saw. I shall have to put
a wedge in somewhere. Now where's my pencil disappeared to?"

"Behind your ear," Beth said.

When he had finished and was packing his tools,
a cloud of bees flew into the orchard and began to
look for a place to swarm.

"Lumme!" he said. "A swarm in June is worth a
silver spoon.—That's what Goody always says."

"There's some old skeps in the barn somewhere."

"Ah. Your grannie kept bees at one time of day.
You run and fetch a skep, then, and I'll see about
settling the swarm."

Beth ran to the barn and fetched a skep. When she
returned, the bees had swarmed in the crutch of a
plum tree, and Walter, below, was beating the blade of
his saw with a hammer.

"They're settling," he said. "Laws, I never saw anything like it! Now you take these and keep up a good
ran-tan while I get a ladder."

She took the saw and hammer and kept up the
noise, while more bees, coming into the orchard,
zoomed past her to join the swarm. Walter brought a
ladder and set it up against the tree. He climbed up,
with his cap in his hand, and eased it gently under
the bees.

"Come on, little beggars. Gently does it, that's the

style. They like the music you're making down there. They're humming to it, can you hear?"

The clamour had brought the men from the workshop. They stood at the orchard fence and watched, and one or two offered mocking advice.

Walter came down with the swarm in his cap, but some of the bees were flying about, buzzing wildly, and many crawled on his arms, face, and neck. Beth dropped the tools and took up the skep. She held it at arm's length while Walter lowered the swarm inside. He shook his cap and pushed at the bees with his free hand.

"Mind! You'll get stung!" Beth said.

"What, with my tough hide?"

He picked the bees from his face and hair as though they were nothing but butter-burrs, and when they clung to his fingers with sticky feet, he flicked them off, gently, into the skep.

"The queen's in, so the odds and bobs'll soon follow." He took the skep and turned it over onto the box he had used as a workbench. "They'll soon cool down when we find them a nice little place in the shade."

Kit Maddox called from the fence:

"Are you stung yet, Walter?"

"No, not me! Not that I know of, anyway."

"No sense, no feeling,—that's what they say."

"They say so best who say so knowing," Walter retorted.

He carried the beeskep on its box and set it down by the orchard hedge, where the damson trees hung over and gave it shade. He turned the skep till the bees' doorway faced south.

"Not east," he said, "or they'll get up too early and catch a cold in the morning dews. Just southward, that's best."

"How do I take the honey?" Beth asked.

"Glory be, you're in a hurry, ent you?"

"No. I just don't know about bees at all."

"Well, remind me in the back-end of the year and we'll see what's what then, shall us?" He leant down

and put his ear close to the skep. "They're all right.
They're right as ninepence. It's nice to have bees
about the place. And Goody always swears they're
lucky."

Always, after that day in the orchard, Walter and
Beth were close friends. Whenever she wanted anything done, however trivial, Walter would always do
it for her. He cut her a prop for the clothes-line. He
made little feeding-troughs for the hens. He helped
with the bees. And he made her a ladder, small and
lightweight, for her to use when picking the fruit in
the orchard.

Often, when Walter was with her, Grandfather
Tewke would work himself into a rage.

"Izzard! Come here! You're wanted in the workshop."

"All right, gaffer," Walter would say.

"Running round after that blasted girl! Who's pay-
master here, I'd like to know?"

"Why, you are, gaffer. You surely know that."

"Then look slippy, you glib streak, or I'll turn you
off."

"You'd better go," Beth would say to Walter. "Don't
get into trouble on my account."

"Don't worry. Your grandpa's been threatening to
turn me off for twenty odd years and it ent happened
yet. Now, then! See if you can carry that ladder without a sweat. All right, is it? Nice and easy to lug
about? Good! You'll be round them fruit trees in
no time at all."

The orchard at Cobbs had never done well, and
Grandfather Tewke was always threatening to fell
the trees. "Same old story, year after year! Plenty of
blossom! Plenty of show! And no more fruit than'd fill
an old wife's apron!" And it was true. Beth had seen
it during her first three summers at Cobbs. But the
year 1889 brought a great change, for the bees had
been at work on the blossom, and the fruit had set,
both the plums and the apples.

In August that year, Beth worked hard to pick all

the plums in due time, and Kate worked, too, bottling and jamming. In October, Beth was busy again, picking apples day after day. Her grandfather know she was working at it from dawn to dusk, but he never sent help, and she was too obstinate to ask him. Walter was working away at Norton. Kate was too nervous to climb a ladder. So all the picking fell to Beth.

When picked, the apples filled every shelf in the hayloft, and Beth was proud, taking the credit because of her bees. There were three stalls in the orchard now, for she herself had taken two casts. She no longer feared them, for, having been stung once or twice, she knew it was not such a terrible thing after all. She liked to see them coming and going about the garden, working away, hum and suck, in the scarlet runners under the wall. She would stand and watch them squeezing in and out of the flowers.

When Walter helped her to take the honey, she would not allow the bees to be killed. She preferred to save them, setting a new skep against an old one, tap-tap-tapping, quietly, patiently, with her fingers, until all the bees had moved from the old skep into the new. And she made sure they had enough honey to last them through the winter months. "They do the work. It's only right they should be cherished." Her own harvest was rich enough even then. The crushed combs hung in a muslin bag in the kitchen, and the honey ran, pale and clear as golden sunlight, into the big earthenware bowl.

That winter, Walter was ill, and because he was often away working in distant places, a month went by before she knew. Then, as soon as Timothy Rolls had told her, on a wet day near Christmas, she put some things into a basket, and borrowed her mother's waterproof cape. On her way out, she met her grandfather crossing the fold.

"Why didn't you tell me Walter was ill?"

"What've you got there? You taking my food to give to Izzard?"

"The eggs and honey are mine," Beth said. "And as

for the jam—I picked the fruit so I reckon that's half
mine as well."

"Is that so! And whose grain feeds the hens?"

"Yours. But you get free eggs every day."

"And whose damned trees gave the fruit?"

"They only gave it because of my bees."

"Hah! I wonder how I got on before you came! I
wonder how I struggled along!" He looked at her with
a sudden sly gleam. "I'm going to Upham to fetch a
load of deal. You can come along for the ride if you
like."

"No," she said, "I must see Walter."

"It's three miles out to the Pikehouse. And a mucky
day for walking."

"I shan't melt for a drop of rain."

"Suit yourself. Though why you should trouble
about Walter Izzard is a mystery to me."

"But he's one of your men," Beth said.

"Not any more. He's licked for good."

"What d'you mean?"

"Just that. He's coughing his guts out. He's making
his will! A pity, I know, but I can't pretend he's much
loss to me. A ham-handed hedge-carpenter, that's all
he was, fit only for work on the farms."

"You made good use of him all the same," Beth
said angrily, "squeezing extra hours out of him every
week without a penny extra on his wages."

"Dammit, you're too fond of chipping me!" the old
man said, showing her a threatening fist. "Your tongue
is too sharp, as I've told you before."

"I keep it sharp for speaking the truth," Beth said.

It was open country out past Norton fork, and the
Pikehouse stood at the edge of the old pike road, its
garden cut neat and square from a sweep of wasteland known as the Chacks. Eastward, the road ran
with the woods of Scoate House Manor. Westward,
the wasteland rose gradually, and Eastery church
looked down from the ridge. "The church mice are
our nearest neighbours," Walter had said. "Them and
the folk in the churchyard, sleeping." The Pikehouse,

built of brick and whitewashed with lime, was a tiny place with a thatched roof. "A queer shape," Walter had said, "like a little oblong with two of its corners sliced off."

He was sitting up in a narrow bed in the down-stairs room when Beth went in. His face looked bonier than ever, and his skin was grey. His breathing came in jagged gasps, and when he coughed, his chest emitted a dreadful noise, like bellows blowing under water.

"Fancy you coming through all this rain!"

"I'll soon dry off by this nice fire."

"The kettle's on. You can make some tea. The pot's in the hearth and the caddy's up on the mantelpiece. Make it good and strong. There's plenty more in the cupboard there."

But Beth, who knew the price of tea and what it meant in a household such as Walter's, merely put in a single spoonful.

"I brought a few things," she said. "Eggs and such."

"We've got hens of our own," he said, "though they ent exactly shifting themselves to lay at the moment, it's true. Honey!"

"How's Goody?" Beth asked.

"Right as ninepence," Walter said. "She's working at Checketts full time now. And so is Jesse."

"What's Jesse doing?"

"Chopping roots at a few pence a day. But we're all right. Goody's a Trojan. And the house is our own, that's something."

"I shouldn't let you talk," Beth said. "It's making you tired."

"It cheers me up, having someone to talk to. I was always one for a good yarn."

He told her how he came to own the Pikehouse.

"My dad was pike-keeper here till the tolls was lifted twelve years ago. Then it looked as if we should be homeless. But he went to Scoate and asked if we could stay on and pay rent. Well, old Mr Lannam had shares in the new road going round by Hallows, and it

seems he wanted it finished double quick, so he said
we could have the Pikehouse for our own if we put
in some time breaking stones at Brinting. Me and my
dad had jobs to go to.—We could only manage a
few hours each day. But Goody and my old mother!
—They was at it sunrise to sunset! They used to take
food in a big basket, and when me and dad went
down in the evening, we had a proper picnic together,
all among the heaps of stones."

"And the Pikehouse was yours after that?"

"Deeds of possession, signed and sealed! And I'm
glad Goody's got the place to call her own when I'm
dead. She's worked hard enough all her life."

"Don't talk of dying," Beth said. "You'll be better
when the spring comes round."

"I shan't get better. I know that. Goody had the
doctor to look at me. But it's no use. I'm all rotten
inside."

'Wait until you see a bit of sunshine. You'll feel a
lot different then."

"I might," he said, just to please her. "I'll send up
a prayer and see what happens."

He began to cough, holding a towel against his
mouth. He doubled over, hunching his shoulders and
folding his arms across his chest, as if only force
could keep his lungs from bursting. Watching him,
Beth felt the strain and pain in her own body, and
when he coughed, she smelt corruption on his breath.

"What can I do?" she asked, frightened. "Shall I
give you some medicine out of that bottle?"

"Don't mind me," he said hoarsely. "I'm used to
these bouts. I've got them beat as you might say."
He lay back, exhausted, against the pillows. There
were dark smudges of blood on his mouth, and his
eyes had a haunting brightness. "You ought to go,"
he said. "It ent good to be shut up with me too long.
But there's one favour I'd like to ask."

"Ask away," Beth said.

"I'd like Jesse to go in the workshop. Maybe you'd
put in a word with the gaffer."

"Yes, of course," Beth said.

But that evening, when she spoke to her grandfather about it, he laughed her to scorn.

"I've just got rid of one Izzard.—I surely ent going to saddle myself with another! That boy Jesse's as slow as snails."

"He could do odd jobs about the workshop."

"The answer's no. And that's all-about-it."

Walter, when Beth went to see him again, tried to hide his disappointment.

"Oh, well! Never mind. It was just my foolishness, that's all, wanting Jesse to take my place."

Beth went every week to the Pikehouse, taking little custards and jellies and cakes. She took her grandfather's old newspapers and read to Walter for a couple of hours at a time. As the weather improved, he grew stronger. He sat in a chair at the open window, watching the larks rising from their nests in the nearby wasteland, and the spring changes coming over the distant fields.

One day at Cobbs, when a cow was calving, Grandfather Tewke came into the kitchen and ordered Beth out to the cowshed. The cow, Minnie, was a young one, and this, her first calf, was giving trouble. She stood in the shed, her legs splayed out, her body contorted, screaming and bellowing all the time. The calf had begun to come, awkwardly, head in advance, and was now stuck in the neck of the womb.

"See what you can do to help her," the old man said. "I've tried, but I'm too big, and we'll lose her if we don't get a move on. You're small. You should be able to manage all right."

Beth stood still, her hands in her pinafore pockets, and stared at the cow. "I'll help on one condition.—That you give Jesse Izzard a job in the workshop."

"God in heaven! You dare to make bargains with me?"

For a moment, it looked as though the old man would strike her, but when he made a threatening

move, her stillness checked him, and his hand fell
against his side.

"You damned wicked bitch!" he said, baffled.
"You'd let the beast suffer just for some crotchet
like this. You'd let her holler! You'd let her die!"

"It's you that's letting her suffer, wasting time
while you swear."

"Swear! I'd swear right enough if I knowed enough
words. Here, where d'you think you're going to,
eh?"

"It's no use my stopping if we can't come to
terms."

"Hell's bells! Ent you ashamed? Just hark at
that cow! Don't that mean nothing to you, hearing
her holler like that?"

"I reckon it means she's near her end. If I'm to
help her, you'd better say the word pretty quick."

"All right! All right!" the old man said. "I ent
stone like you, young miss. I've got some feeling
for poor dumb beasts. Now get a move on and give
her a hand."

Beth pushed up her sleeves and went to the cow.
She eased her hand, her wrist, then her forearm,
into the folds of hot throbbing flesh that pressed
on the calf. Her fingers, exploring its shape and
posture, groped and found a slippery hold, and,
little by little, while bearing down on her other hand,
she turned the calf within the womb. The cow gave a
heave, screaming hoarsely, and went rigid, arching her spine. Beth spoke in a quiet voice.

"Come on, Minnie, there's a good girl. One more
try and it's all over. That's the idea. There's a daisy.
One more push and it's all done."

The cow had a spasm, contracting her sides, and
the calf was suddenly squeezed from the womb. Beth
received it, a hot moist weight, and drew it away.
She let it down onto the litter and rubbed it hard
with a wisp of straw.

Her wrists burnt with a melting weakness. Her
face and body were prickly with sweat. Her clothes

clung under her armpits. She went to the doorway, and the cold fresh wind blew into her lungs.

"Are you feeling twiddly?" her grandfather asked.

"I'm all right now. It's passed off."

The cow was moving, tottering about on shaky legs, leaning one shoulder against the wall while she twisted herself round to lick the calf and nibble the cord.

"Seems you've got a nice new heifer."

"Seems I have," her grandfather said.

"All due to me, so remember your promise."

"What's to stop me taking it back?"

"You're supposed to be a man of your word."

"All right. Get back to the house and clean yourself up. And when you see Izzard, tell him to send his half-baked son on Monday morning, seven sharp."

She went to the Pikehouse the following day, in a changeable wind that bloated her skirts with one gust and wrapped them close round her legs with another.

"A loopy old day," Walter said, as they sat looking out of the Pikehouse window. "March has got all tangled up with April. But glory, there's naught like good news for putting a shine on the day, is there? How'd you do it, I wonder? Did it rain upside down? Or was there a ring round the moon on Sunday?"

"Seems my grandfather changed his mind."

"Jesse'll be all of a heap when he knows. He's out there scaring birds in the Uptops and he comes to the hedge sometimes to wave. Supposing you nip out and tell him?"

"Why not wait until he gets home?"

"Ah, go on. It won't take long, nipping down there."

"All right, if that's what you want."

"Tell him he'll have my bag of tools. And my watch with the strap on it. Tell him——"

"No," Beth said. "I'll leave a few little items for you to tell him."

She went out again, onwards along the old pike road, and into the lane that led to Checketts. There, a little way along, she stopped at a gate and looked into a big brown field that sloped down from the edge of the wasteland. It was newly sown; the birds were there in great numbers; and the boy Jesse ran to and fro from headland to headland, whirling a pair of wooden clappers. Sparrows and starlings flew up and were tossed about like leaves on the wind. Rooks and jackdaws flew up and cruised in circles, dipping their wings.

When Beth called out, Jesse stopped in his tracks, looking around as though puzzled. His face was a fiery red, whipped by the wind, and his fair hair stood up in spikes from the crown of his head. He looked across to the field running up from the far side of the ditch, where a man was ploughing, followed by gulls. He cocked his head, listening intently. Beth called again, and this time he came, plodding across the field towards her.

"Laws, it's you!" he said, relieved, and his chapped lips cracked in an awkward grin.

"The way you gawped, you seemed to think it was some old seagull called your name."

"I was flummoxed, that's all."

"You was always easy to flummox. You used to get tied in knots at school."

"Don't remind me of school! I'm finished with that, I'm thankful to say."

"And what've you got to show for it? Did you reach standard four?"

"No, nor never would if I stopped till domesday."

"Can you read and write?"

"I ent bad at reading. I read all the papers you bring my dad. The almanacs, too.—I like them a lot. Ah, and I like them custards you keep bringing, too."

"They're meant for your dad, not you."

"He shares them with me all the same."

"I reckon you're greedy," Beth said.

"I reckon I am," Jesse agreed. "I'm generally

nearly always hungry. Goody says I must have a hole in my belly."

"Why d'you call her Goody? She's your mother. You should be more respectful."

"I ent never called her anything but Goody."

"Well, I didn't come to preach you a sermon. I came to say you're to start in the workshop."

"Laws! Am I to be a carpenter after all, then? And drive the timber-cart like my dad?"

"You'll have to grow a bit before you do that."

"I'm growing like grass. I am truly!"

"You'll have to spruce up a bit by Monday, too."

"I ent got but this one suit of clothes."

"You can keep them tidy, can't you? And give your boots a taste of blacking. You'll hear from my grandpa otherwise."

"Will he go for me? I've heard he's a terrible man in a temper."

"You'll have to mind your p's and q's, surely."

"I dunno as I want to come," Jesse said, his blue eyes very wide and frightened. "I think I'd just as soon stay on the farm."

"Never mind what you want," Beth said. "Your dad's sick. It's up to you to do something to please him.'"

Jesse was silent, looking away to the far field, where the ploughman was ploughing the rising slope, cutting a clean brown furrow through the acid-green turf. The wind brought the jingle of harness, the blowing of the horses, and, in snatches, the sound of the ploughman singing.

"I had a mind to go to plough myself," Jesse said, "just as soon as I got the chance."

"Well, you can't," Beth said. "Your dad's set his heart on your being a carpenter so just you buck up and look cheerful about it."

"All right," Jesse said. "I'll be there Monday."

"Seven sharp," Beth said.

When she went back to Walter, he could talk of nothing but Jesse.

"He ent too bright, it's true. He takes after me.

But he's a good boy in his way and there ent a ha'porth of harm in the whole of his body."

"He'll have to wake up a bit when he gets to Cobbs."

"Ah. I only hope the men'll give him a fair chance. They're a funny lot sometimes."

"Don't worry," Beth said. "I'll keep an eye on him for you."

She was out in the yard on Monday morning when Jesse arrived, carrying his father's bag of tools. He was late, and Grandfather Tewke, confronting him outside the workshop, pointed up at the clock on the roof.

"Can you tell the time, Jesse Izzard?"

"A bull got out in the road," Jesse said. "I had to go back and tell Mr Mixt."

"Bulls is no concern of mine. Nor yours now you're working for me. Is that clear?"

Jesse nodded. He stood, red-faced and sweating, moving his tool-bag from hand to hand. He looked at the men, who has stopped work and were gathering round him, and he looked again at the workshop clock, where the weathercock, as always, pointed northwards.

"I see you're squinting at our old cock," said Sam Lovage. "I reckon it's got you properly moithered."

"It has, that's a fact, for I could've sworn to a soft south-wester as I was coming along the road."

"Ah, we always get different weather in Huntlip. It's always a couple of waistcoats colder here than anywhere else."

"I see you've got your dad's tools, Jesse," said Bob Green. "Have you done much in the carpentering line?"

"A bit now and then, that's all."

"Well, if you're half the craftsman your dad is, we'll have to look out for ourselves," said Sam, turning to wink at Kit Maddox.

"Oh, I ent a patch on my dad!" said Jesse, and stared in surprise as a shout of laughter went up all round.

Beth, stepping forward, elbowed her way into the circle.

"Take no notice," she said to Jesse. "They'd laugh to see a maggot crawl!"

She glared at her grandfather, standing by, but the waste of time was nothing to him so long as it offered some entertainment, and, perceiving his mood, the men were quick to take advantage.

"Here, Jesse, you ent like your dad to look at, are you?"

"I dunno," Jesse said.

"Well, you're fair-haired for a start, boy."

"I was born at harvest time, that's why."

"I ent seen a head of hair like that since Whitey Newby was round these parts," said Sam Lovage, "and that's funny, really, 'cos Whitey was shepherd at Scoate for a while, wasn't he?"

"Yes," Jesse said. "He was there till last Christmas."

"Laws! That Whitey! The randiest chap in the three counties. They say he was busy, all round Scoate and the Pikehouse and all."

"Yes," Jesse said, utterly guileless. "Specially when the lambing was on."

"Is that so? And Goody was kind to him, being neighbours, eh?"

"I dunno about that," Jesse said. "She wasn't too keen on Whitey. She said he had fleas."

"How'd she know?" asked Bert Minchin.

"She got bitten, perhaps!" said Steve Hewish, and they all laughed.

"Oh, you're so funny!" Beth exclaimed. "Yes, laugh yourselves silly, you great fools!"

"What's up with you?" her grandfather said. "Clucking around like a hen with a chick?"

"Ho, so Jesse's a favourite with Beth, is he?" said Steve Hewish. "Fancy a strapping great girl like her, picking on a little poor little hob like Jesse! Why, he's only thirteen. I bet he don't even know what girls are for yet."

"That's enough!" said Grandfather Tewke. "Time we got down to a bit of work. Izzard, you can put your tool-bag away for today. Your first job is stacking timber. Hopson here will show you how."

The men dispersed, returning to work, and George Hopson, a man of few words, motioned to Jesse and led him away. Beth went indoors, aware that her promise to Walter had proved worthless. She could never stop the men making game of Jesse. He would have to learn to fend for himself.

The following day, when she was cleaning out the dairy, he came to the door to look for her.

"Sam sent me. He said to ask for a bag of holes. Assorted sizes. Urgent, he says."

"Jesse Izzard, you're a born fool!"

"Eh?" said Jesse. "Oh, glory be!"

"They can wait for their laughs," Beth said. "Seeing they sent you, you can help me here."

She kept him busy for nearly an hour, running to and fro with pails of water till the whole dairy was clean and cool and sweet-smelling. Then she gave him a dipper of creamy milk and watched him drink it.

"Why, I ent had such a treat since we lost our old Clover," he said, with a sigh.

"Don't you get milk from Checketts, then?"

"We get a quart, but it's blue beside this. My dad

has a pint of that, cos Goody makes him. Then there's a gill goes to feed our pig, and a gill for us to have in our tea."

"I'll put out a pint for you every morning," Beth said. "You can nip round and drink it at dinner-time. But don't tell the men, else there'll be ructions."

"A pint myself every day? I'll soon be as fat as a landlord, shan't I?"

"You'd better go now. And wipe your mouth or the secret's out. Here, hang on a minute. I've got an idea."

She went to the barn and rummaged among a heap of sacks. She pulled out one that was full of holes and gave it to Jesse.

"They asked for a bag of holes, didn't they? Well, there you are.—You can take them that."

Throughout that spring and summer she visited the Pikehouse twice every week, and Walter was always pleased to see her.

He was growing weaker again now, wasting away to a frail husk. Yet life still burnt fiercely in him, as in a bird with a mortal wound, and on fine days he sat in a chair at the open door, eager for every last sight and sound the earth had to offer.

"I ent going yet!" he used to say. "Not while the summer holds so fine. I was always a great one for sunshine. I shan't go underground yet if I can help it."

That summer, the plum trees at Cobbs gave a heavier crop than ever, and even when the workmen had taken all they wanted, Beth had a surplus of seventy pounds. So she took them in two big baskets, one on each arm, and went to the green to catch the carrier's cart into Chepsworth.

She sold all her plums in the open market and walked home, the empty baskets creaking against her thighs, her pinafore pockets jingling with coins.

"Have you got something to tell me?" her grandfather asked, at supper time. "Or is it a secret, your nipping to Chepsworth to sell my plums?"

"Secret? When Timmy saw me boarding the cart?"

"Traipsing to market like some little badger! Folk'll be thinking I'm on the rocks!" He pushed his mug across the table and watched her struggle to raise the big stone flagon of beer. "Well?" he demanded. "What did you get for the plums, then, dammit?"

"Eight and sixpence," Beth said.

"Is that all? For seventy pounds of best belindas?"

"I'm quite happy with what I got."

"And where is it, what you got?"

"I've put it away," Beth said.

"Along with the pennies you make on your eggs? Did it slip your mind that the fruit was mine?"

"I did all the picking so I reckon the bit of returns is mine. Something put by for a rainy day."

"A little old miser, that's what you are! A grannie skinflint, like old Mrs Bunt."

He finished his supper and sat leaning back in his chair. He watched her narrowly, reluctant to demand the money, yet hating the thought of it in her possession.

"There ent going to be no rainy days for you," he said. "You're safe as the Bank of England with me and that goes for your husband and family when they come along too."

"My stars!" said Kate. "You might give the girl a chance to grow up before putting notions into her head."

"She don't need notions! She's as forward as nuts in May and if I'm any judge, she'll have a couple of brats by the time she's twenty."

"Only a couple?" Beth said.

"You needn't get hoity-toity with me, miss. I'm not against your settling early. The sooner the better as far as I'm concerned, and I'm making my plans accordingly."

"What plans?" Beth said.

"Just you wait!" he said, happy now that he had the last word. "You'll know what they are soon enough."

The next day, at twelve o'clock, when Jesse came

to the dairy for his milk, Beth was waiting and gave him a little bag full of money.

"What's this?" he said.

"It's to buy a few special things for your dad."

"It feels like a fortune. I dunno as I should take it."

"If you don't take it, I'll drop it in the drain there."

"You must be powerful rich, Beth."

"No, I'm not."

"Then I reckon you're good. I do! Honest John! A proper Samaritan, that's what you are."

"I've known what it's like to be poor, that's all. And I reckon I'll know what it's like again one day. Then I might be coming to you for help instead."

"Why should you ever be poor again, Beth?"

"It's just a feeling I get in my bones."

She was feeding the hens in the orchard one morning when a clamour arose in the workshop yard. Grandfather Tewke was out on business. The men were therefore in holiday mood. They had smeared the mortising-stool with glue, smoking hot from the pot on the burner, and were forcing Jesse to sit astride it. Only George Hopson and Timothy Rolls stood aloof. The rest were crowded about the stool, pressing Jesse down on the seat, and tying his boot-laces together under the crossbar.

"Don't you kick, boy, or we'll do to you what we always do to donkeys!"

"Loose him now and see how he rides!" said Liney the pitman.

"Stand back! He's threshing about like Old Nick with two nails. How're you doing, Jesse? Ent you still got nothing to say?"

"He ent talking. He's too stuck up!"

"Whoopsee! He don't look too safe for all we've give him a holdfast saddle."

Jesse swayed, throwing himself forward to keep his balance, and clutching the narrow seat of the stool. His hands were instantly fouled in hot glue, his fingers stickily webbed together, and his skin scalded. He swayed again, rocking about from side to side, and

then, as his knotted boot-laces snapped apart, he toppled and fell in a heap on the ground.

Beth, with her skirts hitched up, climbed the fence
and ran to help him. She took the stool by two legs
and pulled it away. Jesse got up, unfolding slowly
like a hurt crab, covered all over in filth and sawdust.

"Oh, he's dirtied his britches!" said Sam Lovage.
"What a dirty hound it is to be sure."

The men roared, and Beth, in a fury, hurled the
mortising-stool into their midst.

"You'll laugh the other side when my grandfather
hears how you waste your time! The feathers'll fly
pretty smartish then!" Still in a fury, she rounded on
Jesse Izzard himself. "As for you! It's time you woke
up and kept a ha'porth of wits about you! Laws, if I
was a boy, I'd take a mallet and mash a few skulls
before they made a monkey out of me!"

Jesse just stood, stricken dumb. Under his filth, his
face was white, and he stared at Beth with anguished
eyes.

"Jesse, what is it? Has anything happened? Is it
your dad?"

"Dead!" Jesse said, and could say no more.

The men were silent, looking ashamed. Timothy
Rolls removed his cap and one by one the rest followed suit.

"Oh, that's pretty, that is!" Beth said. "If only the
wind could change now!"

"The boy should've told us," Steve muttered.

"Poor old Walter," Sam said. "I'm sorry about it. I
am, that's the truth."

"If you're so sorry, you can think about making
amends," Beth said.

"What d'you mean?" asked Bob Green.

"Walter's widow, that's what I mean."

"You're right!" said Sam. "I was thinking along
them lines myself. But what had you got in mind exactly?"

"I leave that to you," Beth said. "Only don't be
scared of letting the light get into your pockets."

She led Jesse out of the yard, across the fold, and

into the scullery adjoining the house. She filled the
copper and lit the fire underneath.

"Tell me about your dad," she said. "Did he go easy
at the end?"

Jesse gave her a look of horror. He shook his head,
refusing to speak.

"You should talk if you can. It does no good to
stopple things up."

"I can't!" he said. "Oh, Beth, I can't!"

"All right. Nobody's going to make you."

"It was bad!" he said. "Bad as bad. All the night
through. He was too weak to sit up and cough. We
had to hold him, Goody and me. He couldn't breathe,
yet he coughed and coughed, and the blood came up
all over us, him and Goody and me."

"Here, take a hold on yourself, Jesse."

"I never saw anyone dying before. It oughtn't to be
like that, Beth."

"There's a lot of things that oughtn't to be."

"Goody gave him some drops . . . He was quieter
then."

"Did he die while he slept?"

"No, not till morning," Jesse said. "He woke up for
a while and turned his head towards the window. It
was just first light, with bits of pink coming up in the
sky, and he lay quite peaceful, watching them shining
in on the wall. Then he suddenly said, 'I'm off now,
Goody.—I'll see you anon.' In a quiet voice, like he
always said it, going to work. 'I'm off now, Goody.—
I'll see you anon.' And the next thing I knew, Goody
was covering his face with the blanket."

"It's better he's gone," Beth said. "He's earnt his
rest."

"I know that. But I dunno! It seems like nothing'll
ever be the same again."

"It won't be the same. It'll all be changed. But
things don't hurt for ever and ever. That's the one little mercy, I reckon."

"I feel a lot better, talking to you."

"You'll feel better still when you're rid of that dirt,"
Beth said, opening the copper and dipping her fingers

in the water. "It's getting warm. You can start scrubbing. But as for that glue,—only grit and grind is going to shift that."

"Don't I know it! My britches feel like they're made of glass!"

"The next time they start tormenting you, just stick up for yourself, d'you hear? Great fists and knuckles like you've got there! You should be able to uncork a nose or two, so see you do it!"

"I'll try," Jesse said. "But I ent much of a fighter, Beth. You ask Goody. She always says my dad and me couldn't knock the skin off a rice pudding."

When her grandfather heard that Walter was dead, he ordered the men to make a coffin and take it out to the Pikehouse.

"Tell Goody Izzard she can pay when it suits her. Week by week if she chooses. Beth here will make out the bill."

"No need for bills, gaffer," Sam Lovage said, with a large gesture. "Me and the chaps've clubbed together and we're paying for the coffin our own selves."

"Hah! What's up with you all of a sudden?"

"Well, we want to do right by an old butty, don't we?"

Walter was laid in the churchyard at Eastery, up on the ridge, half a mile from the Pikehouse. The village of Eastery lay in a dip, hidden away among the elms, but the little church stood up by itself, its timbered tower a famous landmark, its one cracked bell a famous disgrace. In spring, the steep churchyard was yellow with cowslips; in June and July, it was blue with sheepsbit. The place was a wilderness. Larks had their nests in the long grass, and lizards sunned themselves on the flat stones. The surrounding low walls were covered in ivy, and in the autumn, wasps and hover-flies came in great numbers to the creamy-green blossoms. Wizzlewings, Walter had called them, and the day he was buried, the churchyard was filled with their quiet hum.

The following Sunday, when Beth went to the Pike-

house, Goody was busy cleaning. She had carried the
furniture out to the garden and had scrubbed every
stick and stitch at the pump. The kitchen table, the
chairs and cupboards, the bedstead and settle: all
stood steaming dry in the sun. Strips of matting hung
from the apple tree. Curtains and blankets were spread
on the hedge. The house itself had been swept and
scrubbed, and all the windows were open wide.

"I'm glad Walter's gone before me," Goody said.
"He wouldn't have liked it if he'd been the one to be
left behind. Him and the boy would've moped theirselves silly without a woman to molly for them."

There was no change in her when she talked of
Walter. Her dark little eyes were as quick as ever; her
frown was as fierce; her voice as rough. And while
she talked, she darted about, swooping to pick up the
windfallen apples, sorting them in her apron, setting
the good ones on one side and throwing the maggoty
ones to the pig in his run.

Jesse sat on a bench, blacking his boots, and Beth,
beside him, was mending a rushwork mat with bast.

"D'you believe in heaven, Beth?" he asked.

"I dunno. D'you believe in heaven, Goody?"

"I dunno neither," Goody said. "But if there is,
Walter'll be there, I'm sure of that. And that's good,
'cos it means he can put in a word for me. I reckon I'll
need it, with all my sins."

"Are you such a terrible sinner, then, Goody?"

"I'm just about loaded if anyone is. Snuff for one
thing! I get through a paper of snuff in no time. And
sometimes sooner!"

"You've got to have some bit of pleasure," Beth said.

"Then there's my temper. I swear and cuss and get
in a terrible paddy sometimes. I do! That's a fact."

"You've got to say what you feel, ent you?"

"Then again I ent exactly nice when it comes to
pickings. I often help myself to bits and bobs off the
farm."

"You've got to live," Beth said. "What else after
that?"

"Nothing else. That's just about the sum and total."

Goody shooed a chicken from the settle and sat down
with her hands in her lap. "There ent a lot of choice
for a woman past fifty."

"It's a funny thing," Jesse said suddenly, "but whenever my hands are covered in blacking, my nose
itches!"

Beth, having finished repairing the mat, was putting
Goody's bodkin and scissors away in their bag.

"You go ahead and scratch," she said. "It won't
make no odds 'cos your face is skittered with blacking
already."

She took up the hank of bast and began smoothing
out the tangles.

"Why're you looking at me like that, Goody?"

"I'm looking at you and the boy there, sitting together so right and tight, and I'm wondering if your
grandpa knows you're such good friends with my
Jesse."

"I reckon he knows right enough."

"And does he like it, young woman?"

"I've never asked him," Beth said.

That year, 1890, Beth began picking the apples at
Cobbs on a day in mid October. It was bitterly cold
at eight that morning and the ground was covered in a
dense white mist, but when, on her ladder, she climbed
into the cage of branches, she climbed up out of the
mist, into a gentle brightness above. The leaves were
a bright, pale yellow; the apples a bright, dark red;
and the drops of water were splinters of light pricked
out like silver on the twigs.

She worked quickly, picking with both hands at
once, dropping the apples into her poke-pocket apron,
descending to the ground to empty them into a big
basket, then shifting the ladder and climbing again.

She was high in a tree, reaching up to the topmost
branches, when the ladder was shaken rudely from
below, and she had to throw herself forward quickly,
clutching the rungs. The tree rocked as though in a
gale, its branches springing and bouncing and creaking, sawing together wherever they crossed. Leaves and

twigs came down in a shower, and apples bounced about her head.

When the shock had passed, and the tree became steady again, she turned to look downward, but the mist was still thick on the ground and hid the lower half of the ladder completely. There was no dark shape in the whiteness. There was no sound in the long grass. Beth, however, was not deceived. She took two apples out of her pocket and threw them into the mist below. The first thud brought a grunt. The second brought a burst of laughter.

"I'll pay you for that!" a voice promised, and, the ladder yielding under his weight, Kit Maddox came shouldering up through the mist beneath her. "You very nearly spoilt my beauty."

"Stay still," Beth said, "or I'll dot you again."

"Ah. I can see you've got plenty of ammunition."

"What d'you want?"

"The gaffer sent me to give you a hand."

"I've got two hands already, thank you."

"Shall I start picking up here with you?"

"No. Get your own ladder and start elsewhere."

"All right. You're the one with the say-so here."

He climbed down, vanishing into the mist again, and a little while later she saw a ladder go up in a neighbouring tree. At first he was quiet, but quite soon he broke into song.

"Oh, a lad and his lass they went fishing
On a misty morning in May
On the banks of the Naff in the fair Vale of
    Scarne
Somewhere down Cropley way.

"Now the lad he fished with a lobworm
And his labours came to naught
But the lass she fished with a daintier bait
And alas! the lad was caught!

"Oh, the sun was just about setting,
The shadows were long on the hill,

And Jack his basket was empty,
And Jill her basket was full.

"But that lass she never grew weary;
She said to the lad 'One more cast';
But the lad he folded his rod away
And vowed he had fished his last.

" 'Then go sling your hook!' she cried proudly.
'Take your floater, your plumb, and your gaff!
There's plenty more lads in the fair Vale of
  Scarne
And plenty more fish in the Naff!' "

Kit's singing was one of his vanities, and in the silence that followed, Beth knew he was waiting for her
to praise him.

"There now!" he said, disappointed. "At The Rose
and Crown I'd have got a pint of Chepsworth for
that. Hey, Beth, can you hear me?"

"You'll bruise them apples if you throw them
into your pail like that. You should put them in
softly."

"All right! Whatever you say!"

"What's up with you, all sops and milk all of a
sudden?"

"The gaffer said I was to make myself agreeable."

"Oh, did he, indeed!"

"That's right. His very words. And I'm game to try
it, so what say you?"

"I'd say you was wasting your time," Beth said.

By ten o'clock the mist had gone from the orchard and
the sun was warm. The air was soft and still and filled
with the sweetness of nibbled fruit. Wasps, having
gorged themselves to repletion, lay curled in the
hollowed-out shells of apples, or flopped drunkenly
out of the trees.

Kit had shed his jacket and rolled up his shirt-
sleeves, and now, instead of using his ladder, he
swung about from branch to branch, a showy figure

in red waistcoat and black corduroys. Beth, as always, tried to ignore him, but now, whenever she came to empty her apron into the basket, he was there to empty his pail. If she hung back, he waited for her; if she went first, he leapt to the ground and hurried to meet her. Whatever she did, he was always there, leaning across the big basket, smiling his moody, meaningless smile.

"A great help *you* are!" she said, provoked at last. "You've only got two or three apples in that pail."

"I'm trying to be friendly. That's what your grandpa sent me for."

"I prefer to choose my own friends," she said.

Kit laughed, and, leaning forward across the basket, put out a hand to touch her face. She recoiled at once, and he let his hand fall in such a way that his fingers brushed the front of her dress, lightly tracing the shape of her breasts.

"You're growing up ... Nice and comely."

"Keep your hands to yourself!" she said.

"Ent it time we took these apples up to the hay-loft?"

"Yes. You can start now. You know the way."

"Ent you coming? Well, why not? Don't you trust me?"

"No, I don't."

"Seems to me you've been listening to gossip."

"I know what happened to Rosie Lewis, if that's what you mean. And I know about Lillibel Rye, too."

"You come up to the loft with me," he said, and his fingers closed on her bare arm.

She pulled herself free and hurried past him, but he ran to the ladder to block the way, and so, in exasperation, she snatched up her coat and walked off, leaving him alone in the orchard.

At twelve o'clock, when Grandfather Tewke strode in to dinner, his face was like a thundercloud. He came to where Beth was ladling pot-soup into a plate and dropped his fist with a crash on the table. The plate bounced, and the hot soup slopped from the ladle, spattering into Beth's face.

"What're you playing at, leaving Kit by hisself like that? God almighty! You grumble to me about picking the plums yet when I send someone to help with the apples, you start a morum like today!"

"Kit wasn't helping. He was wasting time."

"Looking you over, do you mean? Well, so what? He's a boy, ent he?"

"Beth's right to keep out of his way," Kate said. "That boy spells trouble."

"Gammon! I've no patience with cant of that sort." The old man's fingers poked Beth's spine. "You get back to the orchard this afternoon and not so much of your damned nonsense."

"I'm not going if Kit's there."

"God in heaven! Other girls would be pleased as Punch."

"Not me. I don't like him."

"I don't believe it. Not one little jot!"

"You don't *want* to believe it," Beth said. "But you can't make me go, so the apples will just have to stay unpicked."

The old man sat down, scowling at her as she passed to and fro. He could not understand her, but he had to give in.

"All right. Kit's too good a workman to waste to no purpose. But you'll try my patience too far one day, miss, and then there'll be ructions!" He broke a crust into his soup and stirred the pieces round and round. "I can be pretty nasty when I like, so you watch out, miss. You just watch out!"

The oak trees at Cobbs, and especially the big oak growing in the workshop yard, seeded abundantly that year, and when, at the end of October, there were several days of high wind, it seemed the acorns would never stop falling.

Beth, returning from church on Sunday morning, was surprised to see Jesse at work in the yard. She went in, and found him shovelling acorns into a barrow.

"What're you doing, working on Sunday?"

"The gaffer's paying me a whole shilling extra to work today. He says the acorns attract vermin."

"What're you doing with them?"

"The gaffer said burn them. I wanted to feed them to the cows, only he said no, it'd curdle their milk. But I'm certainly taking some home to our pig, 'cos Goody says acorns make the sweetest, tastiest pork and bacon ever. And she should know, the pigs she's raised."

"There's enough acorns here to feed your pig for a month of Sundays."

"There is, that's a fact! I've took a load from the sawpit alone. But there! I can't carry more than a sackful."

"No. We'll have to borrow the pony and cart."

"Glory be! Will your grandpa let us? '

"I shan't ask him. He snoozes in the parlour after dinner on Sunday, and I shall be back by the time he wakes up."

At two o'clock, when Beth slipped out of the house, Jesse was waiting in the fold, the cart in the shed already loaded with sacks full of acorns.

"Golly, I'm frightened to death, I am," he whispered.

"You needn't be. My grandfather's snoring like a hedge-hog. Spread this straw and he won't hear a murmur."

"Look," Jesse said, and pointed up at the workshop roof. "I climbed up there and fixed the vane."

Beth looked up, and, sure enough, the weathercock was pointing westwards, moving gently in the wind.

"Are you pleased?" Jesse asked. "You said you wished the vane would work so I climbed up and done it and gave it some grease. Are you pleased, Beth?"

"Yes," Beth said, looking into his eager face. "Yes, I'm pleased."

While Jesse scattered straw on the cobbles, she went to the paddock to fetch the pony, who came suspiciously, lured by a carrot, and had to be coaxed between the shafts.

Cautiously, they drove round the fold and under the archway, hooves and wheels moving almost noiselessly over the straw. Slowly, they creaked along the track that circled the house, and came at last to the village road.

"Whew!" said Jesse, wiping his forehead. "That's the first breath I've drawn in ten minutes. I wish I could be calm and courageous like you, Beth."

"You're all right as you are," Beth said.

As they were crossing the Derrent at Collow Ford, Kit Maddox came sauntering out of the cottage next to the smithy and sauntered down to the slip to meet them. He stood at the edge of the water, blocking the way, and took hold of the pony's bridle.

"I saw you from the window. I wondered what you kids was up to, gadding about in the gaffer's cart."

"Get out of our way," Beth said.

"Does the gaffer know you're out with his yard-boy?"

"Get back to your kennel and leave us be!"

"What's in the sacks? The gaffer's money!"

"Laws, no!" said Jesse, frightened. "It's acorns, that's all. We're taking them home to feed the pig. There's no harm in that. You won't split on us to the gaffer, will you, Kit?"

"I might," Kit said. "Or I might not."

"Get out of my way," Beth commanded.

"Surely! Whatever you say!"

He released the bridle and stood aside, but as the pony and cart moved past him, he reached for a hold and hauled himself up onto the runner.

"Shove over kids!—I aim to drive."

"Oh no you don't!" Beth exclaimed.

"Ent I welcome on this here jaunt?"

"You're as welcome as fleas!"

"Ah, well, you don't get rid of fleas that easy."

"We shall see!" Beth said.

She gave the ribbons a sharp twitch, and the pony trotted, swinging round at the top of the slipway and into the lane that ran for a mile or so with the Derrent.

The wheels jolted over the roots of willows. The cart bumped and shuddered. Yet Kit retained his place on the runner, hands grasping the edge of the buffboard, body lightly riding the bumps.

"Whoopee!" he shouted. "I've had rougher rides on the Porsham ferry!" And he waved one hand to show how sure he was of his balance. "Now then, you kids! I've had enough of riding first class. I'm coming up to sit in comfort."

"Not while I'm here!" Beth said.

She pulled the near ribbon, and Jakes responded, trotting in. The near side wheels mounted the bank, and the cart lurched steeply sideways, just as Kit got a knee on the buffboard. He was jolted backwards and this time he fell. Beth brought the pony and cart to rights again and drove on without a check.

"Christmas!" said Jesse, looking back. "He's gone a most terrible awful whomper. I reckon he's hit his head on a rudge."

"Good," Beth said. "I hope he has."

"He ent so much as stirring a peg. D'you think he's hurt bad?"

"Hurt? Not him!"

"Ent you going to stop and see?"

"No, not me."

"But he might've gone and bost a bone. He might be bleeding. Or even be dead!" Jesse put a hand on the reins and looked at her. His blue eyes were distressed but stubborn. "If you don't stop, I shall have to jump," he said.

"Oh, very well!" Beth said crossly, and drew rein.

Jesse got down and started back along the lane. Beth remained, nursing her temper. She would not trouble herself to look behind, but watched the pony cropping the bank, the wagtails bustling about by the brook, and the willow leaves falling into the water.

After a while, Jesse returned and climbed up beside her, and she flipped the ribbons and drove on.

"Well?" she said, glancing at him. "What's the weather like back there?"

Jesse turned with a sheepish grin, and she saw that his lip was bruised and swollen.

"You was right," he said. "Kit ent dead after all!"

When they got to the Pikehouse, Goody came from the garden to meet them.

"You're putting on style, ent you, boy, driving up like Puss in Boots? I suppose it's tuppence to speak to you today?"

"Fourpence," said Jesse, jumping down.

"How'd you get that lumpkin on your lip?"

"A gatepost hit me," Jesse said.

"There! Fancy! And did you happen to hit it back?"

"Here, Goody, guess what's in them sacks?"

"I can't," Goody said. "I'm blessed if I can fathom it out."

"Acorns!" said Jesse, looking important. "Bushels of 'em! To fatten our porker."

"Would you believe it!" Goody said. "And only this morning I was telling that poor pig he needed a couple of tucks in his waistcoat."

They carried the sacks to the lean-to, and with every sack that Goody emptied, she uttered her own rough blessing. "There's another couple of rashers!" she would say, or, "There's a nice tasty joint of pork!"

Jesse took the last sack direct to the sty, and they all stood around, watching the pig as he ate the acorns and spat out the husks.

"If we die this winter," Goody said, "I *shall* be surprised."

When Beth got home, Kit Maddox was waiting for her in the fold. He sat on the bench, in a patch of sun, at work with a clasp-knife, carving an elaborate wooden spoon. Beth drove around the enclosure, stopped directly in line with the pump, and backed neatly into the cartshed. Kit called out a word of praise, but she ignored him, going briskly about her chores. She took the pony out of the shafts and led him through into the paddock. She put away the sacks that had held the acorns and swept the litter of straw from the cobbles.

"Ent you speaking to me no more?" Kit asked.

"I'm surely not in a hurry," she said.

"Well, don't be too long thinking about it or I might've upped sticks and gone for a soldier. Here, look at this! How's that for a bit of carving?"

He held up the spoon, which was cut from a piece of sycamore wood, very clean and light, the colour of oatmeal. Its bowl was round and shallow, its handle carved in a barley-sugar twist, with a knob on the end shaped like an apple, and all so smooth that the marks of the knife could scarcely be seen.

"That's what I like to do," he said. "Work that a man can put his stamp on, so that folk'll always know it's his. Take that screen I done for the church. —Now there's something folk is always seeing and they say to each other, 'That there screen was done by Kit Maddox.'"

"And the day they stop, you're as dead as mutton, ent you?"

"They don't stop. That's just it. It's always there for them to see. It's like this work going on at Spailes. Just imagine!—Restoring the whole abbey from scratch! There's masons and carpenters there from all over England and the work they do will last forever. Not like the stuff we've been doing lately—all tubs and pails and blasted ladders!"

"Them things is useful," Beth said. "They're a part of life." She gathered up the last of the straw and threw it over onto the midden. "I've got more thanks for the man who makes me a pail than for him who carves grapes and such on my pew in church."

"Get away! Nobody notices a pail from one year's end to the next!"

"I never notice my eyes or my ears but I'm thankful I've got them all the same."

"You don't understand," he said, shrugging.

"But I do!" Beth said, standing before him. "I see into you like a cup of water. It ent enough for you to be clever. You have to be told it over and over again and again. And that'll be your trouble all your days 'cos folk've got other things to do besides fussling over you."

Kit smiled, looking at her through his lashes.

"You don't fussle me, do you, Beth?"

"No, not me!"

"Too much sense, I suppose you'd say?"

"Why so smooth and lardy all of a sudden?"

"Your grandpa thinks a lot of me. We're like a couple of snails in a cabbage. And you know what he says?—The moment you and me get together, he'll make me his partner, with my name on the board at the gate and all."

"There now! Fancy that!"

"It's sense, really. What good is the business coming to you if you ent got a husband that knows the trade? Your grandpa's thinking well ahead. A partner for him and a partner for you, all neat and tidy, like nails in a row."

"Oh, it makes sense, right enough."

"Then why not get on and fix things up? Your grandpa said you needed coaxing, so here's a courting spoon for a start. Go on, you take it. I made it for you."

"I don't want it," Beth said. "You'd better give it to Lillibel Rye."

Kit's face went dark.

"I made it for *you*. Don't you understand plain words?"

"Listen to me! I'll give you plain words! I don't want you. I don't even like you. And it's no use your wheedling me with your come-to-bed eyes and your nonsense with spoons 'cos you're not getting into my grandfather's business by marrying me! Is that plain enough?"

Kit sprang up as though she had struck him. His face was rigid and his eyes looked blind. To Beth it seemed his temper must break out at any moment, but then, abruptly, he turned and walked away, dropping the spoon in the gutter as he passed.

The next morning, while Beth and her mother were

in the kitchen, the door burst open and Grandfather Tewke stamped in.

"Have you seen Kit Maddox?"

"Not since yesterday," Beth said. "Why?"

"The lock's been forced on the workshop door and all his tools is gone from the bench! I've called on his grannie and she says his bed ent been slept in all night. So what's he playing at? You got any notion?"

"That's easy," Kate said, before Beth could answer. "Jeremy Rye's been threatening to haul Kit under the town clock for getting Lillibel into trouble. And Jeremy's sons've been saying they'll tar him."

The old man scowled and turned back to Beth.

"So you saw him yesterday? A Sunday outing together on the sly. Is that it?"

"No, it ent. I met him by chance."

"And did he let on he meant to scuttle?"

"Not exactly. But he talked a bit about Spailes Abbey."

"So that's it! He's gone off adventuring, seeing the sights and spreading his wings, and without a fairy fan to me. I suppose he thought I'd stop him going. Well, well! It might do him good to knock about in strange parts for a bit. He'll see what a damn good pitch he's got here at Cobbs."

"You seem pretty sure he'll be back," Beth said.

"Hah! I give him six months! Maybe a year, if he waits for things to die down with the Ryes. Then he'll be back, large as life and twice as saucy." The old man's anger seemed to have cooled. He was even pleased with the turn his thoughts had taken. "The boy's got nous, going off for a while. It'll maybe bring you to your senses."

Later that day, Beth retrieved the carved wooden spoon from the drain in the fold, and burnt it in the kitchen stove.

"Kit's gone," she said, in answer to Kate's look of surprise, "and I don't want no little remembrances hanging about."

But although Kit had gone, Beth was not allowed to forget him. Grandfather Tewke made sure of that, always finding excuses for speaking Kit's name. "Seems Grannie Maddox has took a lodger. Kit won't like that, finding a cuckoo in the nest when he gets home." Or: "Tell Mr Horton he must wait for that panelling he wanted doing.—My best craftsman is helping out at Spailes."

And later, when Sam Lovage was allowed to bring his son into the workshop, the old man said to Beth: "Don't get smitten on that boy Fred. I've took him on to keep up the numbers but he can't hold a candle to Kit for skill nor never will from now to domesday." Beth, although indifferent to Fred Lovage, was pricked into making an answer to this. "I shan't choose a husband by how he shapes as a carpenter. I'll choose by how he shapes as a man." But her grandfather had the last word. "Either way, Kit's the best bargain you're likely to get!"

That winter, the long hard winter of 1890-91, the Derrent was frozen for weeks on end. The young people were well pleased. So was the blacksmith who made their skates. The pool at Slings Dip, having broken its banks before freezing, became an enormous ice arena, attracting skaters from Middening, Eastery, Norton and Blagg. Every Saturday night, a big fire was lit on the ice, and a few rabbits or hares or even pheasants were roasted there.

Sometimes, Beth went down to join in the games, and once her grandfather went too, taking a bundle of elm loppings and feeding them to the fire with a great deal of show. But even there, watching the skaters, he found an excuse to speak of Kit. "Look at them all, tumbling over, arsing about! No more idea than a pig in pickle. Now if Kit was here, he'd soon show them figures of eight. There's nobody here can't skate like Kit."

The following April, Lillibel Rye's baby was born, and Timothy Rolls, who lived in the cottage next to the grocer's, brought the news to the workshop at Cobbs.

"A daughter," he said. "A bonny thing, though merrybegot, and I for one shan't hold it against her."

"What's she look like?" asked Grandfather Tewke.

"Just the usual little lump, with a dumpling face, like they mostly are."

"But who does she feature, you damned fool?"

"Well," said Timothy, scratching his head, "I reckon you'd better go and see the child for yourself, gaffer, seeing you're so interested in her."

"Interested!" the old man said. "I've got no interest in Lillibel Rye and her mischancements. I'm a busy man."

But later on, one day at the end of summer, when he and Beth were driving home from Chepsworth, he showed his interest all too plainly. The weather was hot, and Lillibel Rye, nursing her baby, sat on a stool at the door of her father's shop. Grandfather Tewke drew rein before her and stared at the baby in her arms.

"Here, hold it up!" he commanded. "I want to see!"

The girl, scarcely more than a child herself, obeyed without question, holding the baby for him to see, and meekly enduring his open contempt. The baby's hair was a golden floss; her skin was fair; and her eyes, dreamily watching the pony's movements, were deep violet.

"H'mm! If that's Kit Maddox's child then I'm an Egyptian!" the old man declared, and drove on, leaving the girl no time to answer.

He was pleased with himself, as Beth could see, and he smirked and nodded to himself all the way home. But then, as they were passing the workshop yard, he became sober and gave an exasperated sigh.

"You know what I think?" he said abruptly. "I think it's high time that boy was home!"

The next Saturday, after eating his breakfast in brooding silence, he rose from the table and shook Beth's arm.

"You get upstairs and pack your night-clothes in a bag. You and me is going a journey. Ah, and get your mother to put up some food."

"So now I'm deaf!" Kate said tartly. "Orders don't come directly to me no more. I have to get them translated to me by my daughter. Now what's all this about a journey?"

"I suppose we're going to Spailes," Beth said. "I've seen it coming like fate since Tuesday."

"That's right," her grandfather said. "And I'll thank you to get a move on, Miss Clever-and-Deadly, for I'm leaving double quick sharp."

"I can finish my breakfast, surely, seeing that other folk've finished theirs?"

"Maybe you don't want to come at all," he said. "Maybe you'd sooner stop at home and twiddle your thumbs?"

"Oh, I'll come sure enough," Beth said. "I ent never been as far as Spailes in my life before."

They drove down, southward and westward, along the winding valley roads and in among the enfolding hills. First the Burlows, then the Stams, then the twin humps, Menna and Marra, and then the Long Men of Clemov, closed behind them, fold upon fold. They drove slowly, stopping often to rest the pony, to

watch the white-splashing waterfalls breaking out of
hillside faults, to speak with passing shepherds, to buy
milk at lonely farms.

At the edge of Seay Forest, in the shade of oaks
and beeches, they stopped and rested for two hours.
Grandfather Tewke, having eaten his pasty, his
buttered crust, and his pickled egg, fell asleep with
his back against a tree-trunk. But Beth, though she
sat, was unable to sleep, for the green and golden
spaces under the trees were too full of movement, the
boughs overhead were too full of sound, the forest
smells were too disturbing and the journey itself
was all too strange.

They travelled on, under the upright, watchful
peaks of The Minders, over the smooth, featherbed
slopes of The Sleepers, and so down into the little
town of Spailes, built on the banks of the River
Ennen.

Saturday, it seemed, was market day in Spailes
when they arrived. The stalls in the square were still
doing trade, and the streets were crammed. Early
evening was always the worst time of a market day,
for now people waited about, hoping the vendors
would sell cheaply. Now the farmers were bringing
their horses and trying to disentangle their carts from
the crush. The last drovers were urging their cattle or
sheep through the narrow roads, and the first
drunkards were leaving the inns in search of a
quarrel. People came to Spailes from both sides of the
border, and Beth, hearing the Welsh tongue spoken
so commonly all around her, felt she had journeyed a
long way indeed.

"What're you smiling at?" her grandfather asked
her. "I don't see there's much to smile at, inching
along through a noisy mob of fools like this."

"I was thinking about my father," she said. "He
was often in these parts, and he used to teach me odd
words of Welsh that he picked up. Horse-talk,
mostly."

"H'mph, your father was always a waster of
time."

They drove down a cobbled street, so narrow that
people had to squeeze into doorways to let them pass.
They crossed the leats and came on the Abbey, its
newly restored tower clean and pink and warm in the
sunlight, standing within its flat green lawns, beside
the skyblue waters of Ennen.

They left the pony and trap at a railing under a
tree, and walked across the springy turf to the Abbey.
Nave and transept were still encaged in scaffolding,
and even now, at six o'clock on a Saturday evening, a
few men were still at work on the roof, pinning
timbers. The thud of their mallets sent echoes
bouncing between the walls, and in any lull, the
men's voices floated hollowly down. Grandfather
Tewke put his hands to his mouth and shouted, and a
face looked over the edge of the wall.

"Have you got a chap called Maddox up there?"
the old man asked.

"I wish I had!" the face called back.

"Then where might he be?" the old man asked.

"I wish I knew!" the face replied.

"God almighty! Can't I get a straight answer here?"

"Try the gaffer, in the cloisters," the face suggested.
"He's got nothing else to do."

They went round into the cloisters on the south
side. There, among the rubble, stood a hut, and a
man came out on the step to meet them.

"Maddox?" he said. "Yes, I did have a carpenter
here of that name, but he's been gone these three
weeks."

"Gone!" the old man exclaimed. "Hell and damnation! Three little weeks! Where's he gone to, do
you know?"

"Is Maddox your son? No? Well, I'll tell you what
happened. He had a fight with another carpenter here
and damn near killed him, pushing him off the
chancel stage. He smashed the man's nose and damn
near blinded him in one eye."

"So you paid him off, is that what you mean?"

"I hadn't the chance. He upped and skipped it
before I had time to see him at all. He knew the

others would skin him alive for what he did to Joel Watkin."

"So you've got no notion where he went?"

"Well, the groundsman saw him that last day, and he was making off in a coracle, down river towards Cleute. Ah, and it turned out he'd helped hisself to the coracle out of Jacky Lewis's garden, so his name is a mouthful round here just now."

"What's down river from here?"

"Radoc and Cleute, that's all. There's nothing there for a chap like him. He may be making for Bristol, of course, but you'll have a job to find him there."

"Seems you're right," the old man said. "I'll call it a day."

He returned to the trap and sat for a while with the ribbons idle between his hands.

"I wonder," he said slowly. "Yes, I wonder if that boy is on his way home."

"Not if he's headed for Radoc," Beth said.

"Ah, but if he was in a spot of bother he'd want to get people off his track, wouldn't he, eh? He'd want to be shut of nosy parkers. You just mark me! That's what he's doing as sure as fate. He's making for home by a long way round. You just mark me! That's how it is."

And having, as always, ordered events as they surely must go if fate understood its business, he drove back to the town centre in search of a lodging for the night.

Beth's father had often talked to her about Spailes. "It's a queer little place, old as the hills," he had said. "It ent quite Welsh and it ent quite English, neither, which maybe accounts for it having a strange sort of feel about it, all of its own." Now, after dark, looking out on the town from her bedroom window, Beth was touched by the same feeling of strangeness, for the streets, lit only by moonlight and starlight, wore a glimmering, waiting look, like streets seen in an old picture, and the dark houses looked as though they were full of secrets. Spailes, her father had often told her, was sly, secret, holy, lawless, and full of years.

The people there talked of the past as though it possessed a living soul, but time itself meant nothing to
them. "Oh, it's a queer little place, sure enough," he
had said, "and it gets in your dreams."

Across the street, in the Talbot Tavern, under the
ruined castle wall, he had once had his pockets picked
and had worked a day and a half in the stables to pay
for his board. A little way down, on the butter-cross
steps, he had seen a big carter swallow a gallon of
beer at a draught, and that carter, it seemed, though
dressed in trousers and smock, was really a woman
called Nance of the Roads. And somewhere out there
at the western edge of the town, where the old drove
road went into Wales, was the place where a tinker
had lain in wait with a knife, springing out on the
passers-by, and accusing them of stealing his wife.
Her father had fought for nearly an hour, and then
the man had run away. Beth remembered her mother
weeping at the sight of her father's wounds, and
begging him never to go to Spailes again. But he had
gone again, for the Welsh horses were best, he said,
and anyway, Spailes had a way of drawing him back.
"It's that sort of place. It gets in your dreams." And
on his return, he swore that a shepherd had found the
tinker dead in the hills.

That night Beth stood at her bedroom window
looking out across the town which was almost asleep
now. The only light came from The Talbot, a smoky
glow from its doorway, shining onto the sign-board
above, and the only noise came from the revellers
inside, one of whom was trying to sing "My Love A
Maiden."

> "My love a maiden;
> My maiden a dove.
> My dove an angel
> Sent down from heaven above."

The last cracked notes were drowned in a chorus of
cat-calls, followed by quiet. Then a concertina began
to play and a different voice began to sing.

"Oh, a lad and his lass they went fishing
On a misty morning in May
On the banks of the Naff in the fair Vale of
 Scarne
Somewhere down Cropley way."

Beth withdrew from the window and sat on the bed.
She stared at the wall and made herself think. The
singer was Kit Maddox. Even at that distance, she
knew the voice and the little tricks he played with the
old song. She got up and opened the door. The house
was asleep. Faint snoring came from behind each door.
Down below, the singing came to an end and the concertina continued alone, playing "Goose and Gander."
She put on her dress and drew a shawl over her head.
Then she crept downstairs and out of the house.

The Talbot had a stable-door, and the upper half
was open wide. Inside, under the dim light of a smoky
lantern, fifteen or twenty men were squashed together,
surrounding a drunken scarecrow of a man who danced
and capered to the concertina, flapping his ragged coat-
tails and scraping his feet on the sanded floor. Beth,
looking in, attracted the interest of two middle-aged
sheep farmers who stood with their dogs just inside the
door.

"Come in! Come in! I'll buy you a drink," said one.
"I think you deserve it if only because you're fresh-
faced and fair and not in the least like the black skinny
wife and daughters I've got at home."

"Or, if you've come to look for your dad," said the
other, "just say the word and we'll shed him out in no
time at all."

"It's not my dad," Beth said. "It's him that was singing a moment ago." She leant in over the door, holding
her breath against the stench of sweat and beer and
bad tobacco. "Him," she said, pointing. "Him with the
blue muffler at his throat."

"Him!" said the farmer. "By God, that's Lucifer,
son of the morning, by the look of him. But if he's
your choice, that's up to you."

Word was sent round, and Kit turned, swaying a little, to peer through the smoke. He stared at Beth for several seconds before recognition finally came, and then, with a shake of his head and a little smile of amazement, he pushed through the crowd to the door.

"Laws, it can't be!" he said. "It's all a dream."

"It's no dream. Can you come outside?"

"I've got a better idea. Supposing you come in."

"I can't talk in a noise like this."

"All right. I'll oblige."

He stepped outside, pulling the half-door shut behind him and leaning against it, still looking at her with the same tipsy, bemused smile.

"What're you doing here in Spailes? Are you looking for me? Oh, laws, what a lark!"

"It's my grandpa's idea, not mine," Beth said. "We went to the Abbey this afternoon."

"Then you will have heard of the miff I had with Joel Watkin."

"Yes. We even heard you was half way down towards the Atlantic Ocean too."

"I might've been at that, but the little cockleshell boat I had went and smashed itself up at Liberty Bridge. So I doubled back here to Spailes instead."

"Ent you afraid of the workmen, after what you done to their mate?"

"Them! They never come near this part of town. And besides, I ent afraid of them. They're nothing but emmets. That's all they are."

"Seems you can't live without making trouble," Beth said. "Did you have to nearly kill the man?"

"I hardly touched him. It wasn't my fault he fell off the stage. But here! What about you and the gaffer?"

"We've got lodgings over there," Beth said, pointing across the street. "Above the butcher's. My grandpa's asleep and has been these two hours or more. I looked out of my window and heard you singing. That's how I knowed where you was."

"Well, I'm jiggered! That's providence, ent it? I reckon it signifies something. I dunno what."

"My grandpa's got it into his head that you're on your way home."

"Whatever gave him that idea?"

"He's like you. He believes what suits him. But it looks like he's wrong. You ent headed home."

"Well, now, that all depends," Kit said. "Here, let's walk on, shall we? I reckon Ellis is shutting up shop and they'll all be tumbling out over us in a minute."

They walked a few paces along the street, as far as the horse-trough, where Kit dipped his hands into the water and splashed his face. He dried himself on his muffler, taking his time, though well aware of her growing impatience.

"Fancy you at the butcher's," he said. "I can't hardly believe it even now. Which window is yours? The one that's open above the porch? Dammit, there must be a providence in it somewhere, your hearing me singing like that."

A few men came out of The Talbot and went off in various directions, and the voice of one of them, commanding the rest to be silent, echoed around the market cross. The two farmers came out together, passing Beth and Kit at the trough, and one of them, peering closely into their faces, stopped to draw Beth aside.

"Are you all right, you and him?" he asked. "No trouble between you? H'mm? Because if you've got trouble, just say the word and I'll put it right."

"No, no trouble," Beth said.

"This young chap looks a handful to me. You want to watch him. Better still, find a different chap altogether, a chap who's got some heart in his guts."

The man went off, whistling his dog, and Kit laughed softly.

"Drunk as a sawyer!" he said. "Sozzled as cork!"

"Are you coming home with me and my grandfather or ent you?" Beth asked. "I'm waiting for an answer."

"I told you, it all depends!" His gaze was no longer bleary, but wide awake, and he looked at her in a considering way. "If you'll marry me, and make me a partner like your grandpa planned it, I'll come with bells on sure enough."

"You're a fool. You should know by now that I'm not the sort to change my mind."

"Then why did you seek me out when you heard me singing? You could easy have turned a deaf ear."

"My grandfather wants you back, that's why."

"If you really cared what he wanted, you'd marry me."

"I don't want to marry you."

"Then I ent coming," Kit said. "I've got a mind to go to Cornwall. There's a new cathedral been built there and I aim to see if they want joiners."

"Then why stick in Spailes?"

"I lost my tools in the Ennen, that's why, and I'm stopping here till I've got the money to buy more. But that won't take long cos I've got a job at the saw-mill here and I get a good wage every week."

"And spend it all at The Talbot."

"I don't. I earn my drinks by singing for them. Ah, and a few extra coppers besides." He put a hand into his pocket and jingled a few coins. "If I had a squeeze-box I reckon I could make a fortune," he said.

"Then you ent coming home?"

"One day, perhaps," he said, grinning. "I'll come back rich, with a nice little dainty Cornish wife, and then you'll be sorry you missed your chance."

"I reckon I'll live through that," Beth said, and turned away.

"Laws, are you going?" he said. "I ent had time to ask for news."

"I'm tired," Beth said. "I'm wanting my bed."

She crossed the street and went in at the door beside the butcher's shop. She stole upstairs and into her room. While she undressed, there came a skitter of gravel against her window, and when she looked out, Kit was standing just below. He put his hands to his mouth and called softly.

"I wanted to ask about my grannie. Is she keeping all right? Hale and hearty and full of beans?"

"She's pretty fair for her age," Beth said. "She's got Billy Ratchet lodging with her."

"Then I've no call to worry about her," Kit said.

"You never have," Beth said, and withdrew inside, closing the window.

When they returned home from Spailes, Grandfather Tewke spent an hour or more clearing the dust and cobwebs from Kit's old place at the workshop bench. He set up new chops and brockets, and he took out the carved oak chest that Kit had left unfinished and set it ready on the stocks. "My new dockerment chest," he called it. "My new dockerment chest that Kit was making to my specifications. Seems I shall have it finished any time now." He expected Kit almost hourly.

But then, as week after week went by, he grew baffled and tetchy. "Damn and blast! What in hell's name does he think he's up to? Wasting time! Playing the fool all round the landscape! God almighty! And to think we missed him by three little weeks. I could kick myself for that. Three little weeks! It makes me render."

The chest remained on the workshop bench, with the dust collecting again in its unfinished bits of carving. The men were not allowed to move it out of the way. They were not allowed to use Kit's place. And when, after a while, they joked about it, referring to "our invisible mate in the corner" and saying, "I wonder how much invisible chaps like him get paid," or, "Let's ask the Thin Lad there for a loan of his drawshave," Grandfather Tewke would swear at them. "Kit'll be back!" he kept saying. "Kit'll be back as sure as domesday." And Timothy Rolls, with a straight face, would say, "So he will, gaffer, so he will. After all, what's a few years more or less to a young chap like Kit?"

During the gales that winter, a great bough broke
from the oak tree in the yard and smashed right
through the workshop roof. It happened at night, which
was fortunate, for several rafters and even a crossbeam
had fallen in, and the stove-pipe was smashed to smithereens.

Timothy Rolls said the time had come for the oak
to be felled, but Grandfather Tewke, having climbed
up and made an inspection, pronounced the tree safe
and sound. The one broken bough was a fluke, he
said, and he sent Jesse up to saw off the splintered
stump and paint the cut with Stockholm tar.

Repairs began first thing in the morning. The wreckage was all cleared by noon, and the new crossbeam,
rafters, and laths were all up before nightfall. Tiling
began next day.

It was bitterly cold, with a murderous wind cutting
straight from the east, and Beth, going out that afternoon, felt shravelled through to the very bone. Up on
the roof, the men worked in the teeth of the wind, handling tiles that were sticky with frost. There was no
warmth coming up from below, for Grandfather Tewke
had not yet returned from the forge with the new stove-
pipe.

"Nippy, ent it?" said young Fred Lovage.

"Ah, cold enough to be winter," Jesse agreed.

"It is bloody winter, you fool!" said Sam Lovage.

"Why, so it is," Jesse said, surprised.

"Ent you cold, Jesse?" Fred enquired.

"Laws," said Jesse, "I'm that cold I don't hardly know which fingers is mine and which is George's."

"Well, I votes we stop!" said Sam, nursing his hands inside his coat. "What say you, Timmy?"

"Not me!" Timothy answered. "I'm cold enough, working, but if I was to stop, I reckon I'd freeze to death where I stand."

"Christ!" said Sam. "I never knowed such a bleeding wicked wind."

"It's an uncivil wind," said Steve Hewish, his mouth full of nails. "It don't step aside for nobody."

"Christ!" said Sam, rocking backwards and forwards. "Oh, oh! Sweet Jesus Christ."

"Are you getting warmer, swearing like that?" Timmy said severely. " 'Cos we've got female company down below."

Sam looked down and saw Beth.

"I think we should stop. It's murder up here. Nobody should have to work in this."

"I reckon he's right," Beth said to Timmy. "You'll be froze to daglets up there."

"There's only a bit more to do," Timmy said. "We'll be finished by dark-fall if we press on."

Beth went indoors and took three bottles of cognac brandy from her grandfather's cupboard under the stairs. She emptied them into a big stoneware jug and set it on the stove to heat. She put in the juice and rind of six lemons, a grating of nutmeg, a few sprigs of ginger, and a few cloves. Then, as soon as it grew steaming hot, she stirred in a pound of clover honey.

"D'you want a tot of my punch, mother?"

"Me? My goodness! You don't catch me drinking stuff like that!"

"Then I'll take it out to them that need it."

"Well, a taster, perhaps," Kate said quickly. "It's a cold old day, sure enough. I'll have just a taste to warm my tongue."

It was getting dark, and when Beth took the jug of punch and twelve mugs on a tray to the workshop, the men were all down from the roof, stamping about on the hard ground and swinging their arms to make themselves warm.

"Here, Beth, what you got there?" Sam Lovage asked.

"Come in and see and light the lamp."

"Glory be, but that smells good," said Bob Green. "It smells like Christmas at Howsells Hall when I went singing carols as a boy one time."

"Is that there jorum for us?" asked Timothy, coming and sniffing at the jug.

"Ah, she's got some good in her after all," said Sam Lovage. "What say you, our Fred?"

Fred nodded, clenching his teeth to stop them chattering. He received his hot mug between his hands and breathed into it, warming his face in the rush of steam, watching intently as Jesse was served.

"Jesse's too young for this," he said. "He'll be falling over his own feet."

Fred, aged sixteen, was only a year older than Jesse, but liked to give himself grand airs. He was a good enough boy in his way, but spoilt by jealousy.

"You got a slice of lemon in yours?" he asked, trying to look into Jesse's mug.

"Yes, and I aim to keep it," Jesse said.

"What name d'you call this drink by?" asked George Hopson, looking at Beth.

"Punch, I reckon," Beth said.

"I call it jorum," said Timothy Rolls.

"I call it toddy," said Liney the pitman.

"Posset!" said George. "Ah, posset! That's what it is."

"Whatever it is, it's certainly loosened your tongue, George," said Bert Minchin. "That's twice you've spoke in as many minutes."

"It ent posset," said Steve Hewish. "Posset is made with curdled milk."

"Bishop, it's called," said Bob Green. "I had it that time at Howsells Hall."

"Here," said Fred, presenting his empty mug to Beth, "let's have a fill-up."

"Is the roof finished?" Beth asked.

"Every cresset!" Timothy said. "There's only the hole for the stove-pipe will want jointing up, that's all."

"That reminds me!" said Fred, and, taking his father's hammer and chisel, he climbed on a stool and began making marks on the new crossbeam.

"What're you doing, our Fred?"

"You'll see in a moment, our dad."

"Don't bring the whole lot down again for God's sake!"

"There!" said Fred, and, raising the lamp, showed them the date he had cut in the beam: Jan: 15: 1892. "How's that?" he said. "I ment be such a wonderful carver as Kit Maddox, God rest his wandering soul, but I've made a good job of that date, now, ent I?"

Sam, like the rest, was silent, for Grandfather Tewke had come in at the door.

"God almighty! What's all this? The aroma in here fair knocks you down."

"Well," said Timmy, in a mellow voice, "we finished the roof in double quick time, you see, gaffer, and the young miss saw fit to make it a proper occasion, as you might say."

"And is that brandy mine you're all so busy pouring down your throats?"

"Yes, gaffer, and I dunno as I ever tasted better."

"Well, if I ent presuming," said Grandfather Tewke, with heavy irony, "perhaps I might be allowed to join the party?"

"Why, here's your mug set ready, gaffer, and now you must do the same as us—toast your new roof-beam, wishing it a long life and a long watch over all the good work going on underneath it."

The old man was pleased, and drank with relish, but he still looked darkly at young Fred Lovage, who had taken the name of Kit Maddox in vain.

"Here, Fred!" whispered Sam, in the boy's ear. "Say something right-putting, quick sharp."

"Gaffer!" said Fred, with a loud hiccup, and raised

his mug high in the air. "Your very good health and damnation! Amen!"

Every year after that, when January came round, the men would draw Beth's attention to the date on the beam and say: "That's nearly time for our bit of celer-beration, ent it?" And every year, Beth would make up the jug of punch. Grandfather Tewke always grumbled about it, but in fact the little custom pleased him, and he took care never to miss it. Anything that marked the stability and importance of the business was pleasing to him, and he liked, also, to throw his generosity up to the workmen, as when, in the spring of 1894, Timothy Rolls came into the office and asked for a rise in wages.

"Rise? Good God, man, you're getting tip-top wages already. Not to mention perks. You get free kindling. You get plums and apples every autumn. *And* there's the brandy-drinking every new year. So don't speak to me about rises in wages!"

Timothy went, and Grandfather Tewke sat scowling at Beth, who was entering figures in the time-book. He snatched up a pencil and began to sharpen it with quick, savage cuts, sending the shavings across her page.

"As for you!" he said, annoyed by her silence: "I s'pose you think I should give it to them?"

"Not if you can't afford it," Beth said. "That'd be daft, to my way of thinking." She blew the pencil-shavings away and turned the page. "I hope they won't blab about it all over the place, however, 'cos it won't help the business if folk get to hear it's feeling the pinch."

"Pinch? Who said we was feeling the pinch? I never said so! I'm damned if I did!" The old man fell silent, frowning into his open cash-box. "Pinch!" he muttered, after a while. "A well-run business never feels no pinch."

He got up and went out, and Beth heard him speaking to Timothy Rolls.

"About that rise. You can tell the men I'll think it over."

The following Saturday, when they came to the office for their pay, he announced his decision: each man's wage would be eighteen shillings and each boy's would be seven-and-six; and, with a great deal of frowning concentration, he began to count out the piles of coins.

"It's what I expected," Timothy said, "for a good little business like you've got here is always bound to look after its men."

"I suppose," said Sam Lovage, watching as his money was counted out, "it'll all pass to Beth, gaffer, when you're dead and gone?"

"A lot'll depend on her finding a husband."

"Fred," said Sam, "there's a chance for you, son." And he pushed the boy against the desk, where Beth was writing up the wage-book. "I know you're sweet on the young miss."

Grandfather Tewke leant forward and planked Fred's wages into his hand.

"If you can win her, she's yours!" he said. "And my blessings upon you both."

When the men had gone, Beth shut her book with a loud thud.

"You know I don't care tuppence for Fred Lovage, so why encourage him like that?"

"'Cos it makes me laugh," the old man said, "watching him and his great sheep's eyes!"

"He's nothing but a nuisance to *me*," Beth said.

Fred was always wanting to help her in the house or garden. "I'll beat your mats," he would say, or, "I'll come and water them taters for you." But when, with some cunning, she asked him to take a cast of bees, swarming wildly in the garden, Fred was alarmed. "Lumme! I ent much of a hand with bees." And later, when she wanted someone to deal with the rats in the outbuildings, Fred fought shy yet again. "Rats?" he said. "I shouldn't know how to start to begin."

Beth was scornful.

"You're no help to me. I shall have to ask Jesse after all."

"It's about all he's good for!" Fred said. "He ent no carpenter, I tell you that. Jesse Slowsides, we call him in the workshop, 'cos he's as thick as Double Gloster."

"At least he ent scared of a rat!" Beth said. "Nor a bee-sting neither."

It was true that Jesse was a poor carpenter. He took after Walter, and his fingers were all thumbs, as he said. He had no judgment, and once, making a dolly for Beth to use in the wash-tub, he whittled it clean away on the lathe. "Fred's right," he would say. "I'll never be nothing more'n a hedge-carpenter, jobbing about on the farms and such." And Beth, seeing his look of sad surprise whenever some cherished piece of work flew to pieces in his hands, would try her best not to laugh. "Somebody's got to do them jobs, fencing and mending stiles," she said. "And as for Fred, he's just jealous.—You know that."

Fred was jealous even of Jesse's strength and was always challenging him to some contest, such as raising a ladder with one hand, or dragging an elm-butt by rope to the sawpit. Jesse had grown, especially broadways: at seventeen, he was the strongest man in the workshop; and when he won these contests, as he did always, Fred would pretend to be contemptuous.

"You're beefy, you are! All beef and no brain!"

Jesse would merely nod and agree. No one could ever hope to provoke him.

"It was milk that made me the man I am," he would say, with a little smiling glance at Beth. "Yes, it's milk that's done it, building me up so broad and strong."

But although a poor carpenter, Jesse, again like his father, was good with the bees, and Beth was glad to have his help, making new skeps and taking the honey, housing and feeding the bees for the winter, and making hackles to keep them warm. He was good with animals, too, and would hold the pony's head while Beth poured a drench down its throat, or would wean an obstinate calf from the cow.

And he had his own way of killing the rats in the outbuildings, setting traps of his own making, each containing a heavy block that fell and crushed the rat in an instant. He would never use poison because it was slow and caused suffering. "And besides," he said, "if the rat goes and dies in some hole in the wall, you've got blowflies and all sorts infesting the place." He preferred to use his big, clumsy traps. "My ratting engines," he always called them.

Fred Lovage could not understand why Beth should make such a favourite of Jesse.

"Such a duff sort of chap, with nothing up top— I dunno why you bother with him."

"Because," Beth said once, "he happens to be worth a dozen of you."

Fred gave a grin. It never occurred to him that she seriously meant it.

That summer, the summer of 1894, Kit Maddox returned to Huntlip. It was in July, early one morning, and Beth was sharpening the kitchen knives at the grindstone in the workshop yard. A dark shadow fell across her, and when she turned, Kit was standing against the sun, his bag of tools slung over his shoulder. It was four years since he had left Huntlip, and his face was thinner, heightening the look of gipsy sharpness. There were shadowy hollows under the cheekbones, and deep lines in the brown skin, and although he had grown a drooping moustache, it could not hide the hard, bitter cast of his mouth. He was twenty-four but looked much older. His glance was withering. His smile was sour.

"Well?" he said. "Ent you pleased to see me?"

"No," she said. "But there's one who will be, and that's my grandpa."

"He damn well should be. I've come a long way."

From across the yard, the men had seen him. They were gathering round.

"The invisible craftsman . . . In the flesh!"

"Glory be! The spook hisself!"

"Here's the old gaffer," Timothy said.

The old man stood at the edge of the circle, looking Kit over from top to toe, and then, aware of his audience waiting expectantly, he took out his watch and compared it with the workshop clock.

"Maddox!" he said. "You're just about four years late for work this morning.—You'd better look slippy if you're going to make up for lost time." He put away his watch with great deliberation and turned directly to face Kit. "And your first job," he said, "is to finish that dockerment chest I need so badly!"

Every evening now, when she went to the orchard to shut up the hens, she knew that Kit was watching her from the darkness under the trees. Sometimes she heard his soft tread in the long grass, and sometimes, out of the corner of her eye, she caught a movement among the shadows.

Tonight, the air was very soft and still, and as she went about, she could feel the prickle of dew on her forehead. Under the trees a great many moths were fluttering, pale presences in the darkness, and overhead the bats were out, peeping and squeaking. Otherwise, the orchard seemed perfectly silent, perfectly still. And yet she felt certain that Kit was there.

She shooed the last chicken into the hut and let

down the door. She took the pail of eggs and walked back, lifting her skirts from the long grass. Just before reaching the gate of the fold, she stopped to place an egg among the nettles growing alongside the cowshed wall, and as she stooped, she heard soft footsteps close behind her. She straightened and turned, and this time, as she moved towards the gate, it squeaked on its hinges, swinging slowly open before her.

"Kit?" she said sharply. "Is that you?"

"The same," he said, and stepped forward out of the shadows.

"You and your tricks!" she said angrily. "Brevitting about! Always mysterious!"

"What was you doing, putting an egg down there?" he asked.

"For the rats," she said.

"No trap nor poison nor nothing?"

"A rat's suspicious if a trap appears in his run suddenly. But he ent so wary if he's had the gift of an egg once or twice."

She crossed the fold and went into the dairy. She groped for the matches and lit the candle on the pricket. Kit followed, lounging about, watching her as she wiped the eggs and placed them in crocks on the cold slab.

"You look a bit bothered. Did I give you a scare just now out there? Laws! You don't never need to be scared of me."

"Don't I?" she said.

"So that means you are? What a lark! To see you scared! That's a flaming marvel."

"What d'you want, hanging around every night? Why don't you clear off and leave me alone?"

"Same old Beth," he said, laughing. "Up in the air at the slightest thing," and he slouched about restlessly, kicking the floor. "Same old place!" he said. "Same old work going on in the workshop!"

"You was glad to come back to it even so."

"I thought I'd give it another chance . . . See if you'd maybe changed your mind."

Beth, drying her hands, swung round to confront him.

"I haven't!" she said. "You can think again."

"Now I wonder," he said. "Just look at you! The way you're built. And not yet married at nineteen." His glance flickered darkly over her body. "Or maybe it's twenty?—I've lost count."

"Get out," Beth said. "I don't want you. Can't you get that into your twisty brain?"

"I'm going to change your mind," he said. "It should be easy enough, I reckon. No girl's an angel, especially you." He reached past her and douted the candle. "That's better," he said, and spoke so close that his breath was warm against her face. "The dark's a lot better at times like this."

Beth turned and ran, out of the diary and across the fold, but he followed close, catching her skirts and pulling her backwards.

"I'm just about out of patience with you!" he said savagely. "The gaffer's right. It's a waste of time. You need to be took in hand and showed what's good for you once and for all!"

He drew her backwards against his body and dragged her, stumbling and kicking, into the barn. There, in the darkness, he put a knee against her spine and sent her sprawling onto the straw, and as she rolled over, trying to rise, he threw himself heavily full-length upon her, covering her body and spreading his thighs against hers.

"There was never a girl yet that didn't want me to love her!" he said. "You'll see! You'll see! Just shut your noise and stay still and you'll soon find out what you've been missing!"

"I'll kill you!" Beth said. "Swine! Swine! I'll kill you for sure if you don't let me go!"

She arched her spine and threw him over on one side, straining against him and clawing at his face and head. But his grip on her arms only grew more cruel, his fingers grinding her flesh on the bone. He was very strong, forcing her down again, underneath him, his body hard and heavy on hers, his booted feet kicking her ankles to keep them still. He laid his forearm across her throat and leant on her with all his weight.

"What's the odds? What's the odds?" he kept saying. "It's got to happen sooner or later so what's the odds? You're a woman, ent you? You're no different from all the rest!" His arm moved away from her throat, and his hands moved down to pull at her clothes, fumbling between his body and hers. "You're no different! So what's the odds?"

She twisted and writhed, and his arm came down on her throat again. She was being choked. Her head was full of splintering pain. But now, as she fought for breath, she became aware of a yellow light growing and blossoming out of the darkness high overhead. The light took shape, revealing the ladder going up to the hayloft, and there, peering down through the open trapdoor, with a lantern in his hand, was Jesse Izzard. She turned her head, painfully, and tried to cry out. Her voice was just a whisper, but Jesse heard, and called to her that he was coming.

Kit sprang up and ran to the ladder. He gave it a jerk and dragged it from the trapdoor, letting it fall while Jesse was only halfway down. Jesse jumped, backwards and sideways, kicking the ladder out of the way, and the lantern went flying through the air. It fell in the straw and Beth swooped, snatching it up before the oil could spill from the can, and setting it on the wall for safety. When she turned, Jesse was rising on all fours, dazed and shaken. She went to help him, but Kit ran forward, shouldering her to one side, and swung his boot at Jesse's head.

"Spying on me!" he said through clenched teeth. "Spying and prying! Hanging around where you ent welcome!" He caught up a batten of wood and swung it at Jesse's head and shoulders. "Great lumping clod! You always had a habit of getting in my way."

Beth went forward again, but he pushed her back, swinging the batten till it broke in splinters on Jesse's head. But Jesse now was on his feet, moving forward with arms upraised. He hit out clumsily, both fists together, and Kit went stumbling, falling against an old heap of lumber and bringing it crashing down about him. When he rose, he held in his hand an old-fashioned barking-spud, rusty but sharp, with a spear-pointed head.

"You!" he said. "You make me heave, the way you come crawling, letting her use you as a foot-scrape!" He began to advance, the barking-spud pointed at Jesse's face. "I'll teach you to get in my way!"

Beth reached for the hayfork stuck in the straw and swung it hard, knocking the barking-spud out of Kit's hand. She stood before him and levelled the prongs at his chest.

"Get out!" she said. "Before I spike you like a cockroach!"

Kit was nursing his bruised fingers, looking at her in pain and loathing. He hated any harm to come to his craftsman's hands.

"I mean it!" Beth said. "Get out this minute, else I'll spike you!"

"D'you think I'd stay?" he said shrilly, and spat on the ground at her feet as he passed.

She fetched lint and iodine from the office and a dipper of water from the pump, and returned to the barn where Jesse waited.

"Sit down," she said, "under the light where I can see you."

She knelt before him and cleaned his face, wetting the lint and mopping the blood from his forehead, his eyes, his lips, his cheekbones.

"Can you still see?" she asked him.

"Ah, just about," Jesse answered.

"And can you breathe through that swollen nose?"

"I reckon I can," he said, sniffing.

"Is your heart still beating?"

"Why, that's ticking away like an eight-day-clock."

"Then it seems you'll very likely live."

"Golly, yes, I'll live to be ninety!"

"What was you doing up in the loft? Setting your rat-traps? That's late, surely, if you've been there since the workshop closed."

"I've been working at Anster and didn't knock off till after seven. Then I cut over here to see to the traps before going home."

"You took your time letting on you was up there."

"Well," Jesse said, not meeting her eye, "the gaffer's been hinting that you and Kit would soon be getting teamed up."

"And you believed it? Knowing how I always hated him?"

"Well . . . Girls've got a way of changing their minds."

"Not this one," Beth said, and began, with a new piece of lint, to dab iodine on his cuts. "Hold hard. I'm going to hurt you."

"That's all right. You go ahead. You're doing me up humpty-dinker."

"Now give me your hands," she said, and winced as she saw them. "You're a mess and a wreckage. You are truly."

Under the dirt and the dried blood, the flesh was scraped back, red and raw, from his knuckles. The skin came off in shreds on the lint.

"Seems to me it's time we got married," she said quietly. "I've been looking after you one way and another ever since I can remember.—I might just as well be your proper wife."

Jesse was looking down at his hands, where they rested in hers. He was perfectly still, and his eyes, half hidden under their fair, almost colourless lashes, seemed emptied of all thought.

"Laws," Beth said. "That little notion's fell in stony ground and no mistake." She folded his fingers into his palms and pushed his hands together into his lap. "I never heard such a silence before in all my days."

"You're having me on," Jesse said.

"And why not indeed? I was always one for a good joke."

"Married!" he said. "I must be twiddly in the head."

"You ent too keen? Well, that's natural, really, I suppose. You're only a green young chap after all. You're only seventeen."

"I'm a man all the same!"

"Seventeen," she said, busy putting things away. "That's a good two years or more younger than me."

"That don't matter, does it, Beth?"

"You tell me!"

"Well, married!" he said. "We've always been friends, you and me, but I never thought of our getting married."

"Then you'd better think now," she said coolly. "You might not get a better offer."

A little smile moved across Jesse's face, followed at once by a wry grimace as the cut on his lip cracked open again.

"I don't understand it," he said, wiping the blood away on his hand. "A girl like you, taking a fancy to a chap like me . . ." He watched her setting aside the bowl of water, the iodine bottle, the packet of lint. "Beth?" he said. "Is that how it is? Have you took a special fancy to me?"

"Now is that likely?" she exclaimed. "A much more clumsier article I never met in a month of Sundays! Nor a slower one neither. As if I was likely to fancy you!"

"Ah, just as if!" he said sadly. "I reckon I knowed you was having me on."

With a little cry, half impatience and half pain, Beth leant forward and drew his head against her breast. She held him close, rocking him roughly yet tenderly backwards and forwards, like a mother rocking a child. She let him go and leant against him, kissing him fully upon the mouth. She felt him tremble and heard him draw his breath in a sigh.

"Here," he said, in a deep voice. "You shouldn't ought to do things like that. It puts ideas in a chap's head."

"I'm glad to hear it. I thought I was making up to a stone."

"Oh, no! I'm a man sure enough. Make no mistake about that!"

He put out a hand and touched her hair, lightly,

shyly, with the tips of his fingers. He looked at her with astonished eyes.

"Why, yes . . . I reckon it's all as plain as plain . . . And yet it's a big surprise just the same. Here, lumme, do you know what?—I shall have to speak to your grandpa!"

"Not just yet," Beth said. "Leave it to me to pave the way."

Kate, looking up as Beth entered the kitchen, dropped her needlework into her lap.

"Goodness, girl, what *have* you been up to, getting yourself in such a mess? And what're them bruises on your neck?"

"Well, they're bruises, ent they?" Beth said.

Her grandfather laid his newspaper on the table and turned himself round in his chair. He looked her over from head to foot.

"Seems like you've been having a tumble!"

"Seems I have," Beth agreed.

"So brazen?" he said, looking at her with a gleam of satisfaction. "Ah, well, so long as it ends the way it ought . . . Have you fixed the day?"

"Not the day, no. Only the man."

"Good! Good! I told Kit it was time he cut rough with you and your nonsense."

"It's not Kit I'm going to marry—it's Jesse Izzard," Beth said.

The old man's face became rigid, the fine nostrils stretched wide, the fine lips pressed together, bloodless and pale.

"Am I hearing you right?" he asked, dangerously.

"Yes, you are, and I mean what I say."

"Then you'd better change your meaning quick sharp or I'll lay you flat on that there floor! D'you hear me, eh?"

"The man on the moon could hear you. There's no need to rant and rave like that."

"You know what I was doing in Chepsworth this morning? I was seeing Baines about drawing up a deed of partnership for Kit and me. Yes, you can stare, girl! Tewke and Maddox!—A good pair of names! And all you've got to do is change from one to the other. God almighty! The business means almost as much to you as me. It's all a matter of family pride and you can't deny it."

"I don't," Beth said. "But why not make it Tewke and Izzard?"

"Izzard!" he said, almost spitting the name in his contempt. "Are you mad?"

"Jesse may not be a craftsman but he knows the trade and he's as honest as the day. As for the business side, I can always manage that."

"Hah! You've got it all worked out, I can see! No doubt you're counting the days till I'm dead?"

"No," Beth said. "It was you that started on about the future, not me."

"I'll be the one to finish too! Now get off to bed! Perhaps a night's sleep will clear your brain."

"I'd sooner we talked it out now."

"I've said my say. Get off to your bed."

"I shan't change my mind. I shall marry Jesse whatever happens."

"We'll see about that! We'll see what a bit of quiet reflection will do for you. Ah, reflection!—When you've thought about saying goodbye to the business, and this old house with its bit of land, and the comfort of having some money behind you. Now get out of my sight! I don't want to hear another word!"

And so Beth, exchanging a glance with her mother, went upstairs to bed.

At breakfast next day, and again at midday, Grandfather Tewke refused to speak. He stumped in, stared through the window all the time he was eating, and stumped out again, grim-faced.

Beth kept away from the workshop all day, to avoid Kit Maddox. Jesse was still working at Anster and would come after work to see to his traps. He had said so. They had planned to meet. But that evening, although she waited for him in the fold, he did not appear, so she went indoors, where Kate and the old man were already eating, and sat down to tea.

"Is Jesse working late again this evening?"

The old man made no reply.

"He said he'd be here to see me at six."

Again, the old man remained silent, pushing water-cress into his mouth and chewing stolidly.

"Well," Beth said. "Seems I'll just have to go to Anster and see for myself."

"Izzard ent there," her grandfather said.

"Then where is he?"

"I went to Anster and paid him off. He'll have been busy today, looking for work."

Beth rose from the table.

"Where d'you think you're off to?" he demanded.

"To the Pikehouse," she said.

"Oh, no, you don't! You stop where you are!"

"I'll do as I choose," Beth said.

"Go through that door, miss, and you go for ever!"

"So be it," Beth said.

"Beth, you can't!" her mother pleaded. "Please sit down and think things over."

"Don't worry!" the old man said. "She knows which side her bread is buttered. She ent leaving."

"But I am," Beth said. "I've got no option so I'll get my things."

"Things," he shouted. "You take no things from out of here! If you're going, you can go the same way you came in the first place, empty-handed and living on air!"

Beth stood for a moment in silence. Then she crossed the kitchen and laid a hand on her mother's shoulder.

"Oh, Beth, don't go!" Kate said, weeping. "Not like this! It's all wrong. You must think things over."

"I've done my thinking," Beth said. "Ages ago, when I first saw this coming."

"At least say some sort of word to your grandpa!"

"No, no words!" the old man said, staring before him. "Let her go to ruin the way she's chose. I don't want no words from her!"

So Beth, in silence, and without looking back, left the house that had been her home for eight years. She took the short-cut across the fields, crossed the Derrent by the stepping-stones, and climbed the steep slopes of Millery wood. She walked along the Norton road, turned onto the old turnpike, and so came to the little Pikehouse, lonely beside the edge of the wasteland, its white walls made pink by the level rays of the evening sun. Jesse was hoeing the garden. He waded out from among the beans and came to meet her.

"Glory! I've been thinking and thinking of you all day."

"Is that why you fled without trying to see me?"

"I was stumped," he said. "The gaffer came to Anster and gave me the push. He said if I saw you he'd cut you off. I'd got to forget what you and me had fixed between us, 'cos you'd gone and changed your mind, he said."

"Oh, ye of little faith!"

"You mean we *are* getting married then after all?"

"I'm sunk if we don't, 'cos I've been sent packing the same as you."

"Glory!" he said. "So you've left all that to come to me?" He leant on the handle of his hoe and looked at her with a radiant face. "And all so quiet and simple, too, like rain coming down, or the sun shining, or the stars winking and twinking at night-time."

"We must talk," Beth said. "You and me and Goody together."

"Why, yes," he said, and flung down his hoe. "A parliament, that's what we want."

Goody was busy gathering seed from the stocks and marigolds and love-in-a-mist that grew in the garden behind the house.

"Oh, it's you!" she said gruffly, straightening up in front of Beth. "I thought I heard a durdle of voices." Her queer little crooked face was hostile. Her eyes glimmered. Her voice was sharp. "And what's the latest freak with you Tewkeses?"

"Did Jesse tell you we're getting married?"

"He told me something. In his cock and bull way."

"You don't seem too pleased?" Beth said.

"It's a mix-up to me, a chap like Jesse, poor as a mouse, marrying into a family like yours. How's it going to sort itself out? Your grandpa ent exactly blessed the notion. Oh, no, not he! He's gone dead against it and Jesse here has got the push!"

"So have I," Beth said.

"Eh?" Goody said. "What's that you say?"

"I've got the push and all," Beth said, "with nothing more than the clothes I stand up in. I'm poorer than you've ever been in your life, Goody, for I'm out on the road."

"That's different!" Goody said, and her dark little eyes searched Beth's face. "You're one of us. Come indoors and eat some supper. This is your home from now on."

In the kitchen, she lit a small lamp and placed it in the centre of the table. She set out a loaf, a wedge of cheese, and a jar of pickles. She set out three old horn beakers, much scratched and dulled, and a stone jug full of small beer.

"Sit up," she said, attacking the loaf with a great curved knife, "and don't be afraid to eat your fill."

"I shan't," Beth said, "for I had no tea."

"Lumme, you must be starved," Jesse said.

They sat together, the three of them, in the circle of light from the lamp in their midst. The crusty bread and the crumbly cheese were the best Beth had ever eaten, and the beer, although its mildness teased her tongue, was the best beer she had ever drunk. She said so, and Goody was pleased.

"The only hunger we've known here is the hunger that gives a savour to plain food. We're a lot luckier than some in this world."

She leant forward and refilled Beth's beaker.

"You'll sleep with me for the time being. Then when you're married, you two shall have the bed upstairs and I'll have the one down here."

"I shouldn't like that, you giving up your bed for us."

"That don't worry me," Goody said. "I'm lost

in that bed since Walter's been gone. It's a good featherbed that we made ourselves when we was first married. It's a pity not to fill it as it's meant to be filled."

"I'm bringing nothing to this marriage. Not so much as a packet of pins."

"You've brought your health and strength, though, ent you? And as it's luckily harvest time, there's plenty of work for everybody. Jesse's already seen Mr Yarby. He starts at Checketts with me tomorrow. And you can go down with us first thing. You ent afraid of field work?"

"Not Beth!" Jesse said. "She ent afraid of nothing on earth."

"You might as well marry as soon as maybe. You can see Parson Chance tomorrow evening."

"Just think," Jesse said. "Beth and me!—Mister and Missus! I can't hardly credit it even now. A chap like me—no looks nor nothing—getting hisself a wife like Beth."

"What d'you mean, a chap like you?" Goody said. "You're a fine upstanding shape, ent you, with arms and legs and all the bits and pieces that make up a man? What more should a woman want?"

"Here we go!" Jesse said. "I've started it now!"

"I've seen worse than you, boy," Goody said, spearing a pickle in the jar. "What's wrong with your looks, apart from them bruises? It's a good enough face as faces go. It's a good strong man's face, with plenty of bone in it, and plenty of chin, and you've got your father's good clean blue eyes. And anyway! When the candle goes out last thing at night, it ent what you look like that matters then, boy!"

"Here!" Jesse said, growing red to the ears. "What a thing to say! Right out like that! In front of Beth."

"You're the one that's ruddling up, boy."

"Ah, well . . ." Jesse said, looking everywhere but at Beth. "You women've got us beat, I know, when it comes to having the last word."

"We've got you beat altogether," Goody said.

The vicar of Eastery-with-Scoate, the Reverend Peter Chance, was known for plain speaking. He stood on his hearth, a tall man with a big brown face and a shock of grey hair, and looked hard at Beth and Jesse, sitting before him.

"How long have you known each other?" he asked.

"Nearly all our lives," Beth said.

"And this quarrel with your grandfather? Who's to blame, you or he?"

"Me, I suppose, for having the nerve to choose my own husband."

"Jesse's made a wise choice," the vicar said. "A wife who's a fighter is worth her weight in gold to a labouring man."

Jesse, sitting perched on the edge of his chair, convinced that its delicate carved legs could never support his full weight, gave a solemn nod.

"Just so long as she don't fight me!"

"You can't have it all ways, Jesse, my boy. Now tell me this. Shall you have children, do you think?"

"Indeed, I hope so," Beth said.

"Why, yes," said Jesse. "Why, yes, indeed."

"How many, d'you think?"

"As many as come," Beth replied.

"Ah," said Jesse, and was lost in thought.

"A wedding it is, then," the vicar said. "But one word of advice to you both. Hot heads and hot words should always be let to cool before bed-time, especially in marriage. Remember that."

Afterwards, walking back down the fields to the Pikehouse, Jesse laughed.

"Mr Chance should know about tempers if anyone does. Why, he got in such a paddy with the verger once, he said he would ring for matins hisself, and he pulled so hard he cracked the bell! He did! Honest John! You won't get melody for your wedding. You'll only get chanks."

"We can always stop our ears."

"He's a card, Mr Chance. Last winter, one time, at evensong it was, when folk was on the fidget with colds and such, he upped and said right out in the prayer, 'Have pity, O Lord, on these thy afflicted gathered here, for a worse lot of snivelling, tissucking folk I have yet to meet in a Christian congregation.' Right out like that, in his parson's voice, as though it was Scripture."

"I'm sure he never said tissucking."

"He did! Honest John! You ask Goody when we get home."

Jesse fell silent, walking along with his hands in his pockets, watching Beth with a sidelong glance.

"What're we pelting along like this for?" he asked, stopping. "We should be going nice and slowly, getting acquainted, as they say."

"We'll soon be tied together for life. There'll be plenty of time for getting acquainted."

"Well, what about something on account?"

Beth went forward into his arms and let him kiss her, and they stood for a while under a thorn tree, where the evening wind was riffling noisily through the leaves. They stood together enfolded in warmth, two beating hearts, two throbbing pulses, their blood moved by the same force. Then she drew away.

"We'd better get home. Goody'll be waiting supper for us."

"We'd better, I reckon, before I get dangerous," Jesse said.

"Three more weeks," Beth said, "and you can be as dangerous as you please."

It was harvest time, and they worked in the fields from first light, when the dew-drenched corn surrendered its strongest scent to the mowers; on through the long burning day; until after dark-fall, when the cooling dew descended again, and the big yellow moon came to light their last labours.

Burning sun was the order of every day that harvest. The fields were on fire with ripening oats and wheat and barley, and the hot brightness dazzled the eyes. Sometimes, bent double, binding the sheaves, Beth felt overwhelmed by the tide of the harvest, the tide of the corn with its waves of hot brightness going on and on. As she stooped and straightened, stooped and straightened, erecting the sheaves, the hot white gold land went tilting madly, the blue sky heaved, and the great tide of brightness threatened to drown her under its waves.

Day after day, her ears were filled with the rattle and whirr of the reaping-machines, the calls of the men, the harsh tseep-tsawp tseep-tsawp of somebody sharpening the blade of a scythe. Day after day, the sun swung round and the circles of light went spreading outwards, wheel upon wheel, radiating, it seemed to her, from the two very sheaves she held in her hands, as she built the corn-cocks up and up and down the fields of stubble, along the paths of sunlight and the paths of wind.

And when a lull came, and the waggons had creaked and rumbled away, and two or three fields were clean and empty, the women would be there, waiting to enter the stubble to glean. Sometimes, in the evening, the men would join them, and Jesse would work beside Beth and Goody. Then the jokes would fly, especially if the three Jimmys happened to be there.

"Does she never laugh, Jesse, this sweetheart of yours?" asked Jimmy Winger.

"Not to your face," Jesse said. "She wouldn't want to hurt your feelings."

"She don't speak English, I don't suppose? Well, she wouldn't, would she, coming from Huntlip as I hear she do?"

"There's good pickings in this field," said Jimmy Shodd. "Some sheaves got forgot this afternoon, so I broke them up and tossed them about a bit all over. Ah, and Mr Yarby catched me at it, though he never said so much as a word. If he had, I'd have answered him straight—it's in the Scriptures, black and white, that if a few sheaves get forgot in the fields they should not be gone back for but left for the sake of the widows and orphans and them that is strangers in the land.

"Jimmy's a great man for the Scriptures," said

Hilda, his wife, working beside him. "The Scriptures and dirty songs.—Jimmy can't be beat for them."

"Was they really forgot, them sheaves you tossed about?" asked Jesse.

"Indeed they was! I was the one that did the forgetting!"

"Yes," said Hilda. "Jimmy's a great man for giving the Scriptures a chance to come true."

Their jokes would fly, but after a while, being bone weary, they would fall silent, inching along, bent double, gathering up the spikes of corn, till the evening drew in, and, in twos and threes, they went from the field.

Beth rarely spoke to Jesse during the day, but their work in the fields bound them together hour by hour, till a current of awareness ran in their blood. The work they did, bringing in the harvest, brought a feeling of richness: the money they earned together was wealth; the corn they gleaned was more than wealth; but the feeling of richness came from something beyond their little hoard of coins and grain: they were reaping their youth and their strength together; they were reaping their lives, and the harvest was a good one.

They were married on the third Sunday in September. Kate was there to give Beth away. There was no congregation, but a number of Eastery villagers, mostly women and children, hurried up on hearing the bell and were waiting in the churchyard when Beth and Jesse came out of the church.

As they stepped out into the sunshine, the bell's flat, dissonant clangour was abruptly stilled, and in the little shock of silence, Goody glared at the vicar.

"What's up with Jack Main? It's a poor bell, I know, but it ought to clank out longer than that for a wedding, surely?"

"Have patience, woman," the vicar reproved her.

Goody, with new yellow daisies adorning her hat, stood scowling ferociously through her veil. Kate clutched her prayer-book and looked nervous, blinking short-sightedly all around. And Jesse, almost a stranger in Sunday blacks and stiff white collar, stood to attention at Beth's side.

"Ah," said the vicar. "Now listen to that!"

Heads cocked, they all listened, and over the fields, faintly but sweetly, came the ringing of Huntlip church bells.

"There, now," said Jesse, in a hushed voice. "They're ringing for us. Huntlip bells."

"Yes," Beth said. "Yes, so they are."

"And why not indeed?" Goody demanded. "The bride's own parish! So they ought to ring!"

"Parson Wisdom and I are good friends,—when we're not falling out," said Parson Chance. "We arranged the ringing as a surprise. Now, if the wedding party will go ahead, I'll follow as soon as I've shed my surplice."

"Right," said Goody, "we'll take it slow."

Arm in arm, Beth and Jesse led the way, receiving a shower of rice and corn from the children ranged along the path. Kate and Goody walked behind. But now, as the little party turned towards the gate that opened onto the field-path, three figures stepped out from behind the yew trees. The first was Kit Maddox, the second Fred Lovage, and the third the Huntlip simpleton, Jumper Lane, who carried a bulging sack on his shoulder.

"What's this?" said Goody, pushing in front of Jesse and Beth and going up to Kit Maddox. "Get out of our way. You don't look right for a wedding to me."

"Well, we are," Kit said. "We couldn't find a sweep so we brought the next best thing instead. Here, Jumper! Let's have the sack!"

The soot, in handfuls, flew through the air. It hit first Jesse then Beth in the face, and spattered down all over their clothes. Goody, with a howl of rage, leapt forward and caught Jumper Lane a resounding smack on the side of his head. He staggered back against Fred Lovage, and the sack of soot fell and burst on the path.

"I'll learn you!" Goody cried. "Coming and spoiling people's weddings! Take that! And that! And you, Jesse, get Beth and her mother out by the lychgate. I'll soon deal with this pack of whelps!"

Jesse took Beth and Kate by the arm. But Beth hung back and would not go.

"No! You know what Kit's like. He'll do Goody a serious mischief if he gets roused."

Kit and his two companions were scooping the soot up from the path and pelting Goody in the face. She was almost blinded, and Jesse was going forward to help her, when out of the church, the skirts of his cassock flying behind him, burst the Reverend Peter Chance, wielding the heavy pastoral staff and shouting out in a great warlike voice as he rushed upon the trouble-makers.

"Out! Out!" he bellowed, and, using the oaken staff as a cudgel, he laid about him with all his strength. "Out of my churchyard! Or we'll dig you a grave where you fall! Out, the lot of you, vicious scum!"

Again and again the sun glinted upon the cross as the staff rose and fell, belabouring shoulders and heads without mercy, driving the three young men down the path. The vicar pursued them, thud, thud, till they broke ranks and ran, out of the lychgate and headlong down the village street, followed by the jeers of the villagers in the courtyard.

"Good!" said the vicar, coming back across the graves. "That's put them to rout, eh, Goody? We two together, like Horatius and Lars Porsena, eh?"

"Ah," said Goody, peering at him with blackened face, through her blackened veil. "Exactly so!"

"Vicar," said the verger, standing by with a long face. "The pastoral staff, sir! Of all things!"

"And what better purpose could the staff serve than driving the Vandal from a Christian precinct? Oh, here you are, man! You can take it. You're a sight too pious for me."

And the vicar turned back to the wedding party.

The table, covered with a blue chequered cloth, was already laid with the wedding breakfast. There was farmhouse cheese, mature and strong, and soft summer cheese, flavoured with parsley, chervil, and chives. There were devilled eggs in nests of lettuce; chicken pasties garnished with cress; and plates piled high with the flat griddle scones, full of currants and raisins, that Goody always referred to as Welshcakes. There was bread of Goody's own making and pale salty butter from Checketts farm. There was strong beer and elder wine.

"You," said the vicar, pointing a finger in Beth's face, "have not been in church these past three Sundays."

"Of course not," said Goody, before Beth could speak. "It's bad luck for a girl to hear her own banns called."

"That's rank superstition, Goody Izzard."

"Is it?" said Goody. "Let me fill your glass."

"That Kit Maddox," Kate said to Beth. "He'll come to a bad end one of these days."

"Now remember, don't let my grandfather put on you, milking the cows and things like that. See that he gets a girl to help."

"Ladies and gentlemen!" Jesse said. "Goody here says I've got to speak. She's right, I suppose . . . But I dunno . . . well, it's like this here, and I'd better begin!" He stood very straight and stiff at the table, squeezing a Welshcake to crumbs in his fingers. "Well!" he said, clearing his throat. "I don't exactly know what to say. Unless it's thanks . . . from Beth and me . . . on behalf of us both, I mean to say . . . And God bless all here!"

"Bravo!" said the vicar. "And I too will speak, pledging your health in this very good beer. May your pitcher never once be empty, and may you know a good old age!"

When Kate had gone, with the vicar to keep her company part of the way, Beth and Jesse changed their clothes and worked in the garden. Jesse dug the winter potatoes and stacked them away in straw in

the shed. He dug the carrots and shallots and onions
and laid them out to dry in the sun. Beth picked the
last of the scarlet runners, setting a few aside for
seed, and taking the rest in to Goody, who sliced
them and laid them in salt in crocks.

The day was soft and warm and misty. The sun
seemed reluctant to leave the sky. They worked on,
Beth and Jesse, till even the twilight had faded away;
till the little lamp was lit indoors and Goody called
them in to supper.

On the kitchen table, the blue and white plates
were set out ready; the old horn beakers and
stoneware jug; and a baked ham with brown sugar
glaze and pale pink meat that came curling off in
delicate shreds as Goody carved with her big sharp
knife. There was beetroot, sliced, in a little dish; crisp
green watercress from the spring; jars of chutney and
Chepsworth mustard.

"My stars," said Jesse, coming to sit beside Beth at
the table. "A feast this morning and another tonight!
It's worth getting married, to get food like this."

"H'mm!" said Goody. "If that's all you expect from
marriage, I must take you aside for a little talk, boy."

"That's enough!" said Jesse, reddening. "You get on
with cutting that ham!"

"Ent you mighty!" Goody said. "There's nothing
like marriage for making a man masterful all of a
sudden."

At nine o'clock she drove them to bed, and they
climbed the steep stairs to the small bedroom under
the roof. The featherbed, made ready by Goody, was
plumped up high and covered over with a patchwork
rug. Beth's nightdress lay on one pillow, Jesse's
nightshirt on the other. The room, so small beneath
its steeply pitched ceiling, held the day's warmth, and
smelt of the day's sweetness and ripeness. It smelt,
too, of warm thatch.

Beth went and leant at the open window, looking
out at the starlit night, and Jesse came to lean beside
her. The window was small. There were wedged to-

gether, shoulder and thigh, and Beth could smell the
clean warmth of his body.

"It's a queer funny thing," he said, "feeling amazed
and yet not amazed at the same time. D'you feel like
that?"

They turned to each other, and she leant against
him, within his arms.

"Jesse, put your hand on my breast," she
whispered.

To Jesse, the sight of his womenfolk working in the
fields was a thing that gave him a sense of wellbeing,
and a sense of pleasure, new every day. "My Two,"
he called them, when mentioning them to the other
workers. "Have you seen My Two this morning?" or,
"My Two are late coming up with the oneses.—I must
speak to them sharpish about that."

In winter, they worked the chaff-cutter in the barn,
or chopped up swedes, or mended sacks. In spring,
they picked stones from the ploughed fields, thinned
the turnips or sugar-beet, or hoed the weeds from
between the rows of drilled corn. In summer, they dug
potatoes and worked on the hay. And he would come
on them, sometimes unexpectedly, sometimes knowing where they would be, but always with the same
little jolt of pleasure that made him laugh to himself,
inside.

Beth, in the fields, stood out among all the other women as a ringdove stands out in a flock of jackdaws. Her shining fair hair was always smoothly coiled about her head, and she carried herself with a certain dignity, free and easy and sure of herself.

He would come upon her, about the farm, when she looked so fine and carried herself with such an air; when her glance was calm and the tone of her voice as cool as water; and through his blood would run a quivering shock of amazement, because she was his. He would come on her with a sense of pride in her coolness and remoteness, but always, underneath, there would be a darker, more secret pride, because of all that lay between them; because he had seen her with tumbled hair, with eyes closed and lips parted, and had heard her voice crying out in need. Wherever he went now, he carried the touch of her hands about him, and the shape of her body imprinted on his. And because of what there was between them; because she had made him aware of himself and his power; now, when he walked about the fields, stalking like a giant over the land, he carried with him a terrible strength and a terrible knowledge.

But there came a time when the sight of her at work in the fields filled him with horror. He wanted to rail at her and drive her out. But Goody said to leave her be, and the three Jimmys offered words of wisdom, each according to his kind.

"It's yourself you should watch," said Jimmy Shodd. "I've been through it and I know. Pain here! Pain there! It's the man that suffers every time."

"You should've took my advice," said Jimmy Winger, "and stayed a bachelor like you begun."

"Don't worry, Jesse," said Jimmy Ling, who had once been a shepherd at Chepsworth Park. "There's always more lambs lost than there is ewes."

Every evening now, Goody drove him out of the house, into the garden to chop wood.

"Off you go!" she would say. "Great solid ornament, lapsing about under my feet. There's plenty for

you to do outside. We'll want good fires this coming
winter. So off you go and work yourself out."

"Shouldn't we ought to get Mrs Tewke?"

"No," Beth said. "My mother's no good at times
like this. It's Goody I trust. She knows what to do."

Jesse nodded, but doubtfully. He had always had
faith in Goody in everything, but now, suddenly, he
was unsure.

"Ah," he said. "I suppose she does."

"No ah about it," Goody said. "Go swing your axe
and work yourself out."

And so he worked, every evening, till the firewood
rose to the roof of the shelter and overflowed on either
side.

The days were open and mild that autumn. The
ground was moist but not wet, and ploughing was
easy, especially on the stubble lands. So mild was the
weather that one day in late October, he saw three
swallows passing over, four or five weeks or more
after the main flocks had gathered and gone. The
date was Friday the twenty-fifth. He had reason to
remember.

He was ploughing the field known as the Outmost,
and whenever he reached the top of the rise, he would
stop for a while to rest his team, and to take a good
long look at the Pikehouse. He could see it plainly,
small in the distance, with smoke rising from its
chimney, with sunlight glinting on its windows, and
with, it seemed to him, a great air of stillness upon it,
alone there in its square of garden, between the lonely
turnpike road and the lonely wasteland. He stood for
a while, watching the house with screwed-up eyes,
then turned again and ploughed down the slope.

It was wheat-stubble land, with a thick growth of
couch-grass and bindweed, and the plough went
through with a loud ripping of roots and stems. The
soil heeled and rippled over, and the pale stubble
vanished beneath the dark wave. With each new
furrow, a new breath of the earth's smell was released
on the air, and the ground steamed in the warm sun.
Going downhill, the two horses, Goldie and Jessamy,

kicked up pebbles that rang on their shoes; they travelled swiftly, with a creaking of harness and a jingle of brass. Behind him, Jesse could hear the crying of peewits coming in to feed on the ploughland, and in the neighbouring field below, Jimmy Shodd was singing a favourite song.

> "I'm only a poor young ploughman
> And I cannot afford to wed
> But I've got a girl who is willing
> To share my barley-straw bed.
>
> "Oh, my sons will have to be working
> And my dear little daughter the same
> Before I can marry their mother
> And give her an honest name."

When Jesse got to the bottom, Jimmy was looking over the hedge.

"Any sign at the Pikehouse?"

"No, nothing," Jesse said.

"You feeling all right? No cramps nor nothing?"

"No, nothing," Jesse said. "How much longer d'you think it'll be?"

"As long as your missus can spin it out," said Jimmy. "They're deadly wonderful people, women, for spinning things out."

Jesse turned and ploughed up the slope, and this time, when he reached the summit, something was fluttering in the Pikehouse garden. It was Goody's signal. She had hung a table-cloth out on the line.

For a moment he stared, and then, scarcely knowing what he was doing, he pushed through the hedge and began to run.

When he burst into the kitchen, Goody was bending over the fire, and she turned on him in a passion of anger.

"What're you doing? D'you want Mr Yarby down on your tail?"

"Can't I see her? Just for a minute?"

"No!" Goody said, pushing him back towards the door. "You just wait till you've finished work."

"How is she, then? Is she all right?"

"You saw my signal, you great noop! That means she's dandy and the same applies to your baby daughter. So get back to work or I'll give you what-for!"

When Jesse went back to ploughing the Outmost, Jimmy Shodd was no longer singing, but plodding along woodenly, intent on his furrow. Jesse looked round and soon saw the reason: Mr Yarby was watching from the gate of the Uptops.

Betony lay in the cot on rockers that Jesse had made during the summer. Her face, just visible under the blankets, was red and wrinkled. Her mouth was open; her eyes tight shut.

"Shouldn't she ought to have a pillow?"

"No. Goody says not."

"She's a nice little baby, ent she?" he said. "All puckered and pink . . . She's a tidy size, too, con-sidering." With a nervous finger, he drew back the blankets an inch or two. "What's up with her hands? They're all tied up in little cosies! There ent nothing wrong with her hands, is there?"

"It's to stop her scratching herself with her nails, that's all."

"Nails," he said, with a little laugh. "There, now. Just fancy that."

He put the candle back in its place and sat down on the stool by the bed. Beth was brushing and combing her hair, twisting it into a smooth golden hank where it lay on her shoulder. While he watched, she pinned it up at the back of her head, then dropped her arms with a tired sigh. Her face was pale. There was sweat like a dew on her lip and forehead.

"Are you all right?" Jesse asked. "Ah, that's all very well for you to nod so serenely, but you've had a time of it, I know."

"It's often hard work with the first, Goody says. But it won't be so bad next time."

"Laws, there ent going to be no next time, surely? Oh dear me no! We ent going all through that again!"

Watching her anxiously, he saw her smile.

"We've done all right, ent we?" he said. "We've got a nice little baby there, and I reckon we'll call it a day now."

Goody came up into the bedroom and went to the cot. She spoke to Jesse over her shoulder.

"Are you going to eat your supper tonight, boy?"

"I ent all that hungry to tell you the truth."

"Great fool!" she said. "Great dromedary!"

"I saw three swallows today when I was ploughing the Outmost," he said. "Swallows, mind, on the twenty-fifth of October! Does that mean anything, I wonder?"

"It means they'll be late getting wherever it is they're going to," Goody said. "Africa, ent it? Some place like that?"

"I thought it might be an omen," he said.

"Omens indeed! Great gobbermoocher!"

"Well, what d'you think of my daughter, then, eh? Gawping into the cradle like that! That's given you something to think about, being a grannie, ent it? So what d'you think of her? You tell me that."

"She'll do," Goody said, "to be going on with."

He was carting muck in the ten acre piece just above the farm. The weather was still open and mild, although it was almost the end of November, and he sweated even in his shirt-sleeves.

Goldie, the mare, did not care for strangers, and when a rider appeared in the next field, she put back her ears and began to fidget between the shafts. Jesse jumped down and went to soothe her. He held her head against his chest.

The next field was a narrow strip of three acres, and was newly planted with spring cabbage. Jesse did not at first recognise the rider, but when she walked her big black mare straight across the cabbages, carelessly treading them into the ground, he knew it was Mrs Lannam of Scoate.

She drew rein a little way off, and sat in silence, waiting for Jesse to meet her glance. She was long-faced and pale, with strange-coloured eyes, almost yellow, set wide apart under pencilled brows.

"What's the matter with that mare? Is she fractious?"

"No, ma'am. She just don't like strangers."

"You're a stranger, yourself. To me, at least."

"Not a stranger, ma'am. I've lived at the Pikehouse all my life."

"Oh! You're Goody Izzard's son Jesse. Yes, I can see it now, though you've changed a lot since I last saw you. Indeed, you've grown into quite a personable man." And she looked him over, with pale-shining gaze. "I heard you had married. Is that so?"

"These fourteen months," Jesse said. "And got a baby daughter too."

"Good God!" she exclaimed. "You make it sound like a miracle, man!"

Jesse blinked and looked away. Her tone of voice, and the mocking way she looked at him, made him feel awkward and ill-at-ease.

"I must call on your wife some time," she said, and rode off past him.

On leaving the field he met Jimmy Shodd, also returning with an empty cart, and they drove down side by side.

"I see you've had company, Jesse, boy. You want to look out or you'll land in a pickle."

"Eh?" Jesse said. "And how's that?"

"Her! Mrs Lannam! She's a bit of a plum. She spells trouble so just you watch out!"

"Get away! You're having me on."

"No, not me. She's after your body. You mark my words."

"I ent listening," Jesse said, growing hot in the face and neck. "Mrs Lannam! A lady like her!"

"D'you like her, then, Jesse boy?"

"Why, no. I can't say I do. I don't care for people riding anyhow over the crops like that. And if I was Mr Yarby I'd speak to her plain."

"He would if he dared. But she's his landlord."

"I'm glad she ent mine," Jesse said.

When they got to the farmyard, Mr Yarby stood on the muck-bury wall, watching the comings and goings of the men.

"Izzard!" he said. "You went ten minutes in front of Shodd so how's it happen you come back together?"

"I dunno," Jesse said, worried.

"It was Mrs Lannam," Jimmy said. "She kept him talking and that set him back."

"Mrs Lannam!" said Mr Yarby, sneering. "So you hob with the high and mighty, do you, Izzard?"

Jesse backed his cart to the bury and began forking in the muck. Jimmy, beside him, spoke in a murmur.

"He's a stinker today. Got up the wrong side. Or else his missus's been on at him again about buying that Turkey carpet."

"Turkey carpet?" Jesse repeated, and his voice, too loud, reached the ears of Mr Yarby, who turned and gave him a hard look.

When his load was complete, Jesse stuck his muck-fork into the heap and climbed up onto the cart. He flicked the reins, and Goldie pulled off with a sharp jolt. But the cart only slewed, its axle screeching, its wheels sliddering in the slime-filled gutter.

"Whoa!" Jesse called. "Easy does it, Goldie girl! Let's try again."

Goldie relaxed, stepping sideways in search of dry ground, and the cart slipped further back. The near side wheel caught the bury wall, and Jesse, looking back over his shoulder, saw Mr Yarby go plunging headlong into the muck.

"Deuce!" Jimmy muttered. "You've done it now!"

"By God!" Mr Yarby shouted, stumbling about, up to the tops of his gaiters in muck. "You did that on purpose, you young swine!"

"No!" Jesse said. "I never did!"

"Great useless clod! I've had about enough of you! You think I'm daft but I saw you leaving the horses up there in the Outmost a few weeks ago!"

"That was the day my daughter was born. I was only gone two ticks."

"You were gone twelve minutes. I timed it myself. I gave you a chance for Goody's sake, but this is the finish! You can damn well clear out right this minute!"

"You surely don't mean that, Mr Yarby?"

"Clear out, I said!"

"Here!" said Jimmy. "That ent hardly fair, master—"

"You hold your tongue or you'll follow!"

"You surely don't mean it," Jesse said. "Not leave my job! Where'd I get another at this time of year?"

"Don't ask me! Just get off my farm! Perhaps Mrs Lannam will look after you, seeing she's such a friend of yours!"

"What about my pay?"

"I'll give it to Goody on Saturday."

Numbly, Jesse climbed down from the cart. He stood for a moment in a daze, resting his hand on Goldie's neck. Then he turned away and reached for his jacket.

"Go to Awner at Noak," Jimmy murmured. "He'll give you a job."

"Thanks, I'll try him," Jesse said.

He took a cut across the fields and followed the turnpike till he came to Noak Hall. He found the farmer clearing a ditch in the home pasture.

"Yarby in one of his puffs, is he? Ah, well, he's a worried man. Aping your betters costs a pretty penny. You know what they say about his kind?—

> "Son learning latin-o,
> Daughters dressed in satin-o,
> Wife at the pian-o,
> All to ruination go."

"Ah," Jesse said. "You may be right. I wouldn't know."

Awner, a sharp-eyed man with a jolly manner hiding a nature hard as nails, was willing to take Jesse on.

"But I can't promise more than the odd bit of ditching. A lot depends what I have to pay you. Will a shilling a day be all right?"

"I reckon so."

"Then when can you start?"

"Now, this instant. Just give me the spades."

That day saw the last of the open weather. The night brought a change, and the wind went round to the coldest quarter. There were a few people, and Goody was one, who awoke some time in the small hours, felt the change in their old bones, and had an inkling of what it portended. The long, mild autumn was gone, and the long bitter winter had come hard behind it, nipping its heels with the first frost.

Every night, on his way through the woods, Jesse picked up dead branches and carried them home, for Goody was right: they needed good fires that winter, and half their firewood was gone already. They needed all the food they could get, too, for their pig that year had died of lung fever.

One night, when he was pulling a dead branch of oak from the tangled thicket, a cock pheasant leapt into flight before him, and instinct sent him sprawling forward, arms outstretched and hands clutching. In one move, he had the pheasant against his chest. In another, he had wrung its neck. The feel of its warm body, limp yet twitching between his hands, filled him with horror, but once the bird was perfectly still, his horror passed. Death was a terrible, terrible thing, but death was nothing compared with dying.

He carried the bird home inside his jacket. Goody plucked it and cooked it that evening, taking care to burn every feather in the fire.

"I'd have liked one or two for my hat," she said, "but a pheasant's feathers tell too good a tale." And then she said: "Poaching is bad, boy, especially here, where the keepers are devils."

"My dad used to say that a bird or a rabbit belonged to nobody until it was catched."

"Well," Goody said, patting her stomach, "there's a part of that bird that's truly mine now."

Jesse worked six days a week at Noak and earned five shillings and sixpence. Goody worked five long mornings at Checketts and earned half-a-crown. But they were lucky, Goody said, for they had their full health and strength, an acre of garden that yielded well, and no rent to pay for the Pikehouse. And Jesse, coming home through the cold and the dark of those winter evenings, to a welcoming light shining out of the window; to a good fire, burning inside; to his two women and tiny daughter, felt that he was lucky indeed.

There was comfort and warmth in that small kitchen. And there would be the day's stew: thickened with oatmeal; flavoured with thyme; swimming with onions, carrots, and parsnips; with potatoes still in their tasty skins; and with little dumplings, each containing some surprise, such as a spoonful of mushroom ketchup or a small cube of brawn. And later, just for an hour or so before bed-time, they would gather round close to the fire: he and Beth side by side on the settle; Goody creaking backwards and forwards in her rocking-chair opposite; and Betony in her cot between them. They would sit with the firelight hot and red on their faces, while outside the circle, the shadows flickered up to the ceiling and the cold wind crept at the walls. Then, if Jesse could get her started, Goody would talk of the old days.

"Go on," he would say. "Tell us the things you used to get up to when you was a girl living at Springs. You and all them brothers and sisters."

And Goody would talk of Bob, who had gone to Australia; of William and Perce, who had gone to New Zealand; of Gret, who had married a prince's coachman and gone to live in a palace in Russia; of Lennard, who had a couple of wives too many and got into trouble with the law; and of Thomas, her favourite, who had died in the first quarry disaster in 1851.

"You'd have liked Thomas," Jesse said, turning to Beth. "He was the best of the whole bunch."

"But you never knew him. He died before you was born."

"Why, yes," he said. "But I reckon I know him just the same. I know them all, as if they was sitting with us this minute." Looking at Beth, he saw her smile. "You're laughing at me again, ent you? Oh yes you are! I saw it plain."

"You do make me laugh sometimes."

"Ah, I reckon that's why you married me, because I'm always good for a laugh."

He liked to see her smiling and laughing. It made him feel very warm and happy, and brought his own laughter bubbling up inside him. Her smile was special, somehow, perhaps because it came so rarely. The sight of it always took him by surprise, and he would watch her until it faded.

Sometimes, however, he was anxious; because he had no regular work; because the worst of the winter was yet to come. Now that the ground was hard with frost, Awner was paying him by the piece, but he dared not grumble, for soon even ditching would come to a halt. Goody told him not to worry. "We shan't starve! Not while we've got our health and strength. We'll have to look lively, that's all, picking up bits and bobs all round."

The weather worsened. There was bitter frost every day and night. The morning Awner paid him off, Jesse tramped twenty miles, looking for work on every farm, but returned without so much as a promise. The next day, he called on a friend, Charley Bailey, who lived in a shanty on Norton common. He left with a ferret and ten nets.

Just about dark, he went to an oak in the older part of Scoate woods, and netted seven holes that ran down between the roots and rudges. He put the ferret into the eighth hole and stopped the opening with a clod of earth. He sat on his haunches and prepared to wait.

Outside the woods, the light was only now fading, the first stars coming up in the sky. But inside the woods, it was already as dark as night, especially here in the oak and beech woods. Jesse never once looked upwards, for the light of the stars would impair his night-sight: he kept his gaze upon the ground, eyes sharp yet relaxed, like a badger's, and from where he crouched, he could see six of the netted holes at a glance.

Beneath him, a slight thrill ran through the ground. He felt it in one of the roots at his feet. He leant forward, ready to spring, and the rabbit hurtled into the net, rolling over and over, pulling the draw-strings tight behind him and wrenching the pegs clean out of the ground. Jesse chopped at its neck with the edge of his hand, and it was dead, with the one blow. He took it from the net and put it into his coat pocket.

The ferret appeared at the mouth of the hole, nose in the air, whiskers twitching. But when Jesse tried to take it, it turned and vanished again down the hole. So he replaced the net and sat on his heels for another wait.

Another rabbit bounded out and he killed it quickly. He put it into his other pocket. He had two does and was well pleased. They were not only bigger but sweeter to eat than the johnny bucks.

This time the ferret was gone so long that he feared it might be lying in. He got down on his hands and knees, put his mouth to the nearest hole, and gave a few little tight-lipped squeaks. The ferret emerged, nosing enquiringly into the net. Jesse caught it behind the shoulders and put it quickly into its bag. He put the nets and pegs in his pockets. Then he stood up and started for home.

The keeper, MacNab, was crossing the clearing, his twinbarrel gun in the crook of his arm, and his dog, a springer spaniel, close at his heels. Jesse stood perfectly still, his back to a tree, while man and dog walked past him. He waited as long as it took to count fifty and then he moved, slowly and cautiously, planting each foot as though walking on eggs.

"Right!" said MacNab, somewhere behind him. "Step out to the clearing where I can see you and don't try any tricks!"

Jesse turned and ran full pelt, away from the sound of the keeper's voice, into the thickest part of the wood. The keeper shouted. The dog barked. The place became full of the trampling of feet and the smashing of old dead timber. Jesse dived at a clump of brambles, just as the keeper fired his first barrel. He received the skitter of shot in his legs, from his feet and ankles all the way up to his thighs and buttocks. He crawled forward, further and further into the thicket, and lay still, resting his face on a bed of dry dead leaves and prickles.

"Right, you!" the keeper shouted. "I can see you fine so don't move!"

He fired again, but away off into the trees, and Jesse, knowing the man was only bluffing, trusted to luck and lay still. He heard MacNab reloading his gun, and heard him beginning to walk away, calling the dog to come to heel. But the dog was pushing into the thicket that gave Jesse shelter. He felt its cold body go brushing past him, then its warm tongue licking his face.

"Floss?" called MacNab. "Floss, where are you? Damn and blast! Can't you come when I call?"

MacNab was returning. Jesse heard him. He knew the dog would give him away. She was wagging her tail and rustling the dry dead leaves on the brambles. He tried to push her away from him but now she was eagerly nuzzling the ferret that squirmed in its bag on the ground at his side.

"Floss?" the keeper called again. "Got a scent of him, have you? Where are you, then, Floss?"

The keeper's voice came very close. His feet trod the brash at the edge of the thicket. His twinbarrel probed the bramble canes. But he dared not shoot because of his dog.

"Damn you!" he said, in his thick Scots voice. "Are you after rabbits, you damned useless bitch?"

Jesse put his arm round the dog and held her against him. With his other hand he released the ferret. Surprised at its freedom, it remained still, sitting up on its little haunches, sniffing the air with quivering nose. It remained so close that its whiskers tickled Jesse's face, and its smoky smell was strong in his nostrils. Then, swiftly, it darted away. The spaniel wriggled and strained to be free, whining and crying in her throat, and after a moment, Jesse let her go.

She broke away from the thicket immediately under the keeper's feet, and the man swore, hurrying off in pursuit. Jesse heard her scrabbling the hard frozen earth of a rabbit burrow, where the ferret had gone to ground, and heard her yelp as the keeper swung at her with his boot.

"Come out of that, you useless bitch!"

Jesse waited, and when keeper and dog had gone off through the wood, he crawled from the thicket and stood up. His legs were very stiff and numb, but when he moved, they came to life again all too quickly. The pellets in his flesh were lumps of fire, pulsing and throbbing, and a few that had penetrated his left instep were scraping like gravel against the bone.

Once he was out of the old oak and beech wood, into the new plantation of pines, he was able to run quickly, making straight for the old turnpike. The moon was up now, white and bright, in its third quarter, and because of it, when he reached the road, he was able to see that a keeper stood guard there, patrolling the boundary of the woods.

Jesse got down flat on his stomach and crawled into the roadside ditch. Its bottom was ice, and he lay upon it full length, with the frosted grasses arching above him. The ice was soothing. Its coldness struck up through his clothes, slowing the pumping of hot blood, quenching the fires that throbbed in his flesh, sending his whole body to sleep. And as his body went to sleep, so did his brain, numbly and coldly, in a dead faint.

When he awoke, the moon was shining fully upon him. He struggled up on deadened arms and peered through the grasses fringing the ditch. The road was empty. The keeper had gone.

Inch by inch, he got on his knees. He struck at himself to bring the blood alive in his veins. He tried to stand up but only rolled over, slowly and daintily, head over heels, unaware of falling until he found himself on his back, staring up at the staring moon. He got on all fours and crawled to the road, and there he tried again to rise.

Something was badly wrong with his legs. He couldn't feel them. They had gone dead. Something was wrong with his head too. It was full of echoing, empty space. He went down again, and this time he lay there, going back to the cold deep sleep. But now there were footsteps coming along the frozen road. Now there were voices calling his name. And now there were arms about his body. Lifting him up. Bearing him on. He was wondering who, and what, and where, when suddenly his head fell back and the white moon put out its light.

He was burning hot. He was burning cold. His body was heavy, a dead weight upon his soul. His body was light and floated on air. It was gone altogether, like melted ice, and his soul was a flame, or two little flames, burning in darkness. He was rather worried about the moon going out like that, because Goody liked to hang her washing out in the moonlight, to make it white, and what would she do if there was no moon?

He could hear voices . . . Beth's and Goody's . . . quietly talking a long way away, but coming nearer all the time; cool words like hands, touching him coolly; drawing the blankets away from his mouth.

"Goody?" he heard Beth say, and her voice was suddenly very close. "He ent going to die, is he, Goody?"

He wanted to speak. To offer some comfort. But

his tongue was locked. He had no voice. And, any-way, what could he say when he himself did not know the answer? He could only lie still waiting for Goody to answer instead.

"Laws! It'll take more than a handful of shot and a bite of cold to kill that boy! Of course he tarnal well ent going to die!"

"Why, no," he said, deep inside himself, down in the burning cold and dark. "I ent going to die. Oh, lumme, no. No lections of that!"

And just before he slipped into sleep, he heard Beth's voice again, close by.

"Goody," she said, *"I saw him smile."*

When he was better and allowed to get up, and he saw the deep snow lying about, he stared in amazement. He felt he'd been gone from the world for ages. He could not believe it was only ten days.

"Snow," he kept saying. "That was all hard frost when I saw it last. I feel I've lost a whole chunk of my life."

"You're lucky," said Goody. "You could've lost the whole lot!"

And when, growing stronger, he wanted to venture out of doors, she went to the mantelpiece, took down a tin that had once held tobacco, and rattled its contents under his nose.

"That's the shot that came out of your body! And a rare old job we had picking it out! So come home here with another load like that, and there'll be ructions, you mark my words!"

"Don't worry. I shan't go down further than the Uptops."

"Bits of nuts and bolts and all sorts we twizzed out of you, boy!"

"And don't I know it!" he said, feeling himself tenderly.

"If that there keeper comes snooping round here, I'll throw all that shot in his nasty red face!" Goody said. "Ho, yes! I'll give him MacNab!"

Jesse walked with a limp now, for two bits of shot

had entered his foot, and although Goody had taken them out and the place had healed well enough, there remained some weakness in the instep, as though the bone had been displaced.

"You should give it time," Beth told him. "Don't be in such a hurry to walk about on it. You've got plenty to do indoors."

"Why, yes, I'm busy as wheels. Look here, what I've made for my daughter, out of these little scraps of wood. That's a cow. That's a horse. And this one here will be a pig when I've finished carving a proper snout."

"I'm glad you told me," Beth said. "Potatoes on legs, they look like to me."

"Well, Betony knows what they are, anyway. She's been lying there, watching me make them. She knows that's a pig. She grunted at it."

As soon as he could walk any distance, he went to Noak to ask for work. Awner had a wheat-stack he wanted threshed. He offered Jesse tenpence a day.

"Tenpence!" Jesse said. "I call that mean, seeing it should be one and six by rights."

He was rather surprised at himself for speaking out so boldly. He had never used such strong words before. But a great many things were coming more easily to him these days.

"Take it or leave it," Awner said

"I can't afford to leave it, as you well know, Mr Awner. That's exactly what makes it mean."

When the threshing was finished he was idle again. There was more snow and he went with Goody every morning to help her dig a way through the drifts.

He was gathering sticks at the edge of the woods one day when Mrs Lannam rode up on her big black mare.

"You're guilty of trespass. Did you know that?"

"With respect, ma'am, we've had the chatting rights in these here woods since the year dot-and-carry-one."

"Well, provided you don't damage the trees . . . or go after game . . ."

"Game? Why, that'd be poaching!"

"Yes, my fine fellow! You may open your eyes as wide as you please, but my keepers are very suspicious of you young men around these farms."

"Keepers is always suspicious. It's what they're paid for. It's their nature, too, especially if they happen to be Scotch."

"I never mentioned MacNab by name."

"No more didn't I," Jesse said.

He stooped and put a few pine-cones into his sack, and a few bits of stick. When he straightened again, she was still watching him with pale, shining eyes.

"I see you're limping. Why is that?"

"I trod on a nail," Jesse said.

"You're not very civil, are you? Don't you take off your cap when you speak to your betters?"

"Not in a cold wind like this, ma'am."

"I think you're a dog!" she said, laughing. "I ought to give you a taste of my crop, but it would be a pity to mark that fine complexion."

Jesse stooped to pick up more sticks. He snatched up dead branches, broke them against his bent knee, and put the pieces into his sack. He found it hard to look at the woman directly. Her eyes were too bright and her glance too inquisitive, flickering over him constantly. And her laugh, too, was very strange. It was not, he thought, a womanly laugh. It was husky and rough and rather hard.

"My word, you *are* strong," she said, pretending to admire the way he broke the brittle branches. "It's disgraceful that a strong young man should be idling about the place like this. I suppose you've been laid off because of the snow?"

"Yes. That's about it."

"Come to Scoate in the morning," she said. "You might be able to help MacNab."

Jesse slung his sack on his shoulder and stood upright, forcing himself to meet her glance.

"I reckon I'd sooner wait," he said, "and take my chance on the farms."

"You mean you refuse?" she said, surprised.

"No, not refuse exactly, ma'am. Just thank you kindly all the same."

She sat for a moment, straight-backed, still watching him with the same bright glance, though her smile had altered.

"I wonder what you're thinking, looking at me so straight and stolid and blue-eyed?"

"I'm thinking, ma'am, that you shouldn't be standing that mare in the cold."

"I don't believe you. I think you're sly. Men of your sort!—I'd give a fortune to read your strange minds."

She brought her horse round sharply and rode away over the snow, staring in at the Pikehouse window as she passed.

In the kitchen, when he went in, Beth was busy making bread, and Betony, lacking attention, lay grizzling quietly to herself. Jesse, without waiting to shed his coat, went at once to bend over the cot.

"What's the matter with my blossom? Is she all wet by any chance?"

"No," Beth said. "She's just having a grouse like we all do sometimes."

"Maybe she wants feeding, then?"

"No, I fed her twenty minutes ago."

"Well, I dunno! The way she's pursing up her lips, I reckon she wants another helping."

"Then you'll have to give it to her yourself."

"Ah, you've got me there, ent you?"

He took Betony in his arms and held her up against his shoulder. The grizzling stopped. She was all smiles. He put his lips against her cheek and blew a raspberry, and she laughed and gurgled, nuzzling her face against his, her skin soft and warm and smelling milky.

"You're a sprucer," he said. "You ent hungry nor you ent wet. You're perfectly come-for-double all the way round."

"I saw you talking to Mrs Lannam," Beth said. "What'd she have to say to you?"

"Eh? What, her? Why, nothing, really."

"She took some time, saying nothing."

"Well, about the bad weather, that's all. The snow and that. And about being laid off at the farm."

"It's a pity she couldn't do something useful, like putting you in the way of some work."

"Ah, well," Jesse said. "She did in a way, in a manner of speaking as you might say. Only I said no."

"You said what!" Beth exclaimed.

"She talked about helping MacNab, you see. But lumme! That's not my kind of work. Not keepering."

"Since when've you been so fussy what you do?"

"That ent fussy. That's common sense."

"Keepering brings in wages, surely? It's better than having nothing at all."

"Maybe. Maybe not." He laid Betony in her cot and went to look out of the window. "But I ent going just the same."

"Oh, you ent? 'Cos it don't just suit you! It ent quite exactly what you wanted?"

"That's right."

"Well, that's a pity, that is, I'm sure! I'm sorry for you! I am, that's a fact. I suppose you prefer going poaching and getting yourself riddled with shot."

"I'd sooner get shot than work with them that does the shooting. And besides—"

"Besides what?"

"Nothing," he said. "Just besides, that's all."

"I suppose it's growing on you, this loafing about, doing nothing? Doubtless it suits you, stalking about with your hands in your pockets, coming and going just as you please?"

"Ah," he said, staring out at the blinding snow. "That suits me humpty-dinker."

"Then take yourself off!" Beth said. "Before I fetch you a clout by the ear! It makes me boil to think of Goody traipsing to Checketts every day while you stroll about like a little lord. I'd be ashamed if I was you! So get out of here before I turn nasty and say something sharp!"

"Ah, I'm going!" Jesse said, and stumped to the door. "Now this instant! No delay!"

The world was very still and quiet in the snow. What few sounds there were travelled strangely, like the smack of axes cutting timber, a sound that bounced in its own echo: chacker . . . chacker . . . all around.

Jesse tracked it down at last, and came to a wood of ash and chestnut. There, at work with their axes, felling an ash tree, were two men: twin brothers, it seemed, for both were black-bearded and hook-nosed and both were equal in size, strength, and temper.

"Is there work here?" Jesse asked.

"No," they answered, speaking together.

"I've done some felling. Not much, but a bit. I worked for William Tewke of Huntlip."

"The answer's still no," one man said, "so sling your hook."

"If I was you I'd have lopped a few branches before I started felling that tree. She's going a terrible lumper when she goes."

The two men stopped work and looked at each other. Then one of them turned, swinging his axe between his hands, till the blade lay flat on his hairy palm.

"Get out," he said, "or I'll split you through from head to foot."

Jesse turned and trudged away, and the smack of the axes started again. Chacker. Chacker. All around.

The world was very quiet and bare in the snow. The uplands were empty. Nothing moved. He went from Strutts to Deery Hill, from Palmer's Cross to the Big Man Stone, from Plug Lane to Litchett and Wadhill, without meeting a single soul.

At Wadhill, some gipsies were camping under the marlbank. Their tent was pitched on a piece of matting, and a baby lay in a basket inside. The mother was cleaning a flannel shirt by rubbing it on her knuckles in the snow. The father sat on a log by the fire and smoked a clay pipe. And three children, a girl and two boys, sat on their hunkers, toasting their naked knees at the fire, where a round black pot hung steaming on a tripod.

Jesse stood, saluting them with open hand, the way his father had always saluted gipsies. But the dark shining eyes in the dark bony faces only stared and stared, without a flicker, until he turned and trudged away.

From the round hill at Checketts, known as the Hump, he could see the farm buildings among the elms; could see when someone moved about the yards; and could see where the cattle, eating the hay put out in the pasture, had trampled the snow till it looked like brown demerara sugar. He could see the whole of the Vale of Scarne, where the Naff ran, a winding ribbon black as ink, between the flat white meadows of snow. He could see to the outermost rim of the earth.

As the day wore on, it grew misty, and at three o'clock more snow began to fall; quickly, excitably at first; then softly and slowly, big feathery flakes that filled the sky and hastened the coming of darkness.

Jesse, trudging along the Checketts track, passed within inches of Mr Yarby, who stopped dead, a dark shape in the flying snow and called out to him by name.

"Izzard? Is that you? Hang it, man! Can't you stop when you're spoken to? I've got something to say to you."

But Jesse was in no mood to answer, and tramped on, his fists in his pockets, his shoulders hunched, while the snow fell and buried the earth.

That she should turn and speak to him so! And look at him with such glittering eyes! She, who knew him and understood him—that she should turn and rend him like that! He could never entrust himself to her again. The bond was broken between them forever.

He was going home because there was nowhere else to go; because his baby daughter was there, claiming him, heart and soul; but he would have to live inside himself in future, where Beth could not reach him.

Somewhere along the old turnpike he fell in with Goody, and they entered the Pikehouse kitchen together. The warmth of the place gave him gooseflesh. It made him shudder throughout his frame. He stood by the fire, utterly blind and indifferent to Beth, but watching Goody, who was fumbling underneath her skirts, drawing out the string bag which she wore hidden, tied round her waist, and in which she brought home the "bits and bobs" picked up on the farm.

"One turmot, a few bits of tops, and some sprigs of corn I pulled from the stack. And how did you get on today, boy?"

"Well, I brought in a sack of kindling this morning."

"So you did!" said Beth, much struck, standing, hands on hips, before him. "You must be properly fagged, doing that!"

"What's up with you?" Goody demanded.

"He wants to watch out for hisself," Beth said. "I shouldn't like him to overdo things."

Goody gave a little sniff, turning from Beth, who was now busy stirring the stewpot, to Jesse, who stood like a stock on the hearth.

"Mr Yarby sent a message. He says he'll take you back again. Soon as the weather's cleared up."

"Did he?" said Jesse. "Ah. There now."

"You don't seem all that bucked about it."

"Maybe it don't quite suit him!" said Beth, throwing the words over her shoulder.

"Here!" Goody said. "What's up with you, girl, all curds and whey?"

"Ask your precious Jesse there! Seems work and him ent all that good friends. Mrs Lannam offered to help him and he was so grand he cocked his nose!"

"What sort of work?" Goody asked.

"Keepering," Jesse muttered.

"Well," Goody said, and sat on the settle, her hands in her lap. "You must be a fool, Jesse Izzard. You could be in clover down there at Scoate, with nothing much to do but keep Mrs Lannam warm in bed."

"Eh?" said Beth. "What's that you say?"

"Aw, be quiet," Jesse said. "The pair of you! Just hold your tongues!"

"Mrs Lannam?" Beth said. "Gone and taken a shine to Jesse? I don't believe it!"

"Why not? You went and took a shine to him your own self."

"But she's gentry. Or supposed to be."

"The gentry's no different. They're maybe more so if anything."

"She's married, too."

"Mr Lannam's over seventy, and frail as a lath. He keeps to his room in winter, they say, and only comes out in summer time to catch a few butterflies in his net."

"I don't believe it," Beth said. "A woman like her! Running after a man like Jesse."

"Oh, yes! There's many a promising lad has been set up for life after working at Scoate, and it wasn't keepering with MacNab that done it, I can tell you. Ask that husband of yours standing there. He'll have heard a few tales around the farm."

"Don't talk to *me*," Jesse said. "I ent listening. I've closed my ears."

"Then mind out of my way," Beth said. "How can I cook while you stand straddled across the hearth?"

Jesse went and sat at the table. He waited in silence for Beth to serve him, and he ate in silence from beginning to end. There was no savour in the food. He ate only to quell the shivers that racked his inside. He would not look at Beth, who came and went as if nothing had happened. He would not meet her glance when she sat opposite, eating her supper. But he could not close his ears when she spoke, and the sound of her voice, so brisk and cheerful, giving Goody the day's news, made him shrink inside himself, dreadfully. It made him harden against her. It turned him to stone.

And when he lay in bed that night, in the little

room under the roof, lit only by the glare of snow outside, he would not watch even her shadow as she
undressed, but lay on his back, cold and stiff, and
made no move to welcome her when she slid, shivering, between the sheets.

"Still sulking?" she said, lying beside him.

"Ah. That's right."

"What a waxy great fool you are, ent you?"

"If you say so. You ought to know."

"You just want to punish me, sulking like this,"
she said. "You hate me, and want to pay me out."

Not knowing how to answer, he remained silent.
No, he didn't hate her, but hatred was there, certainly,
because she had plucked down his bright shining
pride, and because the good thing that had been between them now lay in ruins, and trust was gone.

"Jesse, I'm cold," she said, with a shiver.

"Ah," he said. "It's a cold night."

"Jesse, I'm sorry!" And the words came as though
from a child.

"Ah, well, and so you should be!" he said roughly.

"I've always had a quick tongue. You know that.
And you'd try the patience of Job sometimes . . . But
there! I've said I'm sorry and I mean it too."

He turned towards her, a tremendous warmth moving throughout him, melting his bones and turning
his blood to tears in his veins. He got on one elbow
and leant towards her. His hand moved over her body
and came to rest in the warmth of her armpit, and
she drew him down to her, pressing his head against
her breast.

"Ah, and so you should be sorry!" he said.

To Jesse, a ploughed field was the loveliest sight in the world, and if he himself had done the ploughing, his joy in the sight was manifold.

The moment he walked his horses onto an old grass ley or a stretch of stubble, he was lord of a little kingdom of acres, and nothing could ever pull him down. From the moment the ploughshare made its first cut, on to the time when the whole field lay brown and bare, he would not change places with any man in the three counties. He walked tall, and his shadow, falling across the sunlit earth, was something to see.

There was something neat and clean and perfect about a field newly ploughed. The sight of it was its own reward, for there a man could see his work made manifest indeed, when nothing came between it and the sky. The soil on these uplands was good loam, overlying clay and marl and gravel. In a drying wind, its surface was tawny. Under sunlight, it looked red. And after rain it became a rich dark brown, like strong tobacco. Jesse liked to see the ploughed fields looking clean and neat and empty. He almost resented the advance of the green corn across his kingdom of brown acres.

He never wanted to be a champion and win the ploughing matches at Chepsworth Park as Jimmy Shodd so often did. His pride lay in the work itself.

It lay in the feel of the stilts in his hands, and the motion of the plough as it ran the furrow. It was enough that he did a man's work; had charge of a team of good horses; and was left alone in the quiet fields in the two best seasons of the year.

"I ent clever," he said to Beth, "but ploughing is something I *can* do and not too badly, neither, it seems."

As Betony grew from a baby into a child, he would take her on his shoulders and carry her around the fields in the evening, pointing out the birds on the ploughed land, the charlock yellow among the corn, the pollen blowing from a field of flowering grasses, or the tracks of a hare under the hedgerow. And Betony, fat little legs astride his shoulders, fat little hands entwined in his hair, would sit like a graven image above him, looking on the world with solemn eyes, as though understanding every word.

Beth often laughed at the way he talked to Betony. "You'd think her a hundred, the way you go on." But once, instead of laughing, she accused him of favouring Betony too much and leaving their new daughter out in the cold.

"Why!" he said, feeling very guilty. "It's only that Janie is still such a morsel, that's all. But if she wants to come along with me, then come she may, for I've got two shoulders and Betony'll have to make do with one so's little Janie can sit on the other."

He lifted them up, first one, then the other, and there they sat on high together, each held secure by a great square hand.

"There! Your dad's a regular beast of burden now, ent he? And what'll happen when your little brother or sister arrives, eh? I can't manage three. I shall have to make a little cart!"

From up on the ladder, where he was at work, white-washing the Pikehouse walls, Jesse could see a puff of dust moving along the Norton road. He stopped work to watch it: a pony and trap; wheeling round onto the turnpike; drawing up at the Pikehouse gate.

With his paint-brush swimming about in the bucket, he climbed down the ladder and hurried to his women-folk, who were planting potatoes.

"Company!" he said. "Seems your grandpa is coming to call."

Beth, who was big with their third child, straightened slowly, one hand pressing against her side, and looked towards the gate.

"So he is," she said calmly.

"My stars," said Goody, coming forward with her apron full of potato seed. "Lord Sawdust hisself!"

The old man came clumping along the path, his shoulders held stiffly, his head erect, his hat well forward over his brow. He came to a halt in front of them, crossing his hands on the knob of his stick, and looked at each of them in turn, stubbornly resolved to face them out.

"Hah! I've struck you all of a heap, I can see! You didn't expect a visit from me, did you?"

He turned and looked at the two little girls: Betony, watching from among the currant bushes, and Janie, crawling about the path.

"I always said you'd quicken easy. But why does it have to be girls, girls? Still, by the look of you, there's another due directly, so maybe you'll have a son this time."

"Maybe I shall," Beth agreed.

"I suppose you're wondering why I've come? Well, it's because I've got a proposition. No, I shan't step indoors. I'd sooner stand and get it done."

"Just as you please."

"I want you to come back to Cobbs," he said. "You and your husband Jesse here. I'll make him my partner, all drawn up by Baines the lawyer, and his name can go on the gate and waggons,—Tewke and Izzard, the way you wanted it in the first place."

"What's made you change all of a sudden?"

"That ent sudden. I'm getting old, and there's no one to follow me in the business, so I've got no choice but to humble myself to you, have I? I borrowed a leaf out of your book and done like you did when you was a youngster and came to me for help that time. You remember that?"

"I remember."

"Well, there you are,—the mountain has come to the mommet," he said.

"What about Kit Maddox?" Beth asked. "Ent he in favour no more?" Her grandfather gave her a shrewd glance.

"Don't you get all the news from your mother? She comes to see you often enough."

"She said Kit was drinking, if that's what you mean."

"Drinking! Hah! He soaks like a sponge, that boy, and he's tarnal well ruined hisself as a craftsman. Such hands as he had! And such an eye!—All lost now with drinking and fooling about all round. He's took up with some slut he brought home from Chepsworth, and they're living together bold as brass, and got a child, though nobody ever seems to see it. Ah, he's gone to the bad, that boy, and it's all your fault for letting him down the way you did."

"He always was bad," Beth said, "like an apple with the maggot in it."

"Ah, well! It's history now. So what d'you say to my proposition?"

"I can't answer straight out like that. I'll have to talk to Goody and Jesse."

"What! What! Yes, maybe so. Well, there's no hurry. No hurry at all! You talk it out and let me have your answer directly." The old man turned and looked at Jesse. "You seem pretty fit, young man, and my granddaughter, too. She don't seem to've suffered nothing from marrying you. So let me shake you by the hand to show what's past is past between us.

Jesse wiped his hand on his trousers and gave it to the old man to shake. He tried to speak, but was given no chance.

"As for you, Goody Izzard! You needn't stay here in this little box of a house by yourself, you know. There's plenty of room for you at Cobbs. But I must be off and leave you to talk the matter over. I'll expect your answer as soon as maybe."

"Old snake!" Goody muttered, as they watched him drive off.

"Laws," Jesse said. "We ent going to pull ourselves up by the roots like that, are we?"

"Not me!" Goody said. "I ent leaving my little box of a house for nobody. But that don't stop you two from going if you want to."

"We shouldn't want to leave you by yourself, Goody," Beth said.

"That's nothing. It's yourselves you must think of. Not me."

"Then it rests with Jesse," Beth said. "But goodness, man, what's up with you? You look like you've swallowed a lump of camphor."

"Yes, well," Jesse said, staring into his pail of whitewash. "You're asking me to give up going to plough, ent you?"

"When?" Beth demanded. "When did I ask you? I don't recall asking you nothing!"

"But you think we should go, though, I dare say?"

"Not if you don't want to, boy. Oh dear me no! We'll put the matter out of our minds and let my grandfather know according."

"I never said I didn't *want* to go, exactly."

"My stars!" Beth said. "It's hard to know what you do want, the way you durdle and get nothing said! Suppose you get on with whitening the house and try unpicking the knots in your brain while you're at it? Then perhaps we'll know where we stand."

"Ah," Jesse said, and went back to his ladder.

When he had finished, and the walls were a dazzling new white again, and he had washed himself under the pump, Goody called him in to supper. He sat at the table and watched Beth cutting the bread.

"I've thought," he said, having waited in vain for her to ask him. "I've thought about it and I reckon we'll go. I've been counting all the different points."

"That's a marvel, that is. Let's hear what they are."

"Well, a carpenter gets nearly twice what a farm labourer gets, for a start."

"That's true. We'd be rich, very nearly."

"Then, again, I shouldn't be laid off at Cobbs as I am oftentimes at Checketts when things is bad in winter."

"Another point, true as the first. You've sorted your thoughts out pretty nicely."

"Then, again, if our third child should chance to be a son, well, that's a wonderful start for any boy, to be born into a trade like that."

"True again," Beth said. "Any more points to come?"

"Well, not exactly," he said, fidgeting with a knife on the table, "except that your grandpa shook me by the hand."

"So he did, to be sure! I saw it myself, large as life."

"It's all very well, laughing at me so solemn and all, but just you think!—A partner in a proper business! Tewke and Izzard, your grandfather said. Just think of that! I reckon they go pretty well together, don't you?"

"Like stew and dumplings!" Goody said, setting the teapot down with a thump beside him. "Like liver and lights! Or fleas and hedgehogs! They go together humpty-dinker. Now move your elbows, Tewke and Izzard, and make room for me."

"Goody," Beth said. "Are you sure you don't mind our leaving you?"

"Not me!" Goody said. "Why should I indeed? With my own featherbed to sleep in again and no crying babbies to wake me up? I'll be in clover and no mistake."

She rattled a spoon onto the table and whisked the cosy from the pot. She looked first at Beth and then at Jesse, treating each to a sharp little frown.

"You mean to visit me sometimes, I suppose, and bring the children to see me in my little box of a house? Right you are, then! You get on and fashion your lives and never mind about studying me. Why, I can hardly wait to see you go!"

Jesse had never been inside the house at Cobbs before, and secretly he found it daunting. There were too many rooms and too many passages; too many staircases everywhere; he lost his way often at first, and Kate, hustling him out of the stillroom or pantry, or out of the passage that led to the cellar, seemed to think he was queer in the head.

"But there!" she said, talking to Beth in front of him. "It's not what he's used to, a great house like this. We must make allowances, I suppose."

He was rather frightened of Kate: she used so many unfamiliar words. Furniture at the Pikehouse had always been simple, with simple names such as dresser or cupboard or shelf or stool. But here at Cobbs, according to Kate, he must say "chiffonier" and "whatnot" and "pouffe."

"Your mother is desperate grand," he whispered, alone with Beth in the parlour, before tea the Sunday they arrived. "She's rather a lady, ent she, the way she talks?"

"It's the house," Beth said. "She got grand ideas when she came here and they've grown worse while I've been away."

"What was it she called that there chest when she was talking just now?"

"A commode," Beth said.

"A commode. That's right. I heard it plain." He looked at the polished mahogany chest, with its three big drawers and its shiny brass handles, and shook his head in perplexity. "I always thought a commode was something else entirely," he said.

Kate's greatest joy on their arrival was in the two children, Betony and Janie, and she kept swooping upon them to give them biscuits or knobs of sugar. Grandfather Tewke also paid them a lot of attention and had them up to sit on his lap. He let them examine his silver watch-chain; his coins with the head of King

William IV; and the watch itself, with its two little doors and pretty engraving.

"I'm told you can talk," he said to Betony, "so you ought to be able to call me granddad."

"Say granddad," urged Jesse, whispering into Betony's ear.

"Dad-dad," she said.

"D'you call that talking?" the old man demanded. "Oh, you do, do you? Then we'll have to take your word and your nod, shan't we?" He let them slide down from his knees and watched them as they went to Beth. "I've got nothing against girls. They've got their uses like anything else. But it's that there boy I've set my sights on. Oh, yes, I'm counting on him!"

"Supposing it's another girl?"

"Get away!" he said. "Nobody don't have girls forever. It ent on the cards. No, this third one coming will be a boy. I can feel it in my bones."

Jesse's worst moment was on Monday morning, when he walked into the workshop yard and saw by the men's faces that they had not been warned of his coming.

"My grandson-in-law," said Grandfather Tewke, and allowed his words to fall with full weight: "my grandson-in-law's come back, as you see, and from now on he'll be my partner and right-hand-man."

There was a silence, and a few of the men exchanged glances. Steve Hewish was leaning against the workshop wall. He took his pipe from his mouth and looked thoughtfully into the bowl.

"I suppose, in that case, we'd better call him Mister Izzard?"

"Laws no!" Jesse said. "I've never been nothing but Jesse here, nor never will be, I shouldn't think."

"You've always been Jesse Slowsides to us," said Sam Lovage. "But now you're Jesse Sideways, I reckon, if we call you by your limp. What happened to you? Was you trod by a heifer?"

"Ah, we heard you'd gone back to the farm,"

Steve said. "What made you give up? Too much brain work for you, was it?"

"Enough of that!" Grandfather Tewke said sharply. "Jesse here has got to be treated with proper respect. Is that understood?"

"Proper respect,—yes, surely," said Sam. "After all, he married Beth."

"Christ!" said Kit Maddox. "We all know why she chose him! She likes her own way, that's why, and wanted a mudscrape to wipe her feet on whenever she felt inclined that way. She wanted a man who'd always be putty in her hands."

In looks, Kit had changed. With his drooping moustache and thick streaks of grey in his black hair, he seemed middle-aged, although not yet thirty. He had grown lantern-jawed, and his skin was furrowed from eyes to mouth. He still dressed in a showy way, and wore a thick green leather belt, much adorned with shiny clips and badges, but his clothes were not smart as in days gone by: they were ragged and dirty and ill-fitting.

"Well?" he said. "I'm speaking the truth, ent I? We may as well have it out in the open. What say you, Jesse Sideways?"

"I don't much mind *why* she married me," Jesse said. "She just did and that's all-about-it."

"It's certainly shot you up in the world. Partner! Hah! Don't make me laugh! You wouldn't be nothing if it wasn't for Beth."

"Maddox!" said Grandfather Tewke, in a warning voice. "I won't have none of you talking to Jesse in that way, so mark it, man, or you'll get the push!"

Kit shrugged. He said no more, but walked away to the side of the yard, there to open his trousers and make water against the hedge.

That first day in the workshop was the longest Jesse had ever known, and there were many more such days to follow. After so long away from carpentering, his work was poorer than ever, and Grand-

father Tewke was constantly at him for wasting his time
and timber and nails.

"Laws, gaffer," Steve Hewish would say at these
times, "your right-hand-man is only a left-handed sinner after all, I'm sorry to say."

The men had always been quick to make game
of Jesse, but now that his name had gone up on
the sign-board, jealousy made them extra spiteful.
They withheld advice, letting him finish a piece of
bad work before they pointed out the errors, and
then, when they did speak out, it was always in
front of the old man, and always with a false polite-
ness.

"Mister Izzard,—or Jesse if I might presume to
call you that—did you honestly mean to put that
there fingle on upside down?"

Once, when he was shaving a bar for a sheep-
crib, he leant clumsily on his draw-knife and broke
the blade with a loud crack. He caught a few smiles
on the faces around him and heard Bob Green make
some remark. But no one spoke to him directly.
They were waiting, as always, for Grandfather Tewke
to bawl him out. And then, as he was bending over
his toolbag, with a great bitterness rising in him, a
shadow fell across the ground and a new draw-knife
was laid on the stool beside him. He glanced up,
and there was George Hopson, the gloomiest, most
taciturn man in the workshop, already walking away,
without waiting for a word of thanks.

Kit was an open enemy from the start and was
always trying to provoke a quarrel; by elbowing
Jesse out of the way, allowing timbers to fall on
his foot, or making remarks about Beth.

"I saw Madam in the orchard this morning. She
looked through me as if I was glass. That made me
laugh, I can tell you, 'cos she was sweet on me at
one time."

Jesse said nothing, but went on working.

"D'you hear me?" Kit said, "or are you dummy
as well as daft?"

"No," Jesse said. "And if you're wanting to use

the lathe, there's no need to jostle 'cos I'm just finished."

Early in May, they were all out at Middening, felling timber in Sudge woods. The days were cool, with
short sharp showers that made the air smell fresh
and sweet, and a brisk wind that kept the white
clouds moving swiftly high up in the spring-blue sky.
   The timber was oak, all well-grown trees, tall and
straight and thick in the stem. Work started at seven
in the morning and stopped when the light had gone
from the woods, and all day the passing time
was told and measured, not by a clock as at the
workshop, but by the smack of the axe, the whang-
ing of the two-handled saw, the ring of the hammer
hitting a wedge, and the crash of a tree as it fell to
the ground.
   Every day, a fire was lit in the middle of the
clearing, to burn the brash and the worthless loppings, and the smell of the wood-smoke would
drift strong and sharp on the rain-washed air. Jesse
carried the smell of the wood-smoke home with him,
in his clothes and hair, and the stain of the oak-
brown on his hands. "I smell like a rasher of bacon,"
he said once to Beth. "Or a kippered herring—I ent
sure which."
   He had more joy in those days in the woods than
he had known since returning to Cobbs. They were
good days, and he worked well. He came to know
the balance and swing of his axe, and the feel of
the smooth hickory handle, fitting exactly into his
hands, as though it were but a part of himself. He
learnt to let the weight of the axe be master of
the weight of the stroke, and he came to judge the
bite of the blade to a shaving. The work was good,
and its strong rhythm got into his blood, leaving
him somehow free and clear-eyed.
   The men, too, enjoying the change of surroundings and the change of work, were all in good humour, and Timothy Rolls, who was often Jesse's

partner in stripping the bark from a fallen tree, now talked to him in a friendly way.

"The smell of the woods is a proper tonic. And that ent just a manner of speaking.—I mean it like gospel. It's snuffing the smell of the juices that does it. Cleans your lungs out all the way through!"

Every morning now, it was Jesse's job to fetch the two horses from Anster and follow Grandfather Tewke to Sudge woods. But one morning, a Wednesday in May, Kate ran after him across the fields.

"It's Beth!" she said. "She's fell on her back on the bedroom floor."

"Laws!" he said. "Is she hurt bad?"

"No, no, but it's started her pains and she's asking for Goody to come and tend her."

Jesse left the horses and ran with Kate towards the house.

"I'll take the trap. I'll be quicker that way. You go in and look after Beth."

He drove straight to Checketts and brought Goody back at a rattling speed.

"Should I ought to fetch the doctor?"

"I'll tell you that when I've seen your Beth."

At half past ten he was allowed upstairs to the bedroom, and as he went in, Goody came to him with his child in her arms.

"You've got a son and I'm told his name is William Walter."

He took the child and moved to the bed. His head spun: he was trying to look at his wife and son at once. Beth lay very still and watched him, her eyes very pale, as if shock and pain had washed out their colour. Yet her gaze was as clear and calm as ever, and just as steady: it always astonished him, the calm steady look of her clear eyes.

"Are you all right, then?" he asked gently.

"Right as ninepence," she said in a whisper.

"Goody?" he said. "Is she telling the truth, this wife of mine?"

"She's as right as she can expect to be after turn-

ing somersaults on that mat," Goody said. "She should
take things easy for a while, however."

"And my son? Is he in good order too?"

"He's all there, if that's what you mean. A bit
quiet, maybe, but so he might be, with his mother
shaking him out so rudely, before he'd sent word he was
ready to come. But he'll be all right. We'll see
to that."

"Wife, you gave me a turn," Jesse said.

"You ought to go. My grandpa'll be wondering
where you've got to."

"I ought, I suppose. I've left the horses out there
somewhere. Here, who'll take my son?"

When he arrived at Sudge, the men had stopped
for their elevenses. Timothy Rolls sat on a log,
toasting a piece of cheese at the fire, and Fred Lovage
was warming his tea in a tin mug.

"Where the hell have you been?" asked Grandfather Tewke, as Jesse arrived with the horses. "We
can't hardly move here for want of carting these
butts away."

"It's Beth," Jesse said. "She had a fall and it's
brought the baby double quick."

"God almighty! Why didn't you say so? Is she all
right? Eh? Is she? And what about him?"

"A boy sure enough, and doing all right, Goody
says. And he's going to be called William Walter,
after you and my own dad."

"D'you hear that, Lovage? D'you hear that, Rolls?
I've got a great-grandson,—William Walter he's going to be called—to inherit the business when I'm
gone." And Grandfather Tewke went striding about
from one to another, striking each of them on the
back. "By God! It's a change to have something
the way I want it for once. A great-grandson! Just
think of that!"

"Well, I congratulate you, gaffer," said Steve Hewish. "Though come to think of it, Jesse here done
all the work."

"Ah, I'd never've thought he had it in him," said
Sam Lovage.

"Jesse," said Fred. "You can share my tea!"

"And my Welsh rabbit," said Timothy Rolls.

"Did you get Dr. Wells?" asked Grandfather Tewke.

"Goody said there wasn't no need."

"Well! All's well that ends well! And Goody shall have a whole drum of snuff from me for this."

"I'd say this calls for a celebration," said Timothy. "What're you going to do to mark the occasion for us, gaffer?"

"You can mark the occasion by getting a move on to do some work! Grandson or no, we've idled enough for one day, so eat them elevenses and get off your backsides, quick sharp! I'm taking the horses to pick up the crab."

All except Kit Maddox had come to shake Jesse by the hand. He now drew near for the first time.

"Funny, ent it, the way we're so different? I never went to hold my wife's hand when my son was born."

The men fell silent. Most of them drifted slowly away.

"Jesse Sideways?" Kit said. "I'm talking to you!"

"You're spitting a bit, too," Jesse said, wiping his hand across his eyes.

"So what? Is that something?"

"Look," Jesse said. "I know you're jealous of me but it's no use trying to start a quarrel 'cos I shan't play my proper part."

"Jealous! I've got no cause to be jealous of you!"

"Fine. That's humpty-dinker, then, ent it? We can get back to work."

"Don't tell *me* when to get back to work!"

"I've told you,—I ent a fighting man, so it's no use your crowding me up like this."

"If I was to hit you, would that make you fight?"

"It might," Jesse said. "Or it might not. I can't be sure. But I ent scared of you if that's what you mean, 'cos I'm about twice your weight and build, and my hands don't shake so bad as yours, neither. So you hold your tongue and leave me be and I'll do the same for you exactly."

He turned and went to the lock-up chest where the tools were kept overnight for safety. He took out his knee-pads; his two small axes and rubbing-stone; and his big American axe with the curved handle. He bent over to put on his pads.

The quarrel was almost gone from his mind. He was thinking of Beth and his baby son. But now there was a shout of warning, from two or three of the men at once, and when he looked round, still stooping, fastening a strap, he saw that Kid had taken a burning branch from the fire and was bearing it, smoking fiercely, across the clearing. Jesse was too slow in moving. The burning branch was laid across the back of his neck and held there an instant before he was able to squirm away. The men came running and gathered round, keeping a safe distance from Kit, who threatened them with the burning branch. But Grandfather Tewke, descending on them in a passion of rage, snatched the branch from Kit's hand and threw it back onto the fire.

"You're sacked!" he said. "Get out of these woods before I whip you out as you deserve!"

"Sacked?" Kit repeated. "You can't do that, without proper warning nor nothing. I ent going to take it! You've got no right!"

"If you don't get out, I'll send for the law and you'll go to gaol for assault, boy!"

"What about my pay? You owe me three days!"

"Get out of my sight," the old man said, "and don't let me see you at Cobbs again."

Jesse, in pain, was on his knees on the ground, fighting a heaving wave of sickness. He saw, dimly, that Kit was collecting his tools to go.

"Jesse?" said Grandfather Tewke, just above him. "Can you hear me, Jesse? Timmy's going to put some plantain leaves on that there burn for the moment. Then we're getting you home. D'you hear that?"

"Ah," Jesse said. "I hear all right."

He felt Timmy's fingers like tongs of hot iron upon his neck, and braced himself as his collar was peeled from his burnt flesh. He sucked in his breath between his teeth, and fell forward in a dead faint.

They carried him home unconscious to Cobbs, where Goody roused him and gave him a drink of weak tea. She cleaned the burn with soap and water, put on a dressing and bandaged him up, and made him lie down for a while in the parlour, with the curtains drawn to shut out the light. Only then would she let him go upstairs to Beth.

"How d'you like my smart new stock?" he asked, as he sat, stiff-necked in his bandages, on the side of the bed.

"You should have known better than turn your back on Kit Maddox."

"What'll become of him, now your grandpa's gave him the push?"

"Don't grieve for that," Beth said fiercely.

During the next few days, the men were full of gossip concerning Kit Maddox, and Liney the pit-man, who lived near Collow Ford, had something to report every morning.

"He ent paid his rent, and when old Trigg called down on Monday, Kit ran him up onto the foot-bridge and pitched him over into the brook."

"Kit's still got no work," said Bert Minchin. "He plays his squeezebox in the public every night and passes his cap round after. But he don't get much in it 'cos folks is turning against him on all sides."

"I hear his wife's just as bad," said Sam Lovage. "Well, I say wife for decency's sake, 'cos I hardly know what else to call her . . . But she's a Tartar, too, so I've heard, and there's terrible rows in that cottage sometimes."

Kate, hearing these stories, would shake her head and say what a mercy it was that old Grannie Maddox was not alive to see how Kit went on. And Goody, who was staying at Cobbs to look after Beth and the new baby, would just as surely say: "It's Kit's baby son I think of mostly. What a life he's got com-pared with our young William Walter!"

A week later, Jesse began carting the oak-bark from Sudge woods to the tannery at Chepsworth Bridge. He made three journeys the first day, and was driving home through Huntlip that evening when he heard a commotion at Collow Ford. He jumped from the cart and hurried down Withy Lane, and several boys rushed past in the dark, whirling clappers and cans of stones.

Outside Kit's cottage, a crowd of twenty or thirty people were gathered, hammering on the door and on the shutters locked across the window, beating saucepans and dustbin lids, and shouting to Kit to come out. A few carried lanterns hung on sticks, and by their light, Jesse saw that foremost among the crowd was Emery Preston, the young landlord of The Rose and Crown. Jesse turned to question the smith, Will Pentland, who stood at his door, watching with set-faced approval.

"What's he done!" Will repeated. "What *ent* he done would be more like it! He went into The Rose and Crown and knocked old Mrs Preston against the wall because she denied him drink on credit. That's what he done. And her nearly eighty-three years old! Why, I'd leather him silly if I was to catch him, but it's Emery's privilege to do that and he means to have it sure enough."

Someone had brought a baulk of timber and given it into Emery's hands. He was telling the crowd to stand back while he rammed the door. Immediately after the first blow, the crowd grew silent, watching Emery at work. The second blow broke through the door, and the baulk became lodged in the jagged hole, and then, as Emery struggled to pull it away, the casement above was thrown open and Kit leant out over the sill.

"I ent coming out! Nor you ent coming in neither! I'll see to that!"

He turned back into the bedroom, but reappeared at once, to lean out over the window-sill, holding his twelve-month-old son in his hands, high above the heads of the crowd.

"One more try at that door and I'll toss the boy onto them cobbles! I shall! I mean it as sure as hell is hell! And you'll be to blame, Emery Preston, so just you mark it!"

The people were utterly silent now, and their up-turned faces, perfectly still, had a strange likeness one to another, horror casting them all in the same mould. The child, in short cotton frock and muslin napkin, kicked his naked feet on the air and flailed about with his thin arms. In the light of the lanterns, his face seemed all eyes, very dark and deep and round, gazing upon the crowd below. His mouth was drawn down at the corners, and as his father gave him a jerk, raising him up even higher, he gave a long and drawn out cry, in a thin voice almost too small to hear, so frail was it, and so tired.

"Well?" Kit shouted. "Are you lot going and leaving me in peace or must I toss him down like I said?"

"Rubbish!" a voice called from the back of the crowd. "He won't do it! Not his own child! Take no notice, Emery Preston! Bost down that door!"

"No, not I!" Emery said, and cast the baulk of timber aside. "I've had enough! I'm going home."

"Me too," said Martin Coyle.

"And me," said Oliver Rye.

"We're going now!" Billy Ratchet shouted. "So take that babby inside where he's safe, and may the Lord inflict you for treating him so!"

"Get moving, you sanctimonious old swine, you! You and all your party there! Get off my doorstop or I'll drop him yet, by God I will!"

The people began to move away, and Jesse with them, but, looking back at the cottage window as Kit was withdrawing inside, he saw, in the dark room behind, a shadowy figure waiting and a woman's white arms reaching out for the child. Then Kit reappeared again.

"Hey, you! Jesse Sideways! Tell old Tewke he owes me my wages. Three days' work, the damned skinflint, and I want it quick sharp, so tell him from me!"

"Yes, I'll tell him," Jesse said.

On Saturday, when Jesse knocked at Kit's cottage, the window was still shuttered and barred, and the hole in the door was stuffed with sacking. After a while, there came the sound of furniture being dragged back inside; then the sacking was plucked away and a woman's face appeared at the hole. Jesse, bending to speak to her, could see only a pale-lipped mouth and a small, sharply pointed chin.

"I've brought Kit's wages. Is he in?"

"He's in, yes. Upstairs on the bed. But he won't come down to see anybody."

"Then give him this," Jesse said, and handed the money through the hole. "How's your baby? Is he all right?"

"He's right enough."

"Have you been shut up like this since Monday? Laws, it ent good for you nor your baby to stay shut up in the dark like that. Nor Kit neither."

"I know that!" she said. "I keep telling him so but he won't let me open the door or the window, not even to get a breath of air. I'm near going mad, shut up like this. I'm near as mad as Kit himself!"

"But he's got to come out sooner or later. He can't stay locked in there forever."

"He's scared to come out because of the people. Will Pentland says he'll be safe enough now, but Kit won't believe it. He knocks on the wall for Hesper Tarpin to bring bread and milk to the door."

"Ent there nothing I can do?"

"No, nothing. Only——"

"Only what?"

"Pray for me and the boy," she said, and withdrew from the door, replacing the sacking in the hole.

By the following Monday, the woman was dead, and Kit had vanished with the baby. Liney Carr was the first to bring the news to the workshop, and each of the others, on arriving, had something to add. The smith, Will Pentland, had tried Kit's door at five that morning, and it had opened. Inside, the woman lay

stretched on the floor with her head against the bars
of the grate, and with terrible marks on her throat
and forehead. Kit must have stolen out in the night,
taking the baby with him, but although many people
had searched the district, not a trace could be found,
and now a policeman from Chepsworth was in
charge.

The carpenters talked of it all day, but quietly,
soberly, all very subdued. And in the house that
evening, the women talked in the same way.

"I always said I'd be sorry for any girl that tied up
with Kit," Beth said, "but I never thought to have
such cause as this."

Jesse awoke from a deep sleep to find Beth sitting up
in bed beside him.

"What is it?" he said.

"I heard a noise outside in the yard."

"It's the rain, that's all. It's coming down like bows
and arrows. Just hark at it against that pane."

"No," she said. "It sounded like somebody shifting
timber. There! Did you hear it then?"

Jesse listened, but heard only the sound of the
rain.

"Your ears is sharper than mine," he said, getting
out of bed, "so I'd better go down and see what's
what."

He put on his trousers and went downstairs to the
kitchen. He lit a lantern and took it with him, through
the office and out to the yard. The rain was a cold
and steady downpour, in straight white shafts,
bouncing off the ground. He took a few steps and
was soaked to the skin.

"Who's there?" he called, in a loud voice.

He went on, between the big square stacks of
planking, out to the space in front of the workshop.
He held his lantern down low, moving forward,
slightly stooping, looking for footmarks in the mud.
He heard sounds behind him and swung round, but it
was only Grandfather Tewke, clad in oilskin and
sou'wester, squelching across the mud in his

gumboots, with his old-fashioned shotgun under one arm.

"Beth roused me up. She says we've got burglars. By God! They'll get what-for if I catch them stealing my goods and timber! D'you see any sign?"

"Somebody's been here," Jesse said. "The mud's all poached up along here."

He turned again, taking another few steps forward, still searching the ground for marks. He stood upright to peer about through the rainy darkness, and as he raised the lantern higher, a pair of booted feet swung slowly round in front of his eyes. His nerves gave a twitch along his arm, and the flame of the lantern flickered and leapt. He felt the old man come up behind him, and he raised the lantern as high as he could, to show how Kit had hanged himself in the big oak tree.

There was a ladder against the bough, and Jesse went up and cut the rope, and brought the body down to the ground. He knew by the awful lolling of the head that the neck was broken, and when he felt the dead hands flopping against him, his own live flesh coldly shrank on his bones.

Grandfather Tewke had gone ahead with the lantern, to open the workshop and light the way. Jesse carried the body in and laid it on a trestle table. He forced himself to remove the noose from the neck, to push the wet hair back from the forehead, to wipe the rain from the dead face, and to fold the hands together on the breast.

Grandfather Tewke held the light, looking down at Kit in frowning anger. He watched as Jesse covered the body over with canvas, and then, as though released from the fascination of Kit's dead face, began to move about the workshop.

"The lock on the door was broke," he said. "Kit's been in here. Now I wonder why? Ah, I thought as much! Come here and look."

It was Kit's old place at the workbench, and there Kit had laid his baby son, wrapped round in a shawl that was pinned close with a pewter brooch. The child lay unnaturally still, eyes closed, lips parted, seeming scarcely to breathe at all.

"He's alive, just about," the old man said, and bent over to sniff the child's mouth. "He's been put to sleep with a sup of brandy. Let's take him indoors."

Jesse picked up the child and carried him quickly into the house. All three women were in the kitchen, and Kate was reviving the fire with the bellows.

"Kit's gone and hanged hisself in the oak tree," the old man said. "We've just been laying him out in the workshop."

"Is he dead?" Kate gasped.

"Of course he's dead! It's what you'd expect after hanging, ent it?"

"Laws," said Goody, seeing the child. "Is he dead, too, the poor mite?"

"Dead drunk!" the old man answered. "Set on early by his father."

"Give him to me," Goody said. "What a poor little nottomy scrap of a babe! He's hardly more than skin and bone. Who knows what he's been through these past few days?"

She sat down with the child in her lap, close to the stove, where a handful of sticks were now burning. She undid the brooch and opened the shawl, and as she did so, a piece of paper flew to the floor.

"A note," she said. "Pick it up and read what it says." And, holding the child in the curve of her body, she began rubbing his arms and legs. "Well, Jesse? What's Kit Maddox had to say in his last will and testament there wrote down?"

Jesse frowned at the scribbled note but could not understand it. He gave it to Beth, who took it under the lamp to read.

"It's about the child. It says, 'My son is not to go in the Institution.'"

"No more he shan't!" exclaimed Goody. "Institutions indeed! He's fell in with us and with us he stays or my name ent Goody Izzard. Here, Jesse!— Warm me that milk. I think the babe is waking up."

The child was certainly opening his eyes, slowly

and stickily, because the eyelids were rimmed with scurf. The light at first made him recoil, and he hid his face against Goody's bosom, but then he rolled over and lay against her arm, gazing around with filmy eyes that rolled and swivelled in their sockets.

"Drunk, sure enough," Goody said, and, taking the cup of warm milk, held it for the child to drink. "There, that'll soon quench the poison inside you."

She took off his frock and vest and the three-cornered napkin that was tied in a knot about his loins: all were filthy and specked with blood from the many flea-bites that mottled his skin, and Goody, having screwed them up in disgust, threw them into the fire to burn. Jesse brought her a bowl of warm water, a tablet of soap, and some soft lint. Beth brought a bundle of baby clothes, and Kate brought a jar of elderflower ointment.

Tenderly, Goody washed the child's face, his hair, his body, his thin-fleshed limbs. Then she dried him, anointed his sores, and dressed him in the clean warm clothes. And all the time, he was perfectly quiet, perfectly still, his body slack within her grasp. But at least there was some touch of colour in his cheeks now, as he sat on her lap in the glow of the fire. And his eyes were losing their filmy look, growing steadier, with intelligence in them; beginning to follow Goody's movements.

They were so very deep and dark, these eyes, that they resembled the eyes of a sad-faced snowman: looking on the world in a hollow fashion; blank as coal-knobs; expecting nothing, yet very watchful in a still, deep way, as though they were keepers of unfathomed knowledge.

"Shall we be keeping him, then?" asked Jesse. "Bringing him up with our own?"

"No," said Goody. "You've got three children already. You don't need no more. This little nottomy's going to be mine, to keep me company out at the Pikehouse."

"Gracious," said Kate, "can you manage a baby at your time of life, Goody?"

"Will you be allowed to keep him?" asked Jesse.

"I'll get Parson Chance to speak for me. He'll soon sort it out."

"That's good," said Beth, smiling at Goody, nursing the child.

"What's his name?" Goody asked.

"Laws," Jesse said. "I've never heard it, I don't believe."

"Nor me neither," said Grandfather Tewke. "The blasted kid!—that's all Maddox ever called him. And I know when Parson Wisdom went down in March to chivvy Kit and the woman about the boy's baptism, they laughed in his face and said they weren't yet decided what name to give him."

Goody was shocked. She drew the child close and rocked him gently, her brown wrinkled face full of rage and pity. That a child past twelve months should still be nameless!—Why, even a cat or a dog fared better than that. She had never heard of such a thing in her life before. Such an unchristian thing. No, never! Never! And then at last she calmed down.

"I'll see Mr Chance first thing in the morning and we'll have a christening as soon as maybe." She set the child on his feet on her lap and held him upright, looking into his deep dark eyes. "I shall call him Thomas, after me brother that died," she said. "He couldn't be named after a better man. It'll maybe make up for all he's been through."

There came a day when Betony, aged four and a half, could not be found in the house or garden; the orchard, the fields, or the workshop yard. Beth said she must have wandered out to the road, and Jesse, thinking how easy it would be for a small girl to stumble into the Derrent, ran along the bank as far as the village, searching the waters as he went. But Betony was perfectly safe. She was with a crowd of people that had gathered to watch a platoon of soldiers drilling on the green.

That was the first summer of the war in South Africa. The platoon, belonging to the Three Counties Infantry, based at Capleton Wick, was marching southward, collecting recruits as it went, and Betony, hearing the beating of the drum, had followed them all the way to the green. She could scarcely be bothered to glance at Jesse as he arrived and joined the crowd. She had eyes and ears only for the tall sergeant and the marching soldiers and the little drummer in red-flashed helmet and red sash. And Jesse, swinging her up into his arms, was also happy to stay and watch.

A last command rang out, the drumbeats stopped, and the soldiers, drawn up in a block of fours, stood at ease on the green. The sergeant turned toward the crowd and his glance happened to light on Jesse.

"Ah! Now you're the kind of man we want exactly!"

"What, me?" said Jesse, with a burning face. "Laws, I shouldn't be no sort of use as a soldier!"

"You surely have some care for your queen and country, haven't you, young fellow?"

"Why, yes, I suppose, but——"

"You can't have Jesse," said Oliver Rye. "He's lame in one foot."

"Oh! That's different! That's no use to us. And no one expects a lame man to volunteer as a soldier."

The sergeant was casting about again, looking for more likely material, when old Dr Mellow, who had once been a great scholar at Oxford, but who now lived like a tramp on Huntlip common, pushed to the very front of the crowd and spoke out in his splendid voice.

"Why should any man, lame or not, fight in a war that doesn't concern him and which shouldn't have been begun in the first place?"

"Why?" said the sergeant. "Surely every man in England must want to protect his interests from the thieving Boer?"

"What interests are those?" the doctor asked, and turned to Mattie Makepiece, standing beside him. "Have you got a gold-mine in Cape Province?"

"Not unless my uncle Albert's gone and left me one in his will," said Mattie. "And that ent likely, 'cos that was the Arge-and-nines he went to, I believe."

"And you?" said the doctor, turning to old Mark Jervers, the roadmender on his other side. "Have you got a diamond-mine in Kimberly?"

"Not now," Mark said sadly. "I had to sell it to pay for me boots."

"Then, sergeant, what interests are these you're asking the men of this village to fight for?"

"England's interests are yours and mine, sir!" the sergeant said angrily. "They're what make us rich."

"Rich?" cried Billy Rachet. "There's nobody here richer than four-pence! It's them that own the gold-

mines and such that should go and fight for them if
they've got a mind to! Not our boys here!"

A wave of approval ran through the crowd, and one
or two women began to shout abuse at the sergeant,
who turned abruptly and faced his platoon. At the first
command, they stood to attention. At the second, they
turned to the right in fours, towards the road. The
drummer stood ready, drumsticks up, touching his
nose, and the sergeant paused for one last remark to
the crowd.

"I never thought to find a village in England that
wasn't willing to do its bit!"

"Get away!" said Annie Wilkes. "My eldest boy's
been gone from the start."

"And my boy Dave," said Queenie Lovage.

"And two of mine," said old Jim Minchin. "And
others besides."

"Then I hope they don't die for want of support
from home," said the sergeant, and in the silence that
followed his words, he turned and signalled to his
drummer. The drum-beats rang out, and the soldiers
marched smartly away.

Jesse withdrew from the crowd and set Betony down
on the ground. He took her hand and started for
home. But she, hanging back, was still watching
the soldiers, and as they vanished along the road, she
suddenly burst into storms of tears.

"Gone!" she said, sobbing. "Soldiers all gone!"

"Why, yes," Jesse said, getting down on his
haunches and drawing her against his knees. "They
couldn't stop on the green forever, could they?"

"I want to go too!"

"What, and leave your poor dad all alone by hisself?"

"No!" she said, choking, and her sobs became more
anguished than ever.

"Laws," Jesse said, "you mustn't cry like that, my
blossom. Just look at that starling watching you from
Mrs Merry's garden."

"Don't want to look!"

"That's a pity, that is, 'cos it ent often you see a

pink starling just sitting like that as bold as brass."

"Pink?" she said, forgetting to cry. "Where is he, pink?"

"Why, there, on that laylock. Ah dang it! Now it's flied away!"

"Was it really pink?"

"Pink as piglets," he said, drying her eyes with a corner of her apron. "And with little spectacles on his nose, to see you all the plainer with."

"He wasn't!" she said, striking his chest with her small fists. "It's not true!"

"How d'you know if you never saw him? Why, I bet that pink starling has flied off to Cobbs. He was heading that way right enough. And when we get back he'll be sitting perched on the workshop roof. You mark my words!"

A few days later, Betony was missing again, and this time he found her in the school classroom, a slate on her lap, a chalk in her fingers, and a look of rapture on her face as she squeakily traced a large pot-hook, helped by eight-year-old Agatha Mance. At sight of Jesse, the storm-clouds gathered at once on her brow, and her legs entwined themselves round the bench. Miss Likeness suggested that she should stay, and Jesse, with some misgiving, gave in.

Betony was four and a half. There were many younger than she in the class. But it grieved Jesse to see her going to school, so small, such a baby, yet already growing away from him, making a separate life of her own. He felt he had lost her. He felt she would never be the same again. And he used to slip away to meet her coming across the fields, expecting to find a little stranger. But Betony, although enjoying her new life, was just as close to him as ever. Her day was not complete until it had been unfolded to him. Her joys shone all the more brightly, and her troubles dwindled, the moment he shared them.

"Glory be!" he used to say. "You make school sound like a picnic. I could almost wish myself back on the bench."

The habit he formed, of going to meet her after

school, went on a long time, even when he had
ceased to be anxious. It went on because they both
liked it,—it was their special time together, out of
the day—and the path across the fields of Anster became woven with certain events, some small, some
large, that occurred in their lives.

Here, at the stile by Tommy Trennam's cottage, he
met her with the news of Roger's birth. Here, beside
the copse of birch and rowan, he pulled her from a
snowdrift during the blizzard that came so suddenly
one day in April, 1901. Here, in the field called Big
Piece, they came on the mare, Flounce, giving birth
to the foal, Jingle, and watched from a distance,
through the hedge, so as not to disturb her. And there,
in the cowslip links, Betony wept on his shoulder
after a quarrel with three children from Middening
Bank.

"They set on Rosie Rye and me outside the gate and
said we was all foxes or hounds who live here in
Huntlip!"

"Well, that's nothing for you to get in a pucker for,"
he said. "The Middening kids used to say that same
thing when I was a boy and went to school, and before that, too, I dare say, right back to the beginning
of time. And the Huntlip kids always said that the
Middening kids smelt of the midden."

"Yes, I know. That's what Rosie said to Libby
Potten."

"Why, there you are then. That makes you quits.
It's nothing for you to get upset for. You're too quick
to take things to heart. Lumme, there's sayings like
that for all the villages round about, as I remember.
Blagg, for instance. We used to say 'The people of
Blagg all dress in rags.' And about Horton we used to
say 'They're not quite right, the Horton folk, and
they've gone and boughten a pig in a poke.' "

Betony laughed. Her sorrows were easily van-
quished in these days. And they walked on.

"What else?" she asked, skipping beside him, over
the cowslips. "What other things did you used to say?"

"Well, there's Eastery, now, where I used to come

from. That's a tiny place, you see, and there was a rhyme that said, 'The people of Eastery and what they own could all stand together on a staddle stone.' "

"What else? What else?"

"Well, there's Chepsworth town, where the mustard is made. The folk there is said to be daft, and if we met someone from Chepsworth we used to ask him who blew on the mustard to make it cool."

"But that's not a rhyme!" Betony said.

"Why, no, it ent. It's just a saying, that's all, to stir people up, like the one about Scarne, where they cut down the pear trees to get at the fruit."

"What else? What else?"

"Laws," Jesse said. "I don't know no more."

"What about Capleton? What about Springs? What about all the places over the hills?"

"I dunno," Jesse said. "I've never been further than Scarne in my life."

Betony, as she grew older, was always wanting to know what lay beyond the hills, or over the river, or at the end of the long high roads. She went with Jesse everywhere, in the cart to fetch timber from Porsham wharf, out to the farms to deliver gates and fencing, into Chepsworth to buy tools or nails or hinges. But she never wanted to go with her great-grumpa Tewke, however far afield into strange and exciting places he might be travelling. It was always her father she wanted. Adventures were nothing without him. And Jesse could never overcome his amazement that this bonny, spirited thing, with her quick and ready tongue, should prefer his company to that of anyone else in the world.

"If I was to walk and walk and walk . . . where should I come to at the end?"

"Well, now," he said, "a lot'd depend which way you was going."

"South, of course!—Nobody ever goes north!" she said.

"Then you'd come into Gloucestershire," he said.

"And after that?"

"You'd come into Wiltshire."

"And after that?"

"What, still walking and walking and walking?"

"That's right. Where would I come to?"

"You should ask these questions at school."

"But this is the holidays," she said. "And anyway, I'm asking *you*."

"Ah, I know, and I've got my thinking-cap on, too."

"Don't you know, then?" she asked, surprised, with just a little touch of scorn. "Don't you know what comes after Wiltshire?"

"Dorset!" he said, with a grunt of triumph. "That's where you'd come to, sure enough! And you'll have to watch out now, my blossom, or the rate you're going you'll walk right over into the sea."

"The sea? But we ent come to London yet."

"Why, no, that's right. No more we ent."

"Then where is it?" she asked, frowning.

"I dunno. It's down there somewhere. You must ask your mother."

"Is the sea very big?" she asked him.

"Fairish," he said. "Yes, pretty big, really, all told."

"Is it bigger than Slings Pool?"

"Why, that's only a puddle compared with the sea!"

"Have you ever been in a ship?" she asked.

"No, nor never want to, either," he said.

"Have you seen the sea?"

"Seen it?" he said. "What, seen the sea? Why, not in so many words, exactly."

"Have you or haven't you?"

"No," he said. "But your mother's seen it, I believe. You must ask her.—She'll tell you all about the sea."

But Betony rarely talked to her mother. She preferred him, even when his answers failed to satisfy her.

When the other children began to go to school, he went less and less often to meet them coming across the fields. They had one another. He was not needed. So he went only on special occasions, or when an old impulse moved him.

Janie, a year younger than Betony, was at first her

devoted slave. She had no life of her own,—no thought, no wish—except by reflection. She was the moon to Betony's sun. But later on, when Betony grew dictatorial, Janie withdrew from her and moved closer to William instead, and Jesse, who saw it happening, feared that Betony would be hurt. She was different from all the rest. She took things to heart so passionately. But he need not have worried, for the younger children, though clinging together, forming a separate group of four, still looked to Betony as their head. They were the little sheaves of corn, bowing to the big sheaf of corn in their midst.

They formed a group for the sake of the strength the union gave them, and because they were all of one kind, while Betony was different. But they depended on her to guide them, to protect them, to help with their lessons, and even, sometimes, to direct their games. It was only when she grew too fierce and demanding that they withdrew from her. It was only when she was unkind that they closed their ranks against her completely. They were rarely unkind to her.

One wet Saturday in winter, when he was all alone in the workshop, making a coffin, he looked up to find Betony watching him with a stiff white face.

"I don't like you making coffins!"

"Somebody's got to make them," he said.

"Not you! Not you! Promise you'll never make coffins again."

"I can't promise that," he said, smiling.

"You must!" she said, and her terrible passion made her voice very rough in her throat. "You must! You must!"

"Well, I shan't," he said. "That ent for you to must at me, my blossom."

Betony turned and ran out, but a little while later, as he was tidying up the workbench, she came back with the four other children and marched them straight to the finished coffin that stood on end against the wall.

"There, look at that!" she said to them. "That's for

poor old Mrs Sharpey, lying dead in her house at
Blagg. They'll nail it down tight and put her into a
hole in the ground for the worms and beetles to eat
her up."

Janie and William turned away. Roger went white,
and Dicky, the youngest, began to cry.

"That's nothing yet!" Betony said. "Wait and see
what else I'll show you!"

She took Dicky's arm and began pulling him away,
prodding the other three before her.

"Where're you off to?" Jesse asked, stepping directly in her path.

"To see the hole they've digged for Mrs Sharpey."

"Oh, no you don't!" Jesse said, and made her release little Dicky's arm.

He sent the younger ones back to the house. Then
he took hold of Betony by the waist and lifted her up
to sit on the workbench.

"Ent you ashamed of yourself, my blossom, frightening your sister and brothers like that?"

"No! I'm not!"

"Nor sorry for making Dicky cry?"

"No! I'm not!"

"Well, I'm ashamed *for* you, even if you ent
ashamed for yourself. I am! That's a fact! A big girl of
nine, frightening a poor little chap like Dicky . . . I'm
more ashamed than I know how to say."

"I don't care if you are or not!"

"Don't you?" he said. "Then you'd better run
along, I reckon, 'cos I don't love you when you're like
this. No, not a morsel! So you'd better be Miss Sally
Forth."

He began to be busy, taking a hand-brush and
sweeping the shavings off the bench, but he could see
Betony, sitting just where he had put her, her hands
in her lap, her head and shoulders beginning to droop,
her chin sinking against her chest. He could see the
last of her stubborn defiance lingering on in tight-
closed lips and flaring nostrils.

"What, not gone yet?" he said, as though in surprise.
"It's no use sitting there like that, you know, 'cos I

meant what I said.—I don't love you when you're naughty. What is it, then? D'you need help in getting down?"

He put out his hands, but without touching her, merely waiting for her to move. And now, as she looked towards his waiting hands, her little face went to pieces. Her lips quivered, her eyes crumpled and closed tight, and she became unbelievably small, her face and body melting against him, her hands groping upward about his neck.

"There, there, don't cry," he murmured, and rocked her gently within his arms. "Of course your dad loves you! He loves you as dearly as dearly can be!"

He took her up and bore her about, holding her close, trying to draw the throbbing heartache out of her and into himself. For he was the guilty one. He was the one that ought to suffer. He was the one whose heart should break.

"There, there! It's all over now . . . Shall we be sensible people again, you and me, before someone sees us in all this mess? Eh? Shall we?"

The cause of the trouble was almost forgotten. His only concern was to comfort the child and bring the blue light back into her eyes, where the grey tears had quenched it. And that was how it always was, whenever there had been trouble between them.

He knew he sinned by denying his love, and each time he paid for it in dark guilty shame. Yet whenever she was haughty with him, flouting him and tossing her head, he was lured into the same dark sin all over again. He had to bend her; to break her defiance; to keep her bound to him in smallness, as she had been bound to him from the first. The words would be said:—"I don't love you"—and only when he had brought her to him, creeping, small, into his arms, did the guilt follow.

Once or twice every month, on a Sunday, Jesse drove out to visit Goody, bearing gifts of honey and jam from Beth, and taking his tools to do odd jobs about the Pikehouse. And sometimes Betony went with him.

When she was young Betony loved the Pikehouse because it was so amazingly small. She liked the steep stairs, almost a ladder, and she liked the tiny window under the eaves, where, in the springtime, you could watch the sparrows pulling the straws from the thatch, and the martins building their nests underneath. She also liked the strange shape of the house, with its two flat corners at the road end, and the funny recess where once a board had announced the toll fees.

"Why did people have to pay?"

" 'Cos the road belonged to Mr Lannam and he had to keep it in repair," Jesse told her.

"Why don't they pay now?"

"A new road was made, going round by Hallows, and nobody hardly uses this road now."

"How much did it cost for a pony and trap?"

"Sixpence," he said.

"Then we shall pay . . . just like the people long ago."

So Goody had to come to the gate, while Betony stayed sitting up in the trap, pretending to search her drawstring purse, and at last dropping a clammy sixpence into Goody's waiting hand.

"Good day, Mrs Izzard," she said, primly. "What fine weather for the time of year. I hope your floppy-docks is doing well?"

Betony liked the Pikehouse garden because of all its different scents. Lavender, rosemary, sage, thyme, all grew in amongst the peas and beans and carrots and marrows. There were sharp-smelling marigolds, sweet-smelling pinks, and a bush of lad's love, as Goody called it, which, when you rubbed the feathery leaves in your fingers, smelt sharp and sweet at the same time.

At first, whenever Jesse and Betony went on these visits, the boy Tom would not be there. He had only to see them driving up and he would be off, across the turnpike and into the woods. It was always the same, Goody said.—Whoever called, Tom would never stay to see them. His only friend was Charley Bailey, living in his shanty on Norton common: he had plenty to say to Charley, it seemed, but nothing to say to any-one else.

Betony was full of curiosity concerning Tom. She asked Goody endless questions.

"He's not your grandson, 'cos his name is Maddox and not Izzard, so why d'you let him call you grannie?"

"Tom's adopted," Goody said. "What else would he call me if not grannie?"

"Does he go to school?"

"Yes, he goes to Norton. When he goes at all."

"Here!" Jesse said. "You ought to make him go to school, Goody."

"You're one to talk! My goodness me!"

"Ah, and look at me now. Biggest dunce this side of Ennen."

"Tom's all right," Goody said. "He likes to work on the farm with me, and he's learning plenty, even if it don't come out of books."

One Sunday in winter, as Jesse and Betony drove to the Pikehouse, they were caught in a cold down-pour of rain. Jesse drew up the cape and they kept dry enough, but he was worried, on arriving, to see Tom go running into the woods as usual, clad only in trousers and shirt.

"The boy'll catch his death," he said to Goody. "Keep Betony here while I go and fetch him."

It was cold and wet even in the shelter of the big pine trees, for the rain was heavy and drove through the branches, rattling down on the matting of needles that covered the ground. Jesse went quietly through the wood, and found the boy sitting under a tree, his back to the trunk, where the rain streamed darkly down, his knees drawn up under his chin, and his arms folded about his shins. He seemed not to care that he was soaked from head to foot, that his hair dripped into his eyes, that his shirt clung like a rag to his shoulders. He seemed scarcely to feel the cold, but kept himself knotted hard against it, sitting still, with-out a shiver, looking into the wood.

When Jesse spoke to him, he started up at once

like a deer, and would have run off but that Jesse caught him by the arm.

"You've no reason to run from me. Why, I've known you since you was a little tucker dressed in frocks. You wasn't scared then. Nor you ent now, surely, are you?"

"No," Tom muttered, but his arm was rigid in Jesse's grasp.

"You come home and get dried out before you catch your death of cold."

"No. I don't want to. I'm fine as I am."

"There! And I was hoping for news of Charley Bailey. He's a friend of yours, from what I hear, and so he was mine when I lived at the Pikehouse."

"I know," Tom said. "He mentions you sometimes."

The boy fell in beside Jesse and together they returned to the Pikehouse. At sight of Betony, sitting perched on the settle, he was ready for flight again, but Goody sent him upstairs to change, and when, in answer to her call, he came reluctantly down again, she flung a towel over his head, pressed him onto the stool by the fire, and held him there while she dried his hair.

Beth had sent Goody a parcel. It contained a fruit-cake, a bottle of brandy, a screw of snuff, and a large tin of drinking-chocolate. Goody now took the chocolate and made them each a beaker full. Tom sat hunched on his stool, the towel still over his head, his steaming beaker between his hands. In the firelight, his newly dried face was a smooth dusky brown, shiny about the nose and cheekbones, but shadowy at the jaws and temples, where the thin flesh went hollowly in. His eyes, with the flickering flames reflected in them, seemed almost black.

Betony, sipping her chocolate, studied him for a long time.

"Are you a gipsy?" she asked suddenly.

Tom merely stared into the fire.

"Can't he speak?" she asked Jesse.

"Why, yes. But he's shy, you see, and you've got to give him a bit of time."

"Is he a gipsy? He looks like one."

"Of course he ent. He's just dark, that's all."

"How old is he?"

"Well, try him again," Jesse said, "and see if he answers you this time."

Betony leant a little forward, as though she thought the boy might be deaf.

"How old are you?" she asked loudly, and, when he stayed silent: "Don't you *know* how old you are?"

"Tom," said Goody, in a quiet voice. "Betony's speaking."

Tom's glance flickered to Betony's face.

"Nine," he muttered, and looked back at the fire.

"Can you read and write?" Betony asked him.

"Anyone can," Tom muttered.

"How much can you read?"

"Solomon Grundy. Reynard the Fox."

"Is that all?" Betony said, and, as he fell silent again: "D'you know your tables? D'you know your sums? Do you know how to do division?"

Jesse put his hand on her arm.

"You're going too fast. Try talking to Tom without putting him through the hoop. Ask if he'll take you and show you the badger's earth when you come next time."

"Will you?" said Betony, again leaning forward towards the boy.

"If you like," he said.

"Will the badgers be there?"

"You wouldn't see them. Not in the daytime."

"Then why go?" she said, staring. "Where's the point if there's nothing to see? I call that silly. I do indeed!"

The boy looked at her for an instant, and then away, and she could get nothing more out of him for the rest of the visit.

Driving home afterwards, Jesse took her gently to task.

"Tom's younger than you. You should go more slowly and try to bring him out of his shell."

"I don't think he's right in the head."

"Oh yes he is! He's just wild and shy and unused to strangers. He ent got a family like you, remember. He's only got his grannie Izzard. But you could help him if you had a mind to. You could teach him things and be his friend."

"Yes," said Betony, much struck. "I shall teach him things and be his friend."

Thereafter, when she went with Jesse to the Pike-house, she made an effort to be friends with Tom. She persuaded him to take her exploring in the woods, and she gave him small presents, such as a tracing of a map of Great Britain, a blue-whorled pebble out of the Derrent, and a piece of candy from Capleton Mop. Tom, in turn, gave her a sheep's horn picked up on Norton common, a man-shaped potato dug from the garden, and a lark's egg, beautifully shaded and speckled in brown. Betony received these presents with grave appreciation but threw them away on the journey home, and on the third occasion, Jesse, having seen from the boy's face what it cost him to part with the lark's egg, was very much grieved.

"What d'you do that for? Poor Tom would be sad to see his lark's egg thrown away like that."

"But he didn't see! And what do I want with a smelly egg?"

Jesse was silent a short while, staring thoughtfully at the pony's ears.

"Ah, well," he said at length. "I dare say Tom does the same with the things you give him."

Betony stared. Such a thing had never occurred to her.

The friendship lasted perhaps a year, and then came to a sudden end. Betony, playing schools with Tom, became angry because he could not recite the poem she had set him to learn on a previous visit. She rapped his knuckles with a little cane and ordered him to stand in the corner. He refused and there was a quarrel.

"You're hopeless!" she said. "You never want to learn anything!"

"What was it she wanted to learn you, Tom?" Jesse asked.

"Poultry," Tom said. "Bloody dancing daffodils."

"There!" said Betony. "That's fine expressions, I must say! And it's not the first time he's used them neither!"

She looked at Jesse, and then at Goody, who was sitting opposite, darning a sock.

"He don't only swear. He poaches too. And he goes to see a smelly old man who lives in a hovel and keeps ferrets. His name's Charley Bailey and it's him that teaches Tom to swear. Well? Ent you going to give him what-for?"

"Laws," Jesse said. "Poaching! Lumme!" And he winked at Tom.

"Poaching is stealing!" Betony said. "Little thieving toad!"

"You be careful who you're miscalling," Goody said. "Keep a civil tongue in your head, young miss, or else a still one."

"I shall speak if I want to. It's only the truth. Tom is a poacher. I've seen his snares."

"So are others I could mention, and I needn't look further than your own dad."

"My dad is no poacher!" Betony said.

"He was, though, at one time of day." Goody got up and went to the fire-place. She took down the tobacco-tin full of shot and rattled it under Betony's nose. "Ask your dad where them pellets come from! You ask him. Go on!" She put the tin back and returned to her chair. "Ah, and ask how he got that wonky foot!"

Betony came to Jesse and stood leaning against his knees.

"Shall we go home now?" she said.

"Why, no. I aim to stop another hour or two yet."

"I don't want to stop any longer. Not in this

tiddly house. I don't like it. I think it's queer.
Tiddly little house it is!"

"Hah!" Goody said. "Tiddly it may be, but you
was glad enough to be born in it, however."

"I wasn't born here! You're telling lies!"

"I should know, seeing I brought you into the
world."

"You didn't! You didn't! It's all lies!" Betony tug-
ged at Jesse's jacket. "I want to go home. Now.
This minute!"

"Then you'd better start to walk, my blossom,
'cos I ent coming. Not until I'm good and ready."

"I'm not walking! It's too far!"

"Then you'll have to wait for me, that's all. And
no more tantrums, mind, or I shall get cross and
then there'll be ructions!"

He took hold of her and lifted her onto the
settle beside him, and there she remained, in silence,
for the rest of the visit. She would not have tea
when they had it. Nor would she say her farewells
when she left. And Jesse, glancing at her pale,
tight-clenched face as they drove home, feared she
would not easily forgive Goody for humbling her
pride.

Sure enough, a fortnight later, when he was setting
out for the Pikehouse, Betony did not want to go.
And the next time the same. And the next after
that. He went alone, or with Beth, or with one of
the younger children. Betony went on other journeys, but never to the Pikehouse.

At about this time, she became even more devoted
to learning. She was top of the school in all things
and could do no wrong, either in the eyes of the
vicar, who taught her the Scriptures, or in the eyes
of Miss Likeness, who invited her home for special
coaching.

"Miss Likeness wants me to sit for exams, to go
to the Grammar School, Lock's, in Chepsworth."

"The Grammar School! Lumme! And how long
will you be there, then?"

"Until I'm sixteen. Or seventeen, perhaps."

"Fancy all them years at school! That'd never've suited me. I'd have bost a blood-vessel at the thought."

"Bost!" she said. "What a word to use!"

"Why, what's wrong with bost, you odd little article, you?" he demanded.

"Liddle aarticle!" she said. "Zackly so! Sure nuff!"

"Ah, you're getting too grand for me," he said, turning back to work. "Seems I can't never say the right thing these days. Or else I say it all countryfied. I reckon us two shall soon be strangers."

But at sight of the sadness coming into her face, he knew she was no stranger after all. She was still his favourite, and he was still all in all to her.

He had the pony and trap standing ready in the fold, and was dropping his tool-bag in, when Betony hurried out of the house, putting on her hat and coat.

"Great-grumpa says there's a barge gone aground on Sidley Ait. Can we go and see them hauling it off?"

"I was going to see your Grannie Izzard."

"Oh, but the barge'll be gone by this evening," she said, "and I wanted to write about it in school tomorrow."

"All right," he said. "I can go to the Pikehouse next Sunday instead."

But the next Sunday, Betony wanted to attend the dedication service in the newly restored church of St John's in Dingham, and they had to start out soon after dinner. The next Sunday again, she and he were invited to tea with Miss Likeness, to talk about the Grammar School. And the Sunday after that, when the bad rains had come, and the Idden had burst its banks at Upham, Betony wanted to see the floods.

"Here!" he said, as they stood together on Woolman Bridge. "Are you keeping me away from the Pikehouse on purpose?"

"On purpose?" she said. "Why should I do that?"

"I dunno. I just wondered, that's all."

Looking at her, he could not be sure if she lied or not. Her stare was so straight, so surprised, so puzzled. And, even if she lied, he could not be angry because in his heart there was always a pleasant warmth that undid him. It was his weakness, that he liked to be all in all to her; that he liked her clinging, possessive ways.

There were other people on the bridge, and he saw how often their eyes came to rest on Betony's face, how often they smiled at the things she said. It was not that she was wonderfully pretty. But she was so very harvest-fair. Her hair was so bright, her skin so golden, her eyes such a wonderful shade of blue. And then, too, there was her smile,—her mother's smile, but more frequent—that came unexpectedly, springing into being out of nothing at all, casting its warmth and brightness all about, so that other people broke into smiles as well.

She seemed not to notice the glances that came her way, and Jesse was glad, for she was brightest and best when she could forget herself like this: watching the swans swimming along the streets of Upham; the boys with rods and lines, fishing pots and pans from the flood-water; watching farmers in boats, rescuing cattle.

When they got home, and were talking of all the things they had seen, Beth interrupted with a sudden attack.

"Ent it time you went to see Goody instead of gadding about the country?"

"Yes, I reckon it is, and I shall be going just as soon as maybe."

"Why not next Sunday?"

"Ah, well, me and Betony planned taking some clothes and toys and such to Upham next Sunday, for the poor little mites that are flooded out of their homes down there."

"Then when will you go and see Goody?"

"I shall go, don't you worry, just as soon as there's time."

But somehow another three weeks went by, and Beth drove out to the Pikehouse herself, taking the younger children with her.

"Well?" Jesse said, when they came back. "Any message from Goody?"

"No, nothing," Beth replied.

"What, nothing at all?"

"Why should Goody send you a message? She's probably forgot you even exist."

"Did you tell her how busy I am just now?"

"I told as good a tale as I could make it."

"And didn't she have nothing to say to that?"

"Just nodded, that's all."

"Well, dammit!" he said. "What's the news at the Pikehouse, then, or must I squeeze you like squeezing a cow?"

"The news is all right," Beth said, busy bringing food to the table, "except for the rain coming in through the roof."

"What's that you say?"

"There's two or three holes in the thatch," Beth said. "You said so yourself some months back."

"But are they got bad, then, since I was there last?"

"Goody ent complaining. She's got it all worked out to a tee. If the rain's in the west, she puts her bed under the window. If the rain's in the north, as it has been lately, she puts her bed alongside the stairs. The drips ent too bad there, so long as she covers the bed with canvas."

"Dear Lord!" Jesse said. "I'd no idea things'd worsened that much!"

"Are you interested, then?" Beth asked, surprised. "I thought you was too busy gallivanting to worry yourself about your mother."

"Aw!" Jesse said, and shifted uncomfortably in his chair. "I didn't know things'd got so bad with that there roof-thatch. I'll take the day off and go first thing."

"Oh no you won't!" said Grandfather Tewke, looking up from his supper. "You've got that threshing-floor to finish at Outlands."

"Then I'll go on Sunday," Jesse said. "But by golly! Fancy that roof gone as bad as that! Somebody should've said something sooner."

"There's plenty been said," Beth retorted. "It's the doing that's in such short supply."

"Ah!" he said. "That's right, surely."

And, looking at Betony, who sat as though deaf to what was passing, he knew he had been too weak with her, letting her rule him as she pleased.

On Sunday morning, he loaded the cart with spelks, twine, and trusses of straw, and hoisted the cover to keep things dry. It was raining hard, as it had done endlessly all that autumn, and he wore his mackintosh coat and cap, prepared for a wet day's work on the roof of the Pikehouse. Betony watched him from the dairy.

"Must you go on a day like this? So wet? So cold?"

"Yes, my blossom, indeed I must. Won't you change your mind and come with me?"

"No," she said, and turned indoors as he drove off.

The Pikehouse garden was a puddle of mud. Seedling cabbages, flooded out of the ground, lay in the gutter along the path. Sodden potato-haulms lay in a heap, and the potato-ground was all churned about, where Goody had laboured to salvage the crop. The beans on their sticks were laid low in the mud and sodden onions floated on scummy water in the hollows.

Looking up at the roof, he saw how rotten the thatch had become since his last visit; how the holes had widened, especially round the chimney. He saw, too, how sooty the smoke was that rose from Goody's fire.

In the little porch, there stood a box of windfallen apples, very green and wet, and a box of carrots covered in slime. Goody's old overcoat hung from the nail, and her boots, plastered thick with yellow clay, were on the mat with their toes turned in, as though she had just that moment stepped out of them to go indoors.

When he entered the kitchen, she was sitting in her rocking-chair, fast asleep, her chin on her chest, her hands tucked inside a fold of her apron. He touched the back of the chair as he passed and set it rocking gently. It creaked a little, as always, but Goody did not awake to the sound as she always had done in the past. She remained asleep, with her head bowed, rocking gently to and fro. Jesse went round and stooped to look into her face. He touched her hands, and they were cold, like the leaves of a lily. He touched her forehead, and knew she was dead.

When he checked the rocking of the chair, the whole room became very hushed, for the clock on the mantelpiece had stopped, and the fire in the hearth was only a heap of wet, smoking sticks. Jesse drew up the three-legged stool and sat by Goody, looking at her, with his elbows resting on his knees. He sat for some time, in the hushed stillness, because he wanted to look at her and keep her company, to think about her, and talk to her, quietly, in his head.

Then he went out to look for Tom.

The scarecrow, in sacking skirts and shawl, with a turnip face and with yellow daisies in its hat, stood up in the hedge in the fields at Anster, and Betony often went to see it. She made it her friend, telling it things that would otherwise have remained untold, and it always listened, its head a little on one side, the daisies nodding on their wire stalks.

She could no longer talk to her father, because of the change in him. Whenever she sought to draw him apart, he would look at her in a strange way, with a strange and sad shake of his head. Often he seemed not to hear her at all. So she talked to the scarecrow.

It stood high in the hedgerow, guarding two big fields at once, the eighteen acre on one side, the twenty-six acre on the other. All the land about was still as sodden as could be, the flood-water lying in great pools wherever you went. The eighteen acre field had been sown with barley, the twenty-six acre with wheat. The wheat came struggling up bravely, small blades of brightest green, standing up from the puddled soil. But the barley rotted away in the ground.

"The farmers reckon they're likely ruined, and my great-grumpa says he's never known such everlasting weeks of rain. Some folk in Upham have got a foot of water in their kitchens again, and there's a baby been drowned, too, so I hear this morning."

The scarecrow listened. Its stillness was friendly and sympathetic. It knew she wasn't to blame for the floods; for the people made homeless; for the baby drowned in that Upham cellar.

After a time, however, the scarecrow invaded her dreams at night, and instead of being her only friend, it turned against her. She dreamt she was walking in a narrow lane, and the scarecrow was with her, always a little way in front, up in the hedge, against the sky. She could not escape. She could only go faster,—walking and walking—until her legs felt ready to break.

And when at last, weeping with weariness and anger, she stopped and stamped her foot, the scarecrow would turn very slowly round and would look at her under the brim of its hat. And now its eyes were live, human eyes, looking down, full of human thought, at Betony standing there below.

"Looking! Looking!" Betony shouted. "Why are you always looking at me?"

She stopped going to visit the scarecrow. She tried talking to her mother instead.

"Are you sorry Tom has come to live with us?"

"No," said her mother, busy ironing. "Why should I be?"

"Are you glad, then?"

"You should be helping Janie clean your bedroom."

"I've done my half," Betony said. "D'you think Tom is right in the head?"

"Right as ninepence! Maybe righter."

"I'm not so sure. I think he's queer. He never looks me straight in the eye."

"Perhaps he don't care for what he sees there."

"I think he steals," Betony said.

"So do you," her mother answered. "You stole fourpence from your granna's purse a week or two back and ten sheets of paper from your great-grumpa's office on Tuesday."

Betony stared at the steam rising from Roger's shirt as the iron travelled to and fro. Then she looked at her mother's face, which was calm and unclouded, with no trace of anger in it; no trace of threat.

"That wasn't stealing. Not *proper* stealing. Besides, I never spent the fourpence nor used the paper 'cos someone went and stole them from *me*."

"There now, just fancy," her mother said, going to the stove to change the irons. "That someone was me."

Betony sat, aware of the temper stirring her blood.

"If I'm so bad as everyone says, why don't you tan me?" she demanded.

"I might if you was to get any worser. But you've got sense if only you'd use it, and sensible folk give over stealing once they know they've been catched out."

"Sensible! Sensible!" Betony said, and slid from her stool. "I'm going out of this stupid house and I'm staying away for ever and ever!"

"Very well, don't slam the door," her mother said.

Outside, in the workshop yard, Betony watched her brothers at work, filling the big basket with sticks. William was doing the chopping as always, being proud of his skill with the little chopper, and as he went chop-chop-chop very quickly, the sticks flew about on all sides. Roger and Tom picked them up, and Dicky made them tidy in the basket.

"Tom Maddox!" Betony said, as he stooped to pick up sticks at her feet. "Take care how you lumber into folk, you clumsy thing!"

"Then stand clear," William commanded. "You're in our way."

"Tom Maddox, my mother don't like you," Betony said. "She thinks you're tenpence short of a shilling!"

Tom paid no heed. He went on gathering up the sticks and dropping them into the basket. But William stopped work and stared at her.

"Did mother say she didn't like Tom?"

"Nobody likes him," Betony said. "He's too black by half. Just look at him there, sticking out from all of us fair ones as though he'd been dipped in a bag of soot. He don't belong here. He's not one of us!"

Glancing behind her, towards the workshop, she saw that her father had come to the door.

"Betony!" he said, in a warning voice.

"Go back where you came from!" she said to Tom. "With the gipsies and tinkers. We don't want you here! You're too black for us!"

Her father's hand struck hard across her buttocks, and the shock and pain were a kind of lightning, that burnt through her flesh and melted her bones. He had never so chastised her before. He was changed completely. And she fled from him in shame and outrage; in terrible hatred; in terrible, unforgiving wrath; and ran headlong from the workshop yard. She ran without pause, along the road and over the bridge, down onto the bank of the Derrent and along to the place where the flood was at its worst.

Under the willows, downstream, two men in a punt were spearing eels. One was the idiot, Jumper Lane; the other Dr Mellow, the Oxford scholar who lived like a tramp. They looked at Betony on the bank, and Jumper, grinning from ear to ear, held up an eel for her to see. She sat on a log and pretended to fasten her buttoned boots. Then she took out her prayer-book and pretended to read.

The punt was moored by a long rope tied to a stake among the rushes. The two men allowed it to drift to the limits, then hauled themselves back and drifted again. Betony watched, growing colder and colder, for the air was thick with wet weeping mist, and the willows dripped on her from above. She told herself the cold was nothing. Soon, very soon, she'd be past it for ever. Past care, past care.

The punt went backwards and forwards again and again. The two men showed no sign of growing tired of their sport. And now Tommy Trennam had come to the sluice with his rod and line and was settling there for the afternoon.

Betony leapt to her feet with a shiver and turned towards home. She would not be able to drown herself today. There were too many people at the brook.

"Come to the table," her mother said, "or aren't you hungry for your supper?"

"No, I'm not hungry. Not a bit."

"Maybe you're sickening for some sort of chill?"

"She's sulking," said William. "Our dad gave her a smack."

"Betony's very well able to speak for herself. Are you ill, girl? If so, you'd be better in bed."

"I'm all right," Betony said.

"Then come to the table as you're told."

Betony sat between William and Janie and looked at the food set out on the table. She saw sticks of celery standing up clean and white in the beaker; she saw a big wedge of pale Welsh cheese; and she saw her favourite spiced liver sausage, already sliced at one end.

"Cheese or sausage?" her mother asked her, standing with knife and fork poised.

"Sausage, please," Betony said.

In bed that night, when her mother had been to say goodnight, Betony relit the candle and sat up to write in the blank leaves at the back of her prayerbook.

"What're you writing?" Janie asked. "Is it a diary, like before?"

"Mind your own business," Betony said.

"Mother will notice the candle burnt down. She always notices, you know that."

"Dear, dear! What a terrible thing!"

"I suppose you're practising a tidy hand?"

"Oh, be quiet, and go to sleep."

"Fancy!" said Janie. "The best scholar in the school, yet she can't write a tidy hand!"

"If you don't be quiet, I'll singe your hair," Betony threatened, and held the candle above Janie's head. "That's right, Miss Poke-and-Pry, hide yourself under the bedclothes and shut your noise or you'll be sorry!"

She had not looked at her father all through supper. She would never look at him ever again. It was her resolution, recorded now in the back of the prayer-book, and nothing would ever make her change her mind. She had set it down in her best hand.

It was all too true that her writing was untidy. Miss Likeness said so every day.

"You write good sense, Betony Izzard, and your spelling and punctuation are fair. But your handwriting! How do you expect to win a scholarship to Lock's with handwriting like that?"

"I shall try to do better," Betony said.

"Betony, you must give more attention to work," said Miss Likeness, "and less to playing games with your sister and brothers."

"I never play games," Betony said.

Janie, who heard her give this answer, took her to task about it at home.

"Just look at you now! What're you doing if not playing games?"

"This isn't a game. It's an expedition."

"Where to?" William asked. "What're you tying the toasting-fork onto that pole for?"

"You'll see when we get there," Betony said, and turned to Tom, who was standing nearby. "Not you!" she said. "We don't want you with us."

"If Tom ent coming, neither am I," said William.

"Nor me neither," Janie said. "Not if Tom ent concluded as well."

"What, that little melancholy, casting a damper on all us others? He don't never talk nor laugh nor nothing."

"He still misses his Grannie Izzard."

"What, that old witch? Why, she's not even dead, I don't believe!"

"She is," Janie said, in a shocked whisper. "She's been buried at Eastery these many weeks gone by."

"Who says so? Who really knows? We're never there when all these things are said to be done, are we?"

"Mr Hemms went out to put the words on the stone," said William. "I heard my father say so hisself."

"A stone is nothing! Just words, what are they? Grannie Izzard is still alive. I've seen her myself so I ought to know!"

"Betony, don't be silly," Janie said, and they all murmured against her like bees. But Tom said nothing, merely looking at her with his deep dark gaze.

"I'll show you," she said. "If you don't believe it, just come with me."

She laid the toasting-fork on the bench and crossed the fold to the gate of the paddock.

"Well?" she said, looking over her shoulder. "Are you coming or not?"

She pushed through the gate, and they followed slowly. She crossed the paddock, the pasture, and the hazel copse, and turned along the hedge that formed the boundary with Anster. When she reached the stile, the children were coming more closely behind her.

She crossed the footbridge over the Derrent, plodded up the meadow bank, into the swamp of the eighteen acre, and led the children straight to the scarecrow;

"There!—What did I tell you?" she demanded,

giving Tom a little push. "There's your grannie, like I said!"

Seeing his face, she was suddenly frightened. His eyes were such unfathomed hollows. His stillness was almost more than she could bear. But then he turned and darted away and went running down the steep field and meadow, with the flood-water flying from under his heels.

"Betony, you're wicked!" Janie said. "A nasty, horrible, wicked thing!"

"Leave her alone," William said. "Let's get home and talk to Tom."

"Don't you want to go spearing eels, then?"

"Eels!" said William. "So that's what the toasting-fork was for! And where do we borrow a boat, eh?"

"I know where," Betony said.

William and Janie exchanged a look.

"No," William said, decisively. "We've had enough of you today. We're going home to look for Tom."

She could take them with her just so far, these three brothers and one sister, but once they rebelled against her tyranny, they stood like stones and she could not move them.

"Oh, very well!" she said, some days later. "It's no odds to me if Maddox comes too. But don't blame me if he scares off the eels!"

They went to the Derrent after school. Betony pointed out the mooring, almost hidden among the reeds, and William hauled the punt to the bank. But as they eagerly scrambled in, Tom hung back, his hands in his pockets.

"I ent coming. I ent too keen. Nor I don't think you should go neither."

"Laws," William said. "After all that swither!"

"I don't trust that water. Not after the floods. And the sluices is open, higher up."

"A punt is as safe as the Bank of England. It couldn't capsize if it tried till domesday."

"I ent coming all the same. I'll stay here and watch."

"Suit yourself," William said. "Seems five is enough in this little punt, anyway."

He dropped the rope into the water and pushed away from the muddy bank. The punt drifted, slowly at first because of the reeds; then faster as it gained the middle stream. William reached for the brass fork, tied with string to a five-foot pole, but Betony refused to yield it.

"It's my turn first. It was my idea."

"Hah!" said William. "You ent likely to spear an eel! You've got no muscles, being a girl."

"Mind yourself," Betony said, "and give me room."

The three younger children sat together on one thwart, little Dicky safely wedged between Roger and Janie, while William and Betony stood erect.

"Well, get a move on!" William said. "We're nearly run to the end of the rope."

"You've got to look for the likely places," Betony said, with a little sniff.

Standing at the very edge of the punt, she gazed over into the brook, which was brown and soupy, marbled by swirling yellow mud. There was a greater depth of water than she had thought, and its power thrilled in the boards at her feet. Watching the dimples in the surface, she was held enraptured by their speed, and felt a dizzying pull towards the water, just as the waters and tides of the earth were said to pull to the changing moon.

There came a jerk as the punt reached the end of its mooring. She threw out her arms to keep her balance, and sat down heavily in the bows.

"Laws!" William said. "We shall do marvels at this rate, shan't we?" He took up the rope and began to haul the way back to the bank. "Let me try this time. We'll be here till dark if we wait for you."

"Very well!" Betony said. "Since you're so clever, let's see you try."

They drifted again, William now standing with feet wide apart, leaning out over the water, the fork held aloft in his right hand. Janie and Dicky were beginning to splutter. The sight of William so fierce and warlike, with his round sturdy rump stuck out so boldly and his stockings going to sleep in his boots, was too much for them. They broke into giggles, and Roger and Betony followed suit.

"Shut your noise!" William whispered. "You'll scare every eel from here to Middening."

He plunged the fork into the water, letting the pole slide through his fingers but grasping it firmly again at its end. Then he leant back and drew the fork clear.

"Bost it!" he said. "The fuddy thing don't touch the bottom! You should've got a longer pole."

"I told you, you've got to look for the likely places," Betony said. "Dr Mellow worked closer in."

He tried again, and the fork touched the bottom, stirring up a cloud of mud. He leant back, withdrew the fork in great triumph, and swore to himself as he saw that the prongs were still bare. The punt jerked to the end of the painter, and they returned again to the beginning. William made try after try, but all he speared was an old leather bottle.

"Some people," Betony said, "aren't so clever as they seem to think."

"D'you want to try?" William challenged, without taking his gaze from the water. "You're welcome enough if you think you'll do better."

"You say that now! After bending the fork like you have!"

"Lumme, I saw one! I did! Honest John! I must've just missed him and stirred him up!"

Desperate with excitement, he thrust the fork with all his might into the water. The prongs speared the bottom and stuck fast, and William, stretching too far to tug at the handle, toppled over into the brook.

Betony fell on her knees and reached out to clutch at his hair. But her fingers only scrabbled water. William had sunk to the muddy bed.

The three younger children sat huddled together, whimpering and moaning, and Betony sprawled, wriggling out further and further, her thighs on the gunwale, her feet hooked under the thwart. Her chest and her chin were touching the water. Her arms reached out . . . reached out . . . to save. But when William came to the surface, he was already several yards away. The Derrent had never before seemed so wide, nor its drift so rapid.

The punt reached the end of its painter and jerked to a stop among the reeds. William swept past, his fair hair showing like a handful of straw in the water. Betony wriggled back into the punt and tried to unfasten the rope. The wet knots defied her. So she stood up and began to shout.

"Tom!" she shouted. "Tom! Where are you?"

Tom was running along the bank, making downstream towards the sluice. She saw him go wading into the water; saw him leaning over the sluice-gate, facing upstream, with arms hanging; and saw him clasping her brother by the collar, holding him up against the hatch. Tom had no strength to lift William bodily over: he could only hold on, keeping William's face above water.

As Betony hauled the way back to the bank, she saw that help was coming quickly, for Bert Tupper, working at Luckett's, had heard their noise and was racing to the sluice-gate. When she and the other children got there, William lay face down on the bank, and Bert, astride him, was squeezing the water out of his lungs.

"Is he going to die?" Betony whispered, frightened by William's closed eyes, by the queer look of his pallid skin, by the mud trickling forth between his lips.

"He'll be all right. But we've got to see he don't take a chill." Bert took off his jacket and wrapped William round in it, close and tight. He stood up with the boy in his arms. "Can you run?" he said to Roger. "Then race off home and tell your mother to warm a bed for this young tucker and a sup of something to scald out his guts."

Roger ran off, and Bert followed, hugging William close to his chest, with the other children trotting beside him. But when they reached home, and their

mother came to meet them, Betony withdrew from
the bustle and stole unnoticed into the barn. She
mounted the ladder into the hayloft.

There, she climbed on the stacked hay, into a space
between two trusses. It was warm and dry in there,
and smelt of summer. It smelt of clover dried in the
sun. With her legs drawn up, her arms clasped round
them, and her chin resting upon her knees, she filled
the little space completely. She fitted it, like a nut in a
shell. She merged into the warmth and darkness.

She did not go to sleep, and yet she had dreams, of
spring and sunlight. She dreamt she was being carried
on her father's shoulders, riding along between the
apple trees, her head among the blossoming branches,
the pink and white blossoms reaching into the blue
sky. She saw them and touched them, and the pollen
was yellow on her brown fingers.

Then she was slipping from her father's shoulders,
slipping and sliding down his back, and as she slid
down, she saw the scar on the nape of his neck,
where the flesh had once been badly burnt and had
healed in terrible mottled puckers. No, it no longer
hurt him, he always told her. He scarcely knew it was
there now. He no longer felt it. But Betony felt it, a
silent screech through her head and body, whenever
she happened to see the scar.

Down below, Janie was calling from the fold.

"Betonee . . . Are you up there in the hayloft
again? Betony? Mother wants you."

Betony stayed perfectly still, hearing only the blood
in her ears, and the silence that fell when Janie had
gone.

Then her father's voice came calling, and this time
her heart went up in flames. She moved and nudged a
truss of hay till it teetered over and flumped on the
floor. Her father heard it. He called out at once.

"Betony! I know you're up there, so come on
down! You're acting like a silly mommet."

A pail rattled. The pump-handle creaked six times.

"Suit yourself!" he shouted to her. "If you want to
starve, that's up to you!"

She heard him limping across the cobbles; heard the house door close with a slam; and knew now, truly, that he no longer cared if she lived or died, for he had left her alone in the darkness, cold and hungry, at the mercy of the rats.

Once again she heard the silence; endlessly, endlessly; until a step rattled the ladder, and someone came up into the hayloft, straight to the little place in the hay.

"Come along," said her mother's cool and quiet voice. "It's past eight o'clock and you've eaten nothing for seven hours."

Betony gave herself up, a prisoner, and her mother's hands led her home.

"You can hide!" granna said. "Going off on such missums and nearly getting your brother drowned!"

"Ent you ashamed?" asked great-grumpa. "Suppose young William had catched a fever? I think you should ponder on that, girl, I do indeed!"

"She's pondered enough," her mother said.

"Is William bad, mother?" Betony asked.

"Ha, he's just about beside hisself with consequence, that young man,—sitting up in bed, with everyone running round after him, including your father. You needn't worry about William. He's making the most of today's mishap."

"Well, cheer up, Betony," granna said. "It's all over now. You needn't look so full of woe."

But Betony, though relieved that brother William was unharmed, could not be cheerful. She was to blame for what had happened. She was always to blame, and the world was against her. She knew she would never smile again.

William, having been kept in bed three days, was allowed up for supper on the third day. He looked very pink and clean in the face—like a choirboy, Janie said—and his hair shone, smooth and yellow, brushed close to his head.

By supper-time, he was crimson with excitement, for everyone, on coming into the kitchen, made a great fuss of him, asking tenderly after his health and bringing him presents.

"Come on, mother!" he shouted, rapping his knife and fork on the table. "Where's this special supper granna says we're having? Is is haddock with parsley sauce?"

"Be patient," Beth said. "I'm waiting for your father to settle down."

"What me?" said Jesse, taking his place. "Why, I'm as ready as ready, I am! I'm just about fammelled for that there good smell."

"Then I shall dish up," Beth said.

She opened the oven and removed a deep earthenware basin that steamed and sizzled and smelt of fish. She brought it to the table and set it down in their midst, and when they leant forward, peering into the steaming basin, they saw it was filled with stewed eels.

William's face was a picture. His jaw had fallen. His mouth was ajar.

"Well, my son?" Jesse said gravely. "Ent that exactly what you desired?"

"Laws! Shall I like them?" William said, and when they all laughed: "Yes, I shall! I shall! I shall!"

"Of course you'll like 'em. It's a dish for a king."

"They give you brains," granna said, ladling a helping onto a plate.

Betony, catching her father's eye, felt a ripple inside her. His glance, for her, had not been so merry and warm for a long time. And she felt herself growing in stature again; felt she could do many wonderful things and be wise and clever and good and kind. And then, suddenly, Janie had to open her mouth and speak about something that didn't concern her, and the moment was spoilt, the warm good feeling was all undone.

"Fancy," said Janie. "Look at Betony, actually smiling! She said she'd never smile again."

"I didn't! I didn't!" Betony cried.

"Oh yes you did. You wrote it in your prayer-book. I saw it myself and so did Roger."

"Sneaky little toad!" Betony shouted, and, leaning across in front of William, she slapped Janie's face.

"Betony, go to bed at once!" her father said in an awful voice.

"Here, she ent had her supper," Beth said. "Betony, say you're sorry for hurting Janie, then eat up like a sensible girl."

"I shan't say I'm sorry nor I shan't eat up!" Betony shouted, and bounced from her chair. "I'd just as soon go to bed and starve!"

She ran out, slamming the door, and went stumbling upstairs without any candle to light the way, pulling off the chaplet her father had given her on her birthday and hurling it at the clock on the landing.

"Eels!" she said, groping her way into the bedroom. "Horrible, stinking, slimy things!"

She took her prayer-book from under the mattress and tore out the pages, letting them flutter in shreds to the floor, where they lay glimmering in the darkness.

"There now!" she said, as she stripped off her clothes. "Verily now I shall go to hell!"

She crept into bed and lay, stiff and cold, with her nightdress wound tight round her legs like a shroud. Tonight, when at last she should go to sleep, it would be for ever. Her spirit willed it. She would die peacefully, and be taken from her bed, and be laid in the waterlogged earth in the churchyard, in a small coffin made by her father. And a silence would fall over all the land.

But although she slept, even before her sister had crept into bed beside her, it was not for ever. She awoke, as always, to the misty flare of the candleflame in the morning darkness, the splash of water from jug to bowl, and Janie's little whimpering cry as she braced herself for the cold wash. The morning had come. The day must be lived through.

Life knew best, after all, for time put sorrow further and further behind, until, looking back, you saw it growing small in the distance; and there were other things—little healing things—to set beside it. There were even times of merriment, like the day her father took to smoking a pipe, when everything was again as it should be.

It was after supper one wet cold evening, the time of day when great-grumpa turned his chair to the hearth and took up his paper, and the children were allowed to gather round the fire, to toast themselves before going to bed. At these times, while granna made the kitchen tidy, and their mother searched the dresser drawers for stockings that wanted mending, their father would sit and talk to them, asking about their day's lessons. But this evening, having settled himself comfortably into his chair, he suddenly produced a pipe and tobacco and, without a word, began smoking.

They were dumbfounded. They stared and stared. Plenty of other men might smoke tobacco, including most of those in the workshop, but never their father! The thing was undreamt of. It made them all cry out at once, and granna, emptying sugar into a basin, whirled around with her hands at her breast.

"Whatever's the matter, screeching out, little devils, like that?"

"I dunno, I'm sure," Jesse said, blowing smoke at the ceiling, "unless it's my pipe that's causing the up-roar."

"Pipe?" said great-grumpa, looking at him over the paper. "Since when've you took to smoking a pipe?"

"Since today, at one o'clock."

"Where did you get it?"

"It was presented to me by Owner Jackson when I was at Upham, fetching a load of deal off his barge."

"Do you like it?" Roger asked.

"Why, yes, I do. It's a nice little pipe and I took to it like a dog to a bone. It was made in Seay Forest, carved out of birchwood, and still got the bark on the bowl, d'you see? Ah, bost it! The damn thing's gone out."

"Let's see you light it again," said Janie.

"Ah, that's something to see, ent it, eh? There's a

lot of skill goes to lighting a pipe. It ent just a question of puff and blow."

"Why d'you hold the match-box over the bowl like that?" asked William.

"That's the proper way. It acts like a damper and gives me a good strong mighty draw. Ah, and I get a nice little tune on it, too, don't I? Can you hear it, Dicky, piping away?"

"Is that why it's called a pipe, dad?"

"It might be. I hadn't thought of that before. But here! You're making fun of me, ent you? You're playing me up the garden wall!"

"Why, no," said William, who could mimic his father exactly. "Not us! Not likely! Oh dear me no!"

Jesse was working furiously at his pipe, looking around the circle of faces, with a great show of not watching what he was doing, when the box of matches fizzed into flames. He jumped up and forward in one move, shooting the match-box into the stove, and the children gaped as it burnt up prettily in the fire, while great-grumpa, rustling his paper down again, glared fiercely at Jesse.

"Are you determined to burn the house down?"

"Why, no," Jesse said. "Not determined exactly. Oh dear me no!"

The look of surprise still remained on his face, as though he could not quite believe in such a calamity happening like that, a box of matches alight in his hand. And the look was so fixed in his round blue eyes that the children again broke into laughter.

"Here!" he said, turning to point his pipe at Tom. "Are you gone against me like all the rest? Eh? Have you? I reckon you have. You're laughing at me the same as these others."

Tom blinked, uneasy at finding himself the centre of attention. He looked away with his slow, shy smile. He was sitting perfectly still as always, hunched on his stool, with his arms folded upon his knees. He sat with the rest of them, a part of the family, listening to all they had to say, and yet he was still a stranger among them, the strangeness lying in what he was, in the way he was made, the way he kept so quiet and still.

His stillness vexed Betony. It made her feel, often, that she had been caught showing off, noisily, stupidly, like a child, and that was wrong, for she was the elder by eighteen months. She was wiser. She knew more things.

She would do her best, she thought, as she half listened to William and Janie arguing across her: she would try to be kind and helpful to Tom, if only because her father wished it. Her father was good. She wanted to please him. She wanted to be like him in every way.

"Well, Betony?" her father said, out of the noise all around her. "Am I to be allowed another box of matches?"

"Yes," she said. "I'll go and get them."

The long wet season ended at last. Christmas brought wind, giving the land a chance to dry, and the new year brought frosts, which lasted until the beginning of March. The children made a slide at Sitches Bottom, but Betony never went sliding now. She hurried home straight from school, having homework to do every day. The chimney-corner was given over to her use, a quiet place, out of the way, where she could sit with her writing-box on her knees and work.

"Betony's studying," William would whisper, and would make much ado of going on tiptoe, leading the others back and forth, back and forth, until Betony called on her mother to drive them away.

Sometimes, the boys used to hide her satchel, or rub out the notes she had made in her notebook, or sharpen her pencils at both ends. They sewed shirt-buttons onto her sampler and painted her pencil-box red, white and blue.

They teased granna, too, putting sticky burrs into her mittens, or tying knots in the sleeves of her nightdress. Once they hung a dead owl in place of a partridge in the larder, and granna, whose sight was poor, took it out and started to pluck it, when their giggles warned her that something was wrong. "Ah, well, boys will be boys," great-grumpa would say, laughing, and granna would retort angrily: "That's exactly what I've got against them!"

Then, one day, Roger borrowed the old man's watch, which he found hanging from the knob of the corner cupboard. It was a Sunday, and great-grumpa was having his afternoon nap in the parlour. Roger sat down at the kitchen table and carefully took the watch apart. He studied the parts through granna's lens, cleaned every one with a tiny paint-brush, and carefully put them together again. Sadly, the watch no longer went. Nor would its casing quite close as it should. So Roger hung it back on the door-knob and hoped for the best.

Great-grumpa's fury was something to see. He seemed to the children to grow enormous, and looked as though he would smite them to the floor.

"Ah, well, boys will be boys!" their granna said.

On Monday, their mother took the watch in to old Mr Hines, in Chepsworth. She delivered it back in good order that evening.

"There's no damage done. And I'm the one that paid the bill."

"I should damn well think so!" said great-grumpa.

"Mr Hines said Roger'd done well for a boy his age. He said we should put him to learn the trade."

"Did he?" said Roger, bright-eyed.

"Why in God's name go to a clocksmith when you've got a trade on your own doorstep?" great-grumpa demanded.

"I dunno that I want to be a carpenter," Roger said.

"Hell's bells! You're talking rubbish!"

"When the time comes, Roger shall choose for his-self," Beth said.

"Glory!" said Jesse. "That's different from me, then! You made me be a carpenter whether I liked the idea or not." And he looked up, laughing, as Beth passed his chair. "You did, wife, and don't you deny it!"

Betony, watching her father and mother together,

saw the bright glance that flickered between them, and the hint of annoyance in her mother's face. And afterwards, when she had her father to herself, she talked to him about it.

"What would you have been if not a carpenter?"

"I'd have been a labourer on a farm."

"Why d'you do as my mother tells you?"

"She generally knows what's best, that's why."

"But you're a man. You shouldn't always be giving in. My mother's too fond of her own way."

"So's somebody else I could mention."

"Not me! Not me!"

"Yes, you, little peewit. You're just the same. It's the Tewke in you."

"I wish I was all Izzard, then, that's all!"

"You wouldn't have much of a head-piece in that case," he said. "You'd be a dummel like me."

And Betony, though she denied it, knew her father spoke the truth. She knew she had her mother's quickness, both of temper and of brain.

It was not easy to like Tom. He was too strange. He did such mysterious and meaningless things, such as stealing salt from the dinner-table.

Betony, in her chimney-corner, had the kitchen to herself, for her mother and granna were busy next door, sweeping up the ants that had invaded the store-room. The kitchen table was laid for dinner. A mutton stew steamed on the hob.

. She was sitting there, biting her pencil, when Tom came in and stood looking intently at the table. He was quite unaware of her presence in the corner, perhaps because it was Saturday morning, when she was usually cleaning her bedroom. He looked at the table for some seconds, listening, head cocked, to the noises in the store-room; then he took a small pill-box out of his pocket, filled it with salt from the pewter salt-pot, and went out again, very quietly, although wearing hobnailed boots.

Betony followed. She stood in the dairy and watched through the window. Tom crossed the fold

and went into the cartshed. He climbed on the cart-
wheel and hid the pill-box up on the ledge of the shed
wall, in the worm-eaten space at the end of the crossbeam. Then he left the shed and went off to the orchard, where the other boys were trimming the hedges.
Betony went into the cartshed. She had to discover.
She had to see. But there was nothing more to learn
about Tom's secret. The pill-box was just a pill-box.
The salt was just salt.

The following morning, before church, she saw him
go again to the cartshed; saw him take down the pill-
box, open it to look inside, and put it back again in
its place. She stood waiting, and watched him grow
pale as he turned and found her standing there.

"It's salt," she said. "I saw you take it."

He said nothing, but stood still, hands in pockets,
staring into space.

"Why salt?" she asked. "Where's the point? What
use is it?"

"Nothing," he muttered, and walked off.

That evening, the pill-box was gone, and Betony
never saw it again.

One frosty evening, when the younger children
came in from sliding, they bore signs of having been
fighting. Dicky's coat was torn at the seams, the other
boys had bruised and dirty faces, and even Janie,
so trim and correct, had lost the ribbon from her hair.

"I hate Prudie Green!" said little Dicky. "She
called me a pudding-face! Oh yes she did!"

"And how did it start, all this name-calling?" his
mother asked. "Was it you or Prudie Green?"

"It was Archie Slewton, saying things about our
Tom," said Janie, and, catching a quelling glance from
William, would say no more.

"Well, all you children go outside and play for a
while longer, 'cos I want a little talk with Tom. Yes,
you too, Betony."

"*I'm* not going outside!" Betony said. "I'm doing
my homework."

"Do as you're told," her mother said.

Betony went to the barn with the others, and they

crouched in a circle, warming their hands at a lantern placed on the floor in their midst.

"Well? What's the mystery, then?"

"Don't tell her!" William said. "She'll take it out on Tom."

"No, I shan't! I swear it solemnly, Bible oath."

"All right. You'll hear it from them lot at school, anyway, sooner or later."

"Whatever is it, for goodness' sake?"

"Seems Tom is a bastard," Janie said. "That's what Archie Slewton said. So did Tibby Lovage."

Betony gave a little shiver and reached further forward, spreading her hands very close to the lantern.

"Laws," she said. "Is that all?"

"There's worse than that," William said. "They say Tom's father was a murderer and murdered Tom's mother down in the cottage next to the smithy. People went down with pots and pans and treated him to the rough music and the policemen came and hanged him in a tree."

"I don't believe it!" Betony said.

"No more don't I!" Janie agreed.

Tom came into the barn, and they all stood up.

"What did mother say?" asked William. "Did she say it was true, about your father being a murderer?"

"Yes," said Tom.

"I expect he had a brain-storm," Janie whispered, "like Maisie Morgan did that time."

Tom said nothing, but seemed to shrug. Betony picked up the lantern and raised it so that she could see his face.

"Don't you care that your father murdered your mother and got hanged for it?"

"No," Tom said. "That's nothing to me."

"Haven't you got any feelings, then?"

"No. I haven't."

"That's what I thought. You're made of stone."

"Betony! Remember your promise!" William said.

"I shan't torment him! I've wasted enough time already. I'm going indoors to get warm."

In the following days, however, the new knowledge was almost constantly in her mind, and she watched every chance of catching Tom alone.

"What's it feel like, being a bastard?" she asked, waylaying him one day in the paddock. "Does it make you feel bad inside? And being the son of a murderer? —Does it give you nightmares?"

Tom said nothing, but kept on the move, across the paddock, into the pasture.

"I shan't torment you," she said. "I just want to know what it feels like, that's all. I'll be sympathetic if only you'll let me."

Again he said nothing.

"Does it hurt?" she asked. "Do you blame God?"

But Tom just kept walking, faster now, feet crunching the frosty grass, making towards the open fields.

"I think you're silly!" she shouted after him. "You can't go on like that forever.—Always stepping aside to get out of my way. Not forever, you can't! Forever is a long time!"

But it seemed she was wrong. Forever was nothing to Tom. It was no hardship to him to go off on his own for hours on end, if that was the only way to escape her. The order of things was set between them. Time made no change. He would talk to the others, but not to her, and when they were all gathered together in one circle, it was no hardship for him, as it would have been for Betony herself, to make himself nothing and take no part in the quick flying talk.

And if all else failed to protect him from Betony's probing, he would go to Beth and attach himself to her without a word. He would help her feed the hens and collect the eggs, or would sit in the cowshed and watch her milking the two cows. He knew he was utterly safe with Beth, like a blackbird sheltering under a thorn.

It was four miles to Chepsworth, even the short way, over the fields, and Betony, walking to and fro every day, always looked forward to crossing the railway at Stickington Halt, for it marked the half-way point in her journey. There, too, in the morning, Nancy Sposs would be waiting for her, and the rest of the walk would be nothing at all. It would simply fly.— There was so much to say. And in the evening, they often stood at the level crossing for as much as an hour, to resolve an argument or finish a story before parting.

Nancy was three years older than Betony. She had been one of the first ten pupils to enter the Grammar School, Lock's, with one of the new scholarships for poor children. She would speak in her blunt, matter-of-fact way of the early days in Miss Mussoe's form, when the scholarship girls were kept apart with a screen around them to prevent their smell, their germs, their lice, from spreading among the "daughters of gentlemen."

"It's different now," Nancy would say. "There are more of us . . . and not enough screens to go round."

At first, Betony found Nancy Sposs repellent. She thought her too gruff, too hard and masculine in her ways. Nancy's body was thick and solid. Her face was coarse-skinned, and her hair grew very low on

her forehead, giving her the brutish, scowling look
that she herself called her "donkey beauty". But behind that low forehead there lay a keen and logical
mind, perfectly disciplined, yet full of energy and
imagination. She had warmth, too, and Betony found
her a good friend.

Nancy was top of the school in all the sciences and
in English. At fifteen, she founded the school debating
society, and led her team against the boys' school,
engaging pupils and masters alike in debating com-
pulsory religious instruction, the Montessori experi-
ments, and women's suffrage. She knew exactly what
she wanted from life, and her sights were fixed on a
Cambridge degree, a career in chemistry, and a
vote. Yet in spite of her high-flown ambitions,
Nancy's feet were on common earth. She came from
a poor home, and her family was always her first
consideration. Her father was a linesman on the railway. Her mother took in washing. If her father fell
ill, which happened often, Nancy went gardening at
Chepsworth Park, thus making up for his lost wages.
If her mother fell ill, Nancy stayed at home to deal
with the wash. And she always found time to help
her schoolboy brothers, who hoped to become clerks
on the railway.

Once or twice every summer holidays, Nancy would
spend a day at Cobbs. She was interested in everything: in all the old buildings; in the work going on
in the workshop; in the men themselves. But most of
all she was interested in Tom.

"He's somehow alone . . . Even with your family,
all such a crowd together, he still seems alone. And
he never talks to *you* at all. Now why is that?"

"I wasn't very nice to him when he first came. I
was cruel to him.—I realize that now. I feel guilty
about it sometimes."

"So you ought," Nancy said.

"Oh, it's true I'm bad!" Betony cried. "I'm all the
things I least admire! D'you know that? I'm all the
things I least want to be!"

"Poor little soul," Nancy said tartly.

"Can people change?"

"If they want it enough, they can work marvels. But you don't really want to change. You don't really think about other people. You don't even see them except in relation to yourself."

"Thanks very much! Sometimes I wonder why I'm friends with you."

"I'm your conscience," Nancy said.

When Nancy left Lock's to go to Cambridge, Betony was completely lost. Looking about her at school, she realized how little she had seen for herself, how little she had thought about her surroundings. She had been looking through Nancy's eyes and relying on Nancy's thinking for more than three years. She had worked well enough, but like a pony, between blinders, content to nod sedately along, relying on extramural contact with Nancy to stimulate her own ideas. Looking about her, she thought the other girls dull and insipid, and, worst of all, feared that she herself must be like them. She made friends in time, but there was never anyone else like Nancy.

One summer day, at the level crossing, she met Geoffrey Danville, who had come to the Halt to collect a parcel of books for his father. A train went past, the Slow Train from Here to There, as Nancy had called it, and Geoffrey remarked that it was running late. They stayed talking a little while, and thereafter, every evening, he came on purpose to walk with her a little way along the old drove road.

Betony then was fifteen. Geoffrey was older by eighteen months. His father was rector of Woody Layton and a canon of the cathedral, and his mother was related to Mr Champley of Chepsworth Park. Betony thought Geoffrey the most handsome boy she had ever seen. He was so tall and graceful; his hair was a beautiful chestnut brown; his features sensitive and refined. Even his name was beautiful: an aristocratic name, she thought; and Geoffrey himself did not deny it.

Through Geoffrey's eyes, she caught many glimpses

into a new and exotic world: a world of vast drawing-rooms, with Persian carpets on the floors, and Worcester china in use every day; where silk-vested clergy conferred in groups, grave-faced from the burden of sacred duties, while their ladies drifted serenely about from terraced garden to croquet lawn. And she heard many interesting things, such as how the young viscount could scarcely write his name, and why the dean's daughter had gone to live in Cheshire.

She wanted to share Geoffrey with her sister and brothers; to give them a chance of seeing into the larger world; but when Geoffrey came to Cobbs, the visit did not proceed as she had planned it.

The trouble began when they were showing him round the orchard, for he trod in a very wet cowpat. His distress, and the trouble he took in cleaning his shoe, brought them all to an astonished standstill. They were first baffled, and then enchanted, and, lastly, full of helpful ideas. William offered to ask for a loan of his granna's jemimas. Roger fetched the garden barrow and offered to wheel Geoffrey about in style. And Janie repeatedly rushed forward, making great play with her pinafore, flicking liquid manure from Geoffrey's face and person.

"I'm afraid you think me fastidious," he said, retreating before her.

"Laws, no!" Janie assured him. "You're a fusspot, that's all."

"Don't the cows make muck at Woody Layton?" asked William.

"Not," said Geoffrey "in the Rectory garden."

"Then you don't grow much rhubarb, I don't suppose?"

"No rhubarb, I'm afraid."

"What're you afraid for all the time?"

"That is merely a figure of speech."

"Ah, a figure of speech," William said, nodding solemnly all around. "Merely. Yes. Quite so, I'm afraid."

"Stop it!" said Betony, pinching William's arm.

"Don't you know how to behave when we've got company?"

"Comp'ny?" said Roger, and, putting his hand inside his shirt, began scratching under his armpit. "Lumme, no!" he said, wriggling. "Comp'ny indeed! Whatever next? Jumper Lane's the one for that!"

"Let's go on the common," Janie suggested, taking pity on Geoffrey for Betony's sake. "We might find some mushrooms."

Janie fell in on one side of Geoffrey and Betony on the other, both seeking to protect him from the boys.

"Betony says you come from a very old family. She was telling us, the other day."

"Well," said Geoffrey, "my ancestors came over to England with the Conqueror."

"Ours were already here," said William, deliberately treading on Geoffrey's heels.

"And your dad's a parson?" Janie prompted.

"Rector, yes. As a matter of fact, he's very friendly with your man here, Mr Wisdom. They were up at Oxford together, you know. He's a nice fellow, isn't he? Wisdom, I mean?"

"He's all right," Janie said. "We like Mr Chance of Eastery best."

"Ah, yes, Parson Chance. A good enough man, my father says, but rather indulgent with the common people."

"I dunno about indulgent!" said William, angrily, from behind. "We have a saying, that more gets done by Chance than Wisdom in these two parishes, and it's true, too!"

"Oh, tes frères colériques, Bétoine!" said Geoffrey. "Qu'est-ce que je fais pour les fâcher? Parlons en français. Ainsi on pourrait peut-être éviter d'autres disputes."

"Très bien," Betony said. "Ainsi soit-il!"

With only two terms of French behind her, however, she soon foundered, while Geoffrey swam on in full flood. She could but tut in the gallic manner, picked up from Mademoiselle Jones, and hazard a reckless affirmative when Geoffrey's tone seemed to demand it.

The boys were delighted, and pranced in front.

"Ooley mooley vooley voo!" William said to Roger.

"Kesker petty wetty bong!" replied Roger. "Wee! Wee! Widdley wee!"

And they danced in front, capering, gesticulating, clapping one another on the shoulder, then pretending, by mime, to be onion-sellers pedalling along on their bicycles.

"Oker della looner! Monna me Peru!" sang William. "Pray tomato bloomer! Poorer queerer moo!"

"Mong Jew! Mong ong-yongs!" shouted Dicky. "Wolla cherry bee-cee-clett!"

"Ting-a-ling, ting-a-ling!" shouted Roger. "Scoozer, scoozer! Silver play!"

"Oh, really!" Geoffrey exclaimed, stopping abruptly in his tracks. "Betony, I beseech you! Can't you stop their silly behaviour?"

"Well, I think you'd better stick to English," Betony said, rather snappishly.

"It may have escaped your notice but I *am* speaking English now."

"Ting-a-ling, ting-a-ling!" shouted Roger. "Scoozer! Scoozer! Silver play!"

"Take no notice," Betony said. "They'll soon get tired if you ignore them."

But Geoffrey only grew more fractious, until he was on the brink of tears. He went |home early, and Betony, going with him as far as Tupton, tried half-heartedly to make amends.

"I'm sorry about my brothers' behaviour. But it's only their fun, you know. They don't mean any harm."

"I'm sorry, too," Geoffrey said, sniffing. "I'm not accustomed to that kind of thing."

Betony pitied him, knowing he had suffered; yet she wanted to laugh at him, too, because he was such a Mary Ellen. When they said goodbye, she knew she would never see him again, but she felt no regret:

only shame at having been so bedazzled by him, and
guilt that her feelings had changed so quickly.

"Shall you go to university, Betony, and try for your
cap and gown like Nancy Sposs?"

"No."

"Why not? You're clever, ent you?"

"Not clever enough," Betony said.

She had never faced the question squarely before,
and now, in doing so, she knew she was accepting another hard and uncomfortable truth.

It was all a necessary part of growing up, this coming to terms with imperfection. She remembered how
shocked she had been, years before, on hearing great-
grumpa refer to George Hopson as the best carpenter
in the workshop. Surely her father was best? It was
quite unthinkable that he should only be second-rate.
But as time went on, she was forced to see it. She
was forced to find comfort in reminding herself that
skill was not everything.—Other things mattered as
much, if not more, and her father was a good man in
a great many ways. But acceptance was difficult, always hard-won.

In scholastic achievement, Nancy Sposs had served
as a buffer, for Betony, always top of the village
school, might have expected a similar destiny at
Lock's if she had not perceived at once that Nancy's
powers and self-discipline towered far above her own.
Here, acceptance had come almost unnoticed, eased
by friendship. It was enough for Betony that she
had made friends with one of the cleverest girls at
Lock's. It mattered nothing that she was not to be
numbered among them. She hardly thought about it
at all.

Now, in answering Roger's question, she had accepted another truth. She had taken another step forward.

It was her habit to note the progression, because
it seemed so dreadfully slow. She felt herself somehow
lagging behind, for her sister and brothers were all so
certain, knowing exactly what they would do. Janie,

fifteen, was courting Martin Holt: they planned to
marry in three years' time. William and Tom were
established in the workshop, and Roger, though still
determined to be a watchmaker, had agreed to serve
two years with great-grumpa so that he had "something behind him." And Dicky, at school, counted
the days impatiently, eager to join his brothers at
the workbench. They were all so clear-eyed and self-
assured: beside them, Betony felt herself blind and
muddled; felt herself falling slowly to bits.

She did well enough at school. She was average
in maths, geography, biology, but shone in history,
English, and art. She never behaved badly in class;
was never a rebel; and never questioned any rule,
tradition, or piece of information; all of which made
her a favourite with her teachers. This gave her no
pleasure. It only depressed her. Nancy Sposs had
never been tame and predictable, and Betony wished
she were like Nancy Sposs. But it was no use wishing. She must be herself, once she knew what that
self might be. Meanwhile, she was just a sponge.

Miss Maiberry used to invite certain girls to breakfast or tea in her rooms in Chepsworth, for she
believed in Small Improvements. She taught them
the use of sugar-tongs during afternoon tea, and how
wrong it was to cut toast with a knife at breakfast.
She gave advice on pressing their clothes, and, most
important, on how to accomplish a creaseless sleeve.

Betony now wore the regulation dress of the senior
pupils: long skirt of navy blue serge; black leather
belt with silver buckle bearing the school insignia;
white blouse with tight cuffs and high collar; dark
red tie with fine pink striping. Her mother ironed her
blouses to perfection, and Betony had always been
proud of the straight sharp crease in each long
sleeve. Now, however, perceiving how grave had been
her error, she hurried home from Miss Maiberry's
demonstration, heated the irons on the kitchen stove,
and showed her mother how a sleeve ought to be,
beautifully rounded, and innocent of creases.

Beth was impressed. She watched admiringly.

"My word! If I'd known you was such a dab at ironing I'd have let you take over long since. But there! It's never too late to make amends so finish them shirts of the boys' and then get on with this basketful here."

"But I can't! I've got homework to do this evening."

"First things first," Beth said. "There's plenty of time."

Thereafter, the family ironing frequently came Betony's way, and thereafter, too, she was careful to keep any new accomplishments to herself.

Miss Maiberry was nice but it was Miss Neott, the headmistress, whom Betony most admired. Miss Neott, aged fifty, was handsome and hawklike, with peppery hair impeccably trained about her ears. Her voice was soft but rather compelling, and endowed the simplest words with richness. Betony often emerged from Miss Neott's lessons resolved to speak the most perfect English, though the resolution failed as soon as she was at home again.

When Betony was half way through her seventeenth year, Miss Neott asked her if she had any ambitions.

"I suppose you're not obliged to seek employment? No doubt there's plenty to do at home?"

"Oh, but I don't want to stay at home! I want to see something of the world."

"The world?" said Miss Neott, with a little gleam.

"Well, England, that is."

"Ah, you don't mean to emulate Miss Gertrude Bell?"

"No, I'm not so ambitious as that," Betony said.

Miss Neott said nothing more just then, but during that term she asked Betony to help some girls who had lost time during the influenza epidemic. In the end-of-term tests, the girls did well, and Miss Neott praised Betony's coaching.

"A teacher's work can be very rewarding."

The word dropped delicately into Betony's mind, like a small pebble dropping into a pool.

"If I'm to teach, I suppose I'd better think about going to college."

"Not necessarily," Miss Neott said. "I may be able to help you there. We both know you have teaching ability, and if we nurture it in the next twelve months well,—at the end of that time I may be able to do something for you."

From then on, Betony studied with set purpose, and when, at seventeen, she won her school diploma with honours, she was called to Miss Neott's room to discuss plans for the future.

"I remember, Betony, that you wished to see the wider world. If you still feel the same, I can write to a friend of mine, Miss Telerra, who is headmistress of a private school, the Oldbourne and Simsbury High School for Girls, in the suburbs of London."

"Oh, thank you!" Betony said.

"Miss Telerra requires an assistant teacher and I think if I write to her she may accept you without a preliminary interview. You will write, too, of course, and I will help you compose your letter. Miss Telerra's school is similar to Lock's. Does it appeal to you?"

"Oh, yes!" Betony said. "London! My goodness!"

"The *suburbs* of London," Miss Neott said.

"Yes, of course!" Betony said. "The suburbs of London. Yes, indeed."

At home, when she told her news, Janie and William seemed put out.

"D'you truly want to leave home?" asked Janie. "Go to London? All alone?"

"Of course! Everyone wants to go to London!"

"I don't think you ought," William said. "Mother, she shouldn't ought to go to London, our Betony, should she?"

"Betony's old enough to suit herself. She's a sensible girl. She'll take good care, I'm sure of that."

"Well, I wouldn't go to London," said William. "Would you, Tom?"

"No," said Tom. "I'm well enough here."

Jesse said little or nothing throughout all this, but

later, walking with Betony in the orchard, he looked at her with sad reproach.

"Don't look like that!" Betony said. "I shan't go anywhere if you look like that."

"Don't mind me, my blossom. You must do as the spirit moves you, even if it does mean going to London."

"The *suburbs* of London," Betony said.

"Seems you're going to be something special, what with letters coming and going by post and all."

"I'll be a teacher, that's all."

"That's special, ent it? Not like your dad, a dill-aderry sort of chap, who's never been nowhere in all his days."

Betony put her arm through his.

"Miss Neott's waiting to hear from Miss Telerra. It'll all take ages yet, I dare say."

But Miss Neott received an answer within a matter of days, and Miss Telerra, it seemed, was pleased to offer Miss Izzard a post on her staff, to teach history and English throughout the school, at a salary of thirty-six pounds per annum. Because of her need, and because she trusted Miss Neott's judgment, Miss Telerra would waive the customary personal interview, and would be glad if Miss Izzard could take up her appointment at the start of the summer term. Miss Neott helped Betony to compose her letter of acceptance, and confirmation arrived by return.

The kitchen at Cobbs seemed suddenly filled with bolts of cloth. Granna was never without her spectacles, never without needle and thread and some half-made garment between her hands, and the two flat-irons were never allowed to grow cold.

Jesse, busy making a travelling-box, said it would never hold all the clothes that were being made, and if he were to make a bigger one, no train would be able to carry it. The travelling-box was made of ashwood, covered in canvas, painted dark green, with Betony's initials in black on the lid.

It had rope handles and leather straps, and a shiny brass lock that locked with a tiny figured key.

The time passed terribly slowly, yet when it was gone, she wished she were able to call it back. And at the last, saying goodbye to her family, she found herself wondering all sorts of things about them, thinking of questions she wanted to ask. She had left it too late, and felt she would never now have a chance to know them.

"There's three-pound-ten," said great-grumpa, putting a purse into her hand. "Not for wasting, mind, but for necessary needments."

"Be sure and always air your clothes," said granna.

"Write us a letter every week," said Janie.

"And picture-postcards!" said the boys in chorus.

"Remember, Betony," said her mother, "if you don't like it there, don't delay in coming home."

"Of course I shall like it!" Betony said.

"Goodbye, Betony," said Tom.

"Good riddance, too?" she said gaily, and Tom shrugged.

Her father drove her to Chepsworth station, and saw her safely onto the train. He stood on the platform, filling his pipe, packing the tobacco much too hard, gazing at her as she leant from the window of the carriage door.

"Got your box?" he asked abruptly.

"Yes. You carried it aboard for me."

"Got that address wrote down, have you, where there's a room bespoke for you?"

"I've got all Miss Telerra's directions written down, father."

"What's her name, where you're going to lodge?"

"Mrs Bream."

"Ah, I knowed it was something to do with fish. Here! Look at that! That guard has gone and got off the train!"

The whistle blew, and the train began very gently to move. Betony leant still further out of the window, and her father began to walk with the train.

"Lumme!" he said. "Seems you're going any minute now. I seen that guard nipping on and off, the one with bright buttons and the little green flag. He's a caution, he is! But I daresay he knows what he's about."

"We're moving now!" Betony cried. "We're moving properly this time! Goodbye, father! Goodbye, our dad!"

"You take care up there in London!" he called out, walking faster, dragging his foot. "Take care, my blossom, and don't get trampled to death in them crowds!"

The train gathered speed, and he was left standing on the platform. Betony watched him and went on waving to the last. He looked very lonely, standing there.

That last glimpse almost spoilt her journey, saddening her, making her feel that she had done wrong in leaving him. But then resentment arose in her, and she cast off the guilty sadness, telling herself that she had a right to enjoy the new life now beginning.

As far as Long Stone, she had the compartment to herself, but there two middle-aged men got in, sat down in opposite corners, and put up their papers. Betony marvelled. She looked at them for signs of pretence. That people could actually board a train and be rattled along at high speed, yet show no more feeling than if they were taking a stroll down the road! It was amazing. The two most be seasoned travellers indeed. Some day, perhaps, she would be the same. But for the present she was content to be a new scholar and wonder at everything she saw.

Surely the primroses growing along the embankments were bigger than any at home? Surely the sky over Oxfordshire and Buckinghamshire was different from any sky seen over Huntlip? And surely the towns she passed through were peopled with beings more real, more important, possessed of a higher cast of mind, than any she had left behind her? The towns were exciting. The towns were where great things got done. And London was the apogee, the capital city over them all. Surely the people who lived there shaped the world?

The journey ended all too soon, and when she saw the grey city smoking under the blue sky, she experienced a sighing, dying-away feeling inside her, for now the miracle of this first moment could never, never come again. She stood up, face pressed against the window, and watched the railway lines opening out, wider and wider, more and more rails, running together and parting again, a zig-zag complex of glistening steel. The train ran in under shelter, and the daylight took on an underwater shade of green. Was this London? It was indeed. "Paddington! H'all change!"

A porter carried the box to an exit, and Betony boarded a northbound bus. She paid a fare of fourpence, and, after travelling fifteen minutes, was set down outside The Panting Hart, at a five-road junction in Stanton Broadway. There, as she stood with her box at her feet, again consulting her written instructions, a man approached and touched his cap.

"Carry your trunk, miss? Anywhere!"

"Matlock Terrace," Betony said.

"No distance at all. Just ten minutes across the park." The man, although small, cheerfully took the box on his shoulder. "Charge you a bob," he said, tentatively.

"Thank you. That's very kind."

"New to London?" he asked, as they walked. "Up from the country? I thought as much. Come for a holiday, I suppose?"

"No, I'm going to teach at the Oldbourne and Simsbury High School for Girls."

"Well, I'll go to Putney to see the boat race! My eldest girl's a pupil there. She got a scholarship three years ago. Florrie, her name is. Florrie Smith. What's your name, miss, so's I can tell her when I get home?"

"Miss Izzard."

"I'll tell her I met you. She's a good girl, Florrie. You'll like her, I know." He walked a little way in silence, glancing often into Betony's face. "I expect you're wondering," he said, "at an out-of-work chap like me having a daughter at the High School?"

"I wasn't wondering anything," Betony said.

"You won't say nothing about it, will you? At the school, I mean.—That you seen Florrie's father out tootling for coppers? Better not. They're a very superior class of girl at the High School, and I don't want them making things hard for Florrie."

They were crossing the park, and he pointed towards the eastern boundary.

"The school's over there. See the white wall behind them aspens? You'll be nice and handy in Matlock Terrace."

They passed between two tall iron gates, and crossed a curved road to the terrace of houses on the other side. Number fifty was at the centre. It had net curtains in loops across the windows, and stained-glass panels in the door. The man carried the travelling-box up the steps and set it down inside the porch. He looked pained as Betony offered him his shilling, but took it from her and once again touched his cap.

"All the best, Miss Izzard, and if you should hear of anyone wanting a carpenter, you might remember Joe Smith."

"A carpenter?" Betony said.

"That's my trade—*when* I can get the work," he said, and went off with a last salute.

Betony turned and pulled the bell, and the clangour of it echoed through the house. A curtain moved at one bay window, was held back by jewelled fingers, and, after several seconds, allowed to fall.

Mrs Bream, who came at last to open the door, was a stately woman with corkscrew curls at her temples, a large face, and large strong teeth, very white and square. She was stately and slow in all she did, and she stood in the hall, her hands folded upon her stomach, looking at Betony's travelling-box as if it presented a grave problem. It seemed the maid, Ruby, had chosen that moment to scald herself with a saucepan of milk, and was still busy in the basement, dressing her arm with bicarbonate paste. Mrs Bream, therefore, was obliged to call her daughter, Edna, to help Betony with the box. It was no trouble. The fault was the maid's. Ruby was rather a clumsy girl.

"Of course, Miss Izzard, I wouldn't ordinarily have taken a guest unseen, but for Miss Telerra's personal assurance."

Betony, following with Edna, under a looped velvet curtain and up the stairs, was not sure how to answer. She made a polite noise in her throat. On the landing, where an oriel window gave good light, she and Edna inspected each other across the box. The girl was lively and fresh-faced, with rather prominent green eyes, and all the time her mother talked, she kept making faces and glancing skywards.

From the landing, they climbed another flight of stairs to the attic, where Mrs Bream opened a door and led the way into Betony's bedroom. The room, being high, was full of sunlight, and the casement window looked on the park.

"I've given you a front room, as you see. The view is a large part of this house's charm, I think, and all my guests agree, I'm sure."

She spoke as if her house alone enjoyed the view, instead of sharing it with ninety neighbours, and again the girl Edna sucked in her cheeks and rolled her eyes derisively.

"It's a very nice room," Betony said, and, divining from Mrs Bream's silence that this was scarcely an adequate tribute, she added warmly: "I shall like it here. I shall indeed!"

"Edna is at the High School," Mrs Bream said. "You are much of an age, so I'll leave it to her to make you feel at home here."

The moment her mother had left the room, Edna collapsed onto Betony's bed.

"Poor mother! She's no idea how funny she is!"

"Funny? I didn't think her funny at all."

"What *did* you think of her, pray?"

"I thought her rather dignified."

"That's her transformation! She dare not make a careless move for fear of upsettting those little curls. But let's talk about you! How old are you? Eighteen? I'll be seventeen on June the twelfth. But I'm old for my age, don't you think? I'm very mature, mother says, and Mr Thorsby thinks so, too."

Betony herself was only seventeen, but thought it wiser not to say so.

"Mr Thorsby?" she said instead.

"One of our lodgers. Whoops!—I mean guests! And the only one worth troubling about. He's a surgeon, and rather fine. But what about you! Fancy you teaching at Old and Sims. You must be very clever."

"Only ordinary," Betony said.

"Have you got to see Telerra in the morning?"

"At nine o'clock."

"Sooner you than me! But she's not so bad, considering. Now tell me—where would you like to go this afternoon? We've got plenty of time to wander round town, so what would you like to see?"

"Anything and everything!" Betony said.

For the residents of Stanton Rise, all journeys began and ended at the Broadway, and so, from outside The Panting Hart, they took a bus to Marylebone. They went to the wax works of Madam Tussaud; walked along Oxford Street, gazing into the shop windows; and went to Robini's for tea and gateaux. They then travelled by bus to Chelsea and walked along the embankment there.

"It's lucky you've got some money," Edna said. "I spent my allowance ages ago. Are you sure you don't mind paying for everything? I'll take my turn when I'm in the dibs."

"Of course I don't mind," Betony said.

"That young man was looking at you. The tall one with the dark moustache. They've got dreadful sauce, some of these men. Did you see him stare?"

"No. I'm still seeing the Kings and Queens of England."

"What? Oh, the waxworks! Aren't they splendid! All so real! Now what did you want to see next? Oh, yes, I remember! Let's ask the way."

Outside a tobacconist's shop, a woman in slippers was sweeping the pavement, and they asked her the way to Dr Johnson's house.

"Dr Johnson?" the woman said. "There's nobody here of that name. If you want a doctor, you must go to Walker's Mews and see Dr Snell."

They nodded primly and walked on, but once out of earshot, they clung to each other and sputtered with laughter. It was too delicious, Edna said. The old woman had made her day.

They returned home for dinner at seven, and Betony met her fellow lodgers. Miss Wilkings, who sold flowers from a stall outside The Panting Hart; Mr Lumbe, a plump young man of twenty-two, who worked in a bank in Oldbourne; and Mr Thorsby, a severe-looking man in his late thirties, who seemed to Betony to be cold and remote and absent-minded. She also met the head of the household, Mr Bream, who said she must not expect him to be clever, for he was only a businessman and only knew "how to manage the works". The works being a steam laundry in Simsbury Green.

Edna, describing the fruitless search for Dr Johnson, was scolded by Mrs Bream, the last to take her place at the table, for leaving a tureen of soup to grow cold on the dumb-waiter. Her father defended her. So did Mr Lumbe. Mr Thorsby said nothing, but sipped his glass of water and stared into space.

"What d'you think of London, Miss Izzard?" Mr Bream enquired. "Dirty old place, eh? All smuts and smoke?"

"Oh, no!" Betony said.

"Paved with gold, then, is that it?"

"Paved with history," Betony said.

Briefly, she felt embarrassed by what she had said, but Mr Bream's "Bravo!" and Mr Lumbe's "Hear,

Hear!" set her mind at ease, and she saw that among these civilized people, a little flamboyance would not come amiss.

"Well, Miss Wilkings?" said Mr Lumbe. "How were things at the market this morning?"

"There's a glut of narcissus," Miss Wilkings said. "Specially jonquils. Don't ask me why."

"Oh, but I must!" said Mr Lumbe, with his plump-faced smile. "I simply must ask why jonquils are glutting!"

"Early spring, no frosts," Miss Wilkings said. "Pass the bread, Mr Lumbe, please."

"Mr Thorsby, you aren't finishing your soup," said Mrs Bream.

"Yes, I am," said Mr Thorsby, coming out of a dream and resuming his soup-spoon. "It's very good. Very good indeed."

And those, Betony noted, were the only words Mr Thorsby uttered throughout the meal.

Later that night, when she was preparing to go to bed, Edna came up to the attic room.

"What do you think of Mr Thorsby?"

"He's very silent," Betony said. "Rather stern. Rather reserved."

"He's always silent, except when he and I are alone together. Then he talks. Oh, heavens, yes! But he *is* reserved with other people, and he's often thinking about his work."

"Yes, of course."

"Don't you think he's handsome, Betony?"

"He is. Very. But, Edna, isn't he rather old for you?"

Edna nodded. Her face was tragic. There were tears in her eyes.

"He's twenty-one years older than me, and he feels it dreadfully, poor man. That's what stops him, you see."

"Stops him?"

"Well, if I had my way, we'd be married tomorrow!" Edna said. "And I don't care who knows it! But Edward doesn't see it as I do, unfortunately. Oh, he's

never said so, but I can read him like a book. He has
such pride! And an iron will. He'd sooner deny himself every last chance of happiness than risk exposing
me to gossip."

"Does your mother know?"

"Well . . . She wants me to marry Rodney Lumbe.
But I couldn't! He's soft and pudgy and wears yellow
spats."

"Has Mr Lumbe proposed to you?"

"No. I won't let him. But he follows me round all
the time and he's always trying to get my attention.
Had you noticed?"

"Yes, I had. He hangs on everything you say."

"Edward is much more reserved," Edna said. "It
makes me want to cry sometimes, knowing how he
suffers underneath. But I've got faith and I know everything will come right for him and me in the end.
Don't you think so?"

"I'm sure of it," Betony said, with warmth.

"Oh, you are such a friend!" Edna exclaimed. "I'm
so glad you've come to live with us!"

At nine in the morning, Betony presented herself at
the High School, and met the headmistress. The school
was a square, clean-looking building, its white ashlar
façade successfully hiding the absence of architec-
tural style behind it. Inside, it was rather dark and
smelt of polish, except for the head's room, which
smelt of hyacinths and daffodils. Miss Telerra was a
sombre-looking woman, her face loose-boned, her hair
jet-black, and her skin swarthy. She looked very foreign, but her speech was as English as any Betony
had ever heard.

"Are you settled comfortably in Matlock Terrace?
I'm so glad. I'm sure you'll be happy with Mrs
Bream."

"I'm sure I shall," Betony said.

"The school is not large," Miss Telerra said. "One
hundred and eighty pupils, twelve to eighteen, all of
them day girls. Mostly, they are not ambitious, but

there are two scholarship girls of exceptional ability, one of whom may go on to university."

"Florrie Smith?" Betony said.

"You know her?" Miss Telerra asked.

"No, but I happened to meet her father yesterday, when I arrived."

"Florrie is an exceptional child, although coming from a poor home. You'll know her by her red hair and her hot enthusiasm for work."

Miss Telerra smiled, thus transforming her dark face, and Betony liked her.

"Well, Miss Izzard, there are many things I must tell you about the school and your place in it, and then, when the rest of the staff arrive, I want you to sit in at our meeting. I trust it's convenient for you to stay?"

"Oh, yes! I'm looking forward to it."

At ten o'clock, however, when the room filled with staff and the meeting began, Betony knew a moment of panic. She counted fourteen people in the room, and thought of the hundred and eighty pupils arriving next morning: how could she memorize so many faces and names at once? And the subjects now under discussion: how could she master the endless elaboration of administrative and academic detail?

But as the meeting went on, and she learnt the identity of each of the staff, she became calmer; and by one o'clock, when the meeting ended, she was cheerful again. The rest would come. She must give it time. And each new problem must take its turn.

Miss Telerra had introduced her in a general way, with a little speech welcoming her onto the staff, but now, as the meeting ended, most of them left without a glance in her direction. Only two young women, Miss Crabbe and Miss Horslam, spoke to her as they walked to the gate.

"I hear you're special," Miss Horslam said. "A personal friend of the King of Spain's Daughter."

"Horse means the head," Miss Crabbe explained.

"But I've never met her before today. Miss Telerra knows my headmistress at Chepsworth, that's all."

"I expect you're cheap, then," Miss Horslam said.

"Horse," Miss Crabbe said apologetically, "is not so delicate as her name suggests."

"I meant no offence," Miss Horslam said, meeting Betony's gaze with sleepy composure. "You may be a super-excellent teacher for all I know. But you aren't an M.A. Cantab., are you?"

"Indeed I'm not," Betony said.

"I am. And Crabbe hails from the other place with almost equal distinction. Which means we'll be out neck and crop as soon as cheaper substitutes can be found."

"Oh, surely not!"

"Don't worry. It's a cross we career women have to bear. The school must pay its way and it's only common sense that the head should staff it as cheaply as possible."

"Are you with the Breams?" Crabbe asked. "Yes, I thought so. Your predecessor was there too."

"Watch out for Edna," Horse advised. "She's a handful, that girl, and stuffed with morbid romantical nonsense."

"So, having cheered you up to the best of our not inconsiderable ability, farewell!" said Crabbe. "We meet in the morning—loins girded for the new term."

They were at the school gate, and from there, the two young women went in one direction, Betony in another.

From The Panting Hart, she travelled on top of an open bus to the city. Edna was spending the afternoon with her dressmaker, and would not be free until four o'clock. She had asked Betony to wait for her, but Betony, glad of a chance to be alone, had made excuses. She wanted time to think and absorb; to drift according to her own inclination.

The day was damp, mild, and fitfully sunny. She leant against the rail of the bus, and, looking down at the traffic in the roadway and the lunch-time crowds filling the pavements, she felt a little drunk and dreamlike, enjoying the noise of the motor engines, excited by everything she saw.

She saw a tiny liveried page run down the steps of a large hotel and go weaving through the crowds and traffic. She saw a horse and dray drawn up outside a public house, and the draymen rolling barrels into the cellar. And she read the hoardings everywhere; the billboards on buses; the sandwichboards: Pear's Soap; Nestle's Milk; Hope and Parker's Menthol Snuff; Brand's Essence; Bawley's Beers.

Suddenly, more light, more space—the buildings pushed back—trees, fountains—pigeons in flight—and there was Nelson on his column in the sky. Betony blinked. She could not believe it. She looked at the passengers sharing the deck, and thought they must all be slumbering. She wanted to rouse them: "Look! Behold! It's Nelson's column, Trafalgar Square!" But their eyes, amazingly, were open. It was only their souls that had gone to sleep, lulled by custom. She alone sat up and burned, looking down on London city, laid out so casually for any passer-by to see.

When she alighted, she was setting foot in a place built of dreams; a concrete chronicle of past and present: legend manifest in mortar, brick, and stone; where people even now were treading out the aching human fates that would make tomorrow's history.

She walked and walked, without knowing where she was going, and because she gave herself up to the city in this manner, it sprang its surprises upon her again and again. Here was the river, and a tug-boat folding its funnel to pass under London Bridge. Here was the Monument and its ball of fire. And here was the Tower, perfect and lovely; the Middle Ages seen at a glance, with scarlet pennants aflame in the wind.

She walked and walked, this way and that, through narrow passages and little courts; through Black Bear Alley and Playhouse Yard; Griffon Buildings and King Pin Walk. She saw pans of sausages frying on gas-jets in a cafe window, and was made hungry by the smell of soup coming up from a grating in the pavement. She went in, down the steps, into an underground room full of people. She ate sausages, onions, and mashed potatoes, and afterwards drank a cup of coffee, made from coffee-beans ground in a little machine on the counter.

She walked again, and came on another space between buildings, and there was St Paul's: the phoenix cathedral; the great convenant forged from fire; the City of London's act of Faith; its dome moulded to the shape of the heavens as seen by the human eye.

"Look," she said, to a newspaper-seller standing nearby. "There's St Paul's!"

"Gorblimey, where?" he said, wheezing.

"There," she said, pointing. "Up on that hill."

"Ho, yus! That's been there some time. Well, ever since I can remember, anyhow." He looked at her with sharp eyes, unsmiling, straight-faced. "Don't you touch it!" he said hoarsely. "Or you'll have the king's horses and all the king's men after you. Ho, yes! The whole Magna Carta!"

As she journeyed home, the day drew in and the lamps were lit along the streets. She saw the lamplighters going about, busy with their long poles, and once she saw one of them poking a tuft of dry grasses out of a lamp where birds had begun to build a nest. All the lamps entranced her. The evening became a beautiful thing. The fuzzy rounds of pale splintered light were everywhere, dancing and glancing in the damp air, all the way home to Stanton Rise.

At dinner-time, when Betony entered and took her place at the table, Mr Bream greeted her with a sigh of relief.

"Well, Miss Izzard! You're back at last. We were worried about you, out alone in the great city. We feared you might be lost."

"*Were* you lost?" Mr Lumbe enquired.

"I was, for a while, this afternoon, in a maze of little entanies behind St. Paul's. But only on purpose, to see the city."

"Lose yourself," Mr Lumbe agreed, "and you get to know the heart of a place."

"Entanies?" said Mr Thorsby, looking at Betony with an interest so unexpected that it made her jump. "What are entanies exactly?"

"Yes, whatever are they?" Edna asked.

"An entany is a narrow passage. It's what we always call it at home."

"Ah, a dialect word," said Mr Bream.

"A nice word, entany," said Mr Thorsby. "It sounds exactly what it is."

"How did you get on with the King of Spain's Daughter?" asked Edna.

"She was most kind and helpful," Betony said.

Mr Thorsby, next to Edna, looked at her with a dark frown.

"I think it's unbecoming in you, young woman, to speak of your headmistress by anything but her proper name."

"But everyone calls her the King of Spain's Daughter! Even the staff!"

"You are not staff," Mr Thorsby said.

"No," said Edna, suddenly chastened. "I ought not to say it, and I shan't again, ever, I swear."

Edna's forearm, on the edge of the table, lay touching Mr Thorsby's sleeve. Betony noticed it, and the way Mr Thorsby, after a moment of deep thought, gently withdrew his arm from the table and turned to speak to Miss Wilkings. She noticed, too, how flushed and happy Edna was for the rest of the evening.

The attic room was a pleasant place to be in the evenings, when she had lessons to prepare, or her diary to write, or a letter home. If she sat at the window, she was able to catch every last gleam of light from the north western sky, and when she could no longer see to write, she often sat watching the sunset colours changing. She watched the first stars getting up and the last birds flying home to roost, and when darkness really filled the room, she got up and lit the gas bracket on the wall by the door.

In her letters home, she wrote of the things she did and saw. "Last Saturday, Edna and I went to the museum. Next Sunday, we go to Kew." But, somehow, she could never write about the school, or the pupils, or her work as a teacher. And there were things about the Bream household, too, that she preferred to keep to herself.

One of the first things she did was to buy a diary, but three weeks went past before she found time to write in it, and by then her memory was playing her false. Only the first day at school remained perfectly clear in her mind, and two lessons clearest of all.

The first was with a class of the fourth standard, girls of fourteen and fifteen years old, though they seemed older. They were quick and sharp, eager to know if she were flesh and blood, and one girl, Leonie Siddert, led the rest in a little trial.

"Oh, heavens! We're not still on that boring Middle English? I thought we'd done all that with Miss Scott."

"Can't we get on to something exciting? Like *Moll Flanders* or *Tom Jones*?"

"Or something modern, like *Ann Veronica*?"

"Or Elinor Glyn!"

"Or *The Woman Who Did*!"

Betony, wincing under the onslaught of noise, was extremely angry.

"Be quiet at once!" she said fiercely, and, having surprised them by the trenchancy of her voice, she went on coolly: "I shall give the lesson I have prepared, and if the material is already familiar, well, you'll be doubly sure of it when writing your essays in a few days' time."

The lesson continued without further disturbance. Leonie Siddert appeared satisfied. And Betony had learnt how useful it was to have so much of her mother in her.

Later that day, she gave a history lesson to a class of older girls, and among them she found Florrie Smith, whose father had carried her travelling-box the day she arrived. Florrie was sixteen, a plain girl with ginger hair and flat, freckled face, her plainness redeemed by wide-awake eyes and an easy, unaffected smile.

The lesson worried Betony, for whenever she sought to stimulate discussion by asking questions, Florrie Smith was the only one with anything to say. The others were silent from start to finish, though they listened intently enough, and made endless notes. After school, meeting Miss Crabbe on the stairs, Betony mentioned the matter to her.

"It's Florrie Smith," Miss Crabbe explained. "They look down on Florrie and won't demean themselves by competing with her."

"Are they so special, for goodness' sake?"

"Their fathers are all great men, you see, such as stock-brokers or importers of tea."

"Great men?" Betony said.

"To themselves, certainly, and to their daughters, for they Pay Fees while Florrie Smith is a scholarship upstart without two pennies to rub together."

"But aren't they ambitious? Don't they *want* the education they pay for?"

"Their greatest ambition is to marry as soon as possible after leaving school, to pay a visit here in a motor car, and to flaunt their wedding-rings in the faces of their former school-friends. As for education —it's the done thing. They expose themselves to it just as they go every year and expose themselves to the sea air at Brighton or Clacton. The polish education gives them is on a par with the tan they get from a fortnight's sunshine, also paid for by their doting papas."

"So we just won't get them to take an active part in discussions?"

"There's a golden rule," Miss Crabbe said. "Never ask: 'Can anyone give the cause of the Luddite riots?' because Florrie's sure to answer and the others will just look down their noses. Instead, you point directly to a chosen victim and say: 'Louisa, relate the events preceding the Repeal of the Corn Laws."

Betony smiled.

"I've learnt more than I've taught on my first day of term."

"Is it only the first day? I feel I've been back a lifetime already!"

Miss Crabbe and Miss Horslam were Betony's friends. Sometimes she went to tea with them in their rooms in Oldbourne, but they would never come to Matlock Terrace, because, they said, they knew from her predecessor that Mrs Bream frowned upon visitors. Betony liked them better than anyone else on the staff, and was soon calling them Crabbe and Horse.

"Not Horse and Crabbe, because Horse never really pulls her weight," said Crabbe. "And that's a hackneyed joke if you like!"

"I warn you," said Horse. "Friendship with us

carries certain penalties. Miss Sylke will automatically detest you."

"I don't much care for *her*. She's always so sneering about the other staff. Why does she call Miss Tweet and Miss Snubbs the Twins of Lesbos?"

"Izzard," said Crabbe, "you have a nice mind."

"Have I?" Betony said, surprised.

"Well, compared with Sylke, certainly."

"To Sylke," said Horse, "relations between the two sexes are disgusting, and relations between the same sex are more disgusting still. It's all in the eye of the beholder, and Sylke's eye is full of disgust."

"She's quick to put people in the wrong," Betony said. "I've offended often."

"I told you," said Horse. "You're friendly with us."

Betony first offended Miss Sylke by mounting the school platform before her one morning at assembly. Next, in the staff-room, she offended by sitting in Miss Sylke's chair. And next, most serious of all, she dared to say that King Charles the First was an obstinate man. Miss Sylke, it seemed, was devoted to Charles.

"As head of the history department, Miss Izzard, I am the one to pronounce on such matters."

"Divine right," Crabbe murmured.

One day Miss Sylke came storming to Betony with a piece of paper in her hand. Again it was in the staff-room, for she liked an audience when she staged her scenes.

"This notice you put on the board, Miss Izzard, concerning the visit to Windsor Castle. It reads obscurely and I don't understand it. 'Girls to apply to Miss Sylke by May the sixteenth, bringing their fare of one-and-sixpence and a packed lunch if they so wish.' Am I to expect, Miss Izzard, that I shall be inundated with packed lunches to be kept from the sixteenth to the twenty-ninth?"

Betony took the piece of paper and rewrote the notice on the reverse side.

"There," she said, handing it back. "Now it's plain even to the meanest intelligence."

Miss Sylke flounced out, and the staff-room door slammed behind her.

"You've done it now," Crabbe said. "You'll never be asked to see Sylke's collection of birds' eggs."

"Did she lay them herself?"

"No, no, the dear little robins and wrens did that. It's the one touch of nature Sylke permits, and that's only because she thinks it's done by parthenogenesis."

"I must speak to her," Betony said, "on country matters."

She might have been lonely at school, sometimes, had it not been for Crabbe and Horse.

Sometimes, in the room below hers in Matlock Terrace, Mr Thorsby played his violin. He played Mozart and Mendelssohn, and old folk tunes like 'Barbara Allen' and 'Afton Water.' Once, meeting her on the landing, he asked if his playing disturbed her, and when she said no, that on the contrary, she enjoyed it, he went into his room and closed the door quickly, as though afraid she might follow him in.

Once, when Edna was with Betony in the attic, he played 'Drink To Me Only With Thine Eyes,' and Edna was dreadfully overcome by tears.

"He knows it's my favourite, and he knows I'm up here with you, listening. Oh, dear, you'll think me so silly! But he does make me sad."

Another evening, when Betony went out to the post-box, Edna was standing outside Mr Thorsby's room, listening to him practising scales. The girl shrank back, into the shadows, and Betony, pretending not to have seen her, went on down the second staircase and out of the house. When she returned, Edna had gone, and Mr Thorsby was playing a Mozart sonata.

On Whit Sunday, she and Edna walked in the park. There was hot sunshine. The holiday-makers were out in crowds, and among them, walking dreamily by the duck-ponds, Edna perceived Mr Thorsby.

"There's Edward!" she said, and, taking Betony by

the arm, hurried her towards the ponds. "I thought he might come. He knows I like to hear the band."

Mr Thorsby was coming towards them, but gazing absently all around. As Edna and Betony drew near, his glance flickered briefly towards them, and then away, to where some children were chasing a ball. And he walked past, his hands behind him, his head in the air.

"Oh, really!" Edna exclaimed. "Edward is very trying sometimes. To walk past like that,—sulking—just because I'm not alone! It's always the same, you know.—If anyone's with me, he turns away."

Betony walked along in silence. To her, it seemed Mr Thorsby had not even seen them. His thoughts, as always, had been elsewhere.

"Edna," she said, after a while, "are you quite certain of Mr Thorsby's feelings?"

"Certain?" said Edna, stopping abruptly and staring at her. "Do you think I've been telling lies?"

"No. I thought you might have been mistaken."

"Then you think me a fool, obviously!" said Edna, and her white-gloved fingers kept twisting the parasol on her shoulder. "I must be one or the other!—Either a liar or a fool! I don't see what else you can mean."

"Please don't be silly," Betony said.

"I won't!" Edna said. "I won't be silly another minute! You can walk by yourself, you school-ma'am, you!" And she hurried away up the green slope, towards the south gateway and Matlock Terrace.

Briefly, Betony considered following, but then she shrugged and walked on. Edna's problems must wait until later. The day was too perfect to spend indoors.

Up on high ground, three children were flying a kite, and she stood and watched it, a bright yellow shield, now straining its string as it rose on a current of hot air, now falling and swooping as the air failed. And then suddenly it was caught in an oak tree.

Not far away, a young man was also watching. He spoke to the children and went to the tree. He climbed up into the branches, out on a limb, among the thickening foliage, and down again, bringing the kite safely with him. The children took it and ran off, away to where there were fewer trees, and the young man collapsed onto the grass, bent double as though in pain.

Betony went closer and looked at him. He now lay flat on his back, his hands folded over his stomach. His eyes were closed, his thick black brows met in a scowl, and his thin face was covered in sweat.

"Are you all right?" she asked, just above him. "Or are you ill?"

He opened his eyes, and sat up slowly.

"I climbed a tree and gave myself a bit of a stitch." He stood up, wiping his face with a grubby handkerchief. "It's over warm for such exertions today," he said.

He was quite young, probably in his early twenties, though his hair was unusually streaked with grey. He was very thin, and his shabby brown clothes hung loosely on him, as on a scarecrow. His voice was strange, with an accent she had heard once before, and which, somehow, made her smile.

"What's funny, then?" he asked.

"It's the way you speak. I think you come from Yorkshire."

"Where else?" he said, and stood with his hands in his jacket pockets, looking at her with a straight, steady stare. "Runceley!" he said. "And I doubt if you've even heard the name."

"Runceley," she repeated, and thought for a moment. "West Riding town, on the River Tibble, worsteds, woollens, corduroys. Population 45,000. Annual rainfall 86 inches."

"Good God!" he said. "You must've had the blue ribbon in geography when you were at school."

"Quite the reverse. I was inattentive and the teacher made me write up the towns of Yorkshire as a punishment."

"The old bitch!" he said roundly. "Why Yorkshire?"

"She came from Bradford."

"Eh, she can't have been too bad, then. And where are you from?"

"The three counties," Betony said.

"What, all three?"

"My home village, Huntlip, likes to boast of having a foot in all three. But our nearest big town is Chepsworth."

"Chepsworth," he said. "Cathedral . . . River Idden . . . Leather gloves."

"*Three* rivers," Betony said. "The Idden, the Ennen, and the Naff. And three big brooks, the Swiggett, the Derrent, and the Shinn."

"It sounds a very watery place."

"It can't compare with Runceley for rainfall."

"Why should it indeed?"

While talking, they had walked together down the slope to the central gardens, where lay the last of the three duckponds. Now Betony leant on the railing and looked at the ducks.

"Why must there be fences round every pond?" she asked in exasperation.

"To stop the foxes getting the ducks," he said.

"Foxes? Here? Right in the town?"

"The town's grown up round them, and a few survive, getting their living as best they can. Three weeks ago, a fox ran out from under the band-stand, and a lot of daft folk chased it right across the park. Didn't you read about it in *The Gazette*?"

"No, I didn't. But surely a fox could dig down under these railings?"

"Nay, they were sunk deep on purpose to stop him. It was all in the paper a while back." The young man leant on the railings beside her. "Don't you ever read *The Gazette*?"

"No," she said. "But you evidently do."

"Aye, well, I help to write it."

"You're a journalist, then?"

"If you call it that.—Writing up band concerts and foxes seen in public parks."

"Why do it if you don't like it?"

"I'm serving my time. An apprenticeship, like. But

one day, I'll write for a paper with something to say
for itself, and choose the subjects that really want
airing."

"Which subjects?" Betony asked.

"Children of twelve working in Runceley mills . . .
Conditions down the pit in the Yorkshire coal-fields
. . . Girls in paint factories, dying of lead poisoning
by the age of twenty-four . . . I've a tidy few things
to write about when I get started."

"Will people want to read about them?"

"Nay. They prefer something pretty. And I shall
oblige them! Oh, aye! I'll begin by describing Lord
Soak's soirée, where the flowers alone cost four hundred guineas. Then I'll happen describe a Yorkshire
collier, digging coal for a twelve hour stretch, up to
his chest in poisonous waters."

"You're a radical?" Betony asked.

"I'm a Voice," he said.

Betony was reminded of Nancy Sposs.

"You're somebody's conscience, then, perhaps?"

"Aye. Yours for a start."

"Why mine? I can't help it if people are poor."

"That's what they all say!"

"It must be nice, being Conscience. Rather like
being God."

"God?" he said richly. "I could run things better
with my eyes shut and both hands tied behind my
back! And don't look at me like that, woman!—You're
no more shocked than those ducks and drakes on the
water there."

"How d'you know I'm not shocked?"

"You're too well founded. You're like one of those
little lamps with a loaded bottom.—You might get
knocked sideways now and then but you'll never go
down. Aye, and you'll keep a trim wick and go on
burning whatever happens, I dare say."

Betony laughed.

"Only so long as my oil lasts out."

"I've pleased you," he said. "You like the thought
of yourself as a little lamp."

"If you can be Conscience, can't I be Light?" Betony said, and then: "Is Utopia possible?"

"It should always be the aim. A goal kept constantly in sight."

"But surely there must always be poor people?"

"Why?" he demanded, and turned towards her. "Why must there always be poor people?"

"I don't know."

"Oh yes you do!"

"All right. I know what you want me to say. Because there are rich."

"And you don't want to change it because it's what you've always been used to, and you've never known what it is to starve."

"My parents have known poverty."

"But not you?"

"No, not me."

"That girl across there," he said, nodding. "She's staring at you. Is she a friend?"

Betony, looking across the pond, was just in time to see Edna walking away from the opposite bank.

"I must go," she said. "We had a disagreement, you see, and I want to catch her to put things right."

"Aye. Well. Goodbye."

"Are you sure you're feeling all right now?"

"So long as I don't climb any more trees."

"Goodbye, then," Betony said, and hurried off in pursuit of Edna.

"I came back to apologize," Edna said, "but found you otherwise engaged."

"I apologize, too," Betony said. "Let's forget we ever quarrelled."

"Who's your young man with the fierce eyebrows?"

"I don't know his name. We just got talking."

"Shall you see him again?"

"I shouldn't think so. Unless by chance."

"Was he romantic, Betony? Charming? Witty?"

"No, none of those things," Betony said.

His name was Jim Firth. He was twenty-three, the youngest of six children, and the only one to survive childhood. His mother was dead, and his father lived alone in Runceley, publishing a weekly newspaper there.

"Doesn't he mind your coming to London and leaving him there all alone?"

"He sent me," Jim said, "to stir things up a bit here in the sawny south."

"So you and he are two of a kind?"

"Rank socialists, the pair of us! Aren't you afraid of talking to me?"

At first, they met neither by chance nor arrangement. He came to the park every evening to escape his lodgings in Gasworks Grove, as he called it, and Betony, too, all through the hot May and June of that summer, could not bear to be indoors, but took to the park the moment she was free to do so. Each would have been there, anyway, but each, once there, looked out for the other. And so, almost always, they met. And, almost always, they argued.

"Why do you dislike your mother?"

"I never said I did."

"She sounds a remarkable woman to me."

"You and she would make a good pair!"

"Meaning something nasty?"

"You're both so cocksure that you know what's right."

"Is that all that's wrong with her?"

"Well . . . I've never understood why she married my father. I'm sure she doesn't love him."

"What makes you think so? Is he unhappy?"

"No. He's perfectly happy. He's that sort of man."

"Does he think your mother loves him?"

"I suppose so."

"Well, he must know best. And there are five children. You can't all have been conceived in indifference. The trouble with you is, you never look below the surface."

"It's a funny thing!" Betony said. "I always make friends with people who tear me in little pieces!"

"They're the best kind, are friends of that sort, if you've the stomach for home truths."

"Suppose I were to start on you?"

"Go right ahead. It's only fair."

But Betony, though she tried hard enough, could find no fault in him. All the things that might have been faults, such as temper, impatience, the assurance that he was always right; his rough tongue and rude manner: all were so closely linked with one another, with his beliefs and essential being, they could not be considered faults at all. To censure him would be to censure a fox for its cunning or a wild bird because it had wings.

She tried to explain to herself why this should be so, but could think only of negative things, his lack of falsity, lack of self-interest. It was only later that she realized the positive thing about him: his love for everything on earth that lived.

"Tell me why you came to London," he said.

"Because it's the centre of the world. Because it's romantic. Because there are so many things to see."

"And what have you seen exactly?"

"St. Paul's. The Tower. Westminster Abbey. Madame Tussaud's."

"Is that all?"

"I think so."

"By gow! I'll have to take you and show you the sights, for you've seen nothing yet, that's plain. How about Friday? I'll have a few coppers for a bus by then."

"Friday, yes," Betony said. "But I'll pay my own fare."

And so, now, they met by arrangement. They went by bus to the Edgware Road, and then walked, into a maze of back streets, this way and that. It was after nine o'clock in the evening, because Jim had worked until late that day, reporting a fire at Simsbury Junction. The night was hot, and they walked slowly, feeling they would melt at the slightest exertion.

"Where are we going? We've walked miles . . . We're leaving all the lights behind."

"There's plenty to see all the same," he said, as they turned into a long narrow street called the

Fullway. "Here, for instance. You've got an eye for architecture. Say what you think of the buildings here."

"I suppose you're joking," Betony said.

She looked at the cliffs of tall black houses, where many windows lacked glass, where cobwebs and dirt were the only curtains, and where, here and there, women and children sat out on the sills, exchanging remarks with others who sat on the doorsteps below.

"I don't believe these houses were built. They look as though they had festered from dirt-heaps. And they smell abominable."

"Aye, well, there's only one tap in each house, shared between thirty or forty people, and the water's cut off at eight o'clock. And the drains, such as they are, run straight down into the footings."

They turned again, into an alley, passing along the open back yards of shops and cafés. In one café yard, children were searching the dustbins for food. In another yard, in the darkness under the wall, a man and a woman lay on the ground, two bodies forming a single writhing shape, boots scrabbling against the cobbles, while other men waited nearby. And, in the alley itself, an old man, smelling of meths, went shuffling along, bent double, picking cigarette stubs out of the gutter.

Betony came to a sudden stop.

"Are these the sights you said I should see?"

"The romantic city!" Jim said. "Wasn't that what you said?"

"Oh!" she said, raging. "D'you think I've seen nothing at all in my life? We've got sights like this in Chepsworth! In my own village, too, if you know where to look!"

"Does that make it right, then?"

"I never said so! But what am I supposed to do about it?"

"You! With your miff-maff about romantic London! I decided you needed waking up."

"Oh did you indeed!"

"Aye, and there's plenty more to see yet."

"I'm not going another step!"

"Aren't you?" he said, amused.

"Not an inch!" she said, standing firm.

"Then you'd better return the way you came. *I'm* going on along here."

He walked on, along the alley, towards the better-lit street at the end, and Betony stood uncertainly, clutching her purse against her breast. She knew she would never be able to find her way back. She could not even face it alone. And so, tight-lipped, she followed Jim.

He had turned the corner into Cord Street, and there, where the street-women paraded up and down, he was being accosted from all sides. A bone-thin woman, all frizzled hair and odds and ends of clothing, stepped out from a doorway; two girls, young and pretty, turned in their tracks and walked with him a little way; another stepped out from a crowd outside a public house; and to each of them, Jim politely raised his cap.

Betony, following a few steps behind, was hot all over with indignation. He knew she was there, for now, as well as raising his cap, he was speaking to each of the women in turn, making sure his voice would carry.

"Not tonight, chuck, thanks all the same . . . Nay, not tonight, for I've had a hard day . . . Aye, I believe you!—I'll tell my friends."

But after a while, Betony began to laugh quietly. She couldn't help it. He walked in such a dignified manner, wearing his shabby clothes with an air, gallantly raising a cap much worn and frayed at the edges. She could not be angry. It was too absurd. And then he turned and caught her laughing.

"Well, fancy! You still here?"

"I could hit you!" she said. "I could smack you hard."

"You mustn't brawl in the street or you'll get clapped in gaol, and what'd they say at the High School then?"

They walked on together, and he drew her hand into his arm.

"There, the hussies won't trouble me now," he said. "They'll see I'm already suited."

"Where are we going now?"

"Seeing you've come to my rescue, I'll take you to have a bite to eat. There's a place along here where you can get pie and potatoes and peas for fivepence."

"I'll pay," Betony said.

"Eh, you're a good lass, in your funny way."

That was how it was between them. There was nothing loverlike about it. They had come together purely by chance; and because they were strangers in a strange country, each a long way away from home, they created another country between them, and thus were natives of a single climate, sharing a native kindness and warmth.

She would never let him spend money on her. More often than not, when they went about together, it was she who paid, for she knew he was poor, and she knew that all too often he was underfed.

Once, when they met at a bench near the children's playground, and he was eating his frugal lunch, a girl of nine or ten came and stared at him, watching every bite he took. He broke a bread roll, divided his cheese and pickles in two, and gave half to the eager child, who carried it in triumph back to the swings.

"Why d'you do it?" Betony asked, exasperated. "Why d'you give your money and food away? No wonder you're always so tired and worn!"

"Hush, woman," he said mildly.

"She was begging shamelessly, the greedy thing! She's probably been taught by her parents to beg like that."

"It's a parent's duty to teach survival," he said, munching his own piece of roll. "And that lass is passing the lesson on."

The child had joined her small brother, and the two of them, sitting together on a swing, were shar-

ing the bread and cheese and pickle. Each in turn
took a small bite of bread, a nibble of cheese, and
one lick of the pickled onion, then chewed slowly,
making each mouthful last a long time. At the end,
they shared the pickle,—one bite each and it was
gone—and sat swinging gently to and fro, staring
dreamily into the distance, preserving the memory to
the last.

"I wouldn't call her greedy," Jim said.

"You're very secretive," Edna said.

"No, I'm not. There's nothing to tell."

"You've never even told me his name, let alone
anything about him."

"Edna, pass that folder from the shelf there, will
you?"

"I suppose I'm interrupting your work?"

"Yes. But I don't mind talking if you'll make do
with half my attention."

"As a matter of fact," Edna said, playing with the
curtain at the window, "I happen to know his name is
Jim."

"There, now," Betony murmured, still intent on
her work, "that's clever, I'm sure."

"You'd be surprised what I get to know."

"No, I wouldn't," Betony said.

From the room below, came the sudden scraping
of Mr Thorsby's violin, and Betony, glancing at Edna,
saw the hot colour flooding her face. Mr Thorsby was
tuning up. The harsh sounds continued a while. Then
he began playing 'The Ash Grove.'

"Damn!" Edna said. "And I've promised to go with
my mother to a whist drive!"

"If you're passing a post-box, perhaps you'd post a
letter for me?"

"Of course," Edna said. "Another letter home to
Huntlip, I see. Oh, well, I'd better go down, I suppose,
before mother begins to shout. Shall I knock on Edward's door and tell him you're working?—I'm sure
the music must disturb you."

"Do no such thing!" Betony said. "It doesn't disturb me in the least."

"Perhaps you enjoy it," Edna said tartly, as she went out.

Betony wondered how Edna knew Jim's name. She had always avoided speaking of him, aware that even the most trivial detail would be magnified and shared with the other girls at school. But caution, it seemed, was no protection once Edna's curiosity was aroused, and the following day, when Betony was out in the school gardens, during morning break, two girls approached with a programme of well-rehearsed questions. One was Leonie Siddert, and the other, an older girl named Julia Temple, was Edna Bream's particular friend.

"Miss Izzard, is friendship possible between the sexes?"

"I don't see why not," Betony said.

"But speaking from your own personal experience, Miss Izzard?"

"I took the question to be academic, Julia."

"Well . . ."

"If not academic, it's very impertinent," Betony said.

Julia was for a moment abashed, but, determined to impress the younger Leonie, recovered herself and tried again.

"Are you courting, Miss Izzard?"

"No, Julia."

"Not even slightly?" Julia asked.

"Not even slightly," Betony said.

The two girls, with knowing looks and a splutter of laughter, were turning away to rejoin their friends when Betony called them back and told them to follow her. Taken off guard, they obeyed without question, following her across the garden and through the French window into Miss Telerra's room. Betony knocked as she went in, and the headmistress looked up in surprise.

"I'm sorry to disturb you, Miss Telerra, but I'd like a moment of your time," Betony said, and turned to Julia. "Julia, you asked me a question just now. Will you please repeat it?"

Julia was silent, looking as though she would rush from the room.

"Well, Julia?" Miss Telerra said.

"It was nothing," Julia muttered. "Really. Nothing."

"Come, come," Betony said. "You weren't so shy in the garden just now."

"I only asked if Miss Izzard was courting!" Julia said, with a toss of black curls.

"I see," Miss Telerra said. "Well, Miss Izzard, if you will leave us, I will discuss the matter with Julia and Leonie."

Betony returned to the garden, and when she next saw the two girls, they were careful not to meet her eye. But the damage was done, and Betony, foreseeing further annoyances, knew exactly who was to blame.

"Edna," she said, when next the girl came up to the attic, "you mustn't discuss my affairs at school."

"Affairs?" said Edna. "What affairs are those?"

"You know best what stories you've told."

"I never told any stories at all! Why should I? D'you think I've got nothing to talk about but you and your peculiar young man?"

"Edna, I'm speaking to you as an adult person, so please don't behave like a stupid child."

"It seems to me you must be ashamed of him, whoever he is. I can't think of any other reason for all this secrecy!"

"There are no secrets," Betony said, "because there's nothing to have secrets about." And, as a gesture of peace, she put out a hand and touched Edna's arm. "Come, now," she said. "We're friends, surely? Which means we must each respect the other's reserve."

"But I'm never reserved!" Edna blurted, and great shining tears came squeezing out of her prominent eyes.

"Neither am I, really," Betony said. "It's a storm

in a teacup, all this, so let's make it up and be friends, shall we?"

Edna nodded, smiling bravely through her tears.

"I know I'm silly," she said, sniffing. "I'll try to be sensible in future, I promise. Won't you come down for a game of whist?"

"Well—"

"Oh, do come, please! It gets so dull downstairs sometimes."

"All right," Betony said.

Whist was a passion with Edna and her mother, and because Mr Bream was so often out in the evening, they were always desperate for someone to make up a table. Mr Thorsby would never play; nor would Miss Wilkings, who claimed she could not tell aces from "clumps or tubs or whatever they're called"; but the amiable Mr Lumbe would play, to please Edna, and Betony was often pressed into service as a fourth. She could never enjoy it, for Mrs Bream, who remembered every card that passed, would take her to task after every game, pointing out her criminal errors, and frowning at her flippancy in the face of loss.

"It's no good laughing, Miss Izzard. You'll never make a good card-player if you don't concentrate on what you're doing."

"Oh, well, it's only a game, isn't it?"

"To some, perhaps," Mrs Bream replied. "To some, certainly. Just a game."

Betony once described these games to Jim, and he laughed, saying Mrs Bream should meet Mrs Packle, his landlady in Gasworks Grove, who was also a demon for Norfolk whist.

"They'd make a pair, Mrs Packle and her. But, of course, your Mrs Bream would never be seen around Gasworks Grove. It's barefoot territory down there!"

"Is it really called Gasworks Grove?"

"Nay! Some wit went and christened it Borrowdale Gardens, and the streets across it are Wensleydale Grove and Malhamdale Avenue and such. Just imagine! Some of the wildest, sweetest country in the north and they name the slums of Simsbury after it!"

"But presumably it wasn't always a slum?"

"With the houses built back to back as they are, all round the gasworks, and as near the railway line as a cat can spit!—With inadequate water systems and inadequate drains!—Yes, it's always been a bloody slum! Right from the drawings on the board!"

"Don't you ever think of anything but social problems?"

"Sometimes I do. Sometimes I think about taking off like a gipsy and wandering forever in green places. Sometimes, especially these hot days and nights, I think about stripping and taking a bathe in a pool of cold water surrounded by trees. And I think of a cottage garden I know, miles from anywhere, down in Wiltshire, with an old leaning apple tree by the door."

"Whereabouts in Wiltshire?"

"A place called Midlinger, under the downs. I take a bicycle and go there sometimes. It gets the smoke out of my lungs."

"I can't believe you'd want to escape forever, though," Betony said. "I think you love your dark territory down in the slums.'"

"Happen you do come to love a pain if it's with you long enough."

"Pain? What pain?"

"That," he said, with a wave of his hand, out towards the slums of Simsbury, lying under the smoke. "The dark territory, like you said."

Outside The Panting Hart, when she was buying a newspaper, a man came up and addressed her by name. It was Joe Smith, who had been her porter on the day of her arrival, and whose daughter, Florrie, was at the High School.

"I've been hoping to see you, miss. I wondered if I might ask a favour."

"Yes, surely," Betony said.

"It's this notice in *The Gazette*, about the High School wanting a groundsman. That's a job that'd suit me nicely. I've had some experience with gardening and that. So I wondered if you would put in a word for me with the headmistress."

"I will indeed," Betony said.

"Smith's a pretty common name," he said. "No one need know I'm Florrie's dad."

But, in the morning, Betony found that Miss Telerra had too good a memory to be deceived.

"As I remember, Miss Izzard, from something you said previously, this Mr Smith is Florrie's father."

"Yes. But does it matter?"

"I make it a rule never to employ anyone connected in any way with one of the pupils. And in this particular case, it would be most unwise."

"Why?" Betony asked sharply. "Because the family happens to be poor? Because Florrie is a scholarship pupil?"

"Miss Izzard, it's Florrie I'm thinking of primarily. You know as well as I do that the girls here come from middle-class homes and that there is a certain tone maintained throughout the school."

"Snobbery, yes. I know all too well. But do we condone it, Miss Telerra?"

"Snobbery can't be eradicated by edict, Miss Izzard, and Florrie could be made extremely unhappy if her father worked here as groundsman."

"I do see that," Betony said. "And I'm sorry if I was rude. But need the relationship be known?"

Miss Telerra gave her sombre smile.

"There are few secrets kept in a girls' school, Miss Izzard, as you have already learnt for yourself."

"Yes, that's true," Betony said.

At the first opportunity, she spoke to Florrie Smith alone, and explained the matter to her.

"It wouldn't worry *me* if dad worked here," Florrie

said. "I don't care what the girls say. I'm used to their sneers."

"Well, Florrie, I can't do much more," Betony said. "And Miss Telerra was only thinking of you, you know."

Florrie gave a little smile, as if she placed no faith in Miss Telerra's solicitude.

"Thank you for trying, Miss Izzard. I'll tell my father."

Some weeks later, when the matter of the Harriet Thame Prize came up, Betony remembered Florrie's sceptical little smile.

The prize had been founded by a former head-mistress: it was given once every three years for the best history essay written by a senior girl on a subject approved by the staff, and consisted of a credit-note to be redeemed at The Study Book Shop. That year there were six entries, and Florrie Smith's was unquestionably the best. Miss Sylke and Betony were for once in full agreement, and Miss Lazenby, head of the English department, also concurred. Their decision was delivered in a note to Miss Telerra, but nothing more was heard until suddenly, at the end of term, Miss Telerra announced during morning assembly that the prize had been awarded to Miriam Charcomb."

"Why, why?" Betony asked, in the staff-room, later. "Miriam's essay was nothing at all!"

"Miriam's father is one of the Board of Governors," Miss Lazenby said.

"It's not the first time," Miss Sylke exclaimed, "that something like this has happened here!"

"Isn't it?" Betony said.

"No," said Horse. "My predecessor resigned because of a similar piece of nepotism in the classics department."

"Can't we complain to the head?" Betony asked.

"The King of Spain's Daughter," Miss Lazenby said, "would merely persuade us that hers is the only proper decision."

"That woman is probably descended from Torquemada," said Horse.

"Florrie Smith!" said Miss Sylke, still raging. "The only girl in the school who has a brain and wishes to use it! And what use has Miriam Charcomb for a credit-note at The Study Book Shop?"

"None," said Horse. "Her father will probably have it framed."

A bell rang, and Betony went to give a lesson. The afternoon seemed very long, and whenever she thought of Florrie Smith, her mind was darkly overcast. The school that day was dreary to her. She felt thankful the end of term was at hand; the long summer holiday lying before her.

"What will you do with yourself?" Jim asked, as they walked in the park one evening. "Will you go home?"

"No," she said. "I'm staying here. There are lots of things I want to do."

"Sight-seeing?" he said, to tease her.

"That's right. Why not?"

Every day, she left Matlock Terrace after breakfast and was out until supper-time or even later. The feeling she had when exploring London was not so intense now as it had been. It was muted and calm. It was even tinged with melancholy, springing, she supposed, from her sense of smallness, her utter anonymity, as she walked the streets with the famous names.

One evening, when she went to meet Jim in the park, she found him asleep on a bench in the sun, and she sat beside him, watching the twitching of his eyelids, and listening to the tired little groans in his breathing. When he did at last wake, and saw her there, he struggled stiffly to sit up, stretching cramped shoulders, and looking sheepish.

"It's the heat," he said. "I've been shut up all day in the Magistrates' Court in Oldbourne."

"Isn't it time you had a holiday?"

"You're right. It is. I'll have to see about getting

a Saturday to put with my Sunday. Then I'll go down
and see Auntie Jig."

"Auntie Jig?"

"She's the old woman whose cottage I stop at,
down in Midlinger." He sat up straight, shivering,
and pulled his waistcoat tidy in front. "Have you
got a bicycle? No? Well, happen you can borrow
one for a couple of days, then we'll go down together. Saturday next. Or the one after. D'you
think you can cycle so far in a day?"

"If you can, I can," Betony said.

She borrowed a bicycle from Margaret Crabbe.
She met Jim at five in the morning, and they rode
out of London in a soft white mist that lay shallowly
over the land. After Twyford, they went by quiet
country roads, avoiding even the smallest towns,
and stopping often to rest, to eat, or to look around
them.

It was September, and when the mist lifted, there
before them were the harvest fields, some with corn-
cocks still standing, and some quite empty, with the
sunlight glancing along the stubble. In many places,
especially further west, the stubble was burning,
and when, on top of Rumble Hill, Jim and Betony
sat eating their lunch, they looked down on ridges
of thick black smoke, now and then lit by leaping
red flames.

The smell of burning came up to them on top of Rumble. It was rough in their nostrils, and in their mouths, and it flavoured every bite of food. It was with them constantly when they travelled on, through Snifford, Lamsborough, Sneep, and West Hole: a smell from the very beginning of time; the smell of cleansing and purification; the smell of one earth-year as it died and of another earth-year in the offing.

"They burn the moors at home where I come from," Jim said. "They burn the old heather and gorse. Then the new comes up, bright green in the black ashes."

He had not spoken much during the journey, and Betony, watching him now as they pedalled along side by side, saw that he was pale with fatigue.

"Shall we have another rest?"

"Nay," he said. "We're nearly there now."

They rode through Midlinger village and out again at the far end. They came to a cottage, very small and crookedly built, with a lopsided thatch overgrown with moss, and with very small windows of old, dim, yellowing glass. They left their bicycles against the hedge, and walked up the path, and Jim knocked on the door.

The old woman who came hobbling out was the ugliest Betony had ever seen. Her grey skin was shrivelled and none too clean; her upper lip had long silver hairs, like a cat's whiskers, sprouting from three or four little black moles; and she had one solitary yellow tooth sticking out from her upper jaw. She came in a temper to answer Jim's knock, and glared at him ferociously, but then, as she recognized him, she waddled out onto the step and dropped shapeless hands heavily on his shoulders.

"You, you villain!" she said, cackling. "You haven't been near me for six months or more!"

"I'm near enough now, though! And you smell of tobacco, you old stove-pipe!"

"Stove-pipe yourself!" she said, shaking him roughly

to and fro. "Grudge an old woman her one bit of pleasure, would you?—You come-to-Jesus streak of sanctomy, you!" She humped herself round and stared at Betony with milky-blue eyes. "Who's this you've brung with you?"

"This is Betony," Jim said.

"Betony? I've got betony in my garden! It's good for all sorts of aches and pains. I make it up in ointments and such."

"Aye!" Jim said. "I'm well aware you're an old witch!"

"Don't shout! Godsakes! I'm not deaf, you silly fella!" Auntie Jig was still studying Betony. "Betony," she said. " 'Sell all you have and buy betony.'—That's what they say. It's one of the bestest herbs there is. Did you know?"

"No, I didn't know," Betony said.

"Betony tea! It'll cure you of death, or very nearly. And you, young miss! Are you any good for aches and pains? Eh? Are you? Are you any good for giving men their ease?"

"No, she's not!" Jim said loudly. "She's a respectable girl, not a flighty piece like you, you old muck-wife! So don't be so busy trying to put her to the blush."

"Hah! Cowpats! But you'd better come inside, I suppose."

"We'd sooner go through to your back garden and sit under your old apple tree in the shade."

"Please yourselves! Please yourselves!"

She led them through the dark little cottage and out into the back garden.

"Are you stopping the night? Oh, you are, are you? And what'll I give you for supper tonight? You tell me that!" She stood, hands on hips, and surveyed the chickens that pecked about where they pleased, in the house as well as the garden. "I'll have to take a chopper to one of *them*."

"No," Jim said. "There'll be no murder done on my behalf."

"Nor mine," Betony said.

"Then you'll have to have eggs. Eggs and cheese and a few potatoes baked in their skins. Will that do?"

"Couldn't be better," Jim said.

He and Betony sat on the grass and looked at the apple tree leaning low, its old scabby boughs borne down by the apples, all ripening a rich russet red. Auntie Jig waddled to and fro, bringing tea and fruit-cake and plum tart with thick yellow cream.

"Auntie Jig's pastry is the best on earth," Jim said. "It's because she makes it with dirty hands."

"You're a flaming liar!" the old woman said. "My hands are spotless. Pink and clean as a baby's bum."

"They come clean, making the pastry."

Jim, when he had finished eating, stretched himself out on his back on the grass and was almost instantly asleep. Auntie Jig stood over him, looking down at his tired face.

"That's how I found him the first time he came. Him and that bicycle, all in a heap on the grass in the lane. I thought he'd fell off and cracked his skull. But he was just sleeping, that's all, and planned to sleep out all night, too, to save spending money on a lodging. So I brought him back here and put him to bed on my landing. He's been here often since then and he's always tired out like this."

"He works too hard," Betony said. "And neglects himself. He's always giving his money to beggars."

"Silly fool!" Auntie Jig muttered.

When Jim awoke, and raised himself on his elbows, he found the two of them sitting there quietly, Auntie Jig in a chair, knitting, and Betony, on the grass, winding up a skein of wool.

"I must've dropped off. Did I snore?"

"Snored your head off!" said Auntie Jig. "The girl and me couldn't hear ourselves thinking."

"Just as well, probably."

"What d'you aim to do now? Have another nap?"

"No," he said, getting up stiffly. "I've brought a towel and I'm off to bathe in Luting Pool."

"What, again? You did that last time you were here.

If you're not careful, you'll wash yourself away, slosh-ing about in that old pool."

"Betony, are you coming with me?" he asked.

"Of course she's going with you!" said Auntie Jig. "She surely don't want to stop here with me."

Sitting among the reedmace and rushes, while he splashed about, a white fish in the middle of the water, Betony felt herself soaking up the essence and texture of the place and the day.

The pool, so blue wherever it reflected the sky, so silver and gold when splashed up and broken catch-ing the sun, so olive-black under willows and alders, so green-surrounded; the reeds so sweetly and greenly scented, cool harbours for moorhen and duck, who plip-plopped quietly into hiding; and a lark singing from the ground somewhere not very far away; she was so full of all these things that she knew what it felt like to be a drop of water and flash in the sun; to be cool and green, a reedblade slenderly bending, giv-ing way to the movement of ducks; and to be a sky-lark,—warm tiny body, warm tiny feathers under warm wings—sidling through the stubble forest, throb-bing, throbbing, to sing from the nest.

"Don't look round!" Jim called, wading out of the pool into the reeds a short way away. "You'll make me bashful."

"Get yourself dried!" she called back. "The sun's not so hot as you seem to think."

She watched him drying himself with his skimpy towel. His nakedness was nothing to her, except that his thinness made her want to cry. Nobody should be as thin as that: the flesh so sparely stretched on the bones, and the bones themselves so sharp and frail, like the bones of a bird. Without his clothes, he looked as though he would snap in two. Even with his clothes, he was but a shadow compared with her sturdy brothers at home.

"I feel as good as new," he said, coming and sitting down beside her, combing his hair. "You going to bathe? Nay, it's awreet for you! You've plenty of water in Matlock Terrace."

"Yes. The maid, Ruby, brings it up in a big copper jug. Silly, really, seeing the cistern is in the attic, right next to my room."

"Ruby," he said. "Is she like a ruby?"

"Not really. Her eyes are red-rimmed and her hair is mousey."

"Aye, well! I dare say Ruby is precious to somebody."

"She is. The baker's boy is courting her. But they have to be careful because of Mrs Bream. So, if the coast is clear for him to stop and talk, Ruby gives his horse two lumps of sugar. If the coast is not clear, she only gives one. And they smuggle notes to each other in the basket with the loaves and muffins."

"How do you know so much about it?"

"Sometimes, when Mrs Bream is not about, Ruby and I gossip together. Sometimes she asks me how to spell words for her letters to Matthew."

"It's not the spelling that counts, tell her. And speaking of spelling, I'd a long piece on the subject of pensions published in Barcoe's last week."

"You might have told me before this!" Betony said. "Have you still got a copy of the paper?"

"No. But you don't need to read it. It's only what you've heard me say oftentimes before."

"I'd like to have read it all the same."

"Just because it was in print?"

"Because it was in a paper that goes out all over Britain. Surely you're pleased with yourself about it?"

"Well, it's a start," he said.

Later, as they walked back slowly across the fields, she noticed how often he stopped to ease his back and shoulders.

"Aren't you stiff yourself, after cycling so far?" he asked.

"Not particularly."

"You will be!" he said.

It was twilight by the time they returned to the cottage, and colder, too. Auntie Jig had lit the lamp in the kitchen, and there was a good fire in the stove. The kettle steamed on the hob, and the baked potatoes whistled and piped, buried in the ashes. The table, innocent of cloth, was set with yellow plates and mugs, a big round loaf with poppy seeds on its shining crust, and a wooden bowl full of tomatoes and greenstuff from the garden.

"Are you hungry?" asked Auntie Jig, as she made tea.

"Aye, famished! There's nowt like a swim for making you hungry."

"I'll take your word for that," she said.

First of all, she brought them eggs, which she called cocottes: eggs broken into a stoneware dish, into a pool of hot melted butter, sprinkled with parsley and pepper and salt, and allowed to set beside the fire. Then she brought the potatoes, still in their skins, which split open at a squeeze and revealed their crumbling white mealy middles, steaming hot and smelling like chestnuts, Betony said. And lastly, she pressed on them cheese and apples and rich raisin scones.

"No more," said Jim, leaning back in his chair, "or I'll have bad dreams."

"That reminds me," said Auntie Jig. "Are you two sleeping together upstairs, nice and cosy, or sleeping apart with an extra blanket instead?"

"Apart!" Jim said. "You wicked, immoral old woman, you!"

"Only asking, boy! Only asking!"

"You think everyone's as bad as yourself."

"The trouble with you," she said, poking him as she passed his chair, "you don't eat enough, so you've got no good red blood in your veins."

"Never mind my blood, woman. Just watch your tongue in front of a decent girl."

"You young folk today! You're a strait-laced lot to my way of thinking. But if you prefer to die wondering . . ."

Later, she went upstairs, and they heard her rummaging about above.

"Don't mind her," Jim said. "She likes putting people out a bit, just to see what happens."

"You seem more put out than me."

"With my Wesleyan upbringing, what d'you expect?"

"Has Auntie Jig ever been married?"

"Off and on, I gather. *And* got some offspring scattered about."

Auntie Jig came down with a load of bedding: a straw pallet, three blankets, and a linen pillow stuffed with hops. Jim got up to take them from her.

"Betony was asking if you'd been married."

"Well, I've had a few husbands at different times."

"Other people's, I suppose?"

"We can't all be fussy, boy!"

"I'll tell you this, Betony.—She's done pretty well out of her husbands, what with this cottage and its three acres, and another bit of land across the road."

"Shows what you're missing, girl," the old woman said.

"She's missing nothing," Jim said, busy making his bed on the floor, "for I'm as poor as a chapel mouse."

"Damn fool!" said Auntie Jig. "Damn fool, if you ask me!"

"Stop your noise," Jim said. "I'm ready for bed."

Betony slept in a small bunk bed on the landing. Her pillow, too, was stuffed with hops, and she slept deeply. She awoke to full sunshine, and the distant sound of church bells, rung in changes. Midlinger church was famous for its bells, Jim told her when she got down, and for its ringers.

They had breakfast with Auntie Jig, and spent the morning helping her in the garden, gathering carrots, lettuce, and marrows, which she would take to market on Monday. At twelve o'clock, Jim said they must start back, and she packed great parcels of food for the journey.

"D'you have to go so soon?"

"It's a long ride."

"Well, come again, and sooner next time," the old woman said, grimacing at him with her one yellow tooth stuck out. "And you!" she said to Betony. "Bring him down once a month to be fattened up."

"If I can, I will," Betony said.

On the journey home, Jim was quiet, and Betony, knowing how tired he was, made sure they had long and frequent rests.

In the fields, the stubble fires were still burning, and the smoke drifted on all sides. When evening came on, the smoke vanished under darkness, and the tides of flame were seen instead. Jim and Betony, stopping to rest and eat their supper, sat in a field on the Snifford uplands, and, looking back the way they had come, could see a number of fires at once, burning in the distance, red tidal waves of flame on earth, just as, on the horizon, there were red waves of sunset flame in the sky.

Betony opened the packets of food: bread and butter, hard-boiled eggs, lettuce and radishes, screws of salt and pepper mixed. She opened a tin and found scones, tarts, and apple pasties.

The evening was cold. A sly little wind was blowing up. So she and Jim sat back to back, leaning against each other for rest and warmth, shoulders hunched, collars turned up against the wind They sat together, eating their food and drinking tea from a stone bottle, hardly speaking, but watching the fires and breathing the smell of burning straw. There was great comfort in sitting back to back like this, and much warmth passed between them. They were two animals, wise in blood and bone, and sat in a warmth of their own making, under the wind.

"These are the times I dream of escaping," Jim said. "Going off for ever and ever . . . always free like this . . . never again imprisoned in towns."

"I feel the same."

"You? In love with the city as you are? You must be overjoyed at returning."

"Not at this moment," Betony said. "At this moment, I don't want to go back at all. I feel as you do. I'd like to be free like this for ever and ever."

When Betony got to Matlock Terrace, and was carrying the bicycle down the area steps, she slipped and cut her hand on the chain-guard. The cut was not serious but bled freely, and Ruby, having let her into the basement, went rushing upstairs to the sitting-room, shrieking out that poor Miss Izzard was bleeding to death.

The basement swiftly filled with people. Mrs Bream came down with Edna, followed by Mr Bream and the two male lodgers. Mr Thorsby took charge at once. He washed the cut with carbolic and bound the hand in a thick bandage. He scarcely glanced at Betony throughout. He was purely professional and utterly silent. But Betony, going upstairs on her way to the attic, caught a gleam of jealous anger in Edna's eyes.

A few days later term began and Betony was busy again. She scarcely thought of Edna at all. And then, suddenly, late one night when she was in bed, she was woken out of a deep sleep by a noise of shouting and screaming below. She got up, opened her door, and stood listening. Downstairs, Mr Thorsby burst from his room, strode across the landing, and hammered loudly on the Breams' bedroom door.

"Mrs Bream! Will you kindly come and remove your silly little bitch of a daughter from my room? Because if not I shall be obliged to drag her out by the hair!"

His voice was unexpectedly powerful. It could be heard throughout the house. Betony withdrew into her room and closed her door. She returned to bed and drew the clothes over her head, shutting her ears to the commotion below.

In the morning, Edna did not appear for breakfast. Nothing was said about her. The meal passed almost in silence. Mr and Mrs Bream pretended not to see Mr Thorsby, and he, although looking as if a single word would ignite him, ate with as good an appetite as ever and would not be hurried from the table. Edna did not walk with Betony to school that morning, but was there, in assembly, looking peaked and pale.

At supper that evening, Edna was present and her father took pains in making conversation, but Mr Thorsby was not there, nor was his place laid at the table. No one asked why. No one ever mentioned his name. He was not at breakfast that following morning, not at supper again that night. The room below Betony's was now silent, and when she looked in, discreetly, on her way down one morning, she saw that all his things had gone.

The room remained empty week after week, and then, somehow, it became understood that Edna and Mr Lumbe would have it as part of a suite when they were married, perhaps at Easter.

Edna hardly spoke to Betony now, at home or at school. She had confided her secrets too freely and spoken contemptuously of Mr Lumbe, and she seemed to fear that Betony might repeat the things she had said.

"Edna, we all make mistakes," Betony said. "I don't see why we can't still be friendly."

"I have nothing to say to you, I'm sure," Edna said. "But excuse me, please. I'm very busy at the moment."

Betony smiled. She found it easy to forgive Edna's rudeness. She thought it a mood that would soon pass. But she was mistaken, and forgiveness was not so easy when, a week or so later, she found Edna in her room, reading her diary.

It was a Saturday evening in October. Betony had been to the park to meet Jim. She had waited a while, but he had not come, so, as the evening was damp and cold, she had returned home unusually early. Edna was taken by surprise. She had no time even to put the diary back in the drawer, but stood with it hidden in her skirts, looking guilty and defiant.

"What are you doing here?" Betony said. "I thought you had no time for me these days."

"My mother wants to know if you need clean sheets."

"Don't tell lies, Edna. You saw me go out. We passed each other in the hall. You've got my diary, haven't you? And not for the first time, either, I think."

"This!" Edna said, in a sudden temper, and threw the diary at Betony's feet. "You needn't worry! I couldn't read your terrible scrawling writing, anyway!"

"Get out of my room," Betony said, "and don't come again when I'm not here."

"I certainly don't want to come when you are!" Edna said, and slammed out.

Betony picked up the diary and looked inside. Edna had spoken the truth, she thought: the writing *was* a terrible scrawl.

From that time on, Edna's hostility became active, and it influenced a part of the household. Mrs Bream was barely civil to Betony now, and Mr Lumbe grew distinctly cool. Mr Bream behaved normally enough, but he was rarely at home in the evenings, and Betony was beginning to understand why. Only Miss Wilkings remained friendly, and Ruby, the maid, though she dared not speak now when passing Betony in the hall, would blink her sore eyes in a signal of sympathy and understanding.

At school, Edna was even more active. She and two friends, Julia Temple and Phoebe Davies, whenever they were in Betony's classes, made a point of sitting in front and staring at her throughout the lesson. They would look her up and down repeatedly, or stare at some particular part of her clothing. They would look very knowing, and they often whispered together, taking care that she heard certain words, such as *bicycle* and *weekend with friends*. And sometimes they mimicked the way she spoke.

"Where exactly do you come from, Miss Izzard?"

"Why, Julia?"

"You speak so very broad, Miss Izzard. We wondered what region your accent belonged to."

"Is your father really a carpenter, Miss Izzard?"

"Confine your questions to the subject of the lesson," Betony would say, coldly and calmly, in a bored voice.

But often, underneath, especially when they jostled her in the corridors, her temper was only narrowly held in check.

She had not seen Jim for almost a month, and because of the 'flu epidemic sweeping London, she was anxious about him. So, on a cold wet Saturday afternoon in October, she went down into the slums of Simsbury in search of Borrowdale Gardens.

The street was a long one, and she did not know the number of the house. All she knew, recalling remarks Jim had made, was that he lived on a corner and that the railway ran at the back of the house. It gave her a choice of six houses.

At the first corner house, when Betony knocked, the door was opened by a woman completely bald except for a single plume of long fair hair growing up from her smooth shining crown.

"Mr Firth? No, not here. You've got the wrong house, dear."

"Mrs Packle, then?" Betony said. "She takes lodgers."

"That's nothing. We all do round here. I don't know no Mrs Packle."

At the next corner house, the woman who came to the door had a grey parrot perched on her shoulder, and carried a poker in her hand.

"No! There's no Mr Firth in my house. Nor I don't know Mrs Packle neither."

"Somebody knocking!" the parrot screeched. "Somebody knocking! Let the sod in!"

"Perhaps you've seen him," Betony said. "He's thin and dark-haired, with black eyebrows. He works as a reporter on *The Gazette*."

"No," said the woman. "I don't know him. Try her next door."

"Bloody trains!" the parrot screeched. "Waterloo! All change for Watford!"

At the third house, there was a notice, Rooms to Let, in the window. The woman who answered Betony's knock was small and white-haired, with a tough, pugnacious nose and jaw, and sharp eyes.

"Yes? That's right. I'm Mrs Packle. Have you come about the room?"

"No. I wanted to see Mr Jim Firth."

There was a silence, and the woman came out onto the doorstep.

"Gawd! Mr Firth! He's been gone these three weeks or more."

"Gone?" said Betony. "Gone where?"

"Dead!" Mrs Packle replied hoarsely. "He was took ill all of a sudden, on the Friday, three weeks ago. Oh! But it was a terrible shock to me! I had to go and fetch Dr Sweeting. But it wasn't no use the ambulance coming. He was already dead when the doctor and me got back to the house. Appendix, it was. Peritonitis, the doctor said."

Betony nodded. Peritonitis. Something that killed.

"They carried him out on a stretcher, dead, right through this door, like I'm standing now. Oh I *was* upset, I can tell you! I was nearly ready to drop myself."

"And the funeral?"

"Last Tuesday fortnight. His father came down as soon as I wrote him the sad news. Poor man! The last of all his children to go, he told me."

"Where is he buried?" Betony asked, and was thinking: three weeks ago; on the Friday; that would have been October the third.

"Why not come in?" Mrs Packle suggested. "I can see it's been a shock to you. It was to me, I don't mind saying, but I think I could talk about it now."

"Thank you, no," Betony said. "I won't come in. But could you tell me where he's buried?"

"Simsbury cemetery. Down the junction. Such a nice little chapel of ease. Are you sure you won't come in?"

Betony was walking away. No, thank you. Perfectly sure. Simsbury cemetery and railway junction. Waterloo. H'all change.

The cemetery, acre on acre of white marble, chilled and appalled her: a lunar city, built in

straight, sharp lines, hard enough to resist the working of time. The sharp lines threatened, as though
they were knives, and the screaming whiteness was
paralysing, shrilling coldly along her nerves.

At home, in Huntlip, the old churchyard was grey
and green, quiet and restful to the eyes. The stones
were sandstone and the weather soon ground them
down at the edges. They sank comfortably into the
earth, drew the ivy over their shoulders, and opened
their grain in little fissures, to give the beetles and
emmets a home. The churchyard at Huntlip, and
those at Eastery, Middening, and Blagg, were places
where flowers grew and birds sang. They were places
of rest, for those in the earth, and for those who
tended the wilderness above.

But at least Jim's grave, when at last she found it,
had no glaring marble slab. It was only a mound of
dark earth, soaking up the soft small rain. Soon the
grass would cover it over, and it would be green for
evermore.

After leaving the cemetery, she walked about, hour
after hour, going deeper and deeper into the region of
chimneystacks and cooling-towers; railway sidings
and railway wharfs; the canal cutting and the sewage
farm. In this dark region, the dwelling-houses were
squeezed in, back to back, row upon row, wherever a
space occurred between factories; between gasworks
and power station; or round the smoking refuse dump.
The rain went on falling steadily, and in this region it
brought the smoke and fumes down with it, till the
puddles all smelt of oil and sulphur.

The streets after dark made her think of things that
crawled and crept, and she thought how, if the rows
of houses were lifted by the hand of an inquisitive
God, thousands of people would be revealed like
maggots crawling on a heap of compost.

The darkness between the houses was more than
just an absence of light: it had a texture of its own; it
was like the corruption felt in the veins when the
blood moved under primal compulsions; when there
came a dark will to destroy; a will towards deeds of

cruelty. It was like the feeling that came on seeing a flock of crows rise from their work of devouring carrion. It was like that dark territory in the mind, disputed by two conflicting forces; the will to survive at all costs, and the will towards self-destruction. The streets after dark were full of these forces; the houses, and the spaces between the houses, were sick and corrupt, yet full of squirming, pulsing life. This dark region was both the carrion and the crow.

She had walked herself into a weary stupor. Now she ached in every bone. She wanted to find a place to rest, but went on aimlessly, street after street, for her brain no longer commanded her actions.

A man was walking close behind her. She hastened her steps to shake him off. She took several turnings, but still he followed close behind. She hastened again, into a street where there were lights and traffic and noise. The man also hastened, coming beside her, his rubber mackintosh rattling and creaking as he walked. When she glanced up at him, into his face, he was grinning down at her, showing his teeth, a regular pattern of black and gold.

"Here are you, walking the streets," he said softly, "and here am I, feeling lonely, so what about our pairing up?"

"Go away!" Betony said.

"Now that's not nice. And you don't mean it. You've been leading me on for miles."

"Go away!" Betony said.

"But you looked at me," he said, injured, and put up a hand to take her arm.

On a corner, there was a public house called O'Leary's. The public bar was crammed to the doors, and a great many people were drinking outside, standing about in groups on the pavement, in the rain. One such group, seeing Betony pulling away from the man's grasp, spread themselves out to block her way, and one, a woman, screeching with laughter, pushed her into the man's arms.

"You two been having a bit of a barney? Well, let's see you kiss and make it up!"

Betony saw the ugly teeth: one black, one gold; one black; one gold; and caught the smell of the man's breath.

"Let me go! I don't know him! He's been following me!"

"That's different!" one of the women said at once. "Hoi, let her pass, you drunken pigs! Can't you see she means what she says? And she's soaked right through, the poor little soul! Here, Queenie, get out of the way! And you, Clarence,—give that bastard a piece of your mind!"

They kept the man back, and Betony escaped at a run. She got on a bus and was carried towards The Panting Hart. She felt her clothes, which were indeed sodden with rain. She began to shiver, all through her body, and had to keep her teeth tight-clenched.

At home, on the way upstairs to the attic, Edna passed on her way down. She looked at Betony's wet clothes,

"Been to meet your paramour?"

Outside her room, Betony found a letter from home, and the sight of it reminded her that today was October the twenty-fifth. It was her birthday. She was eighteen.

Winter set in early that year. November was a month of fog and frost. There was no fire-place in Betony's room, and the evenings there were bitterly cold. Mrs Bream had promised the loan of an oil-stove, but weeks went by and nothing was done, and when Betony mentioned the matter again, talking of buying a stove herself, Mrs Bream said she did not want the attic ceiling blackened by fumes.

"There's always a fire in the living-room, Miss Izzard. You're welcome to spend your evenings there."

But Betony was not welcome. If she worked at the living-room table, Edna would play bagatelle with Mr Lumbe, and would jog the board, spilling Betony's ink on her papers. If she sat reading, Edna talked in a loud voice, passing repeatedly to and fro, leaning

across her to open a cupboard, or making her rise so
that her chair could be searched for a lost nail-file.
So, however cold, Betony preferred to stay in her
room, wearing a coat, and wrapping her legs in the
blanket taken from her bed. And when it grew too
cold to bear, she would put on her cape, her woollen
scarf, and the thick leather gloves granna had made
her, and go for a walk, quickly and briskly, until her
blood was moving again and life came back to her
hands and feet.

It was so cold at night that she went to bed wearing
two nightgowns, and her woollen scarf wrapped round
her feet. She had only one blanket on her bed, so she
spread her coat and cape on it, and then the rag rug
from the floor. Once she asked Mrs Bream for extra
bed-clothes, and that evening, on going to her room
after supper, she found one small blanket outside her
door.

But it was during the evenings, when she had school
work to do, that she felt the cold most badly. Her
body, hunched against the draughts, would be stiff
and aching. She would shiver inside, feeling the cold
creeping down into her chest and stomach. She had to
get up and move about, swinging her arms vigorously,
and sometimes, when her fingers were cramped from
holding a pen, she had to hold them close to the
gaslight before she could open them out again.

One evening, when she was correcting test papers,
someone came up the attic stairs. She sprang to her
feet, reluctant to be found sitting hunched in blankets,
and moved about quickly before going to open the
door. It was Mr Bream, all smiles, and he walked in
carrying a small oil-stove, with a can of oil and a tin
funnel.

"For the cistern," he said. "My wife is afraid the
pipes will freeze."

He opened the door into the roof-space, and, bent
double, vanished inside with the stove.

"There!" he said, reappearing, brushing the
cobwebs from his sleeves. "That should safeguard us!
We don't want burst pipes all over the place, do we?

I'll leave the oilcan with you, Miss Izzard.—Perhaps you'll superintend the stove and refill it when necessary? It'll save us a journey up the stairs."

As he was going, he looked back, without quite meeting Betony's glance.

"It's cold up here, Miss Izzard. You will come down if you want to, won't you?"

"Yes, I will," Betony said.

Later that night, when she was about to go to bed, she opened the door and peeped in at the little oil-stove, burning in the darkness under the roof. The sight was cheering; so was the faint breath of warmth in her face; but the smell of the oil was saddening to her, because it made her think of home. She closed the door and went to bed.

December came in colder than ever. Night after night there was hard frost. And one evening, so shrammed with cold that she contemplated swallowing her pride and going downstairs, she thought of the oil-stove in the roof. She went in, treading cautiously along the joists, and brought the stove back to her room. She turned it up high, to a big blue flame, and sat over it, reading a book, until bed-time. Then she carried it back to its place. When she undressed, the smell of paraffin was strong in her clothes, so she hung them close to the draughty window, hoping the smell would be gone by morning.

Every night after that she borrowed the stove for two or three hours and then returned it to its place. She felt no guilt, for the pipes and tank remained unfrozen, and every night she climbed on a chair to wipe the smudge from the bedroom ceiling. But then, one night, when she was in the roof-space, she lost her balance and put one foot through the laths and plaster between the joists, penetrating the ceiling of the room below.

The room was the empty one, once Mr Thorsby's, and when she looked in, quietly, on her way down next morning, there, sure enough, was the terrible hole in the ceiling, with the splintered laths sticking out like ribs and there was the plaster and dust on the floor.

What a shame, she thought, to have made such a mess in Edna's future bridal suite! She closed the door and went down to breakfast.

"Ugh!" said Edna. "You smell most dreadfully of paraffin! It quite makes me sick."

"It's the stove in the roof," Betony said. "I filled it last night, as your father asked me, and perhaps it does make me smell, rather."

"It's surely no trouble," said Mrs Bream, "for you to fill the stove, Miss Izzard?"

"None at all," Betony said. "It was Edna who complained of the smell, not I."

In the school hall, now that Christmas was drawing near, stood a model of the nativity, lit by candles in coloured glass jars. In front of the model stood a large open packing-case, into which the girls dropped gifts of discarded clothing, destined for the orphanage at Oldbourne Hill.

Betony, passing through the hall one afternoon, discovered a group of older girls, including Edna Bream and Julia Temple, gathered about the packing-case, rummaging through the bundles of clothes.

"Look at this!" Julia exclaimed, and held up a muff of grey astrakhan. "It's positively *made* to go with my coat! It's just exactly a perfect match. My coat is grey and has grey astrakhan on the collar and hem. Whoever gave such a beautiful muff to the orphans? It's hardly been used!"

"If I were you I should keep it," said Edna, running a hand over the muff.

"I shall, don't worry! It's absolutely made for me!"

"Julia," said Betony, approaching the group, "put that muff back into the box."

"Why should she?" Edna demanded. "Whoever gave it would just as soon Julia had it if they knew she wanted it so badly."

"Yes, why should I?" Julia said. "I'll never find anything so perfect again."

"Put it back," Betony said.

"No!" said Edna. "Take no notice of her, Julia. She's not the headmistress."

"Perhaps you'd like the head to be fetched?" Betony suggested.

"I don't care!" Edna said. "I'm sure she'd agree to Julia's having the muff."

"Yes, imagine an orphan in grey astrakhan!" said Julia. "Whoever gave it was out of her mind."

"Put it back," Betony said, "or I'll go at once and report the matter to Miss Telerra."

"Oh, all right! You can take it and welcome and damn you so there!"

Furiously, Julia flung the muff back into the packing-case. Then, with a sob, she snatched it half out again, deliberately catching it on a nail and ripping a hole in the astrakhan.

"There!" she said. "Now the orphans are welcome to it!"

Betony's own temper burnt hot and strong. Her hand flew up and slapped Julia's face.

Walking away, she felt divorced from everything around her, but for once it was the world that seemed unreal, not her own inner self. She went straight to the head's room, knocked in a rather perfunctory way, and walked in.

"I'm leaving the school," she said calmly.

"I think you'd better sit down, Miss Izzard, and talk the matter over," Miss Telerra said.

But Betony would not sit down. She had made up her mind and no discussion would ever change it.

"Nevertheless," Miss Telerra said, "I'd like you to give the matter some thought. Is it the Breams? Because if so, I could easily find you a more congenial lodging."

"It's partly the Breams. But not them alone. It's everything, including the school."

"The school?" Miss Telerra said, as though such a thing could not be believed.

"The prize that went to Miriam Charcomb.—It should have gone to Florrie Smith."

"Miss Izzard, I believe you're going home for

Christmas? Well, I suggest you think carefully during the holiday, and, if you feel the same when you return, I will then accept your resignation."

"No. I won't be returning after Christmas."

"But you must! A term's notice is obligatory. You know that as well as I do."

"I don't care," Betony said. "I'm not coming back." Miss Telerra's face became very stiff.

"Are you aware that the school could sue for a term's salary in lieu of notice?"

"I'm still leaving, whatever threats you make."

"You're lucky to be able to treat the threat so lightly, Miss Izzard. There are many people in the world too poor to share your rather casual contempt for money."

"Don't speak to *me* about poverty."

"I beg your pardon!" Miss Telerra said coldly. "I think perhaps you've said enough."

"I think so, too," Betony said, and went to the door. "But there's one other thing you ought to know.—I've just slapped Julia Temple's face."

During a lesson that afternoon, when she was looking through an Early English textbook, she came on these lines:

> Smale birds on plowed londe;
> A man sowing sede;
> Softe wind bryngen rain:
> God lette these abyde
> Till I come againe.

Small birds on ploughed land! She saw them plainly all the afternoon. The words were with her constantly, reminding her of home. A man sowing seed! Everything now made her think of home, and in four days' time, she would be there. God let these abide . . . till I come again.

On the last day, she took formal leave of the headmistress, a few civilities passing like splinters of ice between them. She sought out Crabbe and Horse, to say goodbye, and she sought out Florrie Smith with a farewell gift of books. The rest of the school she ignored completely. And her departure from Matlock Terrace was equally cold.

"I shall not be returning," she said, as she settled accounts with Mrs Bream.

"Very well, Miss Izzard," Mrs Bream replied.

"Goodbye, Ruby," Betony said.

She wanted the train to hurry, hurry. She wanted the journey to be at an end. For now, travelling through the grey frosty landscape, she feared she might again be too late: that home and family, and everything belonging to her past life, might have been destroyed in some awful catastrophe. What proof had she that they were still there? Her letter home, giving the time of her arrival, had merely been an act of faith, and her thoughts now were a constant prayer. Let them abide . . . till I come again.

When the train ran into Chepsworth station, and she saw her father standing there, smoking his pipe, just as she had seen him last, it was as if the intervening months were only a long and complicated dream. Yet there *were* changes, for then his face had been long and glum, whereas now it was rounded out in smiles. Then she had actually *wanted* to leave him, whereas now his very existence was a marvel, and his great bursting smile was as warm on her as a burst of summer sunshine.

"I thought you was never coming!" he said. "I've been waiting here I dunno how long."

"The train was only five minutes late."

"Was it? It seemed like hours."

He shouldered her box, and they walked together along the platform. He took her ticket and gave it to the man at the gate.

"My daughter here is home from London. Ah, London. That's right. She's a teacher there."

The feeling that she was taking part in a miracle was with her still. The sound of their footsteps ringing out on the hard-frozen ground; the pony's little whicker of welcome and the way he nuzzled her with chaff-coated nose the instant his food-bag was taken off; the drive home, with a tartan rug over her legs, a hot stone bottle under her feet, and her father's warm solid body beside her; and his great importance at bringing her home through Huntlip, revealed in the way he sat up straight and made himself tall: all these things were a miracle to her, as though she had long been blind, and now saw; had long been deaf and dumb and unable to smell the pure cold smell of winter, and now had all these senses restored.

"Winter's put in early this year, freezing so hard," her father said. "But there! It's the best way, I always say.—Early winter, early spring!"

Sometimes, lately, she had wished with passion for it to be spring, with birds on ploughed land, and a man sowing seed. And sometimes she had wished it were summer, with the apple trees leaning low in the orchard. But now, knowing that spring and summer *would* come again,—her father had said so; it must therefore be true—she was content with the cold grey frost and mist, for the winter, too, was miraculous in its way.

"How long you home for, blossom?"

"For good," she said. "At least, I'm not going journeying again for a while yet."

One day, perhaps. But not yet. One day, she would go to Midlinger and tell Auntie Jig that Jim was dead. One day, she would go to Runceley and see Jim's father. But now, at present, she needed time to rest and think and recover her strength.

"Not going back!" her father said. "Why, wasn't you suited with things there?"

"No. That's right. I wasn't suited."

"How was that, then, blossom?" he asked.

"I'll tell you some time. But not now. I just want to enjoy coming home."

She could see that he was disappointed. His dreams had been vague, but dreams there had been, on her behalf, as she well knew, and in his heart, he had expected to hear her name come echoing out of the great city, to cause some stir throughout the land.

He said no more, but his feelings were plain in the way he kept looking at her, puzzled and frowning. He could not understand her, because she was changed. He felt that she had let him down. He thought she was shutting him out from things that mattered, and he was inclined to be hurt about it. The misunderstanding was saddening to her: the one smudge on the day's brightness.

But her mother, hearing she was home for good, asked no questions. Not even one. Her mother's eyes looked into hers, read something there, and remained perfectly clear and calm, as always. Her mother's nod was one of acceptance, and the things she said in her cool, calm voice were homely, practical, comfortable things that created a great feeling of safety. And to Betony, at that moment, her mother's acceptance was pure balm.

"It can't last," she said to herself, "but at this moment, I am *good*."

"I wrote you a letter," Janie said. "On your birthday, two months ago. But you never answered."

"I'm sorry, Janie," Betony said. "But now I'm here myself instead."

"There's rabbit stew for supper," her mother said. "The boys went out for the rabbits this morning, because they know it's your favourite stew."

"Did they? Did they?" Betony said.

Everything was exactly the same. Yet everything had a fabled beauty. And the kitchen became the heart of the world. The black beams overhead, the mellow red tiles underfoot; the fire so fierce in the stove when granna opened the damper; the smell of rabbit stewing with onions and carrots and parsnips and swedes and little dumplings flavoured with thyme; the blue and white china being set out, and the old horn mugs that had come from the Pikehouse; the light of the oil-lamp spreading out over the room; even the simple act of drawing the curtains, shutting out the cold grey dusk, shutting in the warmth and light:— everything was just the same, yet miraculously different.

And the boys, too, coming lumbering in from the workshop: all awkward grins and shyness at first; then all clamouring excitement and horse-play, eager to prove that they had grown to be men in her absence: they, though made of solid flesh and bone, were creatures lit by the beauty of fable. Even great-grumpa, clomping in, barking at her in his great voice, barking at everybody because he was growing a little deaf: even he brought a feeling of godlike warmth and safety. And Tom, hanging back from the rest of the boys, the odd one out as always: so dark and thin where they were all so blond and broad: so quiet, so still, watching her with his deep dark gaze: she had only to look at Tom to love him utterly, as her own, and to know that this love would be her punishment, evermore, for treating him cruelly as a child.

"Fancy not seeing the king and queen!" said Dicky, disgusted.

"Nor the lord mayor!" said Roger, laughing.

"Betony," said William, "I want you to teach me some geometry."

"Betony," said Janie, "I want you as bridesmaid when Martin and me get married in June."

"Seems to me you look thinner, blossom," her father said. "Your mother will have to fatten you up."

"Have another dumpling," granna urged.

The miracle lasted. She awoke every morning to find it intact. She went about, through the house and buildings, the orchard and the fields, and everything was precious to her.

Yet there *were* changes, especially in the workshop. Timothy Rolls had died, aged eighty, and Steve Hewish had retired, aged seventy-six. And the oak tree had gone from the workshop yard.

"Three hundred years," William said, as they stood looking at the great stump. "We counted the rings, Roger and me, and we both made it three hundred years."

"Why was it felled? Was it dying?"

"No. Great-grumpa wanted to catch the timber at

its soundest, so's we can use it and give it another life, as he says."

She went with them and looked at the timber the oak had given, the trunk and great limbs, all piled up in a distant corner of the yard. Where would she be, she asked herself, when that timber came under the carpenters' hands? ·

"Shall you be here for the brandy-drinking, Miss Betony?" Sam Lovage asked her.

"Of course she'll be here!" great-grumpa shouted. "She's come back home, where she belongs, and here she'll stay, you mark my words!"

She was home. She would stay. How good was great-grumpa's faith in the matter! Life itself was an act of faith.

On Christmas morning, she and the boys were out early, gathering holly from the hedges, mistletoe from the orchard trees. The house became as green as a forest, great-grumpa said, and the frost, melting from the holly on the beams in the parlour, dripped on granna's neck when she was busy polishing the table.

They carried in scuttles of coal and baskets of logs, and kept great fires burning all day, in kitchen and parlour. All morning, the house smelt of roasting goose and sage-and-onion stuffing, plum pudding and brandy-sauce. All afternoon, it smelt of roasting orange peel, which they toasted in front of the parlour fire and ate with brown sugar, just as they had when they were children.

Her present from her brothers and Janie to her was a new diary, and a week later, sitting in her old place in the kitchen with her desk on her lap, she opened it and pressed down the first stiff clean white page. The miraculous feeling would fade in time, but, for the present, it was strong as ever, and had to be captured. There were so many things that were precious to her. She wished to record them; to have them down in black and white. So she took up her pen, licked the new nib clean of its grease, dipped it into the bottle of ink, and began to write.

"My great-grandfather, William Henry Tewke, was

born in 1831, the year of King William's coronation, and the year the railway came to Chepsworth. He is now eighty-two.

"My grandmother, Catherine Rose Tewke, formerly Firkins, was born in 1853. My grandfather, John Tewke, was born in 1852, and died in 1885, killed by a horse on Huntlip common.

"My other grandfather, Walter Izzard, was born in 1833, and died in 1890. My grandmother, Goody Izzard, was born in 1837, and died in 1906, during the bad winter floods.

"My father, Jesse Izzard, was born in 1877, at the Pikehouse, near Eastery, and my mother, Elizabeth Kate Izzard, formerly Tewke, was born in 1875, in a cottage on Huntlip green. They were married at Eastery in September 1894.

"I, Betony Rose Izzard, was born in October, 1895, and my sister, Jane Elizabeth, in November 1896, both at the Pikehouse. My brother, William Walter, was born in May, 1898; Roger John in August, 1899; and Richard Jesse in April, 1900: all here at Cobbs. My foster brother, Thomas Maddox, was born in 1897: the exact date is not known, but we keep his birthday on March 1st . . ."

Betony paused, and dried the ink. She turned over to a new page, and wrote again.

"This book was given me by my sister and brothers to keep as a diary. I here promise that all events recorded in it will be true in every particular, and written in a good clear hand; beginning today: New Year's Day, 1914."

BOOK TWO

Back to 1891 . . .

On cold wet mornings his knee still gave him trouble, and climbing the ladder to cut hay from the stack was a slow, painful business. He was half way down, with the heavy truss balanced on his head, when he saw that the farmer was watching from below. But he took no notice, sensing from past experience that Dennery was in a bad temper.

'What's wrong with you—creeping paralysis?' Dennery asked, following Jack as he limped across the yard to the cow-pens. 'You're supposed to be loading mangolds in the clamp-yard.'

'I shall get there, don't you worry.'

'Your old war-wound playing you up? Is that your excuse for swinging the lead? By God, I've seen old women move faster than you do!'

Jack said nothing, but moved from crib to crib, shedding the hay out as he went.

'Mercybright?—I'm talking to *you*!' Dennery shouted. 'You don't mean to tell me that leg's still dicky after all these years 'cos I don't believe it!'

'Then don't,' Jack said. 'It's no odds to me.'

'Not exactly a hero's wound, neither, was it, eh? The way you got hit? Breaking into your own stores?'

'Did I tell you that?' Jack said, surprised, and remembered an evening spent with Dennery at The Drum and Monkey in Aston Charmer. 'I must've had more than a few that night, if I told you that story.'

'It'll teach you a lesson not to get drunk, won't it?'

'It'll teach me to be a lot more fussy who I get drunk with, more likely.'

'Not a *Boer* bullet!' Dennery said. 'Oh, no! An English bullet, that's what gave you that crooked leg, warnt it, eh? That's what you told me. Ent that so?'

'Boer or English, a bullet has pretty much the same effect on a man's knee, all in all. Except that the Boers would've got me in the guts, I reckon, 'cos the way they shoot, they can pick the pip from a cherry without even stopping to take aim.'

'The hero of Majuba!' Dennery said. 'Something to be proud of evermore! I bet they gave you a medal for that, didn't they? I bet they gave you the bloody V.C.!'

'No, they gave me a month in the cells,' Jack said, and returned to the stack for more hay.

While he was up on the ladder, Dennery was called away into the house by his wife, and Bob Franks, the cowman, having been listening in the milking-sheds, came out to the yard to speak to Jack.

'What makes men behave like pigs, I wonder?'

'I dunno. Worry, perhaps. The times is pretty bad for farmers.'

'Hah! *He* don't go short of nothing, does he? Nor his missus neither. It's the likes of you and me that suffers. Dud Dennery don't go short of nothing. Oh, no, not he! Yet he don't even fork out to pay for his pleasures.'

'What does that mean?'

'My cousin Peggy, skivvy to the Dennerys this twelve-month past, that's what I mean. Don't tell me you hadn't heard?'

'I know the Dennerys turned her out, and I know Peggy's got a baby, but are you telling me Dennery's its father?'

'Bible oath!' Bob said. 'Cross my heart and hope to die! And although Peggy Smith is no better than she should be, I reckon a man ought to pay for the trouble he brings on a woman, don't you?'

'Why don't her father see about it?'

'What, my uncle Sydney? He wouldn't ask you to tell him the time! And what'd Dennery likely do? He'd laugh in Syd's face just as surely as pigs see wind.'

'Ah, he's a mean bastard,' Jack agreed. 'There's no better side to *his* nature.'

And he walked away, wondering why a young girl like Peggy, pretty enough to take her pick among the young men of Aston Charmer, should have let a middle-aged sot like Dennery get near her.

When he got to the clamp-yard he found that the farm-boy, Noah Dingle, had already filled the cart with mangolds and was trying to urge the old horse, Shiner, up the steep track towards the pasture.

'Can't budge him!' he said. 'I been trying a good ten minutes but he won't budge no more'n a fraction!'

'Your load's too heavy,' Jack said. 'Poor old Shiner will never pull that.' He climbed onto the load of mangolds high in the tip-cart and began pushing at them with a pitchfork, so that they rumbled out onto the cobblestones below. 'How would *you* like to have to pull a load the size of this lot here?' he asked.

'Mr Dennery said pike 'em up well. He said to save on too many journeys.'

'You don't save much if you kill the horse.'

Jack had the cart about half emptied when the farmer came into the yard from the dairy and began shouting at the top of his voice.

'What in hell's name do you think you're doing? I told that boy to fill to the cratches and when I give an order I want it obeying!'

Jack took no notice, but went on forking out the mangolds. A few of them rolled to Dennery's feet and he had to skip smartly out of the way.

'Do you hear me, blast you, or are you deaf as well as idle?'

'I hear you,' Jack said, 'but I only listen when you talk some sense and you ent talking much sense this morning, master. Shiner's too old to pull big cartloads. He ent got the strength nor the breath neither so why break his heart?'

'Christ Almighty!' Dennery said. 'We'll see if he's got the strength or not! I shall soon shift him—just you watch me!'

He went to the horse, took hold of its tail with both hands, and twisted it sideways. Shiner gave a loud whinny of pain and danced a little on the cobbles, but, being a prisoner between the shafts, could not escape his tormentor's hands.

'Another bit more?' Dennery shouted. 'Will another twist shift you, you lazy brute, 'cos there's plenty more if that's how you want it!'

Jack got down from the back of the tip-cart and caught hold of Dennery by the arm, swinging him round in a wide circle. Then he hit him full in the face and sent him sprawling against the cart.

'If you want to twist someone's tail,' he said, 'go ahead with twisting mine—I've got used to it these past two years.'

'By God, that does it!' Dennery said, wiping a smear of blood from his nostrils. 'That flaming well does it, believe you me! You've done for yourself this time, I can tell you, and no two bloody ways about it!'

'I was thinking the same thing myself,' Jack said, 'almost to the very words.'

'You're sacked off this farm! As from this minute! You can drop what you're doing and get moving without delay!'

'Suits me. I dunno why I ent gone sooner.'

'Then get off my land, you useless limping swine, you!'

'I'm going, don't worry.'

'Then what are you standing gawping for?'

'I was wondering if I'd fetch you another clout, that's all, before I got moving.'

'You touch me again and I'll have you up for assault, man, and Dingle here shall be my witness.'

'It's all right. You can breathe easy. It ent worth scraping the skin off my knuckles for. But ent you got a sleeve to wipe your nose on? You're getting blood all over your waistcoat.'

Jack went to the cart and began unharnessing the horse, Shiner. He undid the traces and let the cart-shafts fall to the ground. Then he took off collar, pad, and mullen, and gave them to the boy Noah Dingle, who stood with eyes and mouth wide open.

'What do you think you're doing with that there horse?' Dennery demanded.

'I'm taking him with me,' Jack said.

'Oh no you're not! I'll see you burning in hell first!'

'Oh yes I am. I'm buying him off you for ten pounds.'

'Ten pounds? Don't make me laugh! Where would *you* get ten pounds?'

'I've got it right enough and it's money just as good as the next man's.'

'I should want to see it, though, before I let you take that horse off this farm.'

'You won't never see it 'cos I'm paying it over to Peggy Smith. You know the whys and wherefores, so don't ask awkward questions or the boy here will learn a bit about your private business. If he don't know all about it already.'

'I'll have the law on you, Mercybright, for stealing that horse from off my farm!'

'Do,' Jack said, 'and maybe the law'll be interested to know about Peggy's misfortunes at the same time.'

Dennery glared. He was swearing quietly under his breath.

'What's your interest in her?' he asked, sneering.

'The same as most men's?'

'No,' Jack said. 'I've got enough weaknesses one way and another but women ent one of 'em, thank God.'

He took a hold of Shiner's halter and led him round towards the gateway.

'You're not going to get away with this!' Dennery shouted, following half way across the yard. 'I'll fix you good and proper, you lopsided swine, you, and you'll be sorry for today's doings, believe you me! I'm pretty well known in these parts, remember, and I'll see to it you never get work on none of the other farms around here, not if you try from now till Domesday!'

Jack did not stop. He merely glanced back over his shoulder.

'Then I'll have to try farther afield, shan't I?' he said, shrugging.

He went to his lodgings at Jim Lowell's cottage, put his few clothes into his old canvas satchel, and took his savings from under the mattress. Mattie Lowell saw him off at the door.

'Off again, wandering?' she said to him. 'It's time you settled, a man your age, instead of always on the move.—Settled and married to a sensible wife.'

'I shall have to keep my eyes open,' he said, and kissed her fat cheek. 'If I find one like you, I'll snap her up straight away.'

When he called at the Smiths' cottage, Peggy was alone there, except for the big ungainly lurcher bitch, Moll, and the month-old baby boy, Martin, asleep in a clothes-basket on the settle. The kitchen was steamy and smelt of hot bread.

'Ten pounds?' Peggy said, suspiciously. "How come Dennery sends me ten pounds?'

"I've walked off with Shiner,' Jack said, 'and I'm paying for him by paying you.' He dropped the money into her pocket. 'It's all quite genuine, every coin.'

'I don't want Dud Dennery's money! Nor yours neither!'

'It ent a question of what you want. You think

of your baby for a change. That's money put by for him when you need it.'

'Him!' Peggy said. 'Little mullocking nuisance!' But her sullenness melted as she looked at the baby in its cot. 'Money for him, the trouble he's brought me!'

'You've brought him as much. More, maybe.'

'Oh, is that so? And what does he know of trouble, I wonder? All he ever does is eat and sleep!'

'He'll know it soon enough, the start you've given him.'

'And what about me? Who'll marry me now, saddled with Sonny there all my days?'

'Some chap will marry you, sooner or later.'

'Not you, I don't suppose?'

'I've just bought a horse. I can't afford a wife as well. Besides which, I'm on the move.'

'And where are you heading for, looking for work?'

'I dunno. Wherever the fancy happens to lead me. Then it just depends what offers.'

'That won't be much at this time of year, but I wish you luck of it all the same. Is there anything I can do for you before you go, Jack Mercybright?'

'Yes,' he said. 'You can give me one of them hot new loaves and a tidy hunk of cheese to go with it. I shall be fammelled by the time I've walked a mile or two.'

'Why walk, for goodness' sake? Can't you ride Shiner?'

'Ah. So I can. That's a good idea.'

People stared at him, sitting up on the old grey's back, going at a walking pace through the village, and one or two even nodded a greeting. But nobody spoke to him. Aston Charmer was that sort of place. He had come to it only two years before and now, leaving it, he was still a stranger.

At Charmer's Cross he had a choice of six roads. He took the one going due southwards. And as he went he turned up his collar against the cold rain blowing behind him.

A dozen times during the day he stopped at farms to ask for work, but it was a bad time of year and he met with refusals everywhere. So he travelled on, along the narrow winding lanes, between dripping hedgerows, looking out over the wintry landscape, featureless under the wet hanging greyness.

At about dusk, he came to an old derelict cottage, lonely beside a bend in the road, and decided to shelter there for the night. The garden was a wilderness and beyond it, through a little rickety gate, was an old orchard of perry pear trees, planted on steeply rising ground. He let Shiner into the orchard, then he entered the cottage and lit a fire on the open hearthplace.

There was plenty of wood about the place and he built a good blaze, sitting before it, on the floor, eating a portion of Peggy Smith's bread and cheese and drinking beer he had bought along the way. And gradually, as his clothes dried, the heat of the fire worked through his body, thawing him out and easing his cold, stiff, aching muscles. Once warm, he buttoned himself into his jacket and lay down full length on a bed of straw, heaped against the driest wall. He fell asleep in a matter of minutes.

Some small sound awoke him: light footsteps crossing the threshold; hands fumbling against the doorpost. He raised his head and saw, dark against the open doorway, the shape of a girl dressed in a long hooded cape.

'Bevil?' she whispered, and then, a little louder: 'Bevil? Are you there?'

Lying perfectly still, Jack heard her soft exclamation of anger, with a little sob of disappointment in it that told him she was very young. For a moment she stood there, peering all round into the darkness, and tapping her foot on the stone step. Then, with another angry exclamation, she turned and swept out again, her cape brushing the briars at the doorway.

Jack turned over and went back to sleep, only to waken a little later as another step crossed the threshold. This time a youth stood framed in the doorway: small, slim, with a shock of untidy light-coloured hair.

'Nenna?' he said, and even at a distance of ten feet

or so, Jack caught a strong smell of drink on the air.
'Nenna, are you there?'

And, receiving no answer, he also departed from
the cottage. But whereas the girl had gone away angry
and disappointed, the young man went out with his
hands in his pockets, singing aloud as he sauntered
down the lane.

> 'Oh, Mary had her hair down;
> It reached her knee below;
> For she was afraid, this pure young maid,
> Her nakedness to show . . .'

The voice faded and died in the distance; silence
came back to the ruined cottage; and Jack settled down
again as before.

'Perhaps now,' he said to himself, 'a man may be
able to get some sleep!'

In the morning, while his can of water was boiling,
he walked about inspecting the cottage. It was very
old, built with a sturdy timber framework and clay
infilling, now mostly fallen out, so that only the criss-
cross beams remained. The thatch was almost all
gone from the roof; so were the floorboards of the
upper storey; but the brick-built chimney stood intact and the oak framework was perfectly sound, and
in his mind's eye he saw it as it must once have been:
its timbers well tarred, its panels whitewashed, its
casements gleaming in summer sunlight: all trim and
neat among its fruit trees.

Across the garden, there were two brick-built
sheds and a lean-to, with tools and a ramshackle cart
inside. So the cottage, it seemed, had once been the
farmhouse, displaced, probably, by some larger, more
modern building elsewhere. He could not see where,
because grey wet mist still curtained the landscape.

While he walked about, trying the timbers with his
shut-knife, a peremptory voice called out to him, and
two women came down the orchard. One, very young,
dressed in a dark red hooded cape, was the girl Nenna

of the night before. The other was a woman of perhaps thirty, with strong features and a high colour in her cheeks, and dark hair severely braided over her ears. They came through the gate into the garden, and the older woman spoke sharply.

'You're trespassing here. Do you realize that?'

'I do now you've told me,' Jack said.

'This land is mine. This cottage is mine. I don't like tramps lighting fires in my buildings. You might very easily have burnt the place down.'

'I ent, though, have I, as you see for yourself?'

'Is that your horse up there in my orchard? What right have you to make free with my grazing?'

Jack took his hand from his trousers pocket and offered her twopence.

'D'you think that'll pay for the thistles he's eaten?'

The younger girl smiled but the older one looked more haughty than ever.

'What is your name? Where have you come from all of a sudden? What are you doing hanging about in my cottage?'

'My name is Jack Mercybright. I've come from Aston Charmer, up Woeborough way, and I'm travelling about in search of work. Is there anything else you'd like to know?'

'There's no work here. I'm laying men off at this time of the year, not taking them on. And you'll get the same answer everywhere else about here, especially as—'

"As what?'

'Especially as you seem to be lame.'

'That don't stop me working.'

"Well, I'm sorry,' she said, 'but I can't help you.'

For a moment she looked at him, hesitating, almost as though she might change her mind. But suddenly her glance fell away and she pushed past him into the cottage. He was left with the girl, who made a wry face at him, repudiating her sister's behaviour. Then she came closer.

'Were you here last night?' she asked in a whisper.

'Yes,' he said. 'I didn't speak—I thought it'd scare you.'

'I knew I smelt woodsmoke, but I thought perhaps Bevil had been here before me.'

'He came a bit later. I reckon he must've mistook the time.'

'Don't say anything to my sister. She doesn't approve of Bevil, you see. At least, she wouldn't approve of my slipping out at night to meet him.'

'Why don't you tell her to go to the devil?'

'I couldn't do that.'

'Why not?'

'Well, I'm under age, and she's my guardian. We're not really sisters, properly speaking—Philippa's father married my mother—and I'd have no home if it weren't for her. The whole of the property is hers, you see.'

'Aye, I heard her say so,' Jack said, 'two or three times.'

The older woman came out of the cottage, shaking the dust from the hem of her skirt.

'Been checking?' he said. 'Been making sure I haven't damaged the straw or sacks or the few old hurdles you've got stored in there?'

'I suppose I'm entitled to safeguard my own property?'

'Since you value your property so much,' he said, 'why let it fall to rack and ruin?'

Again she gave him a long hard look, and it was some time before she answered.

'Let me give you a word of advice!' she said then. 'If you're looking for work, as you say you are, you'd be wise to keep a curb on your tongue. No employer will stand for impertinence and a man of your age ought to realize that. As for me, I'll thank you to get out of my cottage and on your way as soon as possible.'

'All right. Just as you say. I'll move on when I've had my breakfast.'

And he watched them walking away up the or-

chard, where the younger girl paused to pat Shiner's
neck in passing.

When he was gathering his things together, packing
his satchel, he found a bracelet on the floor, which
the woman had dropped while searching the cottage.
It was solid silver, in hinged halves, and, among some
delicate tracery, was engraved with her name: Agnes
Philippa Mary Guff. Jack hung it up on a nail in the
wall, where it was bound to be seen at once, but then,
on second thoughts, he took it down and put it into
his pocket instead, deciding to take it to the farm.

On his way up he saw how neglected the fields were:
pastureland rank with reeds and mare's tail; hedges
and headlands so overgrown with briar and bramble
that they measured fifteen feet across; and, in the few
poor acres sown with winter corn, the sparse blades
were labouring up, sickly and yellow, choked by
weeds and poisoned by the rabbits infesting the hedgerows.

The farmhouse was a big square building of grey
roughcast walls and brown paint-work, its windows
much curtained with lace and velvet, giving it a look
of closeness and darkness. He made his way through
the back yard, between tumbledown barns, cowstalls,
sheds, and arrived at the back door of the house. But
as he put up his hand to the knocker, a white bull
terrier sprang growling from its kennel under the
mounting-block and hurled itself at his outstretched
arm.

The dog's big teeth went right through his sleeve
and sank into the flesh of his forearm, penetrating as
far as the bone. Jack hit out with his left fist, but the
dog only growled more ferociously, closing his eyes
and laying back his ears, impervious to the blows on
his flat hard skull. The brute was tugging with all his
strength, growling and snorting, his jaws clenched as
he tried to bring his teeth together through flesh,
muscle, sinew, bone.

Jack looked round and saw an old riding-crop hanging up on a hook on the wall. He took it down, thrust

it under the dog's collar, and twisted it till the collar tightened. The dog snarled, trying to shake Jack's arm as he would a rabbit, but the collar was now pressing his windpipe. He was gasping and choking; his eyes were rolling, showing their whites; and another twist made him lose his senses. The flat head lolled, the jaws relaxed, and he gave a cough deep in his throat. Jack took out the crop and threw it aside. He took the dog's upper jaw and eased its teeth out of his flesh. The animal slumped down onto the cobbles and lay on its side, its legs rigid.

Jack took off his jacket and rolled up his shirt-sleeve. He was walking across to the cattle-trough when the house door opened and the older sister came out on the step.

'What have you done to my dog?'

'What's he done to me, more like!'

'You shall pay for this, I promise!' she said, and then saw his arm, where the blood was welling up from the punctures. 'You'd better come in,' she said quickly, and led him into a kind of wash-house.

'Your dog's unconscious, that's all, though he's lucky I didn't choke him to death. I was in the mood for a moment or two.'

'You must have taken him unawares. We don't get a lot of visitors here.'

'With him as a pet, I'm not surprised.'

'Roy's a good house-dog. It's what he's there for. But I'm sorry you've been hurt, all the same.' She ran a tap into the sink and held his arm under the icy cold water. 'Stay like that. I'll get some ointment.'

She went through into the house. He heard her voice in the passage. The girl Nenna came into the wash-house but stood a little way away, white-faced and wincing. Seeing her without her hood, he realized she was young indeed, probably not more than sixteen.

'What's up with you? Don't you like the sight of blood?'

'No. I hate it. It makes me feel sick.'

'I ent all that keen, neither, specially when it's my

own,' he said, 'and I'm making a fair old mess of your nice clean slopstone.'

The older woman came back again. She turned off the tap and dried his arm. She was quick and efficient, smearing the wounds with carbolic ointment, binding them round with a thick cotton bandage, tying the ends in a neat knot about his wrist.

'Why did you come here, anyway? I thought I told you to take yourself off?'

'I found this,' he said, and gave her the bracelet. 'You dropped it on the floor of the cottage.'

'Did I? How extraordinary! I'd no idea. The catch must be faulty. I shall have to take it to be repaired.'

She put the bracelet into her pinafore pocket and became preoccupied, rolling up the spare strip of bandage, replacing the lid of the ointment jar, swilling the last of the blood from the sink. Her manner amused him. He could read her thoughts. He was not surprised by her next words.

'I believe you mentioned you were looking for work?'

'Ah. That's right. But you said you had nothing to offer me.'

'Well . . . there's not much to do at this time of year.'

'There is on this farm,' he said bluntly. 'The state it's in, you certainly shouldn't be laying men off.— You ought to be getting them out stirring. Your ditches want cleaning and your hedges want laying and that's nothing more than a bit of a start-off.'

'I can't afford to employ a lot of men.'

'You can't afford not to, the way things are. Another two or three years of neglect and this here farm will be useless to you.'

'Yes! Yes! It's just what I tell them!" she said, in a little burst of passion. 'But the labourers here all take advantage, knowing they're dealing with a mere woman.'

'Even when that woman is you?'

'I can't *force* them to do things, can I? I can't stand

over them with a whip! And, anyway, I don't know enough to decide what's best.'

'I know enough,' Jack said. 'Take me on and I'll set things to rights.'

'You're very persuasive.'

'I need to be—I'm down to my last eighteen pence,' he said.

'I can't afford to pay a bailiff's wages.'

'A labourer's wages will suit me.'

'Perhaps I do owe you something,' she said, 'seeing my dog has done you such damage.'

'You owe me nothing!' Jack said. 'Let's get that straight before we start. You'll be paying me my wages for the work I do, not as compensation for a dog-bite.'

'Very well. I'll take you on for a trial period and think again in a month from now. At least I can be fairly sure you're honest, since you brought my bracelet back to me.'

'Aye, that's why you left it there, warnt it?' he said. 'To see if I was an honest fellow?'

'Rubbish!' she said, the colour flaring even more redly on her cheekbones. 'You flatter yourself, I do assure you! Do you think I would risk losing a solid silver bracelet just to test a labourer's honesty?'

'Not much risk, considering how easy it would be to trace me . . . a limping man with an old grey horse . . . travelling about in search of work. You'd have had your bracelet back in no time.'

'Utter rubbish, I do assure you!'

'Just as you say,' he said, shrugging. 'Have it your own way. You're the gaffer.'

'Yes,' she said, and looked at him with hostile eyes. 'Exactly so, Mercybright, and I counsel you to re-member it always!'

His arm was so swollen that it stretched the sleeve of his jacket tight. He could scarcely move it. It was stiff to the shoulder and the slightest touch was agony. For three days he could do no work, and spent the time tramping about all over the farm, till he knew every acre from boundary to boundary.

One afternoon, while inspecting the lower fletchers, he met a man named Joe Stretton. It was getting dark, and Jack was prodding the flooded ditch with a long pole, when he sensed someone watching from the opposite side of the hedgerow. The man stood perfectly still, a grey shape in the grey dusk, his head seeming to rest on his shoulders, so short and thick was his huge neck.

'Who're you?' he asked, as Jack stood up and looked straight at him, in between the tall thorns. 'You the chap that's been strolling about, poking your nose in everywhere, acting as if you was God Almighty?'

'Ah, that's me,' Jack agreed. 'And who might you be?'

'My name's Joe Stretton. I work on this farm and have done for nigh on forty years. Except I've been laid off this past two fortnights.'

'Are those your snares I seen about the fields?'

'Yes. What of it?' And Stretton raised both his arms up high, above the level of the overgrown hedge, showing the rabbits dangling in bunches from each hand. 'You got something to say about it, have you?'

'No. Nothing. There's too many rabbits about the place so you go ahead and keep them down.'

'Who are you to have such a say-so? You a foreman or bailiff or what?'

'I'm just a labourer, same as yourself.'

'But why've you been took on here at all, that's what I should like to know? You!—A stranger!—When I've been laid off and others like me?'

'That's just my good luck, I suppose,' Jack said.

'And how long d'you reckon your luck'll hold?—From Christmas to Easter, if I know the missus who runs this farm, and then you'll be out on your ear like us others. God Almighty! It makes me spew! I've got a sick wife, did you know that? I've got four children still at school and I've been on this farm since I was a tadpole yet *you* come along and take my job! So what's that Miss Philippa think she's doing?'

'I dunno,' Jack said. 'You'd better ask her.'

Later that day, returning along the edge of Hew Meadow, he caught his foot in one of Stretton's snares and measured his length in the wet mud, falling on his swollen arm. The snare was the usual kind set for rabbits: a running noose of copper wire fixed to a peg stuck in the ground; but the noose was twice the size used for rabbits, the wooden peg twice as strong, and Jack felt sure that the snare had been set on purpose for him: a warning to him that he was not wanted at Brown Elms Farm.

He had set himself to clean out the big main watercourse known as the Runkle, but although he got the waters moving, running clear over the pebbles, the field-ditches remained choked, for the drains and outlets had all fallen in. So he set to work to clean out the ditches, starting in the big Bottom Meadow, working from the bank with the long-handled graffer.

"Still puddling about, making mud pies?" Miss Philippa said, coming to see what he was doing. 'When will you start doing something useful?'

'First things first,' Jack said, 'and that means drainage.'

'I hear you're still sleeping at Perry Cottage. You don't need to do that, you know. I could get you lodgings with one of the cowmen.'

'Thanks,' he said, 'but I'd just as soon stay as I am.'

'What, sleeping rough like that, in this sort of weather?'

'I'm all right. It don't worry me.'

'I might even have a cottage for you, if you prefer to be alone. Up at Far Fetch, beside the wood. You may have seen it.'

Jack stood up straight, his legs straddling the wide ditch, his feet wedged in the mud at the sides. He looked up at her, standing above him, among the alders.

'I know the cottage. It's Joe Stretton's. What would you do about him and his family?'

'Stretton would have to go, of course.'

'You'd give him the push?' Jack said. 'Turn him out to make room for me? Now why is that? Because you think I'm better value?'

'Stretton is a surly malcontent. He's a trouble-maker and always will be. He's been here so long he thinks he ought to be in charge of the farm.'

'Then why not *put* him in charge as a proper bailiff? If he's an old hand, he deserves it, surely? A farm runs better if the men have someone to look to for orders, and each one knows exactly where he stands.'

'*I* give the orders on this farm.'

'Ah. I know. That's why it's gone back the way it has done.'

'I warned you before, Mercybright!—I won't be spoken to in that manner by you or by any other man I employ!'

'And I warn *you!*' Jack said, growing impatient. 'If you sack Joe Stretton, you lose both him and me together, 'cos I don't want your blasted cottage nor any lodgings with your cowmen neither! I'm fine and dandy

as I am so leave me alone and let me get on with what
I'm doing.'

He stooped again over the ditch and began shovelling sludge from the bottom, flinging it up to the top of
the bank, careless whether it splashed the woman's
skirts as she stood above him among the alders. He
was tired and wet. His knee was giving him a lot of
pain. His arm still ached where the dog had bitten him.
And he was suddenly so out of patience that one
more word would have set him on his travels again.
But the next time he glanced upwards, Miss Philippa
was no longer there.

Sitting at his fire in the ruined cottage, he ate his supper of bread and boiled bacon and drank a mugful
of strong milkless tea. The night was a wet one. Rain
dripped through the floorboards above and squeezed
through the walls to trickle down, glistening darkly,
inside the crumbling plasterwork. His bedding of straw
and sacks was soaked, because there was now no dry
place to put it, and as he sat eating, two rats crept
out of the deeper shadows to drink from the puddle in
the central floor.

He got up suddenly, and the rats vanished. He
heard them scampering overhead. He shovelled ashes
over the fire and pushed the heap to the back of the
hearth-place. Then he put on his oilskin, pulled his
cap over his forehead, and went out into the rain, making for Niddup, a mile away down the lane.

The Bay Tree was a small public house, no more
than a cottage, standing a hundred and fifty yards or
so up on the bank of the River Ennen. Inside, there
was light and warmth and tobacco-smoke, a smell of
beer and spiced rum, and the sound of a group of
bargemen singing, accompanied by one who played
the taproom squeezebox.

Jack ordered a rum and a pint of Chepsworth. He
drank the rum in one go and carried his beer to the
fireside. He sat in a corner of the big settle. The group
of bargemen had stopped singing. Their audience
broke up and a fair-haired youth of about eighteen

came, glass in hand, to sit in the arm-chair opposite
Jack.

'I see you drink wisely,' he remarked, and, pointing
to Jack's mug: ' "Rum after ale makes a man pale,
but ale after rum is good for his tum." '

'All men drink wisely when they first begin. It's
later on they run into trouble.'

'You speak like a man of some experience.'

'Seeing I'm probably twice your age, you may well
be right, young fellaboy.'

'Is your name Mercybright by any chance? I thought
it must be! Then you're the new bailiff up at Brown
Elms. Allow me to make myself known also. My name
is Bevil Ames.'

'I'm no bailiff,' Jack said. 'I'm a plain labourer and
get a labourer's plain wages.'

'And you skulk in Perry Cottage, eavesdropping
slyly on Nenna and me . . . It's a good thing I was
late for my assignation that night or you might have
been party to a lovers' meeting.'

'That girl Nenna is only a child. D'you think it's
right to lure her out of doors after dark?'

'Nenna is the one that does the luring. She thinks
it's romantic. My own feelings run more with yours.
That's why I'm often late for the meetings.'

'If you don't care for the girl,' Jack said, 'why the
hell don't you leave her alone?'

'But I *do* care! Heart and soul! She's the one person in all the world who tries to understand me. Besides which, it's only right and proper that a man
like me should have an attachment.'

'A man like you? And what sort is that when it's at
home?'

'Oh, when it's at home it's a dull dog indeed, for it
has a father who insists that the law must be its pro-
fession. But the truth is—at heart I am a poet!' And
the young man, making mock of himself, bowed
gravely, one hand pressed against his breast, the
slender fingers delicately stretched. 'Yes, a poet!' he
said. 'A man endowed with much sensitivity and re-

finement of spirit. And yet, as you see, fate constantly thrusts me among the barbarians!'

'Aye,' Jack said, glancing at the company gathered in the taproom, 'yet they seem to bear it cheerfully enough.'

The young man laughed, head thrown back, shaggy fair hair rippling over his collar.

'Drink up, Mr Mercybright, and I'll join you in another. You look as though you could do with a really thorough warming and I know just the thing to do the trick. Come with me and we'll get Sylvanus to make us a jug of his hot rum flip.'

While they stood at the counter, waiting, Joe Stretton came in and flung down five or six brace of rabbits. Sylvanus Knarr whipped them away and passed a few coins across instead. No word was exchanged throughout the transaction, but Stretton, finding Jack standing beside him, gave a loud grunt and spat in the sawdust on the floor.

'This used to be a pretty good place for company,' he said to Sylvanus, 'but it's going off sadly by the look of things.'

'If you two chaps've got a quarrel, take it elsewhere,' Sylvanus said, and reached for the malt-shovel hanging from one of the beams above. 'Otherwise, a fight occurring, both parties get batted with this and my missus here follows it up with a pail of cold water.'

'No quarrel,' Jack said. 'I'd even buy the man a drink if that'd wipe the sneer off his face.'

'I'm taking no drinks with *you!*' Stretton said, and walked out.

"Seems you've made an enemy,' Bevil said.

'It's a knack I've got,' Jack said, shrugging.

When he left The Bay Tree late that night, the rain was falling as hard as ever, but, hunched inside his oilskin cape, he was almost indifferent to it, warmed by the spirit in his veins. And when he lay down on the straw in the cottage, sleep came to him in an instant.

After Christmas, there were two or three weeks of dry, open weather. Jack felt better when the weather was dry; his knee scarcely troubled him at all; and the sight of the teams out ploughing the slopes above the Runkle made the farm seem alive and meaningful for the very first time since his coming there.

When the frosts came, ploughing was halted. Jack had the fields to himself again. He was working on the overgrown hedges in the Home Field now; cutting them back to the very bone; laying the thorns and pleaching them; burning the brushwood in heaps on the stubble. Miss Philippa came there twice a day, stamping the ground with booted feet, fretting because the frosts persisted.

'You see what I mean about the men here?' she said once, warming herself at Jack's fire. 'There were four ploughs out at the beginning of the month.—Fourteen days' work done altogether.—Yet all they managed was about forty acres!'

'It's not their fault. It's the state of the ground. And that won't improve till you've got your drains all running again.'

'How many years will it take,' she asked tartly, 'before you've got them cleaned and dug out?'

'How many years did *you* take,' he asked, 'getting them all choked up as they are?'

She was silent a while, watching him as he forked more brushwood onto the fire.

'You're perfectly free to offer advice, you know, if it's worth hearing.'

'Advice is easy. When the frosts ease off you should set more men to work ditching. Joe Stretton, for one, who's been laid off for God knows how long.'

'I shall take Stretton back when I see good reason.'

'There's work crying out to be done all around. Ent that a good reason? Then I hear his wife's took a turn for the worse. Ent that a good enough reason for you? Not to mention he's got four children!'

'That wife of his is sick in the mind. She ought to be put away in a home. I told Stretton that two years ago and he chose to ignore me. It's his own fault he has no work. Still, I'll think over what you've said, and I'll see what other men I can spare for ditching.'

And she went away.

Stretton was often about the fields, going the rounds of his rabbit-snares, helping himself to turnip-tops and spring cabbage, and openly raiding the clamps for potatoes. Sometimes, too, he was at the cottage, bent on mischief. Jack never caught him, but once when the pump in the yard failed to work, he found clods and pebbles stuffed up the spout, and once he came home to find his tea-kettle hammered flat, nailed to the lintel above the back doorway.

There was an old two-wheeled cart in one of the sheds behind the cottage, and a set of old harness, and one Saturday afternoon, Jack put Shiner into the shafts and drove the six miles into Egham-on-Ennen. He returned with a load of thatching-straw, three balls of twine and a pot of tar, shears, a rake, and a new bill-hook. He spent the evening splitting hazel spars and withies. He had made up his mind to repair the cottage.

By the end of a week, he had cleared the last of the old rotten thatch, brushed the beams and rafters clean, and replaced those laths that were riddled with worm. On Sunday morning he started thatching and in the afternoon he had a visitor.

'What are you doing?' a voice asked, and, looking down, he saw the girl Nenna standing below at the foot of the ladder.

'What's it look like I'm doing?' he said. 'I'm putting a new roof on this cottage, ent I?'

'Do you mind if I watch you?'

'Suit yourself. It's all as one to me.'

'You seem to be good at this work,' she said.

'Well, I worked with a thatcher at one time of day, years ago when I was a boy.'

'Does Philippa know you're repairing the cottage?'

'I daresay she does. She don't miss much of what goes on around her property.'

'You'll have to watch out or she'll soon be asking you for rent.'

'She can ask. She won't get it.'

'She might even sell it.'

'She might so. I couldn't stop her.'

He came down from his ladder to fetch more straw, and the girl watched him as he wet it and combed it into yelms. She sat on the staddle-stone nearby, her hood thrown back, her hair a bright red-gold in the sunlight. Her face was rather beautiful, the features small and neatly made, the skin very pure and honey-coloured, the eyes and lashes unexpectedly brown. Although so young, she had a direct way of looking at people, and the set of her chin suggested a strong and resolute will.

'Doesn't it worry you,' she asked, 'that you might have all this work for nothing?'

'I like having something to do,' he said. 'It keeps me from moping.'

'Why should you mope?'

'Don't you, ever?'

'Yes. Sometimes.'

'Then don't ask silly questions.'

'But it's different for a man. You can do what you like. You're independent.'

'Doing as you like always costs you something.'

'Does it?' she said. 'Yes, perhaps it does. But aren't you willing to pay the price?'

'Maybe. Maybe not. The trouble is, we never know what the price is until afterwards, and then it's too late to change our minds.'

'I must go,' she said, moving suddenly. 'I'm meeting Bevil down by the river. He's taking me on a barge to Yelland.'

'And is he bringing you back again?'

'Of course,' she said, laughing. 'More's the pity!'

When she had gone, he climbed the ladder with the yelms of straw in a piece of sacking, and set to work on the 'eyebrow' arching over the second dormer. He had worked since first light, and, looking along the stretch of shaggy yellow thatch, now almost covering this side of the roof, he was well pleased.

About mid-afternoon, from his perch on the roof, he saw Joe Stretton going home across the orchard with a bundle of firewood on his shoulder. Jack was suspicious, for Stretton had woods at the back of his own cottage, and he watched till the man went out of sight among the bushes behind the cartshed. He was still looking out, wondering what mischief Stretton was up to, when something came hurtling through the air and flashed past him. It was a blazing bundle of birch twigs, with a four-pronged hook at one end, and, the hook catching in the dried-out thatch, the whole roof was ablaze in an instant, the flames whoomphing out to scorch Jack's face and set his shirt and waistcoat burning. The heat was such that even the newly wetted straw was set alight between his hands.

He slid down the ladder and ran to the cartshed, but although it contained a great variety of tools, there was no swat-pole or thatch-lifter to be found among them. All he had was an old pitch-fork and already, when he returned, the new thatch was shrunk to a mat of black ashes, burning through the thick oaken laths, which were dropping in flaming charcoal fragments into the inner part of the cottage. Sparks had fallen in the loose straw strewn about the yard, and now this went up, licking high about the ladder, scorching his boots and the legs of his trousers.

It took two hours and twenty buckets of pump water before he felt sure that every last spark was douted. He sat on the edge of the water-trough, with the stinking wet straw smoking blackly all around him, and rested himself, counting the damage. The cottage was now in worse case than ever. The laths were gone. The rafters were blackened. He had wasted eighteen hours' work, lost a week's wages in thatching materials, and been badly burnt into the bargain. He rose and took a drink of water. Then he set out for Stretton's cottage.

As soon as he knocked, heavy footsteps clattered down the stairs inside, and the door was wrenched open by Stretton himself. Jack took hold of him by his waistcoat. He thrust him against the passage wall.

'I've had about enough of you, Stretton! The time has come to sort things out! So how would it be if I took you and broke your thick ugly neck?'

'Leave go of me!' Stretton bellowed, and shook himself in Jack's grasp, his face contorted. 'Leave go and help me for pity's sake!'

Jack stared, appalled at the tears splashing off the man's face. He relinquished his hold and saw that Stretton was smothered in blood. Upstairs, a woman was sobbing.

'It's my wife!' Stretton moaned. 'She's in one of her fits and she's cut her wrists open with my razor. God! Oh, God! What next, what next?'

There was a scream and a loud crash. Stretton ran back along the passage and Jack followed him, up the steep stairs, into the bedroom, where the sick, demented woman knelt on the bed, plucking at the rags tied around her wrists.

'Lucy, no!' Stretton groaned, and leant across her, holding her arms and trying to tighten the knotted rags. 'Leave them alone, will you! Will you leave them alone, for Christ's sake!'

The woman's face was a terrible colour. There were black circles about her eyes, like terrible bruises, and her lips bore the red raw marks of her teeth, where she had bitten herself in her frenzy. The shift she wore was brown with blood. Her throat and chest were lacerated. Staring at Jack, she wrenched herself free of Stretton's grasp and moved on her knees across the bed, reaching out with her nails as though she would claw at Jack's face.

'I don't want *you*! I know who you are, you cunning devil! You've come to have me put away!'

Jack took hold of her by the arms, forcing her backwards until she lay down. He kept her there while Stretton re-tied the rags on her wrists.

'Have you got any laudanum in the house?'

'I've got some, yes, but she's had a few drops and I'm too damned scared to give her more.'

'Get it,' Jack said. 'She's more danger to herself like this than the laudanum will be.'

Stretton went away and returned with a cup. Together they forced her to drink the contents, and gradually she became quiet. The fierce tension went out of her body, and her eyes, from being stretched unnaturally wide, became heavy-lidded.

'Have I been naughty again, Joe? Have I been giving a lot of trouble?'

'You had one of your turns,' Stretton said, gently stroking her arm with his fingers. 'You was sick again, warnt you, my girl, like you was the last time?'

'I had that pain in my head. I didn't mean to cause no trouble. I sent the children over to Ivy's. *She* don't mind their screaming and yelling but it hurts me, Joe, when I get this dothering in my head.'

'Never mind, old girl,' Stretton said. 'You're a lot better now and Joe is here to see you get your proper rest.'

'Who's this man here? It ent the relieving officer, is it, Joe?'

'No, no. This here's a friend. He called in to see how you was faring.'

'That's nice,' she said. 'We ent got a great many friends, like, have we? I suppose it's because I get so fractious.'

'Have you sent for the doctor?' Jack asked Stretton.

'There was no one to send. She seen to it the kids was gone and out of the way before she started. When I got home—'

'I'll go,' Jack said. 'You stay with her and keep her quiet.'

He hurried out and took the short cut across the fields to Niddup. He delivered the message to Dr Spray and waited to see him set out on his pony. Then he went home and began clearing away the mess he had left there.

There was a small coppice of oak about half a mile

down the lane from the cottage; he went in the evening and cut what he wanted; carried the poles home in bundles and split them into laths. Sometimes, up on the roof late at night, working by lamplight, nailing the laths into place, he disturbed the rooks in the hedgerow elms nearby, and they floated above him in the darkness, quietly cawing their disapproval.

On Saturday, when he got home after work, he found a new load of straw in the cartshed, together with twine, spars, withies, and nabhooks. He was washing himself under the pump, still wondering where they had come from, when Joe Stretton walked into the yard-place.

'I sent 'em,' he said, 'in place of what I burnt last Sunday.'

'It's twice the amount of straw that got burnt.'

'Is it? So what? I've got a cousin in the trade.' He did not try to meet Jack's glance. He stared instead at the roof of the cottage, where the new laths were now all in place. 'I'd offer to give you a hand,' he said, 'only I ent much of a mucher at thatching.'

'How's your missus?' Jack asked.

'She's dead,' Stretton said. 'Yesterday morning, about nine. I thought you'd have heard about it by now.'

'I've heard nothing. The men don't speak if they can avoid it. But I'm sorry about it all the same.'

'She warnt a bad old girl, really. There was lots worse than my old Lucy. It was only since she got knocked down by that horse and dray in Rainborough that time. She was always a good wife to me before that.' He stood for a moment, kicking at the cobbles with the toe of his boot. 'The burial's on Tuesday morning,' he said. 'Niddup church, eleven o'clock. I thought maybe you'd come along.'

'Ah,' Jack said. 'All right. I'll be there.'

When Stretton had gone, he went to the shed and brought out the trusses of new straw. He set about combing it into yelms. It was good wheaten straw, grown on heavy land: tough and even: the best to be

had. It would last twenty or thirty years. He brought
out the rest of the new tackle and climbed the ladder.
He was ready to begin thatching again.

Towards the end of March he was out with the
other men, ploughing the end field below the Runkle.
They watched him with interest, for, being a
newcomer, he had the worst plough on the farm:
an old-fashioned breast-plough, heavy, cumbersome,
badly balanced, that seemed to possess a will of its
own. Joe Stretton was also at work and so was his
eldest boy, Harvey, a cheeky sprig just twelve years
old, helping to lead his father's team.

'How d'you like your plough, then, Jack?' Harvey
asked. 'Or ent you properly acquainted yet?'

'Well, I've ploughed with some funny things in my
time, but I never did come across the likes of this
here. It must've been made for a man with three
hands and wrists like tree-trunks.'

'Out of the Ark!' Stretton said. 'Like most of the
tackle on this farm. And *she* expects us to work with
such rubbish.'

'Why not ask for a new plough, Jack?' Harvey
suggested, winking and nodding. 'Seeing you and
Miss Philippa seem such good friends? Ah, and while
you're at it, ask if I can have a half day's holiday into
the bargain, to go to the sale at Darry Cross.'

'I'll ask if you can ride along with her in the trap if you like. I believe she means going to look at some heifers.'

'Oh, no!' Harvey said. 'I reckon that's your place, Jack, not mine.'

Later that day, when Jack knocked off ploughing and led his team home into the stable yard, he found Harvey Stretton giving an imitation of him, watched by Eddie Burston and the two Luppitt brothers. The boy was limping along grotesquely, jerking his body this way and that, pretending to wrestle with an imaginary plough. Jack took no notice. He walked past with Diamond and Darky. But Joe Stretton, coming out of the stables, cuffed the boy and sent him reeling.

'That's enough of that, Clever Dick! Get back to work before I tan you.' And to Jack he said, 'You've got to watch these youngsters nowadays. Give 'em an inch and they'll take from here to Constantinople!''

Now that the evenings were drawing out, Jack was able to spend more time repairing the cottage. He had finished thatching the main roof. He had made a start on the little wing containing scullery and wash-house. But sometimes he had to wait a while, until he had money to buy materials, and in these between times he worked on the walls: knocking out the old clay and wattle and putting in new, dealing with two or three panels at one time.

He had cut down the hemlock and nettles and tall dead grasses in the garden, and now had two pigs there, cleaning the ground. He also had a goose and a gander keeping Shiner company in the orchard.

One evening in May Miss Philippa drove up the lane from Niddup and stopped the trap outside the cottage. She had often driven that way before; she had seen him working on the cottage; but never once had she mentioned the matter. This evening, however, she was plainly in a difficult mood. She sat in the trap and called out to him in a loud voice.

'Did it never occur to you to ask my permission before interfering with my property?'

'I took it you would've told me pretty damn smartish if you didn't like it. You've seen me at it often enough.'

'Perhaps you'd be civil enough to ask me now.'

'No, not me, 'cos I hardly know what civil means.'

He was up on the ladder, his bucket of moist clay in one hand, his trowel in the other. He turned a little and looked at her fully.

'If you tell me to stop, I shall stop,' he said. 'If you don't tell me, I shall carry on.'

'Where did you get those two weaners?' she asked suddenly, changing tack.

'I bought 'em,' he said. 'Three shillings the two, from Mr Ellenton up at Spouts Hall. And I got the geese from the same place. Why do you ask?'

'*Bought* them?' she said. 'The same way you bought that old grey horse you've got in my orchard?'

'So that's it!' he said. 'You've been hearing stories, ent you?'

'I was over at Woeborough market this morning and I met a Mr Dennery, whose farm you were on at Aston Charmer. His story was that you took that horse without so much as a by-your-leave, to spite him when he dismissed you for idling.'

'Dennery's a liar. I paid ten pounds for that old horse, but I gave the money to a girl by the name of Peggy Smith, that Dennery had got into trouble. Did he happen to mention them little details?'

'No. He didn't. And it's only your word against his.'

'That's right,' Jack said. 'It's up to you to choose, ent it?'

'I shall ask Mr. Ellenton when I see him, whether he sold you those pigs or not, for I'm not at all sure I can trust you, Mercybright.'

'You don't trust nobody,' Jack said. 'But you go ahead and check by all means. It'll give you something to pass the time.'

She flipped at the pony and drove away. Jack turned back to his work on the cottage. When he saw her again the next morning, and in the days following, the matter of the pigs was not mentioned. She had no doubt checked the truth of his story: she was that sort of woman; but she never troubled herself to say so.

All through that summer, the young girl Nenna came to the cottage two or three evenings every week to meet the boy, Bevil Ames, and often they stayed a while, sitting together on a makeshift bench, watching Jack as he pounded wet clay in a wooden bucket, or split green hazel-rods with his billhook.

'I've put you out a bit, squatting here in your meeting-place, I reckon. But no doubt there's barns and such you could meet in together if you had a mind to be really private.'

'Tut-tut!' Bevil said. 'What are you suggesting, Mr Mercybright? Barns indeed, for a well-brought-up girl like Nenna, here? Whatever next!'

'You are my chaperon,' Nenna said to Jack.

'Am I indeed? Who would've thought it!'

'You never finished telling us about the Battle of Majuba Hill,' Bevil said. 'About your Irish friend in the Army.'

'Ah. Well. He fell in front of a shunting engine. Lost both his legs and got scalded all over in a rush of steam. He was lying in the hospital, screaming for something to stop the pain, but the M.O. said he had nothing to give him.'

'Wasn't it true?' Bevil asked.

'Of course it wasn't bloody well true! They expected Paddy to die any minute. They warnt going to waste their drugs on him.'

'So you broke into the medical stores?'

'I tried to break in, but the sentry shot me in the knee.'

'What happened to Paddy?'

'He died three days later, still in pain.'

'Were you with him?'

'No, not me. I was laid up and behind bars.'

'What made you join the army in the first place?'

'I couldn't find work, that's why. Not once I'd finished my bout of navvying on the new canal at Borridge. Then Paddy said to me, "Let's join the

Army," and the next thing I knew we was on our way out to South Africa.'

'So you never actually saw any fighting?'

'Not a stitch,' Jack said. 'It was all over by the time they let me out of gaol.'

'I would never let Bevil join the Army,' Nenna said. 'I think it's all wrong for people to go and fight in wars.'

'There, now!' said Bevil, slapping his knee. 'The very thing I had in mind!'

'No! I won't let you! You'd be sure to get hurt!' And she sat with his hand held tight between her own, as though she feared he would go that minute. 'I shall never let you go away from me. Never! Never!'

Bevil leant forward and kissed her lightly on the mouth. He drew his hand away from hers and got up from the bench, taking his watch from his waistcoat pocket and looking at it with a frown.

'I must go, Nen,' he said, sighing. 'I promised my father a game of chess and the poor old man does depend on me so. But I'll walk with you as far as the farm.'

They went off together, arm in arm, and Jack stood watching them, thinking what strange young lovers they were: like two sedate children, moving through courtship as though through the steps of some slow, formal, old-fashioned dance.

Later that evening, when he went to The Bay Tree for a drink, Bevil was there, standing on his head on the taproom floor, singing a song with ten long verses, encouraged by the usual Friday evening crowd of villagers and bargemen. Jack took his drink out to the garden and sat on the seat beside the bay tree, looking across the quiet river to the Ludden Hills strung out in the distance, charcoal-coloured against the yellow sunset glow. After a while, Bevil came out and sat beside him.

'Be sure your sins will find you out!'

'Playing chess with your father, I think you said? Why do you tell that girl such lies?'

'Ah!' Bevil said. 'Why do we ever lie to women?'

'You tell *me*. I know nothing at all about it.'

'To spare their feelings, of course, what else? Would it be kinder, do you think, if I told her straight out that I better prefer coming down here to spending the rest of the evening with her? A man must be free! He's a lapdog, else. And women, God bless them, however lovable and loving they may be, do stifle a man most dreadfully, don't they? But perhaps it's not the same for other men? Perhaps it's merely because I'm a poet!'

'D'you feel more free in a village public? And does it make you more of a poet?'

'Why, yes, I compose my best lines when I'm drunk!' Bevil said. 'The trouble is, I forget them all by the time I'm sober.'

He became silent, sitting perfectly still on the seat, his brandy glass between his hands. The night was a warm one. Gnats were flying and the smell of the river was strong on the air. Behind the distant hills the sky was still a lemon yellow, but overhead it was already a deep night-blue, with a few stars throbbing in it.

'Do you ever wonder,' Bevil said, lounging backwards until he was staring directly upwards into the sky: 'do you ever wonder what lies beyond the most distant stars?'

'Sometimes I do,' Jack said.

'And what do you see?' Bevil asked. 'In your imagination, I mean?'

'I dunno. More stars again, I suppose, and maybe another moon here and there.'

'More stars and moons . . .' Bevil murmured, and then, declaiming:

'Stars unknown, a universe undreamed of,
And gods, perhaps, that out-create our own!'

He sat up suddenly and turned to look into Jack's face.

'But what beyond that?—Even the stars must finish somewhere! What do you see, beyond it all, at the very last ultimate finish, when you're lying in bed in the small hours, just you and the sky outside your window?'

'If you was a labourer on a farm, always on the go from dawn to dusk and out in all weathers, you'd have more sense than to ask that question. It's sitting all day dozing on your clerk's high stool in that stuffy lawyer's office of yours that keeps you awake in the small hours, my lad.'

'But aren't you afraid?' Bevil asked. 'Of whatever worlds might lie beyond?'

'I'm more concerned with what happens in this one.'

'Oh, yes, that too,' Bevil said, shivering. 'All the terrible things that happen on earth . . . birth and pain and sickness and dying . . . don't all those things make you afraid?'

'Everybody's afraid of dying.'

'And are you afraid of living too?'

'I can see why you drink!' Jack said. 'You've got a problem and no mistake!'

But the laugh Bevil gave was not his usual cheerful laugh. It sounded sickly. And Jack, looking closely in the dim, fading light, did not attempt to tease him further, for the fair face had an unnatural pallor and the eyes were like those of a small boy awaking from a nightmare.

'Sometimes I feel myself changing in texture. I feel myself growing thick all over and my lips feel numb and warm together, as though my flesh were made of clay. Then a cool light rain starts falling and passes right through me, and I have a feeling of immense relief, as if everything is now all right and the worst is over.'

Bevil paused, tilting his glass and peering in at the drop of brandy, rolling like an amber bead at the bottom.

'Do you think death is like that?' he asked.

'If it is,' Jack said, 'it don't sound all that bad, does it? I shouldn't mind the rain going through me, not once my bones had stopped aching.'

'Sometimes I wish it would come and be done with,

because then I need never be afraid again. No more
fear or pain or disgust . . . or self-pity because of other
people's disgust . . .' Bevil emptied his glass and leant
towards Jack. 'I shall never be able to marry Nenna.
It's as much as I can do to face up to life, myself, let
alone look after a wife and family.'

'A good wife would look after *you*.'

'Oh, my God! Nenna's as much a babe as I am!'

'Together you'd be strong, like a bundle of sticks,'
Jack said. 'Women've got more faith in life than us
men, somehow, I often think.'

'I'm getting cold!' Bevil said, and jumped up
quickly, putting on gaiety as though it were a coat.
'Let's go in and join the party. I can hear Angelina
playing her squeezebox.' And then, going in, he said
suddenly: 'I'm not a thorough liar, you know—I *did*
go home and play chess with my father.'

The two cowmen at Brown Elms were brothers named
Peter and Paul Luppitt. One morning when Jack arrived, they were in the farmyard, looking at two new
cows in the paddock.

'Where did they drop from?' Peter asked Jack.

'I dunno. They're both strangers to me.'

'They must've arrived late last night, then, that's all.
Miss Philippa must've bought 'em at Hotcham.'

'She's off her hinges,' Paul said. 'I've seen more milk
on a three-legged stool than we'll ever see on them
eight legs there.'

'Watch yourself,' Peter muttered. 'The missus is
with us.'

Miss Philippa came out of the house, and the two
cowmen went off to the cowshed.

'Well, Mercybright, what do you think of my two
new purchases?' she asked.

'Why not ask Peter and Paul? They're your cowmen.'

'I prefer to ask you. Can't you give me a straight
answer?'

'Well, the roan has got a withered quarter, and I'd

say the black will go the same way. But, of course, if you got the two for next to nothing . . .'

'I paid eighteen guineas! Surely you don't call that next to nothing?'

'No,' he said, 'cheap always comes dear in the end, I reckon.'

'They looked all right when I saw them at Hotcham.'

'You was dazzled by the notion of getting a bargain.'

'So you think they're useless?' she said crossly.

'Not useless exactly,' he said, shrugging. 'They're pretty to look at, the pair of them, and they'll make the shed look a bit more fuller!'

A week later, when she was going to a sale at Ludden, she took Jack with her in the trap. And again in June to another sale at Darry Cross. And then again to a sale of sheep at a farm near Boscott. It was his duty to look at the animals in their pens, mark those he favoured in the catalogue, and nudge her unobtrusively if he thought the bidding went too high. Afterwards, when the sale was over, she would go off to take tea and seedcake with her neighbors, leaving Jack to settle with the agent and find a drover.

'Mercybright will see to it!' she would say, in a voice always just a little louder than was needed. 'Mercybright is acting on my behalf!'

'You should take Peter Luppitt by rights,' he said once, driving home from Darry Cross. 'And Will Gauntlet when you go to Boscott on Friday.'

'Don't you like attending the sales?'

'I like it all right, but Peter Luppitt's your senior cowman, and surely the shepherd should choose his own ewes!'

'I don't trust them. I've known them longer than you have, remember, and I'm sure they would cheat me at every turn.'

She drove a little way in silence, sitting erect, her back very straight, looking too hot in her thick black skirt and jacket, for the day was a close one.

'I trust *you*,' she said abruptly, and, as though seized by embarrassment, she cut with her whip at the brambles growing out from the hedgerow. 'Whose hedges are these? They're a rank disgrace! My new varnishwork is quite scratched to ruins!'

For two weeks in June, the cornfields became a bright acid yellow as the wild mustard bloomed in the sun, the flowers growing up very tall, overshadowing the sickly corn just as the ears were breaking out of their papery sheaths. Then the mustard flowers died and the mauve dog-thistles bloomed in their place, swaying with the corn in the hot July winds, and spreading their strong, sweet, almondlike scent.

'It breaks my heart,' said Joe Stretton, working alongside Jack in the hay-fields. 'Every year the place gets worser. In old Guff's time this farm was a winner, every acre as clean as a bean-row. But what do women know about farming? All they know is eggs and poultry!'

The hay, too, was poor stuff, thin and sour, with a great deal of sorrel and rattle in it, for the meadows were all sadly neglected.

'She grazes heavy all the year round and still expects to make good hay!' said Jonathan Kirby, coming to a halt, and he spat contemptuously, holding up a pitiful wisp on the tines of his hay-fork. 'Look at it!' he said, 'I've seen better stuff poking out of a scarecrow!'

'Have you ever told her?' Jack asked. 'About grazing, I mean?'

'Hah!' Stretton said. 'What good is that? It's like blowing on mustard to make it cool. She don't choose to listen to the likes of us. A farm this size needs twenty men and it had 'em, too, in her father's time, with every man in his proper place and proud to say he came from Brown Elms.'

At the end of August, when the first twenty acres of corn was cut, Miss Philippa herself was there in the field, binding and stooking in the wake of the reaper. Sometimes Nenna was there too. The two sisters worked together. But there was always a clear space around them, for the laborers' womenfolk and children liked to keep their distance if they could.

The thistles in the sheaves were now dry and deadly. The women and children sometimes cried out in pain, stopping to remove the sharp spines from palms and fingers. But Miss Philippa always worked in silence, without even wincing, and frowned severely at Nenna if she grumbled. She thought it beneath her dignity to betray any sign of suffering, and she wished to convey, too, that the thistles were nowhere near so bad as the labourers pretended.

All through harvest, she was about from first light to last, eager and watchful, quick to pounce if the reaping machine missed so much as an inch between swaths, quick to scold if she caught the children nibbling the grains. She would walk the same field again and again, her gaze going hungrily over the corncocks, almost as though she were counting the sheaves.

'But it won't make the crop any bigger or better, will it, now?' Oliver Lacey said to Jack. 'However much she gawples at it!'

And as soon as the last load of barley was carted, safely under thatch in the stackyard, she wanted the first lot of wheat threshed and measured, so that she could take a sample to market at Yelland on Wednesday.

'Aye, that's what she likes!' said Joe Stretton. 'Gadding to market, playing the grand lady farmer! And the way she watches her precious stacks! You'd think she had the bestest corn crops this side of the Luddens!'

But Jack, coming into the barn after the threshing, found Miss Philippa there alone, counting the sacks and biting her lip in open vexation.

'Which field is this from and what is the yield per acre?' she asked him.

'This lot came off the South Wood Field, so it's just about thirteen or fourteen bushels.'

'That's poor, isn't it?'

'It's worse than poor. It's tragical. And, what is more, a lot of that seed is probably mustard. Land like you've got in the South Wood Field would likely give you as much as forty bushels to the acre if only that was in good heart. But you've took too many corn crops off it and you've let the mustard get too strong a hold. Not to mention the docks and thistles.'

'*I* let the mustard get a hold? And what do I pay the men for, I wonder, if not to see the fields are weeded?'

'Did you give orders to hoe the corn?'

'I don't know. I don't remember. Do I have to tell them every single thing? Surely they know when a field wants weeding!'

But the long, hot, anxious days of harvest had tired her, and there was no strength in the angry outburst. Tiredness and disappointment together had brought a hint of tears to her eyes. She looked worn and defeated.

'What must I do, to put the land into good heart?' And she stood over one of the sacks of wheatseed, running the grain through fingers roughened, swollen, torn, after her weeks of labour in the fields. 'When my father took samples of corn to market, the dealers welcomed him with open arms. But now, when I go, I see them sniggering up their sleeves.'

She closed the sack and brushed the chaff-dust from her fingers. She turned to Jack with a look of appeal.

'Tell me what to do and I'll do it,' she said.

'I don't like it!' Stretton shouted. 'I'm the one that ought to be top man here by rights. I've been here the longest. And if I warnt your friend, Jack Mercybright, I'd knock you into that there furrow!'

'Here, Dad, are you going to fight?' Harvey asked. 'Shall I hold your jacket?'

'I ent fighting, you silly fellah. I'm holding a friendly confabulation. So get back to them hosses before I belt you.'

'I get the same wages as you do,' Jack said, 'so how come you call me a top man?'

'More fool you, then, that's what I say. You wouldn't catch *me* working as bailiff just for the buttons. Oh, I know it's *her* that shouts the orders, but they're coming from you in the first place, ent they?

They wouldn't make sense the way they do if they was all her own idea. Well, I don't like it, and I'm telling you outright so's we know where we stand. Now how would you like a chew of tobacco?'

'No, thanks. I'm a smoker, not a chewer.'

'All right,' Stretton said. 'When I've finished chewing you can have my quid to smoke in your pipe.'

By late September most of the stubble grounds were ploughed, and a week or so later the soil was a gentle green all over, where the mustard seed, shed in the harvest, grew apace in the soft moist weather. The ground was then ploughed again and the mustard turned in, a green manure, and then a little later on, the tangled couch-grass was harrowed out, to be burnt at the foot of each field, filling the air with sweet-smelling smoke.

'This is all very fine!' Miss Philippa said, coming to inspect the work in progress. 'I can't afford to bare-fallow so many precious acres all at one and the same time! And all this labour!—Ploughing the same land over and over while other work gets left undone—'

'Get more men. That's the answer.'

'Is that what you're up to? Creating more work for the benefit of your own kind?'

'God creates the work, not me.' Jack said. 'I'm only the go-between. But have a look at this bit of paper. I've wrote down some notes for a cropping rota. I ent much of a hand at writing but I daresay you'll make out what I mean well enough.'

'Rye?' she said, scanning the paper. 'My father never grew rye in his life! And fifty acres of new grass ley! Have you any idea what you're suggesting?'

'Right you are,' Jack said, shrugging. 'You tell me what to do instead and we'll go on the same old way you have done for years, raising rattle and thistle and mustard!'

Miss Philippa turned and walked away, taking the piece of paper with her. She was shut in her office for three mornings running. But the following

week there were two new men employed on the
farm, and a month later, on entering the barn one
afternoon, Jack saw that the grass- and clover-seed
had come, as well as the turnip-seed and rye-seed.
And Miss Philippa was there, checking the items
against her list.

'The clover is all Dutch White,' she said. 'It's
what my father always preferred. The grass is mixed
as you recommended. As to the artificials you asked
for—they are being sent over from Stamley on Monday.'

Now that the evenings were drawing in again, Sunday was a precious day indeed, and he divided it
evenly in two, spending the morning on the garden,
the afternoon on the cottage. He had turned the pigs
into the orchard, to feed on the fallen pears and
apples, and the old horse Shiner, disliking pigs, had
gone to graze in the Long Meadow.

He had dug all his ground and planted a couple
of rows of cabbage. He had cut the hedges and
pruned the fruit trees. Now he was re-laying the
old flagstones that paved the yard between the
two wings of the cottage.

Nenna had brought him an apricot tree, grown
from a stone planted in a pot on her fourteenth
birthday. It was now three years old and twenty-

seven inches tall, and she had planted it under the south wall of the cottage. He did not really want it. He cared nothing for apricots, and there were too many trees in the garden already. But Nenna would not take no for an answer, so there the tree was, and whenever she came she watered it carefully and removed any weeds that grew around it.

'I thought you'd feel you really lived here, if you had a new tree planted in your garden.'

'I *know* I live here,' Jack said. 'I live nowhere else!'

'Jack has no soul,' Bevil said, watching Nenna as she tied the tree to a stake for support. 'At least . . . he hasn't got my poet's soul.'

'No, well, it wouldn't look right on me,' Jack said.

Nenna was kneeling on the grass path, and Bevil put out his hand to help her, smiling at her as he pulled her up. There was great sweetness in the boy's smile sometimes, and today he seemed to be treating the girl with especially tender gallantry.

'A man who jeers at apricot jam is not worth troubling about,' he said, and Nenna laughed, suddenly flinging her arms around him and laying her head against his chest.

'Oh, Bevil! I do love you so! I shall miss you most dreadfully while you're away!'

'Away?' Jack said. 'Why, where you off to?'

'I'm going to London, to spend six months in my uncle's office. He's in law, too, and my father thinks it will be good experience for me.' Bevil touched the girl's hair, smiling at Jack over her head. 'Nenna and I have never been very far apart in our lives before. I rely on you to look after her for me.'

'All right. I shall do my best.'

'Wouldn't it be terrible,' Nenna said, drawing away from Bevil's arms, 'if you met some beautiful woman there and never came back to me at all?'

'Or fell among thieves and was murdered,' he said. 'London is a place for terrible murders, you know.'

'When do you go?' Jack asked.

'Next Saturday. Ten in the morning. I get a train from Kevelport.'

'I shall come and see you off,' Nenna said, 'whether your father likes it or not!'

There followed a week of north-westerly gales, with four dark days when the rain lashed down without pause, turning the ditches into torrents, the fields into marshes. On Friday evening, though the rain had eased off, the gale blew harder than ever, going round a little till it blew straight from the westerly quarter.

Nenna and Bevil were with Jack. They had nowhere else to go, it seemed, for the girl was not welcome at the boy's home, and the boy was not welcome at Brown Elms. So they spent the evening in the cottage, sitting in front of a fire that blazed ferociously, drawn by the wind whirling and thumping in the big chimney.

'I hate this weather!' Nenna said. 'We had an apple tree down in the garden last night. It fell and crushed the old summer-house. It frightens me, when the wind is this fierce.'

'But it's wonderful!' Bevil said. 'It makes me feel very wide awake. It fills me with power and energy. I fancy I must have been born on a night of storm and tempest like this. Just hark at it roaring out there in the orchard! Doesn't it fill you with excitement?

'What a noise of wind in the trees on the hill
In the wild, wild land of Never-Go-Back!
What moonlight and starlight and swift-flying
    clouds!
And, in the day-time, what suns, what suns!

'I shall remember tonight's clean gale when I'm stuck in smoky Cheapside, listening to some old Moneybags discussing how best to do down his partners. I shall write you poems full of nostalgia and send them to you tied up in lawyers' green silk ribbon.'

'I hope you will write me letters too.'

'Of course I shall! Every day, I promise.'

At nine o'clock, Bevil took Nenna home. At half-past nine he was back at the cottage.

'I'm going to The Bay Tree. Are you coming with me?'

'At this time of night? And in this weather?'

'Sylvanus expects me. Angelina, too. It's by way of being a farewell party. Oh, come on, Jack, don't be a spoilsport!'

So Jack went with him, leaning forward against the wind, under a sky where moon and stars looked down now and then between the frayed black clouds rushing eastwards.

Down at Niddup the gale was worse. It screamed upriver for a mile and half with nothing much to break its force. The inn on the bank got the full blast. The tiny place shuddered repeatedly, and all the pewter tankards, hanging in rows along the rafters, swung very gently on their hooks.

'It's a good thing we've got a full house tonight,' said Sylvanus, 'or The Bay Tree would likely get uprooted!'

'I'm the one that's being uprooted,' Bevil said. 'At this same time tomorrow night I shall be in London.'

'Try The Dolphin at Deptford,' Sylvanus said. 'I used to go there when I had a spell on the Thames lighters. It's a good house, The Dolphin.—Poets and painters and all sorts go there.'

'Poets and painters and singers of songs!—I must keep in practice!' Bevil said, and, borrowing the squeezebox from Angelina, the landlord's wife, he played and sang his favourite song:

'Oh, who will grieve for Jimmy Catkin,
Buried with his seven wives?
How many more would lie there with him
If Jimmy had had a cat's nine lives?

'What if each wife had had ten children
And each of them had had ten more?

The Catkin family tree would number
Six thousand, nine hundred, and ninety-four!'

The crowd in the taproom sang the chorus: 'Oh,
iddle-me, tiddle-me, riddle-me-ree!—The Catkins
hang thick on the crack-willow tree!'; and the noise
they made singing together even drowned the noise
of the gale.

Towards midnight, two drovers came in, bringing
with them such a gust of wind that the smoke came
puffing out of the fire-place.

'Ennen's rising fast,' one of the men said to Sylvanus. 'There's folk in the Dip will have two or
three inches in their kitchens by morning.'

'Ah, that's rising like yeast,' said the second man.
'I ent seen such waters in a month of Sundays. And
there's folk upriver that ent been very clever about
it, neither, for there's dead sheep and hen-coops and
privvies and all sorts getting washed down from
Dudnall or somewhere. We seen 'em as we come
across the bridge.'

'Let's go and see!' Bevil suggested, and Stanley
Knarr, the landlord's son, turned at once towards the
door, his pint-pot held high as he pushed his way
through the crowd.

'Who else is coming?' Bevil shouted. 'Reuben?
Jim? Henry Taylor?' He drank the last of the flip
from his mug so that Angelina could fill it again.
'Up to the brim, if you please, Angelina, for this
is the bard's farewell to Ennen! Are you coming,
Jack?'

'Might as well, I suppose,' Jack said. He was feeling just a little drunk. 'I ent seen much of this Ennen
of yours when it's running in one of its famous spates.'

The noise of the water was as loud as though it
came off a weir. Ennen was in full spate indeed,
and, rushing round the circular sweep known locally
as the Dudnall Loop, it hurled itself into the narrow
channel at Niddup with such force that it broke its
banks there and flooded out over the meadows. And

the gale coming up the straight stretch from Egham whipped at the waters as though trying to hurl them back.

There were twenty men crowded together on the bridge. The young ones were singing bawdy songs, but broke off now and then to cheer some dark object as it came rushing down on the foaming torrent.

'What is it, what is it? A Kevelport dumpling, do you think?'

'Maybe it's Dudnall's big bass drum!'

'Here's somebody's dinghy! Whatever's the matter with the folk upriver? Didn't they see this flood a-coming?'

'Watch out, here's an elm! That'll give us a bit of a knock, I reckon.'

There were quite a few tree-trunks coming down-river, and often they got caught up at the bridge, pounding against the cutwater walls until at last, re-leased by a sudden swirl in the water, they found their way through one of the arches.

'Plenty of firewood there!' shouted Stanley. 'Enough to warm The Bay Tree forever!'

'The Bambridge folk'll get most of that,' said an old man standing next to Jack. 'It'll fetch up against the lock at Mastford.'

The water was rising all the time, flowing over the banks at either side and looking, Jack thought, like a great tide of fermenting beer, frothing creamily at the edges as it washed out shallowly over the grass of the big flat meadow known as the ham.

'We ought to start back!' Jack said, shouting into Bevil's ear. 'Otherwise we shall have a wet walk!'

'Not me! Not me!' Bevil answered, waving the tankard in his hand. 'What will the Thames be to me after Ennen?'

'Well, *I'm* going,' Jack said. 'I don't care for get-ting my feet wet.'

He was in the act of turning away when another tree-trunk came down-river and hit the central but-tress like a battering-ram. The whole bridge shud-dered and the tremor lasted a long time. He could feel

it in the brickwork underfoot; he could feel it in the
parapet under his hand: a kind of humming that passed
right through him. So he turned back again and looked
down over the side, and where the cutwater should
have been there was now nothing but foaming water.

'Get off!' he shouted, shoving at Stanley Knarr, beside him. 'For God's sake get off!—The bridge is going!'

But Bevil and Stanley, still singing at the tops of
their voices, merely caught hold of him by the arms
and danced him round a pace or two, trying to lift
him onto the wall.

'We're used to these floods!' Stanley shouted. 'We're
Ennen men born and bred—there's freshets in our
marrow!'

'Get off the bridge! The water's breached us! Can't
you feel it, you stupid fools?'

There came a loud crack and another shock ran
through the brickwork, which opened in fissures at
their feet. And then the bridge was falling away from
underneath them, the stone-built pillars heeling over,
the huge stones toppling one from another as though
they were nothing but great cubes of sugar crumbling
and melting away in the foam. And the noise of it
all—the stone bridge collapsing, the voices screaming
—was lost in the noise of wind and water.

The moment the river closed above him, Jack was
sure it meant his death, for he was half drunk and no
swimmer. But the torrent tossed him about like a cork
and once, by a lucky accident, almost, his left hand
caught hold of a slim willow branch and he was able
to hang on, dinked up and down, up and down, every
moment, sucking in air and water by turns.

Another man's body was swept against him and he
caught it up over his shoulder, his right arm around
it, his fingers entwined in a fold of clothing. He had
no way of telling who it was. He did not even know
if the man was dead or merely unconscious. He could
only hang on, with the extra weight gradually bearing him down, so that grey moonlit water kept breaking in splinters over his head.

Then the willow bough began to bend, letting him down deeper and deeper, until it snapped from its root altogether. His burden was wrenched clean out of his arms and he himself was swept a hundred yards further downstream, to fetch up again among the arched roots of an elm tree, still on the Niddup side of the river.

His rescuers took him back to The Bay Tree. Sylvanus was out, looking for Stanley. Angelina was there alone. She stripped off Jack's clothes, wrapped him in a thick brown blanket, and put him to sit inside the big fire-place. She brought him hot tea with brandy in it and when he had drunk it he sat, half dozing, still with the sick sensation of water washing coldly through him, as though the river had got into his blood.

Once he got up to peer out of the window, and could see the lanterns flickering small and blurred in the distance, all along the course of the river, where rescuers searched for those still lost in the swollen waters. He returned to the fire and after a while fell asleep, sweating inside his thick blanket.

When he awoke grey daylight had come, and three other men sat like himself, hunched in blankets around the inside wall of the fire-place, their heads in their hands. Angelina was sweeping the floor of the tap-room. Sylvanus was bringing more logs for the fire.

'What's the news?' Jack asked.

'They're all accounted for now,' said Sylvanus. 'There's sixteen left alive all told. Twelve of them are at home in their beds. Then there's four of them dead, lying out there on the grass in the garden.' He stood back from the fire and jerked his head towards the window. 'Including our Stanley,' he said in a flat, calm voice, and went to Angelina, who had stopped sweeping and was bent double over her broom.

Jack put on his clothes and went outside. He was met by a cold pale glare of light, for the whole of the ham was flooded now, out as far as the eye could see, and the big sheet of water reflected the cold grey morning sky. The wind still blew strong, and the tarpaulin stack-cloth that covered the bodies was weighted at the edges with big stones. He removed three of these and turned back the stack-cloth, looking at the four dead faces revealed. Stanley Knarr. Jim Fennel. Peter Wyatt. Bevil Ames. The youngest ones. The children of promise. Each one less than half Jack's age.

He covered them up and put back the stones.

'Why?' Miss Philippa said harshly. 'Why should Nenna want to see you? What comfort can you possibly offer?' But, changing her mind, she stepped back further into the passage. 'Very well,' she said. 'You'd better come in. Wipe your feet—the maid has only just swept the carpet.'

She showed him into the front parlour, a room not much used, evidently, for the heat of the fire had drawn out the damp from furniture and curtains, and it hung on the air like winter fog, filling the air with a strong smell of mildew. Nenna sat on the edge of the couch, her hands folded over a letter, her face towards the fire, though quite unwarmed by it, and still as a statue.

'Mercybright has come to see you,' Miss Philippa said, ushering him in. 'He means well, I'm sure, so I hardly liked to turn him away.' She remained standing close by the door.

'I was there when it happened,' Jack said to Nenna. 'I was on the bridge with Bevil and the others. I thought I ought to tell you about it.'

'Why did you let him?' Nenna asked. 'Why did you take him to The Bay Tree at all?' She spoke without moving. She was still staring into the fire. 'Why did you let him go on the bridge?'

Jack was silent, not knowing how to answer. He stood with his fists in the pockets of his jacket, holding it tight around his loins. His clothes were still damp. He shivered inside them.

'Look at that clock!' Nenna said. 'I would just be seeing him onto his train . . . We'd still be talking,

Bevil and his father and his aunt and me, if you hadn't taken him to The Bay Tree.'

'I didn't take him. Going there was his own idea. The Knarrs was giving a sort of a party.'

'Couldn't you have stopped him going on the bridge?'

'It wasn't just him. There was lots of men on it. Twenty of us altogether. How could we know it'd get washed away? Bevil was drunk. He'd been drinking pretty well all the evening. He might've stood a chance, otherwise.'

'Who got him drunk?' Nenna demanded, and turned to him for the first time, her eyes overflowing. 'Who got him drunk if it wasn't you?'

'Don't you blame *me!*' Jack said fiercely. 'Don't you blame *me* for them four boys dead! I ent having that! Oh, no, not me!"

"I *do* blame you!' Nenna said, sobbing. 'Why should all the young ones die and all the old ones be left alive? It's all wrong and I *do* blame you! I *do!* I *do!*'

Jack turned and walked out of the house. Miss Philippa followed him to the back door.

'I told you!' she said. 'I told you it wouldn't do any good—'

But he was walking quickly away, determined to put the farm well behind him. He was chilled to the bone and walked without pause till he came to The Pen and Cob at Bittery, six miles upriver, where nobody knew him.

He awoke with a smirr of small rain tickling his face, and opened his eyes to a sky that moved. He was lying on his back on an old barge, chugging along a narrow canal, with scrub willow trees at either side and yellow leaves drifting into the water.

He got to his feet with some difficulty and limped along the deck to the stern. The bargeman and his wife were strangers to him, but seemed friendly and knew his name.

'What damned canal is this?' he asked them.

'Well, it ent exactly the Grand Union, but it ent

all that bad as canals go. This here's known as the Billerton and Nazel and it links old Ennen up with the Awn.'

'How did I get here?'

'We picked you up at The Burraport Special. Day before yesterday. Half past noonday.'

'What day is it now?'

'Thursday, November the twenty-second,' the bargeman said, filling his pipe, 'in the Year of Grace, eighteen hundred and ninety four, though what bloody grace there might be in it I'd be hard put to say.' He lit his pipe and flicked the match into the water. 'You've been on a blinder, ent you?' he said. 'You don't hardly know if it's Christmas or Easter. You said you wanted to go to Stopford but maybe you've gone and changed your mind?'

'I reckon I have,' Jack said. 'I reckon I ought to get back to Niddup.'

'It'll take you more'n a day or two, butty, but Owner George'll see you right.'

They put him onto the next passing barge, which carried him back to The Burraport Special. From there he travelled on a Kevelport snaker all the way to Hunsey Lock. By Friday night he was back in Niddup, and on Saturday morning he was out in the eighteen acre field at Brown Elms, singling mangolds.

'So you're back, are you, without so much as a word of explanation?' And Miss Philippa stood on the headland behind him, her arms full of teazles and dead ferns, gathered from the banks of the Runkle Brook. 'Did you hear me, man? I asked you a question!'

'Yes, I'm back,' he said. 'Or someone like me.'

'And what explanation have you got to offer?'

'No explanation. I'm just back, that's all.' And he worked on without stopping. 'Seems I've got a lot to catch up on.'

'Do you realize how long you've been away? You've been missing from work for a whole week! And then you come sneaking back here without a word, hoping,

I suppose, that your absence hadn't even been noticed.'

'I surely ent as daft as that.'

'And what makes you think your job is still open? Doesn't it occur to you that you may very likely have been replaced?'

'If I'd been replaced, these here roots should ought to've been singled, but they ent been, have they, so just leave me be to get on with the job.'

'Just look at you!' she said, disgusted. 'Dirty! Unshaven! Your clothes all covered in alehouse filth—'

'Do I smell?' he asked.

'Yes, you smell like a pig in its muck!' she said.

'Keep away from me, then, and that way you won't suffer nothing.'

He went on steadily down the row, aware of the field stretching below him, so many steep wet muddy acres still to be hoed.

'Our young Miss Nenna's gone away,' Oliver Lacey said to Jack. 'She's gone to stay with a school-friend of hers somewhere up near Brummagem. She went straight after the young man's funeral.'

'It's a pity Miss Philippa don't go too,' Peter Luppitt said, swearing, 'instead of always treading on our tails the way she does.'

'Who'd pay our wages then?' said his brother.

'Yes, it's nice to be Jack, coming and going as cool as you please, taking a holiday when he's a mind to and nobody saying so much as an echo. How do you manage it, Jack, old butty? How does it come that you and Miss Philippa's such close friends?'

Jack made no answer. He walked away. He was still in a mood when too much talk made him impatient. All he wanted was to be left alone.

Although he would not allow Nenna to blame him for Bevil's death, he did blame himself, because now, whenever he remembered the man he had held in his arms in the water, it seemed to him it must have been Bevil.

He saw the boy's face all too plainly: the eyes closed and the pale lashes glistening wetly; the short upper lip drawn back a little, as though in a cry; the fair hair streaming out in the water. And as he remembered, his muscles would clench throughout his body as though now, if only he were given the chance again, he could find the strength to hold on, to bear the man up with him out of the torrent. As though *now* his determination would never fail.

At other times he faced the matter with more common sense; knew he could never have saved the man in his arms; felt sure, even, that the man had been dead already. But Bevil haunted him nevertheless. It was something he had to wrestle with. He kept himself busy to drive away the phantoms.

He was working now on the south wall of the cottage. He had taken the old filling out of the panels, tarred the inner sides of the timbers, and was now putting in the new wattlework; four round hazel rods slotting upright into each panel, then the split rods in a close weave across. It was work he enjoyed. He

338

was almost happy. The old cottage was gradually taking its proper shape again.

The day was a mild one at the end of November, and the yellow leaves, quitting the plum trees in the hedgerow behind him, were drifting down to brighten the ground throughout the garden. Two or three blackbirds were busy there, turning the leaves in search of grubs, and under the hedge a thrush was hammering a snail on a stone.

'Poor snail,' a voice said sadly, and Jack, looking round, found Nenna behind him. 'How they must wish there were no such things as stones!"

For a moment her face remained averted. She was watching the thrush. But then she looked at him directly, studying him with thought-filled eyes, as though seeking something in his expression, or reminding herself of something forgotten.

Jack turned back to his work on the panel. He inserted a round rod into its hole in the beam above and bent it until it slotted into the groove below. He stopped and picked up a handful of split rods.

'What do you want with me?' he asked. 'I'd have thought you'd said all you had to say to me when I saw you the last time.'

'I said too much. I didn't mean it. I'm sorry if I hurt you.'

'Ay? So you're sorry. And now you've got that off your conscience nicely perhaps you'll go away and leave me alone.'

'Is that what you want? Just to be left alone always?'

'Yes,' he said. 'I like it that way. It means less trouble.'

'But you must want company sometimes.'

'When I do, I go out and look for it, don't I?'

'At The Bay Tree, you mean, or some other village public?'

'That's right. Why not? You walk in . . . you meet a few folk and chat with them . . . and when you've had enough you walk out again with no offence on either side.'

'And is that all you ever want from life?'

'It's quite enough, just to keep me going. I'm past the age of worrying overmuch about anything.'

'You talk as though you were an old man.'

'I *am* an old man! You said so yourself.' And he rounded on her. 'It's what you called me, don't you remember?—The young ones all drowned. The old ones left alive.—That's what you said if I ent much mistaken.'

Meeting his gaze, her eyes were suddenly filled with tears, and he relented. She was too much a child to be punished for words spoken at such a time.

'Ah, never mind!' he said roughly. 'Never mind what you said! It was true, anyway, every word.' He took a split rod out of the bundle and went on working, weaving it in between the uprights. 'I'm a man of thirty-seven with a gammy leg and more than half his life behind me. Of course you'd gladly swap me for Bevil, just as the Knarrs would swap me for Stanley. The trouble is, life ent arranged so's we can make bargains over this and that, and I can't pretend I wish myself dead, poor specimen though I may be.'

There was no answer, and when he turned round he found he was talking to himself. Nenna had gone. His only companion was a cock blackbird still pecking about among the yellowing leaves.

She was back, however, the following Sunday, feeding crusts of bread to Shiner and hanging a necklace of bryony berries round his rough neck.

Jack was at the top of his ladder, up against the south wall, and saw her making a fuss of the horse in the orchard. He felt impatient, wishing she would keep away. He had nothing against her—she was just a child—but her presence there was an irritation; he felt she was making some claim upon him; asking for comfort he could not give. He dipped his trowel into his bucket and slapped the wet clay onto the wattle.

A little while later, going to the pump for more water, he found her looking at the old stone trough, where Bevil had scratched her initials and his own.

'Why do you come,' he asked, wearily, 'when everything here is bound to make you sad?'

'I don't know . . . I can't help it, somehow . . . I suppose, when sadness is all you've got left in the world, it becomes almost precious in a way.'

'That's morbid,' he said. 'It ent healthy.'

'I get lonely at home. I get so tired of listening to Philippa grumbling all the time. And *I* can't go to The Bay Tree, can I?'

'You ought to have friends. Young folk of your own age. Your own sort, not people like me. Miss Philippa ought to see about it.'

'We never have company up at the house, except John Tuller of Maryhope, and the old Barton ladies now and then. Philippa doesn't much care for having people visit the house. Anyway, I like coming here, because I can talk to you about Bevil.'

'What is there to say?'

'I don't know—just things,' she said. 'I think of those evenings we had round your fire and all the talk we had together . . . Bevil liked you. It makes a link. And then I don't feel quite so lonely.'

'I don't think it's right, all the same. You're a lot too young to dwell on the past.'

'I shall never marry, if that's what you're thinking.'

'Yes, you will,' he said, gently. 'One day you will. You mark my words. You'll meet some young chap and learn to love him and then you'll get married and raise a few children. All in good time. You'll see.'

'No,' she said, shaking her head. 'I shall never marry.'

'All right, have it your own way, but I must get a move on before my clay dries out again.'

'Do you mind if I stay and watch you?'

'Please yourself. It's no odds to me. After all, you used to come to this old cottage long before I happened along, so what right have I to turn you off?'

'Is there anything I can do?'

'Ah. Maybe there is. You can chop up that straw on the block there. Little bits, about half an inch long. But mind you don't go chopping your fingers. I sharpened that hatchet only this morning.'

She came often after that, and one Sunday she brought him the deeds of the cottage to look at, having taken them secretly out of the safe in Miss Philippa's office. Jack had difficulty in reading the old, faded, elaborate writing. Nenna had to read it to him.

'It was built in sixteen hundred and one, by a man named Thomas Benjamin Hayward, and was known in those days as New Farm, Upper Runkle, near the township of Niddup-on-Ennen. The farm was then about two hundred acres. Mr Thomas Hayward is described as a yeoman, and the house is described as a "handsome new dwelling house of two bays with a fifteen foot outshot standing at the south western boundary of the holding."'

'So it is handsome,' Jack said. 'It's a lot more handsome than the big new house you live in up there.'

'Three hundred years,' Nenna said, looking up at the cottage. 'I wonder what people were like then.'

'Not all that different, I shouldn't think. What's three hundred years under the sun?—Nothing much more than a snap of your fingers. And if you picture six old grannies, hand in hand across the years, it brings it all up pretty well as close as close, I reckon.'

'Why grannies? What about all the grandfathers?'

'Oh, they will have played their part, I daresay. But in my particular bit of experience, it was always the grannies that mattered most. My parents died when I was a babby. She was only a little hob of a woman, and us five boys was great big slummocking ruffians nearly twice her size, but if we done wrong, which happened often one way and another, she would put on a pair of heavy hobnailed boots and kick us round the kitchen till we howled for mercy.'

'Rough measures,' Nenna said.

'They worked well enough. We had great respect for my grannie's boots, specially when her feet was in them.'

'But wasn't there any tenderness at all?'

'No. None. Just a feeling that we mattered, that's all. And I never had the feeling again, not after she'd gone.'

'What happened to her?'

'She died when I was about eleven. My brothers went off—emigrated—and I was put in an orphanage. I didn't care for it over much. I ran away after three months or so.'

'And you've been on the move ever since?'

'I suppose I have. It must've got to be a habit.'

'Do you like the life of a wanderer?'

'I dunno that I like it exactly. I'm always hoping for a good place to settle. The trouble is, I seem to fall out with folk, somehow, after I've been with them for a while.'

'You're quarrelsome, then?'

'No, not me,' he said, straight-faced. 'It's the other folk that are quarrelsome. Never me.'

Just before Christmas, Jack was sent to Maryhope Farm to fetch a number of dressed geese, and when he returned to Brown Elms, Nenna came out to help him carry them into the dairy, where Miss Philippa received them, pinching each one and weighing it carefully before laying it out on the slab. It was the custom at Brown Elms that each man employed there should be given a goose for Christmas.

'But why buy from Maryhope?' Jack asked. 'Why not raise your own here?'

'I don't have much luck with geese,' Miss Philippa said, 'not since my father died, that is.'

'Then why not give them a good fat chicken instead? You've enough of *them* about the place.'

'In my father's time, it was always a goose,' Miss Philippa said, rather stiffly. 'The men would not like it if the custom were changed after all these years.'

Jack turned away with a little smile. He knew how the men regarded the custom. 'A Maryhope goose,' he had heard them say, 'is a loud cackle with feathers on it!' John Tuller's produce was poor stuff always.

'Well, no goose for me if you please,' he said. 'It would be a waste, me being alone.'

Miss Philippa, in spectacles, was frowning at the figures on the spring balance. She made a note on the list in her hand.

'I didn't order a goose for you, Mercybright, as it so happens. You couldn't easily cook it on your open fire, could you? You will therefore have your Christmas dinner here with us this year.'

'Here?' he repeated, stopping dead on his way to the door.

'That's right. At twelve o'clock precisely. I've spoken to Cook and it's all arranged.'

Jack was astonished. He hardly knew how to answer. And, looking at Nenna, he saw that she was just as astonished as he was.

'Well, I dunno,' he said, awkwardly. 'Joe Stretton has asked me up to his place—'

'Oh, do come to us!' Nenna said. 'Joe Stretton won't mind. He's got his children *and* his sister's family, whereas Philippa and I are all alone. Do come to us, Jack, I beg of you!'

Nenna's tone was warm and excited, and Miss Philippa, turning, treated her to a long, hard, considering stare, over the rims of her spectacles. She seemed to be thinking very deeply. It was fully a minute before she spoke.

'Twelve o'clock sharp,' she said to Jack. 'We have it early so that Cook can get home to her own dinner.'

'Ah,' Jack said. 'Right you are, then. Twelve o'clock, like you say.'

But outside the dairy, fetching more geese from

the cart in the yard, he wished he had voiced his refusal more firmly. He was not happy about the invitation. He would just as soon have gone to Joe Stretton's.

'At the farm?' Joe said. 'With the Missus and young Miss Nenna? Hell's bells, whatever next! You'll soon be wearing little kid gloves and walking about with a smart Malacca!'

'I'll punch your head in a minute,' Jack said.

'At least you'll put on your grey frock coat? I shall take it amiss if you let the side down by not dressing proper.'

'Shut your rattle and pass that besom.'

'You must mind and take all the condiments with your meat, you know, and not make a noise when you blow on your pudding. Ah, and be sure to say, "Pardon!" after belching or they'll likely think you ent got no manners.'

'Are you mucking out here or resting your shovel?'

'I'm giving you a word of advice.'

'It's a hell of a long word, ent it?'

'Knaves on the raight and forks on the left, unless you happen to be left-handed, of course, in which event the case is altered. Then there's the matter of saying grace . . . always speak through your nose and make it snappy or the apple sauce gets tired of waiting.'

Still leaning on his shovel, Stretton watched Jack sweeping out the piggery.

'I wonder what it is you've got about you that makes the two misses single you out from all us other manly chaps?'

'Whatever it is, I'd just as soon I hadn't got it.'

'And shall you be here to milk a cow or two on Christmas morning, the same as us more common mortals?'

'I needn't do much to do a whole lot more than you,' Jack said, 'if your labours here is anything to go by.'

Just before twelve on Christmas Day, in his best cap and suit of black serge, with a collar and neck-tie bought on purpose in the village shop, he walked up the orchard and fields to the farmhouse. His boots were polished; his face clean-shaven; his hair was slicked down with a little of Shiner's embroca-tion; and he had a white handkerchief in his pocket. But otherwise, he said to himself, he was Jack Mercy-bright just the same.

The house looked as dark and gloomy as ever, the blinds pulled down in the upper windows, the curtains half drawn in the lower ones. The only brightness showed at the back: a red glow in the window of the kitchen, where the cook, Mrs Miggs, was busy at her stove.

He was crossing the yard when Nenna darted out of one of the buildings and hurried to meet him. She looked distressed and very angry.

'What's up?' he asked. 'Didn't Father Christmas fill your stocking?'

'Come with me and I'll show you!' she said.

He followed her past the house door, into the long open passage that ran between wash-house and dairy, and along to the room that was known as the office. There, the desk was covered with a chequered cloth, and a dinner-place was laid for one, with knife, fork, and spoon, a mug and a beer-jug, and a white linen napkin in a ring.

'This is where you're to have your dinner!' Nenna said, striking the desk with both her fists. 'Mrs Miggs has just laid it under Philippa's orders. And *I* thought she meant you to have it with us!'

Jack stood staring at the blue and white cloth, crisply starched and beautifully ironed, and the sil-ver salt-cellar, beautifully polished.

'At least she ent put me to eat with the pigs!'

'I wouldn't stay if I were you,' Nenna said. 'I'd just walk out and leave it be! You needn't think I shouldn't understand. I should feel exactly the same as you do.'

Jack considered doing just that. Then he shook

his head. Underneath, he was very angry. It was just the kind of position he hated. But it was too late for withdrawal now, and he blamed himself for his own unwisdom.

'I reckon maybe I'd better stay.'

'Then I'll eat here too. Oh, yes, I shall! I've made up my mind! I'll get my things and ask Cook to serve mine out here with you.'

'No,' he said. 'It'll only make trouble all around. I don't want trouble. I only want to be left in peace.'

Nenna's face was a bright scarlet, her dark eyes blazing, looking into his. He had never before seen her so angry.

'Very well,' she said. 'If that's how you want it. But I don't know how I shall get through dinner with Philippa now. I'm sure I shall never be able to speak to her from start to finish!'

'She means well enough. It was you and me that got things wrong. Now get back indoors in the warm before you catch your death of cold. Tell Mrs Miggs I'm ready and waiting.'

When Nenna had gone he hung up his cap and sat down, and a moment later Mrs Miggs came in with his dinner.

'Smells good,' he said, as she put the plate in front of him. 'And I see it's done nice and crisp and brown on the outside. I like a bit of nice crisp brown skin.' He spoke up loudly, for Mrs Miggs was very deaf.

'I've gave you a leg, Mr Mercybright, and the first tasty bits off the breast, too.'

'Shall I be able to eat all this great lot here, d'you suppose?'

'Of course you will!' And she set another dish on one side, covered over to keep it warm. 'That's your plum-pudding, Mr Mercybright.—Go easy as you eat it 'cos most of the silver threepenny bits is in that portion I cut for you.'

Left alone, he tucked his napkin into his waistcoat and began eating his Christmas dinner, staring at the old, faded, mould-freckled field-map hanging up on the wall before him. He ate quickly, so that he should be done with it and gone from the place as soon as might be, and when he had finished his plum-pudding, he left the four silver threepenny bits shining along the edge of his plate.

On leaving the farm he went for a long brisk walk across country, to settle his stomach, unaccustomed to the rich food. There was a touch of frost that day; the ground was crusty underfoot; the air faintly foggy, blurring the landscape; and, walking about for two hours, he had this grey, unlit world to himself entirely.

He went home to the cottage and stirred his fire to life on the hearth. He set up a rough trestle work-bench before it and began making frames and casements for the windows.

His work on the cottage was now a quiet passion. Every penny saved from his wages went to buy lime and tar and lead sheeting; carpenter's tools, nails, and oak planking. He was always on the alert for bargains. When an old barn was pulled down at Hotcham, he got the beams and boards and tiles for a few shillings. When a greenhouse fell down at the vicarage in Niddup, he got the glass for a few pence.

The tiles went to roof the cartshed and toolshed and the lean-to. The glass he cut into small panes and joined together with strips of lead for his casements. And the old oaken beams and boards were just what he needed for rebuilding the steep staircase, rising in a curve behind the fire-place.

'You're good at carpentry,' Nenna said, watching one day as he screwed a casement into place.

'Not bad, I suppose . . . I worked for a year or two with a carpenter, once, a long time ago, when I was a youngster.'

'Is there anything you have *not* done?'

'Well, I've never sailed the Arctic in search of whales . . . Nor I never played in a brass band . . .'

'But you've been a thatcher . . . soldier . . . a black-smith, once, I remember you told me . . . and a miner in the Forest of Dean . . .'

'Jack of all trades and master of none, that's me to a shaving, ent it?' he said.

'Didn't you ever have any ambition?'

'Ambition? Yes. When I was a boy I wanted to drive the Royal Mail from Brummagem to London.'

'I was being serious,' Nenna said.

'So was I serious. I saw myself in a curly-brimmed hat and a coat with five or six shoulder-capes on it, sitting up on the box as large as life, flipping away at six black horses, It grieved me sorely, I can tell you, when they took that there mail coach off the road.'

'But didn't you ever want to *do* something with your life?'

'Just live it, that's all.'

He was trying the casement, swinging it to and fro on its hinges. He glanced at her and saw exasperation in her face.

'You vex me!' she said. 'You're too good a man to be just a labourer on the land.'

'The land needs good men. Where should we be if they was all bad ones?'

'You could be a farm bailiff if you wanted to be.'

'I was one, once, on a big estate farm up near Kitchinghampton, but I didn't care for it over much. I was either sitting at a desk all day long or riding about on the back of a horse, and I'm too bony about the rump to spend so much time in a chair or a sad-dle.'

'You ought to be bailiff here by rights, with Philippa using you as she does. You could be, I'm sure, if you wanted it.'

'I *don't* want it,' he said firmly. 'I better prefer to stop as I am. So don't go putting no hints about on my behalf, or there'll be ructions, just you mark me!'

Sometimes in the evenings, especially as the days lengthened and spring was in the offing, the other men would stroll down to Jack's cottage to see how the work was going on. They were interested in it. They were al-

ways offering their advice. And one April evening he
had three of them there at one time: Joe Stretton,
Percy Rugg, and the shepherd, William Gauntlet,
whose flock was in the Low End pasture, just a field
away to the east of the cottage.

'If I was you,' said Percy Rugg, watching Jack as he
mixed his whitewash in a bucket: 'if I was you I'd
give it a couple of dips of the blue-bag.'

'I shall when I get to the last coat or two, but that
won't be for a long while yet.'

'How many coats do you aim putting on, then,
Jack?'

'As many as I've got time for, I reckon, and maybe
a few more extra, too, on those walls that get the worst
of the weather.'

'I'd say you was doing a good job,' said William
Gauntlet, 'though I wouldn't have done them panels
with clay, myself. I'd have filled 'em up with good
brick nogging.'

'I ent got the money for bricks,' Jack said. 'The clay
costs me nothing but the labour of digging it out of the
ground.'

'It's a nice little cottage now you're getting it
patched up a bit,' said Joe Stretton. 'You wouldn't care
to swap with me for mine, would you? No? Ah, well!
I always knew you was a mean sort of bastard the moment I clapped eyes on you down the fletchers.'

'This here chimney,' said William Gauntlet, prodding it with his long stick, 'ent you going to whitewash
that?'

'No, I judge it's better left as it is. The bricks is a
nice warm shade of red, and the fire would be sure to
discolour it if it was whitewashed.'

'Ah. Well. If you say so, of course. But I wouldn't
have left it bare, myself.'

'I see you got your taters heled in already, Jack,'
said Percy. 'A bit early for that, ent it?'

'A lot too early,' Gauntlet said. 'Taters go in on
Good Friday. Anyone will tell you that. I wouldn't
never dream of putting them in no earlier, myself.'

A pony and trap came up the road from Niddup,

with Miss Philippa driving and Nenna sitting up beside her. At sight of the men gathered together outside the cottage, Miss Philippa stopped and spoke to them in her loud clear voice.

'I see you're admiring Mercybright's labours. I think you'll agree that it's really very commendable indeed. It might even inspire you other men to make more effort in keeping your own cottages in better order.'

The three men said nothing. They put on the blank, absent-minded expression they habitually wore in Miss Philippa's presence. Stretton chewed his quid of tobacco. Gauntlet picked at the mud on his sleeve.

'If there's anything you want, Mercybright, you know you have only to ask,' she said. 'I always believe in helping those that are obviously willing to help themselves.'

She drove off, and Nenna, looking back over her shoulder, gave Jack a friendly salute, secretly, while her sister looked elsewhere. The men watched the trap for a little while as it drove round the bend embracing the Low End pasture. It was half visible above the hedgerow. Then it vanished over the rise.

'Lumme!' said Percy. 'It's well to be Jack, ent it, eh?' And, doing his best to mimic Miss Philippa's ringing tones: 'Anything you fancy, Mercybright, and I'll have it brung you on a silver platter!'

'She says things different,' Jack said, 'when she ent got an audience listening in.'

'There's only your word for that, though, ent there?'

'It's up to *her* to keep the farm cottages in repair, not up to us!' said Joe Stretton. 'And it's people like Jack here that makes it more harder for the rest of us, ent it? It's all right for him! He's got nothing else to do but slave his guts out all the time but if she thinks I'm going to do the same for that rotten pig-sty me and my kids've got to live in she's got another think coming!'

'All the same, I reckon he's done a good job on this cottage, give him his due,' said Percy Rugg. 'But it don't seem all that likely to me, somehow, that a man should go to all this trouble just for hisself alone, like, does it? So when are you thinking of getting married, Jack?'

'I'm not thinking about it at all,' Jack said.

'What, not ever?' Stretton asked.

'No. Not ever. Neither now nor never after.'

'Laws, somebody's in for a disappointment, then, poor soul, ent she?'

'Is she?' Jack said. 'And who's that?'

'Laws!' Percy said, opening his eyes very wide. 'D'you mean there's more than one likely hopeful dangling for you?'

'The trouble with you two,' Jack said, 'you both talk too much damned blasted rubbish.'

'That's right, so they do!' said William Gauntlet. 'I wouldn't listen to them, myself. They need a few knots tying in their tongues.'

One afternoon when the men had just come in from the fields and were unyoking their teams in the yard, Nenna came to the door of the cheeseroom and called for someone to go and raise the old heavy press, which had fallen over on its side. Jack pretended not to hear her; he was busy removing Spangler's harness; Martin Mossmore answered the call.

A day or two later, Nenna wanted help in the washhouse, where a jackdaw's nest was blocking the chimney. Jack ignored her yet again and Charlie Foster went instead.

'Are you avoiding me?' Nenna asked, seeking him out when he was alone in the office one morning. 'You always used to be so helpful. What have I done that you should turn your back on me whenever there's something wanting doing?'

'You ent done nothing. It's just that I reckon it's wiser, that's all. You know what the men are like here—always ready with their smart remarks.'

'What remarks? Because you and I are friends, you mean?'

'That's right. They've got runaway tongues, the lot

of them, and they're deadly clever at ferreting out things that ent even there.'

'What do I care for their stupid gossip?' she said, scoffing. 'It's nothing to me! Not so much as a split pea!'

And, as though to prove it, she called on him at home that evening.

He was in the garden, earthing up his early potatoes, and when he took a rest at the end of the row, he saw her coming slowly down the orchard, carrying something in her arms. He went to meet her and found she was bringing an old Windsor chair.

'It's for you,' she said. 'Philippa threw it out weeks ago, just because two slats are broken. I thought you might mend it.'

'I could, I daresay. But I don't want you bringing me things from out of the farmhouse. I'd just as soon not be beholden.'

'This chair has been out in all weathers. It would only rot away in the end. Just look at the state it's in already—there's scarcely a scrap of varnish left on it.'

'All right,' he said, and took it from her. 'But no more presents after this, remember.'

He repaired the chair a day or two later and rubbed it down with glass-paper. He stained it dark with permanganate of potash and polished it with best brown boot-polish warmed at the fire. It was now a fine old handsome chair, and Nenna made him a flat cushion, with tapes for tying it to the slats at the back.

'There!' she said, setting the chair at a little angle beside the fire-place. 'Now you'll have somewhere comfortable to sit when you want to smoke your pipe in the evenings.'

'Yes. The place is getting to look quite homely.'

'With just one chair?' she said, laughing, and glanced about at the brick floor, which, although scrubbed and reddled, was still quite bare. 'You need a few mats about the place to make it warmer. You need a table and cupboards and then some pegs to hang your coats on—'

'Yes, well, all in good time, I dare say. Rome

warnt built in a day, you know. And don't go bring-ing me things from the house or your sister will say I'm preying on you to my own advantage.'

'You don't like Philippa, do you?'

'Not much,' he said, 'though I sometimes feel sorry for her, in a way.'

'She wouldn't care for that, your feeling sorry for her. That would be a blow to her pride indeed.'

'I shan't tell her. Nor will you. So she ent likely ever to know it.'

Every evening now, while the daylight lasted, he worked on the outside walls of the house, adding coat upon coat of lime wash to the clay-filled panels. Then, after dark, he worked indoors by firelight and lamp-light: plastering the inner sides of the panels; re-newing pegs in the beams where needed; laying new floorboards in the upper rooms. And sometimes, as a change, he made furniture for the kitchen.

'I suppose you were once a joiner, too, as well as a carpenter?' Nenna said, holding the lamp for him one evening.

'No, I'm no joiner, and anyone looking at this here table would pretty soon know it, too,' he said.

'Why, what's wrong with it, I'd like to know?'

'Well, the timber's good, so it looks a lot better than the work that's in it, and a bit of polish will do the rest. Anyway, it's good enough for the likes of me to eat his dinner off of, ent it?'

While he was working, a rat ran across the kitchen floor and passed right over Nenna's foot. She gave a loud scream and almost dropped the lamp she was holding. It made Jack jump, and his chisel slipped, cut-ting the palm of his left hand. The rat ran out through the open doorway; Jack gave chase and cornered it as it tried to run up the side of the cottage; he killed it with his hammer and threw it over into the pig-run.

By the time he returned, the cut in his hand was bleeding badly, and Nenna turned away from it with a shudder. The sight of blood always made her feel faint. But still she insisted on washing it for him and tying it up with a handkerchief.

'You're always in the wars,' she said to him. 'You're always doing yourself some kind of damage.'

'I must be clumsy, then, I suppose.'

'I'm sorry I screamed, but I hate rats.'

'There were dozens here when I first came. They used to run over me while I slept. But they've mostly disappeared since I started cleaning the old place up and generally creating a big disturbance. That one tonight was the first I've seen in more'n a twelve-month.'

He cleaned the rat's blood from the head of his hammer, and took the chisel in his bandaged hand. He looked across at Nenna, who was casting around with the lamp before her, still nervously scanning the floor.

'I never used to trouble about the rats before,' he said, "but they're going to notice a big difference now I'm a chap with a chair and a table.'

Spring that year was soft, warm, and damp. The new leys grew apace, and the meadows, under improved management, were lush with broad-bladed grass and clover. Summer came in full of promise and mowing started earlier than usual, but the year turned out to be one of exceptional thunderstorms, so that in the end haymaking durdled on and on until long after the cuckoo had flown.

'Is it wise to cut?' Miss Philippa would ask, waylaying Jack as he entered a meadow. 'There's another storm threatening, I'm almost sure.'

'I think cut, storm or no storm. Better to have it in the swath, getting wet, than beaten down so's we can't cut it.'

'I suppose so,' she would say, frowning. 'Yes. Yes. I suppose so.'

She was on the go all through haymaking, out at all hours, working in a fever; fretting at every slightest delay; scolding Nenna if she came late into the hayfield.

'The way she goes on,' Joe Stretton muttered to Jack, 'you'd think she ate hay for every meal.'

'Maybe she does,' said Peter Luppitt, overhearing. 'A nag always likes a fat hay-bag.'

The three of them were in Longsides Meadow, at work with their scythes, cutting a pathway from the gateway round, so that Jack could get in with the reaping machine. In the parallel meadow, known as Horner's, the hay was already cut and made and the rest of the men, with their wives and children, were hurrying to get it safely cocked before the next storm broke and descended. Miss Philippa was with them and her voice could be heard even at that distance, berating little Archie Gauntlet because he had broken a tooth in his hay-rake.

In the middle of the afternoon, the reaping machine seized up, for the toughest grasses had wound themselves round the end of the axle that drove the blades. Jack got down, took a few tools out of the toolbox, and went to put the matter right. He was bending over the old machine when lightning flashed in the dark southern sky, followed at once by a crack of thunder, and big raindrops came slopping down. Stretton and Luppitt went at once to push their scythes in under the hedgerow. Then they ran for shelter in the old milking-shed at the top end of Horner's.

'Come on, Jack!' Stretton called in his great bull-like voice. 'It's going to be a real drencher!'

Jack dropped his spanners and hammer on the ground and followed Stretton to the shed, where all the haymakers were already gathered, packed close together at one end to avoid a leak in the roof at the other.

'We've finished our lot,' Archie Gauntlet said to Jack, and pointed out at the rows of haycocks ranged along Horner's Meadow. 'Just about in the nick of time, warnt it?'

'My bonnet's out there,' said his sister, Phoebe, with great sadness. 'It fell off when I started running.'

And she hid her face in her mother's apron as lightning again lit the sky and thunder splintered overhead. As the thunder quietened, the white rain fell faster, blanching across the green landscape and filling the air with a loud angry swish that seemed to foretell the end of the world.

It was all over in a few minutes. Then the sun came out again. Phoebe was running to retrieve her wet bonnet and the rest of the haymakers were trooping through the open gateway into Longsides Meadow. And the smell of drenched hay, steaming hotly, was now so sweet that it made a man giddy, Peter Luppitt said.

Jack went back to the reaping machine. He saw that all was not as it should be. Three of the blades were badly buckled; twisted into crazy curves until they were almost touching each other. The tools he had left in a heap were now scattered, the two spanners quite three yards apart, the hammer under the machine itself. He smelt burning and then became aware that the ground was smoking all around him, where the lightning had gone through the wet grass.

'Christ!' said Joe Stretton, just behind him. 'It's a lucky thing you came when I called you or you'd be a goner by now, sure as fate!'

"Ah,' Jack said, and stooped to pick up the long-handled hammer, the head of which was still warm. 'Would you believe it! It's a lucky thing, like you say.'

He went to the mare to comfort her, for her ears were back and her eyes rolling, and she was covered in a froth of sweat. She would not be fit for more work that day. She was scouring badly and her legs would only just support her.

The haymakers were gathering round the reaper, some of them bravely touching the blades, others keeping their hands in their pockets, safely. There was a buzz of excitement among them. They looked at Jack as though he had suddenly sprouted wings.

'You should've covered the machine over,' said Joe Stretton. 'That's asking for trouble, that is, with them blades there shining so silver bright.'

'I reckon I should've,' Jack agreed, 'but I never brought no canvas with me.'

He undid the traces and let the swingletree fall to the ground. He went again to Dinkymay's head. He was still trying to comfort her, speaking to her in a quiet voice, when Miss Philippa came along with Nenna and pushed a way through the little crowd. Nenna looked at the twisted blades of the reaper and touched one gingerly with the tips of her fingers. She looked at Jack with incredulous eyes.

'You might have been killed,' she said, shocked.

'He would've been, too,' Stretton said, 'if it hadn't been for me calling him to come away when I did.'

'Oh, really, this is too bad!' Miss Philippa said, seeing the damage done to the reaper. 'Everything seems to be against us this summer. We shall never be done with haymaking at this rate. How long will it take to repair, do you think?'

'I dunno,' Jack said. 'If we get it down to the forge right away, Tom Andrews might have it done by morning. It all depends how busy he is.'

'See to it, then, will you?' she said. 'Get Andrews to hurry. Tell him we're desperate.'

'That's the penalty,' Stretton said, 'of only having one old reaper!'

Miss Philippa pretended not to hear him.

'Meanwhile, Mercybright, set the men to mow here by hand.'

'Right,' Jack said, but he made no immediate move to obey, and Miss Philippa, in the act of walking away, stopped and looked back.

'Well, man, where's the point in delaying the matter? Why are you making a fuss of that mare?'

'I'm getting her home in a minute or two. She's in a pretty bad state of nerves. But it's no good trying to chivvy her up.'

'Don't talk such nonsense! We've wasted enough time here already. You can use that mare for getting the reaper down to the village.'

'Not Dinkymay. She needs rest and quiet. She needs a bit of coddling up. She came a lot nearer to death than I did.'

Miss Philippa's lips were pressed tight together, and her eyes glittered, but, knowing he would not give way before her, she thought it best to argue no further. Instead, she gave vent to her temper by sneering at him.

'You're making a great deal of capital out of this, I must say! You and all your fellows here! Perhaps you would like me to declare a half holiday all round? But surely there's nothing so very extraordinary about a bolt of lightning, is there?'

She walked away, and Joe Stretton, in huge delight, treated Jack to a powerful shove.

'So that's put you in your proper place for once and no error! It's no good you thinking you're something special just 'cos you had such a near miss. Oh dear me no! No lections of that! It's as common as pass-the-jug-round-and-find-it-empty. Now if you'd been *struck*, that'd be different. The parson would've preached a special sermon over your poor dead remains and the details would all've been put on your tombstone.'

'I'd sooner be a live Nobody than a dead Somebody,' Jack said, and led the quivering Dinkymay slowly homewards.

They were playing catch with the weather right onto the end of July, but the hay was all got in at last and was all well made. Only one stack, up in the meadow at Far Fetch, had to be opened and dried out because of heating.

'Well, we shan't have to buy hay from Spouts next winter, shall we?' Peter Luppitt said to his brother, making sure Miss Philippa heard him. 'Nor shall we have our cattle turning up their noses at the home-grown stuff as they have done in years gone by, poor souls.'

The storms continued into August, and some of the corn in the upper fields was laid low under the onslaught. Miss Philippa fretted worse than ever. She was always calling Jack's attention to some new examples of the weather's depredations. She behaved almost as if he were to blame.

'Just look at this!' she said, taking him into a field of twenty-seven acres known as Long Pitch, under Tootle Barrow. 'Just look what has happened here overnight!'

For the hot boisterous wind, blowing in at the south east corner, had carved a long corridor through the oats, all the way down beside the hedgerow.

'Yes, I noticed it this morning, first thing. It looks for all the world as if someone had left the gate open up there, don't it, and let the wind in?'

'It's even worse in the Round Wood Field. The barley is lodged in great patches all over. And the Home Field too.'

'Ah,' Jack said. 'It's these here hot squalls.'

'You don't seem very worried about it.'

'What can I do? Stand it all up again, is that what you want?' He plucked a few grains from a ripening oatspray and rubbed the husks off in his palm. 'Worrying won't make matters better. It'll only turn your hair grey, that's all.'

'It's easy enough for you to say that! You get your wages whatever the weather does to the crop! It's no odds to you one way or the other!'

'You'll still get a good enough harvest,' he said, nibbling the oatseed. 'Better than you've had these many years past.'

The thunderstorms ended eventually, and when harvest began in the middle of August, they were visited only by short light showers falling out of a pale sky. The workers were glad of these little showers. They would turn up their faces to receive the cool drops.

As Jack had predicted, the harvest that year, although not good, was better than the farm had yielded for a long, long time. Miss Philippa was pleased. She was in great spirits. For once she welcomed all the itinerants who came to Brown Elms in quest of work, though she afterwards worried about the gypsies camping in the birchwoods, close behind the farmhouse.

'So long as they're close, you're all right,' Jack told her. 'Gypsies never steal near home. It's your neighbour John Tuller at Maryhope that'll likely lose his eggs and poultry.'

'Well, they'll grow no fatter on *that*!' she said, and he glanced at her in some surprise. He had never known her to make a joke before. A smile wrought wonders in her rather severe and hard-boned features.

Towards the end of August, the weather turned exceptionally hot, and the harvesters, pledged as they were for every ounce of their strength and endurance, became more silent day by day. The sun's passion was already a burden upon them. Now its demands were cruel indeed.

A man with sweat in his eyes is blind to everything but the need to keep going. He sees only the corn not yet cut, and his blade going through it. He is deaf to everything but the sound of his own blood pounding in his head. He waits for the short night's sleep that stills it. Such a man has nothing to say. His tongue is swollen in his mouth. His lips are burning. He has mortgaged every bit of strength and survives on a budget. Speech is one of the first things to go and no one resents it. They are all as one in this at least.

But the day comes when the silence is broken. A man with a scythe makes one last wide embracing sweep, and the last of the corn goes down before him. Another takes it in his hands; a third steps forward to tie it round; and up it goes for all to see: the last sheaf.

'That's the one! The best of the lot! The one we've been looking for all through harvest!'

The silence is broken. The dumb men find their tongues. The sheaf is held aloft and goes round the field to the sound of cheering and rough laughter. And because the custom has come down from the very earliest ages, the words the harvesters use are old.

'The neck! The neck! Make way for the neck! Here come we, fine chaps one and all!—Make way for us! We bring the neck!'

Ten days later, with the weather still scorching hot, the last load was ready for carting from the Hole Hill Field at Far Fetch. It stood on the brow, with a couple of ropes tied over it for safety, and with Minta, the big roan mare, between the shafts.

The younger lads were gathered in a little circle, making up a special sheaf of barley and oats and wheat together, with scarlet poppies entwined in the bond. When they were done they went to Joe Stretton, the Lord of the Harvest, and put the sheaf into his hands. There was much nodding and winking among them; much whispered argument and banter; and they kept glancing towards Nenna, who stood waving a branch of elder to keep the flies out of Minta's eyes.

'Right you are!' Stretton said. 'We'll go and ask her.'

With the others behind him, he walked up to Nenna and touched his cap.

'The lads would like you to ride on the load, miss. Bringing in the luck, as you might say. And they've made up a special harvest sheaf for you to carry in your arms.'

'Up there?' Nenna said, looking at the load rising above her. 'It's very high.'

'You'll be all right, miss. It's well roped down, don't worry, and we shall see to it that you get a smooth ride.'

'Very well,' Nenna said. 'I wouldn't want to spoil the luck.'

She stuck the elder branch into the hames of Minta's collar, took the sheaf presented to her by Joe Stretton, and climbed the ladder onto the load. She settled herself comfortably, spreading her blue skirts out around her, and slipped one hand in under the cross-rope.

'All right, Miss Nenna?' Stretton asked. 'Feel nice and comfy and safe, do you, and ready to go?'

'Yes, I'm ready. I'm holding on.'

'Right you are, then! We're just about off. No need to be frightened. You're as safe as houses with us, I promise.'

Stretton went and took the mare's bridle, and Percy Rugg got up on the runner, where he could reach the brake when needed. The ladder was removed; the chocks kicked away; and the word given. The waggon started with a little jolt and moved off slowly down the slope, with Nenna sitting up aloft, the harvest sheaf cradled in her arm.

The harvesters walked at either side of the load, and Jack, coming down the field with Joybell and Spangler, stood for a while to watch it go past. Nenna smiled down at him, inclining her head in a regal manner, playing the part expected of her. She even let go of the rope for an instant to give him a wave, but quickly took hold of it again as the load seemed to surge and sway beneath her. She was wearing a big straw hat with a brim, and pinned to the ribbon there was a bunch of artificial cherries, gleaming redly in the sun.

'Make way! Make way!' Paul Luppitt shouted, and all the others took up the call:

> 'Make way, make way,
> And let us pass!
> We sowed it!

We growed it!
We hoed it and mowed it!
Now come we home—
Pray let us pass!'

As they were moving down the field, the harvesters repeating their rhyme for the third or fourth time, more loudly than ever, Miss Philippa appeared in the open gateway. She stood staring, putting up a hand to shade her eyes. Then she hurried forward and stepped directly into Joe Stretton's path. The mare stopped dead; Percy Rugg put the brake on sharply; and Nenna, sitting up high on the load, received such a jolt that the bunch of cherries fell from her hat. It plopped down into the stubble and Harvey Stretton snatched it up.

'Nenna, come down!" Miss Philippa commanded in a loud voice. 'I will not have you making a spectacle of yourself like this, behaving like any cottager's hoyden! Have you no sense of what is fitting? Don't you think it's time you conducted yourself like a grown woman?'

"It's only our fun, ma'am,' said Percy Rugg. 'It was us lot that put Miss Nenna up to ride, so's we could shout the last load home in proper style. We meant no disrespect, ma'am, I assure you truly.'

'Aye, what's wrong with keeping up the old-fashioned customs?' Joe Stretton asked, his chin out-thrust. 'We always *did* used to shout the harvest home in the old days.—Going back, that is, to when the harvests was *worth* shouting!'

Miss Philippa's face was a mottled red. The hot weather disagreed with her, so that she was more than usually peevish today, and Stretton's remark put paid to her temper. She pushed past him and went close to the load.

'Nenna!" she said. 'Come down at once!'

'We can't get Miss Nenna down now,' said Bob Chapman, ' 'cos somebody's gone and took away the ladder.'

'Not unless she was to jump, of course, and we was to catch her,' said Percy Rugg.

'D'you reckon that's wise?' Peter Luppitt asked gravely. 'It's a pretty long way from up aloft there to down here below with us, I would say.'

'Well, I dunno, I'm sure, it's a bit of a pickle, ent it?' said his brother Paul, scratching the side of his sunburnt nose.

'We sowed it! We growed it!' shouted Harvey Stretton, peeping round from the back of the waggon. 'We hoed it and mowed it so why can't we pass?'

'I reckon my boy's got a point,' Stretton said, swaggering up to Miss Philippa. 'The way I see it, we've all got a right to insist upon it that this here procession be allowed to continue.'

'I'm warning you, Stretton! If you don't quickly get out of my way—'

'Yes?' Stretton said. 'And what then, if?'

Miss Philippa was glaring at him. She found it hard to meet his ugly, insolent gaze and was using all her will-power to do so. The air was highly charged between them and Jack was about to interfere when Nenna leant over the side of the load.

'I think I'd like to come down now, Stretton. Would someone please go and fetch the ladder?'

The danger, if any, passed away. Somebody went and fetched the ladder and Nenna came down it, cautiously, bestowing her corn-sheaf on Harvey Stretton, who mounted and took her place on the load, with her crimson cherries pinned in his cap.

'Well, you ent so pretty as Miss Nenna, boy, but I reckon you'll just have to do!' said Joe Stretton, and pulled at Minta's bridle.

As the load moved off, Miss Philippa was already railing at Nenna, and her words could be heard by every man and boy in the field.

'How dare you behave in such a fashion? Don't you realize the consequences of being so familiar with the men? They take advantage enough already without any undue encouragement from you! You're not a child any longer, you know, and it's time you learnt a little decorum!'

She then went off up the field in a hurry, making for the brow, where a few women and children were gleaning, without having first obtained her permission. In another moment, she was venting the rest of her temper on them.

Nenna turned and looked at Jack. He was still standing with the two horses. He saw the trembling of her lip and made a face at her, showing that he was sympathetic. Then, leading the horses, he started after the loaded waggon, and Nenna went with him.

'That's not the first time she's made me look foolish in front of the men. Sometimes I feel as though I could kill her!'

'You didn't look foolish. It's only her own-self she makes look foolish.'

'I felt it all the same! Being scolded like a naughty child! Having to come down off the wagon! In front of them all! In front of *you!*'

'She won't change,' Jack said, 'so the best thing is to take no notice.'

'That's easy for you! You don't have to live with her!'

On the following Saturday, the men stopped work at two o'clock in the afternoon, in spite of dark looks from Miss Philippa.

'We've always finished early on the Saturday after harvest,' Joe Stretton said to her, 'and I reckon we've earned it this year, surely?'

Jack went home and ate a quick dinner of bread and cold bacon. He stripped to the waist and scrubbed himself clean at the pump in the yard. He was shaving the thick growth of stubble from his chin, with his piece of mirror propped up on the spout, when Nenna came in by the orchard gate, wearing gardening gloves and a rough hessian apron.

'I passed here this morning and saw what a mess the garden was in. Your onion patch is a proper disgrace.'

'I've had no spare time all through harvest.'

'I know that,' she said. 'That's why I've come to give you a hand. Your potatoes want lifting. So do your carrots. I thought I'd help you to make a start.'

'I'm doing no work today,' he said. 'I'm going to the fair at Kevelport.'

'Oh!' she exclaimed. 'Can I come with you and see them roasting the great ox?'

With his razor in his hand, poised close to his white-lathered jaw, he turned towards her. Her face was as eager as a child's.

'Well, I dunno . . .'

'Oh, do let me come! I haven't been since I was a child, when my step-father took me and bought me a monkey on a stick.'

'The other men'll be going, remember. There's bound to be talk if they see us together. You know what loose-hinged tongues they've got.'

'What does that matter? I don't care!'

'We should have to tell your sister first . . .'

'We can call and tell her on the way.'

'All right,' he said. 'So long as you're sure, come by all means.'

Nenna pulled off her gardening gloves and threw them down onto the flagstones. She took off her apron and whirled herself round and round on her toes, letting her skirts billow out around her.

'Oh, do hurry up and get yourself ready!'

'That's a risky thing, trying to hurry a man when he's shaving, and if you go on spinning about like that I shall very likely cut myself from ear to ear.'

'Then I'll stop,' she said, and sat down primly on the staddle-stone, watching him as he finished shaving. 'You're a handsome man when you're properly shaved. You ought to do it every day.'

'Then I'd look no different on special occasions.'

'You ought to do it all the same.'

'Ah, well, there's lots of things I ought to do, I daresay, if I did but know it.'

'Yes. There are. You should take more pride in yourself altogether. You could be somebody if you wished it. You could cut a fine figure and win respect.'

'You're buttering me up a bit today, ent you? I reckon you must have an eye on my harvest money! You want me to buy you another monkey on a stick!'

'No, I want to have my fortune told, and I want to see the dancing bear.'

'D'you think he'll be there after all these years? He might have died since you was there last.'

'Oh, no!' she said, stricken. 'Surely not!'

'We shall have to see, then, shan't we?' he said.

He went indoors and changed into his best clothes. He put on his only collar and tie. When he emerged, he handed Nenna his old clothes-brush and she brushed him down, removing cobwebs and bits of straw.

'I was thinking what fun it would be if we could go in the pony and trap.'

'Crying off?' he said. 'Because you've remembered it's five miles to walk?'

'Oh, no! Certainly not!' And she gave his arm a sudden squeeze. 'I'd still want to go if it was twenty!'

'I'm not so sure that *I* would.'

'This jacket of yours! It looks as though you've slept in it!'

'It isn't me that's slept in it. It's that tabby cat of yours from the barn. She had her kittens on this jacket!'

They were standing thus, with Nenna brushing hard at his shoulders, when the orchard gate opened and shut and Miss Philippa appeared before them.

'So this is where you've got to?' she said to Nenna. 'I might have known it! Do you realize that I have been searching all over the farm for you, my girl? Do you realize you left the tap in the dairy running and flooded the place right out to the door?'

'I'm sure I didn't,' Nenna said. 'I'm sure I remember turning it off.'

'Do you also remember leaving the milk-pans filthy dirty? And yesterday's cheese-cloths still in soak? Not to mention letting the chickens get into the granary?'

'I said I was sorry for that, Philippa. I thought it was all over and done with. As for the milk-pans—'

'Am I supposed to do everything myself while you gad about like a giddy school-girl? Don't I deserve some consideration? Surely it's not too much to expect that you should do something towards your keep!'

She was goading herself into a fury. The blood burnt in red spots on her cheekbones, and her eyes were glittering. She was careful not to meet Jack's gaze directly, but her glance kept flickering contemptuously over him, noting that he wore his Sunday blacks and his best boots with polished toe-caps. Suddenly she snatched the clothes-brush from her sister's hands and thrust it savagely into his.

'Surely he can brush his own clothes, can't he? Do you have to wait on him hand and foot? It's a fine thing, I must say, when my sister runs after one of the farm hands and makes herself cheap by skivvying for him! Do you think I can't guess where you are whenever you're missing from the house? Oh, I know well enough! You've always been bone idle at home yet you come down here and work in his garden—'

'Go away,' Jack said, in a quiet voice. 'Go away, Miss Philippa, you've said enough.'

'How dare you speak to me like that? What right have you to interfere between Nenna and me in the first place? Sometimes, Mercybright, I regret that I ever took you into my employ at all and one of these days will very surely be your last!'

'Why not today? Why not send me packing this instant? Or ent I outworn my usefulness to you, trying to set this farm on its feet?'

'I wonder that a grown man like you doesn't feel the awkwardness of such a situation,' she said. 'I wonder you aren't embarrassed by it!'

She swung away and left them. The gate slammed, and they watched her walking quickly up the orchard, vanishing among the perry pear trees. Nenna was pale. But she had in a way become hardened against her sister's outbursts.

'It's not true that I never do any work at home, but

I don't see why I should work all the time and never have any pleasure at all. What do I care for her precious dairy? I hate it and every single thing about it! It's nothing but slavery all day long.'

'I know,' he said. 'I've been in that dairy. I'd say it ent altered since the year dot. She likes to do everything the hard way, that sister of yours.'

'Well, I don't and won't!' Nenna said. 'Whatever I do is never right. If I'm slow she grumbles, but if I'm quick and get finished early, she makes me do everything over again. And she's *not* my sister!'

'I know,' he said. 'I know all that. Still, I think there's something in what she says, and I think perhaps you ought to go.'

'Go?' she said, staring. 'Back home, do you mean?'

'Ah. That's right. To get things sorted out between you. There'll only be trouble otherwise.'

'Right now this minute? And not go with you to the fair at all?'

'Better not,' he said, and looked away, busy plucking the fluff and hairs and straw from the clothes-brush. 'She's right, really. You shouldn't ought to be here with me. It ent seemly.'

'Don't you want me?' Nenna asked.

'It's not that. Don't be silly.'

'But you're sending me away.'

'No, I ent. Well, not exactly.'

'Yes,' she said. 'Oh, yes, you are. You're sending me away.' And there was a child's flat dismay in her voice, coupled with a woman's dignity. 'I suppose I embarrass you, as Philippa suggested. Well, I won't hang around you any longer, I promise, or cause you embarrassment ever again.'

She picked up her gardening gloves and apron, and walked away without another word. She did not look back, not did she stop to pat old Shiner as she went back home across the orchard.

On his way to the fair he got a ride with two of the gypsies who had come to Brown Elms in time for the harvest. They were still camping in the birchwoods. They had permission to stay there till winter. The two in the cart were a middle-aged couple named Boswell and as they drove along the wife remarked that 'the gentleman a'got a lucky face.'

Jack gave a shrug. This was the gypsies' stock-in-trade. They thought every gaujo liked to hear it.

'I ent aware,' he said, 'that my luck is anything much to write home about.'

The gypsy man turned and looked him over. Then he looked back at his pony's ears. He was chewing tobacco.

'There's a lot of folk in this world that always chooses to step aside and let good luck go past 'em,' he said. 'It's a funny thing, that, but I seen it often.'

Sometimes, when he was out ploughing, he would see Nenna a long way off, coming out of the woods with the dog Roy or throwing a stick for him up on the slopes at Far Fetch. Once he saw her out with a basket, picking mushrooms in the lower meadows, and once he saw her running with a message to Will Gauntlet, ruddling his tups in the yard at Low End. But she never came to the cottage now. Never sought him out while he was working. Never popped out of the barn or dairy to speak to him when he came in from the fields with the horses. She had cut herself off from him completely.

There were many days of cold white mist that autumn: days when, especially in the low-lying fields, he could see no further than Joybell's ears as she plodded ahead in front of Spangler. He had to use the swap-plough. There was nothing else for it. He and the horses went by instinct, ploughing a path through the dense whiteness, which then closed in again, swirling behind them, shutting them off from the rest of the world. And somewhere out in the white darkness were the small voices of the peewits crying.

The mists seemed immovable. They hung about all through September. There was no wind to blow them away.

One Sunday morning, working in his garden, he heard a sound at the orchard gate. He turned around expecting Nenna, but it was only the old horse, Shiner, disliking the loneliness of the mist and coming to the gate for company. Jack pulled up a couple of fat, bolted carrots and took them over, and Shiner munched them noisily, awkwardly, having few good teeth left to chew with.

About the middle of September, Miss Philippa took a few samples of corn to market. Jack was with her and saw the look of surprise on the dealers' faces as they weighed the samples in their little pocket balances. Miss Philippa pretended not to notice. She engaged the clerk in conversation. But afterwards, driving home with Jack, she was flushed with satisfaction.

'Did you see their faces? Did you see Harry Swallow look down his nose and then look again with a bit more interest? Oh, they saw that Brown Elms Farm is far from finished, today, surely!'

'That corn wasn't all that special. It was only one up from the bottom grade.'

'But we shall go on doing better! Next year and the year after—there'll be an improvement every harvest. I shall see to it! Mark my words!'

'Aye, if you say so . . .' he said dryly.

'I know a lot of it is due to you, Mercybright, and I'm very grateful, I do assure you. Indeed, if there's anything you want, I shall be pleased to think it over.'

'Thanks, but there's nothing.'

'Nothing new in the way of tools?'

'There's a long list of the things that are needed on the farm and it's hanging up on your office wall. It's been hanging there for a good long while now but nothing much is ever forthcoming.'

'I meant something more in the personal way. Some help with the cottage, possibly, or some plants for your garden.'

'No, there's nothing. Except that you might give Nenna a message.'

'Oh? What is it?'

'Tell her the bear *was* still dancing when I went to Kevelport Fair that day. Spry as a two-year-old he was, tell her, and the old chap with him in pretty good shape too.'

'Yes,' she said. 'All right. I'll tell her.'

'Ah, and tell her there's six or seven apricots on that little tree she planted.—They ought to be eaten. They've been ripe a good while now. Tell her she ought to come and pick 'em.'

'Yes. Very well. I'll give her your message, certainly.'

The apricots, however, fell to the ground and were eaten by birds, and no Nenna came to the cottage. The sweet williams and wallflowers she had planted in the border under the windows had withered now and gone to seed. Jack pulled them up and burnt them on the bonfire, and dug in the seedlings that had sprung up like mustard-and-cress all around. Nenna, he thought, had probably never been given his message.

On wet evenings now, he sat in his chair beside the fire, his feet on a log inside the hearth. The dresser he was making in the far recess remained half-finished, and his tools lay about there, thrown down anyhow among the shavings.

His injured knee was badly swollen. It was always at its worst when the cold wet weather first set in. So he did nothing; only sat and smoked, enclosed in a kind of obstinate stillness; alone with the pain, as if listening to it.

He got up one evening and hurled his clay pipe into the fire-place. He made the fire safe in a mound of ashes and walked out, putting on his cap and jacket as he went and drawing his collar up to his ears. He told himself he was going to The Bay Tree. He wanted the cheerfulness and the company and he needed to buy a few new pipes. But somehow his feet took him up through the orchard and across the fields towards the farmhouse.

The rain had turned to sleet. It struck hard and cold out of the east. The house was in darkness on every side, no flicker of life even in the kitchen window. So he trudged on into Felpy Lane, and met the trap coming up from Niddup. Miss Philippa was driving and Nenna was with her, the two of them huddled beneath an umbrella. Jack stepped back into the hedgerow, leaning against the trunk of an oak tree, and watched the trap go slowly past him. A little while later a light went on in the kitchen window and glimmered wetly through the night. Then the curtains were drawn and the place became dark again, as before.

He began walking towards Niddup. He got as far as Maryhope Farm. Then he changed his mind and returned to the cottage, and there he found Nenna, sitting on the staddle-stone, waiting for him.

'I saw you,' she said. 'I saw you up in Felpy Lane, skulking under the old oak tree.'

He led the way indoors and blew the fire to life with the bellows. He put on more wood and got it burning. Nenna wandered about the room, noting the work he had done in her absence: the two oak stools beside the table; the tall corner cupboard; the basket-work chair; the unfinished dresser. She shed her wet cloak and came to the fire-place, shivering a little as she spread her hands before the blaze.

'I feel I've come home when I come here,' she said, and looked up at him with the fire reflected in her eyes, her face and throat warmly lit by the flames. 'Don't ever send me away again, will you?' she said to him in a quiet voice.

He moved towards her clumsily, and she came to him without any fuss, giving herself up to him, small in his arms.

"Nenna, are you mad?" Miss Philippa demanded. 'A man twice your age! One of the labourers off the farm! A tramp who came here from God knows where, with nothing but the clothes he wore on his back!'

Nenna was silent, standing with her hand inside Jack's arm. She was smiling to herself as if nothing her sister said could hurt her.

'Have you no pride, girl, with your upbringing? You could marry any one of a dozen gentleman farmers' sons in the district or into one of the professional families—'

'How could I, when I've never met them?'

'Is that the trouble? You never said so. That's quite easily remedied, I assure you.'

'It's a bit late now,' Jack said. 'She's settled for me.'

'You! Oh, yes! You've wormed your way in very cleverly, haven't you, winning my trust and enticing Nenna away from me? A girl of eighteen! Scarcely more than an ignorant child! But if you hope to get your hands on this property you're going to be very disappointed, for it's all mine,—every stick and stone on every acre—and Nenna hasn't got so much as a penny piece to call her own!'

'Good. You'll know I'm not marrying her for gain, then, won't you?'

'What *are* you marrying her for, pray?'

'I love her, that's why. What other reason would there be?'

His simple answer seemed to take Miss Philippa by surprise. She stood looking at him for a long time, with frowning eyes, her anger apparently melting away, and when she spoke it was with a tired sigh, as though she admitted herself defeated.

'I was afraid something like this would happen,' she said. 'I ought to have done something more about it.'

She did not ask if Nenna loved *him*. She merely approached the girl and kissed her, rather formally, sorrowfully, as one who believed in doing her duty. Then she shook Jack's hand.

'You mustn't mind the harsh things I said. It's only because I'm anxious for Nenna. I stand in place of both her parents.'

'That's all right. I'd just as soon you spoke your mind.'

'You'll be married from here, of course. I will make the arrangements.'

'Well,—'

'This is Nenna's home, you must remember.'

'Right you are. Just as you say.'

He left the house feeling rather suspicious. He had expected more difficulties. But Miss Philippa, it seemed, having resigned herself to the situation, was determined to improve it as best she could. She had him drive her to market every week and on errands to neighbouring farms, and she made a great point of treating him with marked respect.

'This is Mr Mercybright, my bailiff,' she would say. 'He runs things for me at Brown Elms. He is shortly to be married to my half-sister.'

And she told him, in private, that after the wedding he would receive an increase in wages.

'I've been promoted!' he told Nenna. 'I'm *Mister* Mercybright now, mark you, and going to get a bailiff's wages.'

'I should think so too!'

'Is it your doing? You been speaking on my behalf?'

'No. Not a word. But now that you're marrying me, you see, family pride requires that she raise you to an acceptable level.'

'Ah. That's it. She's making the best of a bad bargain.'

'She's letting us have a bed, did I tell you? And giving us a brand new kitchen range as a wedding present. Oh, and Mrs Ellenton of Spouts is giving us a lamp with a pretty frosted globe on it, and flowers engraved all over the glass.'

Nenna was at the cottage every day now, bringing in oddments of china and glass and cutlery unwanted at the farmhouse; screwing cup-hooks into the shelves of the dresser almost before the varnish was dry; measuring for curtains and making thick warm mats for the floors. Miss Philippa talked in vain of the pans standing dirty in the dairy and cheeses that needed turning in the cheese-room.—Nenna had time only for the work that had to be done in the cottage, and when Jack was free, they worked there together. The wedding was set for January the fourth. Sometimes it seemed all too close.

'Shall we be done in time?' Nenna asked. 'Shall we? Shall we?'

'Done?' Jack said. 'The rate we're going, we could just as well have been married by Christmas!'

There came a day when the last window was in and painted, and he stood back to admire his work. He put aside his paint-pot and brush and walked all round outside the cottage. It looked very trim and smart, he thought: the claywork panels a dazzling white; the beams and windowframes painted black; the thatch now thoroughly darkened by weather and the big redbrick chimney neatly re-pointed from top to bottom; and he called Nenna to come and look.

'When the paint on that window is dry,' he announced, 'the house is finished!'

'Finished?' she exclaimed. 'When there isn't a door on it, front or back?'

Jack was speechless. He felt himself gaping. He had grown so used to the curtain of sacks hanging up in the porch that it seemed the most natural thing in the world.

'If you think,' Nenna said, laughing, 'that I'm going to live in a house without doors you're much mistaken, Jack Mercybright!'

'H'mm, some folks is fussy,' he said, recovering, 'but I suppose I shall have to do something about it.'

And he went off to see what timber there was left in the out-house.

The two doors were made by the end of December; hung and painted on New Year's Day; and furnished with snecks, locks, and bolts on the morning of the fourth, the day of the wedding.

'A near thing,' Jack said to Nenna. 'I reckon I came pretty near being jilted!'

They were married in Niddup, in the big old church above the river. There was snow on the ground that afternoon and more fell as they drove in the trap to Brown Elms.

'A white wedding,' Nenna said, and squeezed his arm against her body, looking at him through snow-flecked lashes. She seemed warm enough and very happy, enchanted with everything, especially the snow.

The wedding party took place at the farmhouse, in the best front parlour, where a huge fire burnt for once in the fire-place, drawing the mustiness out of the furnishings and bringing the perspiration out on the red faces of the wedding guests crowded close together there.

'By golly, ent it hot in here?' Jack said, in Nenna's ear. 'Don't your sister ever open the windows?'

'Our house will never smell musty,' she murmured back. 'I shall see to that!'

'Now, then, you two!' said Joe Stretton. 'You'll have plenty of time for whispering together in the years to come. It's your guests that ought to be getting your attention now, poor beggars!'

'You know what you are, don't you, bailiff?' said John Tuller of Maryhope Farm, pushing Jack and

Nenna together. 'You're a cradle-snatcher, that's what you are, marrying this babe beside you here!'

'Ah, you'll have to watch out with a bride as young as that, Jack,' said George Ellenton of Spouts Hall. 'They're full of mettle when they're under twenty and pretty soon put years on a man if he doesn't take good care about it.'

'I hope he knows, that's all,' Paul Luppitt remarked to Peter.

'Knows what?'

'How many beans make five.'

'I can tell him that—it's six!' said the young boy, Harvey Stretton.

'Drink up, drink up!' said James Trigg of Goodlands. 'The nights are long at this time of year.'

'I *would* drink up,' said Percy Rugg, 'if it warnt that my glass didn't seem to be empty.'

'I daresay Miss Philippa will have gave Miss Nenna some advice worth hearing.'

'She can't have took it, though, can she, or how come we've got a wedding on our hands like this?'

'Lock and key,' said James Trigg of Goodlands. 'Lock and key was the sound advice my father gave me when I got married. Keep things under lock and key.'

'How come our wives warnt invited, I wonder?'

'I reckon Miss Philippa better prefers keeping all us big manly chaps to herself, that's why.'

'And who can blame her?' Ellenton said.

Miss Philippa, going about with the jug of ale, turned a deaf ear to these remarks, though the redness in her cheeks showed that she heard them all too plainly, and the way she glared when Peter Luppitt tipped her elbow showed exactly where she laid the blame. The neighbouring farmers from Maryhope and Goodlands and Spouts Hall were respectful enough in the ordinary way, but now, finding themselves in the company of her labourers, they allowed their own coarseness a loose rein and talked as they would in field or cowshed.

'What about you, Miss Philippa?' George Ellenton

said to her. 'The nights will be long for you, too, now you'll be all alone in the house, eh?'

'Miss Philippa can call me in,' said John Tuller, offering his glass for her to fill. 'I'd have married her years ago, and well she knows it, if I didn't have a wife already.'

'Maybe Miss P. will follow Miss Nenna's example,' said Joe Stretton, 'and choose a husband from off her own farm.'

'Well, Joe,' said William Gauntlet, 'you're the only single bachelor chap now left here unmarried.'

'I know that. I ent simple nor tenpence short!' And Stretton, leaning forward in a familiar way, thrust his face as close to Miss Philippa's as he could. 'How about it, Miss P? You've always had rather a soft spot for me, ent you?'

Miss Philippa bore it all in silence, with the air of one who, though her sufferings were due to others, would always do right by them, come what might. Her sister Nenna had brought this upon her, but she did her duty nevertheless and kept the labourers' glasses brimming.

'Why don't you leave her alone?' Jack said. 'Instead of baiting her all the time?'

'I'm making the most of things,' Stretton said. 'Tomorrow morning she'll be back in the saddle again and I shall be trampled underfoot!' He drank his beer and wiped his mouth on the sleeve of his jacket. He was looking at Jack with wicked eyes. 'It makes me laugh. It does, honest. I'm as bucked as a doe about the whole thing. You! One of us! Brother-in-law to Miss High-and-Mighty! And her there, looking as if she's swallowed a beetle!'

'You can have a lie-in tomorrow, Jack, seeing it's Sunday,' said Peter Luppitt. 'Paul and me will do your share of the early milking.'

'No need,' Jack said. 'I shall be there, the same as always.'

When he and Nenna were ready to leave, there was talk of the party going with them, 'to see them tucked up' as Lacey said, but the joints of cold mutton and beef not yet eaten and the second beer-cask not yet broached were a stronger attraction and kept the wedding guests behind. So Jack and Nenna were allowed to leave peacefully and went arm in arm, treading carefully over the crisp bright sparkling snow to the cottage at the laneside.

The fire was laid in the brand-new shiny kitchen range and while Jack got it going, Nenna went about her wifely duties, filling the kettle ready for the morning and setting the breakfast things out on the table. Then, while he was outside pumping more water, she made porridge and left it in its pan beside the hob.

A little while later, bringing in an armful of logs for the basket, he found the place empty. His working-boots stood on the hearth; his working-shirt was hung up to air; the candle in its holder was burning ready to light the way upstairs to bed. But Nenna was out in the cold night. He followed her foot-prints in the snow and found her standing out in the lane, looking at the cottage with the firelight flickering in its leaded windows and the smoke rising against the stars.

'I wanted to see what it looked like,' she said, 'to anyone passing up the lane.'

She came closer, and her face in the starlight was a child's face, the skin clear and pale, the eyes enormous, the cheekbones delicate and frail-looking. He was suddenly frightened, and she sensed it in him.

'Jack? What's the matter?'

'God, what have I done, marrying such a child!' he said.

She was very small, leaning against him, but she reached up with strong, wilful arms until he submitted and bent his head. The wind blew cold. Light snow began falling again. She shivered a little and he took her indoors.

During the fierce gales that winter, he would sometimes take the lamp from the table and go about inspecting the walls, to see if the rain was driving through them. But the work he had done on the cottage was good. It was proof against every kind of weather.

'Seems the old methods ent so bad after all. That there dobwork is quite as hard as any bricks and a lot more wet-proof into the bargain.'

'Come back with that lamp,' Nenna said, waiting at the table with her scissors poised above a length of shirting, 'or I'll end by cutting your collar crooked.'

'Like you done with the last one? And the one before that?'

'You!' she said. 'I've half a mind to give you a haircut!' And as he set the lamp on the table, she made a threatening move with the scissors, going snip-snip-snip close beside his ear. "And your eyebrows too! Great bristly things! I've half a mind to trim *them!*"

'You just get on with making my shirt, so's I look smart in church next Sunday.'

'Then you are coming after all?'

'I might,' he said. 'It all depends what hymns they're having.'

'You ought to go to church sometimes,' Nenna said. 'A man in your position . . . it's only seemly.' She finished cutting out the second collar and placed it carefully aside. 'Just this once, anyway.'

'Why this once?' he asked, amused.

'Well . . . now we know there's a baby coming . . . it seems to me it's only right.'

'Why? Doesn't the Lord know we're married? He damned well ought to! We was joined together in his sight, according to what the parson said.'

'Shush!' Nenna said. 'That's blasphemy.' But she laughed all the same. 'What would Philippa say if she heard you?'

'If I go to church,' he said, watching her as he lit his pipe, 'shall I wear my new worsted suit and my soft boots and my smart new wide-awake hat?'

'Of course! Of course!'

'And the spotted silk stock you got for me, too, and the handsome stick-pin?'

'Yes, of course! Where else would you wear them if not to church?'

'Aye,' he said, waving away a cloud of smoke, 'that's why you want me to go, ent it, just to show me off in my smart new clothes?'

'Well, what's wrong with that? Oughtn't a wife to be proud of her husband?'

'I could go in corduroys and still be your husband.'

'Now you're just being awkward, aren't you?'

'Or send my new clothes along by theirselves.'

'You could go to please *me*,' Nenna said crossly, and her scissors moved at a great rate, cutting along a black stripe in the shirting.

'Here, steady on, or that there shirt'll end up an apron!'

'Well, will you, then? Go to church to please me?'

'I daresay I shall. Anything for a quiet life. And there's no fool like an old fool, as the saying goes.'

'You are *not* old.'

'Oh yes I am. I've got bristly eyebrows. Not to mention a gammy leg . . .'

Nenna threw down her scissors and rushed at him in a little passion. She snatched his pipe from between his fingers and threw it in under the stove, where it broke in fragments on the hearthstone. She beat at his chest with clenched fists.

'Another tantrum?' he said, laughing, and put his arms around her waist, drawing her close until she was helpless. 'That's the third clay pipe you've smashed for me in a fortnight, woman.'

'Serves you right!' she said, clicking her teeth at him, like a puppy. 'You ought not to smoke so many pipes. Tobacco is weakening, Dr Spray says.'

'Who's weak, I'd like to know?' and he lifted her up against his chest, till her feet were some distance from the floor. 'Am I weak, woman? You answer me that!'

'Don't squeeze me so hard!' she said, gasping. 'You must think of the baby!'

But when, alarmed, he set her gently on her

feet again, she clung to him with her arms round his neck.

'No, don't let me go, Jack! Just hold me and love me. I want you to touch me . . . I want you to carry me up to bed . . . like you did the first time, the night we were married.'

This was the time of year he hated: the wet and cold coming together: endless weeks of it, turning the farm into a quagmire; when every steep track became a rillet, and the tumbrils got stuck in mud that reached to the very axles; when the ditches, overflowing, stank of rotting vegetation; and still the rain fell, day in, day out. And in this weather his leg gave much trouble.

He disliked the idea of Nenna seeing his swollen knee; he tried to keep its condition a secret; but one evening when he got home, after a day spent sweeping the floodwater out of the cowsheds, he was limping so badly that Nenna was anxious. She made him sit in his chair by the fire and she knelt before him, turning his trouser leg up to his thigh. The knee was ugly and misshapen, the flesh puffed up, darkly discoloured, like an over-ripe damson, the pus discharged from it drying in a scab.

Nenna sat back on her heels and wept. She looked at him with anguished eyes, and the tears trickled slowly down her cheeks.

'Poor leg, poor leg!' she kept saying, and she wanted to go at once for the doctor. 'There must be something he could do!'

'No, there's nothing,' Jack said. 'I've had this here wound about fifteen years now and any number of doctors've seen it, but nothing they do is ever any good. They all say the same—it can't be mended.'

'There must be something!' Nenna said. 'Surely? Surely? There must be something!'

'It's the wet and cold that does the damage. It seeems to get in between the bones. The rest of the time it ent too bad. I can even forget it when summer comes round.'

'But surely there's something? Some ointment, perhaps, or some kind of lotion? Didn't the doctors ever suggest anything at all?'

'Nothing they did ever made any difference.'

'But there must be something! No one should have to suffer like that. I can't bear it for you!'

Her distress was such that Jack began casting about in his mind.

'Well, I dunno . . . unless we should try out some sort of poultice . . .'

'Was that something a doctor suggested?'

'Not a doctor, no. It was some old dame I talked to once when I was up at Aston Charmer.'

'Did you ever try it?'

'Why, no, I didn't. I forgot all about it until this minute.'

'What kind of poultice?' Nenna asked.

'I dunno that I remember. It was two or three years ago. Maybe more.' But at sight of her bitter disappointment, he gave the matter further thought. 'Bread!' he exclaimed. 'That's what the old dame recommended.—Bread boiled to a sort of pulp, with a lot of linseed oil in it, and a good pinch of soda. Then you spread it out on a piece of cloth and tie it round the bad place. But I dunno if it really works—'

'It must!' Nenna said, and got up at once to set a saucepan on the hob. 'You sit and watch me and tell if I'm doing it right.'

When the poultice was made and wrapped round his knee, held in place by a cotton bandage, Nenna began preparing his supper. But all the time as she moved about the kitchen she watched him closely.

'Is it better?' she asked. 'Is the poultice working?'

'I reckon it is . . . I reckon it's taking some of the heat out . . .'

'Are you sure?' she asked. 'Do you really mean it?'

'Cross my heart!' he said, getting up and taking a few trial paces. 'That's a marvel, that is! I ought to've tried it a long time ago, only I was too lazy to take the trouble. Why, that's very nearly as good as new!'

He said it to please her. The poultice made no difference at all. And yet there was something as she ministered to him every evening thereafter, that made the pain more easy to bear. It was her tenderness when she touched him; the way she suffered at sight of the wound; the way she cared for him, tireless in doing whatever seemed best. But the poultice itself was nothing much. It was her touch that brought relief.

The doubts he had had in marrying Nenna were now removed. Only a kind of wonder remained. Because of his leg, he had expected her revulsion. Instead, he was cherished all the more. Because he was so much older than she and because he had known a great many years of self-denial, he had thought the roughness of his man's desire might frighten her. But Nenna's passion was as rough as his own. She was eager for him. She wanted him always.

Often during those winter nights, when the rain rattled like grapeshot at the windows, she would draw up the bed-clothes until he and she were covered completely and there in the close warm darkness underneath they would lie on their sides, face to face, two naked children enjoying each other. They had secrets to share. There was laughter between them. They would talk over the happenings of the day together. Until, soft word and soft touch leading at last to hot words and urgent caresses, they would call on each other for the wild union that shut out the black wet winter night completely; obliterated pain; eased away weariness and brought the deepest sleep.

To please Nenna, he now went to church once a month or so, wore the fine clothes she had bought for him, and lingered with her after the service, exchanging gossip with their neighbours. To please Nenna he now shaved every day of the week; had his hair cut regularly; kept his fingernails neat and clean.

'By God!' said Joe Stretton, waiting in the farm-yard one afternoon when Jack returned from Kevel-port. 'You're that smart it hurts! I suppose you'll be having the mayor to tea before very long? Or the Lord Lieutenant?'

'What, riff-raff like them?' Jack retorted. 'Here, give me a hand with this, will you?'

'What the hell is it, for God's sake?'

'It's a butter-making machine, that's what. Miss Philippa ordered it from John Jackson's.'

'I daresay she needs it, too, now lately, seeing Miss Nenna is so busy mollying after you that she's got no time to spare for the dairy.'

Stretton helped to unload the machine and then walked round it, looking under its canvas cover, tilting the table this way and that, and kicking at the framework.

'I don't hold with machines,' he said, 'putting poor people out of work the way they do.'

'If you want a job as dairymaid, you've only to ask.' Jack said. 'But you might as well get used to the notion of machinery on this here farm 'cos there's going to be a whole lot more of it in the future days to come.'

'And that's your doing, I suppose?'

'What if it is? You're always saying yourself that this place is right behind the times so why grumble if we start catching up?'

'Where's the Missus get the money, that's what I should like to know?'

'That's none of my business. Nor yours neither.'

'Oh yes it is!' Stretton exclaimed. 'If she's got money to spend on machines, why ent she got it to pay our wages instead of laying us off work?'

'But you're not laid off.'

'Oh yes I am! She told me so this afternoon.—— While you was out doing her shopping! She's got four wheat-stacks there wanting threshing but will she give 'em to me to do? Oh, no, not she! She better prefers to hang on and hoard 'em, hoping she'll get a top price in the summer. Ah, and then she'll likely have the traction, seeing she's so smutten on machinery all of a sudden. But it's all wrong, you know, and you as bailiff should ought to tell her.'

'Yes, I'll tell her,' Jack said, and went in search of her straight away.

At first she refused even to listen. She liked to see her yard full of corn-stacks. Her pride in them was beyond belief. She was always sorry to see them go.

'But if you hang on to 'em too long,' Jack said, 'that'll likely be money down the drain.'

'How d'you make that out?' she asked sharply.

'The talk is of more and more grain coming in from America, not less, so you'd better look out or you're going to be left feeling pretty silly.'

'Where did you hear this?'

'I heard it in Kevelport this afternoon.'

'I'm not too sure I believe you,' she said.

But the following morning, the big barn resounded to the noise of flails, and Jack, looking in, found Stretton at work there with his son Harvey.

'I'll say this much for you!' Stretton shouted, without once pausing in his swing: 'You've certainly got the measure of that damned woman!'

'He's got the measure of both of 'em, ent he?' Harvey chipped in. 'Seeing Miss Nenna's in the family way already?' Then he gave a great howl, for his father, by shoving him sharply in the ribs, had caused him to falter, and the swingle of his flail had come down hard on the top of his skull. 'What'd you do that for, Dad?' he demanded, feeling his head very tenderly. 'You damn near done for your boy Harvey!'

'She ent Miss Nenna to you no more. She's Mrs Mercybright and don't you forget it. Now get on swinging and not so much fussle. So long as it's only your head that gets dowsed you won't reach much harm, seeing it's mahogany all the way through.'

The butter-machine was something of a wonder; even Nenna wanted to see it working; but it was forgotten when the new winnowing-machine arrived, and the new horse-rake, and the new wide drill.

'Laws, ent we modern all of a sudden?' Peter Luppitt said to Paul. 'It makes me giddy, watching all this change, honest.'

But the greatest excitement was in July, when the new reaper-and-binder arrived, brand new from the Kevelport foundry. It stood in the yard and the men gathered from all over the farm to see it.

'Reaper *and* binder?' said Joe Stretton. 'I've heard of such things but I still don't believe it.'

'Is there hands on them shafts,' asked Peter Luppitt, 'with fingers on them?'

'That's right,' said his brother, 'and they're that clever once they get moving that you've only got to watch a minute or two and out pops a nice big crusty loaf of bread!'

'Does it malt the barley into the bargain?'

"Aye, and passes out a jug of beer!'

'What happens, then, when you put it in to cut the oats?'

'Out pops a Scotchman in a kilt!'

'Does it talk to us and tell us when it's time for oneses?'

'Does it sing?' asked Lacey. 'I was always one for a good tune.'

'What *I* should like,' said William Gauntlet, leaning forward on his shepherd's long stick, his long body steeply inclined, 'is an engine that stays up at night while I'm sleeping, delivers my lambs and snips their tails off, then pays me my wages for doing nothing. How about it, Jack?—Could you get me one by next spring?'

'I wouldn't trust it, myself,' said Percy Rugg, borrowing Gauntlet's own favourite phrase. 'Supposing it never knowed when to stop? That tail-snipping bit would have me worried.'

'Who's going to drive this reaper-binder?' asked Joe Stretton. 'Who's going to have the first go?'

'I am!' said Harvey. 'I ent scared of an old machine!'

'Oh no you don't!' Stretton said. 'If anyone has first go it's me, not a green sappy half-man like you, boy.' Then he turned to Jack. 'Unless you want first go, being bailiff,' he said.

'No, you go ahead,' Jack said. 'Try it out on them oats above the Runkle.'

Harvest that year went forward like clockwork. It was over and finished in record time. The weather stayed open and ploughing was easy. Jack had been nearly three years at Brown Elms now, and each year had seen an improvement, yet Miss Philippa was far from satisfied.

'How long,' she asked him, 'before we get rid of the reeds in the Middle Nineteen Acre?'

'Two or three years, most probably. Four, even.'

'So long? So long?'

'It takes a lot longer to clean the land than it does to get it soggled up.'

'How long before Rummers can be sown with a corn crop?'

'The same, most likely. Two or three years. It's good enough land but sour as a cesspit. It needs nursing and the only answer is time and patience.'

'Patience!' she said, and gave an angry sigh.

'There are no short cuts,' he said, 'not once you've let the land go back so badly.'

'It's not my fault this farm's gone back. There was no one I could trust until you came along.'

But, having given him her precious trust, she expected miracles in return.

'That sister of yours!' he said to Nenna. 'She seems to think I'm some sort of magician. She expects me to work wonders for her.'

'You *have* worked wonders,' Nenna said. 'Nobody else would have worked so hard.'

As far as Nenna was concerned, plainly he could do no wrong. She was fiercely protective if she thought he was being put upon, and would take her sister to task about it.

'It was after ten again when Jack got home from work last night. Do you have to run him around as you do?'

'I pay him good wages. Surely he doesn't expect to get them for nothing?'

'That's not what I said.'

'Does he talk about me?' Philippa asked. 'Does he tell you things, about what I want doing on the farm?'

'Of course he talks to me!' Nenna said. 'What do you expect between man and wife?'

She looked at her sister in some surprise, and Philippa turned away to the window.

'And does he complain of the way he's treated?'

'No,' Nenna said. 'Jack never complains about anything.'

'Oh, doesn't he indeed! You're talking rubbish. Your husband, let me tell you, is quite capable of looking after his own interests. *He's* never backward in coming forward or he wouldn't be where he is today.'

'And where is that?' Nenna asked scornfully.

'Married to *you*!" her sister said.

It was true that Miss Philippa liked to run him around, and often she kept him after work, calling him into the poky office to talk farm business by the hour. He rarely refused her. He thought she was probably very lonely now that Nenna was no longer with her.

One autumn evening she asked him indoors, into the best front parlour, and gave him a glass of Madeira wine. He was at a loss. He could not understand her. And then John Tuller of Maryhope Farm came in, obviously expected, and he too was given a glass of wine.

'Jack, I think Mr Tuller would be glad of your advice in improving his grassland. Do talk to him about it, will you?'

But the whiskered Mr Tuller, looking down his

handsome nose, could scarcely be bothered even to answer Jack's nod.

'I came to see *you*, Miss Philippa, and well you know it.'

So Jack drank up quickly and took his leave, noticing that Miss Philippa's colour was heightened, though her manner was dignity itself. He could not decide whether she had invited him in for support or merely to show him that she had an admirer. Either way, he was sympathetic, but Nenna, when he told her, was extremely angry.

'That terrible man? I can't abide him! His wife scarcely cold in her grave, poor soul, and he's already casting about for another!'

'It might not be such a very bad thing. I daresay your sister would prefer to be married and if she likes him—'

'Not John Tuller! He only married his first wife to get his hands on Maryhope Farm and over the years he's bled it dry! He'd do the same for Brown Elms and drive poor Philippa out of her mind. Drinking and hunting—that's all he cares for!'

'Maybe you're right,' Jack said, knowing Tuller's reputation, 'but I dunno that it's any business of ours exactly.'

'Yes, it *is* our business,' Nenna said. 'What would become of us, do you think, if Tuller were lord and master here?'

Jack laughed. He had never seen her so indignant. But, failing to jolly her out of her temper, he tried to comfort her instead.

'If the worst should come to the worst,' he said, 'I should just have to look for a job elsewhere.'

'After all the work you've put in on this farm, pulling it together the way you have? Oh, no! I wouldn't hear of such a thing!'

'We'll cross that bridge when we come to it, then. Though I don't see what you can do about it, anyway.'

'I can do plenty. I can speak to Philippa for a start.'

'Ah, that'll make everything dandy, I daresay.'

'Are you laughing at me?' Nenna demanded.

'Good gracious,' he said, 'as though I would!'

'*I'm* not laughing, let me tell you.'

'I can see that.'

'Oh, you do make me cross sometimes, you do, really!'

'Hush a minute and listen,' he said. 'Did you hear that?'

"No. What?'

'My belly rumbling. It's wondering why I'm late with its supper.'

'Oh!' she exclaimed, and rushed to open the door of the oven. 'There, would you believe it? Just look at my patty!' And she showed him a pie somewhat charred at the edges.

'I like 'em like that, nice and crispy. What's it got inside? Meat and taters? Ah, I knowed it was, the instant I smelt it.'

'You!' she said. 'A lot you care what it's got inside it, you old bread-and-cheese, you! You're just wanting to change the subject.'

'What subject was that?' he asked vaguely.

'You know well enough what subject it was.'

Nenna brought a dish of carrots and cabbage to the table, and a jug of gravy. She sat down and began cutting into the pie.

'I'm thinking about the future,' she said. 'The farm could belong to our children one day. You surely don't blame me for keeping their interests in mind, do you?'

'No, I don't blame you. At least, not exactly. But you don't expect your sister to stay single all her life just so's our children should get the farm?'

'No, of course not,' Nenna said, shocked. 'But, after all, she is well past thirty. She's not very likely to get a great many chances now.'

'She's got John Tuller. Or so it seems.'

'He'd bring her nothing but humiliation. And how would you feel if the farm became Tuller's when it might very well have come to your son?'

'This is too much for me,' he said. 'It's looking too far into the future.'

That Nenna should be so calculating was a thing that amazed him. This jealousy on behalf of her young, for the rights and possessions accruing to them, must be something that came with motherhood, just as extra strength came to the heavily burdened body, and milk to the breasts. He looked at her with new eyes, and Nenna looked back without shame. She was now very big and sat with dignity, arranging the folds of her smock in front with a care that made him smile anew.

'How come you're so sure it's a son you're carrying? Did your gypsy friends up in the birchwood tell you?'

'Yes!' she said defiantly. 'You may scoff if you like but gypsies often know these things and Mrs Rainbow read my face.'

She put a small piece of pie into her mouth and chewed carefully. Everything she did now was done with great care, on account of the baby.

'Besides which, I *want* it to be a son,' she said.

'Ah, that just about settles it, then, and no question!'

But the child born to them that autumn was a daughter, and was named Linn, after Nenna's mother. Nenna wept at first with disappointment. She would not have the cot placed anywhere near her. It had to stand against the far wall. But then, seeing Jack's delight in the baby, she recovered and asked for it to be placed in her arms.

'You never said you wanted a daughter.'

'I didn't know myself till I got her,' he said. 'I left that part to the Almighty.'

'Do you think she'll forgive me for being disappointed?'

'It depends how you treat her from now on.'

'I shall give her lots of brothers and sisters,' Nenna said. 'She shall never be a lonely little girl as I was.'

On a working day late in October she brought the baby, wrapped in a woollen shawl in her arms, up to the farm for the men to see and give their blessing.

'She'll do well,' said Peter Luppitt, 'born with a waxing moon as she was.'

'Peter's right there,' said his brother Paul. 'I always plants my cabbages when the moon is waxing and you know what mighty things they always grow to.'

'Married people should always get their children with a waxing moon,' said Peter. 'It's only common sense.'

'That ent always easy,' said William Gauntlet, with a slow and solemn shake of his head.

'She ent going to open her eyes at us, is she? I reckon she knows we ent much to look at.'

'I don't wonder she's sleeping,' Jack said. 'She was up half the night screaming her lungs out.'

'Got a tooth coming through, I shouldn't wonder.'

'More likely wind,' said Oliver Lacey.

'You want to go to old Grannie Balsam up at Goodlands. She makes the best gripe-water in the district.'

'Have you took her up to Tootle Knap?' asked Gauntlet. 'You should always take a new born babby up on top of Tootle Knap. It's the highest point in the parish, you see, and gives the child a good start in life, like being baptised or having a mole on her left elbow.'

Jack only smiled, but Nenna wanted to go at once, so he went with her to the top of the mound known as Tootle Knap and there among the elm trees, with the yellow leaves flit-flittering down, he took the baby between his hands and held her up as high as he could.

'There you are, Linn Mercybright! What do you think of the air up here, then? Suit you nicely, eh, does it?' And on the way down again he said to Nenna, 'At least she can't say we didn't do all the right things for her!'

'Don't you believe in luck?' Nenna asked.

'I ought to,' he said. 'The way things are going for me just lately, I never see a magpie without I see two!'

He went back to work drilling wheat in the Sliplands, with Harvey Stretton up behind in charge of the seed-box, and a little while later John Tuller came across on his way to the farmhouse.

'I've been wanting to talk to you, bailiff, about those gypsies you've got camping here. I don't approve of it one iota. You shouldn't allow them to hang about for weeks on end.'

'They come every year to help with the harvest. They'll be moving on soon to their winter camp in the quarry at Ludden.'

'That's not soon enough to suit me! I'm losing chickens every day.'

'Then you'd better see Miss Philippa, I reckon.'

'I shall, never fear. I'm on my way.'

Tuller strode on, smart in breeches and Norfolk jacket, keeping carefully to the headlands. Jack flipped at the horses and they moved off again up the slope, while Harvey Stretton, perched up behind, gave a squawk of laughter.

'Them chickens he's lost!—They most likely fell down a crack in the ground, poor things!'

That afternoon, when Jack led the horses into the yard, Tuller was standing there, deep in conversation with Miss Philippa, and had a basket of eggs in his hand. He was well known for being a cadger.

'I've settled the matter of the gypsies, bailiff. Miss Philippa is sending them packing in the morning.'

Jack was surprised. He glanced at Miss Philippa's blank face. Tuller, it seemed, had influence with her.

But a good many mornings came and went and the gypsies continued to camp in the birchwoods, coming and going just as they pleased.

'I thought you was sending them packing,' Jack said, and Miss Philippa gave a little shrug. 'Why should I?' she said. 'They do me no harm and they'll be moving on anyway in November.'

So she liked to keep Tuller on a string, plainly, and Jack wondered why. It was quite impossible to guess her thoughts or feelings.

As autumn wore on into winter, Tuller was seen more and more at Brown Elms, striding about over the fields and poking his head into the buildings. Jack took care to keep out of his way, sure that meetings would lead to trouble, but the other men fared badly. They complained that Tuller spied on them and carried his tales to Miss Philippa. He had waylaid the Luppitts after work one evening, demanding that they open the sacks they were carrying, and had then confiscated the two brace of pheasants and the hare and rabbit he found inside. So Joe Stretton, every night after that, carried home a sack full of stones, intending, if challenged, to drop it hard on Tuller's toes.

'But Farmer Tuller keeps clear of *me!* And well he might, too, or I should try straightening his long twisty nose-piece!'

'That's all very well,' said Peter Luppitt, 'but what if he ups and marries our Missus?'

'If that ever happens I shall emigrate,' Stretton said. 'I shouldn't stay on under Farmer Tuller.'

'Emigrate?' said young Harvey.

'Ah, that's right, over the water!'

'What water's that, Dad? The Atlantic Ocean?'

'Ennen water!' Stretton said. 'There's some pretty good farms over the other side from Niddup.'

John Tuller was warmly disliked and held in great contempt, too, as the title 'Farmer' showed very plainly. For whereas James Trigg of Goodlands and George Ellenton of Spouts Hall, farming their land in the best tradition, were each known as 'Mister,' the master of Maryhope, frittering his substance away on drink, was everywhere known as 'Farmer Tuller.'

'Just imagine,' said William Gauntlet, 'selling *land* to pay for *bubbles!*'

Jack, however, could not always keep clear of Tuller, and one day late in November, when he had five teams out ploughing the Placketts, Tuller came up and asked for the loan of two horses.

'I've seen Miss Philippa about it and she says I can have them.'

'Has she indeed? It's the first I've heard.'

'I want the loan of a man, too. Perhaps you'd be good enough to oblige me. I want some coal fetched from the station.'

'It'll have to wait,' Jack said. 'I ent wasting good weather like this. Carting coal is a wet-weather job.'

Tuller was angry, but made an effort and kept his temper.

'When you've finished, then. I don't much mind so long as it's today.'

'It won't be today, no lections of that. When these horses finish this afternoon they'll have done their stint for today, Mr. Tuller, and they'll be entitled to shut up shop. But I'll think about it as soon as maybe.'

'Damn you to hell!' Tuller said, and this time his temper went for nothing. 'Come back at once and ask your Mistress! She'll soon tell you what your orders are!'

'It's no odds to me one way or the other. I'm bailiff here, not Miss Philippa, and I'm the one that says what the horses do or don't do.'

'We'll see!' Tuller said. 'Oh, yes! We shall see about that, I promise you, man!'

He hurried off across the rough ploughland, and Jack continued up the slope, while, further on along the Placketts, the other men were all agog. A little while later, Tuller returned with Miss Philippa, and they stood together on the lower headland, waiting for Jack to plough down towards them.

'I hear you've refused Mr. Tuller the horses.'

'I didn't refuse. I only postponed it.'

'Is it really necessary for all the horses to be out ploughing at the same time?'

'This weather's a bonus. It won't last much longer. If we go all out for the next few days we shall get the Placketts and the Brant sown with dredge-corn. That's a lot more important to my way of thinking than lugging coal for your neighbours' fires.'

Tuller's face was now ugly. He turned to Miss Philippa and thrust out his chin.

'When I first asked you this small favour, your answer was yes, as I recall.'

'Only if the horses were not needed here, Mr. Tuller. I said that plainly.'

'Are you lending or are you not? I don't much care for haggling about it!'

'When Mr Mercybright says they can go, you can have them by all means, Mr Tuller.'

'So! You allow yourself to be ruled by your bailiff?'

'I am ruled by no one,' she said stiffly. 'Not even by friends such as you, Mr Tuller.'

'No?' he said, sneering. 'Well, I wouldn't let any labourer of mine speak to me as this lumping clod does to you, madam!'

'You're forgetting, I think, that Mr. Mercybright happens to be my brother-in-law as well as my bailiff. He is therefore something more than a mere labourer.'

'Not to me, he isn't! And I'm glad I've come to my senses in time!'

Angry at being brought down before his inferiors, Tuller was determined to have his revenge, and made a great show of looking her over from head to foot.

'By God!' he said, in a voice that carried across half the field. 'I had plans for making you my wife, madam, but as I've no stomach for welcoming ploughman and pigman at my table, I'm thankful this day has gone as it has done!'

He then walked away along the headland, taking the short way home to Maryhope, and Miss Philippa turned her wrath on Jack.

'I hope you will always remember,' she said, 'that for your sake I fell out with a neighbour and gave him cause to make me look foolish.'

'My sake?' Jack said, but she also was walking away.

The men were well pleased with the outcome of the clash that morning. Oliver Lacey had heard most of what had been said and had passed it on to all the others. For once Miss Philippa found favour among them.

'She told him, didn't she, eh, Jack? She put Farmer Tuller in his place all right *and* sent him off with a flea in his ear-hole. Oh, yes! She took him down a peg right nice and tidy.'

'It'd been a lot better,' said Joe Stretton, 'if she'd never rizzed him up in the first place.'

That was Jack's opinion, too. Tuller, he felt, was probably a bad man to quarrel with. There was sure to be trouble. And sure enough, about three weeks later, the dog Roy was found dead in the sunken track dividing Maryhope land from Brown Elms.

'He was after my pheasants,' Tuller said, 'so my keeper shot him.'

There was no evidence either way. Tuller's story was well prepared and his keeper confirmed it. All Jack could do was to be on his guard against further incidents and warn the men to be equally watchful, especially the shepherd, who had three dogs.

'If they kill my Snap or my Pip or my Patsy,' William Gauntlet said grimly, 'I shall kill them and no bones about it.'

And the old man, a fearsome figure when he chose to stand upright and make the most of his six-feet-six-inches, went up to Maryhope straight away to deliver his threat in person.

'You harm my dogs,' he said to Tuller and the keeper, 'and I'll hang both your gutses with the rest of the vermin on your own gallers!'

There were no more dogs killed on the farm, but Tuller was never at a loss how to make trouble, and scarcely a month went by thereafter without some fresh example of his spite: field-gates broken and the hinges levered out of the gate-posts; ballcocks weighed in the cattle-troughs so that the water overflowed; an old scrub bull allowed in to run with the Brown Elms heifers.

'There's nothing worse than a bad neighbour,' Peter Luppitt said to Jack, 'unless, of course, it's two bad neighbours.'

One Sunday morning, after church, as Jack and Nenna stood talking to Philippa in the churchyard, Tuller jostled Jack in passing, turned to glare at them all in contempt, then pushed past to speak to Mrs Carrington Wilby of Halls, presenting his back to the Brown Elms party.

The incident was noticed by almost all those gathered in the churchyard. Philippa and Nenna were both upset. But a moment afterwards Mr Tapyard of Ennen Stoke, an important landowner and a magistrate, came up to them and raised his hat.

'How are things at Brown Elms? Fat and flourishing, from all I hear, and improving all the time under Mr Mercybright's supervision. It's a pity there aren't a few more farmers like you, Miss Guff, with cattle and sheep and pigs on their land instead of a handful of half-starved pheasants.' And without much pretence of lowering his voice he then added, 'If you have any trouble with that fellow Tuller, *don't be afraid to take him to law.*'

Miss Philippa was comforted by Tapyard's show of sympathy and she found the other farmers round equally friendly. There was not much regard for John Tuller. He was too well known as a spendthrift and a scrounger.

Still, Miss Philippa was a solitary creature, and Jack felt sorry for her, going home to eat her Sunday dinner in the cheerless farmhouse, with only the stone deaf cook for company.

'It's her own fault,' Nenna said. 'She could easily make friends if she wanted to but she just doesn't try.'

'All the same, I feel a bit bad about it, having took

you away,' he said. 'I reckon we ought to do some-thing about her.'

'Such as what?'

'Such as having her here to eat dinner with us on a Sunday, so that you and her can enjoy a bit of a chat together.'

'Yes,' Nenna said. 'That's a good idea. And perhaps she will then believe that I really do know how to cook.'

The visits were not a success, however, for Miss Philippa was always finding fault with the way Nenna brought up the baby.

'What a terrible mess that child is making, sucking that piece of cheese,' she said. 'Was it you who gave it to her or was it Jack? Ought she to have it, a child her age?'

'I don't see why not,' Nenna said. 'It's quite plain she likes it.'

'And does she always have what she likes?'

'So long as it's wholesome, certainly.'

'She's going to be very spoilt, then, I can see.'

'She's going to be happy,' Nenna said.

Miss Philippa sniffed, watching the child crawling across the floor towards her. She sat sideways in her chair, her skirts drawn in about her legs, determined to elude the sticky, clutching fingers. Jack leant for-ward and lifted Linn onto his lap.

'She's got four teeth, had you noticed?' he said. 'And another two on the way.'

'That's nothing extraordinary in a child of seven months, is it?'

'I wouldn't know. I never had a baby before.'

And, catching Nenna's eye, he exchanged a little smile with her. It was difficult to share what they had with Philippa—the more they tried, the more they seemed to shut her out.

Nenna, on the whole, was patient under her sister's criticisms. She had made up her mind to endure them calmly. But acts of interference she would not allow, and one day there were words between them.

It was a warm Sunday morning in summer, and

Linn, now nine months, was crawling about the floor barefoot. Nenna went out to the garden for a moment to pick fresh mint and to tell Jack that dinner was very nearly ready. She returned to find Philippa holding the child down hard on her lap, forcing on the second of her tiny shoes, over a twisted, much-wrinkled stocking. Linn was crying bitterly, and Nenna, snatching the child up into her arms, took off both the shoes and the stockings and flung them into a corner of the settle.

'It's none of your business!' she said fiercely. 'How dare you make the poor child cry?'

'She shouldn't be going about barefoot like that. On this cold brick floor! On the rough garden path! She'll do herself an injury.'

'It's none of your business!' Nenna repeated. 'You have absolutely no right to interfere. If you think you know so much about raising children and caring for them, it's time you got married and had your own, before you find you've left it too late!'

Jack came in to an atmosphere that sparked and prickled. He stood glancing from one red angry face to the other. Then he went forward and lifted Linn out of Nenna's arms.

'Them there taters is boiling all over the stove,' he said. 'They'll put the fire out in another minute. Here, come to your dad, Miss Mercybright, and he'll give you a ride like Jack-a-Dando.'

He sat down in the basketwork chair with the child on his knees, facing towards him, and jiggled her about until she laughed.

'Jack-a-Dando rode to Warwick
With his newly wedded bride—
Bumpety-bump up and down,
Bumpety-bump from side to side—
Jack-a-Dando's famous ride!'

Linn was now croodling and blowing bubbles, leaning towards him, hands clutching at his waistcoat pocket, where she knew she would find a pod of green peas. Nenna smiled from across the kitchen. She liked to see Jack and the child together. But Miss Philippa took much longer to thaw, and was still rather cool when she left after dinner.

'Well?' Nenna said, defiantly, confronting Jack afterwards. 'Whose child is she I'd like to know——hers or mine?'

'Mine,' he said, to avoid disagreement. 'You can tell she's mine by the way she's so fond of her bread and cheese.'

Often that summer, when Nenna went out to help in the hay-fields, she would take Linn with her and put her to sleep in the shade of the hedgerow, somewhere nearby, where she could keep a watchful eye. And at harvest-time, too, Linn would be out in the fields all day, safe in the charge of the older children, playing in a corner, well away from the reaping machine and the mowers at work with their sharp scythes.

One hot day young Bobby Luppitt caught a large grass-snake and carried it across the harvest field to show it to the other children. Nenna ran up in some consternation, for Linn was awake and would surely be frightened. But when she arrived, Linn had the grass-snake in her arms and was trying to cuddle it against her body, enchanted by its warmth and the way it wriggled in her grasp. She was laughing and gurgling all the time, and cried only when the snake escaped her, vanishing into the shady hedgerow.

'Dolly?' she called, crawling along on hands and knees. 'Dolly? Dolly? Cheep, cheep?' Every pet or plaything was 'dolly' to her.

She was a forward child from the first, and a happy one, as Nenna had promised. She was pretty, too, and had fair hair with more than a hint of red in it, which Nenna herself kept trimmed short, so that it grew in little fine feathery waves all over her head. Her eyes and lashes were dark, like her mother's, and her skin golden.

'Someone I know is a bobby-dazzler,' Jack would say, lifting her up till her hands touched the rafters. 'Someone I know is as bright as a button. Now I wonder who it is? You got any idea, have you?'

'Dolly! Dolly!' Linn would say. "Dolly Doucey! Bobby-dazzler!'

She could say many words by the time she was fully a twelvemonth old.

Towards the end of harvest that year there were five days of heavy rain, holding the harvesters back, fretting, and beating down the corn still standing uncut on forty-five acres. And when Jack went up with the other men on the sixth day, determined to cut the oats and barley in the Top Ground, however wet, he found that Gauntlet's sheep had got in from the rough grazing above. The field was a nightmare, the sprouting corn all trodden into the miry ground, and the sheep with their bellies so distended that they lay about, unable to move, having gorged themselves on the undersowing of grass and clover.

'They warnt here last night!' Gauntlet said. 'I was up here going the rounds at ten and they was all safe in the leazings then. It's Farmer Tuller that has let 'em in here, or one of the scum that dirties for him!'

When Miss Philippa saw the state of the field, she stood for a time with the tears glistening in her eyes. It really hurt her to see the corn ruined. But then anger got the upper hand.

'I'll have the law on Tuller this time, as Mr Tapyard said I ought.'

'There's not enough evidence,' Jack said. 'Farmer Tuller has seen to that. It's our own sheep that have got in and he's took good care that them holes in the hedge should look as if they was accidental.'

'Then what can we do?'

'We can see that it don't happen again.'

So every night after that he patrolled the boundary, armed with a double-barrelled shotgun, and one night he challenged a man who was creeping across the sunken trackway. The man turned and ran, and Jack fired one barrel into the branches of a nearby oak tree.

'Tell your master,' he called out, 'that the next man he sends won't be half so lucky!'

The message, it seemed, went home; there were no

more intruders after that; but Jack, working all day to
finish the harvest and patrolling five or six hours every
night, was in danger of wearing himself to a shadow,
and Nenna complained to her sister about it.

'Is it my fault?' Philippa said. 'I never asked him to
patrol, did I?'

'Then perhaps you'll ask him to stop,' Nenna said,
'before he kills himself with lack of sleep.'

'I shan't stop him. Not until the harvest is safely in.
After all, it was all through Jack that I quarrelled with
Tuller in the first place, so no doubt he feels himself
somewhat to blame.'

The harvest was got in at last without further damage. Jack was able to sleep at nights in his own bed,
and to put John Tuller out of his mind, at least until the
Top Ground fields had been ploughed and re-sown.
Then, perhaps, there might be a need for vigilance
again.

That autumn, however, there was a change that removed the problem. Maryhope Farm was put up for
sale. Jack was driving home from Hotcham and saw a
man in the act of nailing up the poster, on the trunk of
a tree in Felpy Lane. 'Maryhope Farm: two hundred
acres of freehold land, with dwelling-house, barns,
out-houses, byres, and sundry other buildings pertaining: to be sold by auction on Thursday, October 28th.,
unless previously sold by private treaty.'

Jack went in search of his sister-in-law and found
her in the dairy, up to her elbows in the cheese-tub.

'Seems your friend Tuller is selling out. I've just
seen a poster in the lane. Maryhope Farm is on the
market.'

'Yes, I know, and I'm going to buy it,' she said
calmly. 'I've seen Mr Todds about raising a mortgage
and he will be arranging the whole transaction for me.'

Jack was struck dumb. He stood watching her bare
white arms as she swirled the curds to and fro in the
tub. She looked at him with a little smile, enjoying his
surprise, making the most of her moment of triumph.

'Are you mad?' he asked.

'No,' she said. 'I don't think so.'

'With farming going downhill all the time? And no sign of any improvement?'

'It means the land is going begging. I couldn't afford it, if it weren't cheap. And things can't stay bad for ever and ever. You've said so often enough yourself. Farming is bound to pick up in the end and when it does this will be one of the finest holdings in the country.'

'That land of Tuller's is in worse case than this here land of yours used to be. He's bled it white and you damn well know it. It'd take years to put it back into heart again. Five years at least. Probably longer.'

'That's where you come in,' she said.

'Ah, I thought it might be. I had this feeling in my bones.'

'I hoped you'd be pleased, having a bigger farm to manage.'

'I'm happy enough as I am,' he said.

'But you will take the Maryhope land in hand, too, won't you? I can't do it without your help.'

'Yes, well, I'll do my best about it, surely.'

At home that evening, when he passed the news on to Nenna, she was at first inclined to be angry.

'Philippa puts on you,' she said. 'I will not allow it!'

But the very next time she mentioned the matter, after discussing it with her sister, she spoke of it as a settled thing.

'The farmhouse at Maryhope will be sold separately and will keep the name,' she said. 'The land will become part of Brown Elms and a new field-map is drawn up already. It'll really be quite a sizeable holding now.'

'You've changed your tune a bit, ent you?' he said.

'It will be for the best in the end,' she said, 'seeing the farm will pass to our children.'

'Oh? Who says so?'

'Philippa says so. She never intends to marry, she said, so our sons will inherit the farm.'

'What sons?' he said, to tease her. 'Have you been keeping something a secret?'

'No, I haven't!' she exclaimed. 'I only wish I could say otherwise!'

'Well, lumme . . . it's early days to be tamping about it. We ent been married two years yet—'

'But Linn came so soon! It was all so easy in every way! I can't understand why other babies haven't followed.'

Nenna longed for more children. She felt a hungry impatience for them. And it made her angry that she should be denied.

'Why is it?' she asked. 'Why don't I ever get my own way? It isn't a wicked thing to wish for, is it, so why should God deny me more children?'

'Don't worry yourself about it,' he said gently. 'I daresay they'll come when they're good and ready.'

So now he had charge of six hundred acres, a holding which, if he stood at the top of Tootle Barrow, was laid out all round for him to see, spreading its slopes to the south and west.

'Aren't you proud,' Nenna said, 'to be bailiff of such a farm as this?'

'I shall be a lot prouder when the Maryhope lands is in some sort of fettle,' he said.

It all took time. There were no short cuts to salvation on the land. There was only labour. But changes were wrought, little by little, and at the end of two

years those changes could be seen plainly: as the wet
pastures were drained and sweetened; as the poor
starved arable grounds were manured and rested; as
the rough grey leazings were cleared and ploughed
and sown anew, and slowly, with patience, coaxed into
kindliness, the new grass growing close and thick together, bright green and glistening under the spring
and summer sun.

'It warms my heart,' said William Gauntlet, 'to see
this land all smiling again.'

Jack was somebody nowadays. Farmers sought him
out at market and sometimes drove up to Brown Elms
to see the improvements he was making there. They
asked his advice about grassland and stock and machinery and the use of artificial manures. He was
known by name for some miles around and held in
some regard, too, and he was pleased because of
Nenna. She took such pride in all he did that he could
not help but be proud himself. He had never been so
cared for before. He had never known such warmth
and comfort and satisfaction.

Sometimes, when he worked in the fields nearest
the cottage, he would see Nenna's duster fluttering out
of an upper window, or would see her going about the
garden, scattering corn for the hens and the geese.
Sometimes, resting his team at the end of a furrow, he
would take off his cap and wave to her, and she would
wave back, lifting Linn up to do the same.

Sometimes Nenna and the child would come hand
in hand across the fields to see him, bringing his midday meal in a basket, with a big stoneware bottle full
of cold sweet tea. If the day were a mild one, they
would stay in the field and eat with him, sitting on a
rug beneath the hedge, and on these occasions, Linn
would bring her very own dinner, wrapped in her own
red chequered napkin and carried in the tiny chipwood
basket that had her initials done in pokerwork on the
handle.

'What've you got for bait today, then?' he would ask
her. 'It's not bread and cheese by any chance?'

And it always *was* bread and cheese, for she had to

eat whatever he ate, and would even have had a raw onion, eating it with a knife as he did, but that she knew it would make her cry.

When her dinner was eaten, she would wander off, stepping carefully from clod to clod, to speak to the horses and offer them her last crust. Jack had to watch her, ready to order her away, for she had no fear and would if allowed have passed to and fro under the horses' bellies or gone behind them to pick at the mud drying on their fetlocks. She thought they were all like old Shiner at home, whose tail she swung on and whose poor, split hooves she polished every day with a little boot-brush.

Shiner always let her do just as she pleased and would stand looking down at her over one shoulder as she rubbed spit on a wart on his leg or pulled the sticky-burrs out of the long coarse hairs on his feet. He would come to her with a little whicker of welcome the moment she squeezed through the bars of the gate into the orchard. She and Shiner were great friends. He knew she always brought him something. All the loaf sugar would have gone to him, had Nenna not kept her cupboards fastened.

Linn wanted to be friends with every living creature on earth and would run after the geese in the garden, her small bare arms outstretched towards them, calling out: 'I'll catch you, geeses!—I'll catch you, geeses!' And would then stand forlorn, on the brink of tears, because they would not stay and let her embrace them. The tears seldom came. Something would certainly happen to distract her: a jackdaw perching on the pig's back, or an apple falling, smack, off the tree, and she would be rocking with laughter instead.

When Jack was at home, she hardly ever left his side, but wanted to watch whatever he was doing. Everything he did was such a splendid joke.

Every six months or so, he cleaned the chimney with four long beanpoles tied end to end and a big branch of holly as a brush. Linn would be out in the garden, waiting, and when the 'brush' shot out of the chimney, she would go off into fits of trilling laughter.

'Again?' she would call to Jack, indoors. 'Dad? Dad? Do it again?'

In wintertime, whenever there was a hard frost, he would lift her up so that she could reach the icicles hanging along the eaves of the thatch. She would break one off and lick its point.

'Ooo! Brr! It's cold. It's cold.'

'Well, of course it's cold! Whoever heard of a hot daglet?'

'I did!' she said, tilting her chin, saucily. 'I seen 'em, too.'

'Oh? Where was that?'

'Not going to tell you!'

'That's because it ent true.'

' '*Tis* true!' she said, and held her icicle against his throat, threatening to drop it inside his shirt. 'Shall I?' she said. 'Shall I drop it down?'

'You do,' he warned, 'and I shall put one in your drawers!'

'You wouldn't,' she said.

'Oh, yes, I would.'

'It'd melt on me. It'd make me wet.'

'And jolly well serve you right, too—you with your yarns about hot daglets!'

'How do they come? The icicles?'

'Drip, drip, drip, that's how they come, and get catched in the act when the weather turns frosty.'

'Why does the weather turn frosty?'

'Now we're off! We're in for it now—why? why?— sure as Worcester shines against Gloucester. Supposing you ask why little tongues must always waggle?'

'Why must they?'

'Ah. Why? You've got me there. I reckon they must want something to do.'

In the springtime one year, when the birds were nesting, he climbed his ladder to put a 'cat' on the cottage roof, to scare away the sparrows making holes in the thatch. The 'cat' was made of old velveteen, stuffed with straw, and had two green glass beads stuck in for eyes. It had a humpty back and looked ferocious. But its long upright tail was soon pecked to pieces; its glaring eyes disappeared; the birds were just as busy as ever.

'Damn and hammer it!' Jack said to Linn. 'I reckon you told 'em that cat warnt real.'

'Not me,' she said. 'I never told 'em.'

'Who was it, then, if it warnt you?'

'A little bird told 'em!' she exclaimed.

She was always laughing. Everything was a joke to her. Even when she was being scolded, she always managed to turn it aside.

'Whose little dirty black hands've been here?' Jack demanded, pointing to the five tell-tale smudges on the white wall.

'Don't know,' Linn said, considering the matter.

'Then let's have a look-see who fits, shall we, and maybe we shall learn something.'

He took hold of her hand and put it up against the wall, fitting thumb and then fingers into the smudges. But long before the fourth and last finger was pressed firmly into its place, the child was already wriggling and spluttering with delighted laughter. This was the best joke of all: to see her own hand fitting the imprint on the wall.

'Someone,' he said, 'is proved to be a dirty rascal.'

'You,' she said. 'Dirty lascal!'

'Someone was told to go to mother and get herself washed in time for bed, warnt they?'

'Did wash. Two times.'

'I reckon you're telling me tales,' Jack said. 'Black paws like them! I reckon you must've been up the chimney.'

'Holly bush! Up the chimney!'

'Just look at your pinny, the state it's in. How is your mother to get that clean? And your frock too—I reckon you've been huggling the coal-man.'

But the more he frowned at her, keeping his face perfectly straight, the more she spluttered at him, finding him irresistibly funny.

'Old eyebrows!' she said. 'Tobacco-face!—Puffing away!'

'Who're you talking to?' he demanded.

'Talking to *you*,' she said, doubling over.

'You're getting too saucy, Miss Mercybright.'

'Grrr!' she said. 'Saucy your own-self. Old vexatious!'

'Your mother's calling, so you run along before she gets cross and has to fetch you, otherwise there'll likely be ructions, 'cos you've got an appointment with soap and water.'

Linn's life was like a bird's: she was always happy to go to bed; always happy to get up in the morning; and in between times she was never at a loss how to fill the hours.

But there were sorrows even for Linn, as when the old horse Shiner died, on a snowy morning in the middle of April, 1900.

It was a Sunday. Jack was lighting the fire in the stove and Nenna was laying the table for breakfast. They had got up in darkness and not yet done more than glance briefly at the outside world. But Linn, upstairs, waking to the sight of the snow falling, tumbled out of bed and went straight to the window, looking out over the garden to the orchard. And there was Shiner, lying stiffly on his side, a dark grey shape on the whitened grass, with the powdery snow falling upon him.

Linn came downstairs sobbing fit to break her heart and threw herself into Jack's arms. He could not understand it. Nor could Nenna. They stared at each other over the child's head.

'What is it? What is it?' he asked, distraught. He had never heard her cry before. 'Did you hurt yourself? Did you have a bad dream?'

'It's Shiner!' she said, her voice muffled against his chest. 'Shiner's dead! Out there in the snow!'

'Ah, no?' he said, and went to the window with the child in his arms. 'He surely ent? Not our old Shiner?' But a glance outside was enough to convince him, for the horse's head was stretched back and his mouth was open. 'Poor old boy,' he said sadly. 'Poor old Shiner, he's gone, right enough. And only last night we was talking about him being so sprightly, warnt we?'

The child would eat nothing all day long, but went about like a small ghost, refusing comfort. When Jack took her out to say a last farewell to the horse, she wanted to stay and sweep the snow from the body; wanted Jack to bring the old horse back to life. And at bed-time that night she cried and cried into her pillow, so that even Nenna got out of patience.

'You'd better go up to her,' she said. 'I can do nothing with her. She won't go to sleep and she'll make herself ill if she goes on like this.'

So Jack went up and sat on the edge of Linn's bed, and her small face accused him wanly.

'Why did Shiner have to die?'

'He was old, that's why. He was tired and frail and and he'd got so's he wanted a good long sleep. You don't grudge Shiner his sleep, do you?'

'When'll he wake up again?'

'I dunno about that exactly. Not for a while, I don't suppose. But when he does wake up in the end, why, he'll be a new horse all over again.'

'Mama said he'd gone to heaven.'

'Ah, that's right, in heaven,' he said. 'That's where he'll be when he wakes up. He'll have all his teeth in his head again, and a good clover ley growing all round him, and a bin of oats every morning and evening.'

But she was worried because the old horse had died out in the cold, in the snow.

'Why wasn't he in his shelter?'

'I dunno. I suppose he preferred to die out in the open. He never thought much of that shelter I built him. He only used it to scratch hisself on. He always preferred to be out and about under the trees, winter or summer, rain or shine.'

He could bring no brightness to the child's face, but as he talked to her, quietly, her eyes closed little by little and sleep claimed her.

In the morning, he brought in a basket containing

seven baby chicks, to keep them warm beside the stove, and when Linn came downstairs she was attracted at once by their chirping. In the afternoon, Nenna took her to have tea with Amy Gauntlet, to be out of the way when the knacker came for Shiner's carcass. And the following day, she went with her Auntie Philippa to see some new calves at Spouts Hall Farm.

Time did the rest. The child was only three-and-a-half. There were many things to see and do. Shiner stepped back a pace or two and was soon wrapped round in mist and shadows.

All through the spring of 1900, when the newspapers were full of the war in South Africa, the men would come to Jack and discuss the latest news with him. They plied him with questions. They expected him to know all about it.

'This here Modder River, now,' said Peter Luppitt, 'whereabouts would that be, precisely?'

'Search me. I dunno much more than you do.'

'You was out there, warnt you, back in 1881?'

'It's a big country,' Jack said.

'Seems to me you was only wasting your time when you *was* out there,' said Joe Stretton, 'Seeing we've got it all to do again by the look of things.'

'Ah, why didn't you finish the Boers good and proper while you was at it?' asked Oliver Lacey. 'Instead of leaving them to breed?'

' 'Cos they finished us, more nearly, warnt it?'

'Well, we didn't lose to them, exactly, did we?'

'We certainly didn't win, did we?'

'Did you kill a few?' asked Percy Rugg.

'No, none,' Jack said.

'What, not even one or two extra big ones, them you couldn't hardly miss?'

'No. Nurra one. Not so much as a Boer rabbit.'

'I bet I shall bag a few when I get out there,' said Harvey Stretton, bright-eyed.

'You?' said his father, with great scorn. 'They ent taking half-pint boy-chaps yet, are they?'

'I'm going, though, as soon as I reach my full nineteen.'

'It'll all be over by then, you fool. Another month and the Boers'll be beaten.'

'D'you think it will, Jack?' Harvey asked.

'I dunno, boy. You'd better write and ask Lord Roberts.'

In June that year a recruiting party came to Niddup and drilled for an hour or two on the ham. Harvey gave his age as nineteen and received the Queen's Shilling, along with nine other Niddup lads, and a few weeks later he was walking about in his uniform, showing off to his father and the rest of the men on the farm.

'It's a natty little hat,' said Jonathan Kirby, drumming with his fingers on Harvey's pill-box, 'but it ent going to keep the sun off your noddle much, is it?'

'What're them stripes down the sides of your trousis for?' asked Peter Luppitt. 'So's the Boers can see you better?'

'I shall have a pith helmet to go out there,' Harvey said, 'and a khaki uniform with puttees.'

'I hope they're giving you a rifle,' said his father, ' 'cos you certainly ent having my old shotgun to go with and you needn't think it!'

'I go into barracks on Sunday night and I start training on Monday morning.'

'Leffright, leffright, leffright, leff!' Percy Rugg bellowed suddenly. 'Ten!—Shun! All fours!'

'I wouldn't have volunteered, myself,' said Will Gauntlet. 'Fancy leaving your Dad like that, and your younger brothers.'

'Hah!' said Stretton, clapping Harvey on the shoulder. 'Somebody got to go, ent they, and I shall be thankful to see the last of him for five minutes. It'll maybe make him buck up his ideas a bit.'

Harvey went off with the nine other Niddup volunteers, and his place on the farm was taken by his brother Ernest, aged thirteen.

'I shan't be moving, neither, when Harvey comes back,' Ernest said. 'He'll have to make do with being second ploughboy under me.'

Heifer calves born on the farm that year were given names such as Ladysmith and Bloemfontein. 'And as if that ent bad enough,' Jack said to Nenna, 'the Peter Luppitts is calling their new baby son Kimberley!'

'Another baby son?' Nenna said. 'They have three boys already, surely? Why should the Luppitts have so many?'

'Ah, well, that's the way it goes,' Jack said. 'It's all meant, I daresay.'

He was angry with himself for mentioning the matter. He could have bitten out his tongue. For it was a great sadness to Nenna that the sons she longed for never came, and in recent months, especially, she had been growing strangely moody. She was always fancying herself with child and then, when she had to admit that she was mistaken, she would fall into a kind of fretful sullenness, when even Jack could not get a word out of her.

'Don't *you* want a son?' she said once. 'Of course you do! It's only natural. All men want sons.'

'I'm quite happy to take what I'm given.'

'Well, I intend to give you a son, and I shall, too. I'm determined on it.'

'Have you been talking to Amy Gauntlet? Listening to her and her old wives' tales?'

'Why not? She's had eleven children, didn't she?'

'That's because old Will is a shepherd. Shepherds always have a lot of children. They're used to dealing with flocks, you see.'

'*I'm* not laughing,' Nenna said. 'It's no good making jokes with me.'

'And what did Amy suggest this time? Tinkertations under the moon? Or a glass of parsley wine at bedtime?'

But although he teased Nenna about it, he was often worried, deep down inside, for he too had his superstitions and he felt, somehow, that to ask too much of Providence was to turn it against you.

'We're all right as we are,' he said. 'I ent worried about having a son so just you forget it and leave well alone.'

But Nenna only looked at him with a sly smile, as though she had something up her sleeve. She was young. She was strong. Dr Spray had said she was perfectly healthy. It was wicked that she should have had only one child in four and a half years of marriage.— She was therefore resolved to do something about it. And at harvest-time that year, when the gypsies came as usual to camp in the birchwoods behind the farmhouse, Nenna was up there everyday, talking to Mrs Zillery Boswell.

'How many pegs do they make you buy in exchange for them potions?' Jack asked. 'Seems to me we could easy supply the whole of Niddup!'

They were out with Philippa in the Home Field, testing the wheat with a view to cutting, and one of the gypsies had just galloped past on a skewbald pony.

'She ought not to go there,' Philippa said. 'It encourages them to be familiar. You're her husband—you ought to stop her.'

'I shan't stop her,' Jack said, laughing. 'I'm a man that likes a quiet life.'

But there came a time, not all that long after, when he felt obliged to change his mind.

It was a day near the end of the harvest. The men were all up in one of the old Maryhope pieces, cutting the last thirty acres of dredge-corn. They worked late, wanting to get it all up in stooks, because there were showers in the offing. So it was quite dark by the time Jack went home, and as he walked down the fields of stubble he saw a red glow, somewhere up behind the farmhouse.

He turned aside and went on up into the birchwood and there, in the middle of the largest clearing, he found a gypsy waggon burning. The fire from its roof leapt as high as the treetops. The timbers blazed; the paint-work blistered and then crackled; the big red sparks flew up and drifted about overhead. The gypsies stood around, watching the blaze with sombre faces, and Jack saw one of them step forward to throw a set of harness into the very heart of the fire.

'Who's dead?' he asked, going to Mrs Zillery Boswell.

'Old Hananiah,' Zillery said.

'What was he sick of, do you know?'

'He was eighty-three. That's a pretty good age for any man. I wouldn't say he was sick exactly.'

'How long was he ailing?'

'A few days or so. I couldn't say, not exactly, but it warnt overlong, anyhow. He was an old, old man. He said his Rosanda'd been calling for him. You remember Rosanda? She died a while back, when we was at Dingham.'

'Did you have a doctor?' Jack asked.

'No doctor, no. There's no cure for old age.'

Mrs Zillery's face was closed against him, and the faces around were so many graven images, redly lit, staring at the burning waggon, now beginning to crumble inwards. Jack turned away, knowing he would learn nothing further from them, but stopped once to call out a warning.

'See that fire don't catch them trees! If there's timber ruined I shall have to run you off the farm!'

And when he got home he spoke very firmly to Nenna about it.

'Keep away from the gypsies. There's sickness among them. Old Han has died and they're burning his waggon.'

'What sort of sickness?'

'I dunno. They wouldn't say. But they fetch their water out of the horse-pond and there's no one else would drink such stuff. So be sure to keep away in future—it's always best to be on the safe side.'

Nenna nodded. She was frightened of sickness. She went at once to burn all the clothes-pegs the gypsies had sold her.

The following Saturday, Jack finished work at three o'clock, but when he got home, Nenna and Linn were not there, so he went in search of them, guessing that they had set out to meet him and had missed him somewhere, crossing the fields.

He came upon Nenna in the Long Meadow, sitting with her back against a willow, close beside the lower brook. The day was warm and airless, and she was asleep, her hat and scarf thrown down beside her, and a basket of mushrooms nearby. Linn was wading about in the brook, gathering buttercups and cresses, the muddy water washing over her shoes and stockings and wetting her frock whenever she stooped to pick a flower.

Jack pulled her out and scolded her gently, wringing the water out of her frock. He was more severe when he scolded Nenna.

'You should be more careful! The child has got herself drenched all over. And supposing she'd got herself stuck in the mud? It's three feet deep or so, just below. You'd never've heard her calling you, sleeping so fast as you was, neither. I had a job to wake you my own-self.'

'I came over tired,' Nenna said. 'The day is so terribly close and stuffy. But I didn't mean to go to sleep. I only sat down to watch the linnets in that poplar.'

She picked up her hat and scarf and basket, and they walked home together, Linn between them, swinging from their hands. Nenna talked of the ketchup she intended making. She had a new recipe from Amy Gauntlet and was going to try it that afternoon.

'Mushrooms are good for you. Good as meat, Amy says.'

When they reached home, she stood for a moment outside the porch, looking up at the roof, where a wagtail was busy running about. She put her fingers up to her forehead.

'I feel rather strange all of a sudden. My head is gone all numb and muzzy.'

'It's sleeping out-of-doors has made you feel like that. Come inside and drink a drop of your barley water.'

He was intent on changing the child's wet clothes for dry ones, a task that took him a good ten minutes. When he turned again to Nenna, she was standing on the hearth, bent almost double with her arms folded across her stomach, and as he went closer to look at her face, he saw that her skin was grey and yeasty, wet all over with perspiration.

'Here, you're poorly!' he said, frightened. 'Sit down in this chair and take things easy.'

He made her sit down in the basketwork chair, with a couple of cushions behind her head, then he covered her over with a warm blanket. Her eyes were filmy. Her jaws were clenched hard together. She was shivering all over.

'You sleep for a bit. That's the best thing. I shan't be gone more than a jiffy.'

And he turned to Linn, who stood at the window, setting out her flowers along the ledge.

'Don't you move,' he told her sternly. 'You stay as you are till you see your Auntie Philippa come in at that door there. Understand?'

He went to the farmhouse as fast as he could and sent Miss Philippa down to the cottage. Then he went to Niddup to fetch Dr Spray.

'She will need nursing,' the doctor said. 'And I warn you it may be a long illness.'

'Ought she to go to the Infirmary?'

'I think she's better staying here, where she's isolated, at least till we know for sure what's wrong.'

'Then I'll come and stay and nurse her for you,' Philippa said, her hand on Jack's arm.

'No, no, I'll nurse her myself. You take Linn back home with you, if you please, and keep her there till it's all over.'

'How can you nurse her, with so much work to do on the farm?'

'Damn the farm! It can go to hell!'

'What use is a man, anyway, at a time like this?'

'I think it's better,' the doctor said, 'for Mr Mercybright to nurse his wife, so long as he follows my instructions, of course.'

'I'll do whatever you tell me,' Jack said. 'Anything. Just tell me what.' And a little later, seeing the doctor off at the door, he said: 'What's wrong with her? What illness is it?'

'I have a suspicion it's typhoid fever. But I can't think how she should have come to contract it.'

'I can,' Jack said grimly, and told the doctor about the gypsies. 'One of 'em died. Didn't you have to sign a certificate?'

'I wasn't summoned. I know nothing about it. It was probably Dr King from Hotcham—He'd sign anything when he's half seas over. I shall have to look into the matter myself. Meantime, well, I'll call on Nenna first thing in the morning.'

'Yes. All right.'

'She's a strong young woman. She should be all right. She'll pull through—I'm sure of that.'

Jack was left staring. It had never occurred to him to doubt it. He went inside and closed the door.

Nenna's illness lasted a full eighteen days. Jack was with her day and night. The doctor came every morning and evening. A nurse came every afternoon.

During the last four or five days, Nenna often lay unconscious. Her poor wrung-out body was thus relieved, though the fever continued to rage in her brain. Jack could not understand most of the things she said in her delirium. It was a perfect stranger talking, and sometimes the words themselves had no meaning.

Only once did she open her eyes and look at him and speak to him, knowing who he was, and that was a few hours before the end. Even then her mind was wandering: she thought she had given birth to a child; and she looked at him with a little smile not of this world.

'It's a boy this time, isn't it? I knew it would be. I told you I'd give you a son, remember, and I've kept my promise as a good wife should. I always knew you wanted it, really, although you would never say so outright. And I shall have more. You'll see.'

On his way up towards the birchwood, he passed alongside the Home Field, where the men had already begun ploughing. They saw him passing and Joe Stretton came running up to the corner gateway.

'Hey! Jack! Hang on a minute. We been wanting to ask you—how's your missus?'

Jack made no answer but tramped on up the rise and into the birchwood. The gypsy women were at their fires, with their stewpots steaming, cooking supper ready for their menfolk. The gypsy children gathered round, offering him baskets of damsons for sixpence, but he pushed past them and went to Mrs Zillery Boswell.

'Where are all your menfolk?' he asked.

'At Egham Horse Fair, mostly, I reckon.'

'Then send and fetch them back at once. I want all of you off this land by darkfall. Every last pony and every last waggon! Do you hear what I say? Do you understand me? Never mind your suppers,—that's nothing to me—just get the rest of your tribe together and clear off this farm as soon as maybe!'

'But the gentleman surely don't mean it really—'

'If you ent all gone by the time I come back in a couple of hours I shall speed you on your way with a couple of barrels of gunshot!'

Reading his face, the gypsies believed him, and a boy was sent off on a pony to Egham. By dusk that evening, the clearing in the wood was quite deserted, and the procession of waggons was creaking on its way, down the steep track into Felpy Lane, curved roofs and smoking chimneys just visible over the hedgerow.

As Jack stood watching at the top of the track, Miss Philippa came up with Stretton. She glanced at the shotgun under Jack's arm.

'Why are the gypsies moving already? They don't usually go till winter.'

'I told them to, that's why,' he said. 'I sent them packing, bag and baggage.'

'What right have you to give such orders without so much as a word to me? This land is mine, not yours, remember, and if there are people here who are not wanted it's up to *me* to order them off!'

'I've saved you the bother, then, ent I?' he said.

'They're not responsible for Nenna dying. You can't

blame them for what has happened. For God's sake pull yourself together!'

'Get out of my way,' Jack said. 'Get out of my way, the pair of you, both. I ent in the mood for arguments.'

He went into the wood to see that the gypsies' fires were douted.

Sometimes, ploughing the big steep fields up at Far Fetch or around Tootle Barrow, he turned up old skulls and bones and pike-heads and a number of small thick metal coins. The skulls and bones he put into the hedgerow. The rusty pike-heads he ploughed back into the ground. And the coins he took to Sylvanus Knarr at The Bay Tree, where they were cleaned and used in the making of hot rum flip, 'to put a bit of iron into our blood' as old Angelina was fond of saying. According to her, the old coins were better than new ones. They had more virtue in them, she said.

Sometimes, that autumn, the clouds came so low over Far Fetch that they swept along the slopes of the fields, bearing down on him as he trudged, until everything was blotted out around him. He would come to a standstill, blind and helpless, wondering if he should go for the swap-plough; but then the cloud would pass on by, rolling across the ribbed brown field, leaving him soaked as though by a shower. In another moment he would be able to pick out his marker on the far hedge.

He would click up the horses and trudge on, the plough-share travelling through the moist earth with a sound like the hissing of an angry goose.

It was very cold all through October. The fall of the year was swifter than usual. Summer seemed to slip straight into winter.

One day, when he was spreading muck in the Placketts, Miss Philippa came up behind him.

'Linn has been wondering where you've got to. She's asking whether you've gone away. What am I to say to her?'

'Tell her I shall be calling in to see her. Tomorrow, perhaps, or the day after when I ent so busy.'

'That's what you said the last time I asked you. And the time before that. Why do you say things if you don't mean them? And what am I to do with her?'

'She's all right with you, ent she? She ent sick nor pining nor nothing?'

'She's in perfect health, if that's what you mean, and I daresay she's as happy as can be expected in the cir-cumstances. But that's not the point.'

'Then maybe you want me to come and fetch her and take her back home again to the cottage?'

'No,' she said quickly. 'I don't want that, the child is better staying with me.'

'Well, then!' he said. 'Why all the fuffle?'

'I want to know when you mean to see her.'

'I'll be along, don't you worry, just as soon as I find the time. You tell her that. Say I'm coming as soon as maybe.'

'You ought to come to us for your dinner. I'm sure you're not eating properly by yourself, and what use is that, neglecting yourself and getting run down as you surely will? You need a woman to look after you—to see that you eat good nourishing meals. Come on Sun-day at one o'clock. I'll tell Mrs Miggs to count you in.'

'Right you are. Just as you say. Sunday dinner at one o'clock.'

'You'll come, then?' she said, surprised.

'Might as well. I've got to eat somewhere, like you say, so why not at your place?'

But he said it only to be rid of her. He had no intention of going to the farmhouse. He would just as soon go to The Bay Tree.

'By the way,' she said, 'Dr Spray was looking for you.'

'Oh? Was he? What'd he want? I paid his bill, didn't I?'

'He wasn't best pleased at your driving the gypsies off as you did. He'd been keeping an eye on them up here, he said, in case there were any more outbreaks of fever. He wanted them kept in one place.'

'They'll be in the quarry at Ludden all winter. It ent all that far for a man with a pony. He can keep an eye on 'em there if he wants to.'

He turned his back on her, forking the manure out over the stubble.

He gave himself work in out-of-the-way parts of the farm. It suited him to be alone. He wanted no one. When the men needed orders, they sought him out. When he had to be with them in the cowshed or barn or working on the threshing-machine, they would speak to him briefly now and then, but the rest of the time they left him to himself.

He wished Miss Philippa would do the same, but she was always appearing to him, seeking him out in remote places, and one day she came to the Twenty Five Acre, one of the old Maryhope fields, where he was laying an overgrown hedge.

'I want to talk to you about the stone.'

'Stone? What stone?'

'The headstone, of course, for Nenna's grave. The ground should be settled enough by now and it's time something was done about it. I want you to help me choose the words.'

'You're going to get wet, standing there.'

'And whose fault is that?' she asked, raging. 'If you came to the house as I wanted you to, we could talk things over and get them settled. We could even behave like civilized people! But oh, no,—I have to traipse about the fields in all weathers before I succeed in tracking you down. The other men never know where to find you, or so they pretend at any rate, so perhaps you'll be kind enough to give me your attention just this once and settle the matter here and now!'

'You attend to it,' Jack said. 'Put whatever words you like.'

'It's you that ought to see the mason. Whatever are people going to think?'

'They can think what they like. It's no odds to me.'

'That's all very fine. Everything left to me as always! You were Nenna's husband, remember, so why should I have to do it all?'

'You're the one that's wanting a stone.'

Jack was working with his back to the wind. He wore a sack folded in half, corner into corner, making a hood of double thickness, and was thus well protected. But Miss Philippa stood on the opposite side of the newly laid hedge, with the sleet driving sharply into her face.

'I don't suppose you would care if Nenna's grave remained bare and nameless?'

'That's right. I shouldn't care tuppence. What good is a stone? It won't bring Nenna back to life, will it?'

'Do you think your behaviour will bring her back? Skulking about at all hours, dragging your tail through muck and mire like a stricken fox in search of a hole? Just look at yourself! Have you no sense of pride whatever?'

'No. None.'

'Then you should have!' she said. 'For your child's sake—and for mine!'

'Yours? Why yours?'

'I *am* your employer,' she said tartly, 'even if I'm nothing else.'

'If I was you I should stand well back. You might get a wood-chip in your eye, else.'

'Coming and going like a thief in the night! Avoiding me at every turn! The only time you set foot near me is when you want me to pay your wages.'

'I work for them, don't I? So I might just as well pick them up?'

'Oh, you work, certainly! Even the ox must be given his due. But what do you do when you're not working? Where do you go and what sort of company do you choose? You revert to nature and spend your nights sleeping in the sawdust on the floor of a common village public house!'

Jack ignored her. He bent down a thorn with his gloved hand and sliced at the stem with a chop of his billhook. It was easy enough to pretend the woman was not there. He had only to turn his head a little, till the keen east wind was riffling at both sides of his hood, for the noise of it to cut her out completely. And the east wind it was that eventually drove her away.

One morning he awoke to find himself lying on a heap of hop-waste outside the kilns at Ennen Stoke. He could not remember how he had got there. All he could remember was leaving The Bay Tree with a traveller from Brum and setting him on the road to Egham.

It was still dark when he awoke, but there was a cloudy moon shining. He went straight to the farm and arrived in time for early milking. Joe Stretton had already started. He was on his way out with two full pails.

'By God, you look rough! And you smell like you came down the brewery drain-pipe!'

'It's the hops,' Jack said, sniffing his coat-sleeve.

'I know damn well it's the hops, man, and they'll be the ruin of you yet! You look a lot worser than old Nellie Lacey's stinking tom cat and I couldn't say fairer than that by no man!'

Jack sat on his stool and put his pail under Dewberry's udder. He pulled his cap down over his eyes and leant his forehead against the cow's side. And it seemed to him that her body yielded, melting away to nothing beneath him, letting him down and down and down, into a heaving dung-coloured darkness.

'You asleep, Jack?' asked Peter Luppitt, looking in at the end of the stall.

'By God, he is!' said Jonathan Kirby, looking over

Peter's shoulder. 'He's forty-winking, I do declare, and poor old Dewberry there nearly bursting!'

Jack opened his eyes and the cow's body became quite still. He put out his hands,—his fingers closed over the teats,—the milk went spurting into the pail. Luppitt and Kirby moved away. Joe Stretton appeared instead.

'Yes, what?'

'Did you have any breakfuss?'

'No. I warnt hungry.'

'You look more than just a little bit comical to me. I reckon you've got a fit of the jim-jams. Ent there naught I can do for you?'

'Yes. There is. You can leave me be.'

'All right. If that's how you want it. But there must be easier ways of killing yourself, I reckon, even if they ent all so clever as this one.'

Stretton still stood, hesitating. He seemed anxious.

'I was going to tell you about the letter.'

'What letter?'

'From my boy Harvey. He's coming home. He wrote me a letter from a hospital-place somewhere near Gloucester. Seems he's been wounded in the arm. I couldn't make out every word exactly—he was never much of a hand at writing—but it can't be too bad 'cos he's coming home any minute directly.'

'Good,' Jack said. 'I'm glad to hear it. That's good news for you, your boy Harvey coming home.'

A little while later, carrying two full pails across the cowshed, he slipped and fell on his back on the cobbles, the milk from both pails slopping over him, soaking through the sack he wore as an apron and wetting his jacket and trousers underneath. Joe Stretton helped him up and made him sit on a stool in the corner.

'You just sit there and take it easy. Seems to me you're about gum-foozled. Be quiet a minute while I get you a bunnel.'

He went to the house and returned with a mug full of hot sweet tea.

'I was in luck. They was just getting breakfuss. I

saw Mrs Miggs and she sent you this. Drink it up and you'll feel a lot better.'

Jack sipped at the tea, breathing heavily into the mug, and the steam rose up in a cloud to his face, moistening his stubbled jaw and cheekbones and forming a drop on the end of his nose. The tea warmed him. He could trace the course it took inside him, a tingling furrow of heat in his guts. But his head was still an empty vessel; his limbs and body were a burden to him; so he sat for a while and smoked his pipe.

While searching his pockets he came across a trinket bought the night before from the Brummagem traveller: two tiny Dutch clogs, carved out of pegwood, each the size of his small finger-nail, threaded together on a piece of red ribbon. He got up stiffly and went to the back door of the house. When Miss Philippa answered he gave her the empty earthenware mug and held up the trinket.

'I got this for Linn. Is she up yet?'

'She's up, yes. I'll give it to her.'

'Where is she, then? I'd better prefer to give it to her my own-self. Can I come in for just a minute?'

'In that condition? I think not! *I* have some thought for Linn's feelings, though you yourself evidently have none.' And she looked him over in disgust. 'Have you no idea how the child would feel—have you no idea how it makes *me* feel—to see you so drunken and degraded?'

At that moment, Linn came along the passage behind her and stood, half hidden, peeping out from behind her skirts.

'Here,' Jack said. 'I've got something for you. Two little clogs like they wear in Holland. I bought them specially last night. How do you like 'em?'

Linn inched forward and looked at the trinket dangling from his fingers. She reached up and took it without a word, stepping back at once into the shadows. Her small face was blank. Her frown was suspicious.

'Well, Linn?' Miss Philippa prompted. 'What do you say when you're given a present?'

'Thank you very much,' the child whispered.

'That's all right—I'm glad you like 'em,' Jack said.
'I reckon it's time you had a present, seeing it's very
nearly Christmas. And how are you going on here
lately? You keeping nicely? Everything fine and
dandy, is it?'

The child made no answer; only stared at him with
Nenna's eyes; and after a moment he turned away.
But before the door was closed upon him, he heard her
voice as she spoke to her Auntie Philippa.

'Who is that man? He's not my daddy, is he, auntie?
That dirty old man is not my daddy . . .'

The day was a wet one and in the afternoon Jack took
four horses down to be shod at the smithy in Niddup.
Waiting his turn he leant in the doorway, looking out
across the dip to where the three main roads came
down, meeting in a little open place called the Pightle.

At three o'clock the carrier's cart arrived from
Egham, and a young soldier climbed out, shouldering
his kit-bag. It was Harvey Stretton and as he turned
into Felpy Lane, Jack saw that the boy's right sleeve
was empty, folded and pinned to the side of his tunic.

The smith was having some sort of trouble. The
Ridlands Hall carriage was in for repairs and was taking longer than expected. He called out to Jack, saying
he would have to wait even longer.

'All right,' Jack said, 'I'll go for a bit of a stroll
round.'

'Ah, and have one for me while you're at it, will
you?'

But although Jack started towards the river, he did
not turn right towards The Bay Tree; he turned left
instead to the old church, standing at the upper edge
of the ham. It was almost dusk, but he found Nenna's
grave easily enough, and was able to read the name on
the headstone: Henrietta Ruth, beloved wife of John
Mercybright: died September 26th., 1900, aged 24.
The mound was covered in new grass, little straight-
standing blades, very fine and pointed. Soon, he
thought, it would want cutting.

Inside the church, someone was moving, carrying a

light. Jack stood watching it, glimmering first in one tall coloured window, then in the next, until it reached the eastern end, where it blossomed out in quiet splendour as the bearer lit the candles on the altar. Outside, in the rainy darkness, Jack shivered and turned away.

On Sunday morning he set about cleaning and tidying the cottage. He swept and dusted everywhere, beat the mats on the hedge in the garden, scoured the floors till the red bricks showed their colour again. He even black-leaded the kitchen range and polished all its bits of brass, before lighting a fire in the stove.

He heated the copper in the little wash-house, stripped off his clothes, and scrubbed himself hard all over, using a tablet of strong red carbolic soap. When he came to shave, the ten weeks' growth of beard proved stubborn. It took time; he had to keep on stropping his razor; and when he was finished, his skin felt tender and soft, like a baby's. He found he had a narrow scar, only recently healed, running along the edge of his jaw, and a small cut on his left ear. It was so long since he had last looked into a mirror, the face he saw there was almost a stranger's.

He put on his best Sunday suit and cap and his best soft boots, and, smelling of camphor and boot-polish, set out for the farmhouse. Mrs Miggs let him in and showed him into the front parlour, and there, in another moment or two, Miss Philippa came to him, wearing a full-skirted dress of black silk. She was clearly astonished to see him looking clean and tidy. A little gleam appeared in her eyes. But she stood stiffly, her hands folded in front of her, the fingers entwined.

'Where's Linn?' he asked.

'Why d'you want to know? Have you come with more cheap gew-gaws to give her?'

'No, I've come to fetch her and take her home.'

'Don't be ridiculous!' she exclaimed. 'How can you possibly take her home? The state the place is in—it's worse than a pig-sty!'

'Not now, it ent. I've been sprucing it up.'

'And who would look after her? Surely not you?'

'I don't see why not.'

'You can't even look after yourself properly, let alone a child of four. Oh, you're well enough at this very minute—quite the respectable gentleman, I'm sure—but how long is that going to last, I wonder?'

'I'd like to see Linn, if it's no odds to you. Will you fetch her for me?'

'No!' she exclaimed. 'This is all wrong! I will not let you drag the poor child away from me just to suit your whim of the moment. The idea is monstrous. She's better here.'

'She's *my* daughter. Not yours.'

'Rather late in the day for remembering that, isn't it, seeing you've ignored her all these weeks past?'

'Late or not,' he said, 'I mean to have her.'

For a while she stared at him, hazel eyes very pale and bright, the blood dark on her prominent cheek-bones. Then she moved away to one side of the hearth and spread her hands towards the fire.

'How can a man look after a child? It isn't natural.'

'It's natural enough, when the man is her father.'

'You'll be working all day.'

'Linn will go to school with the Gauntlet children. They'll be calling for her on the way down. She's been wanting to go this twelvemonth or more and now I reckon it'll do her good. Then Cissy Gauntlet will stop with her at the cottage after school and look after her till I get home.'

'Cissy Gauntlet is only thirteen.'

'I know that. But she's good with little 'uns and Linn likes her. I'd trust Cissy Gauntlet anywhere.'

'It seems you've got it all arranged.'

'That's right, I have. I seen the Gauntlets yesterday evening.'

'But why can't Linn stop here in the daytime and then come to you after work?'

'No,' he said. 'It's better my way.'

'And what about when you go to The Bay Tree? What happens to Linn when she wakes up at night and finds herself all alone in the cottage?'

'I shan't be going to The Bay Tree,' he said.

'So you say! So you say!'

But it was the last feeble shot in her armoury, thrown off at random. Her expression already showed her resignation. She knew he would never neglect the child—not now he had given his promise.

'Very well,' she said. 'I'll send her to you.'

She went out of the room and a little while later Linn came in, small and pinched-looking, creeping forward as though afraid. She stared at him for fully a minute, her gaze going over him, taking in the familiar clothes, the familiar watchstrap fastened across the front of his waistcoat, then returning at last to dwell uncertainly on his face.

'Well, Linn Mercybright, don't you know me?'

The child nodded but remained quite silent, withdrawn, unsmiling. There was no hint of welcome in her face; nothing of her usual small bright spirit; nothing of the old warmth and fondness. Was she paying him out for his desertion in the past ten weeks? If she was, he deserved it, he told himself, and it was his task to win back her favour.

'I've come to take you home, and about time too, I expect you'll say. I want you to help me make the dinner. We're having a bit of boiled beef—Cissy Gauntlet got it for me—but I ent too sure how to make the pudden. You'll help me, won't you?—You'll give me a hand?'

Still nothing more than a slight nod, but when he made a move towards the door, holding out his hand towards her, she put her own hand into it at once and went with him unquestioningly.

Miss Philippa's face as she saw them off at the back door was difficult to read. She seemed genuinely fond of the child; her fingers rested for a moment on the small fair head; yet her manner was just as severe and abrupt as ever—what warmth she had seemed always to be well battened down.

'Don't be a nuisance to your father, will you? No naughty tricks? No disobedience?'

'Linn'll be good,' Jack said. 'She's going to help me get the dinner.'

With a tiny knife, not too sharp, Linn scraped at the lump of suet, sitting opposite him at the table as he stood peeling the onions, carrots, parsnips and potatoes. The big saucepan hummed on the trivet, and the kitchen was filled with the smell of boiling beef.

'What next?' he said, dropping the vegetables into the saucepan. 'A handful of barley? A good whoops of salt?'

'Yes,' she said, stopping work to watch him.

'How're you getting on with that there suet? Shall I give you a hand? Take a turn, shredding?' He took a sharp knife and scraped the suet into shreds. 'And now I must make this roly pudden. Two handfuls of flour. One handful of suet. Salt and pepper and a good mix round, then make it sticky with this here skim milk. Am I doing it right, do you think? Making a proper molly job of it, eh?'

'Yes,' she said, watching as he plumped the piece of dough on the table.

'Jiggle it all about in the flour . . . roll it into a roly-poly . . . and wrap it round in this nice clean cloth. Ah, and how do I do up the ends, I wonder? Do I tie 'em up with bits of blue ribbon?'

'No,' she said, and a little breath of a laugh escaped her.

'What, then? Boot-laces?'

'Silly,' she said. 'You have to tie them up with string.'

'String!' he said, snapping his fingers, and went to search the dresser drawer. 'What a good thing it is I've got you to tell me how to go on. I'd be making janders of it, else.'

While the dinner was cooking and Jack was bringing more logs for the basket, Linn stood on a chair at the gable-end window, watching the birds fluttering and squabbling at the old bacon bone Jack had hung in the cherry tree early that morning. The day was damp and overcast, but with little bursts of sun now and then, slanting down whenever a hole got torn in the clouds.

'Not a bad old day,' Jack said. 'I thought we'd go down the dip after dinner and take a walk along the Nidd. There was herons there a few days ago. Five or six of 'em. Maybe seven.'

'What were they doing?'

'They were standing looking at theirselves in the water.'

'Why were they?'

'To see and make sure that they was tidy. They like to look decent the same as most folk. And then, of course, they'd also be thinking of doing a bit of fishing.'

'Fishing? How can they?' And the frown she turned on him was puzzled, for she pictured the herons with rods and lines.

'Oh, herons is clever at fishing,' Jack said. 'They keep their beaks long and sharp on purpose. Would you like to go down with me and see them? And maybe find some white violets under the trees like we did when we went there once before?'

Linn nodded assent, her eyes wakeful, the glimmerings of pleasure in their depths. She was happy enough in her quiet way. Happy enough to be with him again. As happy, anyway, as he could expect. The old warmth was still missing between them, but that would come back in time, he was sure. It was up to him to see that it did. He must work towards it. He would need that warmth in years to come and so would Linn, for they had nobody but each other.

Every afternoon now, Cissy Gauntlet brought Linn home when school was over, lit the fire and made the place cosy, and kept the child company till Jack got in after work.

Cissy was a fair freckled girl with a long narrow face and something of her father's sorrowful manner. At thirteen she was already a natural mother, delighted to have sole charge of Linn and taking her responsibilities with the greatest seriousness.

Often when Jack arrived home, he would find the two of them going over the twice times table or the words of Our Father or the alphabet, and while he washed himself in the scullery, he would listen to them chanting together.

> 'A for an apple on the tree,
> B for the busy bumblebee,
> C for cat and D for dog,
> E for earwig, F for frog.'

Often, too, he would find Harvey Stretton sitting with them, joining in their childish games. Harvey was a special favourite with Linn. He would bring her sprays of spindleberries, or giant fir-cones, or a mumruffin's nest out of the hedge, or a bunch of feathers from a cock pheasant's tail. And, despite his disability, he was always cheerful, always full of life.

'Where's your arm gone?' Linn asked, touching the boy's empty sleeve.

'Seems I must've left it somewhere.'

'Why did you?'

'Well, it warnt of a lot of use to me, really. I was silly enough to let it get damaged. So here I am like Admiral Nelson, except that I've still got two good eyes.'

'Will it grow again, your arm?' Linn asked.

'Now that's an idea, ent it, eh? I'd like to have two arms again and get two hands on the stilts of a plough. I must hope for the best, mustn't I, and see if this sleeve gets filled up again?'

Harvey was doing odd jobs on the farm, earning only a few shillings, but Cissy Gauntlet had ideas for him. Cissy was an intelligent girl, eager to learn and get on in the world, and her great ambition when she left school was to become a village postmistress. She wanted Harvey to be a postman.

'Well, it's an outdoor job, that's something, ent it?' Harvey said. 'Even if it does mean swapping one damned uniform for another. But it's reading the names on the envelopes—that's the thing that'd flummox me.'

'Can't you read, then, for goodness' sake?'

'I can read all right so long as the words is all printed but I ent much shakes when it comes to what's hand-wrote by folks theirselves.'

'Then I'll have to teach you,' Cissy said.

The boy and the girl were 'great' together, as William Gauntlet said to Jack, and although the girl was not yet fourteen, they were fast becoming 'acquaintances.' It would come to a wedding one fine day and Ciss would be the making of that boy Harvey.

Soon Harvey was calling at Perry Cottage dressed in his postman's uniform and carrying his big canvas satchel. But as it was always at the end of his round, he had no letters to show Linn, and she was bitterly disappointed.

'Why don't *we* get letters?' she asked him.

'I don't rightly know,' Harvey said. 'Not everyone does. Not by a long chalk. I suppose there ent enough to go round.' Then, seeing Linn's face, he said gravely: 'I shall have to speak to the postmaster, shan't I?'

So once a week after that, there would always be a letter for Linn, in a small envelope carefully addressed in capitals: To Miss Linn Mercybright; Perry Cottage; Brown Elms Farm; Niddup, near Hotcham. Harvey would pretend to search his satchel; would draw out the letter and squint at the writing; and would place it in Linn's impatient hands. Then, once she had opened it, it was Cissy's job to read it aloud.

'Dear Linn: I hear as you had a cold in your nose the day before yesterday, Sunday, that is, so take good care and don't go out in this cold east wind without you wear your thick woollen scarf . . .'

'Who's it from, who's it from?' Linn would ask, and Cissy, frowning over the signature, would say, 'This one's from the Lord Mayor of London' or 'Seems it's her Majesty the Right Honourable Queen Victoria writing to you this week from the palace . . .'

Jack, coming home, would hear the three voices upraised in talk, and Linn's light laughter trilling out, and would stand for an instant waiting for the three young faces to turn towards him in the red warm fire-glow.

Then his daughter would run to him, as in the old days,
for him to lift her up to the rafters.

'You had another letter?' he would ask. 'I thought
as much when I heard the excitement. And who is it
this time? The Shah of Persia?'

'Don't look and I'll show you!' she would say. 'It's
wrote on blue paper and there's little drawings of Mr
Gauntlet with all his sheeps and dogs in the paddock . . .'

His life and hers were linked as before. The warmth
was back between them again.

On a dry day in March, when the wind blew, but not
too briskly, they set fire to the steep piece of wasteland
known as the Moor, up on the slopes above the
Placketts. It was a field of sixteen acres, the very worst
of the old Maryhope land bought from Tuller, the very
last to be cleared and intaken.

It was quite unfit for grazing by cattle and even the
sheep got 'scarcely enough to starve on comfortably'
as William Gauntlet said to Jack. It was grown with
great 'bull-pates' as Gauntlet called them: tussocks of
grass so old and tough that no beast would touch them;
and the ground between was so tunnelled by vermin
that a man could twist his leg in a pot-hole two or even
three feet deep.

The fire was lit at the foot of the slope, and, the wind

blowing easy from south and west, it burnt its way slowly and surely uphill, breaking out now and then in a great crackling flare as it caught a thicket of gorse or bramble. Jack was there with Joe Stretton and Jonathan Kirby, each armed with a swat on a long pole, ready to run if the flames at the boundaries threatened the hedges. The black smoke rose up across the sun, darkening what should have been a bright day, and as the heat grew on the ground, hares and rabbits and smaller vermin bolted from their holes and ran uphill, where Ernie Stretton lay in wait with his father's shotgun.

'You've started something now, ent you?' Jonathan Kirby said to Jack. 'We shan't dare budge from here now till this lot's burnt itself out and douted.'

'And what's the use of it?' Stretton demanded. 'This stretch of ground will never be nothing worth it neither. It's been naught but wasteland since time unremembered.'

'All the land on earth must've been rough like this at one time,' Jack said. 'Somebody had to start clearing it somewhere.'

'Now you've got me beat there,' Stretton retorted. 'I don't remember that far back!'

During the morning, Miss Philippa came to watch the burning, and asked to see the slaughtered game. Stretton produced four brace of rabbits, three of hares, and a red-legged partridge that must have strayed over from the Came Court estates.

'Is this all?' she asked.

'Well, there's a few stoats and weasels and a mole or two,' Stretton said, 'but I wouldn't recommend them for eating, exactly.'

'No doubt you've put the best bag aside for yourselves,' she said. 'I know you men here.'

'And we know *you*,' Stretton muttered, as she walked away. 'We ent simple so much as just plain unbewildered.'

Going home that evening, when the field-fire had burnt itself out, Jack was covered from head to foot with fine charcoal dust and black ashes. He looked like a collier and Linn, glancing up as he entered the kitchen, opened her mouth in a little 'ooo.'

'Who's a dirty rascal?' she demanded.

The next morning, when he went up to look at the Moor, the ashes were blowing about on the wind. He hoped for rain and that night it came, a heavy soaker, cooling the ground and settling the ashes.

As soon as the couch-grass and weeds were showing, he and two others went in and ploughed the sixteen acres lengthways. It took six days and was hard going. Then, a month later, when the weeds were showing green again, he mucked the land and ploughed it crossways.

'You'll never get it clean,' Joe Stretton said.

'Oh, yes, I shall, given time.'

'One year's weeds, seven years' seeds,—that's what the old folk always say—so you'll have your work cut out, that's a promise.'

'I depend upon it,' Jack said, 'to keep me out of mischief.'

All that spring and summer, whenever he could spare the time, he went and worked in the sixteen acres, ploughing in crop after crop of green weed seedlings. Or else he went over it with the new cultivator, teasing out the roots of couch-grass and bindweed and thorn and bramble, and burning them in heaps that smoked and smouldered for days on end.

'Where's Jack?' someone would ask. 'Up there ploughing his piece again, is he? He'll be getting the hang of it soon directly.'

And so, since the sixteen acres could not now be called the Moor, it became known instead as 'Jack's Piece' and one of the men wrote the new name in on the field-map hanging up in Miss Philippa's office.

'That's almost as good as having an apple named for you, ent it?' Peter Luppitt said to Paul. 'Or a new climbing rose, say, or a new kind of tater.'

'He won't get much else in the way of rewards,' said Joe Stretton. '*She* won't thank him for working his guts out the way he does.'

Jack only shrugged. He worked hard for his own

satisfaction; because he hated to see land wasted; because he would just as soon work as not. And William Gauntlet, tending his sheep on the high hilly slopes of Tootle Barrow, where he had the best view, noted the changes wrought month by month as the old starved Maryhope lands were given new heart and brought under cultivation again.

'It does a man a power of good to see these fields all *smiling* again.'

And Miss Philippa, too, whatever Joe Stretton might say, seemed well pleased with the way things were going. She and Jack were in Hotcham one day, attending the market, and she left him for a while to go to the bank. When she returned, her face was quite radiant, her eyes gleaming with something akin to gaiety.

'It's the mortgage I took when I bought Maryhope Farm,' she said. 'Every penny is now paid off. Don't you think that's wonderful news?'

'It's humpty-dinker,' Jack said. 'Maybe now you'll be able to afford a few new gates where they're needed.'

'More than that. We shall have improvements everywhere. Those new implements you've been wanting . . . repairs to the sheds and the big barn . . . perhaps a new cowshed altogether . . .'

She was full of energy and plans for the future; more outward-looking; more willing to share her hopes and ambitions than she had ever been before; and as they walked away from the sale-ring, talking, she slipped her hand inside his arm. For once they were equal together, it seemed. A good understanding existed between them; a sympathy; a fellow-feeling; so that the friendly, comfortable gesture seemed perfectly easy and natural between them.

'The men's cottages, too,' she said. 'I know some repairs are badly needed and I mean to make a start before next winter . . .'

Often on fine summer afternoons, Cissy Gauntlet brought Linn up to the fields after school, to where he was working. At hay-making time, the child some-

times rode with him on the reaper, sitting on his lap,
within the circle of his arms, and with his big hands
covering hers on the ribbons.

'Giddy up! Giddy up!' she would call to the horses,
and, when stopping, would lean right back against
Jack's body, saying, 'Whoa, there! Whooooaaa!' trying
to make her voice deep and gruff and manly. Like his,
she thought.

At harvest-time, too, she was there with the other
children: the Gauntlets; the Luppitts; the little Ruggs;
tying up the sheaves until her fingers quickly grew tired
and she wandered instead from corn-cock to corn-
cock, pulling out vetches and purple knapweed, pink
weatherwine flowers and dark red clover, and tying
them up in little posies. And when it came to dinner
time or tea time, she would sit with Jack in the shade
of a hedgerow maple tree, sharing his bread and
cheese and cider.

'How many ears of corn are there in this field?'

'I dunno. You'd better count them.'

'I can't,' she said. 'It's too many.'

'You'll have to make a guess, then, that's all.'

'Hundreds and thousands and millions and billions.'

'Ah, that's about it, near enough, I would say.'

'Why does barley have whiskers on it?'

'Laws, now you're asking, ent you?' he said. 'I'd like
to know the answer to that one my own-self. Nasty
sharp things, getting inside a man's shirt as they do,
prickling him and driving him crazy. I reckon them
whiskers is put there on purpose to make us swear.'

'You mustn't swear, it's naughty,' she said.

'Oh, and who says so?'

'Miss Jenkins says so.'

Miss Jenkins was the Niddup schoolmistress: to
Linn, a person from another world: not flesh and
blood but the Voice of God in sealskin jacket and
black snood.

'Don't she ever swear, then, your Miss Jenkins?'

'No,' Linn said, in a shocked whisper, then put up a
hand to stifle a little spurt of laughter. The idea of it
almost overcame her. 'Not Miss Jenkins.'

'Don't she even say Drat and Bother?'

'No. Never.'

'Ah, well, *she* ent never had barley-ails inside her shirt, that's certain.'

'Miss Jenkins says . . .'

'Yes? Well? What does she say?'

'Miss Jenkins says . . .'

'We shall hear something now. I can feel it coming.'

'Miss Jenkins says *Oh-my-goodness-gracious-me!*'

'Does she, by golly? Now would you believe it?'

'Sometimes she says *Oh-dear-how-teejus!*'

'There you are, then. It's like I said. She enjoys a good swear the same as we all do.'

Now and then, on a Sunday, he and Linn had dinner at the farmhouse, where they had to be on their best behaviour. Miss Philippa held that they ought to eat there every day; she was sure a man's cooking could not be good enough for his own needs or those of a child; but he kept the occasions as few as he could, because neither he nor Linn enjoyed them.

'Auntie Philippa,' Linn said once, 'why ent there any sugar in this here apple pudden?'

'You mustn't say ent, Linn. I've told you before.'

'Why *aren't* there any sugar, then?'

'There's plenty of sugar in that pudding. I made it myself.'

'I can't taste it.'

'Then there must be something wrong with your tongue, that's all I can say about you, little miss.'

'Perhaps there's something wrong with the sugar.'

'That's hardly polite,' Miss Philippa said, frowning severely, and, thinking to teach the child a lesson, she stretched out a hand as though to remove Linn's plate. 'Perhaps you'd sooner go without altogether?'

'Yes,' Linn said, and pushed the plate across the table. 'I don't like it. The apples is siddly. They make me go all funny all over.'

Miss Philippa stared. Her lips were tight-pressed. There was trouble brewing.

'I reckon maybe it is a bit sharp,' Jack said, to save an outburst. 'We've got a sweet tooth, my daughter and me, at least when it comes to apple pudden. D'you think we could have a bit more sugar?'

So a bowl of sugar was brought to the table and the pudding was eaten to the last mouthful. But on the way home that afternoon Linn, remembering, gave a shudder.

'I don't like Auntie Philippa's dinners. They make my mouth feel funny after. They make me feel all *ugh* inside.'

Jack felt a good deal of sympathy with her. The mutton stew had been swimming in grease. The cook, Mrs Miggs, was getting old, but Miss Philippa would never admit it. He did his best to make Linn think of other things.

'Where shall we go to get our blackberries? Up Felpy Lane or down Long Meadow? It's your turn to choose. I chose last time.'

'Up the Knap and round by the Placketts.'

'All that way? You'll be winnelled nearly off your legs.'

'You can give me a ride home on your shoulders.'

'Oh, I can, can I? And who says so?'

'You always do, when I get tired.'

So, on a Sunday, according to the season, they would go berrying along the hedgerows, or looking for mushrooms in the meadows, or collecting fir-cones in the woods at Far Fetch. They always went somewhere, once his stint in the garden was finished, or the clothes washed out, or the house made tidy, and when they returned on cold winter afternoons, he would open the range and stoke up the fire, light the oil-lamp on the table, and see that Linn exchanged her wet boots for dry slippers.

'What would you like for tea today? Welsh rarebit, maybe? Or a nice soft-boiled egg with bread and butter? Or shall we just have a walk round the table?'

'Muffins!' she said. 'That's what I should like for tea.'

'Who said there was muffins? I never said so, I'm sure of that. I never mentioned muffins once.'

'I seen 'em!' she said. 'In the pantry. Under the cover.'

'Laws, there's no keeping secrets in this house, is there? Not with that sharp little snout of yours poking in here, there, and everywhere.'

'It's not a snout.'

'What is it, then, a knob of putty?'

'It's a nose,' she said. 'Only pigs and piglets have snouts.'

'It's a snout right enough when it comes to rootling about in the pantry. Them there muffins was meant to be a big surprise. And who's going to toast them, as if I didn't already know?'

She would sit on the milking-stool on the hearth, draw the kettle-glove over her hand, and take down the polished brass toasting fork with the three curved prongs and the *Cutty Sark* on the end of its handle. As she toasted each muffin and handed it up to him to be buttered, her face would grow very pink and shiny, and she would go into a kind of trance, basking in the heat from the open stove.

Eating the muffins was the grand culmination. She licked each finger afterwards, exactly as he did, with great relish. But it was the toasting of them that mattered most; the encompassing warmth after several hours out of doors; the sharing and the closeness.

Her contentment touched him, so that he was at peace with himself, yet watchful, too. Every evening, when he had seen her into bed,—face and hands washed; hair brushed; prayers said; and a hot stone bottle wrapped in flannel at her feet;—he would stand at the bottom of the stairs, listening, anxious lest fears should come to her with the darkness and aloneness. But all he ever heard was the drone of her voice as she sang to the doll cradled beside her with its head on the pillow: 'Little Dolly Daydream, pride of I dunno . . .' After the singing there was only silence. She had very few terrors in her life.

The farm was doing well these days. They had the threshing-machine in November, and all the corn-crops weighed out heavy. Miss Philippa took pride in her neat, clean, orderly fields, and in the produce garnered from them, knowing it could scarcely now be bettered throughout the county.

She was in high spirits and at Christmas that year she went about visiting her neighbours more than she had ever been known to do before. She was more at ease. She talked more freely. She held her head high, proud in the knowledge that she was now a farmer of some repute. And often on these visits she insisted that Jack and Linn should go with her.

'You and the child are all I've got left in the way of family now. It's only right that we should be seen to be united.'

The new year came in cold and wet and continued so for weeks on end. February not only filled the dykes but had them overflowing everywhere, and in Niddup village, the river came up to the very foot of the The Bay Tree garden. It was just the kind of weather Jack hated and all he wanted was a dry place in a corner of the barn where he could get on with repairing tools and machinery and harness. But Miss Philippa, spending money more freely now, was always sending him off to sales.

One day she sent him to a farm sale somewhere near Egham in the hope of his picking up a corn drill and a horse rake cheaply. But at Nelderton Dip the river was up over the road and a notice announced that the sale had been postponed, so he returned homewards with an empty cart. The early afternoon was dusk-dark, the rain falling in a cold steady downpour, out of a sky full of thick black clouds.

As he drove homewards, through the mud of Hayward's Lane, just before reaching Gifford's Cross, he noticed an elm in the right-hand hedgerow that seemed to lean out of the greyness above, slanting sharply across the roadway.

'That's funny,' he thought, 'I don't remember that there elm tree leaning so much when I drove this way earlier this morning.'

He decided it was probably just his fancy—the tree

looking bigger in the rainy darkness——but as he passed beneath it he heard its roots groaning and creaking and heard the plop-plopping of loose clods dropping into the ditch below. And when he looked over his shoulder, he could see the tree falling. He jumped to his feet and flipped the reins, calling out urgently as he did so, and the horse, astonished, pulled as hard as he could along the mud-filled ruts and rudges.

They escaped by inches. An outer branch just clawed the tailboard. But the great noise of the elm tree falling behind them——the screeching of its roots tearing out of the waterlogged clay, the crunching of the branches and the shuddering whoomph as the big trunk bounced to the ground——so frightened the horse that he put up his head and bolted at a gallop. He got the bit between his teeth and Jack could do nothing but hang on, while the cart-axle bumped on the ground between the ruts, and the wet mud flew up in spray from the wheels.

A hundred yards on, when they reached Three Corners, the frightened horse took the nearside turn, which was sharp and narrow and ran downhill. The cart-wheels were pulled clean out of the ruts, and the cart went slewing over rightwards, where it crashed with great force against the corner of Winworth's linhay. Jack was thrown right out of the cart and hurled against the linhay wall. He then fell in a crumpled heap in the roadway while the horse and cart rattled on.

For one slow fractional instant it seemed to him he was given a choice: between light and darkness: living and dying. It was only a question of concentrating.——It was up to him to find the strength.——But the darkness claimed him and he fell forward into the mire.

The horse returned home to Brown Elms, trailing the splintered remains of the cart. Joe Stretton and the rest of the men set out immediately to search the back lanes between Niddup and Egham, but it was young Harvey, out delivering letters at Gromwell, who found him and ran to Winworth's for help. By then, Jack had lain unconscious for five hours, with the rain falling on him without pause.

He was taken home to his own cottage. He was still unconscious. Cissy Gauntlet helped to strip off his sodden clothes and to get him to bed wrapped in hot blankets. Linn was frightened by the sight of her father being carried so blue-looking into the house, and Cissy stayed to comfort her while Alfie Winworth went for the doctor and Harvey went for Miss Philippa.

Dr Spray was sure that Jack would die. Pulse rate was critically low. Breathing was almost inaudible. He would send a reliable nurse, he said, to do what little there was to be done. It was probably only a matter of hours. Then the nurse must go to Ridlands Hall.

But Miss Philippa would have nothing of it. She called Dr Spray a stupid fool. She would look for more sense from the drunken Dr King, she said, or old Grannie Balsam with her herbs and simples.

'This man is most certainly not going to die, Doctor, —not if I have anything to do with it! And as for your reliable nurses, you needn't put them to any trouble, —I will nurse him myself, better than they would!'

Sometimes he thought it was Nenna's presence he felt in the bedroom; Nenna's hands sponging his burning face and body; Nenna's eyes watching over him at all hours. At other times he remembered clearly that Nenna had been dead for seventeen months and was buried under the chestnut tree in the church-yard at Niddup. The woman in the room must therefore be a stranger.

Once he thought he was drowning in the muddy, chopped-up waters of Ennen. The bridge was crumbling underneath him, the stones tumbling as though they were nothing but a child's building-blocks, kicked from underfoot. The flooded river would have him this time, and he didn't really mind, for it took too much strength to swim against such an angry current. He would have to give in. He would let his lungs fill with cold water.

'No! No! You are *not* to give in! I am not going to let you! Jack? Do you hear me? You must think of your daughter.—What would become of her, do you think, if you gave up now?'

So the woman was not such a stranger after all. She knew all about him. She called him by name. Yet the calm, perfect face was quite unknown to him, leaning towards him in the soft lamplight. And her quiet voice, speaking with such strength and assurance— surely he had never heard it before?

'Philippa?' he said once, and the quiet voice answered him: 'Yes? I'm still here. Drink a little of this barley water.'

Sometimes the pain in his chest was such that he wished he knew how to stop himself breathing. The pain was everywhere more than he could bear. He wished the quiet voice would release him, give him leave to slip down into the darkness, where the cold river waters would ebb and flow throughout his frenzied blood. But then a picture came into his mind, of a small child in a blue frock, wandering all alone in a meadow, lost among the buttercups and ragged-robin.

'Linn?' he said, leaning forward, off the pillow. 'Where's Linn?'

'Linn is all right. She's with Cissy Gauntlet down in the kitchen. I shall bring her to see you as soon as you're well. Tomorrow, perhaps, or the day after.'

'Tell her,' he said.

'Yes? Tell her what?'

'Just tell her,' he said. 'Tell her I'm here. Tell her I'm going to get a lot better. Tell her I shall see her soon.'

Sometimes, when Philippa held a cup to his lips for him to drink, or when she leant over him, arranging the pillows at his back, a sense of freshness and strength seemed to pass from her to him. It was in the cool touch of her fingers on his; in the way her arms supported him, holding him up, strong behind his shoulders, as she made the bed smooth and comfortable and wholesome again. And once, when his head lay for a moment against her breast, the scent of lavender that hung about her was like the breath of pure sweet air blowing from a summer garden.

'I can't rightly see you.'

'Then I'll turn up the lamp.'

'What time is it?'

'It's half past seven.'

'Evening or morning?' he asked, puzzled.

'Evening,' she said. 'I've just been seeing Linn to bed.'

'Is it still raining?'

'No. Not now. It hasn't rained for a week or more. There's a brisk wind blowing now and the land is drying out very nicely.'

'A peck of dust in March . . .' he said, with an effort, and fell into a deep, quiet, sweet-tasting sleep.

When he awoke, Dr Spray stood before him.

'You're a lucky man, Mercybright. I have to confess that I myself had given you up as lost. And so you would have been, no doubt of that, if it hadn't been for Miss Guff here. You couldn't have had a better nurse if you'd searched all through England.'

'Am I past the worst, then?'

'Just stay as you are and obey Miss Guff in everything, and you'll soon be up again, breathing God's air without any undue strain.'

That afternoon, sitting up in bed, washed and made tidy and wearing a clean white nightshirt, he was ready to receive Linn, who came on tiptoe to the side of the bed.

'Why, bless my soul, you've brought me some prim-roses, ent you?' he said. 'I bet I can tell you where you got 'em.'

'I didn't get them in Long Meadow.'

'Then you got 'em in the woods at Far Fetch. Am I right? Eh? And I bet they took some finding, too, so early in the year as this.'

He took the primroses and put them to his nose. Their cool creamy· scent was to him at that moment the purest thing in the whole world. He gave them back to Linn and watched her put them in the pot on the table.

'That'll cheer me up, seeing them primroses there beside me, knowing the spring is under way.'

'Why is your voice gone funny, father?'

'Got a frog in my throat, I suppose,' he said.

'Are you better now?'

'I should think I am! I'm very nearly fighting fit. Just another day or two and I shall be up like Punch and Judy.'

'Auntie Philippa's come to live with us now. Did you know?'

'It's only for the time being, while she's looking after your dad.'

'She brought a pallet and sleeps next to me in my room.'

'Ah. Well. And is she comfortable, do you suppose?'

'I dunno,' the child said, shrugging.

'Then you ought to ask her. She's gone to a hang of a lot of swither, you know, looking after me like she has done, and it's up to us to show we're grateful.'

'Why are you growing a beard, father?'

'To keep my face warm in winter,' he said.

'But it's not winter now—it's spring,' she said. 'Mr Gauntlet's got twelve lambs already.'

'Has he indeed? Who would've thought it? But hang on a minute—what's all this 'father' business all of a sudden? You always used to call me "dad." '

'Auntie Philippa said I must call you father.'

'Did she by golly? Well, maybe she thinks it goes a lot better with my beard. But I'd just as soon you

called me dad the same like you have done herebe-
fore.'

The bedroom door opened. Miss Philippa came in.

'You must go now, Linn, before your father gets
too tired. You'll be able to see him again tomorrow.'

Linn stared at Jack for a long moment, then left the
room and went downstairs.

'She ent feeling lonely, is she, d'you think?'

'Oh, no, why should she?' Philippa said. 'Cissy
Gauntlet is down there with her. Cissy is teaching her
how to knit.'

Sometimes, waking up, he would find Philippa sitting a
little way away, in the wickerwork chair from downstairs, with the lamp on the table at her elbow, and a
piece of needlework in her fingers. She always knew
when he was awake, however still he lay there, watching. She seemed to sense his eyelids opening.

The lamplight was kind to her, softening her rather
strong features, giving her eyes great depth and darkness, and shining on her smooth dark hair, the colour
of red-brown sorrel flowers seen in sunlight. There was
something very quiet about her. He found it restful;
reassuring; he had never known her so serene.

'There's a little arrowroot in this basin. I brought it
ten minutes ago. If you take it now, it'll still be warm.'

'I shall be getting to look like arrowroot directly.'

'Perhaps so, but you're not yet ready for bread and
cheese.'

Even her smile had something about it that surprised
him. He sat up in bed, looking at her, and accepted the
basin of arrowroot. He took the spoon.

'How are things doing on the farm?'

'Kirby and Rugg were out harrowing the Breaches
this morning. I shall sow it with beans as you suggested. The others were ploughing in the Upper
Runkle. The weather continues dry, thank God, and
Stretton thinks we shall soon be quite upsides with the
sowing.'

'Has that kale-seed arrived?'

'Yes. And the clover-seed for undersowing in the Sixteen Acres.'

'That'll need a good going over with the roller and harrow first. But I hope I'll be out and about in a day or two.'

'You ought to be. The doctor has given his sanction to it. But you won't worry too much about the work, will you? The farm is all right. You're not to worry.'

'I'm not worrying. Only asking, that's all.'

And it was true. He was not worried. He knew how things went on a well-ordered farm. A man fell out,— his place was taken by someone else, for a time or forever, as the case might be—and the work went forward as before. Yet, although not worried, he kept having the same strange, disquieting dream.

He dreamed he set out to plough twenty acres of barley stubble. He knew the place he was making for. It was close behind Will Gauntlet's cottage and was known as the Scarrow. But when he arrived there, instead of a field of barley stubble, he found a field of yellow wheat, the grains plump and round in the braided ears, crying out with fullness and ripeness. So he turned and went back to the farm for the reaper. But now, on reaching the field again, he found it full of seeding thistles, standing tall and thick, crowded together throughout the whole of the twenty acres, and the tufts of grey down were blowing away on the boisterous wind, which sowed the seed broadcast over all the innocent land around.

He woke up with a shout, and in a moment Philippa was beside him, dressed in her night-clothes, her dark hair twisted into a single plait that hung forward over her shoulder. In one hand she held a candle in its holder. With her other hand she touched his forehead.

'Jack, what is it? Are you bad again? Is there anything I can bring you?'

'It's all right,' he said, feeling ashamed. 'I had a funny dream, that's all, about ploughing the Scarrow.'

'I told you,' she said, 'you are not to worry about the farm.'

'Did I wake the child?'

'No, no, she's still fast asleep.'

'I woke you, though. I'm sorry for that.'

'It doesn't matter. Don't fret yourself.'

Her hand was cool and soothing on his brow. Her fingers pushed back the moist, lank hair from his forehead. He closed his eyes and was gone again, to sleep till morning.

On his first day out of doors, walking over the fields to speak to the men, he felt as though the keen March wind was blowing straight through him.

'My God,' said Joe Stretton, 'you look like a walking ghost, man!'

'I feel like one, too. I feel as though I was made of muslin.'

'Then get back home in the warm for God's sake and don't come haunting us again till you've put a bit of flesh on them there boneses.'

'I wouldn't have come out, myself,' said Will Gauntlet, sparing a moment from his lambs, 'not on a sharp old day like this one.'

'I've got to come out sooner or later,' Jack said.

Within a week he was doing a full day's work again, and within a fortnight he was very nearly his old self. His illness had at least meant a rest for his knee, and for once his left leg was as good as his right one. He decided not to shave off the beard and moustache that had started growing during this time, but trimmed them neatly and let them remain, brindled and streaked with grey though they were, giving him the look, Joe Stretton said, 'of some damned prophet out of the Scriptures.'

'It's to keep his face warm,' Linn explained to all and sundry.

Miss Philippa was still at the cottage. She would stay, she said, until satisfied that he was quite fully recovered. And he had to admit there was much comfort in having a woman in the house again; in finding his supper already cooked when he got home; in having someone to talk to in the evening.

She would sit in the old Windsor chair, with her

tapestry-work or a shirt of his that wanted mending, and he would sit in a corner of the settle, opposite, remarking on the news in the daily paper, or discussing future plans for the farm.

'Why don't you smoke a pipe?' she said once. 'Your lungs are not troubling you now, are they?'

'My lungs is fine. But I had an idea somehow that you was against tobacco smoking.'

'Why should I be? My father always smoked a pipe and I liked to see him looking contented. Besides, a man is entitled to do as he pleases in his own home, surely?'

'Right, then, I will. So long as Linn ent took all my pipes for blowing soapy bubbles with. It's a trick she's fond of.'

'No, they're up on the shelf. I put them there out of Linn's reach.'

'They say there'll be peace in South Africa soon. Did you see it in the paper?'

'They've been saying that since the new year.'

'That's true,' he said, sitting down again, puffing at his pipe. 'But it's got to come in the end, I suppose, when they've all done arguing the toss about it.'

'Jack, I've been wanting to speak to you,' Philippa said suddenly.

'Oh, ah? Well, speak away.'

'It's about Linn . . . I'm sorry to say it but the child has been stealing.'

'Stealing? Good heavens! What *do* you mean?'

'She keeps taking the eggs from out of the larder. It's happened two or three times just lately. I found them under the orchard hedge and when I asked her how they got there, she said she was giving them back to the hens.'

'There, now,' Jack said, straight of face. 'Would you believe it?'

'She takes no notice of me, you know. I'm afraid you've spoilt her. She's very rude and impertinent sometimes.'

'Right, then. I shall have to speak to her about it.'

The next night at bed-time, when he mentioned the

matter to Linn, her face became very set and stubborn.

'How long is Auntie Philippa stopping in our house?'

'Why? Don't you like her?'

'She put sour cream on my porridge this morning and made me eat it.'

'Any more reasons besides that one?'

'This isn't *her* house. Why should she always give me orders? It's your house, ent it, not hers? Why don't she go home and leave us by our own-selves like we was before?'

'You know why she's here. She's been looking after you and me. We'd have been in a rare old pickle, you know, if it hadn't been for your Auntie Philippa coming here. Still, it won't be much longer now, I reckon, before she ups sticks and goes back off home.'

But Miss Philippa continued to stay at the cottage, and the men on the farm were beginning to make remarks to Jack.

'You cosy down there, you and the Missus, tucked in together all this time?' asked Peter Luppitt, winking at his brother Paul. 'Looking after you nicely, is she?'

'All the home comforts?' asked Jonathan Kirby. 'Without the strings?'

'Supposing you just attend to your business!'

'Who would've thought it of our Miss P?'

'Them prudish ones is always the worstest.'

'Sooner you than me, Jack, but everyone to their own taste as the old lady said when she kissed the cow.'

'D'you want to know what I think?' asked Joe Stretton.

'No,' Jack said. 'You can damn well keep your mouth buttoned!'

At home that evening, sitting opposite Philippa as usual, he broached the matter without beating about the bush.

'It seems you've been here long enough. It's beginning to cause a bit of gossip.'

'Oh?' she said, and dabs of bright colour appeared at once on her high cheekbones. 'Among the labourers, do you mean? How dare they gossip behind my back! They've no right whatever to discuss my affairs.'

'You can't stop folk talking. It's meat and drink to most of them. You know that as well as I do.'

For a time she was silent, sitting straight-backed in the Windsor chair, her hands together, resting on the tapestry in her lap. She looked at him with a still gaze.

'In that case,' she said, 'I'll go tomorrow.'

'Yes,' he said. 'I reckon it would be for the best, all told, really. You've done well by me. I'm grateful for it. But I'm perfectly healthy again now, and quite well able to take good care of myself and Linn.'

She watched him intently. There occurred another long silence. He even heard the deep, slow breath she took before she finally spoke again.

'I have a suggestion to make,' she said. 'You may have some inkling of what it is. I suggest that you and I should marry.'

Looking at her,—meeting the stillness of her gaze; trying to see past her composure—there was a moment in which he almost felt something for her. There were lines of tiredness in her face, especially about the eyes: they were there because of him; because she had spent so many vigilant nights at his bedside; he saw the little signs of strain and was touched by them. Then the moment was gone. He knew the feeling for what it was. Gratitude. Nothing more.

'No,' he said, and his glance fell away, seeking refuge elsewhere. 'No. It wouldn't do. Such a thing is not to be thought of.'

'Nenna and I were not really sisters. We had no tie of blood whatever, so there's no impediment, if that's what you mean.'

'As far as I'm concerned you *are* Nenna's sister.'

'That's just stupid. I've no patience with that. A man needs a woman to take care of him and run his household. He's all at sea otherwise.'

'I can manage all right. I have done so far.'

'Can you? Can you?' she demanded. 'Were you able to manage these few weeks past, lying helpless as you were, with only me to care for you?'

'I was pretty far gone. I'm aware of that. I've got a lot to thank you for, and I *do* thank you with all my heart.'

'You were very near death. You should ask the doctor. It was only my nursing that pulled you through.'

'I'm aware of that too. I heard what the doctor said right enough.'

'Then what's the point of boasting that you can look after yourself and your child? How can you think it? You have no one else in the world but me.'

'Philippa,' he said, but could think of nothing more to say.

'Well? What? I'm waiting and listening, as you see, so what is it you're trying to say?'

'Nothing,' he said. 'Nothing more than I've said already.'

'Supposing you were to fall ill again?'

'I shan't, I promise. I shall see to it.'

'How can you be so arrogant? Do you think you have control of the future?'

'No,' he said. 'I don't think that.'

'Then just supposing?'

'I shall cross that bridge when I come to it.'

'No doubt you think I should always be at hand! Always ready to pick up the pieces? Always at your beck and call when needed? Is that what you think? Is it? Is it?'

'No. It ent. I've never thought about it at all.'

'No,' she said, in a quieter tone. 'You haven't thought of it, that's just the trouble.' She threaded her needle into her work, folded it neatly, and put it away into its bag. 'Perhaps we both need time to think . . . to consider the future . . . and perhaps a night's sleep will help us both to think more clearly.'

She rose to her feet and went to the dresser, to put her work-bag away in a drawer. She returned with her candle in its holder and lit it at the fire in the stove. On her way past again she paused close beside him, and allowed her hand to rest on his shoulder.

'We're both of us quite alone in the world, you and I . . . It's worth considering my suggestion . . .'

'I'm not alone—I've got Linn,' he said, and then, perceiving the cruelty of his answer, he put up a hand to cover hers where it lay on his shoulder. 'Ah, no!' he said. 'I didn't mean to say it like that—'

'But exactly so!' Philippa said. 'You've got Linn and I've got the farm! And what I'm suggesting is that we both plan our future lives together around the things that really matter! It's only common sense. I'm sure you must see it.'

A burnt-out log collapsed in the stove and a shower of sparks sprayed out in the hearth-place. Jack leant forward and swept them under with the hearth-brush, and Philippa's hand fell to her side. She thought the withdrawal was deliberate—perhaps it was; he could not have said—and when he looked up again, her hands were folded, holding the candle, and her gaze was entirely without warmth.

'This is a practical proposition, Jack, based on matters of mutual convenience.'

'Aye? I daresay.'

'Good God!' she said harshly. 'Did you think otherwise by any chance? Did you think I was troubled by girlish considerations of love?'

'No,' he said, 'I didn't think that.'

'I don't *love* you.—You needn't worry yourself about that! I'm a woman of thirty-six.—I'm not a foolish, romantic girl of twenty. You mean nothing more to me in that way than if you were just a block of wood! Do I make myself clear to you, I wonder?'

'I get the drift,' he said, nodding.

'Then I'll say goodnight and leave you alone to consider the matter.'

'I ent got nothing to consider.'

'Oh, yes, you have,' she said, quietly, 'if you really put your mind to it.'

The following morning she packed her things and returned to the farmhouse. They had the cottage to themselves again, he and Linn, and the child's satisfaction was plain indeed.

'This is *our* house,' she said to him. 'You're the master here, ent you, and I'm the mistress?'

'That's right,' he said. 'We pull together like a good team of horses. Like Spindleberry and Dinkymay. Like Minta and Maisie. Like Diamond and Darky and Jubilee. And that's the way it'll be always, you and me in harness together.'

It was now the second week in April. There was a softness in the air. The green, growing season was under way. Jack was out in the sixteen acres reclaimed from wasteland the year before, going over it with roller and harrow, reducing it to a powdery tilth, ready to receive its first sowing in more than twenty-five years. He had Ernie Stretton and Jonathan Kirby harrowing with him.

On Saturday morning, in an interval between showers, Miss Philippa came to the gate of the field and leant there watching. Jack took no notice but continued on up the slope, turned at the headland, and descended again, keeping the horses to a slow walk. Miss Philippa pushed the gate open, and, lifting her skirts above the ankles of her buttoned boots, made her way across the field to meet him.

'Have you been avoiding me on purpose?'

'I've been busy, that's all, making up for lost time.'

'It's three days since I left the cottage. I want to know what conclusion you've come to.'

'The same conclusion as before.'

'I don't understand you. I simply cannot make you out.'

'Perhaps you don't try,' he said, shrugging. 'Though, come to that, I don't understand you, neither.'

'It's perfectly simple. An unmarried woman is always at a great disadvantage in this world. I therefore want a husband.'

'If that's all it is, you'll soon find one easy enough, I daresay.'

'But I happen to trust *you*!' she said, with sudden passion. 'You're the only man in the world that I *do* trust! Do you realize that? Have you any idea what a precious gift trust can be between people?'

'Precious, yes, but it still don't buy a man body and soul as you seem to think it does,' he said, 'and the trust has to be on both sides.'"

'Brown Elms would be yours. Do you realize that? A farm of over six hundred acres! You would be its master. Surely that must mean something to you?'

'I'm master now, as far as the work is concerned,' he said. 'I *made* this farm what it is today. That means something, I don't deny, but it's no odds to me whose name's on the deeds.'

'And where would you be if it weren't for me? What were you, in fact, when I first found you, skulking in the old ruined cottage? What were you then—you answer me that!'

'The same as now, just a man,' he said.

'You were nothing!' she said. 'And nothing you'll remain if you go against me, for I can make you or break you just as I choose, as simply as though I were snapping my fingers. Everything comes from me, remember.—The house you live in.—The wages you draw.—Everything you have you get from me!'

'I work for my wages. I don't pick 'em like apples off the tree.'

'Work!' she said. 'What is work to me when I can get labourers two a penny?'

'And d'you think marriage would make us equal? In your own eyes, I mean, not in mine. Do you truly believe it?'

'You would be my husband. What more could you want?'

She turned from him and left the field, and he stood for a moment looking at her footprints, clearly marked in the soft, fine, crumbly brown soil. Then he clicked at the horses and went on down, and the harrow jiggled the footprints out.

When he finished that day, the field was ready for sowing on Monday, and he said so to Stretton in the stables.

'Ah, well,' Stretton said, 'I reckon you'll want to sow them oats yourself, seeing it's your own piece of ground so especially, that you cleared and reclaimed from the very start.'

Jack gave a shrug.

'It don't much matter who sows it,' he said, 'just so long as it gets done.'

At bed-time that evening he said to Linn, 'How would you like to go on a journey?'

'Where to? Where to?' she asked, wide-eyed.

'Well, as to that, I reckon we'll have to see when we get there.'

'Both of us together?'

'Why, of course!' he said. 'You wouldn't go off and leave your poor old dad on his ownsome, would you? Where's the fun in that? We're a team, you and me, like I said to you the other day, and we pull together like a pair of good horses. We shall always stick together, you and me, come rain or shine, thunder or hailstones. So what do you say to my new idea?'

'Yes!' she said. 'Let's go on a journey!' And she gave the bedclothes a little shake, sending them rippling over the bed. 'Shall we go on a train?'

'Not on a train, no. Shank's pony. We'd miss the best places if we went on a train.'

'When are we going?'

'First thing in the morning, if that's all right with you,' he said.

'First thing?' she said, doubtfully, and her eyes opened wider still.

'That's the ticket. Bright and early. Up with the lark while the dew's still falling! And if we look smartish, we shall see the morning daisies growing, yawning and stretching and waking up out of the grass.'

'Shall we?' she said. 'Shall we, honest?'

'Of course we shall! And see all the cockerels perched on their mixens, crowing away to wake the world up. You'll like that, I know, 'cos you was always one for getting out and abroad bright and early.'

'What time will you wake me?'

'First thing, like I said. And we must hope for a fine day, without too many April showers.'

'I'll ask for sunshine in my prayers.'

'Ah, you do that,' he said, 'and then go off to sleep nicely so that you're full of beans tomorrow.'

He woke her in the morning at first light; ate breakfast with her in front of the fire; then packed a few of her clothes and his into his old canvas satchel.

'Can I take my doll?'

'Why, surely, yes! We can't go and leave Dolly Doucey, can we? You pop her in on top of my shirt there, so's she rides nice and comfortable.'

'Are we taking bread and cheese?'

'Lashings of it. Every bit we've got in the house. I never went on a journey yet without I took plenty of bread and cheese.'

He tipped his savings out of the old earthenware jug and put the money in his pocket. He poked the fire down low in the stove and closed the damper. Linn was still sleepy, but became bright and fresh as she stepped out into the morning air.

'Shall we be coming back?' she asked.

'No, my chilver, we shan't be coming back,' he said. 'Neither late nor soon. Not ever nor never.'

He locked the door and pushed the key up into the thatch. The child watched him with uncertain face. Her lip trembled.

'Aren't we going to say goodbye to Auntie Philippa up at the farm?'

'What, at this time of day? She'll still be in bed, tucked up tight and fast asleep.'

'Nor Cissy, nor Harvey, nor Mr Gauntlet?'

'Better not,' he said, 'or we should take all day about it and never get going at all, should we?'

'Do we have to go?'

'I reckon we do. We promised ourselves a journey, remember, and think of the things we shall see on the way.'

'Daisies!' she said. 'Waking up!'

'Right the first time. But we'll have to keep our eyes skinned, won't we, all the time as we're going along?'

He lifted her up and she sat on his shoulders. The gate closed behind them and they set off down the winding lane, between fields still milky-white with mist.

'You comfy up there, Linn Mercybright?'

'Yes,' she said.

'Seems we're lucky with our morning. I reckon it's going to be a fine day.'

'Will it be nice, where we're going? Shall I go to school there and make new friends? Will there be a river and woods and hills?'

'It's up to us to choose,' he said. 'When we come to a place we like the look of, that's where we'll stop, and see what we make of it, you and me.'

'Will there be horses at this place?'

'I never yet saw a place without 'em!'

'And will the people be nice there?'

'They'd better be middling. We shan't stop, else.'

He took the back lanes out past Niddup until he came to Darry Cross. There, a signpost stood in the grass in the middle, and they had a choice of three roads.

'Well?' Jack said. 'Which way would you like to go?'

'That way,' she said, and pointed along the straightest road, where sparrows were bathering in the dust, and where stitchwort flowers were white in the hedgerow at either side.

'Very well,' he said. 'Whatever you say. It's up to you.' He looked at the signpost, which, pointing that way, read: Yarnwell; Cranfield; Capleton Wick. 'It sounds all right. We'll give it a try.'

So he took the road Linn had chosen, and the newly risen sun was warm on his back.

BOOK THREE

1914

Betony and the young Army officer, Michael Andrews, had sat opposite each other all the way from Paddington, but they might never have struck up a friendship had it not been for the scene that occurred between two other people in the compartment: a stout district nurse and a young man who looked like a clerk.

At Paddington the train had been crowded. After Oxford it ran half empty. The nurse got in at Long Stone, the clerk at Milston, and right from the first she fixed him with a stare calculated to discomfit him.

'I wonder you aren't ashamed!' she said, when he was foolish enough to meet her gaze. 'A sturdy young man in the prime of life, fighting-fit and full of beans, yet still wearing civvies! *I'd* be ashamed. I would, honest!'

'It so happens I suffer with asthma,' the young man said, red with embarrassment, and hid himself behind his paper.

'That's what they all say nowadays, but you look healthy enough to me, young fellow, and if you were a proper man you'd be up and doing like the captain there, and all our other gallant soldiers.'

The woman glanced across at Michael. Plainly she expected his approval. Then she leant towards the clerk and rattled the newspaper in his hands.

'It's funny what a lot of asthma there is about lately, not to mention gastric troubles and the odd cases of housemaid's knee, but I could give it another name if anyone was to ask *me!*'

Michael, in his corner, could bear no more.

'Madam, be quiet!' he said sharply. 'Leave the man alone and hold your tongue!'

The woman was shocked. Her mouth fell open a little way, showing teeth stained mauve with the sweets she was eating.

'You've got no right to speak to me like that! If my husband was with me you wouldn't dare!'

'If your husband was with you I hope he'd keep you in better order.'

'Well, really!' she exclaimed. 'Well, really, I'd never have believed it!'

But she leant back again in her seat and remained silent for the rest of her journey, glaring at the newspaper shielding the clerk. Michael turned again to the window, and Betony looked at him with new interest. Straight sandy hair, rather untidy; beaky face and brown skin; tired grey eyes and tired mouth with lines at the corners: the sort of face, young yet old, which she had grown accustomed to seeing in the fourteen months since the start of the war.

The train was now stopping at every station. When the clerk and the nurse got out at Salton, Michael turned to Betony.

'I'm sorry about that,' he said, 'but the damned woman got my goat.'

'It's the new blood sport, baiting civilians,' Betony said.

'If she only knew what it's like over there—if she could see for just five minutes—it would soon wipe the smile from her smug pink face.'

'But somebody has to go and fight.'

'Yes, yes,' he said, with some impatience. 'But everyone here is so complacent! So glib and self-righteous and so damnably bloodthirsty!'

'How would you like us to be?' Betony asked, and he gave her a smile.

'Quiet . . . comfortable . . . calm . . .' he said, 'talking of cricket and fishing and the crops, and whether the hens are laying at the moment . . .'

Betony nodded. Looking at him, she could feel his tiredness. Her own flesh ached, as his must ache.

'You've been wounded, haven't you?' She could see how stiffly he held his shoulder.

'I've been wounded three times yet up I pop again good as new. A charmed life, apparently. I was gassed, too, on this last tour. That's why my voice is rough at the edges. Not badly, of course, or I shouldn't be here to tell the tale.'

'How long is your leave?'

'Until I'm fit. A month, perhaps.'

'And then what?'

'Back again to face the music.'

'How can you do it?' Betony asked, marvelling.

'No choice,' he said, and turned the talk towards her instead. 'Do you travel a lot?' He glanced at her briefcase on the rack above.

'Quite a lot, yes, though not usually as far as London. I've been to a sort of conference there. But mostly I travel around the midlands, seeing to the welfare of women workers in munitions factories.'

'Do you enjoy it?'

'Yes. In a way. At least it's something that needs doing. But I'm always glad to leave the towns and get home to Cobbs where it's quiet and peaceful.'

'Cobbs? Where's that?'

'In a village called Huntlip, near Chepsworth.'

'I live in Chepsworth, myself,' he said. 'It's a nice walk from there out to Huntlip. Can I come and see you sometimes?'

'Yes, come and meet my family,' she said. 'I can't guarantee they'll talk about cricket, but someone is sure to mention hens.'

'There's one good thing about the war. We can take short cuts in making friends, even with members of the opposite sex.'

But he felt she would not have rebuffed him, anyway, war or no war. She was at ease with him; sure of herself; quiet and calm and straightforward. She was also very pleasant to look at: he liked her bright fairness and the clarity of her blue eyes. She had the serenity he longed for.

'Tell me about your family,' he said.

At Chepsworth station, Jesse Izzard was waiting for his daughter, eager to take her bag and brief-case, carrying them for her with a sense of importance. His fair face shone, as it always did when he welcomed her home, and his pride increased when she introduced Michael Andrews.

'Captain Andrews will be coming out to visit us, dad. He wants to see the carpenter's shop.'

'Why, yes,' Jesse said, as he shook Michael's hand. 'Very welcome, I'm sure. Are you Captain Andrews of King's Hill House?'

'That's right,' Michael said. 'Just up there, behind the station.'

'I put a new fence round your paddock once. Years ago, now, when your father was alive.'

'You'll be glad to know it's still standing.'

'Ah, well, it would be,' Jesse said. 'It was good oak fencing.'

His sense of importance knew no bounds. He walked with a very slight swagger. The Andrewses were well-known people. They had lived in Chepsworth umpteen years. But there was a blot on Jesse's day, for, outside the station, instead of the smart little pony and trap, stood the old workshop waggon with sacks of sawdust and shavings aboard and the scruffy horse, Collier, between the shafts.

'It's your great-grumpa's fault,' he said, muttering to Betony. 'He took the trap to go to Upham.' And, clearing his throat, he said to Michael: 'Can we give you a lift, captain?'

'No, thanks,' Michael said. 'I shall enjoy the walk up the hill.'

He stood on the pavement and waved them off. Jesse saluted, rather stiffly.

'D'you think he refused on account of the waggon?'

'No, of course not,' Betony said. 'He's not such a snob as you are, dad.'

And, sitting beside him, she squeezed his arm to reassure him. He did not always know when he was being teased.

The old house at Cobbs was quiet under its oaks and elms. There was no noise from the carpenter's shop, for work stopped at twelve on a Saturday now. Only Great-grumpa Tewke found things to do.

'You've had the sign painted,' Betony said. They were passing the gate of the workshop yard, and the two names, Tewke and Izzard, stood out black and shiny on the white ground. 'The things that happen when I turn my back for a few days!'

'Young Tom done that. He's good with a paint-brush. He gets it from his poor dead father.'

In the big kitchen, as Betony entered, her mother was laying the table for supper. She paused, looking up with a welcoming smile, and her flickering glance delivered a warning—that somebody lurked behind the door. Betony pushed it open wide and squeezed her youngest brother, Dicky, who emerged crestfallen, holding his nose.

'Aw, they told you!' he said, disgusted. 'And I was going to make you jump!'

'You're too fond of making folk jump,' Jesse said. 'Here, take this bag up to your sister's room.'

'No, don't take it up,' Betony said. 'I've got things to show you when everyone's in.'

'She's brought us presents,' Dicky said.

He was young enough, at fifteen, to have waited indoors for his sister's return, but William and Roger, with manly interests to pursue, sauntered in casually a little later.

'Had a good journey?' William asked.

'A slow one, I bet,' Roger said, 'stopping at every wayside halt.'

'What happened in London, when you saw them high-ups?'

'Your sister's been put in charge,' Jesse said. 'She's to superintend the whole region.'

'That'll suit our Betony,' Dicky said, 'telling folk what to do.'

By supper-time, Granna Tewke had come out of the parlour, spectacles pushed up high on her forehead, and Great-grumpa Tewke had returned from Upham, having looked at a stand of timber there and rejected it because of the price.

'Taking advantage!' he said, swearing. 'They're taking advantage everywhere you go nowadays but nobody's going to profiteer *me!*'

'Where's Tom?' Betony asked.

'Late as usual. We'll start without him.'

'I reckon he's courting,' Dicky said.

'More likely drinking in The Rose and Crown.'

'He'll go to the bad, like his father, that boy,' said Granna Tewke, looking everywhere for her glasses. 'Ferrets indeed! What's a decent boy want with ferrets?'

'Our Betony's made a new friend,' Jesse said. 'Captain Andrews of King's Hill House. They was talking together on the train and he's likely coming out here on a visit.'

'What, one of that lot with all the money?'

'All made out of mustard,' said great-grumpa, 'and now they live like landed gentry.'

'The captain's all right,' Jesse said. 'A nice young gentleman, straight off.'

'He'll think hisself somebody,' William said, his mouth already full of food, 'being in uniform and all.'

'And isn't he somebody?' Betony asked.

'No more'n the rest of us,' William said.

'Oh, no, of course not!' Betony exclaimed. '*You* risk your life every day in the workshop, whenever you take up a hammer and chisel!'

'So that's it?' said William. 'Now we're hearing a few home truths!' His clear-skinned face became crimson, and his blue eyes glittered. 'You want me in uniform, out at the Front, living in trenches like a rat!'

'No, I don't,' Betony said. 'I just don't like to hear you sneering at those who are.'

'No more don't I,' Dicky said. 'I'd go tomorrow if only they'd have me.'

'Me, too,' Roger said. 'I'm as big as many chaps of eighteen.'

'Go and good luck to you!' William said. 'You're both too wet behind the ears to know any better!'

He sprang from his chair and would have hurried from the room, but that his mother spoke out sharply.

'Sit down, William, and stop jogging the tea on the table. We'll have no arguments on this subject, nor on no others for the time being. Roger, cut your father a slice of bread.'

William sat down, though still in a temper, and the others talked to cover his silence. Often a word was enough from their mother. She had great-grumpa's forcefulness, coupled with a coolness of her own. It was she who ruled within the household, just as great-grumpa ruled in the workshop.

At King's Hill House, Michael had soaked for an hour in the bath, and now, in his bedroom, dressed in grey flannels and a white shirt, he was combing his hair in front of the mirror. Behind him, on the floor, his uniform lay in a crumpled heap, where he had stepped out of it, trampling it underfoot in the process.

His mother knocked and came in. She watched him putting on a tweed jacket.

'Oh, dear! They don't fit you, do they, your old clothes? You've grown so much thinner.' She turned to the crumpled heap on the floor and picked up his tunic. 'Really, Michael, that's surely no way to treat the King's uniform!'

'The King is welcome to it,' he said, 'and its livestock, if any.'

'Livestock?' she said, and dropped the tunic with a shudder. 'You're surely not serious? I don't believe it!'

'Perfectly serious, mother,' he said. 'Now perhaps you understand why a man likes to get into ordinary clothes.'

'Doesn't your servant look after you properly?'

'It's not his fault. It can't be helped. We're all the same over there—lousy as hedgehogs.'

'But you've been in hospital. Surely—'

'Oh, I've been deloused, certainly, but the eggs survive the fumigator and live to hatch another day.'

'Good heavens!' she said. 'I couldn't bear it if it started here.'

'Neither could I. It's bad enough over there.'

'My poor boy! How thoughtless of me. What must I do with all your things?'

'Leave it to me. I'll take them down to Cook and get her to bake 'em in one of the old wall ovens. A few days of that should do the trick.'

Returning a little while later to the bedroom, he found her at work with a spray of disinfectant. She stopped spraying and looked him over.

'Are you going out, dear? You won't forget dinner's at seven?'

'I won't forget. I'm only going down to the town for a drink.'

'At a public house?' she said, astonished. 'But there are plenty of drinks in the sitting-room.'

'I feel like a long cool draught of beer.'

'I am worried about you, going out dressed like that. People are often unkind to civilians, you know.'

'I know about that. I witnessed a sample on the train today.'

And, having related the incident, he went on to talk about Betony.

'She travels round the midlands, arranging facilities for women working in the factories. It's amazing what girls are doing now. They're really breaking out and showing their mettle.'

'A carpenter's daughter, did you say? How extraordinary!'

'She didn't have tin-tacks between her lips, mother, or a pencil stuck behind her ear.'

'No need to be so touchy, dear. I didn't think she sounded like your sort of girl, that's all, but if I'm mistaken, perhaps you'd like to invite her to tea?'

'Now you're going a bit too fast.'

'Yes, well, perhaps it's not such a good idea. Food is so scarce here now, you know, that meals are becoming quite a problem.'

Michael smiled, having seen the dinner Cook was preparing in the kitchen. His mother, interpreting the smile correctly, gently reproved him.

'Today is rather a special occasion. We don't always eat so well.'

'I'm sorry, mother. Don't take too much notice of me. I'll be less sour in a day or two.'

Walking down into the town he experienced a feeling of well-being so all-suffusing that the pain of his wound almost gave him pleasure. He felt pure and clean and not-of-this-world. Yet his mood was supremely physical, too: the scent of chrysanthemums in people's gardens; the sight of the chestnut trees turning a fiery red-and-yellow; the sound of the great cathedral clock striking as he crossed the close and turned down beside the river: he apprehended all these things in every particle of his body.

And when, drinking a pint of Chepsworth ale in the bar of The Swan, where four farm labourers sat with the landlord and the talk was of turnips and winter wheat, he smiled to himself and listened greedily to every word, till one old man drew him into an argument about the virtues of home-baked bread.

At King's Hill House, his mother, worrying, hoped the war would soon be over. It seemed to be giving Michael a taste for low company.

The orchard at Cobbs was at its best, the apples so thick that many branches were borne down low, and Betony, walking among the trees, often had to bend her head. She had never known such a year for apples. She kept touching them with the tips of her fingers: the big green quilters, the rusty red pippins, and the crimson winesaps much loved by wasps. She was choosing a pippin for herself when she saw Michael coming towards her from the house.

'I met your brother William,' he said. 'He told me where to find you.'

'Was he polite to you?' Betony asked.

'Perfectly. Why do you ask?'

'He's in a sullen mood lately. Anti-military. Anti-war.'

'Then his feelings run with mine exactly.'

'I think he feels guilty at not enlisting.'

'It'll all be decided for him soon, when conscription comes in.'

'Poor William,' she said. 'He so loves his home and his family, and the work he does in the carpenter's shop. He so loves everything to be neat and tidy. He'll hate all the mess and confusion and waste . . .' She looked at Michael. 'Where will it all end?' she asked. 'And when, oh, when?'

Michael shrugged. He knew he ought to say comforting things: that the Germans were beaten and it was only a question of finishing them off. Such was the spirit promulgated by the commanders. But his own feeling was that the war might last for ever and ever. He could see no solution; no victory on either side; no other outcome except complete annihilation. Perhaps it was just that he was so tired. Once he was perfectly fit again, his old optimism was bound to return.

'It's got to end somewhere, sometime,' he said. 'But don't ask me when. I'm no strategist, God knows. I just obey orders—with my eyes shut mostly—and do my best to stay alive.'

They were walking slowly through the orchard and he noticed how, whenever she stooped beneath a low branch, her skirts went out in a billowing flare, sweeping the grass. The dress she wore was a very dark red with black threads running through it in waves, and, watching the way the skirts flared out at every curtsey, he knew he would see the pattern they made whenever he thought of her in future.

'You said you'd show me round the workshop.'

'It's shut up on Sundays. Great-grumpa Tewke is strict on that score.'

But she took him and showed him the workshop buildings—stables, once, when Cobbs had been a farmhouse, long years before—and the yard where oak and elm planking lay criss-crossed in piles, with laths between to let the air blow through and dry them. She showed him the sawpit and the timber-crabs and the store-yard full of ladders, field-gates, cribs and troughs. And she told him all she knew of the business, founded by Great-grumpa William Tewke in the year 1850, when he was a boy of nineteen and had scarcely enough money about him to buy his first tools. Now the workshop employed twelve men. Or would do, she said, if two had not gone into the Army.

They walked and talked until dusk was falling, when her father came in search of them, saying supper was on the table and would the captain care to stay?

In the big kitchen, under the low black beams and rafters, they sat down to eat at a long table covered over with a stiff white cloth. There were nine in the household. A clan indeed. Ten, he was told, if they counted Janie, but she was married to Martin Holt and lived at the neighbouring farm of Anster. Michael, himself an only child, was glad to be sitting with this family. He wished he belonged there, sharing the strength their unity gave them. He had often been lonely in his own home.

At the head of the table sat William Tewke, quick of eye and ear although he was turned eighty-four, and next on his left sat Kate Tewke, his dead son's widow, vague and shortsighted, known to the younger ones as granna. At the foot of the table, Beth, Kate's daughter, fresh-faced and comely, her corn-coloured hair in a braid round her head, looked on them all with a calm blue gaze and saw to it they had what they wanted. Next to her, her husband, Jesse, was just as yellow-haired as she, so that it was no wonder the two of them together had produced children of such harvest fairness.

But there was an odd-man-out among them: the boy named Tom Maddox: black-haired and brown-eyed, with the hollow cheeks and smooth dark skin of a gipsy, and the same slender build. He was very quiet, with an almost unnatural stillness about him, and although he was one of the family, he was yet apart from all the rest, watchful, intent, aware of everything that passed yet speaking it seemed only when some-one spoke to him. He was an oddity indeed; an orphan brought into the family and raised with them from the age of nine; standing out from all the rest like a black-bird in a sheaf of corn.

'You can see he ent one of us, can't you?' said young Dicky, showing off to Michael. 'Mother's never been able to scrub him clean.'

'Tom is courting,' Roger said. 'Did you know that, dad? It's Tilly Preston at The Rose and Crown.'

'Is that really so, Tom?' Jesse asked, assuming a father's gravity. 'And if it is, shouldn't you be asking my advice?'

'No,' Tom said, 'it ent true.'

'Well, Till Preston is sweet on *him*. She drew him a pint of ale for nothing when we was there on Friday night.'

'That's another bloody lie!'

'Now, then, Tom, mind your language in front of strangers.'

'Hah!' said great-grumpa. 'I daresay the captain's heard worse'n that.'

'Yes, indeed,' Michael said. 'It's a true saying, "to swear like a trooper." '

'But you're not a trooper,' Dicky said. 'What are you, exactly, since you ent in uniform for us to see?'

'Infantry,' Michael said. 'Second Battalion, the Three Counties Regiment.'

'Then you've seen some action, probably?'

'Oh, there's plenty of action out in France at present, yes.'

'Them French!' said granna, suddenly, adjusting her glasses to glare at Michael. 'You give them what-for and teach them a lesson!'

'What're you on about?' asked great-grumpa. 'The French are our allies, same as the Belgians.'

'Allies?' said granna. 'I thought they was meant to be on our side!'

'Let's not talk about the war—Michael gets enough of that,' said Betony.

'Don't he like talking about it?—He's different from most, then,' William said.

'Let's talk about the chickens and whether they're laying well lately.'

'Chickens?' said Dicky. 'Why talk about chickens for heaven's sake?'

'It's as good a subject as any other.'

And, across the table, Betony exchanged a smile with Michael.

He was often at Cobbs after that. It became for him a place apart. And the family accepted him, even William.

Having done his duty by his mother, going with her to luncheon parties, allowing her to show him off in his new uniform, he would then change into comfortable clothes and escape on long walks into the country, where he ate bread and cheese in quiet pubs, and drank beer. He could not have enough of days like these and often at the end he would come to Huntlip; to the old house at Cobbs; to Betony, whose day's work ended at six o'clock.

One evening they walked in Millery wood, half a mile away, on the north bank of the Derrent brook. It was just about dusk and as they climbed the steep path they passed a figure standing perfectly still in the shadows.

The man's stillness was uncanny, and immediately Michael was back in France, creeping at night along derelict trenches, where at every turn an enemy guard might loom up darkly. His flesh crept. He almost sprang at the man and struck him. But Betony's voice said, 'Tom? Is that you?' and her foster-brother stepped out to the pathway. Michael's breathing became normal. The sweat cooled on his lip and forehead.

'Yes, it's me,' Tom muttered, and slouched past them, hands in pockets, down the path towards the Derrent.

'Extraordinary fellow!' Michael said. 'What does he mean by it, skulking about in the dark like that?'

'It's nothing unusual for Tom. He's always been a night-creature.'

'Was he spying on us by any chance?'

'Goodness, no!' she said, laughing. 'Badgers, perhaps. Foxes, even. Or he may have been lying in wait for a pheasant. But he'd never bother to spy on people. They don't interest him enough for that.'

'Perhaps he had an assignation. That girl your brother Roger mentioned.'

'I hope not,' Betony said. 'Tilly Preston is a slut.'

She was rather protective where Tom was concerned. Michael had noticed it often before. And he wondered that she should concern herself with a youth whose manner towards her was always surly and indifferent. He had learnt a little of the boy's history: Tom was illegitimate; Granna had spoken of bad blood.

'Bad blood! What rubbish!' Betony said. 'I don't believe in all that. Tom's father had a terrible temper. He killed Tom's mother in a drunken quarrel and afterwards he hanged himself. Tom was a baby of twelve months or so, neglected until he was skin and bone. Then he was raised by my Grannie Izzard, well-looked-after but allowed to run wild. Those are the things that have made him strange. It's nothing to do with bad blood.'

'You're certainly a loyal champion.'

'I was cruel to him at first,' she said. 'When Grannie Izzard died and Tom came to us, I made his life a misery.'

'How did you?'

'Oh, tormenting him about his parents . . . making him feel he wasn't wanted . . .'

'Did your brothers do it too?'

'No. Only me. I was horribly spiteful.'

'That explains why you leap to defend him. You're trying to pay off a debt of guilt.'

'I suppose I am, though there's nothing Tom ever wants from me, and the silly thing is, he bears me no grudge.'

'Are you sure of that? He's very churlish.'

'He still doesn't trust me,' Betony said, 'and I can't really blame him.'

Coming out of the wood, onto high ground, they were met by a big full golden moon shining on the skyline, and Betony's face, when he turned towards her, had the moonlight bright upon it.

She looked serene. Her glance, meeting his, had a smile in it. But when he put out a hand to touch her, intending to hold her back a while, just as she was, with the moonlight on her, she walked quickly past and swung along the ridgeway path.

'I can hear the trains at Stickingbridge . . . that generally means we'll get a shower . . .'

The orchard at Cobbs presented a different picture now. The apples had been picked and the boughs, relieved of their heavy burden, had sprung back to their proper place. The forked supports had been removed; Martin Holt's sheep had been put in to graze; and now the leaves were falling fast, a luminous yellow in the long lush grass.

Michael was aware that the days were slipping through his fingers. His month's leave was almost over. He wished he could choose a specific moment and call for time to stand still. This moment, for instance, with Betony laughing in the sun, standing on tiptoe under a plum tree, trying to reach a globule of gum that hung on the branch like a bead of amber.

Yet what was the use of asking time to stand and deliver? All living creatures must take what they could. There was no fulfillment otherwise. Betony, with her arms upraised, the shape of her breasts inviting his touch—surely she was aware of herself, aware of the sun going round the sky, faster and faster every day?

Feeling him near her, she turned quickly, letting her arms fall to her sides. She was laughing and breathless and flushed with exertion, but as she looked at him and read the sick appeal in his eyes, her laughter faded away to nothing. His hands touched her face, her throat, her hair, and she stepped back a little, pushing him away. Her eyes remained steady. She tried to think of something to say. But it was Michael who spoke first.

'I want you to marry me. Soon. Straight away. I thought I'd get a special licence.'

'No, Michael. It's too soon. I don't really know if it's what I want.'

'I know my own feelings. I've no doubts whatever.'

'How can that be? It's impossible. We've known each other eighteen days! Afterwards, perhaps, when the war is over—'

'There may not be any afterwards for me.'

'You mustn't say that! It isn't fair to say such things.'

'It's true all the same. Do you know what the chances of survival are over there? I'm already living on borrowed time.'

'So you'd marry me quickly just to go off and leave me a widow?'

'No! That's just it! I know it's silly, but somehow I feel if I had your love, it would keep me safe from everything. I'd damn well make sure I got through safely!'

He knew he was playing on her feelings, but when he saw the pity in her face, he became ashamed.

'This is what it does to us!—Turns us into abject beings, preying on people, demanding their love. I'm sorry, Betony. Don't judge me too harshly. Let's forget about it and try to be as we were before.'

He took her hand and drew it into the crook of his arm, and they walked together towards the house, talking quietly of ordinary things. But all the time he wondered about her; tried to guess how she felt towards him; for he had pinned his faith on her and looked to her as his protection.

In the cobbled fold at the back of the house, Jesse Izzard was pumping water, filling two old wooden buckets. He saw Betony walking with Michael through the garden but pretended he had something in his eye. When they had passed, he picked up his buckets and went into the dairy, where his wife was busy bottling honey.

'The captain seems smutten on our Betony. Think it'll come to anything, do you?'

'Maybe. Maybe not.' Beth for once had no sure opinion. 'But Betony's a girl who will find it hard to give herself heart and soul to someone.'

Often when Tom was in The Rose and Crown, someone would bring him a chunk of wood and ask him to carve a bird or a fish or an animal, and today Tilly Preston, the landlord's daughter, had brought out an old maplewood beer-mug, for him to carve her likeness on it.

It took him perhaps half an hour, using only a pocket-knife, but the face on the mug was Tilly's exactly: the wide-set eyes under fine brows; the small straight nose with flared nostrils; the pretty lips parted a little, showing teeth with spaces between them; and the wisps of hair curling down over her forehead.

Tom, as he worked, was shut away from the noise around him, and Roger, watching his clever fingers, wished he had half Tom's skill in carving.

'Why, you've made me look flat!' Tilly complained, when she held the finished mug in her hands. 'Still, I reckon you've earnt your pint of Chepsworth.'

She filled the mug brimfull, and Tom drank it down in one long draught.

"That's the idea, Tom,' said Oliver Rye. 'Up with her until she's empty!'

'Is that all he gets?' asked Billy Ratchet. 'Don't he get a kiss and a bit of a huggle?'

'Go on, young Tom. Tilly's agreeable, I'll be bound.'

'Perhaps he's frightened,' said Henry Tupper. 'Perhaps he don't rightly know the motions?'

'D'you want a few pointers, Tom, lad, from one of us old hands that've had some experience?'

Tom said nothing. He wiped his mouth with the back of his hand. His dark face was flushed, and he couldn't look at Tilly Preston. But Tilly herself was leaning towards him, and when Billy Ratchet pushed Tom forward, she put her arms up round his neck. Her small round breasts rested against him, and her face came slowly closer to his, her lips parting as they touched very softly against his own.

The little gathering sent up a cheer. Glasses were thumped upon the tables. Then, abruptly, there was silence. The girl sprang away from the boy's arms and turned to her father who stood scowling in the open doorway.

Emery Preston was a well-built man. His chest was like one of his own barrels. And, going up to the slim-built Tom Maddox, he looked like a bulldog approaching a whippet.

'If I catch you touching my daughter again, I'll make you sorry you was ever born!'

'Father!' said Tilly, pulling at his arm. 'You mustn't speak to my friends like that.'

'No lip from you or you'll get my belt across your bottom! You're supposed to be courting Harry Yelland. I won't have you meddling with this chap Maddox.'

'Why, what's wrong with Tom?' Roger demanded, hot in defence of his foster-brother.

'I knew his father!' Emery said. 'He was the nastiest-tempered brute in Huntlip and he once hit my mother across the mouth because she refused him drink on the slate.'

'When was that? In the year dot? It warnt our Tom that done it anyway!'

'Like father, like son, so I'm taking no chances,' Emery said. 'Just mind and keep him away from my daughter!'

'Don't worry!' Roger said. 'We'll keep away from you *and* your daughter and be damned to both of you good and all!' And, taking Tom's arm, he led him to the door. 'Come on, Tom, we'll drink elsewhere. There's plenty of places better'n this one.'

Outside the door Tom pulled away from Roger's grasp and thrust his fists into his pockets. He turned along the Straight and Roger followed.

'Take no notice of Emery Preston. Who cares about him? Or Tilly neither?'

'Not me,' said Tom. 'I ent grieving over them.'

'San-fairy-duckwater, that's the style.'

'He was telling the truth, though, all the same. My dad was a bad 'un. There's no doubt of that. He murdered my mother down in that cottage at Collow Ford and then went and hanged hisself in a tree.'

'So what? It's all ancient history, over and done with. You don't want to worry yourself over that.'

'I don't,' Tom said. 'It's other folk that worry about it, not me.'

Sometimes he tried to picture his father: the drunkard hitting out in a rage; the fugitive run to ground by guilt; the despairer saving the public hangman a task. But no picture ever came to mind. It was just a story, and the man in the story was shadowy, faceless.

Could he picture his mother? Yes, perhaps. For sometimes he had a memory of white arms reaching towards him; of warm hands receiving his body into their strong, safe, thankful grasp. But the memory, if memory it was, always slid away when he tried to catch it, and then there was only a pitchblack darkness.

'Let's go to Chepsworth,' Roger said. 'We'll have a drink at The Revellers. They've got a skittle table there.'

At The Revellers, in Lock Street, a coloured poster

hung on the wall, showing the ruins of Louvain cathedral after its capture by the enemy. It was an artist's impression, it said, and it showed the German cavalry stabling their horses in nave and transept. One German trooper was smashing a painted plaster madonna by hurling it against the wall. Another was tearing the sacred vestments. Several others were burning carved wooden statues, including one of Christ blessing the loaves and fishes, to boil a pot of stew on a tripod, while, in the broken doorway, a few Belgian people, mostly old men and women, stood with their faces in their hands.

'I was just thinking,' Tom said, 'supposing that was Chepsworth cathedral, in ruins like that, with soldiers breaking everything up?'

'You ent religious, are you, Tom?'

'No, not me, but I think it's wicked all the same.'

'What about all the people killed? That's a lot more wicked than bosting statues.'

'Ah, well, that's right, of course,' Tom said. 'People is more important than statues.'

But he hated the thought of all those carved figures fed to the flames in Louvain cathedral, just to boil a stewpot for German soldiers.

'You've gone and done *what?*' Jesse asked, openmouthed. 'You surely didn't say enlisted?'

'Ah,' said Tom. 'Enlisted, that's right. Three o'clock this afternoon.'

'And you?' Jesse said, staring at Roger. 'You surely never went in too?'

'They wouldn't have me. They wouldn't believe I was eighteen.'

'God in heaven!' said great-grumpa. 'Anyone with half an eye could see you was only just weaned.'

'They took my name, though,' Roger said. 'They'll be sending for me in due course.'

'Due course,' said Jesse, relieved. 'Why, it's more'n a year before you're eighteen, and the war will surely be over by then?'

'It'd better be!' great-grumpa said. 'It's damn near ruining the business.'

'So Tom is to go? Would you believe it! I can't hardly credit it even now.' Jesse looked doubtfully at his wife. 'Ought we to let him, do you think, or are you going to put your foot down?'

'We can't stop him,' Beth said. 'He's well past eighteen and a grown man. If all I had to do was put my foot down, this war'd have been over before it started.' She looked at Tom, standing before her. 'When d'you have to go to the barracks?'

'They'll be sending my papers, the sergeant said.'

'You done right to enlist,' granna said. 'I'm only glad it ent our William.'

Tom went off to bed-down the pony in its stall, and there Betony found him later, having heard the news from her father and mother.

'Why did you go and enlist like that, without a word to anybody?'

'I just thought I would, that's all.'

'Do you think it's easy being a soldier?'

'I dunno. I ent considered.'

'I suppose you were tipsy as usual.'

'I suppose I was,' he said, shrugging.

She could never get near him, try as she might. He spoke to her only to answer her questions. It had always been so from the very beginning; from the moment he had come to Cobbs, when she had made him feel an outcast and had driven him into himself like a crab. Nothing would change him now, it seemed. He would never believe that she minded about him.

'I can't imagine Tom as a soldier.'

'You seem to be worried,' Michael said, 'yet it's no different for him than for any other volunteer.'

'Tom's known so little happiness. It would be wicked if he were killed.'

'He's been happy enough with your family, hasn't he?'

'But he's known no *joy*,' Betony said.

'How many people ever know joy?'

'Not many, I suppose, and then only in fleeting moments.'

They were walking in the garden at King's Hill House. Betony had sat through afternoon tea and had weathered his mother's interrogation. But her thoughts, obviously, had been elsewhere.

'There ought to be *special* joys in the world for people like Tom,' she said, 'though I've no idea what they might be.'

'You don't seem to mind that he treats you so boorishly all the time.'

'I know I deserve it, that's why.'

'Oh, come, now!' Michael said. 'You can't have treated him that badly.'

'You don't know. You weren't there. Children can be very cruel.'

'It was all a very long time ago.'

'I still feel guilty all the same.'

'I'm glad it's nothing more than that. I was beginning to be afraid you loved him.'

'But I *do* love him!' Betony said. 'I love him dearly and I wish to God I could make him trust me. He's a creature all alone in the world yet I can't get near him —I can't do anything to help him. Oh, yes, I love him. I love him very dearly indeed.'

Then, suddenly, she saw the expression in Michael's eyes.

'Ah, no!' she said. 'It isn't like that! Not *that* sort of love. How can I make you understand?'

And because she could not bear to see him unhappy, she reached up and kissed him, holding his face between her hands.

'You mustn't look like that,' she said. 'You've got no reason to look like that.'

'Betony—'

'Yes, yes, I know.'

'You do feel something for me, then?'

'Of course I do. How can you ask?'

'Are your feelings the same as mine?'

'I think they will be, given time.'

'Time,' he repeated. 'Ah, time!'

But he had her promise, and it was worth more to him than her surrender. He told her so by taking her hand and raising it formally to his lips. His eyes were not so desperate now.

Mrs. Andrews, watching them from the French window, gave a little sigh of resignation. The girl meant to have him. That much was obvious.

Towards the end of his leave, he went before a medical board. The wound in his shoulder had healed well. The effects of gas poisoning were passing away. He was fit for duty.

'You're very lucky,' the elderly doctor said to him. 'You've got an excellent constitution. Still, I'm taking no chances with those lungs of yours, so it's home service only for at least six months. Then we'll have you along again.'

Michael's heart leapt. Six months in England! He could hardly believe it.

'Disappointed?' the doctor asked dryly.

'I think I can bear it,' Michael said.

'You've earnt your respite. I wish I could give it to all the men who pass through my hands, but I have to send most of 'em back out there, like so many pitchers going to the well.'

Michael went home to enjoy the last few days of his leave and await his posting.

'I'm so relieved,' his mother said. 'Perhaps it will all be over soon, before you're ready for foreign service.'

'Perhaps it will. Who knows?'

That was November, 1915. The war must end sooner or later. Why not look on the bright side?

The new year came in, bringing a new determination. 1916! There was a certain sound about it. Great things were expected from the start, and people in Britain were pulling themselves together again, preparing for a new effort.

Michael was now at Yelmingham, attached to the new Tenth Battalion. He was lecturing recruits on trench warfare.

Tom, in training at Capleton Wick, had a weekend

pass every third or fourth week, and the family at
Cobbs grew used to seeing him in khaki. Dicky still
jeered at his skinny legs, bound tight in puttees, but
Great-grumpa Tewke thought him much improved.

'They've smartened you up, boy. They've made you
walk straight instead of lolling about like a ploughboy.
There's something to be said for discipline.'

Early in April, Tom was at home for the last time,
on twenty four hours' draft leave. There were three
other Huntlip boys due to go, and the four were given
a noisy send-off at The Rose and Crown. Tilly Preston
hung on Tom's arm almost all the evening and her
father for once said nothing about it. The family, too,
gave him a send-off, drinking his health in a bottle of
Beth's strong coltsfoot wine, and presenting him with
a pocket-bible.

'Are you sure you don't know where you're going?'

'No, they ent told us, but the chaps think it's
France.'

'Well, wherever it is,' granna said, 'always take care
that you air your clothes.'

Later that evening, Tom was missing from the family party. Betony went out to the fold, where the cobbles were frosty underfoot, and saw a light in the old
woodshed. Tom kept his ferrets in a hutch there, and
when she went in, he had the two of them in his arms.
His stub of candle stood in the draught, so that his
face was lit and unlit ceaselessly, cheekbones and jaw-
bones sharply outlined, deep dark eyes now seen, now
unseen, as the flame leapt and flickered, trying to pull
itself free of the wick.

'Will you look after my ferrets for me?'

'Why me, for mercy's sake?'

'The boys'd forget. They're not keen on ferrets.'

'I'm not keen myself. Nasty smelly things. But yes,
I'll look after them, that's a promise.'

It surprised her that he should entrust this duty to
her. He had never asked a favour in his life before.
It pleased her, too, and she stroked the ferrets in his
arms.

'I suppose you think you're going on an outing?'

'Ah, that's right, a regular dido.'

'Or out poaching with old Charley Bailey.'

'I know what it's like. I read the papers.'

'You'll write to us, won't you, and tell us how you're getting on?'

'I ent much of a hand at letters.'

'Well, I'll write to *you*,' Betony said, 'and that's the second promise I've made.'

Tom merely shrugged. He was feeling a wart behind Nipper's ear. It might be serious and need a spot of something on it. He showed it to Betony and made her feel it, telling her what she must do about it if it got worse while he was away.

Out there in France, in the trenches, however, letters were precious and were read over and over again. They were kept until they wore through at the folds and even then they were sometimes mended. All except the most intimate letters were passed round and shared, and Betony's letters were great favourites, being full of things that made the men laugh. And because she addressed them to 'Private Thos. Maddox' Tom was newly christened 'Toss'.

'We can't call you Tom,' said Pecker Danson. 'We're all Tommies out here!'

'What's she like, this Bet of yours?—Is she well-built?' asked Big Glover. 'I like 'em well-built, with some shape about them. Fair, did you say, and nice-looking? Soft and sweet and gentle, is she?'

'No,' Tom said, and the thought brought a faint smile to his lips.

'Whatya mean, no?'

'I wouldn't call her sweet and gentle.'

'Are you saying she's a Tartar?'

'Well, a bit on the bossy side, you know.'

'We might've known there was snags in it somewhere. God preserve us from bossy women!'

But their disappointment did not last long. They would have nothing said against Betony. They had made her their mascot.

'It's a good thing sometimes, being bossy,' said Bob

Newers. 'I wish we had her out here with us. She might get the rations up on time.'

'Ask Bet if she'll marry me when I get back to Blighty, will you?' said Big Glover. 'Say I'm six-foot-four and handsome with it. Don't mention the mole on my left elbow. I'd sooner keep it as a surprise.'

'She's got a chap already,' said Danson. 'An officer in the Second Battalion. That's right, ent it, Toss? Name of Andrews?'

'Ah, that's right,' Tom said.

'Sod hell and damn!' said Big Glover. 'The officers get all the luck.'

'Stands to reason,' said Rufus Smith. 'Bet ent like Toss. She's educated. You can tell by the way she writes her letters.'

'It makes me laugh whenever I think of it,' Pecker Danson said, choking. 'What she said last time, about the girls at Coventry writing messages on the shells. It makes me wish I was an artillery man. I might've learnt a thing or two.'

Rain was falling steadily. The trenches fell in as fast as the men worked to repair them. They stood to the knees in icy water, filling sandbags with the chalky mud.

'Why don't you never grumble, Toss? Why don't you never cuss and swear?'

'He don't need to, Pecker old son, 'cos you do enough for him and you both.'

'He ent hardly human, the way he never grumbles nor nothing. Don't you feel the cold and wet, Toss, the same as all us other chaps?'

'I try not to think about it,' Tom said.

Somehow he was able to shut out the cold teeming rain and the tiredness. He was able to shut himself up inside, with his own thoughts, while his body moved automatically and his arms went on working. Yet when they asked what these thoughts were, he could never tell them.

'The same as yours, I suppose,' he said.

'You're a dirty little tyke, then, if you think the same thoughts as the rest of us.'

After their spell at Hébuterne, which Danson said was to get them used to shellfire, they marched to billets at Beauquesne. The weather improved. They had ten days of intensive training, mostly in sunshine.

'Why bayonet practice?' Glover said, during a respite. 'Are we running out of bullets?'

'I saw a general this morning,' said Ritchie, 'the first I've seen since coming over.'

'You didn't see the C.-in-C.?'

'I wouldn't know him from Adam, would I, except that he'd be wearing khaki?'

'Who *is* C.-in-C.?' asked Pecker Danson.

'Blowed if I know. Does anyone else?'

'Charlie Chaplin,' Glover said.

'Mrs. Pankhurst,' said Rufus Smith.

'Angus Jock Maconochie.'

'Alexander's Ragtime Band.'

'Here, sarge!' said Bob Newers, stopping Sergeant Grimes as he came by. 'Who commands the B.E.F.?'

'I do!' said Grimes. 'And next after me, General Sir Douglas Haig.'

'Haig,' said Newers. 'Any whisky coming our way?'

The sergeant fixed him with a pitying eye.

'D'you mean to tell me you didn't know the name of the C.-in-C.? You're ignorant, Newers, that's what you are.'

'I am,' agreed Newers, nodding sadly. 'I'm that bloody ignorant they'll give me three stripes if I ent careful.'

'Enough of that!' Grimes said, without rancour. 'Too much sauce and I'll make you caper.'

Not all the instructors were like Grimes. Sergeant Townchurch, for instance, was out of a different mould entirely. He liked to pick on weaker men and humble them before the others, and one such was a Welshman named Evans, a small thin man with sunken chest who had trouble with his breathing: a man, Newers said, who should never have been in the Army at all.

'Evans?' said Townchurch, during a mock attack

one morning. 'A Welshman and a miner, eh? In other
words, a bloody slacker! We've heard about your lot,
going on strike for better pay while we sweat our guts
out fighting the Huns!'

Evans said nothing. His eyes were glazed and his
skin looked like putty. He was almost choking, for
Townchurch had run him about at the double, weighed
down by pack, rifle, entrenching tool, and two canvas
buckets full of grenades.

'How come you're in the Three Counties? Won't
they take slackers in the Royal Welsh? Or even in the
South Wales Borderers?'

'Leave him alone,' Tom said. He was standing next
to Evans and could hear how the man struggled for
breath. 'If he was a slacker he wouldn't be here.'

Townchurch came and stood before Tom. He
looked him over from head to foot.

'Are you another bloody Welshman? No? Perhaps
not. A gipsy, then? It's what you look like. And what,
might I ask, is your sodding name? Maddox. Right.
Be sure I'll remember.'

So Tom and Evans became his victims. Luckily their
stay at Beauquesne was brief. The party in training
broke up, and the Sixth Battalion went into the line,
taking over trenches at Mary Redan. Evans was now
in C Company, in the same platoon as Tom and
Newers, and by a strange unlucky chance, when their
sergeant was injured by shrapnel, his place was taken
by Sergeant Townchurch.

Tom's letters home were few and far-between, and,
although written with immense labour, were never
more than half a page long. 'I am well. I got your
parcel. How are Nipper and Slip and the workshop?'
There was not much to say. The censor would only
cut it out. So he wrote about the yellowhammer, heard
so often in the hedgerows, saying *A little bit of bread
and no chee-eeese,* just the same as it did in England.
And he pressed speedwell flowers and herb robert between the folded sheet of paper. It astonished him

daily that the same flowers grew in Picardy as grew in the fields and lanes at home.

'Things cann't be too bad over there,' Jesse said to Betony, 'if young Tom's got time to gather flowers.'

In England, now, the may was out and the wild June roses would soon be coming. The weather was good. Hay harvest had started at Anster and in the evenings Jesse and his sons were out in the fields, helping Janie and her husband Martin with the haymaking. William had now had his eighteenth birthday. Jesse was rather worried about him.

'Won't you get into trouble, boy, stopping at home now conscription's come in?'

'It's no odds to me. I still ent going.'

'If William was to work on the farm full-time he might be exempt,' Janie said.

'I don't care to be exempt—I just ent going,' William said. 'I didn't start this damned war so why should I down tools and go fighting in it?'

'Yes, but suppose they put you in gaol, boy?'

'They'll tarnal well have to catch me first!'

One day soon after, William and Roger were delivering ladders at a shop in Chepsworth. Roger disappeared for a little while and returned triumphant.

'I've been along to the recruiting centre. They took me this time. No questions asked.'

'Are you gone in the head, you stupid fool? You've got no right! You're still under age.'

'If I look eighteen then I'm good enough to be eighteen. I'm a lot stronger than some of the chaps I seen there today.'

'I'm going down there to get your name took off their list!'

'If you do that,' Roger said, 'I'll run away south and join up there.'

William saw that Roger meant it. He stood for a moment in a quivering rage. Then, suddenly, he was calm.

'All right,' he said, 'if one of us goes, we're both going.'

'But you don't want to!' Roger said.

'I ent letting you go by yourself. A kid like you needs looking after. Besides, what'd I look like, do you think, with my younger brother gone and not me?'

So William and Roger joined together, and together confronted their parents at home.

'Don't worry, mother,' William said. 'I'll take care of Roger for you and I'll make certain-sure we don't get parted.'

Within a month, they were in camp at Porthcowan, training with the Royal Artillery.

'It's not a bad life, considering,' William wrote in a letter home. 'In fact I reckon it suits me fine.' And at the end, in a casual postscript, 'I came out top in the ranging tests yesterday morning. The instructor says I'm a born gunner. I might put in for a stripe directly if everything goes according to plan.'

Being William, now that he had become a soldier, he was determined to be a good one.

One Sunday in May Betony went up to London and spent the afternoon with Michael. He was looking better: stronger; more relaxed; yet when she told him so, his eyes darkened and a shiver went through him.

'I'm practically one hundred per cent, which means I'll soon be posted abroad.'

'Are you sure?' she said. 'Sure you're fit again, I mean.'

'You just said so, yourself.'

'I said you looked it, but I'm no doctor.'

'No, well, we've got plenty of those, and they look me over now and then.' Then he said abruptly: 'How are things in munitions nowadays?'

'Frightening,' she said. 'I was in Birmingham yesterday, where they're making shells. The output is tremendous, and it's just the same wherever I go.'

'That's the stuff! We might get somewhere if we've got things to throw.'

'Is something coming?' Betony asked. 'A big offensive?'

'Shush,' he said, smiling. 'How do I know you're not a spy?'

They were having tea at The Trocadero. He passed his cup across the table and watched her, secretly, as she filled it. There was something about the shape of her face, and her calm expression, that took him by surprise each time he saw her. She seemed so unconscious of herself; of the way she looked, the way she smiled. He had not been mistaken. He wanted her badly.

'Betony,' he said, 'do you have to go back to Chepsworth tonight?'

'Yes. I've got to be in Gridport at eight in the morning.'

'Oh, that work of yours!' he said. 'Couldn't you be late just once in a while?'

'No, Michael, I'm afraid not.'

'Would you have stayed with me, had you been free to?'

'I'm never free for more than one day.'

'You're just trying to spare my feelings. The answer is no, obviously.' His gaze fell away and he stared at the sugar-bowl on the table. 'I'd like you to know,' he said slowly, doing his best to make light of the matter, 'that I don't try it on with every young woman I meet.'

'Do you meet so many, at Yelmingham?'

'You'd be surprised at the number of homes we officers are made welcome in. It's all meant to sustain our morale and there's a certain titled lady at Gaines who takes her task very seriously indeed.'

'Are you trying to make me jealous?'

'Drink up,' he said. 'We ought to be moving if we're to catch that train.'

He drove with her in a taxi to the station, and kept up the same light-hearted conversation till her train pulled out.

'Give my regards to your family,' he said. 'And don't forget to call on my mother. She's very anxious to get to know you.'

Towards the end of May he was pronounced fit for general service and ordered to rejoin his old battalion. He had forty-eight hours' leave and arrived at Chepsworth at eleven o'clock on Saturday morning. After lunching with his mother he walked out to Huntlip, but Betony was not at home. She had gone to Stafford on a special course and was not expected back until Sunday.

'What time on Sunday?' Michael asked.

'We don't rightly know,' Jesse said. 'She didn't go by train, you see. She went in a special motor bus, along with some very important people.'

'Can I get her on the telephone?'

'Laws!' Jesse said, and his blue eyes opened very wide. 'I shouldn't think so!'

So Michael left a note and returned home. His leave slipped away, pointless and empty, with his mother pretending not to notice his silence. She feared for him dreadfully, three times wounded yet returning once more to the battle zone, and she thought it wrong that the same young men should be called upon again and again for duty.

And yet at the same time she took pleasure in the sight of him in his uniform, with the three stars on each epaulette, and the three yellow wound-stripes on the sleeve. She took pride in him because he was her son, and because he had been among the first to answer his country's call for men. She forbore to reproach him for his silence. Her only complaint came at the end, when he refused to let her see him off at the station.

'Is it because of that girl?' she said. 'The carpenter's daughter? Will she be there?'

'I don't even know if she got my message.'

'If she hasn't, you'll be leaving all alone.'

'I'll chance that,' he said. 'I'd much rather say goodbye here.'

'Very well. It's as you wish. I will be praying for you, my son, and thinking of you constantly.'

'Good,' he said, and stooped to kiss her. 'I may be too busy to pray for myself.'

His train left at nine that evening. It was drawing out as Betony ran down onto the platform. She saw him at once and hurried forward, trying to take his outstretched hands as he leant towards her, out of the window. Their fingers were joined momentarily,—a brief exchange of warmth and softness—then the train gathered speed and tore them apart. Betony hurried along beside it, and Michael looked down at her with anguished eyes, his lips apart but no words escaping between them. He wanted to open the door and jump out. She was growing smaller all the time. She had come to a standstill.

'Michael, take care, take care!' she called, and he heard her even above the noise of the engine. 'Come back safely! I'll be waiting for you!'

Staying in London overnight, he heard much talk of the coming offensive, even among the hotel staff. He mentioned the matter to Morris Tremearne, a fellow captain in the Second Battalion, also staying at The Kenilworth.

'Even the bootboy knows there's going to be a push. And now there are hints in the newspapers. We may as well send the Kaiser a telegram, stating the exact time and place!'

'Ah, that's the beauty of it!' said Tremearne. 'The fuss we're making, the Germans'll never believe it's going to happen, don't you know!'

Michael turned away, catching the eye of his new batman. Lovell was discretion personified, but his glance was expressive.

Three days later they were with their battalion in

Béthune. Michael was glad to see men he knew. Six months was a long time. He tried not to think of those who had vanished in the interim. He tried not to keep counting them.

'My God, you look smart!' Lightwood said. 'I hardly knew you.'

'Plenty of new chaps coming up, not all of them hopeless,' Ashcott said. 'This specimen here is a good man.—He's brought the latest gramophone records.' And he waved a hand at the new young subaltern standing beside him. 'His name's Spurrey. We call him Weed.'

'What's the new C.O. like? Big man or small?'

'Big and fatherly and serious-minded. Has a proper respect for flesh and blood. Treats us almost as human beings.'

'What's happening here at the moment?'

'We're up and down the canal mostly. We know it like the backs of our hands. Still, the big push is coming, so they say, and soon we'll be sleeping in the Kaiser's palace.'

'Has he *got* a palace?' Spurrey asked.

'I'm damn sure he doesn't live in a dugout!'

'Four miles,' Michael said, listening to the guns firing at Givenchy. 'It sounds nearer.'

'That's because you've been away. You've got used to the hush at home in England. What did you do with yourself, all that time? Pickle the onions?'

'It's mustard, not pickles,' Michael said. He was used to jokes about the family business. 'But I never go near the factory if I can help it.'

'Mustard! Of course! That explains your famous coolness under fire. You've had it hot and strong all your life, what?'

'Besides, I haven't been in Chepsworth all the time.'

'No, you've been manning a desk at Yelmingham, you lucky devil. Still, I expect you're glad to be back in the swim. It must be pretty dangerous in England now, with all those women driving the trams.'

The next day, they were in the front line, in the Cuinchy sector. Michael had command of B Company, and his sergeant was a man named Bill Minching, a veteran of Mons and Festubert: quiet-spoken; steady-eyed; unupsettable, as Lightwood said. Almost half the men in the Company were new drafts but they looked on Michael as the newcomer.

A working party, under Minching, was out one night digging a new communication trench. Some rain fell and in the morning, when Michael inspected the finished work, there was water at the bottom of the trench. The men slopped about in it, thinking it nothing, but Michael gave orders that duckboards were to be laid down immediately.

'One of those, is he?' a private named Biddle was heard to say. 'Believes in giving us plenty to do!'

Minching tapped him on the shoulder.

'You may have webbed feet, Biddle, but the rest of us are not so lucky.'

Two men were killed by shellfire that day, and two were wounded. One of the wounded was Private Biddle. He was carried away with a deep jagged gash spouting blood from breast-bone to navel, and, passing Minching, he spoke weakly.

'Seems I'm a goner, don't it, sarge?'

'Oh no you're not!' Minching said. 'You'll just be laid up for a bit, that's all. You've got a Blighty one. —Ent that the answer to your prayers?'

Biddle believed him. New hope came into his eyes. He lay back smiling.

'Carry on, my good men,' he said to the bearers, 'the surgeons are waiting.'

'Will he live?' Michael asked Minching later.

'I don't know, sir, but faith can work wonders, so they say.'

One afternoon, during an off-duty period in Annequin, a young subaltern, exploring the ruins of a bakery, set off an old enemy shell that had lain there, rusting, for over a year. He was blown to pieces.

'It's a bad place, this,' Spurrey said to Lightwood at mess that evening. 'I don't like it. It gives me the creeps.'

He was nineteen and had come out in April with his friends Hapton, Challoner, and Wyatt. All three friends were now dead. Wyatt was the man killed by the old 'sleeping' shell.

'Don't like La Bassée?' said Hunter-Haynes, as though offended. 'You surely don't mean it!'

'How about a stroll down to the brickstacks?' Ashcott said, patting Spurrey's shoulder. 'Plenty of souvenirs to be had there . . . such as a bullet in the head.'

'You should look on the dark side, young Weed,' said Spencer, 'then every day is a kind of bonus.'

'Blessed are the meek, for they shall inherit the earth,' said Lightwood, 'though I must say the will is a hell of a long time in probate.'

'You're quiet, Andrews,' Ashcott remarked.

'He's got inside knowledge, I bet,' Lightwood said. 'How do you do it, Andrews, old man? Have you got the colonel's ear?'

'I've got Minching's ear. He's good at sorting out the rumours.'

'And what does the omniscient Minching predict?'

'A move southward in the near future.'

'Nothing more specific than that?'

'I'm afraid not.'

'Ah, well,' Lightwood said. 'I doubt if Staff themselves know very much more. I don't suppose they've stuck a pin in the map yet.'

After their tour of duty in the trenches, they returned to Béthune and had a fortnight's training there, mostly mock battles. They now knew, officially, that the great offensive had begun, thirty miles southward, on the Somme.

'Shall we be in it?' Spurrey asked.

'Up to our necks,' Ashcott said, 'but not yet, I hope.'

'Why not yet?'

'There's a marvellous girl living near the soapworks, and I mean to have her, that's why.'

'You and whose army?' Lightwood murmured.

On July the eighth, after dark, the battalion entrained at Lillers station and travelled southwards through the night. Early next morning they arrived at

Saleux, and from there they marched nine miles to St. Sauveur.

After the coal-pits and slag-heaps of Artois, Picardy was lovely indeed: a district as yet hardly touched by war: a country of orchards and big sweeping fields full of green standing corn, where poppies flared along the roadsides, and the air smelt sweet and fresh and clean.

At every farmhouse, every hamlet, people turned out and watched from their doors. A very old man bowed gravely, straightened and gave a military salute. An old woman wept into her apron. Children ran beside the soldiers.

'Tommee! Tommee! Soldats anglais!'

'Napoo lay boutons!' the soldiers said, as many small hands plucked at their tunics.

'Napoo lay badges!'

'Napoo nothing! Allay bizonc!'

'Après la guerre finee. Maybee. Ah, and viva to you, too, you cheeky monkey!'

But the men were tired. They grew more silent with each mile that passed. The day was a hot one and they marched in a cloud of thick white dust that dried out their mouths and gave them a terrible raging thirst. So at St. Sauveur they stopped for rest, drink, and food, before pressing on another eight miles towards the banks of the River Ancre.

They came at last to Vecquemont, a glimmer of lights in the dusk now falling, and here they stayed, the men flopping down beside the road while the officers went to arrange billets. The people of Vecquemont were not best pleased. They stood about, blank-faced, unmoving. Yet when a battalion of the Glasgow Highlanders marched through half an hour later, with the pipes playing, they were given a rousing cheer.

'That's what we're here for,' one of their officers said to Michael. 'The Scots turn-out is good for morale. It gives the civilians a bit of a boost. And you English fellows, too, of course.'

'Cocky bastards,' Lightwood said, as the Highlander

turned and swaggered away. 'Strutting about in their fancy dress!'

All next day they remained at Vecquemont, giving the men a chance to recover from their seventeen-mile march and make themselves ready. They left early the following morning, and, determined not to be outdone by the Glasgows, marched smartly out of the village.

'We may not have a howling cat to lead us,' Sergeant Minching said to his men, 'but there's nothing wrong with the way we march.'

'Good old Three Counties!' a voice shouted from the ranks. 'Especially Leominster!'

At Morlancourt, eight miles westwards, they rested again for twenty-four hours, and the men handed in unwanted equipment, including greatcoats. They were now within close sound of the guns. No civilians were to be seen. The villages here had all been evacuated some time before. After dark on the twelfth, they marched three miles to Bécordel, close to the old front line of 1914. There they met up with other battalions, and the whole brigade went into camp.

In the morning, Michael rode up with the other company commanders to a ridge called Calou, from whence they could see the new battle zone, a mile or so distant, under bombardment by British artillery. The noise was deafening. The enemy line danced and quivered under the smoke. The air was never still for a moment.

'I feel almost sorry for poor old Fritz,' a man named Logan said to Michael. 'We've been pounding him for three weeks. I shouldn't think he could stand much more. It should be a walkover, when we attack.'

As they rode back again, down onto the fields where the whole brigade lay in bivouac, Michael felt an upsurge of hope. There were two thousand men mustered below, and everywhere else along the line the concentration of troops was enormous. Surely the offensive must carry the war? Official communiqués were encouraging. They told of successes further south. And yet, somehow, sneaking in under the official news,

there were rumours that spoke of bad setbacks everywhere; of terrible losses; of whole divisions cut to
pieces on the enemy wire. How did the rumours get
about? he wondered. Were they, as the colonel stated,
merely the work of German spies?

That night was cold, and because the encampment
was hidden from the enemy by two or three ridges of
high ground, the men were allowed to light fires. They
flickered up everywhere, small ghosts of fires in the
damp darkness, each with its close-packed ring of men.
Some groups told stories. Some sang songs. From a
few came the sound of a mouth-organ playing. And,
going about from group to group, Colonel Nannet in
his British warm, with his collar up and his cap pulled
well down, stopped to exchange a word or two with
the men of his battalion.

Michael, with the other officers of his company,
stood at the opening of their tent. Lightwood was
smoking a large cigar. The scent of it wafted on the
damp air.

'There goes the old man, dishing out his eve-of-
action comfort.'

' "A little touch of Harry in the night," ' said Ashcott. ' "Oh, God of Battles, steel my soldiers' hearts!" '

'Something the poor devils could well do without,'
said Lightwood. 'Still, he's not a bad old cock, really.'

The colonel retired to his quarters at last. B Company officers retired to theirs. Michael sat looking towards the west, where gun flashes lit the cloudy sky,
beyond the contours of Calou Ridge. Underneath, in
the darkness, the camp fires still flickered, kept alive
assiduously with twigs and leaves and bits of grass.
Some of the men were still singing.

> 'When this lousy war is over,
>   Oh, how happy I shall be!
> I will tell the sergeant-major
>   Just how much he means to me. . . .'

From first light onwards, the Allied bombardment was
intensified, all along the enemy lines. It was Bastille

Day and the French guns were particularly active. At ten-thirty, the sun was already very warm, shining down on the columns of men marching along the Fricourt road.

They were among the trenches again; on ground that covered, all too shallowly in places, the dead of two years' warfare. All along the old front line, the bodies of those killed in more recent fighting still lay about, and the stench of corruption was everywhere. Sometimes these bodies appeared to heave, because of the flies seething upon them, and because of the movement of scavenging rats.

At the village of Fricourt, now in ruins, the battalion rested for several hours, awaiting orders. They got food and drink from a field kitchen, but every mouthful tasted of lyddite from the batteries of guns firing nearby. Such news as came was so far good. The enemy line was reported broken and the Germans were said to be giving way. Our Indian cavalry had been in action and were at this moment riding the enemy into the ground. Certainly a great many prisoners had been taken. Whole columns of them kept coming down, eyes staring out of blackened faces; exhausted, shrunken, scarcely able to lift their feet.

From Fricourt the battalion marched to the village of Mametz, now no more than a heap of rubble. Among the ruins stood a column of motor ambulance cars, and there were crowds of British wounded awaiting attention at the medical aid post. They seemed cheerful and said the day was going well.

'We've cleared the way for you up there. You've got nothing to do but go round with the mop.'

'Jerry is running for all he's worth.'

'Bazentin is in our hands . . .'

'Mametz Wood is in our hands . . .'

But one man, with bandaged head, sitting smoking a cigarette, gave a cynical laugh.

'Dead hands, mostly, you'll find,' he said.

Leaving Mametz, the battalion moved down a sunken road, then forked off into a valley. On their right rose a long escarpment. On their left the ground sloped, open, all the way up to Mametz Wood. The noise of the bombardment was almost more than they could bear, for, all across the open area, batteries of British field-guns kept up an incessant fire, and beyond the escarpment were the French seventy-fives. The shriek of shells overhead never stopped, for the British heavies were also at work, some way behind.

The rough road was strewn with dead. Michael tried not to look too closely, for it seemed to him there were many more khaki-clad bodies than field-grey, and now the number of walking-wounded had grown to a never-ending stream. Silent men, trudging past as though indifferent; mere shadows of men, hollow-eyed, the same as the Germans; men whose last remaining strength was needed to carry them along the road.

'What lot are you?' Minching asked, as one group passed.

'Manchesters,' came the brief answer.

'What lot are *you?*' he asked another.

'South Staffords—what there is left of us!' a man said, snarling.

Everywhere along the valley lay the carcasses of dead horses, their heads thrown back, their legs in the air. Some were transport horses, and their smashed limbers lay nearby; but some were cavalry horses with braided saddles and gleaming stirrups, and their riders lay only God knew where.

Down the road now came wounded troopers of an Indian regiment, some leading their terrified mounts, others slumped as though dead in their saddles. One elderly Sikh, having watched his wounded horse collapse, was on his knees beside it, and the tears were running down his bearded face. His lips moved as though in prayer. His hands made a little secret sign. He took his revolver from the saddle and shot the dying horse in the head. He knelt, watching, until it was still. Then he turned the revolver on himself and fell across the horse's body.

'Christ!' said a soldier to his mate. 'Did you see that?'

'No one saw nothing!' shouted a sergeant, determined to keep the column moving. 'Close up, there, Number One Platoon! Keep your dressing by the left!'

The men marched on along the valley, passing between the two flanking storms of the great bombardment, under a sky that shrieked and sizzled with the flying shells.

Logan came up and rode with Michael a little way. He had been talking to a wounded officer of the South Staffords.

'He says he's been here since the big push started. A whole fortnight in the front line. No wonder they all look such wrecks, is it?'

'What's the name of this place, did he say?'

'Seems they call it Happy Valley.'

They came out into the open, among fields of tobacco and turnips and corn, the crops all trodden into the ground. It was now seven o'clock in the evening, and the battalion dug itself in for the night, close beside a wood known, from its shape, as Flatiron Copse. Enemy shells were falling all the time. Eight men were killed before the shelter-trenches were dug. Another six were badly wounded.

Nobody slept. The shelling was too close for that. It was also very cold, and the men, having left their greatcoats at Morlancourt, lay huddled close together for warmth, trying to make the most of their groundsheets. Dawn, when it came, brought some relief, and there was breakfast of a sort, with hot sweet tea and a tot of rum.

The battalion fell in, and the whole brigade moved off eastwards in a thick white mist, forward into the battle area. The ground was broken and badly cratered, littered with debris and dead bodies. There were wounded men, too, who had lain out all night and who now reached up with pleading arms as the marching columns tramped by. One or two soldiers, not yet hardened, stepped out of line, reaching for their water-bottles, but were herded back by a watchful N.C.O.

'Leave that to the stretcher-parties! You'll need them water-bottles yourselves directly!'

The brigade formed up in a valley south of High Wood. The Second Three Counties were in reserve. They held a position at Trivet Spur, beside a rough track known as Windy Lane. The Second Worcestershire were nearby.

A mile to the north, the Glasgows and the Queen's formed the front line, and some of the Glasgows had already been in action during the night, in High Wood itself. Now they were attacking the main Switch Line, where the Germans, contrary to earlier reports, were as strong as ever. High Wood was thought to be safe, but as the Glasgows advanced across the open, they were cut down by enemy machine-guns firing from among the trees.

Michael, watching through his field-glasses, could see it all: the double lines of kilted figures advancing up the open slope; the glint of a bayonet here and there; and then the terrible thinning-out as the Maxims raked them from front and rear. He could see the depleted line pressing onwards, with men of the King's and the First Queen's going up to fill the gaps; could see the line faltering again, the bodies thick in the green corn; and now the live men were falling, too, crawling to the cover of shell-scrapes and craters. He saw the Worcesters go up to help: two companies into the wood; two attacking across the open; and he saw the pitiful remnants returning, dragging themselves back to their line.

'What do you think, sir?' Logan was saying to the colonel. 'Shall we be sent up to help, d'you suppose?'

Michael put down his glasses and turned a little, waiting for the answer, which was slow in coming. The colonel's face was deep-lined, and his eyes were full of angry tears.

'Is that what you want?—To go the same way as those poor devils out there?' But he quickly relented. 'I'm sorry, Logan. I didn't mean to snap your head off. I've no idea what our orders will be. All I know is that it's madness attacking across that space while Fritz still holds that bloody wood. I'm sending along to Brigade H.Q. to tell them so.'

At twelve noon, for half an hour, there was another
bombardment by British guns, but it short-ranged and
the shells fell on what was left of the Glasgows' own
forward line. German shells were exploding in the
southern half of the wood, driving out the Worcesters
and the South Staffords, many of whom were mown
down by their own machine-guns before they were
able to make themselves known.

At four o'clock in the afternoon, two companies of
the Second Three Counties were sent up into the
wood: C Company under Logan and D Company under Tremearne; roughly two hundred men in all. The
other two companies remained in their trenches, with
enemy shells falling close, and at half-past-four orders
came for them to advance up the open hillside.

Colonel Nannet delayed. He wanted to be sure the
wood was safe. He sent up a runner, who failed to return, and was about to send another when a message
arrived from Brigade H.Q.: 'High Wood is ours. Proceed as ordered.' So, at six o'clock exactly, A Company under Ashcott and B Company under Michael
climbed out into the open and began advancing up the
slope towards the enemy Switch Line.

The hillside was strewn with the dead and dying, the
ground was broken everywhere, and black smoke
drifted from left to right as enemy shelling intensified.
Visibility was bad, and the slope grew steeper all the
time, so that progress was slow, but once up and over
the brow, the smoke lessened and it was like coming
out into a brighter light again.

Michael turned his head, first right, then left, to see
how many of his men had gone, falling, unseen, behind the smoke. It seemed to him the line was still
strong, the forward movement still determined, and he
caught a glimpse of his sergeant's face, calm, intent,
open-eyed, under the brim of his steel helmet.

Towards the top of the first slope, crossing a road,
Michael turned aside to avoid a deep crater, and as
he did so, three men with rifles rose from its shelter

and fell in behind him: kilted men of the Highland regiment: survivors of the earlier attack.

'We're wi' ye, laddie! And whoever you are you're doing fine!'

They were out past the corner of the wood now, moving across the wider space, inside the range of the worst shelling, though shrapnel was bursting overhead. A Company was on the right, B Company on the left, the two lines straggling but still moving forward in good order. The ground had flattened out again. The enemy line was only two hundred yards away.

But now, suddenly, from the northernmost boundary of the wood, came a burst of machine-gun and rifle fire, and Michael, glancing back, saw his three Highlanders fall to the ground. Over on his right, A Company had received the first and the worst of the fire, and nearly half its men had fallen. The remainder struggled on, only to meet the same destructive fire from in front, as they tried to reach the enemy line. The task was beyond them and the few men remaining faltered badly, seeking shelter instinctively behind B Company, still advancing. Only Ashcott kept to the front, and, running close beside Michael, sobbed out, swearing:

'The liars said the wood was ours! Why do they tell such lies, the bastards?'

Then, abruptly, he was no longer there. His body was being trampled underfoot. His place beside Michael was taken by Gates. The noise of the Maxims was very loud. Their fire was withering, murderous, keen. Michael felt himself blinking, averting his face as though in a hailstorm, and all the time as he ran forward he felt he was pushing through a great bead curtain of spent bullets. He had the strange fancy that this bead curtain was his protection: that a deadly bullet would not get through: that all he had to do was to keep pushing forward.

Gates was hit and fell with a terrible high-pitched scream. The man who took his place was sobbing and swearing, snorting for breath through wide-open mouth and wide-stretched nostrils. He was hit in the chest and fell headlong, and his rifle was thrown between Michael's feet, causing him to stumble.

Now, whenever he glanced to left or right, there were great gaps all along the line; gaps that were no longer filling up; gaps that grew bigger as he looked. He pressed on, leaping over a huddle of corpses, and as he did so he was hit in the thigh. He fell among the dead bodies.

Twenty yards away lay a crater. He began crawling on his stomach towards it. A man looked over the edge and saw him. It was Alan Spurrey, his new young subaltern, bare-headed, having lost his helmet. Spurrey was wounded in both feet, but he crawled from the crater and wriggled forward, arms outstretched to help Michael.

'Get your head down!' Michael shouted. 'Get down and get back, you bloody fool!'

A machine-gun rattled, and Michael pressed his face to the ground. Bullets struck the turf beside him and ripped on in a curving line. When he looked up again, Spurrey was dead, his head shattered. Michael crawled on into the crater.

It was not a bad wound: the bullet had entered the fleshiest part of the right thigh and had passed out behind; but the bleeding was heavy and soon soaked the dressing, so he used his tie as a tourniquet.

When he looked out over the edge, there was no advancing line to be seen, for those few men who were left alive had sought shelter in the broken ground. He could see some of them nearby, crawling on their stomachs, and after a while two men joined him in the crater, one of them wounded in the chest.

The wounded man, Aston, was in a bad way. Michael helped the other, a corporal named Darby, to dress the wound. He gave him a drink from his water-bottle.

'What a mess it all is!' Darby exclaimed. 'What a stinking awful bloody mess!' He looked at Michael with bitter defiance. 'We never stood a chance of reaching the Germans. Neither us nor the other poor sods this morning. Surely the brasshats should've known?'

'They know now,' Michael said.

'If I get back safe I swear I'll get some bloody red-nosed brigadier and stick him through with my bloody bayonet!'

'Is Aston your particular friend?'

'He's my brother-in-law. He married my sister before coming out. And what'll *she* say when she hears he's hurted?'

'He may be all right. We must get him back as soon as we can.'

'What a hope!' Darby said. 'What a bloody flaming hope!'

A burst of machine-gun fire shut him up. He crouched low in the loose earth. Michael was wondering what had drawn the fire when a man rolled over the edge of the crater and lay down beside him. It was Sergeant Minching.

'You all right, sir? I see you're hit.'

'Not too badly, though I've bled like a pig. It's Aston here who's in trouble.'

Aston was only barely conscious. Minching bent over him, listening to his heartbeats and his breathing. Darby watched him.

'Any hope, sarge?'

'There's always hope,' Minching said. 'The bullet's missed his lungs, I would say, but we'll have to be careful how we move him. Might be better to leave him here—let Jerry find him and patch him up.'

'Hell, no!' Darby said.

'He'd get attention that much sooner.'

'What sort of attention, though, by God?'

'The Jerries aren't monsters. They'd take care of him all right.'

'I'm getting him back,' Darby said, 'even if I have to do it by myself.'

'All right, we'll do it between us, don't worry, as soon as it's dark enough to move.' Minching turned towards Michael. 'What about you, sir? Can you walk?'

'If not, I can always crawl.'

A shrapnel shell burst in the air nearby, and they pressed their faces into the earth, while the balls blasted the crater's edge. When Michael looked up, the smoke was drifting overhead. He called to Minching, who was looking out.

'What's going on out there? Can you see?'

'I can see a bunch of our men, sir, falling back down the side of the wood. They're making a dash for it, back to the line.'

'No sign of their rallying?'

'There's nothing much left to rally, sir. A couple of dozen at the most.'

'What happened to our Lewis-gun sections?'

'Copped it, sir, quite early on. A shell got one of 'em—Mr Rail's—and the gun was useless. I know it was 'cos I went to see. The other lot stopped at the corner of the wood, trying to get that bloody Maxim. They were cut down in seconds. They never even got their gun into action.'

A rifle cracked from the German line, and a bullet struck the edge of the crater. Minching wriggled back at once.

'The colonel was killed, sir, did you know? So were Mr Lightwood and Mr Haynes.'

'And Mr Spencer?'

'Badly wounded in the head. A Company's worse off than us. I reckon they're pretty well wiped clean out.'

Michael turned away and closed his eyes.

Just before darkfall, Minching opened their iron rations. They ate corned beef and hard biscuit. Aston, though conscious, could eat nothing. He asked for water all the time. Darby kept giving him his own bottle.

'Hang on, Fred, it won't be long now. We'll get you back, don't worry. But for God's sake remember to keep mum or we'll have Jerry down on us as sure as fate.'

As evening came on, artillery fire was renewed on both sides, and the air above was filled again with the shrieking of shells; but after a while, as night fell, it eased off and became intermittent; and between the two flashing skylines, darkness settled along the ground.

'Now,' Minching said. 'It's time we started.'

He and Darby hoisted Aston till he hung with an arm round each man's neck. Aston gave a cry but choked it back quickly, sucking his breath between clenched teeth.

'Easy does it,' Minching muttered. 'Hold on, my lad, and bite on the bullet. It's a long way to Tipperary.'

He turned his face towards Michael, who lay trying to bend his knee.

'You coming, sir?'

'No, not yet. Better for you to go ahead.'

'Supposing you was to need help?'

'Don't fuss, man! Just get a move on and do as I say.'

'Very well, sir, but don't dilly-dally too long—the Jerry patrols'll be out soon.'

'I know that. I'm not a fool.'

'All right, sir, and good luck.'

'Good luck, Minching,' Michael said, and watched as the three men stumbled over the edge, vanishing into the misty darkness.

He crawled to the rim and lay listening. All around in the darkness, wounded men groaned and whimpered, and sometimes he heard slithering noises as somebody crawled along the ground, inching his way down the slope. Sometimes he heard tortured breathing. Once he heard a man praying.

Half a mile below, shells were bursting in High Wood, great yellow flashes splintering the darkness between the trees, while, on the horizons, north and south, as the big guns answered each other, the sky flickered, pulsing whitely. Now and then a starshell rose, green-spiked, beautiful, a manmade meteor rising and sinking like a sigh. And every few minutes the bright Very flares blossomed overhead like Japanese flowers, spreading their light over all the earth.

Michael lay back again, looking up at the throbbing sky. He had lost much blood; he was weak and light-headed; a deathlike weariness numbed his limbs. Somewhere nearby he heard voices speaking in German, and heard the tread of booted feet. The first patrols were going out, picking their way among the dead and wounded.

'Ach, du liebe Gotte, was fur ein wüstes Durcheinander!' a voice said, quietly but clearly. Then the voices and the footsteps went further away.

Michael knew he ought to move. His wound was not crippling; he could easily find the strength to crawl; and the doctors at Douvecourt would soon patch him up as good as new, so that he could fight again another day. But his will was paralysed, his soul inert, and his body obeyed its own dictates. So he stayed where he was in the shell-crater and waited for the Germans to come and take him prisoner.

Betony, receiving a letter from Mrs Andrews, went at once to King's Hill House. She was shown into the morning-room, which was full of sunshine and the scent of roses. Mrs Andrews sat straight-backed, her face impassive, but when she began talking of Michael, she broke down and wept and it was some time before she could continue. She felt ashamed, weeping in front of this carpenter's daughter, this girl of twenty whose own eyes were dry, whose manner was strangely matter-of-fact.

'I'm sorry, Miss Izzard, but I haven't yet got over the shock. I didn't expect you to come so soon.'

'Have you heard from Michael himself?'

'Yes, but only one of those printed postcards. A letter is following, it said.'

'Is he wounded badly?'

'The Red Cross people say not. But he's in a German hospital and I cannot believe they will treat him properly.'

'I'm sure they will. The Red Cross are there to see that they do.'

'I wish I could share your confidence, but we hear such terrible tales sometimes . . .'

'At least he's safe. That's the main thing.'

'My son is a prisoner-of-war with the Germans. I find little in that to comfort me.'

'But he *is* alive!' Betony said. 'He *will* be coming back again, eventually, when it's all over. Surely that must comfort you?'

And she thought of the thousands of men who had died since the great offensive had begun, for, travelling about England as she did, visiting factories, she met grieving women everywhere and had lost count of all those whose menfolk lay dead on the Somme.

Mrs Andrews got up.

'I'm glad you're taking the news so calmly. I was afraid you might be distressed. I expect you young women are getting quite hardened, which is probably a blessing in its way.'

'Is there an address where I can write to Michael?'

'Yes. Of course. I'll give it to you.' Mrs Andrews went to her desk. 'He'll be very glad to hear from you, I'm sure.'

All through summer and on into autumn, fighting continued on the Somme. Pozières. Longueval. Delville Wood. Morval. Le Transloy. Then, in November, it ground to a halt. A few miles of territory had been gained. 500,000 lives had been lost. The big push had failed. But the Germans, it was said, were demoralized by their own losses. It was bound to tell on them in the end. Meanwhile there was deadlock again; the two opposing armies dug themselves in; and winter advanced upon them both: the worst winter for twenty years.

D'you think it's as cold as this at home, Woody?'

'Definitely. My missus wrote she was getting chilblains.'

'We're practically strangers, my feet and me, not to mention other members.'

'Anyone here called Winterbottom?'

'Hey, Toss, remember how hot it was at Monkey Britannia? I could almost wish myself back there now. Or Devil's Wood, say, when the trees was burning. I'd sooner've been burnt like poor old Glover and Verning and Kyte than froze to death by bloody inches.'

'How can you talk like that?' asked Costrell, one of a new draft out from England. 'As though it was all a huge joke?'

'It *is* a huge joke,' said Danson. 'A killing joke for some, it's true, and has a lot of the rest in stitches. But you new chaps don't understand.'

Costrell was silent. He thought them callous, ghoulish, disgusting. He could never share their attitude. He was always aware of the frozen corpses lying out in no-man's-land, many of them visible from the front trenches, some quite close to the picket wire, only a few short yards away. And when Danson said, as he often did, 'D'you reckon old Bill could do with a blanket?' or, 'I could swear John Willie has turned hisself over since this morning,' Costrell could not help shuddering.

'It's all right, son,' Bob Newers said to him. '*They*'re all right, the ones out there. *They* don't feel the bleeding cold, or hear the ruddy shells come over, or get told off for san fatigues. They're better off and they bloody well know it.'

'Did you notice that subaltern smelling of scent?' said Pecker Danson.

'Poor sod,' said Dave Rush. 'He's probably plastered with anti-louse cream.'

'Get away!' said Privitt, looking up from the letter he was writing. 'Do officers have chats, then, the same as us?'

'Not the same, no. The chats they got is bigger and better, with pips on their shoulders and Sam Browne belts.'

'What about Fritz? Has he got 'em too?'

'It's him that flaming well sends 'em over. He fires them in canisters, same as gas. It's the Kaiser's most successful weapon.'

Privitt, going back to his letter, wrote for a moment or two in silence. He was having a bit of fun with the censor. He looked up again to read what he had written so far.

' "Dear Brother Humphrey, Last Saturday night I slept with three French girls and their mother. The mother was best though not as good as the Friday before when I spent the night in a high-class establishment kept by a Chinese lady who used to run a laundry in Solihull." There! That'll make 'em open their peepers! When the major reads that he'll be after me to know the address.'

'It isn't true, is it, Privy?'

'Hah! Get away! All I've ever slept with is a woolly rabbit.'

A shell came over and exploded, crump, behind the parados. The men ducked low, and a shower of hard-frozen clods fell upon them, bouncing off their steel helmets. Privitt sat up again, wiping the debris from his notepad.

'The way things are here, I shan't get much chance to graduate, neither!'

'The Lord be thanked for tin bowlers,' said Pecker Danson, adjusting his helmet. 'Or do I mean Lloyd George?'

'Get a move on there!' shouted Corporal Flinders, coming quickly round the traverse. 'Clear that mess away, quick sharp, and no sweeping it under the carpet!'

The men got to work with entrenching tools, shovelling up the fallen earth and tossing it onto the broken parados. They filled new sandbags and repaired the gap.

'Entrenching tool,' Costrell muttered. 'Why can't they call a spade a spade?'

'I'm thinking of changing my name,' said Privitt. 'It's no joke, you know, being called Private Privitt, nor Privy neither, seeing the privies here ent all that private.'

'Say that faster and you'll find yourself in the next camp concert.'

'How many shells has he sent over this morning, Toss?'

'I dunno. I ent been counting.'

'Seems quiet to me. Perhaps he's busy doing the crossword.' Newers, on the firestep, sniffed the air. 'He's got bacon for breakfast again this morning. Smoked, I reckon, the lucky sod.'

The two lines at Brisle were certainly very close together, and there was a live-and-let-live policy there, so that rifle and machine-gun fire was only rarely exchanged, and that, as Corporal Flinders said, just as a sort of formality. No-man's-land was scarcely fifty yards across, and when some Tommy sneaked out and raised a notice there, saying *Trespassers Will Be Prosecuted,* the Germans, instead of blasting it to smithereens, merely pelted it with snowballs. Even the officers turned a blind eye to these unwarlike pastimes.

One freezing night, when the men were huddled in a dugout, warming themselves at a small brazier, Dave Rush got out his wheezy old mouth-organ and began playing popular tunes. The men sang, swaying together from side to side, for the singing and the movement kept them warm. And then, half way through *There's a long, long trail a-winding,* Burston, on sentry, suddenly pulled aside the curtain.

'Shut up and listen,' he said to them, and when they obeyed him they heard the Germans finishing the song.

'Would you believe it!' Rush exclaimed. 'They've got a nerve, pinching our songs. But I'll soon fix *them.* Just listen here.'

He raised his mouth-organ to his lips and played the first verse of *God Save The King.* At the end he stopped and listened again, and across the way, in the German trenches, there was utter silence.

'That's foxed 'em!' he said. 'They're not singing *that,* the saucy buggers!'

'No more ent we,' said Pecker Danson, and, taking the brazier outside, swung it about till the charcoal glowed redly again. 'The new moon is up,' he said, returning. 'Anyone got a franc to turn?'

The Germans now, recovering, were singing *Deutschland Uber Alles.* The Sixth Three Counties retaliated and noisily drowned the rival song.

'Oh, the Kaiser fell in a box of eggs,
Parleyvoo!
The Kaiser fell in a box of eggs,
Parleyvoo!
The Kaiser fell in a box of eggs
And all the yellow ran down his legs,
Inky-dinky-parleyvoo!'

There came a day when Sergeant Townchurch was with them again, after a month in hospital. No one knew what his illness had been, though rumour gave it as 'a bout of German measles and a bad cough.' He himself gave no explanation. He preferred to forget he had ever been ill. And he reasserted his authority by reporting Corporal Flinders, acting platoon sergeant during his absence, for letting the discipline run down.

One morning, after a heavy fall of snow, two excited German soldiers, fair-haired boys of about seventeen, climbed onto their parapet and began making a snow-man there. Tom and Newers, looking through a loop-hole, watched with amusement as the snowman grew to lifelike proportions and was given a field-grey com-forter and cap and a few bandoliers slung over his shoulder.

Sergeant Townchurch came along. He pushed be-tween Newers, Tom, and Evans, and peered out at the two Germans dressing the snowman on their parapet. He unslung his rifle, put it to his shoulder, and took careful aim through the narrow loophole. Newers moved along the bay and apparently tripped on a loose bit of duckboard. He lurched against Town-church and the shot went wide. The two German sol-diers dived for cover.

'Clumsy swine! You done that on purpose! You got friends over there, have you?'

'Sorry, sarge. It's these loose slats. I'll go and get a hammer and nails before someone breaks his silly neck.'

A few minutes later, an arm appeared above the German parapet, and a well-aimed grenade exploded inside the British trench. Then a second and a third.

Costrell and Rush retaliated. Six grenades were returned for three. The sector quietened down again. But Burston and Trigg had each lost a hand and Corporal Flinders had been blinded; and Dick Costrell, hearing this news, would have gone for Townchurch with a pick-axe if Tom and Newers had not restrained him.

Quite soon afterwards, the silence in the enemy lines became uncanny. Patrols going out after dark found the trenches deserted. The Germans had withdrawn, noiselessly, to the strongly fortified Hindenburg Line, ten miles or so behind their old trenches.

'Why not to Berlin while they was at it?' said Dave Rush.

'The Hindenburg Line,' said Bob Newers. 'Is that part of the Great Western?'

'That's right,' said Danson. 'Paddington, Oxford, Cardiff Docks, and all stations to Haverfordwest.'

'If Jerry's gone we can maybe go home—I don't think!' said Dick Costrell.

Two days later they were relieved by the North Warwicks and went into billets at Doudelanville. When they returned to the line again, it was to take over newly dug trenches in the Vermand area.

The weather continued bitterly cold. Men who stood still for a few seconds found themselves frozen to the boards. They could scarcely bear the touch of their rifles, so cold was the metal in their hands, and they fired off round after round at nothing, to warm the barrels and prevent the bolts from freezing up.

But worse even than the cold was when the thaw came, and they lived always in a world of slush, wet through, waking or sleeping. A man named Thompson complained of trouble with his feet. They were badly swollen and had gone numb. He could not get his boots off to rub in the oil that might have brought him some relief.

'Move about a bit more!' Townchurch said. 'Of course you'll get trench feet if you never shift yourself, idle bastard!'

Three days later, when their spell in the forward

area ended, Thompson was quite unable to stand. He had to be carried out of the line, into the rest camp three miles behind, and there he went for a medical.

His boots were cut away and the feet were revealed, swollen and shapeless, the colour of raw meat putrefying, with the woollen socks darkly embedded, making a pattern in the rotten flesh. Thompson, watching, said not a word. He merely swallowed, making a noise. Then he looked away, into the distance, whistling tunelessly between his teeth.

The doctor took Newers on one side. He said Thompson would probably lose both feet.

'Why wasn't he sent before?'

'Sergeant Townchurch thought he was swinging the lead.'

'I must have a word with your Sergeant Townchurch.'

But the doctors at Vraignes were busy men. They worked a twenty-hour day. And when the battalion returned to the line, at Gricourt this time, Townchurch went on as he always had done.

'Evans! Maddox! Newers! Rush! I want you in a raiding party. The colonel has asked for a couple of Boche prisoners. It's up to us to try and oblige him.'

'Why always Evans?' Newers asked.

'Why always *me?*' Townchurch retorted.

Townchurch himself was without fear. Rush said he meant to get a decoration. He had more than once been mentioned in dispatches, and was held in some regard by the C.O. Townchurch knew it. It was only his due. He worked hard and he had courage. He could do great things if only he were given the chance, and he told his fellow N.C.O.'s that he meant to make the Army his career. He wouldn't go back to being coachman at Capleton Castle. The gentry would never wipe their boots on him again. He was somebody now and his great ambition was to gain a commission in the field.

There was hard fighting again that spring. The British were following up the German withdrawal.

They were pushing on towards St. Quentin. The bombardment was heavy on both sides.

In the Gricourt sector, shells were falling with great accuracy, aligned exactly with the front line trenches for a length of fifty yards or so, reducing the earthworks to a mass of debris. The noise of the British guns answering was overwhelming. It was like living between volcanoes. And under the storm, human nerves were stretched and broken, human minds were dislocated.

Tom, in a hole scooped out of the trench-side, felt the earth would never stop shaking. He felt it would open and swallow him up. Opposite him was a man named Lambert, who crouched on the firestep with terrible tremors running through him, and who plucked with his fingers at his lower lip till blood splashed down onto his tunic.

Suddenly Lambert sprang to his feet and hauled himself over the parapet. Tom tried to catch him but was too late. Lambert was already through the wire, running towards the enemy, lobbing imaginary grenades as he went.

'Bloody guns!' he shrieked. 'I'll soon shut you up! I'll shut you up once and for all!'

Tom was following, running like the wind, when Lambert fell dead, a sniper's bullet through his forehead. Tom veered and doubled back. He leapt head first towards the trench and rolled over into safety. His left foot felt as though he had hit it with a heavy hammer. A bullet had taken the heel off his boot.

Sometimes, during a period out of the line, housed in a barn or ruined cowshed, a man might throw himself down in the straw and sleep for ten or twelve hours at a stretch. He slept through anything. The world could end for all he cared. The last trump could sound and he'd never hear it.

But in a day or two he would revive. Hot food eaten in safety; hot tea made with clean water; time to sit and smoke a cigarette; and perhaps after all the end of the world had better not come yet. A wash and a shave could make a new man of one who had thought himself played out. There were things to do. Pleasant things. And if he were lucky he could stroll in places where grass still grew and leaves were opening on the trees; where the air still smelt wholesome; and where, from fields of green corn, larks flew up and hung singing in the blue sky.

'It's funny,' Tom said, 'how many things is just the same as they are at home.'

On the farm where they were billeted, there was an orchard of apple trees, and the blossoms were just beginning to open. Tom sat on the ground and watched the swallows building in the eaves of the ruined farmhouse. Some chickens were pecking about in the grass, and a little way off, sitting on a hencoop, a solemn-faced girl of seven or eight was keeping guard over them.

The house was no more than a broken husk, but the elderly farmer lived there still, with his family of womenfolk and small children. The younger men were away fighting. The old man was up on the roof, nailing canvas over the beams, a short clay pipe between his teeth, a straw hat on the back of his head. The women were working in the fields. One was ploughing with a team of cows.

Tom got up and walked towards the child on the hencoop. She looked at him with frowning eyes.

'You needn't worry. I shan't steal your hens.'

'Comment?'

'Chickens,' he said, and pointed to them. 'I shan't steal them. Nor the eggs neither.'

'Comment?'

'I was watching the swallows, that's all, and looking at the blossoms on the trees. I reckon you'll have a nice crop of apples, so long as there ent no nasty late frosts.'

The child said nothing. She did not understand him. She sat with her hands tucked into her apron and frowned at him harder than ever.

'Look at this here,' he said to her, and took a snapshot from his pocket. It had come with a letter from

Betony and it showed her mother in the orchard at
Cobbs, a straw beeskep between her hands, about to
take a cast of bees that were swarming on the trunk
of an apple tree. 'You know what those are, I'll be
bound. I see you got stalls of your own up yonder.
This is in England. Blighty. *You* know. See the blossom on the trees there? Just the same as you got here.'

The child took the picture and looked at it for a
long time. She handed it back and her hands disappeared in her apron again.

'C'est la ruche,' she murmured, 'pour les abeilles.'

'Ah. Well. Like I say, that picture was took in England.'

Tom walked on. Newers and Danson were coming
towards him. So was Evans. They were stopping to
smell the apple blossom.

'Hello, Toss, been fraternizing?'

'I was trying to tell her I wasn't after her eggs and
chickens.'

'*We'd* be after 'em fast enough if it warnt for her
grandpa. The old devil keeps a shotgun.'

'I wish I could talk to the people here. It don't seem
right, not to be able to talk to them.'

'What's that to you, Toss? You don't hardly talk
much even to us. You was always a silent sort of bastard.'

'I talk when I think of something to say.'

'Ah, Tuesdays and Fridays usually, ent it?'

'Take no notice of Pecker,' said Newers. 'He just
lost his pay in a game of poker.'

Tom had picked up a rounded chump of sweet-
chestnut wood, roughly the size of his own fist, and had
carved the little girl's likeness from it. Whenever he
had a moment to spare he worked away at it, shaping
the neatly rounded head, set so gracefully on the fine
neck, and perfecting the features from memory.

The battalion was under notice to move. The men
were mustering outside the village. Tom walked out to
the old farmhouse and met the child driving cows up

the lane. He took the carved wooden head from his pocket and gave it to her.

'For you,' he said. 'A souvenir. I done it myself, see, with this here knife. I hope you like it.'

The child looked at the carved head, then at Tom. Her face remained blank. She said nothing.

'Well!' he said. 'I've got to go or I'll land in trouble. We're moving in a little while.'

He turned and hurried back towards the village, his boots thudding in the dust of the roadway. When he got to the bend and glanced back, she was still standing, a tiny figure, the carved head clutched against her chest.

At ten o'clock that morning, the whole of the battalion was assembled outside the village, fully accoutred and ready to move. The day was a warm one and the air smelt sweetly of trampled grass. The men sat about on the roadside verges, smoking and talking, awaiting orders. Newers and Danson were throwing dice. Tom was adjusting Evans's pack.

'Hey, Toss!' said Newers, nudging him. 'Ent these the people from the farm?'

An old man and a small girl were coming slowly along the road, scanning the crowds of waiting soldiers. The old man had very white hair and black eyebrows. He wore a blue cap and smoked a pipe. The child wore a pinafore striped white and brown. They came along the road hand in hand, and one or two soldiers called out to them, making jokes in broken French. Suddenly they came to a halt. The child was pointing a finger at Tom.

The old man nodded, puffing at his pipe. He took something from his pocket and gave it to the child. She in turn gave it to Tom. It was a wooden crucifix, six inches long and four wide, with Christ carved very plainly and simply: the sort of crucifix he had seen so often lately, hanging on the walls of ruined houses throughout the district.

'It is for you,' the old man said, in careful English, 'to keep you safe from harm in battle.'

'Laws,' Tom said. 'You shouldn't have walked out all this way—'

'The little one wanted so much to find you. It was important. *Very*. Yes. You are her friend and make her a present. She will keep it always, and remember you. Me too. We will remember.'

'Ah,' Tom said, and rose awkwardly from his knees, aware of the men listening all round him. 'Thank you. Merci.' His hand rested briefly on the child's head.

'Bonne chance,' the old man said. 'God be with you, and with your comrades.'

He and the child went back hand in hand. They were soon lost to sight, for the soldiers were moving now, thronging the road. Tom stood looking at the crucifix, turning it over in his hands, feeling the smooth-worn corners and edges, and the smooth grain. It was carved from boxwood and felt very old.

Sergeant Townchurch came along, shouting orders. He saw the crucifix in Tom's hands.

'What the hell's this? You aren't a bloody Catholic, are you, Maddox?'

'No, somebody gave it to me,' Tom said.

'Some tart, I suppose,' Townchurch said, and passed on, shouting his orders. 'On your feet, all you men! What d'you think this is, a jamboree?'

So the Sixth Battalion marched away, leaving the village of Nobris behind them. Larks sang overhead and sparrows whirred from the roadside hedges. The sun was in the soldiers' eyes. They were marching again to the battle area.

'I *was* married,' Evans said, 'but my wife died ten years ago, and our baby with her.'

'How long was you married?' Danson asked.

'Two years, that's all.'

'Ent you got no family at all?'

'None that I know of,' Evans said. 'There's no one to miss me when I'm gone. That's one good thing.'

'Gone?' said Braid. 'Why, where're you off to, Taff? Monte Carlo?'

Evans gave a little smile.

'I shan't come through this war alive.'

'Oh yes you will,' Newers said. 'I bet you a pound.'

'You got a foreboding, Taff?' asked Dave Rush. 'You're all the same, you bloody Welshmen.—All as superstitious as hell.'

'You was exempt, being a miner,' said Dick Costrell. 'Why didn't you stop down the pit?'

Evans looked up at the blue sky.

'I wanted to come up out of the darkness.'

'You warnt very clever, choosing your moment.'

'It's being afraid all the time, you see. I thought I'd left all that down the pit. I thought, out here, I should either be killed or not killed. I hadn't bargained for *living* with death as though it was a presence in itself. A presence lying in wait everywhere, preying on the minds of men.'

'It's time you put in for a spot of home leave.'

'I have,' Evans said. 'But somehow I don't think I'll ever get it. I've got this feeling all the time, that something is about to give.'

'We all get that feeling,' Danson said. 'It means another bloody button going!'

Evans laughed along with the rest. He leant across and punched Danson's shoulder. But the long period out of the line had not built him up as it had the others. He was white-faced and worn, and his hands, when he lit a cigarette, shook like those of a very old man.

There was heavy shelling in the Seiglon sector. The village was soon a heap of rubble. Both the front line trenches and the reserve were blasted in repeatedly, for the enemy had them registered 'right to the fraction' as Corporal Stevens said to Braid. One morning, early, a shell fell directly on a forward observation post, and afterwards there was silence there. The post had been manned by Lieutenant Bullock and two men, Bremner and Evans.

Tom and Newers crawled across, under fire from a machine-gun. They reached the post and began to dig. The officer and Bremner were both dead, but Evans, buried under four feet of earth, was still alive when they dug him out. His mouth and throat were full of earth; they had to scoop it out with their fingers; it was almost an hour before his lungs really filled with air.

They thought he would die if he didn't have prompt medical attention, and so they decided to run for it, although it was now broad daylight. They lifted him up and started off across no-man's-land. They had about two hundred yards to travel. The German machine-gun opened fire and the bullets perforated the ground behind them. A rifle whipcracked three times. Then, abruptly, the firing stopped. The Germans were letting them cross in safety.

Evans went to the medical post at Rilloy-sus-Coll. The doctor pronounced him a lucky man and sent him back to duty again. A fallen rider should always re-mount at once, he said, and a shell-shock case should face the barrage. Sergeant Townchurch was of the same mind. He carried the principle one stage further. And only forty-two hours later he named Evans for a wiring-party.

'You can't take Evans,' said Corporal Stevens. 'He's a sick man. He shouldn't be in the line at all.'

'All that twitching and jerking, you mean? He's putting that on. He's swinging the lead like he always has done.'

'That man was buried alive in the O.P. on Monday. Newers and Maddox had to dig him out.'

'So what? It's only when he's buried *dead* that he'll be excused his whack of duty. Till then he takes his turn.'

So Evans went with the wiring-party, fifty yards out into no-man's-land, carrying a coil of new barbed wire. There were ten men including Townchurch and during the night they were fired on by an enemy patrol. The party returned with two men wounded. Townchurch reported another missing. The missing man was Private Evans.

'Was he hit?' asked Captain Edman.

'Not him!' said Townchurch. 'He's bloody well skipped it, that's what he's done. I always said he was a slacker.'

Some days later, Evans was discovered sitting in the church at Basseroche, and was brought back under arrest. He went before a court martial, charged with desertion. Sergeant Townchurch gave evidence against him. So did the fox-hunting doctor from Rilloy, who stated that Evans was in good health, physically and mentally. Certainly Evans seemed calm enough now. No longer twitching. Only tired. He was found guilty and sentenced to death.

The battalion moved into camp at Berigny. The weather was broken. There were thunderstorms. The men of Number Three Platoon were digging drains to carry away the surface water. Sergeant Townchurch sought them out. He wanted Tom.

'Maddox!' he shouted. 'Follow me!' And, as soon as they were out of earshot: 'I got a job lined up for you. One of twelve for a firing party. Little matter of an execution, first thing tomorrow morning.'

'I won't do it,' Tom said.

'Not all the guns're loaded live. You might get a blank.'

'It makes no difference. I still won't do it.'

'You don't seem to realize—this is an order. D'you know what'll happen if you refuse?'

'I don't care a sod. You've got no right to pick men out from the same platoon. You won't get none of the others to do it neither.'

'Somebody's got to do these things. I reckon it's better, keeping it in the family as you might say.'

'Let them who sentenced him do the shooting. I came out to kill Germans, not to kill my own mates. Ah, and I sometimes wonder why the hell I should kill *them,* seeing they're people the same as us.'

'Maybe you'd like to join up with them? There's sure to be lots like you in their lines. You'd find yourself at home with Fritz. *Don't turn away when I'm talking to you!* Where the hell d'you think you're going?'

'I'm going back to my platoon.'

'Oh no you're not! I'm putting you under arrest,

Maddox, and tomorrow you'll find yourself up on a charge. It's easy enough to disobey orders. We'll see if you like the consequences.'

Tom was taken to the edge of the village and locked in a cowshed for the night, next to stables occupied by Evans. There was only a wooden wall between, and Evans heard Tom arrive.

'Who's in by there? Someone I know?'

'It's me,' Tom said. 'Toss Maddox.'

'What you been crimed for, Toss, man?'

'I was late on parade,' Tom said. 'Third time this week, according to the corporal.'

'They're going to shoot me in the morning. Did you know that, Toss? Did you hear what happened?'

'Yes. We heard. The chaps was wanting to come and see you but somebody said you'd asked them not to.'

'I'd just as soon be left alone. They weren't offended, were they, Toss? It's just that I need to have time to think.'

'They warnt offended,' Tom said.

'It's nice and quiet here, considering. I can hear a blackbird singing somewhere.'

'You got a window in there, Taff?'

'There's a small round window above the door. I can see the sky, anyway. Looks like we're in for another storm. It'll get dark early tonight, I'd say, but I've got a candle and matches here.'

'You got plenty of cigarettes?'

'Diawl, yes! A tin of fifty. But I was never much of a smoker. Just the odd one now and then.'

'Me, too,' Tom said.

When darkness came, Evans struck a match and lit his candle. Tom sat on his bunk in the shed next door and looked at the cracks of light in the wall. A little while later he lit his own candle. Outside the shed, footsteps sounded occasionally, and men's voices. Further away, north of the village, wheels rumbled on the stone-paved roads as the ration-limbers went up to the line, and further off still was the noise of the guns. In a lean-to shed next to the stable, a few chickens rustled on their perches during the night, querking sleepily now and then and changing places with a flutter of wings.

'Toss?' Evans said. 'Are you awake?'

'Yes, Taff, I'm awake.'

'Are you sitting up with me till the end?'

'Might as well. Company, like. But you don't have to talk if it don't suit you.'

'Have you ever been to Wales, Toss?'

'No, never,' Tom said.

'There's a little village outside Merthyr with a stream running through it and an old crooked bridge over the stream and silver birch trees growing beside it. The water in the stream is so clear that if it weren't moving over the stones you would never know it was there at all.'

'I should like to see that place,' Tom said.

'When I go out tomorrow morning, I shall think I'm going to walk by that stream. It's nonsense, I know,—I've never believed in the life everlasting— but that's what I shall be thinking about, and that's what I'll see in my mind's eye. I'll follow the stream till the ground rises. I've done it often and I know exactly where I'll come to. A green hillside and someone waiting.'

Just before first light, the stable door was unlocked, and the padre entered. He sat on a stool at the makeshift table and looked at Evans opposite. The condemned man, he thought, looked quite composed.

'Well, Evans?'

'I told them I didn't want a parson.'

'I thought you might have changed your mind.'

'I have not changed my mind.'

'Are you a chapel man, perhaps? I can find the Methodist padre if you want him, you know.'

'No, no. I was brought up church,' Evans said. 'But I'm nothing now. I'm an unbeliever.'

The padre was silent, looking at Evans in the light of the candle. His hand, with the crumpled prayerbook in it, was long and slender, like a woman's. His face was childlike. He was trying hard to understand the condemned man's mind.

'Obviously, then, it is lack of faith that has brought you to this sorry state.'

'Go away,' Evans said.

But the padre remained, hesitating. He felt it was his duty to try again.

'You call yourself an unbeliever, yet when you were arrested you were found sitting in a village church.'

'It was quiet there.'

'If you cannot believe in God, can't you at least have faith in your fellow men?'

'I come from South Wales,' Evans said. 'I have seen where certain men have laid their hands, and the place is left black and smoking ever after. I have seen where other men have laid their hands, and the place is greener than it was before.'

'So? What then? It follows that you believe in good and evil.'

'They exist together, and will do always.'

'You don't believe that good must ultimately win a victory over evil?'

'It is a victory that good exists at all.'

'I *could* give you comfort, you know, if only you'd let me.'

'I don't need it,' Evans said.

The padre went. The two halves of the stable door were closed and bolted. Light came gradually in at the round hole above and Evans douted the flame of his candle. He put the stump into his pocket.

Tom, in the cowshed, sat on his bunk with his knees up and his arms clasped round them. He watched the daylight growing brighter through the slatted window. Outside, in the yard, the hens had been released and a cock was crowing. Someone was working a chaff-cutter. Next door, Evans was making himself tidy.

When the escort came to take him away, Evans stood up and knocked on the wall.

'So long, Toss. Look after yourself. Thanks for sitting up with me.'

'So long, Taff.'

Tom got up and looked out through the slats of his window. He saw them marching Evans away. In the straw-littered yard an old woman with a black knitted shawl over her head was scattering a panful of grain for the hens. She came to a standstill, crossing herself, as Evans passed by between his guards. Tom craned his neck and looked at the sky, overcast with purple stormclouds, under which the morning light shone out levelly over the earth. He saw three seagulls flying over, silver-white against the dark clouds. From somewhere not very far away came a quick volley of rifle fire. The old woman got down on her knees.

Tom, appearing before the court martial, was charged with refusing to obey an order. He admitted the charge and was found guilty. Townchurch, of course, had been in the wrong. Tom knew it; the officers knew it; but discipline had to be maintained, so no one asked what the order had been.

He was sentenced to five days' Field Punishment Number One. This meant extra fatigues, parading on the hour in full marching order, and confinement in the guardroom. It also meant that every evening of the five-day period he spent two hours tied to the wheel of a gun limber, stretched crossways with his feet off the ground, his wrists and ankles strapped to the spokes. Sergeant Townchurch was there to see that the straps were pulled tight; he was there again later to see Tom released; and every evening, as the straps were removed, he would ask the same question.

'Well, Maddox? Don't you wish you'd obeyed that order?'

Tom never answered the sergeant's question. He tried to pretend the man was not there.

At the end of July, the Sixth Battalion left the Somme and moved north into Flanders, up to the martyred city of Ypres, under bombardment day and night. A group of signallers stood watching as they marched in.

'Welcome to the capital of the salient!—Kindly leave it as you find it!'

'Come to Wipers and be wiped out!'

'Hope you're nifty, catching whizzbangs.'

'The barracks is over there on your left, or it was this morning.'

'The password is knife. You never get time to say nothing more.'

That evening, Tom and Newers explored the city, once a place of proud spires. They gazed at the ruins of the old cathedral, the skeleton of the Cloth Hall.

'Someone's going to have to do some building here when it's all over. I wonder how they'll ever have the heart to begin.'

'Will you come back?' Tom asked. 'Afterwards, I mean, to see how it looks?'

'It's an idea,' Newers said. 'How about us two coming together? Ten years after the end of the war, say, on a special trip?'

'Right, it's a deal,' Tom said, 'so long as we're alive to do it.'

'If we're dead we'll come in the spirit. There'll be plenty of ghosts wandering through France and Belgium in the years to come.'

Throughout the salient, troops were massing for the new offensive. Every acre of open space was packed with men, horses, guns, equipment. And the enemy, occupying the higher ground north-east of the city, could look down over the bustle below as though looking on a human ant-heap. His observation posts were supreme. His gunners could place their shells as they chose. The bombardment intensified every day.

'Talk about sitting ducks!' Dick Costrell said to Newers. 'What the hell are top brass waiting for, for God's sake?'

'They're finishing their game of bowls.'

'Another day or two of this and there'll be nothing left of us to attack with.'

Costrell spoke bitterly. The waiting was getting on his nerves. Rain had begun falling now. The ground was receiving a thorough soaking.

On the last day of July, as first light came, the British guns redoubled their fire, and all along the salient front the British infantry climbed out of their assembly trenches and, following the creeping barrage, advanced towards the enemy lines. The great new offensive had begun.

The Sixth Battalion was in support. They had orders to push through the line established by the Worcester-shires and press on to the next objective. Tanks were coming up to assist. But the ground had been thor-oughly soaked with rain and the tanks were either bogged down in the ditches or moved so slowly that they were destroyed by enemy shells.

The Sixth Battalion went into the attack but were beaten back by murderous gunfire. They had to dig in short of their objective. And in the evening came more rain. They lay out all night in shallow trenches full of water. The rain continued all next day, and the day after.

On the fifth night they were relieved by a sister

battalion. They marched along the Menin road and went into camp outside Ypres. They were given dry clothes and hot sweet tea with rum in it. Food when it came was bully beef stew ladled piping hot into mess-tins, but, because of the undiminished shelling, it contained a few unwelcome ingredients.

'What's this?' Newers asked, fishing out a piece of shrapnel and showing it to the sergeant cook. 'Iron rations?'

'That's something you leave on the side of your plate.'

While they ate, they tried to glean news of how the big attack was going, but nobody seemed to know for sure. They heard only rumours and some of these were bad indeed, like the post corporal's story of how the British guns had pounded a position already captured by British troops. They heard, too, of a whole company of the Third Three Counties lost for eight hours in the darkness up near Pilckem Ridge. And they heard—was it true?—that the Fifth Battalion West Mercia had lost three quarters of its strength in the action outside Rannegsmarck.

'The bloody Somme all over again,' Pecker Danson said to Tom, 'only bloody worse if anything.'

August was always a wet month in Flanders, but August 1917 was the worst known for forty years.

'It's the guns that bring down all this rain,' Danson kept saying. 'I've noticed it time and time again—get a big bombardment and down it comes!'

They were in trenches near Hooge, soaked to the skin for days on end. There was no sleep because of the shelling. Tempers were short and nerves ragged. Only Newers remained cheerful.

'You should've brought your brolly, Pecker.'

'I should've brought my bleedin' canoe. I can see why Fritz is so keen on his submarines. He'll be using them in the trenches soon.'

'Listen!' said Newers, a finger to his lips.

'What the hell is it?' Danson asked.

'Darkness falling. Stand-to!'

'I'll bloody well brain you in a minute.'

The enemy bombardment, heaviest at dusk, gradually lessened as darkness came. Shells were fewer. More widely spaced.

'Fritz is getting ready for bed,' Newers would say, as the shelling eased. 'He's putting the cat out and leaving a message for the milkman.'

Womp. Womp. Away on the left.

'Two pints,' Newers said.

Womp. Womp. Away on the right.

'He's fallen over the milk-bottles.'

Womp.—Womp.—Womp.—Womp.

'Now he's going upstairs to his missus. She's lying there listening to his steps on the stairs. She's been warming the bed like a good wife should.'

There followed a silence. Newers sucked at his empty pipe.

'I don't like to think what they're doing now.'

Womp. Womp. Very close.

'Seems he's fallen out of bed.'

'Don't you ever shut up?' Costrell shouted suddenly.

'Sometimes I do,' Newers said.

'I'm sick to death of your endless clacking! For God's sake let's have some peace and quiet!'

'All right, keep your hair on,' Newers said. 'I can take a hint as well as the next man.'

Costrell was in a state of nerves. He twitched and trembled all the time. Tom was reminded of Lambert and Evans. He leant across the tiny dugout and offered Costrell a cigarette. Costrell knocked it out of his hand.

'Steady on,' Danson murmured.

The next night, wet as ever, Tom and Danson were on sentry. So was Costrell. Tom heard a commotion in the next bay and went along to see what was wrong. Costrell lay stretched out on the duckboards, a rum-jar beside him, and the other sentries were trying in vain to wake him up.

'He's dead to the world! Where'n hell did he get that jar?'

'What shall we do?' Rush whispered, and there was panic in his voice. 'If Townchurch sees him like this he'll end up the same as poor Taffy Evans.'

They raised Costrell and slapped his face, but he remained lifeless in their grasp. Tom ran back to his own bay and called Newers out of the dugout. Newers came, turning his pipe-bowl upside down, and lifted one of Costrell's hands. He put his thumb-nail under Costrell's and pressed down hard into the quick. There was a sudden loud cry. Rush put his hand over Costrell's mouth and Danson rubbed the boy's wrists. They stood him on his feet and ran him quickly to and fro. He was soon sick and began to recover.

'Where'n hell did you get that jar?'

'I dunno. I won it somewhere.'

'Can you stand now? Can you walk about?'

'Think so,' Costrell muttered.

'You better had!' Danson said. 'You know the penalty for being drunk on sentry, don't you?'

'Christ!' Costrell said, and began crying. 'I feel so ill!'

'Pull yourself together, lad. Townchurch'll be along in a minute.'

'Oh, Christ!' Costrell said, but he stood up straight and took his rifle from Dave Rush.

'If it wasn't for Newers you'd still be out cold,' Danson said. 'We couldn't do nothing to bring you round.'

Costrell's glance slid to Newers.

'Thanks, chum. I'll buy you a drink in 'Pop' on Friday.'

'Chew some of this,' Newers said, and handed him a plug of tobacco. 'It'll maybe soak up the smell of rum.'

Newers went back to his own dugout, taking the half-empty rum-jar with him. A few minutes later, Townchurch came by with the platoon officer, Mr Coleby. All the sentries were up on the firestep. Everything was as it should be.

The low-lying land north of Ypres had long ago been

reclaimed from the sea; it was kept drained by a
series of dykes; but these dykes had been broken
down by the British bombardment and the waters,
overflowing, were turning the area back to swamp.
Over this swamp the Allied forces were attempting
to advance, against the Germans firmly entrenched
on the ground above.

'Talk about Weston-super-bloody-Mare!' said Dave
Rush, dragging one leg from the mire as he spoke.
'It's only sheer will-power that's keeping my boots
on my bloody feet.'

'The continong is not all it's cracked up to be,'
said Pecker Danson. 'I'll stick to Skegness in future.'

'I'll stick to everything after this!'

Newers had been caught in a shell-blast that had
bowled him over into the mud, yet he still had his
empty pipe in his mouth and was blowing through it to
clear out the muck.

'A mud-pack is said to be good for the complexion.
We'll come out looking like the Oxo Boy. There's
ladies in London who spend a mint of money to get
what we're getting here for nothing.'

'I bet their mud-packs don't smell like this.'

'You mustn't mind that—it's only the smell of rotting bodies.'

'Yes, my pal Jim Baker's buried here, somewhere.
He was out in 1915.'

'Well, we won't stop and look for him now, Pecker.
We got an appointment with Fritz in the morning.'

It was towards the end of August, a night of rain
and intense darkness, and they were moving up to the
line, feeling their way yard by yard into the forward
assembly trenches, ready for the engagement next
day.

'What we need,' said Dave Rush, 'is an electric
torch with a black light.'

'No smoking!' came the order, passed along from
man to man.

'I ent ready for this engagement,' Pecker Danson
said to Tom. 'I haven't bought the bleeding ring.'

'No talking from now on!' shouted the corporal, just behind them.

The columns of men filed forward very slowly, slock-slock, through the mud. It was still raining. The assembly trenches were all flooded. The water reached above their knees.

Dawn, when it came, showed itself first in the flood-water lying out in front. No-man's-land was a waste of puddles and the light in the water seemed paler, brighter, than the light in the heavily clouded sky. Rain was falling steadily, a grey curtain reluctantly letting the daylight through, to reveal the desolation on the ground. Ruined field-guns lay lopsided in the mud and smashed tanks were bogged to the turrets. One great tank had lost its tracks. Dead men and horses lay everywhere, sunk in black slime, unrecognizable except that in places, here and there, a hand or a hoof stuck out and pointed to the sky.

'If I get out of this war safely,' Dave Rush said to Tom, 'I never want to see another dawn as long as I live.'

Communications were difficult. They lay out all morning in the rain waiting for orders. At two o'clock the British guns opened up an intense fire. The attacking platoons crawled from their trenches and began pushing forward through the mud, following the barrage as it moved slowly up the slope.

Weighed down as they were with battle equipment, moving through mud which in places reached to the very thighs, their progress was dreadfully, painfully slow.

'It's all right for Jerry,' Danson said. 'He's got the best place up there on that ridge.'

'Then you know what to do—take it from him!' said the young lieutenant commanding the platoon, and pushed forward, his rifle held high.

'Easy, ent it?' Danson said, as Newers drew alongside. 'Nothing to it, if Jerry'll just wait while I get my bleeding feet up, out of this bleeding rotten muck.'

Townchurch, ahead, had stepped up onto a slab of

concrete and was urging the men to make more effort.

'Come on, you grubs! Shift yourselves and get a move on! I want some progress bloody forward! I want my platoon up there in front!'

'We know what *you* want!' Costrell shouted, hardly aware of what he was saying.

'Yes, Costrell, what do I want?'

Costrell was struggling in the mud. Townchurch splashed across to him and helped him on with a shove from behind. Costrell fell forward onto his face.

'I said get a move on!' Townchurch bellowed. 'I said to shift yourselves and show some spunk! You'll get on forward up that slope if I have to push you all the way!'

Costrell floundered onto his knees, choking and crying, trying to wipe the mud from his rifle.

'Just look! Just look! How the hell can I use that? I can't go on without a rifle! What the hell am I going to do?'

'You've got your bayonet!' Townchurch said. 'If you ever get close enough to use it! Now get on or I'll bloody well put you on a charge!'

Tom and Newers helped Costrell up.

'Keep with us,' Newers said, 'and if one of us falls, grab his rifle.'

Townchurch was now splashing forward to another group stuck in the mire.

'Shift yourselves, can't you? I want you up there behind that smoke! If I can move, so can you!'

The barrage, creeping forward, was gradually leaving them behind. They could not keep pace with it, slow as it was, and now, as the smoke around them drifted away, there was nothing to hide them from the enemy. They were out in the open, in a sea of mud, though the enemy lines were still some way off, under the smoke and the driving rain.

'Which way? Which way?' a man was screaming, off his head. 'I don't even know where the Germans are!'

'Nor me neither,' Newers said. 'I'm following them two up there.' He pointed to Townchurch and the subaltern, moving twenty yards ahead. 'Let's hope *they* know where we're going!'

Tom, sharp-eared, heard an order shouted in German, somewhere on the right, not far away. A Maxim opened fire from there, followed by another on the left, and the men in front went down like ninepins. A few that were left crept into shell-holes. Others, stuck, unable to move, burrowed into the mud where they were. Tom found himself treading on a man's shoulders.

The Germans had set up machine-gun posts in shelters of sandbags out in the open, and now the barrage had moved over, they came into action everywhere. The attacking platoons were in an ambush, receiving fire on both flanks, and the second wave went down like the first. D Company had suffered badly: all its officers had fallen and the remnants, pushing on, followed a subaltern of B Company, who had lost touch with his own men. He was calling to them and waving them on when a Maxim opened fire from the main German line, now visible a hundred yards off. He fell, wounded, and lay on his elbows watching men falling all round him.

'It's no good!' he shouted, as the stragglers reached him. 'Save yourselves! We can't get through!'

But Sergeant Townchurch was urging them on.

'Don't listen to him, he's raving!' he said. 'Of course we'll get through! Follow me!'

Then his arms flew up and he toppled over into the mud, and everywhere behind him men took cover in the broken ground.

Fighting continued all day: fierce little battles conducted from shell-holes; and all the enemy machine-gun posts were at length destroyed. But the main attack was not renewed. Those men who were left were too few and too tired; there was no hope of reinforcements; and early darkness put an end to the day. Orders came to dig in. Rain fell harder than ever.

All next day, stretcher-parties were out from both

sides, retrieving their wounded. The big guns exchanged some token fire, but all along the forward area an unofficial truce was observed, and the bearers moved across the open, searching the shell-holes. Enemy losses had not been great, and sometimes the German stretcher-bearers, having rescued British wounded, would set them down near the British lines.

Tom and Newers, with Braid and Costrell, worked on until after darkfall. They moved about the battalion aid post, doing what they could to help the wounded until the doctors could get to them. Townchurch lay groaning out in the open. He was asking for water. Costrell passed him many times, ignoring him, refusing to help him. Pecker Danson did the same. Tom fetched water and took it to him. He held the bottle while Townchurch drank. The man was in great agony. His face was contorted, his eyes glazed. He looked at Tom with slowly dawning recognition.

'Currying favour?' he whispered hoarsely. 'You're wasting your time—I'm a dead man.'

Late that night, Tom was sitting with Newers and Danson, drinking tea from a field-kitchen before going off to get some sleep. A young doctor came out to them.

'Your Sergeant Townchurch has just died.'

'I'm not surprised,' Danson said. 'He was pretty far gone.'

'He was saying some rather strange things.'

'He was always like that, sir, even when he was in the pink.'

'He wasn't delirious,' the doctor said. 'He knew what he was saying and he claimed he'd been shot from close behind.'

'Well, we had Jerry on both our flanks, sir, and if the sergeant was turning round—'

'The hole in his body was definitely made by an English bullet. I can guarantee that.'

'Would you believe it!' Newers said. 'He must've got in somebody's way. One of the accidents of war, sir. I've seen 'em often in the past year.'

'I'll have to make a report of the matter. I can't just let it go at that.'

'No, sir. Of course not, sir. Very sad thing to happen, sir.'

The doctor looked at them each in turn, and went away without further comment. Newers took a drink of tea, breathing heavily into his mug. He was sitting between Tom and Danson.

'It wasn't me, chums, if that's what you're thinking.'

'Nor me neither,' Tom said.

'Accident of war, that's what it was. Lots of chaps've copped it that way, not all so deserving as Townchurch, of course, but there you are. Pity he never got his V.C.'

Three months later, on a foggy night late in November, Tom and Newers, with Danson and Rush, were in an estaminet in Poperinghe.

It was much patronized by British and Colonial troops and the wall was covered with their scribblings. 'Lost, stolen, or strayed: one Russian steamroller,' someone had written, and another: 'On August tenth, at the new St. Wipers nursing home, to the B.E.F., 12 baby elephants, all doing well.' There were other jokes, too, less pure, that Danson said made him blush.

Newers ordered four glasses of wine. Neither he nor the others would touch Belgian beer. They had drunk better stuff from shell-holes, they said.

'Have you seen the Americans yet?'

'I dunno. What colour are they?'

'Much the same as Canadians, really, but maybe more so,' Danson said.

'Watch it, Limey!' a Canadian said from the next table.

'Sure, sure!' Danson answered, through his nose. 'Whaddya know! Ontario!'

'Here, Toss,' said Dave Rush. 'There's two chaps looking in at the window, making ugly mugs at you. I reckon they're trying to get your goat.'

Tom turned in his chair and saw two faces pressed against the glass.

'It's William and Roger! My foster-brothers! Glory be, can you beat that?'

He went to the door and yanked it open. William and Roger sauntered in.

'Catched you, ent we, drinking as usual?'

'We heard your outfit was up here somewhere so we took a chance of tracking you down.'

'Ent that a masterpiece?' Tom said. He could not get over it even now. 'Come over and meet my mates.'

The two Izzard boys were now big men. Even Roger had grown thickset. But they were as fresh-faced and snub-nosed as ever, bright fair hair brushed sleekly down, eyes very blue under colourless eyebrows, wide awake, missing nothing. William was now a bombardier but pretended to think it nothing much when Tom, amazed, touched the stripes on his sleeve.

'Picked 'em up cheap,' he said, shrugging, 'from a chap that didn't need 'em no more.'

'You artillery chaps is full of swank,' said Danson, rising to shake hands. 'So you're Bet's brothers? Fancy that.'

'You know my sister?' William said.

'We know her from snapshots,' Newers said. 'And her letters, of course, that she writes to Toss. She writes a good letter, your sister Bet. We always like it when Toss hears from her.'

The six of them sat at a small table. William ordered a bottle of wine. It was brought to them by a fierce old woman with frizzled hair who glared at them, scowling, as she set the bottle on the table.

'Six francs,' she said, one hand held out to William.

'Get away!' said Newers. 'We've never paid more'n five before, and that's five too many, you old bundle, you!'

'Six francs,' she said, and tapped her palm with an impatient anger.

"Don't pay it, mate,' Pecker Danson said to William. 'She's trying it on 'cos she thinks it's a party.'

'Five francs,' William said, and put the money on the table.

'Non-non-non-non! Six francs! I insist! I insist!'

'Five!' William said. 'And bring two more glasses if you please. You don't expect us to drink from the bottle?'

'Six! Six! I must insist!'

'Bring two glasses, please, madame, and not so much of your ruddy nonsense.'

'Toot sweet,' Newers said, 'and the tooter the sweeter.'

'Non-non-non-non! Six francs. I insist! I insist!'

The argument was attracting attention. The Canadians were laying bets on the outcome, and a group of Gloucesters were shouting abuse at the old woman. She had grown purple in the face and was threatening to remove the bottle when a younger woman appeared on the scene. She came to the table, placed two glasses in front of William, and picked up the five francs.

'Drink up, Tommees, and kill a few Boches for me tomorrow.'

'I'd sooner get rid of your old woman.'

'Don't mind the old one. She is greedy for money to ransom her son. He is a prisoner with the Boches. She thinks she'll be able to buy his freedom.'

'Tell her from me it'll soon be over.'

'Never! Never!' the old woman said, and there were tears in her eyes. 'I do not believe it will ever end.'

'That's cheerful, that is! Are there more like her around these parts?'

William poured out the wine and raised his glass to the old woman.

'Viva la victoree!' he said. 'Viva the happy smiling faces!'

The old woman went, still grumbling, led away by the young girl. William and Roger grinned at Tom.

'If mother and dad could see us now!'

'How come you're here?' Tom asked. 'I thought you was down in the south some place.'

'That's right. Lafitte. But we had to come up to

Armchairs on a course and we thought we'd take the long way back.'

'How're things with you, Tom?' Roger asked.

'All right,' Tom said, and could think of nothing more to say.

'Your lot's been copping it again lately, I heard. Have you been in the new push?'

'We was at Steenbeek,' Tom said.

'And the Menin road,' said Pecker Danson.

'And Passchendaele,' said Dave Rush.

'What was it like?' Roger asked. 'Was it as bad as people say?'

'People!' said Danson. 'What people?'

He and Newers drank their wine.

'I'm going on leave directly,' Tom said. 'Any message for them at home?'

'Wish them all the best, Tom, and say you found us in the pink. Rog and me ent going on leave. Not till we've finished this bloody war. It'd mean splitting up if we went on leave and I promised mother we'd stick like glue.'

'The truth is,' Roger said, 'they can't fight the war without us gunners.'

'Why, are you the only two they've got?' Newers asked, lighting his pipe. 'No wonder it's quiet in Picardy lately.'

'We're two of the best, that's all.'

'You're all the same, you artillery blokes,' said Pecker Danson, 'but seeing how I'm drinking your vin I can't hardly tell you what that is.'

When the party left the estaminet, they met two girls just coming in.

'You buy drinks for us, yes, Tommee? Plentee monee! Buy café rhum?'

'Après la guerre!' William said, walking on, and then, to Tom: 'If mother and dad could see us now!'

Outside the town the group split up, William and Roger going to their train, Tom and the others going to scrounge a lift back to camp. Their voices echoed across the street.

'So long, Bill! So long, Rog! We'll be thinking of

you when we hear them guns of yours lousing off down there at Lafitte.'

'So long!' Tom said, watching the two boys walking away. 'All the best!'

'So long!' they said. 'Be seeing you, Tom.'

Home for ten days' leave at Cobbs, Tom strolled about the carpenter's shop, kicking the shavings that littered the floor and sniffing the old familiar smells of timber, putty, paint and glue. The carpenters watched him with some curiosity.

'Well, young Tom? I suppose you find it pretty tame at home here now? Quiet, like? Nothing much happening in the old place?'

'Ah. Quiet. Just like always, or very nearly.'

'Have you been having a good time? Making the most of things? Getting a bit of experience, eh?'

'A good time?' Tom said.

'Well, you're only young once, that's what I say, and you might never get the chance again.'

'The mademoiselles, that's what Sam means,' said Bob Green.

'Oh, them!' Tom said, and stooped to pick up a knot of wood. 'They're just after your money, that's all.'

'Well,' said Sam, 'you don't expect to get it for nothing?'

'Get what?' Tom said, and went a dark red as their laughter sounded along the workshop.

'Laws, Tom, you ent as innocent as all that?'

'A chap like you, turned twenty, and a soldier in the Army, too! Don't they teach you nothing at all?'

'You ent your father's son, boy, if you're as green as all that.'

'Tom is keeping hisself nice for Tilly Preston. *She's* the mademoiselle for him. Ent that so, Tom?'

Tom merely shrugged and walked away.

In the big kitchen, Beth Izzard sat at the table with writing-pad, pen, and a bottle of ink set out before her. Her husband, Jesse, stood behind her, smoking his pipe. Opposite her, a mug of tea in mittened hands, sat Mrs Clementina Rainbow, a handsome old gipsy from Puppet Hill, where the gipsies had always camped in winter ever since never, people said.

Mrs Rainbow could not read or write. She had therefore come to Cobbs for help. Her son, Alexander, was in the Army, serving somewhere on the western front, and a letter must be sent without delay to his commanding officer, requesting that Alexander be sent home at once, for his poor ma and da had received an enormous order for pegs and Alexander's help was needed.

Beth sat, somewhat self-conscious, aware of her husband standing behind her and the boy Tom sitting quiet in the chimney corner.

'My daughter Betony's the scholar by rights. If you wait till this evening, Mrs Rainbow, she will write your letter for you.'

'You can do it, Mrs Izzard. I seen you writing oftentimes. You done that notice for Georgie's waggon.'

'Very well,' Beth said, and took up her pen. 'What shall I say?'

'Well, about the pegs, Mrs Izzard, please. An immendous great order we've had, tell him, and can't manage without Alexander.'

'They won't send him home,' Jesse said, 'just to make pegs, Mrs Rainbow.'

'You think not, Mr Izzard?'

'I'm certain of it, Mrs Rainbow.'

'Then put in we've had an order for baskets as well, Mrs Izzard, and must have'm ready in time for Christmas.'

'Anything else, Mrs Rainbow?'

'Tell the gentleman-colonel, please, that I seen things last night in the smoke of the fire that mean he's coming into money.'

Beth, straight-faced, finished the letter and wrote Mrs Rainbow's name at the bottom. She put it in an envelope and wrote the address.

'Silly fella!' the gipsy said. 'Going to the Army and

'listing like that. He'll never be the same again, Mrs
Izzard, getting mixed up in this old war.'

'No one'll be quite the same, Mrs Rainbow.'

When the gipsy had gone, Beth looked up and met
Tom's eye.

'I'd like to be there,' he said, smiling, 'when
Alexander's colonel gets that letter.'

'How was William and Roger?' asked Jesse. 'Was
they keeping hale and hearty?' He had asked the
question a dozen times.

'They was fine,' Tom said. 'They've growed pretty
big, the pair of them. William is nearly as big as a
house.'

'Ah, well, he's a bombardier now, remember.'

William and Roger had had their photograph taken
in Rouen and had sent it home. Then, in December,
an old soldier had come through Huntlip, walking
on crutches, having lost his left leg in the fighting at
Mons in 1914. He eked out his pension by painting
portraits from photographs of absent soldiers. He
travelled about, knocking on doors.

'Husbands, fathers, sons, lovers.—If you've got a
photo I'll copy it for you, a proper portrait, done in
oils.'

Beth had given him the photograph of William and
Roger, together with details of their colouring, and
he had copied it, true to life. The portrait hung in
the front parlour, on the wall above the fireplace, and
the two boys looked out on all the family gatherings:
sitting side by side, fair hair greased down, faces
glowing, keen blue eyes looking straight ahead; proud
to be sitting together in khaki, William with his two
stripes, both with their buttons polished to perfection.

'You should get *your* photo took as well,' Jesse told
Tom, 'and we'll get the artist to paint you too.'

He thought perhaps Tom might feel left out, because Granna Tewke, always knitting for William
and Roger, never knitted anything for Tom.

'Not that you miss much,' he whispered once, 'cos
granna's knitting is none too gainly nowadays.'

'What's wrong with my knitting?' granna demanded,

sitting up and glaring at Jesse. Her sight might be poor, but her hearing was perfect. 'What's wrong with my knitting I'd like to know?'

'Why, that glove you made last week had a finger too many, and there was a cap as I recall that was half purple.'

'Young Dicky done that. Changed the wools when I warnt looking.' Granna leant forward and touched Tom's arm. 'I'll knit you something. What'd you like? Socks or gloves or a comforter?'

'Don't you bother. I'm all right.'

'You never did seem to feel the cold.'

'I'm all right,' Tom said. 'I've got plenty.'

Beth and Betony sent him woollens. They saw that he was kept supplied.

'What's the *best* thing to send?' Betony asked him. 'What would you find really useful?'

'A big Dundee cake, like your mother sent in a tin one time. It was packed with fruit and had almonds on it.'

'Don't you know there's a sugar shortage? It's going on ration in the new year.'

'I thought maybe Beth could spare some honey.'

'My mother says she's never known so many people ask so kindly after her bees as they have done lately since sugar got scarce. But no doubt she's got some to spare for you.'

The two of them were alone in the kitchen. Tom sat staring into the fire. Betony watched him.

'You never used to like fruit cake.'

'We're glad of it, though, out there.'

'What do you mean by "we" exactly?'

'The chaps,' he said. 'They always like Dundee cake.'

'And must I make cakes to feed the chaps?'

'Not just them—we share things,' he said. 'We always share what we get in our parcels. It's good stuff, you see, and we're pretty nearly always hungry.'

'But why?' she exclaimed. 'Why on earth don't they feed you properly?'

'A lot of the food gets flogged,' he said. 'There's chaps that sell it to the shops and cafés. Or so I've heard, anyway, and I reckon it's true.'

'But that's terrible! It makes my blood boil to hear such things! There ought to be better supervision.'

'There ought to be, but it ent easy, out there.'

The fire collapsed in the open stove, and Tom leant forward to put on more logs. He looked at her for a while in silence.

'I was sorry,' he said, awkwardly, 'to hear the captain was a prisoner.'

'Yes,' she said. 'I hope the Germans don't treat him badly. He says in his letters he's all right, but I can't help wondering all the same.'

'I don't think the Germans is all bad. Some of them must be, but not all. He'll be all right, Bet, don't you worry.'

'I wish you wouldn't keep calling me Bet! You never used to in the old days.'

'Sorry,' he said. 'I've got the habit off the chaps.' And he went on to explain to her about the letters. 'We share *them* as well. We read each other's. Except when they're private, from wives and that. The chaps always like it when I hear from you. Your letters go round like hot buns. You cheer them up and make them laugh. They always say it's a real tonic.'

'I shall have to be careful what I write.'

'You don't mind, do you, Bet? I didn't think you'd mind about it.'

'No,' she said, 'I don't mind.'

In fact the knowledge gave her pleasure. She felt herself closer to the men out there, suffering, enduring as they were. It was little enough, in God's name, and she must try to write more often.

'Tell me about them, these mates of yours,' she said, and, seeing him smile: 'What's the joke exactly?' she asked.

'I was thinking about Big Glover. He was always talking about you. He said once to ask if you'd marry him.'

'Tell him I'd have to see him first.'

'Big Glover is dead now. He was killed last summer on the Somme. He came from outside Bromyard somewhere. So did Ritchie and Flyer Kyte. Kyte was clever with a jew's harp. Ritchie was always full of tales. They was both good chaps, Kyte and Richie, but they're dead now.'

And so it went on: Tom's own roll of honour: Cuddy; Evans; Mustow; Braid; Verning; Reynolds; Privitt; Smith; all good men but dead now.

'Good God,' Betony said, 'are none of them left alive at all?'

'Not many,' he said, 'but there's new chaps coming up all the time.'

'It's all wrong,' she said, 'that so many men should be sent out to die, cut down like cornstalks in a field.'

'Yes,' he said, 'it's all wrong.'

Looking at him, she thought him changed. He had always had a haunted look, but now he was old before his time. His eyes had seen things no eyes should see.

'Dicky'll be called up next spring,' she said.

'Ah. I know. He was telling me.'

'Where will it end, Tom? Where will it end?'

'I dunno, but it's bound to end somewhere, I suppose.'

'Shall we beat the Germans, do you think?'

'I reckon we've got to,' Tom said, 'or all them lives will've gone for nothing.'

'Take care of yourself,' Betony said, 'and tell your mates the cake will be coming.'

'Don't let the war be over yet,' said Dicky, 'cos I want to be in it and have some fun.'

'Dicky, be quiet!' Beth exclaimed. 'You've got no notion what you're saying.'

'Ah, you jus be quiet, son,' Jesse said, 'and give Tom a hand with that there kitbag.'

'I'll be knitting you something,' granna said, 'just as soon as I find the time.'

'I hope you ent losing your touch as a craftsman,' said Great-grumpa Tewke, thumping Tom's back as he climbed up into the trap. 'You should practise carving whenever you can, to keep your hand in for when you come home.'

And Tilly Preston, waiting outside The Rose and Crown, watching for the pony and trap, ran out into the road and threw a knot of ribbons, red white and blue, into Tom's lap.

'Keep them, Tom, and they'll bring you luck.'

Tom stuffed the ribbons into his pocket. Jesse, driving, glanced at his face.

'D'you like Tilly Preston, Tom?' he asked.

'She's all right,' Tom said, shrugging.

The Sixth Battalion, having moved south into France again, was reforming, absorbing men of the Tenth Battalion, disbanded after heavy losses, and being made up to strength again with new drafts just out from England. Tom and Newers were now old sweats. They felt entitled to give themselves airs. They were veterans. Men of experience. It was their duty, Newers said, to take the new recruits in hand, especially when they got to the trenches.

'See as much as you can, hear as much as you can, and do sod-all about either,' he said. 'It won't be long now. We're dying of boredom on both sides. And what's left of the B.E.F. will all go home in the same boat.'

The new men were teased without mercy.

'Have you brought your sugar card?'

'The sergeant likes you to call him dad.'

'Six months as san-man and you get the D.S.O. Twelve months and you get the V.C. Two years, you retire on a pension.'

One young lad, entering his dugout, was horrified at the number of rats scampering and fighting there.

'Ugh!' he said, drawing back. 'I don't like rats.'

'You'd better *get* to like 'em,' Newers said, 'cos they bloody well think the world of us!'

'Hey, Toss,' said Danson. 'There's a chap here asking to see Jack Johnson!'

'That's nothing,' said Rush. 'I've got one here complaining about his thigh-boots. He says he never takes nothing but number nines!'

The weather turned cold. There was deep snow. The men had been issued with leather jackets. They sat huddled close in the tiny dugouts, woollen comforters pulled down over their ears, sandbags tied like gaiters round their legs.

'I find myself thinking of featherbeds, and my missus beside me, warm as toast, tickling my back,' said Chirpy Bird. 'Pathetic, ent it?'

'I think of my furnace,' said Bert Moore, an ironworker from Wolverhampton, 'and the heat in my face as I push a load in on the jib.'

'I think of summer days and cricket on Pitchcroft,' said Bob Newers, who came from Worcester, 'sitting in the sun in my white flannels, waiting my turn to go in and bat.'

'I think of damn-all when I'm cold,' said Baines, ' 'cos my brainbox is froze and won't work.'

It was very quiet along most of the front during the cold spell early that year. Too quiet, Newers said, and they feared the worst.

'Nip and see what Jerry's doing and tell him not to, will you, Cox?'

'D'you think it's true he's getting ready to give us hell?'

'Nasty rumours are always true. He'll have a go at

smashing us before the Yanks get organized. It won't be much use his trying after.'

The rumours became established fact. German prisoners, coming in, all spoke of a big offensive, and from the forward observation posts, German reinforcements could be seen massing behind their lines, just out of range of the British guns. The weather was improving. March winds were drying the ground. In the little salient near Cambrai, British troops, working to strengthen the defences there, were caught unawares by a heavy bombardment of mustard gas. Two men in three were incapacitated.

Tom, delivering a message at Montevalle, saw a long string of these gassed men, blinded, voiceless, filing hand-in-hand along a zig-zag communication trench, making their way to the rear line. He counted a hundred and thirty-three.

'Will they recover?' he asked an ambulance man at Chesle.

'After a fashion,' the man said.

On the night of the twenty-first, the Germans began an intense shelling of the British line, all the way from Croiselle to La Fère. It was heavier than anything known before, and in the forward defences the British garrisons crouched low under the storm, deafened, concussed, as the earth split around them on all sides.

'This is it,' Newers said. 'Once this stops they'll be all over us like flies on a cowpat, God rot their wicked souls.'

From where they lay they could see British shells exploding in St Quentin. Gunflashes turned the night to day. Some distance away, on their right flank, a machine-gun post was blown sky high, and, further on still, three shells in a row fell into a trench sector.

'Poor bastards,' Newers said. 'That's Wilkie gone up with them emma gees. I liked old Wilkie. I'll miss him a lot. He owed me a shilling from a game of poker.'

First light came, struggling through a thick fog, but

the German bombardment continued all morning. Then at nine-thirty it moved over and the German infantry were seen advancing, grey-clad men coming out of the grey fog. The forward posts opened fire.

The fog was helping the enemy, and they came not in waves but in separate groups, working their way through the weakly manned British defences, then turning on them from flank and rear. The forward posts were soon overwhelmed. The few survivors were falling back.

In the main line, there was confusion. Officers strode up and down the trench, calling to the men to keep their heads. One young subaltern ran to and fro several times.

'Keep calm! Keep calm!' he shouted to the men on the firestep. 'Keep quite calm and choose your target carefully.'

'Hark at *him,*' Newers muttered. 'He's the one that's getting excited.'

But Captain Highet, their company commander, watching over the parapet, was calm and quiet to a degree, ready to give the order to fire. A group of Germans emerged from the fog out in front, coming across at a steady pace. The order was given and there was a burst of rifle fire. The group of Germans disappeared, its place was taken by another, and other groups loomed up behind. Elsewhere, in many places, they had broken through the main line.

The Sixth Battalion, in Artichoke Trench, had the enemy strong on both sides and was in danger of being cut off. Bombers were posted in shell-holes at either flank, to cover withdrawal, and Tom was in the party on the right, with Newers, Danson, Grover and Coombes. The battalion fell back, fighting fiercely as it went, till it reached the safety of Sandboy Redoubt. The bombing parties were the last to leave. They stayed until all their grenades were thrown, and then made a dash for it, every man for himself.

On the way, Tom came under fire from a German machine-gun, and was hit in the calf of each leg. He crawled to a shell-hole and lay low. The machine-

gun was firing from the rim of a crater fifty yards off.
There came an explosion and the machine-gun stopped.
A well-aimed bomb had found its mark.

His puttees and trousers were ripped from the
back of each leg and hung in tatters, sticky with blood
and fragments of flesh. He was trying to open his
field-dressing when a voice spoke and there was
Newers, coming towards him, crouched low, unlit pipe
between his teeth.

'Bloody fool!' Tom said. 'Coming back through all
this!'

'I thought you might have a match,' Newers said.

He knelt beside Tom and broke a phial of iodine
over each wound. The dressings were soaked with blood
instantly, so Newers took off his own puttees and used
them as extra bandages. Tom then fainted and knew
nothing more.

Newers gathered him up in his arms and set out
across the stretch of open ground now overrun by
enemy troops. His only cover was the fog, but he
reached the rear lines unharmed and carried Tom to
the medical aid post at Vraine St Marie, a distance of
almost two miles. When Tom recovered consciousness,
Newers had gone.

Tom spent three weeks in the field hospital at St Irac,
and was then put on a long period of light duty, in
the stores at Aubrille. He fretted, rather, away from
his mates, for the news coming in was grave indeed.
The Germans had broken through everywhere, and the
Allies were falling back all the time, fighting des-
perately over every mile of ground yielded. The
Commander-in-Chief had issued a message to all his
troops. They had their backs to the wall, he said,
and every man must fight to the end.

By the end of May, however, the German offensive
was losing its force, and the British line began to hold.
Hope was reviving, growing strong, and soon there
was confidence in the air.

In the middle of June. Tom rejoined his own battalion, in reserve at Chantereine. Three months had

passed and many friends had disappeared, been killed or sent home badly wounded, but Bob Newers was still there, and Pecker Danson, and Dave Rush was back again.

'And we've still got Fritz with us, of course. That's him over there, across the way, but don't provoke him if you can help it 'cos he's lost his sense of humour lately.'

'I thought you'd got a Blighty one,' Pecker Danson said to Tom.

'Not Toss,' said Newers. 'He's a lot tougher than he looks.'

Twice in June the Germans attacked nearby Bligny, but were beaten back. Afterwards, the attacks died down in that sector, and things were quiet for the Sixth Battalion. Away on their right, the besieged city of Reims still held, and away on their left, the enemy advance had been stopped in the woods on the banks of the Marne. In the middle of July the Germans attempted another thrust, but were checked by Foch and thrown back to the Vesle, and by the end of the month the German offensive had come to a halt everywhere.

In the lull that followed, the Allies had time to nurse themselves back to strength again. They counted their losses and re-formed. Soon they were ready to strike the blow that would end the war. The American forces were building up. The French spirit was on fire again. This time it really *would* be over by Christmas.

August and September saw the turning of the tide. The Allies were advancing, driving the enemy back across France. By early October the Hindenburg Line was in Allied hands.

'What'll you do when you get to Berlin, Pecker?'

'Dance the Blue Danube with the Kaiser.'

'And then what?'

'Catch the next train for Blighty, of course.'

The Sixth Battalion was on the march. They had seen little action in the past six weeks, but now, after careful and strenuous training, they were on their way to the front line again.

At a small town called Vaillon St. Jacques, the people turned out to watch them march through. Women ran forward with cups of coffee for the soldiers to drink; old men wanted to shake their hands; children waved small tricolour flags. At one house, plainly a brothel, a group of women stood on the iron balcony, blowing kisses and baring their breasts.

'Tommees, come in! We give you good time! Soldats anglais, we surrender to you!'

'On our way back!' the soldiers answered. 'Mind you keep the offer open!'

And, marching on, they sang their own version of a popular song.

> 'Keep the red lamp burning . . .
> We shall be returning . . .
> Though a soldier's pay is poor
> He can spare two francs . . .'

Outside Vaillon, as they marched through, they could hear the noise of guns some miles away towards the east, reminding them that the war was not quite over yet.

'Here we go!' Danson muttered. 'Back to the bloody mincing-machine.'

'Only one more river,' Newers said in a comforting way.

In pouring wet weather in late September, they marched through Les Boeufs, Le Transloy, Rocquingny, Chenay. It was a district they knew all too well. Many friends were buried there. They knew the kind of weather too. Did it never stop raining in this country? It was worse than Manchester, Shuttleworth said. A few days later they passed through the ruins of La Bouleau, and, on another dark rainy night went into trenches in the front line.

Their objective was called County Point, a strong-point in the enemy line. C and D Companies were to attack together and press on to the sunken road known as Bull's Alley. A and B Companies were to follow up on their right flank and take the position called Cock's Spur. At five in the morning, first light, the British guns opened fire and the four attacking companies advanced behind the creeping barrage, over slippery ground that rose slightly.

In front hung a curtain of thick choking smoke as the barrage fell, moving forward, perfectly timed. The first wave of troops was now straggling, thrown out by the broken ground, unable to see because of the smoke drifting past in coils. Orders were shouted but were lost in the noise.

Coming out of the smoke, Tom found himself stumbling against a thicket of barbed wire surrounding a German machine-gun emplacement. The gun was in pieces behind the shattered breastwork and the gun-crew were lying dead. He swung to the right, going round the entanglement, and half a dozen men went with him. Two of them fell, hit by snipers hidden somewhere in no-man's-land, and the others went forward at a trot. But the rest of the line had disappeared, somewhere under the drifting smoke, and in front of the few lay a waterlogged wasteland rising to an empty sky. Rain was falling heavily. Visibility was bad. It seemed to Tom they had gone past their mark. The little group stopped to confer.

'If this is the Cheltenham racecourse,' said Bird, 'it seems there's no meeting today, lads.'

'Do we go back or go on?' asked Tom.

'On,' said Brownlee, 'and hope for the best.'

They had gone perhaps three hundred yards when a shell exploded in front of them. The five lay low, then went on again, and now they could see the enemy line, in the dim distance away on their left, marked out by the flash of guns and the puffs of smoke hanging in the rain. They could also see their own men, like ants in a swarm, seething on the slopes there.

'Jesus wept!' Newers said. 'We *have* gone astray and no mistake.'

They changed direction and began to run, the rain

now blowing in their faces, and as they stumbled through the mud a machine-gun rattled from a sand-bagged emplacement on their right, Brownlee fell dead, and Bird doubled over, hit in the stomach. The three remaining men dived for the cover of a shell-crater and Newers got a bullet in the arm.

Tom and Thurrop looked over the rim, trying to locate the machine-gun post. A chance British shell located it, one of six fired from a battery of field-guns at Souane-la-Mare, and the watchers saw it go up in smoke. Tom and Thurrop went out to help Bird, but found him dead, his face contorted. They crawled back to Newers, who sat in the crater, blow-ing through his empty pipe.

'Don't tell me—I know—we're in a hole. We'll be mentioned in dispatches for this and asked to lecture to the rookies. "How to lose your way in a direct charge." Oh, well, I daresay the chaps'll manage without us.'

'You all right, Bob?'

'No, half of me's left, Toss.'

'Let's see that arm. I'll do you up.'

'Go easy, then, 'cos that's the arm I shall use for bowling when I play for Worcestershire next year.'

Tom dressed the badly torn arm and gave Newers his water-bottle. Thurrop was up at the edge of the crater, looking out, his rifle at the ready. There came a sharp crack and he fell back, dead, rolling over and over down the slope till he splashed into the pool at the bottom. Tom went quickly up to the rim and lay looking out. There was a movement in the next hole and he took aim. The sniper heaved and then lay still. Tom stayed where he was, watching.

'Did you get him?' Newers called.

'Yes, but I reckon there's more of 'em out here somewhere.'

'Our own chaps've got it in for us as well. We'd better get to hell out of here as soon as we can find another hole.'

The field-guns at Souane were firing again and the shells were falling very close.

'Stupid sods,' Newers said. 'You'd think they'd know a British-held crater when they saw it, wouldn't you?'

Tom was just turning when a shell exploded within the crater and he was knocked over by the blast. Debris covered him and he felt scorched. He got off his knees and shook off dirt that weighed a ton. Everything now seemed very quiet and when the smoke cleared away he saw that Newers had been blown to pieces. Nothing remained that could be called a man. Yet the pipe from his mouth was quite undamaged, lying in the mud some yards away. Tom crawled towards it and picked it up. He put it in his pocket and buttoned the flap. And then without warning a shell exploded in front of him, a fireworks show inside his head, followed by darkness.

When he became conscious again, he thought it was nighttime, but after a while he realized he was blind. The darkness was in his own head. It was not lit by stars, or Very lights, or the distant flashes of guns. It was darkness thick and absolute, and he was at its mercy.

The upper part of his skull felt numb, yet inside it was full of pain. When he put up a hand, there were hard splinters embedded in his flesh, all over his face and scalp and neck. His uniform hung in ribbons in front, and his body felt small, as though it had first been scorched then crushed; and everywhere, when his fingers explored, he encountered sharp chips of metal and stone, driven into his skin by the hot blast. He had an open wound in his chest, sticky with blood, and he held his field-dressing pressed against it.

He crawled from the crater, out onto flat land. His eyes were hurting him, hot in their sockets, and whenever he blinked he could feel the gritty fragments in them. He crawled on his belly; he had no strength to raise himself up; and he pushed himself on with one arm. His mouth was shrivelled and he drank from puddles, water corrupt, evil, stinking, for dead men had rotted recently in this ground and cordite vapours had spread their poison everywhere.

He came to a trench and wriggled down into its bottom. It was an old German trench, long deserted, and in many places its sides had collapsed. He crawled along it for some way, and then sat still, listening. The sound of gunfire was very faint, and he thought his hearing had been affected. He felt very cold and knew he ought to keep on the move, but before he could make another effort he had passed into a deep faint.

He awoke to a small scrabbling sound, somewhere close at hand. A rat, perhaps, scavenging among the bones. But then he heard a human footfall and the click of a rifle bolt being drawn back.

'Who's there?' he called. He could see nothing.

'Stehen bleiben oder ich schiesse! Hände hoch, du englischer Tommee, keine dummen Geschichten. Du bist mein Gefangener. Verstanden?'

God in heaven! He had crawled right into the enemy lines. How had he managed to travel so far? But the German, it seemed, was all alone: a man like himself, cut off from his comrades, seeking shelter where he could. He saw that Tom was hurt and unarmed, and there was a sound as he leant his rifle against the wall.

'Du lieber Himmel! Du siehst ja schlimm aus. Trink einen Schluck Wasser.'

'Water,' Tom said. 'Yes. Thanks.'

He felt the bottle at his lips and drank from it weakly, his head back. It was muddy stuff, tasting of petrol, but might have come from a clear mountain stream, so cool was it in his aching throat. He was too weak to move and lay where he was, shivering, while the German touched him, looking at his wounds.

'Blown-up? Stimmt's? Dich hat's da draussen irgendwo erwischt?'

'Blind,' Tom said, and put up a hand to touch his eyes. 'My eyesight's gone. Napoo! Kaput!'

'Tut mir leid! Armer Kerl! Sehr unangenehme Sache. Wenn mein Kameraden kommen, können wir uns

vernünftig um Dich kümmern. Wir haben gute Arzte,
die Dir wieder auf die Beine helfen.'

'Kamerad,' Tom said. It was the only word he
understood.

The German had opened his ragged tunic and was
cleansing the open wound in his chest. The unseen
hands were quick, sure, gentle, as they put on a dressing and tied it in place.

'Thanks,' Tom said. 'It feels a lot better, that's
a fact.'

'T'anks? Hast Du Dich etwa bedankt? Vielen
Dank?'

'Ah, that's right, danke schön.'

'Ich heisse Josef. Und Du?'

'I dunno. Search me!' But after a moment he understood. 'Tom,' he said, wearily.

'Tom? Tommee? Führst Du mich etwa an der Nase
'rum?' The German was chuckling, slapping his leg.
'Fritz und Tommee! Tommee und Fritz! Merk'
Dir—ich bin nicht Fritz, sondern Josef.' Then, as Tom
shivered again, he gave an exclamation and got to his
feet. 'Ich werd' Dir was zu essen holen, und veilleicht
was zum Zudecken.'

He was gone a long time. Tom thought he had
gone for good. But he came back with a German
greatcoat and helped Tom into it, wrapping it round
him and turning the collar up to his ears. He also
brought food and a stoneware bottle full of liquor.

'Käse,' he said, and placed a small piece of cheese
in Tom's hand. 'Was heisst das auf englisch?'

'Cheese,' Tom said, putting it whole into his mouth
and sucking slowly. 'Danke schön.'

'Brot,' Josef said, and this time he gave Tom a
crust of bread. 'Was heisst das?'

'Bread,' Tom said. 'I hope you've got some for
yourself. Eh? Have you? Brot for Josef?'

'Richtig. Ordentlich was zu essen für uns beide und
natürlich 'ne Menge Schnaps.'

When Tom had eaten, Josef took his hands and
placed them round the stoneware bottle, helping him

raise it to his lips. The drink was warming and brought some life into Tom's veins.

'Schnaps. Was heisst das auf englisch?'

'I reckon that's brandy,' Tom said. 'It's good. Very good. It's made me feel a lot better.'

'Schmeckt's, ja? Freut mich. Du solltest Dich jetzt aber mal ordentlich auspennen.' Josef was making snoring noises.

'Ah,' Tom said, his head aching. 'Yes, you're right, I'm about done.'

'Leg' Dich hin—so geht's gut. Ich halte Wache. Bisschen später kommen meine Kameraden und wir sehen zu, dass wir Dich zur Sanitäts-Station hinkriegen.'

'Is it night-time?' Tom asked. 'Nach, is it?'

'Nacht? Ja, es ist zehn Uhr.'

'That's just what it feels like,' Tom said.

He lay on his back, staring upwards, but could see nothing of the night sky. Only a kind of throbbing blackness. His eyes were ruined and he was too numb to think about it. He fell asleep like a dead man.

He awoke to a smell of hot coffee and sat up, looking around him. Surely his eyes were not quite ruined after all, for when he looked downwards at the ground, the darkness was greater than when he looked upwards into the sky, and there was the hint of a shadow moving, where Josef was busy preparing breakfast. Only a blurred featureless shape, it was true, but it made his heart leap up with hope. Yesterday, blackness. Today, a grey fog. Tomorrow, perhaps, there would be light.

'Morgen!' said Josef. 'Trocken, sogar.'

'My eyes are better!' Tom exclaimed. 'I can see! I can see!'

'Was war das? Ich versteh' Dich nicht. Kannst Du mich sehen? Kannst Du mein Gesicht erkennen?'

'Eyes,' Tom said, and pointed to them. 'They seem a lot better than they was.'

'Dir geht's besser—Willst Du das sagen? Schön, gut. Gott sei Dank!'

He brought Tom a breakfast of black coffee, faintly
sweetened, and a hunk of rye bread with a slice of
stale cold sausage on it. They sat opposite each other,
with the fire between them, and Tom peered at the
German's outline, a darker shadow against the greyness. He wished he knew what the man looked like.
He wished he could touch the unseen face. And he put
out his hands in such a way that the man understood
him, and, laughing a little, guided the hands towards his
face, allowing Tom to feel his features.

'Bin ich nicht schön? Ich find' mich wunderschön!
Bin ein Bild von Junge, findst Du nicht?'

He laughed again, deep in his throat, and Tom
smiled, guessing the nature of the joke. He now had
a picture of the German's face: square in shape and
broad-browed, the flesh shrunken on the strong bones,
the stubbled skin tightly stretched; and he let his hands
fall into his lap.

'You ent been getting enough to eat. You shouldn't
have shared your food with me.'

'Na? Was war das wieder? Was sagst Du da?'

'Have you got a wife?' Tom asked. 'Frau? Kinder?
Family?'

'Ja, klar. Ich habe Bilder von ihnen. Ach, stimmt
ja, Du kannst ja nicht sehen. Ich hab 'ne Frau, Mar-
garete, und zwei Kinder, Peterlein und Lottchen.
Ausserdem noch einer Hund Waldi.' He made a
noise like a dog barking. 'Hund!' he said. 'Was heisst
das auf englisch?'

'Dog,' Tom said.

'Dog. Waldi. Er kommt gut mit Schafen zurecht'
He made a noise like a sheep bleating. 'Schafen!' he
said. 'Was heisst das?'

'Sheep,' Tom said.

'Ja. Ja. Gut-dog-mit-sheep. Dann werd' ich wohl
bald prima englisch sprechen!'

So the man was a shepherd and lived on a farm.
Why had he left it and come to fight? Were German
shepherds under conscription? Tom had no way of
asking these questions. He picked up his mug and
drank his coffee.

Suddenly there was a noise. Voices talking not far away. Josef sprang up with an exclamation and went running off along the trench. Tom remained sitting, ears strained, trying to interpret the sounds that reached him. Then came the loud-bouncing crack of a rifle, followed by several cracks close together, and, after a pause, footsteps coming to the edge of the trench. An English voice spoke, and Tom answered.

'Good God, there's one of our own lads down here!' said the voice, plainly that of an officer. 'And in pretty bad shape by the look of things. What's your name, man, and which lot are you from?'

'28233 Maddox, Sixth Battalion, Three Counties.'

'I thought you were a German, wearing that coat. It's lucky you spoke up quickly like that or I might have shot you. Can you walk, Maddox?'

'I reckon I can. The only thing is, I can't see too well.'

'Hang on a minute. We'll give you a hand. Cunningham! Dodds! Come and give this man a hand.'

'Where's Josef?' Tom asked.

'What, that bloody German?' said one of the men who came to help him. 'He's bloody well dead, with three or four bullets in his rotten carcass.'

'But he was my friend! He saved my life! He gave me his coat and let me share his food and drink.'

'Did he, by God?' the officer said. 'Well, I'm sorry, Maddox, but he *did* open fire on us first, and he got my man Ross straight through the heart. That made me see red, I can tell you, because Ross was the best servant I ever had.'

As they led Tom away they told him that the battle of La Bouleau had been successful. County Point had been taken, so had Cock's Spur, and eight hundred Germans had surrendered. The whole of that sector was in British hands.

In the crowded hospital at Rouen, a doctor came every morning and evening and examined his eyes, looking into them with a tiny torch.

'Will they get better?' Tom asked.

'Oh, yes, I think so. They're improving already, aren't they?'

'A bit. Not much. I still can't see nothing but shapes and shadows.'

'It's early days yet. That shell must have been a pretty near thing. I'd say you were lucky to be alive.'

The hospital was never quiet. There were over a hundred men in the ward with Tom, many of them in great pain, groaning, whimpering, crying out. The nurses were terribly overworked. Their voices were often loud and impatient, their hands ruthless, plucking dressings from torn flesh. Tom, still in darkness even by day, was often confused by the bustle around him. It hurt his head and made him feel dizzy. He had nothing to say to these brisk white presences talking across him. He was all alone at the centre of a world of noise and movement.

But one day, out of the commotion, a more restful presence, a gentler hand, and a girl's voice speaking in quiet tones beside him.

'Private Maddox? Someone said you came from Chepsworth, where they blow on the mustard to make it cool.'

Tom smiled. The girl's voice was a voice from home. Her accents were his, though not so broad, and she called the town 'Cheps'orth' in the local manner.

'You must come from there yourself, knowing that saying.'

'I come from Blagg, a tiny place four miles out. Do you know it?'

'I should just think I do, for I come from Huntlip, right next door. Why, we're practically neighbours, you and me.'

'The people of Huntlip are either foxes or hounds, they say, so which are you?'

'And the people of Blagg all go in rags!' he answered back, enjoying himself.

'Not me,' she said, 'I get my uniform free of charge.' And he could hear that she was smiling. 'Whereabouts in Huntlip do you live?'

'Place called Cobbs, out towards Middening. There's a carpenter's shop—Tewke and Izzard's.'

'Oh, yes, I've passed it often.'

'What's your name?'

'Linn Mercybright.'

'I don't remember you at school in Huntlip.'

'We've only lived at Blagg these past five years. Before that we lived at Stamley and before that at Skinton Monks. My dad's a bit of a wanderer. He works at Outlands Farm at present and has a cottage in Stoney Lane.'

'I know Outlands. I've been there a lot. But I'd better not say what I was up to.'

'Poaching?' she said. 'You needn't worry. My father's only a labourer there. He'd very likely give you his blessing.'

Tom leant forward a little way, but could see her only as a white shadow.

'I wish I could see you properly.'

'You will be able to soon, I'm sure, but I must go now or Sister will have me on the carpet.'

'Nurse,' he said, anxiously. 'Nurse! Are you there?'

'Yes?' she said. 'What is it?'

'Will you come and see me again?'

'Yes, of course, every day.'

She had been in service at Meynell Hall before volunteering as a nurse. She would go back there when the war was over.

'God willing, of course.'

'It won't be long now, from what they're saying.'

'God grant they're right.'

'Linn?' he said. 'How old are you?'

'Close on twenty-two.'

'Six months older'n me, then.'

'I see you've had a letter from home. And a parcel too.'

'Trouble is, I can't write back. Not a proper letter. All I could do was get someone to fill in a card.'

'I'll write a letter for you, when I get time. Tomorrow, perhaps. It's my easy day.'

Next day when she came, he was sitting out on the terrace. There was bright sunlight and he could see it on her hair, which was reddish-gold and shone like copper, for now, off duty, she wore no cap.

'I can see you better today,' he said. 'You've got red hair.'

'Mrs Winson at Maynell Hall always used to call it auburn.'

'Auburn, that's right. I couldn't think of the right word.'

'I was only teasing you,' she said, laughing. 'Of course it's red, and who cares? The main thing is that you can see it. Has Dr Young been to see you today?'

'Early this morning,' Tom said, and, after a moment: 'Strikes me he's bald.'

Linn, delighted, laughed again. He had never heard laughter quite like hers. He could see her leaning back in the chair.

'You *are* improving, aren't you?' she said. 'Soon you'll be able to see our warts.'

'Warts?' he said. 'What, you?'

'That was just another joke.'

'Are you going to write my letter?'

'Just this once, yes, but soon you'll see to write your own.'

At the end of the week he *could* see. His sight was almost back to normal. He could see that Collins, in the bed beside him, who had lost both his legs, was only a boy of eighteen, and that Beale, in the bed on the other side, was jerking with tetanus. He could see the many men poisoned by the fumes of gas, who lay with faces discoloured and burnt, breathing painfully, with a terrible noise, drowning with their lungs full of foul bubbling foam, whose dying was drawn out day by day.

He could see, too, that the wound in his chest had now healed, leaving a dark empurpled scar; that his face and body were criss-crossed all over with smaller scars; that the dressing on his foot had concealed from him the loss of two toes.

'Seems I came off lightly,' he said, 'compared with most of the chaps here.'

'You'll be going to hospital in England soon.'

'Ah. I know. The doctor told me.'

He could see now that Linn's eyes and eyebrows were dark brown; that her features were small and neatly made; that, suffering as she did with the mutilated men in her care, her cheerfulness often cost her dear.

When his transfer came, he was given only an hour's notice. He packed his few belongings quickly and hobbled off in search of Linn. He found her in the last ward, renewing the dressing on a man's neck.

'Seems I'm for off. Marching orders. They're putting me on the next train.'

'I heard there was a contingent going. I wondered if you might be among them.'

'They don't give much warning, do they?' he said. 'I've been running round like a scalded cat.'

'Hoi!' said the man whose wound she was dressing. 'You go ahead, nurse, and say goodbye to your chap here. I shan't hurt for a minute or two.'

'No,' Linn said. 'I mustn't leave you half done. Besides which, Sister's watching.'

'I'll say goodbye, then,' Tom said. He could see the ward sister, three rows away, frowning severely across at him. 'Maybe I'll see you back at Blagg.'

'Sure to,' she said, and turned to smile at him, looking at him in a searching way. 'You might go to Outlands and look up my dad. Tell him I'm well and looking forward to coming home.'

She turned back to what she was doing, and her patient gave Tom a sympathetic wink.

'I'd let you take her back to Blighty, cock, only my need is greater than yourn, I reckon.'

Tom nodded and walked away.

A month later, after treatment at the military hospital in Sawsford, he was home in Huntlip, discharged from the Army and wearing civilian clothes again.

It felt very strange, sleeping alone in a room of his own, after the crowded hospital ward, and the crowded billets. Often he lay wide awake, listening to the silence, till the small sounds of the household at rest came to him through the deafening stillness. He would look at the window and wonder at the steadiness of the sky outside: its unbroken darkness when there was mist; the constancy of moon and stars when the night was a clear one. He expected the lightning of gunflash and flare to whiten the sky and set it pulsing. It took a long time to get used to an earth so dark, so hushed, so perfectly still.

'Why've you been discharged?' Dicky asked. 'If your eyes is all right again, why don't they want you back in the Army?'

'Seems I ent quite up to standard. My papers've got "shell-shock" on 'em.'

'Is that all that's wrong with you?'

'Leave Tom alone,' Beth said to her son. 'Just be thankful he's back safe.'

'Ah, don't ask so many questions, boy,' said great-grumpa. 'Tom may've lost a few bits and pieces.'

'I've lost the tops off two toes,' Tom said.

'There!' said granna. 'And I was going to make you some socks.'

'He'll still need socks, granna,' Betony said, impatiently.

'What gets me,' Dicky said, 'is Tom's being hurt by a British shell.'

'Them things happen,' Tom said.

Dicky himself was in khaki now. He was based at Capleton and had a weekend pass every month. He had lost all desire to go to the front. Such a muddle it all seemed. He wouldn't have minded dying a hero, but to get blown up by your own side! People said it would end soon, and he hoped they were right.

At The Rose and Crown, when Tom went in with Dicky one evening, Emery Preston was quite friendly.

'A drink on me for you two lads. I always believe in treating soldiers.'

'I knew you'd come back, Tom,' Tilly said. 'I never doubted it. Not once. Have you brought me any souvenirs?'

'No,' Tom said, 'no souvenirs.'

'Show her the scar on your chest,' Dicky said. 'That's a souvenir, ent it?'

'How long d'you think it'll be before it's over?' Emery asked.

'Not long now,' Tom said.

One Monday morning, Tom and Jesse were up on the slopes of Lippy Hill, repairing a field-barn for Isaac Mapp. The day was a cold one, with drizzle blowing on the wind, grey and drenching. Jesse was sawing a new beam, inside the barn, where he was sheltered. He stopped work, thinking he could hear music, and went across to the door to listen.

Brass-bands on a weekday? There must be something wrong with his ears! Yet somewhere down in the greyness below there was certainly a banging, clanging noise of some kind and, as the explanation came to him, a bright sunrise dawned in his face.

'It's the Armistice!' he shouted to Tom. 'That's what it is! It's come at last! The war is over!'

He dropped his saw, snatched up his jacket, and went hurrying down the steep track, leaving Tom behind. He reached the road at the bottom of the hill and there, sure enough, the villagers were out from Otchetts and Peckstone and Dugwell and Blagg, and were marching on Huntlip, armed with pots and pans and biscuit-tins,—anything that would make a din—gathering more people as they went.

'The war is over!' they said to him. 'The Armistice was signed at eleven o'clock. The Kaiser has skipped it and gone to Holland. Our boys'll soon be coming home.'

'Glory be!' Jesse said. 'I knowed what it was the very minute I heard the rumpus! I've got two boys of my own, you know, William and Roger. They'll be coming home! They'll be coming home!'

He fell in with the noisy procession and danced along with it, clapping people on the back and telling them about William and Roger.

'My eldest boy, he's a bombardier, and my second, well, he's a gunner, see. But God bless my soul! To have them back again after such years!'

And, growing impatient to reach home, he took a short-cut across the fields, sending sheep and cattle in all directions.

In the kitchen at Cobbs, when he stumbled in, Beth sat at the table, a cabbage half shredded on the board before her. Great-grumpa Tewke stood at the window. Granna Tewke sat by the fire.

'Ent you heard the news?' Jesse demanded. 'It's the Armistice! The war is over! Everyone's out in the roads, creating, and the din can be heard from here to Scarne. Ent you had word of it down here?'

'Yes, we've had word of it,' Beth said.

'Well, you don't seem too bucked,' he said, laughing. 'I thought you'd be all over the moon.'

Her stillness stopped him, brought him up short, and he saw the telegram on the table, lying open, under her hands. William and Roger had been killed in action. Sunday the tenth. Eleven A.M. Twenty-four hours before the signing of the Armistice.

Only two days before, there had been a letter, written by William: 'We're in the pink, Rog and me, still washing behind the ears and sticking together like you told us to do.'

They had died together, serving their gun, when an enemy shell had fallen directly into their gunpit.

The carpenter's shop stopped work that day. The men were sent home. Dicky, coming on special leave, entered a house of terrible silence. Betony was there and broke the news. He went at once to look for his father and was shocked to hear him weeping aloud in the empty workshop. He crept away, unable to face such open grief, and returned later. His father stood hunched against the workbench.

'Why should my sons've been took from me? Why? Why?'

'You've still got *me*, dad. You've still got me.'

Jesse made no answer, and Dicky went away again, hurt and baffled.

A few days later, a small package came, containing the two dead boys' effects: cap-badges, passbooks, letters, snapshots. Jesse was angry at sight of these things. He wanted to hurl them into the fire.

'What use are they without the boys?'

'No use,' Beth said, 'except just to remember them by.'

She put the badges up on their portrait, pinning them to the ledge of the frame. Jesse gave a groan and left the room, pushing Dicky aside in the doorway. Beth turned and saw the boy's eyes as he looked at the portrait of his brothers.

'You mustn't hate them for having died.'

Dicky was ashamed. How did his mother know his feelings? His father knew nothing. He had shut them all out.

'My dad don't want me nowadays. I reckon he wishes me dead like them.'

'Your father's not hisself at present. It's up to you to be patient with him.'

Betony, seeking to comfort Dicky, went with him

to Chepsworth Park, to the special ceremony held
there. A part of the grounds, about fifteen acres, had
been given to the public by Mr Champley to com-
memorate the signing of the Armistice. A plaque
was unveiled on one of the gateposts; a drinking-
fountain was switched on; doves were released from
the old stone dovecote. It would be known as Polygon
Park and would be a place of recreation for the
people of Chepsworth. The house itself, with the rest
of the grounds, was already a home for disabled soldiers. Mr Champley's only son had been killed in
the battle of Polygon Wood.

'Is it wrong for us to be gadding about?' Dicky
asked.

'No, of course not,' Betony said.

'My dad seems to think so,' Dicky said.

Huntlip itself had almost a week of celebrations, end-
ing after dark on Saturday night with a torchlight procession through the village, up onto the open common.
A straw-stuffed effigy of the Kaiser, with a realistic
withered arm and wearing a genuine pickelhaube
helmet, was carried up with a rope round its neck
and hanged from the old gibbet. A fire was lit underneath it and fireworks secreted in the dummy's body
went off with loud bangs as the dummy burned.

Tom, alone in the outer darkness, stood watching
the yellow flames leaping and the rockets fizzing towards the sky. The Kaiser had dropped from his rope
now, and the gibbet itself was burning fiercely,
beginning to topple into the fire. The dancers and
singers were cheering its fall.

Tom felt withdrawn, a living ghost. The merry-
makers were strangers to him. The night was unreal.
Though the voices shouted, the words meant nothing.
And although a great many people were gathered there
under the moon, reaching out to one another, there
were no pale arms reaching out to him. He was
wrapped in a caul of darkness and aloneness.

'Tom?' said a voice, and Tilly Preston stood beside
him. 'I've been looking for you everywhere. Dicky said

you was here some place. Why ent you dancing like the others? Harry Yelland's arrived now and brought his accordion.'

'I ent much good at dancing, Tilly. I'm none too steady on my pins. But you go ahead and dance if you want to. I'd just as soon stand by and be quiet.'

'I don't care about dancing neither. Great lumping louts they are here. I'd just as soon go for a walk, away from the noise, wouldn't you?'

She slid her arm into his and leant against him, looking into his thin dark face, lit by the bonfire, now burning red. She wanted to touch him, tenderly. She wanted to kiss his poor scarred eyes.

'What're you thinking about, Tom?'

'I was thinking of William and Roger,' he said, 'and all the other chaps that're gone.'

'Don't be unhappy, Tom. Don't look like that. They wouldn't want you to grieve for them, would they, specially not on a night like tonight?'

'I was only thinking, that's all.' And he turned his head to look at her. 'You sure you don't want to join in the dancing?'

Tilly was wearing a hand-crocheted cap of fluffy red wool with a pompon on it, and a long scarf to match, with a similar pompon at either end. She looked very small, in her long winter coat and buttoned boots, like a child going skating on an icy pond.

'Don't you want my company, Tom?'

'I never said that.'

'Wouldn't you sooner go for a walk?'

'All right,' he said, 'let's go for a walk.'

She took him to a barn at New Strakes, her uncle's farm on the edge of the common, and led him up into the hayloft. She undid her coat and was warm against him, taking his hands and guiding them slowly till they covered her breasts, as she drew him down with her into the loose-tumbled sweet-smelling hay. Her breath was quick and hot on his lips. She ached for him and knew she could easily make him love her.

The church bell at Eastery, cracked for more than

thirty years, had been recast in honour of Eastery's war dead, and on the fourth Sunday in November, when people from neighbouring villages came for the rededication service, it rang out tunefully over their heads, in celebration of the new peace.

'When your mother and me was married here,' Jesse said to Betony, 'that there bell made sorry music, but now it's something to hear, ent it?'

Old memories had unlocked his tongue. He was almost himself again.

'That's a wonderful thing to hear the church bells ringing out, after being stopped for so long, and to know they're ringing all over England. Ah, and that's a wonderful thing to know the captain is coming home, too, ent it? Are you sure you don't want me to drive you to the station?'

'No, father. I'd sooner go alone.'

Betony was nervous, meeting Michael after two and a half years. She felt she hardly knew him at all; hardly remembered what he looked like; and could not, however hard she tried, pin down exactly what she had felt for him before the enforced separation.

But when at last he stepped from the train, helped by his mother, and she saw his starved face, with its slow-twisting smile and burning gaze, she knew that even if he were a perfect stranger he would still have a claim upon her love. She had seen so many men like this, their faces sculpted by suffering, and she felt that love should be theirs for the asking, given freely, without meanness.

'Betony,' he said. 'I thought this journey would never end. The train stopped at every station.'

'Michael. Darling. You look so ill.'

'I've had this damned 'flu. It's left me feeling as weak as a kitten.'

When he took her in his arms, she could feel the tension thrumming in him, as though he were wound up tight like a spring.

'Will you marry me, Betony?'

'Yes,' she whispered. 'Yes. Oh, yes.'

'Thank God for that. I have wanted you so. I think I would die if you said no now.'

'I haven't said no. I've said yes.'

'It was the one thing that kept me going. Thinking of you. Knowing you loved me. I remembered the way you looked at me, that last time, on this very station, when you got here just as the train was leaving. Do you remember?'

'Yes,' she said, 'I remember.'

'If you hadn't been here today,' he said 'looking at me in just the same way, I don't know what I would have done.'

'Michael. Darling. I *am* here.'

And she felt the tension easing a little, as he let her go and looked directly into her face.

'Come along, both of you,' his mother said. 'There's a car waiting.'

Their engagement was soon made public, and Betony was often at King's Hill House. Mrs Andrews gave her blessing, but thought they ought to wait a while before marrying. Six months, perhaps, or even a year.

'Don't you think I've waited long enough?' Michael said.

'You're a sick man. Is it fair on Betony to marry her before you're quite well?'

'I shan't take that long, getting well.'

Alone together, he and Betony talked it out.

'My mother says it's unfair on you. Am I such a wreck?'

'Your mother thinks we're not really suited. She thinks if we have to wait a while we shall change our minds.'

'In that case we'll wait!' he said grimly. 'If only to prove how wrong she is. I don't really mind, so long as I can see you often.'

'I don't mind, either. With my brothers only recently dead, it would be better not to have a wedding in the family yet. Also, there's so much work crying out to be done.'

Her work in the factories had come to an end. She

was now at Chepsworth Park, helping at the home for sick and disabled ex-soldiers. There, under the direction of volunteer doctors, men were learning to use new artificial limbs; nervous cases were learning to talk again; husks of men with burnt-out lungs were coming to terms with the remnant of life that was left to them; and those who had nothing left at all were being nursed through their last days of pain.

Betony travelled about the three counties, raising funds, recruiting helpers, buying equipment. And often she worked with the men themselves: washing and feeding those who were helpless; giving her shoulder to a cripple hobbling on metal legs; wheeling men in bathchairs out to a sunny place in the orangery. There were men who stammered very badly and men who spoke only gibberish, and Betony would sit with them, trying to interpret their crazy, tortured utterances.

There was a boy named Johnny Clegg whose brain, it seemed, was tied in knots. He had no family or friends; received no visitors; and frightened everyone at the home by dashing at them, shouting unintelligibly at the top of his voice. He was very wild-looking and, failing to make himself understood, would hurl himself about in a frenzy.

He came to Betony one day, took hold of her arms, and shook her savagely to and fro. He dragged her towards the piano.

'Lanno!' he shouted. 'Lanno! Lanno! Midder-orders-plidder-chewing!'

'Tune?' she said. 'Your mother always played a tune?'

'Assit! Assit! Plidder-chewing-obesit-obing!'

Betony went and sat at the piano and played *Home Sweet Home*. Johnny, beside her, stood perfectly still, listening intently to the end. Then when she turned round on the stool, he threw himself onto his knees before her, hid his face in her lap, and burst into tears.

He was always calmer after that. He had managed, just once, to make himself understood, and Betony, becoming attuned, was able to teach him to speak more clearly.

Tom stood at the bend in Stoney Lane, looking at the small neat redbrick cottage. The door was open, held back by an iron dog, and a few bits of matting lay out on the path. Blue smoke rose from the chimney.

A cloud of dust appeared at the doorway, followed by a man with a long-handled broom. He looked a lot older than Tom had expected and his face was half covered by a crinkly grey beard. He swept the dust out to the garden and stood leaning on his broom, staring at Tom who stood, hands in pockets, outside the gate.

'I seen you before. What're you up to, hanging about round my cottage?'

'I was looking for Linn,' Tom said. 'I wondered if she was home yet.'

'If Linn was home,' Jack Mercybright said, 'I wouldn't be doing my own sweeping.'

He came out onto the path and picked up the mats. Tom saw that one leg was lame at the knee.

'How come you know my daughter?'

'I was in France. In the hospital at Rouen. I live in Huntlip and Linn said to call and say how-do.'

'Then why hang about instead of coming straight to the door? Did you think I'd eat you?'

'No,' Tom said, 'I didn't think that.'

'Well, if you've come to tell me how she is, you ent making a lot of headway.'

'She's all right. She said to tell you not to worry.'

'No message besides?'

'I don't remember nothing else.'

'Well, it's soon delivered, I'll say that!'

Mercybright was turning indoors. He seemed about to shut Tom out. But he paused briefly and spoke again.

'I had a letter from her this morning. Seems she'll likely be home tomorrow. Who shall I say was asking for her?'

'Tom Maddox.'

'Well, you call again,' Mercybright said. 'In a day

or two, when she's got settled. I'll tell her you're coming.'

He went inside and closed the door.

Three days later, when Tom was again loitering in the lane, Linn saw him from the cottage window and ran out to meet him. She wore a dress of dark green, with a collar standing up at the neck, and above it her hair was bright red-gold, neatly twisted into a coil, but with fine-spun strands curling down over her nape. Her dark eyes were shining. She laughed at him in the way he remembered.

'Why don't you come to the door and knock? You surely don't think you aren't welcome?'

She took him by the arm and led him into the cottage kitchen. Her father sat beside the hearth, smoking an old-fashioned clay pipe, the bowl of which was shaped like an acorn. He motioned Tom towards the settle, and Linn sat there, too, perched sideways, watching Tom's face.

'How're your eyes since you've been home?'

'Pretty good, considering.'

'Not giving you any pain?'

'I wouldn't say pain. Not exactly. My head beats a bit now and then, but nothing special.'

'And your foot?' she asked. 'How's that?'

'Pretty good, considering.'

'Seems to me,' her father said, 'you must've been through the mill, young fella.'

'I came out alive, though, that's something.'

'Only just, by the look of you.'

'Take no notice of dad,' Linn said. 'I never do. It's bad for him.'

'Ent there some beer we can give this boy?'

'How should I know?' she asked, laughing. 'I've only been home five minutes.'

But she went out to the back kitchen and returned with two mugs full of frothing beer.

'That's what I like!' her father said. 'Being waited on and mollied after. I missed that a lot while you was away, girl, and I reckon I bore it pretty well.'

He took a deep drink and wiped the froth from

moustache and beard. He looked at Tom with keen eyes.

'That'll come hard on me,' he said, 'when my daughter leaves me to get married.'

When Tom had gone, and Linn was left alone with her father, she sat with her hands folded in her lap, laughing at him. He looked back at her, straight-faced.

'I been making enquiries about Tom Maddox.'

'There, now!' she said. 'Fancy that!'

'Seems his parents warnt never married.'

'You surely don't hold that against him?'

'No. Surely not. But it's always better to know these things. And there was worser stories than that.'

'What stories?'

'His father was a drunkard and killed his mother in a fit of temper. Then he hanged hisself in a tree. Your Tom was a babe about twelve months old.'

'Poor boy,' Linn said.

'There was good things told me as well as bad. They say the lad's a clever craftsman. Does carving and such, at Tewke and Izzard's, as well as first-rate carpentry.' Jack leant forward to light a paper spill at the fire. 'So it's just as well his sight warnt ruined by that shell.'

'D'you like him, dad?'

'It's early days to answer that. He ent got a lot to say for hisself, has he?'

'Not as much as some I could mention.'

'You ent growed less cheeky, since being out in foreign parts.'

'Puff, puff, puff,' she said, watching him as he lit his pipe. 'Old tobacco-face! Always smoking!'

'The real question is, whether *you* like him.'

'I think I do.'

'But you ent sure?'

'He's a strange boy. He reminds me, somehow, of a wild animal. Oh, I don't mean wild in a fierce way, but awkward and shy, like a deer in the forest.'

'I bet they wasn't all shy, them soldiers you nursed over there.'

'No,' she said, 'far from it.'

'It makes me boil!' Jack exclaimed, striking his chair with the palm of his hand. 'It makes me boil that a young girl like you should've had to nurse a lot of rough soldiers the way you been doing these past two years. I'm a man and I know what they're like. They don't deserve to be mollied for by nice young girls of your sort.'

'Father, be quiet, you don't know what you're saying!' she said, and her eyes were suddenly full of tears. 'You've no idea what these men had to go through.'

'I was a soldier once, remember, for a short while back in the eighties—'

'You still don't know what *these* men went through in *this* war. Nobody knows, except those who've seen for themselves, and it's wrong to say they're undeserving. It's wrong, very wrong, and I won't have it! You know nothing at all about the matter.'

'H'mm. It's a fine thing, I must say, when a man is told he knows nothing by his chit of a daughter who knows it all!'

'I saw so much courage . . . so much unselfishness . . . and so much love, among these men. The work I did was nothing at all, and I won't have you grudge it to them, father.'

She leant across and touched his knee. She had thrown off her sadness and was laughing again, teasing him, the tears still glistening on her cheeks.

'Own up,' she said. 'You were only cross 'cos I went and left you to fend for yourself. Now isn't that so?'

'Things ent much improved now you're home, neither.—My mug's been empty this past half hour.'

Often when Tom was at Lilac Cottage, he would fall into a kind of dream, watching Linn as she ironed clothes at the kitchen table or sat by the fire with her knitting or mending. Sometimes his gaze was so intense that she felt herself growing uncomfortable.

'How you do stare!' she said to him once. 'You really oughtn't to stare at people so hard, Tom, especially saying nothing for hours on end.'

'Sorry,' he said, and looked away, frowning at the fire in the stove.

But at the sight of the colour rising in his face, and the fraught expression in his eyes, Linn regretted her little outburst, humbling him in front of her father, and wanted to put the matter right.

'You can stare if you want to. You can stare at me as much as you like! I know what it is. It's my red hair. It's enough to make anyone stare, I'm sure.'

Tom smiled. His glance rested briefly on her face, then flickered away again. He tried to think of something to say.

'Won't be long now. Christmas, I mean. I reckon it's just about eighteen days.'

'You'll have to do better'n that,' Jack said. 'We thrashed that one out an hour ago. Not to mention the chances of snow.'

'Father, please,' Linn said.

'I know I don't talk much,' Tom said. 'The chaps used to say so in the Army. Betony always says so too.'

'I met Betony at Chepsworth Park. I told her I knew you and she said, "So that's where Tom's been spending all his evenings lately." '

'Ah. Well. Now she knows.'

'Is it such a secret, Tom, that you come out here to see us?'

'Not a secret exactly. I wouldn't say that.'

'You haven't told anybody?'

'No. Maybe not.'

'Then it must be a secret, mustn't it, unless Betony's told other people?'

'She wouldn't do that,' Tom said.

'That's all right, then.—The secret is kept.'

'I reckon you're teasing me again.'

'Good gracious!' she said. 'As though I would!'

Later that evening, when Tom had gone, Jack spoke to Linn in a serious manner.

'What's your feeling for that boy?'

'I don't rightly know. It's hard to say. I haven't

known him very long . . . yet I feel I've known him all my life.'

'Do you care for him?' Jack asked.

'Oh, dear! What a catechism! Must I make up my mind tonight?'

She was looking at him with her head on one side, laughing into his bearded face, making fun of his fierce eyebrows. But Jack was not to be deflected.

'It's as well for you to know your mind, 'cos *he* cares for *you* a mighty lot, just as sure as God's in Gloucester.'

'Yes,' she said, becoming serious. 'Perhaps he does.'

'You must mind and not lead him on for nothing.'

'D'you think I'd do that?'

'No, I don't, but I reckon you ought to consider the matter and sort out your feelings as they are so far.'

'Yes,' she said, 'perhaps I should.'

Every evening now, immediately after supper at Cobbs, Tom made himself tidy and left the house. And today, Saturday, he hurried off after midday lunch.

'Where's he get to?' Jesse asked. 'Is he courting, Dicky, do you suppose?'

'I dunno, dad. He don't say nothing to me about it.'

'It's none of our business anyway,' Betony said.

'Ent it?' said Dicky, and rose, grinning, from the table, a piece of bread pudding in his hand. 'Supposing I think it is?' he said. 'Supposing I go and try to find out?'

He left the house and followed Tom to Millery Bridge, taking care to keep out of sight. Just past the Malthouse, Tom turned off along the road to Blagg, and when Dicky got to the corner, he had already reached Shepherd's Cross. There, as he passed the old ruined cowsheds, a girl stepped out and ran to meet him, and Dicky, watching from the Malthouse doorway, saw that it was Tilly Preston.

He returned home in triumph and told his father what he had seen.

'Oh, well,' Jesse said, 'she was always sweet on him, warnt she, that girl?'

But Betony was extremely puzzled.

'Are you sure it was Tilly Preston?'

'Laws!' Dicky said. 'I've seen her often enough, surely?'

Tilly had waited for Tom at the old cowsheds. She was shrammed with cold and shivering. Her face was pinched, red, miserable.

'Are you avoiding me, Tom Maddox?'

'No, not exactly,' Tom said.

'I think you are!' she said, hugging herself and rubbing the upper parts of her arms. 'Oh, yes! I'm certain of it!'

'You'll catch your death of cold, Tilly, hanging about in this weather without a proper coat on.'

'Whose fault is it I'm hanging about? You've got no right, avoiding me, not after all that's happened between us, and I shouldn't have to come looking for you. *You* should ought to be calling on *me*.'

'It was all a mistake,' Tom said. 'It shouldn't never've happened by rights.'

'A mistake? Really? Well, that's nice, I must say! You've made my day for me now, ent you, telling me a thing like that?'

'It *was* a mistake, though, all the same.'

'It's a bit late for saying that, and it don't get us no further forward, does it?'

'No. Maybe not. But I dunno what else to say.'

'You was glad enough the night it happened. You was quite content and don't you deny it, taking advantage like you did. But now you've got other fish to fry, ent you, and don't care tuppence what happens to me?'

Tilly was crying, her eyes almost closed, the tears squeezing out between reddened lids. She was shivering violently, cold to the bone, and she cried with little gasping noises, holding both hands against her mouth.

'You ought to get home,' Tom said, 'or you'll get a chill as sure as fate.'

He put out a hand to touch her gently and she took it eagerly in her own, holding it close against her chest.

'Why not come home with me and see my dad? Why not tell him we're going to be married? I'm sure he'd be pleased.—He's quite changed his mind towards you ever since you went as a soldier.'

'No,' Tom said, and drew back his hand.

'Why not?' she asked. 'Why shouldn't we get married?'

'It wouldn't be right for us, that's why.'

'Supposing we had to?' Tilly said. 'Supposing I was having a baby?'

Tom was silent. He looked at her for a long time. 'You ent, though, are you? No. Surely not.'

'I don't know. It's too soon to say. But I think about it all the time and it makes me so scared I could nearly throw myself into the Derrent.'

'You can't be,' Tom said. 'No. Surely not.'

'Why can't I, for goodness' sake? These things do happen, as well you should know, seeing it's how you come to be born your own self.'

'I know it happens, but is it happening to you, that's the point?'

'I don't know. We'll just have to hope for the best, shan't we? It certainly won't work out that way if I can help it.'

'Don't you go doing nothing foolish!'

'It's too late saying that.'

'You know what I mean.'

'No. I don't. What do you mean?'

'Well, if it should happen there *is* a baby, you won't do nothing to harm it, will you?'

'No,' she said. 'I won't do that, I promise, honest.' And she looked at him from under her lashes. 'You do care what happens to me, then, after all? I knew you did, deep down, underneath. I knew you couldn't be horrid to me.'

'I reckon I'd better see you home.'

'And speak to my father while you're there?'

'No!' he said. 'I got nothing to say to him at all.' And he thrust his fists into his pockets. 'I've got to have time to think things out. I shall need to know about that baby.'

'Meantimes, perhaps, you'll be making up to that Mercybright girl who lives with her dad in Stoney Lane? Oh, yes, you may well look surprised, but *I* know what takes you out to Blagg every moment you got to spare!'

'I've got to go,' Tom said, and walked away, making towards Puppet Hill.

'You'll be hearing from me!' she called shrilly. 'You can't just drop me like an old glove. Not after all that's happened between us! I won't take it. I won't! I won't!'

One evening, a week or so later, Jack Mercybright was in The Rose and Crown, buying a pint of Chepsworth ale and four new clay pipes.

'Quiet this evening,' he said to Tilly, for he was her only customer.

'Too many folk ill in bed with the 'flu, including my dad and two of my brothers.'

'You ent sickening for it, I hope?'

'I hope not indeed. I've got troubles enough, already.'

'I'm sorry to hear it,' Jack said.

'You might be sorrier,' Tilly said, leaning her elbows on the counter, 'if you knew the other party concerned.'

'What're you on about, girl?'

'I happen to know that Tom Maddox is a friend of yours, made welcome in your home.'

'That's right. He's a friend of my daughter's.'

'You ought to warn her,' Tilly said, 'or she might end up the same as me, carrying his baby.'

Jack, smoking, looked into Tilly's watchful eyes. His own face was blank. She would read nothing there if he could help it.

'Does Tom know you're having his baby?'

'I wasn't too sure of it last time I saw him, and he ent been near me since I mentioned the matter.'

'What about your father? Does he know?'

'Lord, no! My father would kill me. He would, honest. He don't think a lot of Tom Maddox. I dare not mention it till the wedding day is fixed between us.'

'You're very free in airing your troubles, young woman.'

'I wouldn't air them to no one else. But you've got a daughter to consider. You wouldn't want no harm to befall her.'

'It ent likely to,' Jack said. 'My daughter is no slut.'

He drank his beer and left without speaking another word.

He went straight home to Lilac Cottage, and there, when he entered the bright, warm, comfortable kitchen, Tom was helping to wind Linn's wool, holding the skein on outstretched hands while she wound it up in a soft ball.

'Gracious,' she said, as Jack stood on the hearth between them, 'you look like murder, dad, you do, really.'

'I've got good reason,' Jack said. 'I've been talking to Tilly Preston and she says she's carrying this chap's baby.'

Tom and Linn were facing each other, sitting close, their knees touching. Linn had stopped winding and was looking at him with unbelieving eyes. He could see the laughter dying in them; could see her face growing slowly cold; and inside himself there was a similar coldness and deadness, together with an immense shame.

'Well?' Jack demanded, angrily. 'Is it true or false that you've been lovering with this girl?'

'What a word,' Tom muttered. 'Lovering!'

'Choose what word you better prefer. I'm only asking if it's true.'

'Yes, It's true. That ent disputed.'

'And you knew,' Linn said, staring at him, 'that Tilly was going to have a baby?'

'Not for sure, no. She was afraid of it, but she wasn't sure.'

'You didn't go to her to find out?'

'No,' he said, and looked away.

'How long is it since you saw her last?'

'A week. Ten days. I dunno.'

'And said nothing at all about it? Came here every evening the same, behaving as always, knowing Tilly was in such trouble? What did you think would happen to her?'

'I reckon I put it out of my mind.'

'How nice for you, having a mind so *very* convenient!'

Linn leant across and took the skein of wool from his hands. She held it loosely in her lap. Her face was pale, and she still looked at him as though she could scarcely believe what she heard.

'Well?' Jack said. 'What d'you aim to do about it? Tilly expects you to marry her.'

'I dunno why,' Tom said. 'I reckon she knows I don't love her.'

'But you must do!' Linn exclaimed. 'Surely? Surely? At least a little? Or are you the sort that takes every girl that comes along?'

'It was the night of the bonfire,' he said. 'A lot of folk was mad that night. But it don't mean I love her. Not enough to marry her. Nor she don't care tuppence for me neither. I'm pretty damn well sure of that.'

'How d'you know? Have you ever asked her?'

'I don't need to. I just know.'

'You haven't thought of her feelings at all. It's too inconvenient. It's something else you've put out of your mind!'

'The way you're talking to me,' Tom said, 'I reckon maybe I'd better go.'

'Yes!' she said. 'Go to this Tilly Preston of yours and do what you know is right by her!'

Tom got up and stood for a moment as though

lost. Then he walked out and they heard his footsteps in the lane. Linn sat staring with hurt, angry eyes. Her father watched her, aching for her.

'And I thought I *knew* him!' she said with sudden self-scorn. 'It was silly of me, after so short a time, but I thought I knew him through and through.'

'I told you before, you're a lot too trusting where other people is concerned, and men ent altogether quite the way you see them.'

'Then no doubt you're pleased, being right as usual!'

'No, I ent pleased. Far from it. In fact I feel sorry for that boy Tom.'

'It's the girl I feel sorry for, poor soul.'

'You needn't worry on that score. Tilly can look after herself pretty well.'

'It's a good thing she can,' Linn said.

Tom went to The Rose and Crown and found Tilly still alone in the taproom.

'You got my message, then?' she said.

'Yes, I got it. That's why I'm here.'

'I've been so worried these past two weeks, I'm nearly going out of my mind.'

'It's definite, then, about your having the baby?' he said. 'Have you been to see the doctor?'

'What, and let the whole district know about it?'

'No,' he said, 'I suppose not.'

'It's definite, you take my word. So what're you going to do about it?'

'Get married, what else? It's the only solution. I'll ask Jesse if we can have the old Pikehouse to live in and a few bits and pieces of furniture.'

'A house of our own?' she said, glowing. 'Oh, Tom, won't that be lovely? Won't that be grand?'

'I'll see the vicar in the morning. If we get a move on, we can be married just after Christmas.'

'My word, you're in a hurry, ent you?' she said.

'There's no point in hanging about.'

At Cobbs, later, when the news was known, only

Betony felt surprise. She took Tom aside and asked
him about it.

'What happened to Linn Mercybright?'

'Nothing happened. I'm marrying Tilly.'

'But for God's sake why? I don't understand.'

'We've got a baby coming,' he said. 'He's forced
our hand, as you might say.'

'Oh, you're such fools, you men!' she said. 'Getting
yourself into a mess like that with a little trollop like
Tilly Preston! I thought you'd more sense.'

'Tilly's all right,' he said, shrugging. 'It ent just
her fault she's having a baby and it's him we got to
think of now.'

He had lived at the Pikehouse as a boy. It was strange
to be back there again now, with some of the same
furniture, given to them by Beth and Jesse, and some
of the same old crockery hanging up in the tiny
kitchen.

'I lived here with my Grannie Izzard. She wasn't my
proper grannie, really, but she brung me up from
about a year old. That old rocking-chair was hers, and
the footstool there, and that little old Welsh dresser.'

'I bet you never thought,' Tilly said, sitting beside
him on the settle, 'that you'd be bringing your bride
home here and setting up house the way you have.'

'No,' he said, 'I never did.'

'I reckon we're lucky, don't you, having a nice little
home of our own, miles away by ourselves like we
are, with no nosy neighbours poking in?'

'Yes,' he said, 'I reckon we are.'

'I shall try my best to be a good wife to you, Tom.'

'And I shall try to be a good husband.'

'Oh, I know you will! I know. I know.'

'I put some wood aside in the workshop yesterday,
ready for making a cot,' he said. 'I shall start work
on that when I've got a bit of time to spare.'

Tilly moved closer and put her arm through the
crook of his, squeezing it hard against his side. She
rested her face against his shoulder.

'The men'll see it if you do that. You know what gossips they all are, specially Sam Lovage.'

'They've got to know sooner or later. You can't keep a baby secret for ever.'

'Tom,' she said, twisting the button on his cuff, 'I've got something to tell you about that.'

'What is it?'

'I made a mistake about having a baby. I'm not going to have one after all.'

'Mistake?' he said. 'How could you have made a mistake when so many weeks is gone past by?'

'You know what I mean. I was frightened to death! I thought you was going to let me down.'

'There wasn't no baby. It was all a lie. Is that what you're trying to say to me?'

'I really don't see it makes much difference. We have been lovers, after all, and men so often need a nudge before they come up to scratch, the wretches.'

Tilly felt the change in him. She sat up straight and looked at his face, and what she saw there made her afraid.

'Tom?' she said, in a small voice. 'Don't look at me like that, Tom. It gives me the creeps. It does, honest. It makes me go icy all down inside.'

Gently, her fingers plucked at his sleeve.

'Surely it's better to be by ourselves for a bit? We're only young once and babies come soon enough I daresay. Why not make the most of things while there's a chance?'

Tom got up and reached for his cap. His shadow leapt, huge in the firelight. His face was that of a graven image.

'Tom, where are you going?' Tilly demanded. 'You can't go out on our wedding evening! You can't go out and leave me alone!'

Tom made no answer. He was already on his way out. A blast of cold air blew into the room, the door rattled shut, and he was gone. Tilly put her face in her hands and rocked herself to and fro, giving vent to small choking sobs. Then she took out her handkerchief and wiped her eyes, aware that her tears were washing the face-powder from her cheeks and would stain the front of her wedding-gown.

The fire had burnt low. She threw on three logs and wiped her hands on the rag-made hearth-rug. She was feeling hungry and she thought of the joint of cold mutton lying on the platter in the pantry. Ought she to wait till Tom returned or would his sulks keep him out past midnight? If so, that was his own fault. It was no reason for her to starve.

She got up and went to the pantry.

Sometimes, at night, Tom would slip quietly out of bed, put on his clothes, and creep downstairs, out of the house. He rarely slept more than three or four hours at a time, for his head ached and there was a splitting of coloured lights immediately behind his eyes. Even his breathing gave him trouble. He had to get out in the keen night air.

Tilly, luckily, was a sound sleeper. She never knew when he left her side She was still in bed when he set off for work at seven But one morning, while he was eating his breakfast, she came downstairs in night-dress and shawl.

'You been out poaching again?' she said. 'Brevitting about in them old woods?'

'I went for a bit of a walk, that's all.'

'In the dark?' she said. 'On cold winter nights like

they are now? You must want seeing to, really, you must.'

'It wasn't dark last night. There was a big full moon about three o'clock, and a sky full of stars.'

'Respectable folk are warm in their beds at three o'clock in the small hours.'

She came behind him and put her arms around his neck, and her face, close to his, was soft and warm like a sleepy child's.

'Don't you love me no more, now, Tom? Aren't you going to try to forget that I told you just that one little lie?'

'I shall get round to it, given time.'

'And will you be nice to me again?'

'I ent aware that I been nasty.'

'I could make you love me again if only you'd give me half a chance. I could make you my slave. I know I could. There was plenty of chaps who was always after me in the old days. Harry Yelland for one. I could twist them all round my little finger.'

'Then why ent you married to one of *them?*'

'I chose you instead, didn't I? Though I sometimes wonder why I did!' She was holding him back against her body, her arms tightening across his throat. 'Tom?' she said softly, into his ear. 'I know I can make you love me again if you'll only let me. I'm your lawful wife. You've got no right being nasty to me.'

'I've got to go. I'll be late at the workshop.'

He rose from his chair and Tilly released him. He began getting ready and she studied him with growing anger.

'Don't forget to ask Jesse Izzard about that new stove. I can't cook on this open fire. I've never been used to it, all my life.'

'My grannie cooked on that open fire. She never found it gave her trouble.'

'Oh, your old grannie was a proper wonder! But I'm not cooking at that there fireplace all my days and you may as well make up your mind I mean it!'

'All right,' Tom said. 'I'll ask Jesse's advice about it.'

One evening when he got home, he saw a new broom with a brown-painted handle standing in the corner of the kitchen, and a new metal dustpan, painted green.

'Where'd they come from, all new and shiny like that?' he asked.

'A man came selling them at the door. From Birmingham, he said he was. I can pay bit by bit for that broom and dustpan, and anything else I care to buy.'

'From Birmingham? And comes all this way?'

'He's got a motor-car,' Tilly said. She looked at Tom with a little smile. 'He offered to take me for a ride round. That's 'cos I said there was no buses. But I told him no, my husband wouldn't like it.'

'It's no odds to me,' Tom said, 'though it's maybe wiser to watch your step with chaps of that sort.'

'Chaps of what sort, I'd like to know? Mr Trimble's a very nice man. He was in the Army the same as you. Out in Egypt with the engineers.'

'All right. You go for a ride if that's what you want. I ent raising no objections.'

'What fun do I get, stuck out here all by myself, miles away from other people? I see old Mould from the lodge sometimes and I see Mrs Awner going past, but otherwise not a single soul do I ever talk to from one day's end to the next.'

'I reckon it *is* pretty lonely out here, after your being right in Huntlip, with all the folk at The Rose and Crown. Why not go in now and then and give your father a hand like you used to?'

'Oh, no!' Tilly said. 'Why should I work in my father's taproom, now I'm married with a home of my own? What'd people say, seeing me back there, serving beer? What d'you think I got married *for*?'

'Look!' Tom said. 'You do whatever it is you want to do and stop going on at me. All I want is peace and quiet.'

'And nothing else matters!' Tilly said. 'You don't never think of me at all!'

She turned away and began crying, great heaving sobs that wrenched her body. She leant against the back of the settle and hid her face in her folded arms. She looked small and frail, and it seemed she would never be able to stop crying.

'I wish I was dead! I do really! You're always so horrid nowadays. I never thought it'd be like this! Hating me, hating me, all the time!'

'Ah, no,' Tom said. 'You mustn't say that 'cos it ent true. You must stop crying or you'll make yourself ill. I never meant to make you cry.'

He put out a hand and touched her shoulder, and straight away she was in his arms, clutching at him and pressing her body against his. The shivering sobs ceased abruptly and when she looked up at him, into his face, he saw she was laughing.

'I knew I could do it!' she said, exultant. 'I knew I could make you love me again if I put my mind to it properly. Men are as soft as dough, really, but they have to be kneaded to bring them round.' She put up her hands and entwined her fingers in his hair, trying to make him bend towards her. 'Your *face!*' she said. 'When I turned just now! If you could've seen it! I had to laugh!'

Tom pulled away from her, jerking his head back, free of her grasp. She clutched at him and he pushed her aside.

'Now what's the matter, for goodness' sake? You're not going out without your supper?'

'Damn the supper and you too!'

The door slammed and she was left alone again, strands of his hair still entwined in her fingers.

'I get the feeling,' said Sam Lovage, toasting his cheese at the workshop stove, 'that marriage don't agree with our butty here.'

'He's quieter than ever lately, ent he?' Albert Tunniman agreed. 'And his work's gone off something terrible.'

'What've you got for oneses, Tom? Don't Tilly feed you, the bad girl?'

'He's got bread and dripping, same as always,' said Fred Lovage, winking at Sam.

'Oh no I ent!' Tom said. 'It's fried bacon.'

'You ent got a motor-car, have you, Tom? A smart little Austin with a hood? No, well, it ent hardly likely, I don't suppose. Yet my girl Lilian swears she seen one, outside the Pikehouse on Friday morning, when she was going to sew at Scoate.'

'It's a traveller-chap, selling brushes. He calls every Friday for his money.'

'I shouldn't like that,' Tunniman said, 'a stranger calling on my missus when I ent there to see what's what.'

'I know about him,' said Sam Lovage. 'He's been through Huntlip, door to door, and tried to sell Queenie a new mop. She sent him packing and a good thing too. There's too many salesmen going about bothering people since the war. Somebody ought to up and stop it.'

'Tom should ought to speak to Tilly. I wouldn't stick it if I was him.'

'It's no odds to me,' Tom said. 'Tilly must do as she thinks best.'

He finished his lunch and went back to the bench, where the screen he was carving lay half done. He selected a chisel from the rack.

'Don't you never rest?' Lovage shouted. 'It wants twenty minutes to one o'clock.'

'I've had all I want,' Tom said. 'I'd just as soon get on.'

The next day, Saturday, Tom had work at Crayle in the morning and finished it by eleven o'clock. The workshop was closed in the afternoon so he went straight home, thus arriving early, perhaps an hour before his time. And, seeing a motor-car in the roadway, he went across to the woods opposite and stood among the trees, waiting for the visitor to depart.

At one o'clock, a fair-haired man came out of the Pikehouse, glancing at his watch, and Tilly followed him to the gate. They stood talking for a little while, and the man had his arm round Tilly's shoulders. Then he got into the motor-car and drove away towards Norton. Tilly turned and went back indoors, swinging the end of the silken cord which she wore tied about her waist. Her heels click-clicked along the path.

When Tom walked in, she was combing her hair before the mirror.

'You're early today, aren't you?'

'Ah. Well. Maybe I am.'

'I've been busy this morning. You'll have to make do with bread and cheese.'

'Suits me,' Tom said.

It was true, as Albert Tunniman had said, that his work was not so good lately. Great-grumpa Tewke said the same.

'You've lost your touch, boy, that's your trouble. You've been too long with a rifle in your hands instead of the tools of your proper trade. You can't go off for three years without it showing in your work.'

'I reckon that's right,' Tom said. 'I shall have to practise all the harder.'

But however hard he tried, it would not come: there was not the old unity between hand and eye; there was not the mastery over the chisel; and often his judgment played him false.

The work he was doing was for Mr Talbot of Crayle Court. A fire had occurred there in December and some old oak furniture had been badly damaged. Tom's task now was to make two replica doors for a cupboard, each one carved with a Talbot hound, surrounded by oakapples, leaves, and acorns, the initials E.B.T. among them. One of the old burnt doors lay before him and he was copying it, using oak Great-grumpa had given him, taken from an old oak pew.

One day, while carving the second door, peering closely to follow the delicate pencil-lines, he had trouble in keeping to the tiny detail. His gouge seemed too big, the tracing too small, and the whole design seemed to swim hazily before his eyes. He stood up straight and looked out of the window. The workshop yard was covered in frost; the cobnut bushes were white-fuzzed; a blackbird quivered on a slim stem. When he looked back again at his work, the tracery seemed smaller than ever, and he suddenly threw down his gouge and hammer.

'I can't do it,' he said to Jesse. 'George Hopson'll have to do it.'

And, pulling his jacket on as he went, he walked out of the workshop door.

'What's up with him?' asked Great-grumpa Tewke, coming to Jesse.

'I don't rightly know,' Jesse said, frowning. 'I reckon maybe he feels it, you know, your telling him he'd lost his touch. It ent like Tom to leave a piece of work unfinished. I must speak to him about that in the morning.'

But Tom was not at work the next morning, nor the morning after, so early on Saturday afternoon, Jesse took the pony and trap and drove to the Pikehouse. His knock brought no answer. The door, amazingly, was locked, and when he peeped in at the window, he could see no sign of life whatever. He returned to Cobbs puzzled and worried and spoke to his wife and daughter about it.

'Nobody at all?' Beth said. 'Not even Tilly?'

'Neither hide nor hair of either of 'em.'

'If Tom's there alone and in one of his moods,' Betony said, 'he may have been lying low when you called, just to avoid talking to you.'

'Why should he do that? To me of all people? Ent I as good as a father to him?'

'I was thinking of him as a little boy and how he always ran off to the woods whenever we called on Grannie Izzard.'

'But he ent a little boy now,' Jesse said. 'He's a grown man. I should like to know what it is that's up-set him.'

'So should I,' Betony said, 'and I mean to find out.'

She went that very afternoon, going on foot to give no warning, and arriving just as dusk was falling. The house was in darkness, silent as the grave, lonely beside the old turnpike road, with only a handful of Scoate House sheep grazing on the surrounding wasteland. She opened and closed the gate with care, walked on tiptoe along the path, and stood for a moment in the porch. The door when she tried it opened before her and she stepped straight into the unlit kitchen.

'Tom?' she said. 'It's me. Betony. Are you there?'

'Yes, I'm here,' Tom said, and got up from the rocking-chair. 'How did you come? I never heard no sound of the trap.'

He struck a match and lit the oil-lamp on the table. The room came to life and Betony closed the door behind her.

'What's wrong with you? Why haven't you been to work? Why didn't you answer when dad called earlier today?'

'I'm taking a bit of a holiday.'

'Just look at the mess in this kitchen! It can't have been cleaned in a month of Sundays. Whatever does Tilly think she's doing?'

'Tilly ent here, she's gone,' he said.

'Gone where, for God's sake?'

'I dunno where. She didn't say.'

'Has she gone back to her father in Huntlip? No, surely not, or we should have heard.'

'I reckon she's gone with another chap.'

'Don't you *know* what's happened to her?'

'I came home from work one day and there was a note to say she'd gone. I dunno no more'n that.'

'What makes you think there's another man?'

'I seen him,' he said. 'A traveller-chap, selling brushes. Once he was here when I got home. I saw them laughing and talking together. Then he went off in a little car.'

'Well, that's a fine thing, I must say, after only a few weeks of marriage! Don't you care where she's gone? Aren't you going to try and find her?'

'No. Why should I? It's no odds to me.'

'It's cold in here,' Betony said, shivering. 'Don't you think you should light the fire? There's plenty of sticks and logs there and *I* don't like freezing even if you do.'

'All right,' he said, and began at once pushing the

wood-ashes back in the hearth. 'Maybe it *is* time I boiled a kettle.'

'What about the baby?' Betony asked.

'There wasn't no baby after all. Just a mistake, Tilly said.'

'You mean she led you up the path?'

'That's about it, I suppose, yes.'

When the fire was burning, piled high, and the kettle hung above the flames, Tom rose from his haunches and crossed the room to hang up his jacket. On the way he stumbled, sending the little footstool flying, and almost sweeping the lamp from the table. Betony gave an exclamation and set the lamp in its rightful place.

'You can't be drunk at this time of day! What's wrong with you for heaven's sake?'

Tom stood quite still, his hands in his pockets. He was looking past her, into the fire.

'Seems I'm going blind,' he said.

After a while, when the kettle boiled, Betony made a pot of tea. There was no milk to be found anywhere; nor any sugar; only a jar of her mother's honey; so she stirred a spoonful into the mug of milkless tea and sat opposite, watching him drink it.

'How long is it since your sight began failing?'

'I dunno. It's hard to say. It comes and goes, like, and sometimes it seems better than others.'

'Have you seen a doctor?'

'Not since leaving the hospital at Sawsford.'

'Then you must!' she said. 'Where's the point in losing time?'

'Will they be able to do something for me?'

'We won't know that till we get there,' she said. 'But it's no use burying yourself away out here, without a word to anyone. What did you hope to achieve by it?'

'I wanted time to sort things out.'

'How did you think you were going to live, stuck out here and not working?'

'I hadn't got as far as that. I just wanted to be by myself and make the most of what sight is left me.'

'And afterwards?'

'I dunno. I hadn't decided. End it, maybe, somehow or other.'

'Do away with yourself, you mean, the same as your father did before you?'

'I'd just as soon die, as go through life in the dark,' he said.

'What rubbish you're talking!' she said, with scorn. 'This is something you've got to fight! You fought over there for nearly three years. You didn't give in so easily then and you certainly mustn't give in now. You must fight back like a proper soldier.'

Tom sipped at his hot tea, and the steam rose, moistening his face. His dark skin was smooth and shining, but still white-flecked in many places, where the shell-blast had scarred him. His deep dark eyes were bright, steady, contemplative, and looked at her with childlike hope. It was hard to believe those eyes could fail him.

'All right,' he said. 'Tell me what I ought to do.'

Her family, when she broke the news, could scarcely believe what she was saying. Tom's injury was four months old. They had thought his sufferings were over.

'Ah, no, not our Tom!' Jesse said. 'After all this time? And what he's been through?'

'Did Tilly know he was going blind when she left him?' Beth asked.

'No, mother. He told no one until today.'

'He shouldn't have married her,' Dicky said. 'I said all along she was nothing worth it.'

'Damnable war!' Great-grumpa said. 'Is there no end to its consequences, even now?'

'No, there's no end,' Betony said. 'I see its evil every day when I visit the men at Chepsworth Park.'

'I'll go out and see him,' Jesse said. 'I'll knock this time till he lets me in.'

'No, don't go yet,' Betony said. 'I think he's better left alone.'

On Monday, early, she travelled with Tom by train to Sawsford. The military hospital stood on a hill and had a fine view out over the town. To Betony it

seemed very busy but to Tom it was quiet compared
with when he had been there last. He was seen by
three doctors and spent half an hour with each in turn.
They were strangers to him but had his medical details
before them and asked him a great many questions.
He was then given X rays and told he would have to
wait some time before they could tell him the results.

'I suggest you have lunch,' the surgeon, Major Ker-
rison, said, speaking to Tom and Betony together. 'The
Fleece round the corner is good. Tell the waiter I sent
you.'

After lunch at The Fleece and an hour spent walking
over the hill, they returned to the hospital and sat waiting. The day was a mild one, with a premature hint of
spring, and in the gardens outside the window, helio-
trope flowered, pink and mauve.

A nurse came into the waiting-room, and Tom
stood up. He was white to the lips and a pulse was
throbbing in his cheek.

'The doctor would like to see Mrs Maddox.'

'I'm not Mrs Maddox,' Betony said. 'I'm his foster-
sister. My name is Miss Izzard.'

'Oh. Well. Come this way, Miss Izzard, please.'

So Tom had to wait again, sitting on the bench with
his back against the wall, while nurses in white and
patients in blue passed to and fro along the corridor.
When Betony came back at last, he knew from her face
that she brought bad news.

'What'd they say? You may as well tell me straight
out.'

'They say there's nothing they can do.'

'No operation nor treatment nor nothing?'

'The optic nerves are too badly damaged. There's
nothing they can do about it. They say it's only a
question of time.'

'Total blindness?' Tom asked.

'I'm afraid so.'

'How long?'

'They don't know.'

'Six months? A year? They must have some notion,
I'd have thought.'

'No. They're uncertain. It could happen soon . . . or it could be as much as two years.'

'I knew it was going to be bad,' he said, 'when they asked for you.'

'The doctor wants to see you too. He has some advice he wants to give you and a letter for Dr Dundas at home. He says you're eligible for a pension.'

'A pension!' he said, hollowly, and went away down the corridor.

Betony sat with her hands on her handbag. She had not told him everything, even now, because she and the doctor had decided against it, and she closed her eyes for a brief moment, seeking in herself some untapped spring of strength and courage. By the time Tom returned, she thought she had found it. She rose and went to him with a calm face.

When they reached Chepsworth and were on their way to The Old Plough, where they had left the pony and trap, Tom stopped suddenly and said he would prefer to walk back home across the fields.

'It's a nice afternoon. You don't mind, do you, Bet?'

'Promise you won't do anything silly.'

'It's all right,' he said, and a rare smile just touched his lips. 'I'm taking it like a proper soldier.'

'You may never lose your sight at all,' she said briskly. 'Doctors have been known to be wrong sometimes.'

She drove home without him, and as she turned into the fold, Michael came out of the house to meet her.

'You're very late, Betony. We're due at my uncle's by half past five but I doubt if we'll get there much before six.'

'I'm sorry, Michael, I'm not coming. There's something important I have to do.'

'More important than keeping an engagement?'

'I hope you'll make my excuses to your uncle and explain that it just couldn't be avoided.'

'I suppose it's something to do with Tom? Your mother said you'd both been down to Sawsford today.'

'Yes, I went with him to the hospital there.'

'How much longer, may I ask, are you going to play nursemaid to that young man?'

'Tom's going blind!' she said bluntly. 'I suppose you'd admit he needs help?'

'Betony, I'm sorry, I'd no idea. Your mother and father should have said. But still, even so, I don't see why *you* should take the responsibility. Not now that he has a wife.'

'Tilly's left him,' Betony said.

'Good God! What a mess it all is!'

'The longer you wait here, the later you'll be getting to Ilton.'

'Yes, yes, I'm going,' he said, but continued to stand there, watching her as she fed the pony. 'You don't seem able to get away from Tom, do you? He haunts you like some guilty dream. You're always trying to pay off a debt for something you did or did not do to him in childhood.'

'Yes, well, perhaps I am.'

'In my opinion, it can't be done. I feel you're only wasting your time.'

'It isn't only *my* debt. Tom was hurt while fighting in France. I think we all owe a debt to men like him.'

'That can't ever be paid either.'

'No, I don't think it can,' Betony said, 'but I think we should try all the same.'

An hour later she drove to Blagg and called on the Mercybrights at Lilac Cottage. Jack was sitting reading his paper. He put it aside as Linn showed Betony into the kitchen, but he made no attempt to stand up, and she saw that one leg lay resting across a stool.

'I wanted to talk to you both about Tom.'

'You'd better sit down. I'm willing to hear what you got to say, and so is Linn, though I doubt if his business can interest us much.'

'Tom's wife has left him. He's all alone. It wasn't true she was having a baby. She led him up the garden path.'

'I ent too surprised,' Jack said. 'She struck me as a

sly piece. But it don't alter the fact that he'd been monkeying with her in the first place.'

'One fall from grace,' Betony said, 'and you'd hold it against him all his life?'

She turned from him to look at Linn, who sat on the edge of an upright chair, her hands still nursing a cup and tea-cloth. The girl was beautiful, Betony thought: delicate features, neatly made; colouring vivid and unusual; dark brown eyes full of thought and feeling. There was a gentle warmth about her, yet plainly she had a resolute will.

'Would you hold it against him for ever?'

'I'm not his judge,' Linn said.

'I'm hoping you might be his salvation.'

'Look here,' Jack said. 'That young man made my daughter unhappy. He hurt her, Miss Izzard, and she done right to send him away.'

'He must have meant something to you, then,' Betony said, still looking at Linn, 'if he had the power to make you unhappy.'

'He chose someone else. It's not my fault if it didn't work out.'

'He never cared tuppence for Tilly Preston.'

'He told me that, but I didn't believe him.'

'You ought to have done. Tom doesn't tell lies.'

'Why have you come to us, Miss Izzard?'

'I've come because Tom is going blind.'

'No,' Linn said, and turned her face away, hiding her pain. 'No! Oh, no!'

'Can't something be done for him?' Jack asked.

'No, nothing,' Betony said. 'He saw the doctors this afternoon. Now he's out at the Pikehouse, alone, facing up to it the best way he can. But there's something else—something Tom himself doesn't know—that nobody knows except myself—and I hope to God I do right to tell you.'

Betony paused. She was trying to read the girl's face.

'He's only got a short time to live,' she said. 'Twelve months at the most, and that only if he takes things quietly. If he had an illness of any kind, or too much strain, death could come sooner, the doctor said.'

Linn sat perfectly still. It was some time before she spoke.

'I remember . . . at the hospital in Rouen . . . they were afraid of brain-damage . . . but then it seemed as if everything was all right after all.' She was perfectly calm, though white as ashes, and she drew a deep, controlled breath. 'I wish I could have known . . . when I first came home and met him again . . .'

'Linn, do you love him?' her father asked, and when she turned to look at him, giving her answer silently, he said, 'In that case, I reckon you'd better go to him, don't you?'

'Yes,' she said. 'I think so too.'

'I'll take you there,' Betony said. 'I'll wait outside while you get ready. Don't be too long. I've already kept the pony standing and the evening is getting a lot colder.'

She went out to the trap and sat waiting, and after a while Linn joined her, carrying a small canvas bag. It was dusk by the time they reached the Pikehouse, and a small rain was sprinkling down, out of a sky the colour of charcoal. The house was in darkness, and Betony sat waiting again while Linn found her way to the door. A few minutes passed, then the lamp was lit and shone through the window. Betony turned in the narrow roadway and drove home through the drizzling rain.

It was a Sunday, and the family at Cobbs were about to sit down to their midday dinner when the back door burst open and Emery Preston walked in, followed by his eldest son, Matthew.

'What's all this?' Granna demanded, bringing a pile of plates to the table, and Great-grumpa Tewke, carving-knife poised against the steel, said, 'This ent The Rose and Crown, by God, and I'll thank you to knock before lifting the sneck of decent folks' doors.'

'Decent folks?' Emery shouted. 'Decent folks, did you say?'

'What d'you want?' Beth asked. 'You can see our dinner's on the table.'

'My business is with your husband.'

'Why me?' Jesse said. 'Why me, I'd like to know?'

'You're the nearest thing Tom Maddox has got for a father, that's why, and I want to know what's happened to Tilly.'

'Yes, well,' Jesse said. 'That ent nothing to do with me.' And he busied himself about the stove, leaving the matter to his wife and daughter. They, it seemed, found nothing amiss with the way young Tom was carrying on. They, therefore, could answer all the awkward questions.

'Tilly's run off,' Betony said to Emery Preston. 'Hadn't you heard?'

'I've heard a lot of funny things lately, but nothing at all from Maddox hisself, so what's he playing at, you tell me that!'

'Seems they weren't happy, so Tilly left him.'

'Then why ent we seen her?' Emery said. 'A girl falling out with her husband like that would surely come home to her own father?'

'Not if she left with another man.'

'I ent having *that!* Not my girl Tilly. She was always a good girl and she certainly wouldn't behave like that!'

'Rubbish!' Beth said. 'Tilly's no better than she should be, and well you know it, Emery Preston.'

'She deceived Tom,' Betony said, 'making believe she was having a baby.'

'She never told *me* she was having a baby.'

'She wouldn't, of course. She knew you'd take your belt to her.'

'Who says I take my belt to my children? And why shouldn't I if they deserve it? I always warned her against that boy. I tried to stop her marrying him.'

'It's a pity you didn't succeed, Mr. Preston.'

'What'd he do to her, the swine, to make her run off without a word?'

'*He* didn't take his belt to her, if that's what you mean.'

'We don't know that! We know nothing at all. He's been acting queer for some time past and I ent the only one to say so neither.'

'Is it surprising, since he's going blind?'

'I know! I know!' Emery said. 'It ent that I don't feel nothing for him. He's been through a lot, I daresay, but it don't excuse his ill-using Tilly and I'm going out there to see him about it.'

'No, don't do that,' Betony said. 'Leave him alone.'

'You needn't worry about my feelings! I know damn well he's got another woman living there with him. It's no good hoping to keep it quiet, even if he does live three miles out. All Huntlip knows about the way he's going on.'

'Huntlip would!' Dicky muttered.

'He didn't waste much time, finding someone to take Tilly's place?'

'She was the one who walked out.'

'I don't know that! That's just his story! It's like this chap she's supposed to've run away with. I don't know he even existed.'

'He existed all right,' said Great-grumpa. 'He came to my workshop, trying to sell me foreign brushes.'

'Well, *I've* never seen him,' Emery said, 'and *I'm* the one that keeps the pub!'

'I've seen him, though,' Matthew said suddenly. 'Chap about thirty, driving a motor, sounded as though he came from Brum. I was parked beside him in the road once and he gave me some lip about my motorcycle.'

'Oh? Is that so?'

'Come to think about it,' Matthew said, 'he ent been around these few weeks lately, though one or two people still owe him money.'

'Why didn't you say so before?'

'It warnt till they mentioned his selling brushes—'

'And it still don't prove nothing, neither, does it?'

'What're you hoping to prove?' asked Beth.

'I dunno!' Emery said. 'All I know is that I don't like it and I tell you straight so's you know how I stand. But I'll say this—if Tilly turns up with this salesman fella, they'll both rue the day, I promise you that!'

He turned towards the door, shoving the boy Matthew before him, and Great-grumpa Tewke looked up from carving the joint of beef.

'I'd ask you to stop to dinner,' he said, his voice laden with sarcasm, 'if it warnt all gone cold while you was so busy showing yourself up for the fool you are!'

When the Prestons had gone, Jesse returned to his place at the table, next to Betony.

'All this talk!' he said, shaking his head. 'I'm disappointed in that boy Tom, causing all this scandal and gossip. Whatever will people think of us? What'll the *captain* think of us?'

'You don't need to call him the captain now, father. He's not in the Army any more.'

'He'll always be the captain to me.'

'Even when he and I are married?'

'H'mm,' Jesse said, 'and when'll that come to pass, I wonder?'

He longed to see her married to Michael. He could not understand why they should wait.

'You're always so busy,' Michael said, looking over Betony's shoulder at the exercise-book she was correcting. 'What with your work at Chepsworth Park and now the school—I hardly see you nowadays.'

'It's only temporary,' Betony said. 'The school, that is. It's only while Miss Likeness is ill.'

'I'm surprised you teach them geometry. I'd no idea village schools were so ambitious. I thought it was all hymn-singing and sewing fine seams on linen samplers.'

'Huntlip's got a *good* village school. All others ought to be like it.'

'I've half a mind, the moment we're married, to whisk you off to South Africa and hide you away on my uncle's farm.'

'You're always talking about South Africa.'

'I had a very happy year out there, when I was a carefree boy in my teens.'

'The trouble is not so much that I'm busy,' Betony said, 'as that you are not busy enough.'

'Would you believe it!' he exclaimed. 'My mother says I need a long rest and you say I need to be active. What's a man to do, between two women offering such conflicting advice?'

'He should choose for himself, every time.'

'I don't seem able to settle down, since coming home from the war,' he said. 'I'm bored stiff with the factory and it runs itself anyway under George Williams. I think what I'd really enjoy is having a farm of my own.'

'Then why not buy one?'

'You make it all sound so simple.'

'Well, isn't it simple, if you've got the money?'

'Would you like living on a farm?'

'Yes, I should, though not in South Africa,' Betony said.

Michael went and stood at the window, looking out at the old orchard. The plum trees were stippled white with blossom; the evening sunlight lit their trunks; and a woodpecker flew from tree to tree. Nearby, in the garden, Jesse was splitting seed potatoes and Beth was planting them in the rows, her back bent in a perfect arch, her gloved hands working swiftly and surely, opening the soil with her sharp trowel and closing it again over the seed in a movement almost too quick for the eye to see.

'I suppose South Africa is too far away from your collection of lame dogs.'

'What lame dogs?'

'Oh, come, now,' he said. 'There's your foster-brother for a start.'

'Why do you always call him that? You know his name so why not use it?' Betony closed one exercise-book, placed it on its pile, and took another. 'Sometimes I feel you resent Tom.'

'Perhaps I do,' Michael said, turning towards her. 'He does claim rather a lot of your attention.'

'You can't be jealous of someone like Tom, knowing he's going slowly blind. It's too absurd.'

'I didn't say I was jealous of him.'

'Then what is all this about, exactly?'

'Oh, I don't know! It isn't very easy to talk to you these days, Betony. You're always thinking of other things.'

'Very well,' Betony said, and swung round to face him. 'You now have my undivided attention, so what is it you're trying to say to me?'

'Yes, you're very good at putting me in the wrong and making me feel ridiculous,' he said. 'You're always much better than I am at any sort of argument.'

'But I don't want to be better at it! I don't want to argue at all. All I want is to understand you.' Looking at him she could see there was something seriously wrong; some awful uncertainty in his face; some fear that lurked and flickered in his eyes. 'Michael,' she said, 'was it very bad in the prison-camp?'

'It wasn't what I would call a picnic.'

'I wish you'd tell me about it.'

'No,' he said. 'There's nothing to tell, and you're mistaken in thinking I want to talk about it. It's the last thing I want. I'm always trying to forget about it.'

Betony rose and went to him. She touched his arm and found he was trembling.

'You'll have to make allowances for me, Michael, when I don't understand things. It was so hard for us at home here to imagine what it was really like. We tried and tried—or some of us did—but we couldn't really understand. And I must admit I stopped worrying—indeed I was thankful in a way—once I heard you'd been taken prisoner.'

'Thankful? Were you? Were you really?'

'Of course,' she said. 'Especially after the uncertainty while you were posted missing. All I could think of was that you were safe. Safe and alive and out of it all!'

'Yes,' he said, in a dull voice, and took her in his arms so that his face should be hidden from her.

The night was unusually warm for May. There were too many blankets on his bed and he lay sweating, unable to sleep, listening to the cathedral clock striking. It was half past two. The room was full of white moonlight.

He rose and put on his dressing-gown. He opened the door quietly and went out across the landing. His mother heard him and called out. Her door was half open, and when he looked in she was sitting up in bed, groping for the light-switch.

'Don't put the light on. The moon is bright enough.'

'What's the matter, Michael, are you ill?'

'No, no. I just couldn't sleep, that's all. I thought a drop of Scotch might do the trick.'

'I'm worried about you, not sleeping. You've been like this for weeks now.'

'My bed's too cushy, that's the trouble. Perhaps I should get a wire-netting bunk.'

His mother patted a place on the bed. He went and sat there, and the two of them were close together, with the moon shining on them, bright as a searchlight. Her grey hair was set in symmetrical wavelets, as orderly as in the day-time, and had the sheen of polished pewter. Her face was pale and her lips in the moonlight looked almost purple.

'Have you got something on your mind?'

'Nothing more than usual.'

'Is everything all right between you and Betony?'

'If it isn't, the fault is entirely on my side.'

'You can't expect me to accept that.'

'It's true all the same.'

'You've been home for five months, yet you grow more nervy all the time. You're drinking a lot. You never used to.'

'That's what it does to us . . . lies in wait and pounces on us . . .'

'Were you ill-treated at the camp?'

'Some of the guards were pretty brutal, but most of them were all right. Hunger was the worst thing we had to bear, and I almost welcomed that in a way, as an expiation.'

'Expiation?'

'Because I felt guilty at being safe.'

'My dear boy! What nonsense you're talking—'

'Don't interrupt me. I want to tell you what really happened. I gave myself up, you see, because I couldn't face any more fighting. I wasn't all that badly wounded. I could have got back to our lines if I'd tried. Minching and Darby wanted to help me, but I made some excuse and stayed behind, where the German patrol was sure to find me.'

His mother was silent, sitting upright against her pillows, her hands lying motionless on the quilt. For once he could guess nothing of her thoughts.

'I liked it at first, being a soldier. I was even good at it, up to a point. Promotion came quickly, as you know. But it all went on so long, so long, and the more one did the more they expected. I began to wish, like everyone else, that I might be wounded and out of it, but I was wounded three times and every time they patched me up as good as new and sent me back again for more.

'It wouldn't have been so bad, I think, if I had been just a private soldier, but I was an officer giving orders . . . blowing a whistle and sending men over the parapet . . . and when we were in a tight spot, I'd see them all looking at me, expecting me to know the answer, expecting me to do the right thing and get them all out of the mess. Sometimes their faith nearly drove me mad. I *didn't* always know what to do. Often I knew no more than they did. And there were one or two among them who were better men than I'll ever be.'

From being hot, he was now shivering. The sweat lay cold on his face and body, and sickness crept on him, reducing him to nothing.

'I forgot when I gave myself up,' he said, 'that I'd have to live with it ever after.'

His mother's face was still impassive, and yet she was reaching out to him, leaning towards him with outstretched arms. And when he yielded his shuddering body, she drew him fiercely into her bed, pressing him close, trying to give him strength and comfort, trying to protect him from the bitterness of self-recrimination. He was her child again, creeping into her warm bed, letting her wrap him round in the bedclothes, letting her press his head to her bosom. He was her child, crying after a bad dream, and her only duty in the world was to him.

'They asked too much of you. Yes, yes, they did! How could you go on for ever and ever? Nobody could. It's too much to ask. You mustn't feel guilty for the rest of your life. What good does it do? None whatever!' And a little later, as the shivering passed, she said to him: 'Have you told Betony about this?'

'No,' he said, 'I'm afraid to tell her.'

'There shouldn't be secrets between man and wife.'

'I'm afraid I might lose her. I couldn't bear that.'

'If she loves you, it won't make any difference. She

will understand you that much better. She'll be able to help you. It's only right that she should know.'

'Yes,' he said. 'It's only right, as you say. I'll tell her tomorrow.'

But in the morning, when he thought of Betony, he knew he would never be able to tell her.

High above the woods of Scoate House Manor a kestrel hovered, taking its ease on the warm summer air, and Tom, returning with Linn along the old turnpike, a bundle of osiers on his shoulder, stood still to watch it, one hand raised against the sun.

'Can you see it?' Linn asked.

'Yes, just about, though I wouldn't have knowed it for a kestrel if it warnt for *knowing,* if you see what I mean.'

'Supposing you tell me what you mean.'

'Well, it's the way he's lazing about up there . . . the way he's concentrating on something below . . . ah, and now the way he's gliding around, before going off, away down the wind.'

The kestrel circled three times and swooped away, racing its shadow over the treetops. Tom turned his attention to a soaring lark.

'I'm a lot luckier than folk that've had no sight at all. Take that there lark, now, up in the sky. That could be a gnat for all I can see to tell me different, but when I hear it singing, well, it means I can see it at the same time, just as plain as I ever did, rising up and up all the time into a sky as blue as blue.'

They had been shopping in Norton village. Tom drew his pension from the post office there, and they rarely went to Huntlip now. He bought his osiers at Washpool Farm and sold his baskets to a dealer who called every other Friday.

The day was a hot one in late July and the sun was immediately overhead. Every few hundred yards or so, Tom dropped his bundle on the grass verge and the two of them sat on it, side by side, among the meadowsweet and sorrel. What wind there was came breathing hotly out of the east, and Linn tried to cool it by fanning herself with a bunch of ferns. Under the brim of her big straw hat, her face was shadowed, and he saw her only as a shape. Yet he knew the day had exhausted her.

'You'd have done better stopping at home. You shouldn't be walking so far in this heat.'

'We spend more time resting than we do walking. It'll likely be dark by the time we get home.'

'Dark or light, what does it matter? We ent catching no train, are we?'

'I left my washing on the line. It'll go too dry for ironing.'

'You just rest,' he said firmly. 'You know what Mrs Gibbs told you. You've got to rest and take things easy.'

When they reached home and were passing through the Pikehouse gate, Linn saw a man standing watching them from the edge of the woods, thirty yards off, across the road. He was half-hidden behind a tree and stood quite still, his hands in his pockets, his cap pulled low over his forehead.

'There's a man over there. Can you see him? He's standing at the edge of the wood.'

'Perhaps it's a keeper,' Tom said.

But then the man stepped out to the open; he crossed the grass verge and stood in the roadway: a short stocky man with a chest like a barrel.

'It's Emery Preston,' Linn said.

'What's he doing hanging about here for?'

'It's not the first time I've seen him about. When I went up to Eastery last Friday, he was standing on the churchyard wall, looking down at the Pikehouse, and he stared hard at me as I went past.'

'I'll go and have a word with him,' Tom said.

Emery Preston stood like a post. Tom went up to him, squinting a little, for he could see better by looking out of the sides of his eyes.

'Do you want to speak to me, Mr Preston?'

'No, why should I?' Emery said.

'Then why are you out here, watching us the way you are?'

'Is there a law that says I mustn't?'

'No, there's no law,' Tom said, 'or none that I know of, anyway.'

'There's laws about *some* things,' Emery said. 'There's a law against bigamy for a start.'

'I ent no bigamist, Mr Preston.'

'You're both a lot worser to my way of thinking, living together, the two of you, with no sign of shame in either of you. I'm a publican and a sinner but I wouldn't carry on like that.'

'What d'you want of us?' Tom asked.

'I'd like to know what became of my daughter.'

'Tilly went off with another chap. I dunno no more'n that.'

'So you say, but I sometimes wonder!'

'What do you mean?'

'Never mind! Never mind! I was thinking out loud.'

'You should try looking in Birmingham. That's where he lived, the chap she went off with.'

'Have you tried looking for her your own-self?'

'No,' Tom said, ''cos I don't want her back.'

'That's understandable, sure enough. A lawful wife is something of a hinderment to the likes of you. You better prefer a looser arrangement.'

Linn still stood at the Pikehouse gate. Emery could see that she was with child. His glance roved over her, full of contempt.

'You yourself was begot in the hedge, Maddox, and it seems it's a thing that gets passed on!'

He turned and walked off towards Huntlip, kicking up a cloud of dust. Tom and Linn went indoors.

'Take no notice,' she said to him. 'Don't let it upset you.'

'It don't worry me, except for your sake,' Tom said, 'and maybe the little 'un's, when he comes.'

'You are not to worry. There's no need.'

It was very strange, the way his sight varied from day to day. Some days, especially when the sun was shining, he could see the poppies red along the roadside, the apples ripening in the garden, the white clouds crossing the blue sky. But other days were bad, and once, out in the empty stretch of wasteland surrounding the Pikehouse, he came to a standstill, lost as though in a thick dark fog.

He was quite alone, and he felt that the rest of the earth had gone; he thought of it as a smoking ruin, crumbling away into a pit, leaving him on the edge of nothing; and he knew a moment of whirling terror. But after a while, putting out his hands, he felt the long feathery grasses that grew high everywhere around him, and their touch reassured him. The earth was still there, unchanged, unchanging, and he must find his way across it, through the gathering darkness. Home was in front of him. Not much more than a hundred yards. He could smell the woodsmoke, and could hear Linn beating a mat. It seemed a long way.

'You should've called to me,' she said, coming to him as he groped along the hedgerow to the garden gate. 'I'm sure I'd have heard you.'

'I've got to get used to finding my way about,' he said.

But Linn rarely left him alone after that. She watched over him and was always at hand when he needed her. Their lives were tight-linked. They shared every moment of the night and day.

Once, when she was rummaging in the cupboard, she said, 'I didn't know you ever smoked.'

'I did smoke, a bit, in the trenches,' he said. 'Why?'

'Cos I found this.' And she put a tobacco-pipe into his hands.

'It belonged to Bob Newers, my mate in the army. I meant to send it home to his people, but what with my getting blown up and that, I never got round to it after all.'

Until now, whenever he had remembered Newers, he had seen only the space left after the shell had burst the crater; had seen only the hole in the ground, and the debris falling, bringing down bits of human remains. But now, as he held the pipe between his hands, he saw Newers as a whole man again; felt his solid bulk beside him; heard his voice; and remembered a day at

Liere on the Somme, when the first tanks had been seen on the road, making towards Rilloy-sus-Coll.

Newers and he, in the reserve line, had been drumming up tea when a new chap named Worth had let out a shriek.

'God Almighty! Take a dekko at these monsters! What the hell are they, d'you suppose?'

'What, them?' said Newers, standing up to look at the tanks. 'They've brought the buns.'

Linn went and sat beside Tom on the settle. She saw he was smiling.

'Newers could always make us laugh,' he said.

Every day now, while the summer weather lasted, Tom worked out of doors, close by the pump where his osiers lay soaking in the trough. He sat on a mat on the paving-stones with a wooden board on his lap, and often when Linn went out to the garden she would stop and watch the basket growing as his clever fingers worked on the rods, or reached for the hammer to rap them home, or took up the knife to trim the ends. Human hands, when they worked and made things, always filled her with a kind of wonder.

'I know you're there,' he said once. 'I can see you plain. Well, plain enough. You've got your blue dress on, and the new pinny with the big pockets.'

'And what am I holding in my hand?'

'I suppose it's that medicine again.'

'You drink it up and no nonsense.'

'All right,' he said. 'You're the nurse. But it won't bring my sight back, I don't suppose.'

'It'll help your headaches, Dr Dundas said.'

'It'd be a miracle if that was to give me back my sight. I'd drink a whole bottle every day.' He emptied the glass and returned it to her. He looked up at her with his sideways stare. 'It ent very likely, is it?' he said. 'Miracles ent all that common nowadays.'

'No, Tom, you won't get your sight back, I'm afraid.'

'No. Well. It's not to be expected, I know that. It's just wishful thinking, as they say.'

One day when Linn went out to the garden, to pick

the last of the kidney beans, she saw Emery Preston again, coming out of Scoate woods. He stood for a while, looking across as though hesitating, then walked off towards Huntlip. She decided not to tell Tom, but the next time her father came to call on them, she took him aside and told him in private.

'I don't know what he means by it. I suppose it's to make us feel uncomfortable. In which case he succeeds all too well, 'cos it worries me, somehow, seeing him prowling about like that.'

'I'll have a word with him,' Jack said. 'I'll tell him to mind his own damned business.'

'I don't think it's wise to quarrel with him.'

'Who said anything about quarrelling?'

'I know what you are, father.'

'It's no use wearing velvet gloves when dealing with men like Emery Preston. You've to tell them out straight.'

Jack went to The Rose and Crown the following evening after work. He spoke to Emery regardless of the crowd in the taproom listening.

"What're you always hanging around the Pikehouse for?'

'It's a free country. I do as I please.'

'Then hear this!' Jack said. 'If you cause any harm to my daughter, or to Tom Maddox, you'll have to answer to me for it, and I'm none too gentle when dealing with ruffians like you, Preston, so just you watch out!'

Jack walked out again. Emery turned to his customers.

'He thinks hisself somebody, that chap Mercybright, don't he, by God? And him just a labourer on Outlands Farm!'

'What's wrong with labourers?' Billy Ratchet said, offended. 'Jack's all right. He's a good sort. I feel sorry for him, with that daughter of his turning out so unexpected, living like she do with Tom Maddox and carrying his bastard, bold as brass.'

'You needn't tell *me!*' Emery said. '*I* know how they're carrying on. I been out there and seen for myself. But it's what they done, the two of them, to get rid of Tilly that bothers me, and one of these days I shall find out!'

'Why, your Tilly's as bad, herself, ent she?' said Norman Rye, calling from one of the small tables. 'Going off with that traveller like she done?'

'That's the story that's been put about! But I've got ideas of my own on that score, and I shan't rest till I know more about it.'

'What do you mean, Emery?'

'You'll know soon enough, when the time comes.'

Emery went and drew himself a pint of Chepsworth. He drank till the glass was three parts empty and froth had given him a white moustache. His three sons watched him. His customers eyed one another in stony silence.

On a warm Saturday in late September, a car drew up at The Rose and Crown, and a young man got out, red-faced and sweating. He locked the car door, made a face at the children gathering round, and glanced at his wrist-watch. It wanted five minutes to closing time. He was very thirsty.

Matthew, in the taproom, called his father to the window.

'It's him,' he said. 'That travelling salesman. You can see the brushes in the car.'

'Are you sure it's the same one?'

'I'm positive,' Matthew said.

When the young man came in, glancing round at the customers, and smoothing his hair with the flat of his hand, Emery stood behind the counter.

'Your name Trimble by any chance?'

'Upon my word! What memories you country folk have got—'

'Is it or ent it?' Emery demanded.

'Yes, indeed,' the man said, and found himself half way across the counter, with Emery Preston's enormous hands twisted in the front of his jacket. 'Good God! What's the matter? Are you drunk or mad or what?'

'Where's my daughter Tilly got to?'

'I don't know what you're talking about.'

'The story is she went off with you, in that dinky motor you got out there, and if it's true, Mr Smarty Trimble, I'll break every bone in your soft greasy body!'

'Of course it's not true! I don't even know your daughter Tilly.'

'You know her all right. You sold her brushes out at the Pikehouse.'

'Did I? Did I? Good Lord, let me see! The Pikehouse, you said? Yes, it does ring a bell. It's that tiny tollhouse out towards Norton. The young lady's name was Mrs Maddox.'

'And what else do you remember?'

'Nothing whatever, I do assure you. I called there three or four times, I agree, and sold Mrs Maddox a few little items, but what you're saying is simply monstrous and I insist you let go of me at once!'

'Monstrous, is it?' Emery said. 'Does that mean you're saying it's a damned lie?'

'Indeed I am! And I'd like to know who's responsible for it! I'm a happily married man. I can show you snaps of my wife and kiddies. I can get people to speak for me—'

'Never mind that,' Emery said. 'Just answer me one more question. Why did you leave the district so sudden, with people owing you money on orders?'

'I was taken ill. I went down with 'flu and very nearly died of it. If it hadn't been for my wife, God bless her, nursing me for weeks on end, I shouldn't be here at this moment.'

'Oh, is that so?' Emery said. 'And now you've come back to collect what's owing? Well, you're hopeful, I must say, after so many months gone by.'

He loosened his hold on the man's jacket, but continued to look at him narrowly.

'You got a business card you can give me?'

'No, no, I haven't,' Trimble said. 'I've had some trouble getting them printed.' He shrugged himself into his ruffled clothes and tucked his necktie into his jacket. He half glanced round at the few customers in the taproom. 'But I'll write my address down if you want it and then you can verify all I've told you.'

'Yes, you do that,' Emery said, and watched as Trimble, with a shaking hand, wrote his address on a scrap of paper. 'Seems I got the wrong man. I'm sorry I rumpled you up a bit but it ent my fault you've been blamed for something you ent done. It's my son-in-law you can thank for that.'

'Is it indeed? I should like to meet him!'

'Don't you tangle with Tom Maddox. I shall be dealing with him myself.'

'Right!' Trimble said. 'All's well that ends well, that's what I say, and no hard feelings either way.'

'Ent you having the drink you came for?'

'No, no, I think not. I'm behind-hand already and I've got an appointment at two-thirty.' Trimble walked towards the door. 'Let me know,' he said, 'if there's anything more I can do to help you.'

He drove away from The Rose and Crown and chugged slowly along the Straight, but once out on the main road he opened the throttle and let her go, eager to put the village of Huntlip well behind him, together with its ugly-tempered, violent people.

At The Rose and Crown, the last customer had now left, and Emery Preston was locking up. He threw the keys to the boy Matthew.

'So now we know where we stand, by God, and it's what I been scared of all along. I warned our Tilly oftentimes against taking up with Tom Maddox, but she wouldn't listen, oh no, not she!'

'You reckon he's gone and harmed her, dad?'

'He's done away with her, that's what he's done, the same as his father done with his mother, only *he's* been smarter about it, the swine, and made sure she ent to be found!'

'What're you going to do, dad?'

'I'm going to the police,' Emery said, 'which I should've done at the very beginning.'

'Detectives?' Linn said, staring at the men who stood in the porch.

'I'm Detective-Inspector Darns, madam, and this is Detective-Constable Penfold. We'd like a word with Mr Maddox.'

'You'd better come in.'

They stepped in after her and the younger man closed the door. It was not yet six o'clock, but the lamp had been lit and Tom sat beside it on a stool, mending a boot on a last in his lap. Linn stood behind him and touched his shoulder.

'It's the police. They want to see you.'

'Ah, I heard. I was wondering what it was all about.' He sat up straight, trying to see them. 'What am I supposed to've done?'

'May we sit down, Mr Maddox?'

'You go ahead. Suit yourselves.'

'We're enquiring into the disappearance of your wife, Mrs Tilly Maddox, formerly Preston. Her father has reported her missing.'

'Has he?' Tom said. 'Whatever for?'

'Is there anything you can tell us?'

'She went off with another chap. I couldn't tell you where she is.'

'What date would that be, Mr Maddox?'

'Early in February,' Tom said. 'I can't say no nearer than that.'

'Did she tell you she was going?'

'No. Not beforehand. Not in so many words, exactly.'

'Can you make that a little plainer?'

'She *did* say she wished she could live in a town. She didn't like it out here. She said it was lonely and drove her mad.'

'I'd like you to tell us how she left.'

'I came home and she was gone. There was a note on the table there. All her things had gone too.'

'Did you keep the note?'

'No,' Tom said, 'I threw it away.'

'Perhaps you can remember what it said.'

'She wrote she was sick of being so lonely. She said she wouldn't be coming back.'

'Did she say she was going with a man?'

'Not in so many words exactly.'

'What *were* her words, Mr Maddox?'

'Well, she said she was tired of the way I treated her, and Mr Trimble would treat her better. He would look after her, she said.'

'So you assumed they'd gone off together?'

'I'm certain of it,' Tom said. 'They was thick together. He was here a lot. I saw them once, laughing and talking. He'd got his arm round her, squeezing her tight.'

'Were you jealous, Mr Maddox?'

'No, not a jot, it was no odds to me.'

'I gather you didn't get on all that well with your wife?'

'You couldn't gather nothing else, after what I just been saying.'

'What was the cause of your disagreements?'

'Everything,' Tom said. 'It was all a mistake, our getting married in the first place. We shouldn't never ought to've done it.'

The two men were sitting side by side, almost filling the small settle. Tom could see them as two dark shadows; their faces were nothing but paler blurs; but he sensed that the young one was making notes.

'You writing it down, what I'm saying?'

'My constable is writing it down.'

Inspector Darns was a man of fifty, quiet-spoken, easy-going. He sat relaxed, his hands clasped on the hat in his lap. He was rather interested in the half-cobbled boot on Tom's last.

'I'm surprised you can see to mend boots. I'd heard you had trouble with your eyes.'

'I can see if I feel,' Tom said. 'But it's true what they said about my eyes. I got blown up during the war.'

'He's going blind,' Linn said.

'Were you going blind when your wife was with you?'

'It had started,' Tom said, 'but she didn't know it.'

'Were you resentful, Mr Maddox, when this misfortune came to you?'

'Wouldn't you have been resentful?'

'You haven't really answered my question.'

'Haven't I? I thought I had.'

'Were you upset, Mr Maddox?'

'I wasn't exactly over the moon.'

'And did you take it out on your wife?'

'Maybe I did. I wasn't too nice to her sometimes.'

'Did you hit her by any chance?'

'No, never.'

'Not even once, in a temper, perhaps, when she was nagging as she probably did?'

'I never touched her,' Tom said. 'Is somebody trying to say I did?'

'Mr Preston is not quite satisfied that his daughter left you for another man. He thinks you killed her, Mr Maddox.'

'He's off his hinges!' Tom said.

'I take it you deny the allegation?'

'I do deny it! It's a bloody lie!'

Tom sat rigid on his stool. He felt imprisoned; trapped by his blindness; and a great anger ran through his blood, threatening destruction. He felt it would break him; that he would go to pieces like a man driven mad; that the darkness would engulf his mind. But he felt Linn's hand on his shoulder again, and her touch steadied him. He wished he could see the two men's faces.

'Why now all of a sudden? Tilly's been gone for months and months. Why don't Emery look for her in Birmingham, together with that Trimble fellow?'

'The man Trimble's been seen in Huntlip. Mr Preston asked him about your wife and the man denies that she went with him.'

'But she must've done! She took all her things. She couldn't have took 'em if she'd gone alone. She couldn't have took 'em if she didn't have a car to drive away in. It's three miles to the nearest bus. Supposing Trimble is telling lies?'

'If somebody's lying, it's up to us to find out, Mr Maddox, and that's what we are aiming to do.'

The two men stood up. They were very tall and their heads touched the rafters. Tom could feel them towering above him.

'You ent arresting me nor nothing, then?'

'Your wife has been reported missing and a certain allegation has been made. We have no choice but to follow it up. That's all there is to the matter at present, Mr Maddox, and I hope we'll succeed in tracing your wife in Birmingham as you suggest.'

'What happens if you don't?'

'We'll cross that bridge when we come to it. But one last question if you don't mind. Do you know the name of the firm this man Trimble worked for?'

'The name,' Tom repeated, and thought about it. 'It was Bruno,' he said. 'Bruno Brushes of Birmingham. It was on the dustpan and broom Tilly bought. You can have a look at them if you like.'

'No need for that,' Darns said. 'It merely confirms what we've already heard. Thank you for answering our questions, Mr Maddox. We'll let you know if we have any news.'

The two men went. Tom and Linn listened as they drove away. He turned towards her.

'*You* don't think I murdered Tilly?'

'Don't be foolish,' Linn said.

'I should like to know.'

'No, Tom, I don't believe it.'

'What about them? Did they look as though they believed me?'

'I think so, yes. In fact I'm sure.'

'Seems like I bring you nothing but trouble. I make a mess of things all the time.'

His hands were still clenched on his cobbling hammer. He was breathing hard, and trembling a little. Linn took the hammer and the boot on its last and put them aside. She knelt before him, taking his hands between her own.

'You must try not to worry about it,' she said. 'The police will soon find her, I'm sure of that. I know how you feel, having Emery Preston spreading this lie, but you mustn't let it poison you. You must try and put it out of your mind.'

Tom made no answer, but drew her gently into his arms.

At The Rose and Crown, when the two detectives entered the taproom, the gathering of customers fell silent. Emery Preston, sitting at one of the crowded tables, got up at once.

'Well?' he said. 'Have you arrested Tom Maddox?'

'Mr Preston,' Darns said, 'I'd like a word with you in private.'

'No need for that. I don't mind my customers hearing. I ent got nothing I want to hide.'

'I'd sooner we were private,' Darns said, and Emery, shrugging, led them into the back room.

'I'll ask you again.—Have you arrested Tom Maddox?'

'No, Mr Preston, for there's no evidence as yet that a crime has been committed at all.'

'Evidence? It's your job to find it! Though there won't be much, I don't suppose, 'cos he'll have made certain of that, you mark my words. Out there in that lonely place, he could've buried her in them woods and no one the wiser, and I'll stake my last penny that's just what happened.'

'If there's anything to be found,' Darns said, 'we shall find it, be sure of that.'

'How long'll it take?' Emery asked. 'From now to Christmas?'

'The only fact so far is that your daughter has disappeared. Everything else is speculation and I would advise you to be more careful in what you say or Mr Maddox could take you to law on a charge of slander.'

'I'd like to see it!' Emery said. 'A murderer taking me to law because I tell the world what he is?'

'What reasons have you for your suspicions?'

'Where's my daughter if he ent killed her?'

'Apart from that, Mr Preston?'

'His father was a murderer. Did you know that?'

'That's no reason,' Darns said, but he was interested all the same.

'It is to *me!*' Emery said. 'I know the stock Tom Maddox comes from. His father was a wrong 'un. Anyone will tell you that. He attacked my poor old mother once and she was over eighty years old. He had a murderous temper always. He turned on the woman he lived with in the end and hit her over the head with a poker. He went and hanged hisself afterwards and saved the hangman a lot of swither.'

'Yes, I remember that case, now you mention it,' Darns said, 'but is the son as violent?'

'Sure to be. It runs in the blood.'

'But he's never actually been in trouble?'

'Not that I know of. He's been away. But he'll have got used to killing, won't he, out there in the war, fighting the Germans?'

'That could be said of thousands. But what I came for, Mr Preston, was to ask for the address of Arthur Trimble.'

'I've got it here,' Emery said, and passed over a piece of paper.

'I'd also like a photograph of your daughter.'

'What for?'

'To help us trace her, Mr Preston.'

'Trace her! Trace her!' Emery muttered, beginning to search a sideboard drawer. 'How'll they trace her if she's under the sod?' But he found a photograph and handed it over. 'That was took on her wedding day and a bad day it turned out to be for her, too, poor girl.'

'She looks very happy in the picture.'

'She didn't know what she was in for, did she?'

Emery followed them out through the taproom and saw them off the premises. He returned to his customers with a scornful face.

'A lot of use *they* are, going about so dilladerry, as though they got all the time in the world. Tom Maddox could vanish while they play about.'

'Have they seen him, Emery?'

'Seen him? Yes! They been passing the time of day with him, just as though they was all good pals, or so it seemed from what they said.'

'That's the way they go about it,' said Emery's cousin, Humphrey Bartley. 'They let him feel he's pretty safe and then when he goes and gives hisself away they pounce on him like a cat on a mouse.'

'If I had Tom Maddox alone in my yard,' Emery said, hard-faced, 'he'd be telling the truth in ten seconds!'

Betony was away in Wiltshire when the rumours started. She returned to find them in full spate.

'Who started all this? Emery Preston, I suppose! And no doubt the village is all agog!'

'No doubt it is,' her mother said, 'but the best thing is to take no notice.'

'Has anyone been to see Tom and Linn?'

'Dicky and me went a day or two back but your father's busy all of a sudden and can't find the time.'

'Yes, well,' Jesse said, not quite meeting Betony's eye, 'what good can I do, going to see them?'

'I always said it!' granna exclaimed. 'I always said he'd end up badly. It's the bad blood in him. He can't rightly help it.'

'So he's tried and condemned already, is he?' Betony said, fiercely angry. 'By his own family too!'

'We ent his family by rights,' said great-grumpa. 'We took him in as an act of kindness.'

'Yes, and it's him that's cut hisself off,' said Jesse, 'living over the brush with the Mercybright girl and making us feel ashamed to know him.'

'I'm not ashamed,' Betony said.

'Don't mind your father,' Beth said. 'Go out and see them. They need to know they've got a few friends.'

'Yes, mother, I'll go now.'

Driving along the main road, she overtook Jack Mercybright, and he rode with her the rest of the way. When they got to the Pikehouse, Tom was sitting in the open doorway, watching the sun going down in splinters of crimson light behind the church on Eastery ridge.

'Can you see it?' Betony asked.

'I should think I can!' he said, smiling, and the sunset colours were bright on his face. 'Such sunsets we been having lately! Almost as good as the winter time. But I don't see much, besides lights.'

In the lamplit room beyond, Linn, big with child, moved slowly to and fro, setting supper on the table. Tom rose from his chair and carried it in. He set it by the table, feeling his way.

'You heard what they're saying about me in Huntlip?'

'I've heard it all right. This fairy tale!'

'You don't believe it, then, Bet?'

'Not a single word.'

'There's plenty that will,' Jack said, and stood lighting a broken clay pipe, watching Tom through the smoke he was making. 'As for myself, well, if you *had* upped and murdered Tilly Preston, I dunno that I'd really blame you. Her sort of girl often asks for trouble.'

Father!' Linn said, rounding on him. 'What are you saying?'

'I reckon he's trying me out,' Tom said. 'The policeman did the same thing. But I ent going to be catched that way 'cos I never touched her, neither by accident nor on a purpose, though I'd hardly admit it if I had, would I?'

'You needn't worry,' Jack said. 'I'd sooner believe what you tell me than anything the Prestons is putting about.'

'The police are trying to trace Tilly, but what'll happen if they don't? What'll they do if she don't come forward?'

'What can they do when there's nothing to go on except a rumour? If you're innocent you got nothing to fear.'

'It's the waiting and wondering,' Tom said, 'and the fact that the rumour might never get scotched.'

'Forget about it,' Jack said. 'Gossip of this sort is not worth fretting over. It's less than the smoke going up that chimney. Meantime, we must look on the bright side, and hope that wife of yours turns up.'

'I don't think she will,' Tom said.

'Oh? Why's that?'

'I dunno why. I just don't, that's all.'

Jack said no more, and Linn at that moment called on him to put out his pipe, for the soup-bowls were filled and on the table. But Betony noticed how, during supper, his gaze often rested on Tom's face, and, driving home later that evening, she asked him if he had any doubts.

'Doubts? Yes. Ent you?'

'I've never known Tom tell a lie.'

'Everybody tells lies, especially when they're in trouble.'

'Then you think him guilty!'

'I never said that. I *don't* think it. I only said I'd got my doubts. I'll have them for ever, I daresay, if that Tilly ent found.'

'They can't be very serious doubts or you'd be frightened for Linn's sake.'

'No, I ent frightened, 'cos it's like I said—if Tom did kill Tilly she very likely drove him to it.'

'I don't think he killed her. He wouldn't, I'm sure.' And she cast her mind back to that day early in the year when she had called on Tom at the Pikehouse: the day he had told her Tilly was gone and that he was beginning to go blind. 'I'd have *known*,' she said. 'I'd have felt it, somehow, in my bones.'

A few days later, Michael called for Betony at Chepsworth Park, and took her to lunch at The Old Plough.

'There's good news about Kingsmore Farm. I'm taking over the lease at Christmas, so by the time we come back from our honeymoon, there'll only be a month or two to wait before we move in. We'll live at King's Hill until then. D'you think you can bear it?'

'If your mother can, so can I.'

'You don't look all that delighted,' he said. 'Aren't you pleased about Kingsmore?'

'Of course I'm pleased. It's just that I'm worried about Tom.'

'Ah, yes, I might have known. So much for my little celebration!' He raised his glass, sardonically, and sipped his champagne. He tried to purge himself of his irritation. 'Is there any truth in the allegations?'

'No, there isn't. None whatever.'

'You seem very sure.'

'It's just wicked gossip. Huntlip has bouts of it from time to time.' And, after a pause, she said: 'I'm afraid this is all very unpleasant for you, Michael. You're not only marrying beneath you—you're marrying into a family that's getting talked about in a hateful way.'

'Huntlip gossip is nothing to me, though I agree it's a very unpleasant thing to happen. Still, I'll have you out of it quite soon, and you'll be able to put it behind you.'

'You don't understand,' Betony said. 'I don't want to be out of it. Not while this thing is hanging over my family. I think we should wait a little longer.'

'Haven't we waited long enough? Hell and damnation! Your vicar has started publishing the banns.'

'It's the going away I don't like.'

'Look,' Michael said, and he was suddenly very angry. 'I'm not giving up my honeymoon for anything or anyone, least of all that foster-brother of yours. He got himself into this God-awful mess and he's only got himself to blame.'

'I don't agree. None of this is his own doing.'

'How can you be sure of that?'

'How can we be sure of anything?'

Betony's anger was as fierce as his. They stared at

each other across the table. But, aware that people were watching them, they ate for a while in complete silence, until they were in command of themselves and could speak calmly.

'If Tom is innocent, you don't need to worry.'

'But he's a sick man. It's the strain and the worry that will do the harm.'

'He's got other people looking after him.'

'Yes. That's true.'

'Can you do more for him than they can?'

'No,' she said, 'perhaps not.'

For a moment she was tempted to tell him the truth: that Tom was now a dying man; but she could not. This secret she shared only with the Mercybrights and old Dr Dundas out at Norton. It was better that it should remain so.

'You're right, of course, there's nothing much I can do for him.'

'Well, then?' Michael said, and reached across to refill her glass. 'Perhaps now I can have a few minutes of your time in which to discuss our future lives? Just trivial things, you know, like the wedding arrangements and the honeymoon and making Kingsmore fit to live in.'

Betony smiled.

'Dear Michael,' she said. 'You're very patient.'

One morning, when Tom awoke, he could see nothing, not even outlines. When he stepped out in the garden and turned his face towards the sun, its light was concealed from him, as though in eclipse. It fell on dead eyes.

He sat on the old backless chair against the wall and yielded to the darkness. He felt it surrounding him, pressing in on all sides, as though it would squeeze him from the face of the earth. Nothing was left of him, only a central bubble of fear, and if that burst he would be destroyed.

Then suddenly the fear was gone. He could not have said why. But it was as though he had been away from his own body, lost in a no-man's-land of nothingness,

and now he had come upon himself again, sitting on
this seat in the autumn sun, with the overgrown garden
all around him, smelling of mint and marigolds and
apples eaten-out by wasps.

'What is it?' Linn asked, finding him sitting there
so still.

'I was thinking of Grannie Izzard,' he said, 'and
how she used to tend this garden.'

'Are you coming in to breakfast?'

'Might as well, if you've got it ready.'

He was reluctant to tell her that the last of his sight
had gone completely. It would only grieve her. But
Linn knew without being told, and she took his arm to
lead him indoors.

Betony often called at the Pikehouse. She brought
him a white-painted walking-stick and a whistle for
him to hang round his neck. She brought things, too,
ready for the baby.

'No more visits from the police?'

'No. Nothing.'

'I was thinking,' she said once. 'It might be as well if
you were to see a solicitor. Great-grumpa's man, perhaps, young Mr Hay. I would go with you if you like.'

'But I ent done nothing,' Tom said.

'Think about it all the same, if the police come
pestering you again.'

'I reckon it's all blowing over now,' he said.

But a few days later, on the fifteenth, the two policemen came again.

'Is it news of Tilly?' Tom asked.

'I'm afraid not, Mr Maddox. There's been no re-
sponse to our poster so far, nor to our enquiries. But
I'd like to ask a few further questions. What, for instance, was Mrs Maddox wearing the day she left
home?'

'I dunno. I wasn't here.'

'But what about in the morning, early, before you
went to work? Can you recall what she wore then?'

'She was in bed when I left the house.'

'And you did say, I believe, that she left no clothes
behind her?'

'Not a stitch,' Tom said. 'Is that all you wanted to know?'

'Unless there's something more you'd like to tell me.'

'No, there's nothing,' Tom said.

Darns turned to Linn.

'Were you acquainted with Mrs Maddox?'

'No,' Linn said, 'I never saw her in my life.'

'Would you mind telling me your name, Mrs—?'

'Mercybright,' Linn said, 'but it's Miss not Mrs.'

'May I ask what relation you are to Mr Maddox?'

'It's none of your business!' Tom said.

'I don't mind answering,' Linn said. 'We live together as man and wife.'

'Thank you,' Darns said. 'It's always a help when people are perfectly frank with us. Were you acquainted with Mr Maddox before his wife disappeared?'

'Yes. I was.'

'How long after her departure did you come and take her place as it were.'

'About a week,' Linn said, and met the man's gaze with only the slightest change of colour.

'I'm just wondering,' Tom said, 'if I ought to see a solicitor.'

'And what do you think he would do for you, Mr Maddox?'

'I dunno,' Tom said. "I dunno what they ever do. Somebody said it, that's all.'

'I shouldn't worry, Mr Maddox. Not yet, anyway.'

'What do you mean, not yet?'

But Darns and his constable left without another word.

Betony, hearing of this visit, became very angry.

'That settles it!' she said. 'I'm going to Birmingham to look for Tilly.'

'There's no point in that,' Tom said. 'If the police can't find her, what chance have you?'

'Perhaps they're not trying hard enough.'

'They've got posters out, or so they told me.'

'I'm going there all the same.'

But although she spent two whole days in Birmingham, tramping all the busiest streets, asking at shops and boardinghouses, she learnt nothing. 'We've been asked already,' a shopkeeper told her. 'The police've been round trying to find that same young woman.' And she saw the posters everywhere, asking for Mrs Tilly Maddox, of the Pikehouse, Eastery, near Chepsworth, to present herself at the nearest police station, as her next of kin were anxious about her.

At the Bruno Brush Company in Hall Street, however, Betony discovered an interesting fact: that the travelling salesman, Arthur Trimble, had left their employ at a day's notice on September twenty-ninth and had talked of taking his family to London. His wife, it seemed, had relations there. Her uncle was offering him a job.

Betony returned home and went to the Pikehouse. She found Tom alone, for Linn had gone up to Eastery, to see the midwife, Mrs Gibbs.

'September twenty-ninth! Don't you see? It means Trimble left Brum immediately after Emery Preston had asked him questions about Tilly. So obviously he must have been mixed up with her, just as you said, and was frightened his wife might hear about it.'

'We're still no nearer finding Tilly.'

'No, she probably parted from Trimble quite soon, and she might be anywhere by now. But at least the police must know all this. They'll know he went off in a terrible hurry and they'll draw the same conclusions as I have done.'

'I hope you're right,' Tom said.

'Of course I'm right!' she exclaimed, and went on to talk of her wedding instead. 'Will you be coming, you and Linn?'

'Better not,' he said, undoing knots in a piece of string. 'What with her being pretty near her time, and the things folk're saying in Huntlip at present, we'd only spoil it if we was there.'

'You could come to Cobbs, though, afterwards. Dicky could fetch you in the trap.'

'Better not,' he said again. 'We ent really wanted there, Linn and me.'

'*I* want you,' Betony said, 'or I wouldn't be asking.' But she knew he was wise to keep away. Only Dicky and her mother accepted him now. To the rest of the family he was an outcast.

'All right,' she said. 'I won't press you if you'd rather not come. But I hope my present is ready in time!'

'It will be,' he said. 'There ent a lot to do on it now.' He was making her a wickerwork chair. 'Jack comes out to watch me at it, so's I don't make janders of it, but that'll be ready in time, you'll see. Honest John! as William always used to say.'

Often, when he was unable to sleep, he would lie on his back, utterly still, afraid of disturbing Linn beside him. He would think of things to make himself sleepy, such as counting the cost of his osier rods, and the profit remaining when he sold his baskets. Sometimes he was back at Etaples during inspection, going over in his mind all the items laid out before him. Respirator. Field-dressings. Iron rations. Mess-tin, water-bottle, Tommy's cooker. Rifle, ammunition, ground-sheet.

Then the names would start coming. Newers. Ritchie. Glover. Braid. Danson. Evans. Privitt. Rush. Until, in a state between waking and sleeping, he wandered alone in a vast empty space, over ground much cratered by shells and mines, looking for men he knew were lost, while a voice kept whispering in his ear: Where are they? Where are they? Where are they *gone?*

Often Linn herself was awake, because of the baby moving inside her, or because she sensed his wakefulness. She had nursed many men during the war; had heard them groaning, sobbing, swearing; had held them, writhing, in her arms while they screamed out the substance of their nightmares. But Tom never tossed about in bed; never moaned or screamed; he lay quite still and silent always, and if she turned her head on the pillow, she would find that his eyes were wide open, twitching a little now and then, intent, it seemed, though they saw nothing.

'Tom? Can't you sleep? Is your head hurting?'

'It's throbbing a bit, but nothing much.'

'What were you thinking about?' she asked.

'Oh, this and that. Nothing special. It's harder to sleep, you know, now that day and night are the same.'

But sleep when it did come was often pure and sweet and clean, and sometimes his dreams were happy ones.

'I was up on Lippy Hill and the sun was shining. The berries was red on the rowan trees, and there was dozens of thrushes there, mostly gathered on just one tree. I had a little lad with me. He brought me some berries that the thrushes had shook down onto the ground and he showed them to me in his two hands.'

'What did he look like?' Linn asked. 'Perhaps he was our son.'

'I never properly saw his face. Just the berries in his hands. Then we was sitting on a little hummock and all the rabbits was out playing. It was evening time. Still and warm. And some of the rabbits came so close, they was eating right between our feet, mine and the boy's, as we sat on the hummock side by side.'

Tom was lighting the fire for breakfast. He liked to be able to do these things, and Linn, though she watched, never interfered. He was always careful, handling the matches, and the fire was always beautifully laid.

'The berries was just as red as red, and the thrushes was yellow, with great fluffed-up chests speckled all over as smart as you please.'

He put a match to the laid fire and it crackled up. He crouched before it, the light of it flickering in his eyes.

'It's a funny thing, but I ent never blind in my dreams,' he said.

One morning, early, when Linn was shaving him and trimming his hair, she thought she heard a dog barking, somewhere in the woods across the road.

'It's probably MacNab's spaniel,' Tom said. 'Maybe he's out after rabbits.'

At half-past-nine, Jimmy Winger's milk-float stopped at the gate, and Linn went out with the quart jug.

'I see you got company,' Jimmy said, and pointed to a car drawn up on the grass at the edge of the woods. 'The police are rooting about in there. I seen 'em as I came round past Tyson's. What're they up to, do you reckon?'

'Haven't you heard the gossip, Jimmy?'

'I might've done,' Jimmy said. 'But I wouldn't stand for it if I was you. There should be a law against policemen.'

Jimmy had once been fined ten shillings for riding his bicycle without lights. Policemen were worse than game-keepers and needed something better to do.

'I'll lend you a loan of my shotgun if you like, so's you can send 'em packing,' he said, 'and if I should meet one of 'em on the road, I shall let old Twinkler ride him down!'

When Jimmy had gone, Linn stood looking towards the woods, but could see no sign of the searchers there. Only, once, she thought she heard the same dog barking, somewhere deep among the trees.

648

She said nothing to Tom about it, but later in the morning another car drew up behind the first, and four policemen in uniform got out. One of them sounded a blast on the horn and after a while the first party emerged from the wood. Detective-Inspector Darns was among them. There were seven men altogether, one of them with a wolfhound on a leash, and they all stood talking for about five minutes. Then the new-comers went to their car and each took a spade and a sack from the dicky. All seven vanished together among the trees.

'What's the commotion?' Tom asked.

'The police are searching the woods,' she said.

His face became bleak. He stood as though turned to stone. Linn went to him and took hold of his arm.

At one o'clock, the searchers assembled at the edge of the wood and sat on the grass, eating sandwiches and drinking tea from vacuum flasks. Tom went across to them, using his white walking-stick and making to-wards the sound of their voices, but they stopped talk-ing as he drew near, and he stood in the roadway, hesitating. Darns got up and went to him.

'Yes, Mr Maddox, did you want me?'

'What d'you hope to find in there?'

'What are you afraid we'll find?'

'You're wasting your time. You won't find nothing.'

'Then there's no need for you to be worried.'

'Who said I was worried?'

Tom turned and walked back home, very slowly, counting the paces. Darns went and sat on the running-board of the first car, and one of the uniformed con-stables offered him a cigarette.

'Is he as blind as he seems, that chap?'

'What a suspicious mind you've got, Ryelands. You're very nearly as bad as me.'

'You got any intuitions, sir, one way or the other?'

'Not reliable ones,' Darns said. 'But if he has done his missus in, well, the sight of us turning the place upside down may well poke a chink or two in that armour of his.'

Towards the end of the afternoon, when the searchers

again mustered on the turnpike, they found they had an audience there: three women and a man, all elderly, who had wandered down from Eastery.

'Is it true,' the old man asked, 'that you've found a grave in them there woods?'

'No, it's not true,' Darns said.

'What *have* you found?'

'I'm afraid I can't answer any questions.'

'Then they ent found nothing,' the old man said to the three women. 'I knowed it was all a pack of lies.'

'Who spread these rumours?' Darns asked.

'Not me, not me!' the old man said.

'Have you got permission to search them woods?' one of the women asked Darns. 'Have you spoken to Mrs Lannam?'

'Yes, and we've got a warrant,' Darns said.

'What, signed by the king and his chancellors?'

'Move away, please!' a constable said. 'Can't you see we're trying to turn?'

As the first car moved off, back towards Huntlip, a tall figure came striding down the field-path from Eastery and stepped out into the road. It was the Reverend Peter Chance, vicar of Eastery-with-Scoate, a big man with a shock of white hair, and he stood waving the car to a standstill.

'What is the meaning of this?' he asked, stooping to speak to Darns through the window. 'Why are you persecuting Tom Maddox? Has he done something wrong? Is there any truth in these wild rumours?'

'It's our job to find out, vicar.'

'Have you questioned the boy? Does he admit harming his wife?'

'People don't generally admit such things, until they're obliged to,' Darns said.

'If he denies it, I'm quite sure he's speaking the truth.'

'But just supposing he isn't, vicar?'

'Then God will punish him, without a doubt.'

'I'm afraid that won't satisfy the law.'

'The law takes too much on itself in these matters. Revenge belongs to God alone. "Thou shalt not kill," the commandment says, and it makes no exception of any kind. The hanging of murderers is therefore wrong.'

'It has one advantage,' Darns said. 'It stops them doing it again.'

He motioned the constable to drive on.

The next day, Saturday the twenty-fifth, was cloudy and dull and rather cold. Tom stepped outside as always, first thing, and stood for a while sniffing the air. The wind was blowing from the northwest.

'Betony's wedding day,' he said, 'and it smells like rain.'

'What time is the wedding?'

'Two o'clock this afternoon. If we listen carefully we may hear the bells, though it ent very likely with the wind as it is.'

'It's certainly a dark old day,' Linn said, 'but perhaps it'll brighten by this afternoon.'

At ten o'clock two cars turned into the old turnpike and parked as before on the wide grass verge. Linn went to the gate and saw the policemen go into the wood. There were five altogether, four in uniform, one in plain clothes. Inspector Darns was not among them.

Linn for once was filled with hatred. She wanted to rush out after the men and pummel them. She wanted to strike their cheerful faces and see them crumple. She wished she and Tom could run away.

'Is it them?' he asked, when she went indoors.

'They're deadly determined, I'll say that, when they once get a notion in their heads.'

'Why must they stop just opposite? They could just as well stop in Tyson's lane.'

'They want me to know they're there,' he said. 'They want to scare me and whittle me down.'

'You mustn't let them,' Linn said.

'I shan't, don't worry. But I wish it was over all the same.'

By eleven o'clock, there was a gathering on the turnpike road of people from Eastery, Huntlip, Middening, and Blagg. Two newspaper men drove out from Chepsworth and took a photograph of the Pikehouse. They talked to all the local people. Emery Preston came with his sons, the four of them packed onto Matthew's motor-cycle and sidecar, so that when Darns arrived at half-past-eleven he was appalled at the gathering crowd. He turned to Penfold.

'Send these people about their business! What the hell do they think this is?'

'I'm taking no orders from you, young fella,' an Eastery man said to Penfold. 'You ent even wearing a uniform.'

But the crowd moved off eventually. The newspaper men drove away. Only the Prestons lingered on.

'Mr Preston,' Darns said. 'I must ask you to take yourself off and your sons with you. You've got no business hanging about here like this.'

'It's *my* daughter you're looking for, remember, and I aim to give you a helping hand.'

'Enter those woods,' Darns said, 'and I'll have you placed under arrest.'

'Why, what've you found, for God's sake?'

'Nothing whatever so far, Mr Preston, but I'm in charge of this investigation and I will not tolerate interference.'

'You can't turn me off the road, however. I've got a right to stand here if I so choose and so've my boys.'

'I thought you had a public house to manage.'

'My cousin's looking after that. I've got more important business here.'

'Was it you that summoned those reporters?'

'What if it was? People got a right to know what's happening.'

'We don't even know if anything *has* happened, Mr Preston.'

'No, nor you never will, neither,' Emery said, 'if you don't shift yourselves better than this!'

Darns and Penfold turned away. Their work was often distasteful to them.

'I reckon he'd *like* it,' Penfold muttered, 'if we *were* to dig up his daughter's body.'

The day remained darkly overcast, and from midday onwards a small rain fell, light but drenching. Emery

Preston and his three boys took shelter just inside the wood, staring across at the tiny Pikehouse, where firelight flickered at the window and smoke blew downwards from the chimney.

'Sitting comfortably by his fire!—The murdering bastard!' Emery said, and turned his collar up to his ears.

At one o'clock, when Darns thought of cancelling further search, Penfold came to him with a cotton scarf, found in the deeper part of the wood, among the oaks and breeches. It had lain in the undergrowth a long time; its printed pattern was almost gone; and it had a dark brown stain upon it that could have been blood.

Penfold had marked the place of its finding, and Darns went with him to look around. Many trees had been felled during the war. Their stumps were still pale and clean-looking, and heaps of brushwood still lay around. Darns gave orders for the search to continue. He wanted the heaps of brushwood moved. Then he and Penfold went to speak to Emery Preston. They showed him the scarf, carefully folded with the stain inside.

'Have you ever seen this before, Mr Preston?'

'Seen it? Yes. It belonged to Tilly.'

'Are you sure of that?'

'How sure must I be? She had one like it. That's all I can say. I bought it myself at the Christmas bazaar last year.' Emery looked from one to the other. He swallowed hard. 'Did you find anything else besides?'

'Nothing else, Mr Preston, and the scarf of course means very little. Your daughter could have dropped it at any time, if she happened to take a walk in the woods.'

'Tilly never walked if she could help it. Not by herself, at any rate.'

'I think we'll have a word with Mr Maddox,' Darns said to Penfold.

'About time too!' Emery said. 'I'll come with you.'

'No, Mr Preston. You'll return home.'

'I ent budging till it damn well suits me, so you might as well get used to the fact.'

'Please yourself,' Darns said, 'but you're not seeing Maddox.'

When Linn let them in, Tom was sitting at the table, finishing a meal of bread and cheese. He pushed back his chair a little way and crossed his legs. Darns put the scarf into his hands.

'We found that in the woods, Mr Maddox. Can you tell us anything about it?'

'I dunno what it is, do I? I can't see it.' Tom felt the scarf between his fingers. 'Is it a handkerchief?' he asked.

'It's a cheap cotton scarf, Mr Maddox, printed red and white, with a stripe at the edge and spots in the middle. Did your wife have such a scarf?'

'I dunno. I don't remember.'

'Mr Preston said she did.'

'Maybe she did, then. He ought to know. Why ask me if he's already told you?'

'It appears to be stained with blood,' Darns said. 'Does that help you remember?'

'It ent Tilly's blood, if that's what you mean. It's the blood of a dog that got catched in a trap.'

'So you do remember the scarf, after all?'

'Yes,' Tom said. 'It's coming back. Charley Bailey was out after rabbits and his dog, Shorty, got catched in a trap. Charley called on me to help and I took that scarf to tie the dog's leg with.'

'But the scarf has just been found in the woods.'

'Shorty must've shook it off.'

'Laboratory tests will show whether the blood on that scarf came from a dog or a human being.'

'If there's human blood on it,' Tom said, 'that'll be mine, not Tilly's, 'cos Shorty took a bite out of my hand when I was trying to get him free.'

'Mr Maddox,' Darns said, 'I'd like you to come with us to the police station.'

'Why?' Linn demanded, stepping between them. 'Why does he have to come with you?'

'He's not obliged to,' Darns said. 'I'm asking for his co-operation.'

'What if I don't?' Tom said. 'What if I refuse to go?' He was very pale.

'It's only for questioning, Mr Maddox.'

'Why can't you ask your questions here?'

'Yes! Why can't you?' Linn exclaimed. 'He's blind and helpless. Why do you have to take him away?'

'It's customary procedure,' Darns said. 'A refusal could constitute an obstruction of the law.'

'But you said he wasn't obliged to go!'

'It's like the Army,' Tom said. 'Our N.C.O's used to say to us, "I want volunteers for a listening party— you five in front will suit me fine!" ' He got up and went to the door. He felt for his jacket and put it on. 'I'm ready,' he said, and stood waiting.

'Can I come with him?' Linn asked.

'I don't advise it,' Darns said.

'No more don't I!' Tom said. 'That won't do no good at all.' His hand rested on Linn's arm. 'You stop at home and don't worry. You must think of the baby— you mustn't let yourself get upset. They'll bring me back. You'll see.'

'But when? When? How long will it take, asking these questions?'

She was looking at Darns, and he found it difficult to meet her gaze.

'It all depends. But we'll let you know if any developments occur.'

'What d'you mean, developments? What developments *could* there be?'

'Come along, Mr Maddox,' Darns said.

'I asked you a question!' Linn said, following them out along the path. 'What developments do you mean?'

'Please! Linn!' Tom said, in distress. 'Don't fret yourself. You must take it easy.'

'Tom, I'm afraid! I don't think you ought to be going with them.'

'Don't be afraid. They can't hurt me. They're just hoping I'll let something slip. You go indoors out of the rain and don't worry. I promise you I'll be all right.'

But Linn continued to stand in the garden, her hands clenched in the pockets of her apron, watching as they led him away.

Outside when they got to the car, the Prestons were waiting.

'Are you arresting him?' Emery asked.

'No, we're not!' Darns said, snapping. 'He's coming to the station of his own free will. He's agreed to answer some further questions.'

'But you will be arresting him when you get there?'

'Out of the way, please, and let us pass.'

They got into the car and drove off, and Emery was left swearing. He hurried over to the motor-cycle and sidecar.

'Come on, you three. There's no sense in waiting here. Matthew, you can drop us off at home first, then go on to Chepsworth, to the police station. I want to know what happens next.'

'But I ent even had my dinner yet!'

'You can buy yourself a sandwich when you get to Chepsworth. But mind you remember what I said!— Don't come away till you know what they're doing with Tom Maddox!' And Emery, waiting while Matthew adjusted his goggles, looked back to where Linn still stood in the rain. 'She should think herself lucky they've took him away, before he turned nasty and done for her like he done for our Tilly.'

Matthew stepped hard on the starter and the engine roared. They drove off towards Huntlip. Behind them, in the woods of Scoate House Manor, the police search continued.

Linn, going back into the kitchen, was struck by its look of emptiness. Tom's chair set sideways at the table; his dinner plate with its few crumbs; his empty teacup askew in its saucer: these things cried out to her like ghosts, and she could scarcely bear to see them.

Sitting upright on the settle, she made herself breathe very deeply and slowly, till the tightness eased from around her heart. She wished with a kind of sick longing that her father were with her, for she felt, as she had always felt in childhood, that he would know just what to do. So intense was her longing that she sprang up and went to the window, convinced she had heard his step on the path. But she was mistaken. He was not there. She knew she would have to go to him.

She got up and put on her coat. She drew a shawl over her head. She stepped into her rubber galoshes. The clock on the mantelpiece said five to two. She went out into the rain.

At Cobbs, when the clock on the workshop roof struck the hour, a crow took off from the weathervane and left it swivelling against the wind. Jesse stood at the parlour window. He watched the crow flying off towards Anster.

'That's two o'clock striking. We're going to be desperate late, ent we?'

'A bride is expected to arrive late. Granna said so. It's the done thing.'

Betony smiled at him, seeing him frowning at his watch. She went forward and took it from him, and slipped it into his waistcoat pocket, where it belonged. She held his hands between her own, to keep them from fidgeting with his collar and tie.

'Just look at that rain!' he said to her. 'That vexes me so's I could bost! Why did you have to choose October?'

'Today is my birthday. I'm twenty-four. It seemed as good a day as any. What does a drop of rain matter?'

'It'll spoil your dress. That's why it matters. Now where's that cloak you're going to put on?'

'It's here, handy, on the back of the chair.'

'Do I look all right in this new suit? Is my parting properly straight? Have I shaved myself nicely, would you say?'

He got his hands free and touched his hair, which was well greased down and shone like straw. He touched his chin, feeling critically for traces of stubble.

'You look very handsome,' Betony said, 'and far too young to be my father.'

'The church'll be crowded. D'you realize that? Folk have been going up forever. I seen 'em as early as twelve noon.'

'I hope there's room for them all to sit.'

'There won't be,' he said. 'No lections of that! A lot'll be standing about outside. The rain won't stop them. You mark my words.'

He turned from her to the dining-table, extended as far as it would go, caparisoned in a white damask cloth, and already spread with the wedding breakfast.

'There's cold roast venison. Have you seen it? Mrs Andrews sent it yesterday.' He took up a spoon and polished it on his jacket sleeve. 'Of course,' he said, 'the men'll be eating in the kitchen.'

'The men from the workshop, do you mean?'

'The table in the kitchen's more fuller than this one. Your mother and granna have worked very hard, and your sister, too.'

'I suppose *you'll* be eating in the kitchen, then, seeing you're a carpenter just like them? Dicky, too, and great-grumpa.'

'Not us! Laws, no! Not the bride's own family!' And, turning away from her teasing glance, he said: 'The men'll be happier, keeping theirselves to theirselves out there. They wouldn't be properly come-for-double, mixing with the captain and his mother and all the guests on *their* side.'

'Michael will see that they mix,' she said, 'and so shall I.'

'Glory be, just look at the time! Where d'you think that boy can've got to?'

'It's only five minutes past, father. Try and relax and stop fussing.'

'That's all very well,' Jesse muttered. 'We should've hired another carriage. Ent I been saying so all along?'

Michael and his mother, with his uncle and aunt from Ilton Lye, and his best man, Major Peter Thomas, had gone to the church in the King's Hill carriage, with a King's Hill servant in livery driving. The Cobbs family had gone in the trap, and Dicky was returning for the bride and her father.

'What's the betting Duffer's cast a shoe?' Jesse said. 'Or gone lame, even. It's always at times like this, ent it?'

A door slammed at the back of the house, and Jesse snatched up Betony's cloak.

'Here he is! Here he is! Better late than never, I suppose.' And as Dicky burst into the room: 'Good heavens, boy, how's it you've been so long a-coming?'

'It's Tom!' Dicky said. 'The police've took him away to Chepsworth.'

'Who told you that?' Betony asked.

'I seen it my own-self. They drove past me as I came from the church. They'd got Tom sitting in the back of the motor.'

'Didn't you stop them and ask why?'

'There wasn't no chance,' Dicky said. 'By the time I realized what was happening, the motor-car had gone right past. I did draw up straight away and while I was stuck there, wondering what I ought to do, the Prestons came up on that motor-cycle. Seems they was out at the Pikehouse all morning and saw our Tom get took away.'

'Did they say he'd been arrested?'

'No, they didn't say that, or not exactly.'

'What *did* they say, for God's sake?'

'They said he'd got what was coming to him. They said we'd be reading it in the papers.'

'What about Linn?' Betony assked.

'Left at home,' Dicky said.

'Laws!' Jesse said, looking anxiously at Betony. 'That this should happen on your wedding day! Was ever anything so unlucky?' He felt he could scarcely look at Dicky. If only the boy had had the sense to keep the news until after the wedding! 'Never mind, my blossom. Try not to let it spoil your day.' He moved towards her with the cloak.

Betony was staring at the clock in the middle of the mantelpiece. Her mind worked with great clarity. The wedding ceremony would take perhaps an hour and a

half. It would all be over by four o'clock. Not very
long, she told herself, if she went from the church immediately afterwards. And yet it was *too* long. Some
part of her said so. Some part of her had already settled all the questions.

In fancy now she saw Michael's face as he waited
for her inside the church. He seemed to know what she
was thinking; his grey eyes were worried, intent on
hers; he was asking her to come to him. Then she saw
Tom's face, his eyes deep and dark and hollow-looking,
staring past her, asking nothing.

'Come on, my blossom,' Jesse said. 'We're late
enough as it is already.'

'No, dad, I'm not going. The wedding will have to be
postponed.'

'Postponed? Are you mad? You surely can't mean
it! It's out of all reason!'

'You'll have to go to the church and tell them. I'll
drop you there on my way to Chepsworth. But first
I must go and change my dress.'

'Betony, no!' he said, outraged, and stepped in front
of her, barring the way. 'You can't go and do a thing
like that! Think of all the people waiting! Think of the
captain and Mrs Andrews! What in God's name are
they going to say?'

'Don't you care what happens to Tom?'

'I care all right. A whole lot more'n he deserves.
But what can you do to help matters?'

'There must be something I can do.'

'Well, afterwards, then, when it's all over. We can
go and see about it then.'

'No, father, I'm going now.'

'I don't understand you!' Jesse said, following her
out across the hall. 'I don't know how you can do
such a thing! I'd never've believed it! You of all people—my favourite daughter!' He continued to shout
at her as she hurried upstairs. 'What if the captain
don't forgive you? I'm sure I shouldn't, in his
place! I shan't forgive you anyway!—You're making
us a byword in this village, you and Tom between you.'

When Betony descended again, having changed into

an ordinary dress, her father sat on the bottom stair
and Dicky stood over him, arguing with him. Jesse's
face was averted from her. He had never been angry
in his life till today. She could see he was sick with
disappointment.

'I ent going to the church to tell them. You needn't
think it.'

'Then Dicky must go instead,' she said.

'That's up to him. I can't stop him. My children take
no account of me.'

'If you won't go to the church, will you go to the
Pikehouse and see Linn? She must be worried out of
her mind.'

'Not me. Oh, no! That young woman is nothing to
me. I'm just stopping where I am.'

'Come on, Dicky,' Betony said, and Dicky followed
her out to the trap.

Driving briskly through Huntlip, they passed little
knots of villagers, who turned and stared as the trap
went past them. Further on, when they got to the
green, she could see the people gathered in the churchyard, standing under the yews and birches, sheltering
from the rain. The bells were ringing out loud, and the
rooks, disturbed, were floating in circles round the
tower. Betony stopped to let Dicky down, then she
drove on towards Chepsworth.

Linn walked as fast as her heavily burdened body
would allow. She tried to keep fear from clawing at her
mind. It was three miles by road from the Pikehouse to
Huntlip, and another two and a half from Huntlip to
Blagg, but by taking the footpath to Millery Bridge
and the old drove road over Puppet Hill, she was able
to cut off a mile.

The rain was now a steady downpour, and she felt
glad of it, soaked though she was, for it meant her
father would surely be at home, sitting with his leg up,
beside the fire. He hated wet days, for his bad knee
became swollen and caused him much pain, and only
the heat of a good fire brought him any measure of
relief.

So strong was her faith that he would be there, reading his paper and smoking his pipe, that when she found the cottage empty she stood for a moment in shocked disbelief. A terrible weakness flooded through her, and a great anger. Why couldn't he be there when he was needed? What business had taken him out of his home on a wet Saturday in October? A boy scaring birds in the field below came to the hedge and gave her the answer.

'Mr Mercybright's gone to Upham. The master sent him to look at a boar.'

'How long'll he be, Godwin, do you know?'

'He said he'd be home by six o'clock. He said for me to light his fire and he'd give me tea when he got in. He generally does on Saturdays.'

'Then I'll write him a message,' Linn said.

She went into the cottage and sat for a while, shivering in her wet clothes. She felt sick and giddy, hot and cold at the same time, and pain burnt in the small of her back, as though her spine were splitting and breaking. She thought of putting a match to the fire; of resting and warming herself for an hour; even waiting for her father; but she was afraid the police might return with Tom to the Pikehouse and that he would be worried at finding her gone. Or, she thought, they might call to say he had been arrested. So she got up, found paper and pencil and wrote her message, and went out again into the rain.

Just past the farm, at a bend in the lane, where it was narrow, she had to stand aside for a herd of bullocks. They had just come down from Puppet Hill, and the man in charge of them, Frank Kendrick, was driving them too fast down the steep track. Linn, though she pressed herself close into the hedge, was bumped and buffeted several times and had to hold tight to a hawthorn branch to avoid being spun out into the lane and trampled under the cloven hooves. But the last bullock lumbered by, and Frank Kendrick came panting behind, his stick on his shoulder, his dog at his heels.

'Bloody cattle!' he said as he passed. 'I could shoot them sometimes. I could. Honest.'

Linn walked on, up the steep track and through the wicket, out onto the open hill. At the top of the rise she stopped to rest, leaning with her back against a tree, her hands on her stomach, seeking to still the throbbing there; seeking assurance that all was well within her womb. Then, having felt her child moving vigorously under her hand, she walked on over the hill.

All the way along Cricketers Lane, where the horse-chestnut trees hung over the hedge, the ground was strewn with the fallen chestnuts, bursting out of their spiky shells. Passing that way earlier she had met not a soul, but now a ragged figure crouched there, shuffling along low on his haunches, the skirts of his overcoat trailing in the mud. Although a man of forty or more, Jumper Lane had the face of a schoolboy, smooth-skinned and pink, with little arched brows over eyes a brilliant china blue. He looked at Linn with a gap-toothed smile and sprang upright, showing her the chestnuts crammed to the tops of his overcoat pockets.

'Yes, Jumper, they're beautiful. You're going to be busy, collecting all these.'

'Look at this one!' he said, and snatched up a chestnut still in its skin, pressing it open to show her the dark-shining nut inside. 'Look at *this* one and *this* one and *this* one and *this!*'

He was shuffling after her, stooping repeatedly to snatch up the chestnuts, then jumping up to thrust them at her.

'Yes, they're lovely,' Linn said. 'But I must hurry. I've got to get home.'

'No need to hurry. The clocks are slow. Stop and help me collect the conkers.'

'Not now, Jumper, I'm in a hurry.'

'You always used to play with me.'

'Not today, however. There's no time.'

'I shall tell on you if you don't stop. I know what you done. You're just as bad as Alice Quinton.'

And, blocking her way, he made his arms into a

cradle, rocking slowly from side to side and uttering croodling noises in his throat. Then, his whole body squirming suddenly, he leapt high into the air, his knees going up like the blades of a jack-knife.

'Can't be helped! Can't be helped! What's done is done and can't be undone!'

'Please let me pass, Jumper,' Linn said. 'I'm tired and wet and I want to get home.'

'Not till you let me have my way. I ent so simple as you seem to think.'

'If you don't let me pass I shall speak to your auntie, Mrs Tupper, and tell her you were behaving badly. You won't like that, now, will you, Jumper?'

'Play conkers, then. I'll thread one for you.'

'I told you before. I haven't got time.'

She had never been frightened of Jumper Lane. There was no harm in him beyond a boisterous playfulness and the lewdness he learnt at The Rose and Crown. She was not frightened even now but she couldn't get past him and tiredness was bringing her close to tears. She made a great effort to keep her composure.

'Look here, Jumper, what about seeing me half way home? I'm passing not far from your Auntie Tupper's. We can walk together as far as the bridge.'

'All right,' he said. 'But people will talk, you know. People will say I'm to blame for the babby.'

'Never mind. Talk never hurts us, does it, Jumper?'

'They was asking me at the public once if I was to blame for getting Alice into trouble. But I ent saying. Oh, no, not me! I ent so green as I'm cabbage-looking.'

Walking beside her along the lane, he kept kicking the chestnuts and leaves on the ground, but now and then he would turn towards her, putting both hands on her right arm and giving it a hard squeeze. He was plainly enjoying his walk with her.

'My auntie's got a mangle. She lets me turn the handle for her. She gives me a penny if I don't turn it backwards.'

'You're always very good to your auntie. I've heard people say so oftentimes.'

'I want watching, though. I'm a dark horse. Joe Wilkes says I'm as sly as the devil. He wouldn't leave his missus with me for five minutes. He said it hisself. So did she.'

'People talk a lot of rubbish.'

'They do, they do, they want sewing up!' Jumper said. 'They want their gobs stopped, that's what I say.'

On reaching the stile at the playing-field, he vaulted over in a single bound, slithering a little in the mud. Linn followed, slowly and awkwardly, and Jumper watched her in some concern.

'The trouble is, you've gone too fat. You're as fat as a landlady, that's what you are. Now, easy does it, that's the ticket. Easy and over and down and round.'

He reached for her hand to help her down, but the moment his fingers closed on hers, he was seized by a sudden spasm of mischief.

'Statues!' he said, and pulled her headlong off the stile, so that she fell with great force, face forward onto the ground.

The pain was worse than anything she had ever experienced. The scream of it echoed on and on, in her mind and her body, shrilling along every nerve. She thought she was going to lose her senses, but she lay on her side in the long wet grass and fixed gaze on a marguerite that hung, drenched with rain, about eighteen inches from her face. She made herself think of it, concentrating with all her will, focussing on it until she could see every clean white petal sprouting from the yellow middle. And after a moment the faintness passed. But the whole of her body shrieked with pain. It was spreading out from the core of her being, where her child lay coiled like a spring in her womb. It made her powerless to move.

Jumper was bending over her, trying to look into her face. His big clumsy hands were locked together.

'I never done it! Oh, no not me! She was climbing the stile and she tumbled off. It's not Jumper's fault she went such a whomper. He warnt nowhere near the playing-field.'

He ran off, whimpering, back along Cricketers Lane, plunging his hands into his pockets and scattering the chestnuts as he went.

When Linn got up, raising herself little by little, he had vanished completely. It was useless calling him back to help her. He would be at the marlpits by now, or even at Outlands, hiding in one of the farm buildings. She stood for a time holding on to the bar of the stile, waiting while the sickness ebbed and flowed; waiting till her sight no longer rippled. Then she went on her way, across the playing-field and out at the gate by Millery Bridge.

Every step she took was a step homewards. Pain must not be allowed to matter. The sensible thing, as she well knew, was to turn into Huntlip and ask for help. Fifty yards off, if she turned left, there was a row of cottages, but she shrank from the thought of appealing to strangers. In half a mile, if she turned right, she would come to Cobbs where she was known, but there, she thought, the wedding party would be under way and her arrival would spoil it all. So she crossed the main street of the village and took the path up through Millery Wood.

But now a new kind of pain took hold of her, and she stood still, as though listening to it, as though her stillness would smooth it away. It was different from the pain she was already suffering: it was one sort of pain underlying another: the sudden clenching of a savage fist and the the slow, reluctant unclenching, leaving nausea in its wake. There was also a terrible liquid warmth and she knew that the waters protecting her child in the womb were breaking and moving.

But if animals could hold back their young without any harm coming to them, then so could she, for her will was surely as strong as theirs? And she went on steadily as before, up the steep slopes of Millery Wood, over the open fields at Peckstone, out onto the Norton road. When the pains came she stood quite still, gripping the fence with both hands, breathing great deep measured breaths. Fear and pain were working together. They would pluck her down if her strength failed, and she would be like a hare in its form or a vixen creeping into its hole.

'Please, God,' she whispered, 'don't let my baby be born at the roadside.'

The Pikehouse was as empty as when she had left it, the fire dying on the hearth. She took a white sheet from a drawer, went out to the garden, and pegged it securely on the line. It was a signal to the midwife, Mrs Gibbs, who lived in a cottage near Eastery church. The cottage could not be seen from the Pikehouse because it was hidden among the trees; nor could the Pikehouse be seen from the cottage; but if Mrs Gibbs stepped out to the churchyard and looked down between the two elms as she had promised to do every morning and evening, she would see the signal very plainly.

Linn went in and closed the door. She reached for the bellows to revive the fire. But then, since darkness was not very far away, she lit the lamp with the pink-frosted shade, took it upstairs into the bedroom and placed it in the window facing towards Eastery church.

'Please, God,' she said, as she turned up the flame, 'make Mrs Gibbs step out to the churchyard.'

She went downstairs again into the kitchen, to rebuild the fire and shed her wet clothes. The pains were coming more frequently now. Fear could no longer be shut out.

When Betony arrived at the Chepsworth police station, she found Matthew Preston sitting on a form in the main hall.

'What are you doing here?'

'My father sent me. He said to wait and see what's happening.'

'Isn't your father satisfied with the trouble he's caused already?'

'It ent my dad that's caused the trouble. It's him in there—Tom Maddox.'

'Tom never hurt anyone in his life.'

'The police don't think that. Or why've they got him in there?'

'Why indeed!' Betony said.

At the desk in the hall sat a uniformed sergeant, writing in a ledger and drinking a cup of tea at the same time. He stopped writing and looked at Betony over his cup.

'Yes, miss?'

'I want to know why Mr Thomas Maddox is being held here.'

'Ah,' he said slowly, and put down his cup, looking at her with sharper interest. 'Are you some relation to the man Maddox?'

'*Mister* Maddox is my foster-brother.'

'And your name is?'

'Miss Betony Izzard.'

'Well, Miss Izzard, Mr Maddox is here to answer questions concerning the disappearance of his wife. Inspector Darns is in charge of the matter, and Constable Penfold is helping him.'

'I would like to see Inspector Darns.'

'I'm afraid that's impossible at the moment. The inspector is with Mr Maddox now and he won't relish being disturbed.'

'That's nothing to me. I insist that you tell the inspector I'm here. It's very important.'

'Very well, Miss Izzard, I'll send in a message as soon as I can.'

'When will that be? After you've had another cup of tea?'

'If you will kindly take a seat——'

'No, no. I'd sooner stand.'

She walked about the hall, reading the notices on the boards. The station was a big one, newly built. A corridor ran from the back of the hall, with five doors at either side. She watched people coming and going for a while, and, with growing impatience, returned to the desk.

'I've got a pony and trap outside. If I'm going to be kept waiting——'

'I'll get someone to see to it for you,' the sergeant said, and beckoned to a constable who was crossing from one door to another. 'There's a pony and trap outside, Simmonds. Drive it round to the stables, will you?'

'I'm obliged to you,' Betony said.

'All part of the service, miss.'

'Is it part of the service to keep a man in custody when he's done nothing at all to deserve it?'

'Mr Maddox is not in custody, miss. He came along of his own free will.'

'Did you send in my message to Inspector Darns?'

'Yes, miss, but I doubt if he'll see you for a while yet.'

'Which room are they in, out of all those?'

'Third on the left,' the sergeant said, and eyed Betony with some suspicion. 'You weren't thinking of just walking in, were you, miss?'

'I might,' she said, 'if I don't soon get satisfaction.'

'I wouldn't advise doing that, miss. It'll only draw things out that much longer. Why not sit down and wait patiently?'

'It's very important that I see Inspector Darns.'

But she went and sat on one of the forms, watched by Matthew Preston, sitting nearby.

The clock on the wall said ten past three. She thought it was probably rather slow but five minutes later the cathedral clock was striking the quarter. At twenty past four a man in plain clothes emerged from a door in the corridor and stood talking to the desk sergeant. Betony rose and went to him.

'Miss Izzard?' he said. 'I'm Detective-Constable Penfold. I gather you're enquiring for Mr Maddox.'

'How much longer do you intend keeping him here?'

'That depends on what he tells us.'

'And what has he told you so far?'

'Nothing much,' Penfold said, 'but it's often surprising what a man will tell us when he's been here for a few hours, and we've had time to wear him down.'

'Perhaps if you wear them down enough, they may even confess to things they've never done!' she said.

'That's hardly likely, Miss Izzard. We don't employ the thumbscrew, you know.'

'Tilly went off with a man named Trimble. Why don't you try finding him?'

'Arthur Trimble is proving elusive.'

'Exactly!' she said. 'Because he had an affair with Tilly and doesn't want his wife to know.'

'Not necessarily. People often take fright for nothing at all. But, of course, it may be that Trimble was indeed having an affair with Mrs Maddox and Mr Maddox took exception to it. In which case, if jealousy was the motive, and provocation could be proved, the charge would be manslaughter, not murder.'

'Aren't you being a little previous?'

'I was theorizing. Nothing more.'

'Mr Penfold,' she said. 'I want to see Inspector

Darns. There's something important I want to tell him.'

'Is it directly concerned with the case?'

'It's directly concerned with my foster-brother. That's all that matters to me. But it *is* important.'

'All right, Miss Izzard, I'll see what I can do.'

Penfold went along the corridor and back into the room on the left. He emerged again with an older man and they stood talking in quiet voices, glancing often in Betony's direction. Then they went off down the corridor and into a room at the far end. Betony took a few steps forward but the desk sergeant stood in her way. She returned in great anger to her seat against the wall.

'Take their time, don't they?' Matthew Preston said to her.

Betony glanced at him but made no answer. He was, with his dark curly hair and thick stocky body, the very image of his father, and she hated him for it.

'Wasn't you getting married today? I thought the wedding was two o'clock. Did you leave the chap standing on account of Tom Maddox?'

'Don't speak to me!' Betony said. 'There's nothing I want to say to you!'

She would not allow herself to think of Michael. Not yet, anyway. Such thoughts would have to wait.

Tom sat in a room that smelt of hot water pipes and floor-polish. It was stuffy and airless, and he wished they would open the window wider, but he couldn't bring himself to ask. The silence, ever since Darns had gone out, was too sweet to break, and he sat quite still in the chair at the table, his ankles crossed, his hands in his lap, his head turned in such a way that the current of air coming in, teasing though it was, blew directly into his face, bringing with it the smell of rain.

He knew he was not alone in the room. He knew that a constable sat in the corner and watched him. But so long as the man remained silent, Tom could pretend he was not there; could pretend the room was utterly empty; could picture the walls receding, receding, until they were gone altogether, giving way to open country where the rain blew like smoke on the wind and the clouds rode low on the backs of the distant hills.

Some little way off he could see the Pikehouse, lonely beside the old turnpike road. He was walking towards it, down the slope from Eastery, across the wasteland known as the Chacks, with the long tawny grasses brushing against him, leaving him dusty with their pollen. He had been on an errand to Mrs Hurst's shop. He carried flour, yeast, sugar, matches, candles, soap, rock salt, in a sack slung on his shoulder, and a can of paraffin in his left hand. Linn would be waiting for the yeast. It being Saturday, she was going to make bread.

Now, in fancy, he saw the tiny Pikehouse kitchen, with its scrubbed deal table and two varnished chairs, its oak settle and corner-cupboard and brass-topped fender round the hearth. And yet there was something that worried him. He could not picture what Linn was doing. The fire was burning brightly enough. The kettle, on its hook, was puffing steam up the chimney. The whole place was neat and trim and spoke of Linn's recent attention, yet she herself was somehow absent, and he heard his own voice calling, 'Linn? Where are you? Are you upstairs?' But although he listened carefully, inside his mind, there was no answer.

'What time is it?' he asked sharply.

'Half past five,' the policeman said. 'Would you like a cup of tea?'

'No, I'd like to go home,' Tom said, and when Inspector Darns came into the room, he sat up straight and turned his head. 'I reckon you've kept me long enough. I've answered your questions. It's time I went home.'

'We'd all like to go home, Mr Maddox, but there are just a few more questions I'd like to ask you before we finally call it a day.'

'A few more? Or the same ones all over again?'

'You saw your wife with Arthur Trimble. You walked in and found them, in your own home, in something of a compromising situation. That's what you said, I think, when I first questioned you some weeks ago?'

'Oh no it ent!' Tom said. 'I never said nothing of the kind!'

'What *did* you say, Mr Maddox?'

'I said I saw them. I never said I walked in. I didn't walk in. I went away.'

'You mean you spied on them, without their knowing?'

'Not on purpose. It just happened.'

'What were they doing when you saw them?'

'She was seeing him off at the gate. He had his arm around her neck. It looked like they was pretty friendly.'

'That must have made you very angry.'

'Not me,' Tom said. 'I was past being angry by that time.'

'But you had been angry in the beginning?'

'When I found out she'd lied about having a baby, that made me angry, right enough. I could've struck her.'

'Quite natural, I'm sure. Any man would have felt the same. But when you struck your wife, Mr Maddox, what exactly did you use? A stick? A hammer? A fire-iron snatched from the hearth?'

'I didn't use nothing!' Tom said.

'Just your bare hands, is that what you mean?'

'No. It ent. I never touched her.'

'Perhaps you only meant to slap her. Just a light blow with the flat of your hand. Or a bit of a push that sent her reeling, so that she fell and hit her head.'

'Seems to me you're getting muddled. You been listening to tales about my father.'

'Did it happen at home or did you persuade her to walk in the woods?'

'No more questions!' Tom said. 'We been over and over it time and again. You won't get me saying nothing different, not if you try from now to domesday.'

'You certainly had plenty of time,' Darns said, 'to decide what story you would tell.'

He drew a chair from under the table and sat down

opposite Tom. He opened a folder and turned over a few of the papers.

'About this court martial when you were in the Army.'

'Yes? What about it?' Tom said.

'You were charged with refusing to obey an order. You were found guilty and given five days' F.P.'

'You should know. You're the one that's looked it up.'

'What was the order you refused to obey?'

'Don't it tell you in my record?'

'The details are sparse. Even at the court martial itself they don't seem to have asked what the order was.'

'No. That's right. It didn't suit them.'

'What was the order, Mr Maddox?'

'I was told off as one of a firing-party.'

'What made you refuse? A delicate stomach?'

'I didn't hold with killing my mates. They'd no right to ask me. They knew that.'

'What about sergeants, Mr Maddox? Did you hold with killing them? Or one sergeant in particular, say, by the name of Townchurch? A man you fell foul of, I understand.'

'Me and a few score others, yes.'

'A man who was mortally wounded in the back, although he was facing the enemy, and who died making certain accusations. Or so I was told at Capleton barracks.'

'I never killed him, if that's what you're saying. It was more than likely an accident.'

'An accident! That takes some believing.'

'Them things happened,' Tom said. 'I was blinded by an English shell but nobody says it was done on purpose.'

'You look a bit groggy,' Darns said. 'Are you feeling ill?'

'I'm all right,' Tom said. 'I'm just wondering what else you're going to try and blame me for.'

'You do look groggy all the same. Perhaps you'd like a cup of tea.'

'T'd like to go home,' Tom said. 'That's all I want. I just want to be took back home.'

Outside the room there was a sudden loud commotion; a scuffling at the door and voices upraised; then a woman's voice ringing out above the rest. Darns got up and went out quickly. The policeman in the corner moved to the door. Tom sat listening as the voices outside slowly died away. His head felt hollow, like an empty shell, and the usual pins-and-needles feeling was spreading out from the back of his skull. Perhaps he was having strange fancies, but he could have sworn it was Betony's voice he had heard outside in the corridor.

Betony and Darns stood facing each other in a small room with barred windows. They were quite alone.

'Well, Miss Izzard, now you've got your way, what is it you have to say to me that's so important?'

'My foster-brother is a sick man. It's very wrong that you should keep him here like this, and I have come to take him home.'

'A sick man? Are you referring to his blindness?'

'It's not only that. Tom was badly blown up in the war and there was some damage to the brain. The doctors who saw him last February gave him a year at the outside. Too much strain could be very harmful and perhaps shorten his life still more.'

'I see,' Darns said. 'And he himself doesn't know this?'

'No, nor mustn't, ever!' Betony said, with great passion.

'Don't worry, Miss Izzard,' Darns said. 'We aren't monsters here, you know.'

'You can check what I've told you by telephoning Dr Dundas at Norton.'

'I may do that, but at present I'm willing to accept your word.'

'Then I can take him home?' she said.

Before Darns could answer, Penfold knocked and looked into the room, waving a piece of paper. Darns excused himself to Betony and stepped outside.

'It's Waring's report on that scarf at last,' Penfold said. 'The blood is animal's blood, sure enough, so we're left with precious little to hammer Maddox with, aren't we?'

'I'm losing the desire to try,' Darns said.

'Feel he's innocent, do you, sir?'

'I don't know. I've got no feelings either way. He certainly isn't easy to rattle.'

'One other thing,' Penfold said. 'Blackmore's back from searching Scoate. He says it's getting too dark to see. But he reckons he'd bet his last penny that there's nothing to be found in those woods.'

'That settles it, then. I'll tell his sister she can take him home.'

A few minutes later, Betony and Tom walked out through the hall. Matthew Preston rose from his seat. He looked past them at Inspector Darns.

'You letting him go? My dad won't like that! I thought you was going to arrest him for murder.'

'There is no evidence whatever against your brother-in-law,' Darns said, 'and you can tell your father I said so.'

'I'll tell him all right, but he ent going to like it! I reckon he'll just about raise the roof!'

Matthew ran out, leaving the glass door swinging, and they heard him ride away on his motor-cycle. When Betony followed, guiding Tom down the steps, the pony and trap stood in the roadway with a caped policeman in attendance, and the two lamps had been lit ready. The sky was very dark now, but the rain was little more than a drizzle.

'Smells good,' Tom said, as they drove off. 'I thought I should likely smother in there.' And, after a while, he said: 'I don't understand about your wedding. I don't, that's a fact.'

'It's perfectly simple,' Betony said. 'It's been postponed till another day. Such things do happen sometimes, you know. There's nothing extraordinary about it.'

As they journeyed homeward dusk became night, although it was not much later than six o'clock. Tom was silent, sitting hunched behind her, and whenever she turned to look at him, his face in the glow of the lamps looked worn, his eyes anxious.

'Are you all right?' she asked once.

'Right as rain,' he said promptly.

'I thought you looked tired.'

'I was thinking of Linn, left alone all this time. She'll be worried sick.'

'We won't be long now. We're almost in Huntlip. We've just passed Steadworth Mill.'

At Carter's Bridge, where the road crossed a bend in the Derrent Brook, a light was glimmering through the drizzle, and as she got nearer Betony saw that a man stood in the middle of the bridge, swinging a lantern.

'What is it?' Tom asked, as the pony slowed to a hesitant walk.

'Someone with a lantern. I don't know who.'

Betony halted and was at once sorry, for out of the darkness stepped four more men, and now she realized who they were. The man with the lantern was Harry Yelland, who had once been 'engaged' to Tilly Preston. The others were Emery and his three boys. They had chosen a good place for their ambush. The nearest house was half a mile.

'It's Yelland and the Prestons,' she said to Tom. 'We're at Carter's Bridge and they're blocking the way.'

'Can't you drive through them?'

'No. I've left it too late.'

She drove forward a little way, up the incline onto the bridge, hoping the Prestons would give ground before her, but Emery caught at the pony's bridle and jerked him to a standstill. Betony took the whip from its socket.

'Step aside and let us pass or you'll be sorry, I promise you.'

'*He's* the one that's going to be sorry. Him there behind you, who murdered my Tilly.'

'The police have sent him home because there isn't

a shred of evidence against him. If they're satisfied, why aren't you?'

' 'Cos I know Tom Maddox better'n they do. I know what sort of stock he growed from. His father was a murderer and everyone knows it and the old saying speaks the truth—like father, like son, every time.'

'If that were true, we'd all be murderers,' Betony said, 'seeing we're all descended from Cain.'

'I'm not wasting time in arguments. Just hand that man over and you can get home.'

'Do you set yourself above the law?'

'He may be able to fool the police, but he'll soon tell the truth when I get hold of him, you may be sure of that, by God!'

'I've already told the truth!' Tom said. 'I've told it and told it and it ent going to change!'

'Supposing you step down from there!' Yelland shouted. 'Instead of hiding behind a woman!'

'This man is blind!' Betony said. 'Have you lost all sense of pity?'

'We know he's blind,' Emery answered, 'but it don't mean he's going to get away with murder.'

'You will not set hands on my foster-brother unless you deal with me first!'

'We mean you no harm, being a woman, but if you choose to hinder us, it's your own fault if you get hurt.'

Emery let go of the bridle and came alongside the trap. He tried to step up onto the wheel. Betony struck at him with the whip-stock and he fell back, swearing, one hand covering his eyes. She flicked the reins and tried to drive on, but Matthew had taken his father's place and was pulling hard on the pony's bridle. The pony reared up and danced a little, the white sparks flying as his shoes scrabbled the smooth-worn cobbles. Alfie Preston got kicked on the knee, and his twin, Victor, was squeezed between the wheel of the trap and the low stone parapet of the bridge.

Harry Yelland set down his lantern and took a stone from the heap he had ready between his feet. His arm went back and the stone flew close past Betony's face. Tom, behind her, gave a cry of pain, and when she turned to look at him, the blood was dark on his left temple. At the same moment, Emery Preston came forward again, but this time when Betony lashed at him with the whip, he caught hold of the thong and wrenched it clean out of her hands.

'Now, then!' he bellowed. 'I've had about enough of this! Come down from that trap, Tom Maddox, or it'll be worse for you in the end 'cos I'm just about running out of patience!'

Approaching the trap, he was trying the whip in his right hand. He looked as though he would use it on Tom. But now, suddenly, there came the sharp crack of a shotgun, which set the pony dancing again but brought the five men to a standstill. The skitter of shot went into the boughs of a willow overhead, and in the little silence that followed, a few spent pellets fell among them, pattering down like extra heavy drops of rain. Then a voice spoke and Jack Mercybright came up onto the bridge, into the light shed by the lantern. His shotgun lay in the crook of his arm, smoke curling from one barrel, and he turned it full on Harry Yelland.

'Come away from that trap, all you others, or he gets the next lot in his guts. Make haste about it! No dilladerrying or trying tricks. The sort of day I've had today, I'm in the right mood to murder someone, and I'd just as soon it was one of you as anyone else I can think of off-hand.'

'This is none of your business!' Emery shouted. 'We've got a score to settle with Maddox and it's no concern of yours whatever!'

'It is now,' Jack said. 'Move out of the way or Yelland gets it.'

His wet bearded face was grim and ferocious. They decided he meant every word he said. Emery twisted the whip in its thong and threw it onto Betony's knees. He motioned his sons away from the trap, and led them back over the bridge, picking up the lantern as he went. Yelland followed, and the five of them stood at the side of the road, watching as Jack climbed into the trap.

Betony gave a flip of the reins and the pony pulled off over the bridge. As the trap passed him, Emery took a step forward, but at sight of the shotgun pointing towards him, he thought better of it and vented his feelings by pounding the panelwork with his fists.

'We'll get you, Tom Maddox, even if we do have to bide our time! No murderer yet ever went unpunished. Your crime will catch up with you, mark my words!'

'Take no notice,' Jack said, and, peering closer into Tom's face: 'Are you all right, boy? It looks like you've had a crack on the head.'

'I'm all right,' Tom said. 'I just want to get back to Linn.'

'We shan't be long now,' Jack said.

'How did you happen to come by just then?' Betony asked, over her shoulder.

'I got a message from Linn, that's how, saying Tom'd been took away, so I set out to go to Chepsworth to see the police like she asked me to.'

'Armed with a shotgun?' Betony said.

'I saw the Prestons come jumbling out of The Rose and Crown and I judged they was up to some sort of mischief. So I went along to the haywarden's office and borrowed this gun from Billy Ratchet.'

Tom, sitting hunched against the rain, could feel the blood from the wound on his forehead trickling down the side of his face. He wiped it away with his handkerchief. The wound was not hurting overmuch, but his whole head ached in a dense way, especially the back of his skull.

'How did Linn manage to send you a message?'

'She brought it herself,' Jack said. 'Godwin saw her.'

'What, walked all that way?' Tom exclaimed, and gave a groan, pressing the knuckles of his fists together and squeezing them hard between his knees. 'But I *told* her not to go out of doors! She had no right to go walking so far! Supposing she was took ill going back? Supposing she was to lose the baby?' And then suddenly from the depths of his darkness and helplessness, he cried out in a great trembling voice, 'For God's sake, Betony, get me home!'

Betony whipped up the little pony and they drove fast through the stinging rain.

'It's all right,' she said, when they came at last within sound of the Pikehouse. 'It's all right, Tom, there's a light in the window so she must be there.'

In the Pikehouse kitchen, Mrs Gibbs removed her soiled apron, wrapped it in newspaper, and stowed it away in her leather bag. She heard the sound of the trap approaching and stood listening for it to stop. She went to the door and opened it wide.

'My dear life!' she said, seeing the blood on Tom's forehead. 'The policemen never done that to you, surely?'

'Mrs Gibbs! How come you're here? Where's Linn?'

'Linn's all right. So's your little baby son. They're both pretty fine, all things considered, and now they're having a well-earnt rest. Here, sit down, young fella, you look as though you're about all in.'

'No, no,' Tom said. 'I want to see her.'

'Well, you can't go up dripping wet, can you? Nor with your head all bloody neither.'

'Of course he can't,' Betony said. She drew him towards the blazing fire. 'A minute or two won't make much difference. You must shed a few of these wet clothes.'

He took off his cap, jacket, and bloodstained shirt, and Mrs Gibbs received them from him. She hung a towel round his shoulders.

'Are you sure she's all right?' he asked. 'You ent keeping nothing from me?'

'I give you my word,' Mrs Gibbs said, and touched his arm.

'How long ago did the baby come?'

'Half an hour or thereabouts, and if he'd come sooner he'd have stood a chance of getting hisself born between here and Blagg.'

'You sure she ent done herself no harm?'

'She's used up every ounce of strength for the time being, but she'll be all right, I promise you.'

'Oughtn't we to get the doctor?'

'Yes,' Jack said, 'I'll go and fetch him.'

'It might be as well, to be on the safe side,' said Mrs Gibbs. 'It's Dr Dundas down in Norton. Second house past the post office.'

'Tell him it's urgent,' Tom said.

'I'll bring him, don't worry,' Jack said, and the door closed behind him.

Mrs Gibbs was warming a shirt at the fire. She gave it to Tom and he put it on. He was trembling all over and his fingers could scarcely fasten the buttons. She had to help him. Betony brought a bowl of water and cleaned the blood from the cut on his temple. He bore it in silence, only dimly aware of what she was doing. He tucked his shirt into his trousers and ran a hand through his hair.

'Am I tidy enough? Can I go up to her now?' he asked.

'Go, you,' Mrs Gibbs said, 'and I'll come in a minute to show you your baby.'

In the tiny bedroom, Linn lay in bed feeling she would never move again. Close beside her, her baby lay in its wickerwork cot, a doll-like shape under the blankets, a smudge of dark hair just showing above. She could hear the voices in the kitchen below, and when Tom came up the steep stairs into the bedroom, she turned towards him, putting out a hand.

'You've hurt your head,' she said, in a weak voice.

'It was an accident,' Tom said. He did not want to tell her about the Prestons. 'I hit myself on a low rafter.'

'You look pale and tired. They had no right to keep you so long.'

'I wish I could see how *you* are looking, after all you been through today.'

'I'm not too bad. Mrs Gibbs was wonderful. Did she tell you we've got a son?'

'Oh, I've heard about *him*. Is he there beside you? Does he like the cot I made for him?'

'Come round,' she said. 'Seems to me he's heard your voice and he's listening to it. He's turning his head this way and that.'

'Is he?' Tom said, and felt his way round to the cot. 'Does he know I'm his father, d'you suppose?'

When he touched the blankets covering his son, and felt the warm body moving, small, under his hands, something leapt at his throat and took his breath away completely. Until this moment the baby had merely been part of Linn's body; a part of the life they had together; something that made him fearful for her. But now as it stirred beneath the blankets, and he felt the warmth of it throbbing against the palms of his hands; felt the shape of it, and the way it squirmed, trying the strength of its small limbs; he knew it had a life all its own, its own heart and soul and obstinate will, its own place under the sun.

'Pick him up,' Linn said. 'He's your own son.'

'I'm afraid to,' he said. 'I might hurt him, being blind.'

The stairs creaked and Mrs Gibbs came into the room. She took the baby out of his cot and placed him, in his blankets, in Tom's arms. And now, with the small warm face nuzzling with such surprising strength against his own, the small hands pushing against him, Tom stood for a while feeling that he and this baby son of his were alone together in the dark. Alone together as one flesh. But, right at the heart of this shared darkness, there was a sunny picture forming.

'I can see you,' he whispered. 'I can see you, little boy, one summer's day, after rain, reaching up with both hands to touch a wild pink rose in the hedgerow, and you're laughing the way your mother laughs, 'cos one or two raindrops is splashing down into your face.'

Mrs Gibbs took the baby and laid it back again in its cot. Tom returned to Linn's bedside and sat with her hand between his own.

'Your father was here. Did you hear him? He's gone to fetch Dr Dundas.'

'Yes, I heard him.'

'You went against me, didn't you? You left the

house and went all them miles to Outlands Farm. That frightens me to think of, your going all that way.'

'Did father come and fetch you home?'

'It was Betony that done that. She put off her wedding, would you believe it? I dunno what she said to the policeman, but they let me go, whatever it was. Then we picked up your father on the way home.'

Tom felt Mrs Gibbs beside him. She was touching his shoulder.

'We should ought to let her rest. The doctor'll be here before long. You can come up again in an hour or two. I'll sit up here while she has a sleep.'

'I reckon that's right,' Tom said. 'I'm gabbling on like an old goose.'

He rose from the stool and leant over to kiss Linn's forehead. He felt her fingers touching his face. He turned and went down into the kitchen.

'How is she?' Betony asked.

'She says she's all right. And Mrs Gibbs don't seem too worried about her, does she? Anyway, Dr Dundas will be here directly.'

'How's the baby?'

'Oh, he's a masterpiece, he is! I daresay they'll let you see him later.'

'Sit down here,' Betony said. 'I'm going to clean that forehead properly.'

'All right,' he said, and sat on the edge of the rocking-chair, his back quite straight, his hands folded between his knees. He was thinking about his baby son. 'Maybe he'll be a carpenter, the same as me. Maybe they'll take him on at Cobbs.' And after a while he said, 'D'you think he'll mind overmuch, having a father that's stone blind?'

'No, he won't mind, I'm sure of that.'

Betony was swabbing the deep cut, wiping away the dried blood.

'I don't like the look of this at all. It's very ugly.'

'It's a funny thing, but I can't feel it. I felt it all right when the stone hit me. I thought I was going to fly to bits. But I don't feel nothing any more.' He put up a hand and touched the wound with the tips of his fingers. 'No, not a thing,' he said, pressing. 'My head just feels numb, that's all.'

'Numb all over, do you mean?'

'Pretty well all over. I ent sure. It's like pins-and-needles inside my skull.'

'I wish the doctor would come!' she said. 'Surely he ought to be here by now?'

'Maybe he was out some place else. Maybe Jack has had to wait. Are you worried about Linn?'

'I'm more worried about this cut.'

'I told you, that's nothing, I don't hardly know it's there at all. I'm a bit muzzy, but I'm used to that.'

'I think you ought to try and rest.'

'Can a man rest when he's just this minute become a father?'

'They haven't all spent such hours as you have, under police questioning.'

'No,' he said, and, after a pause: 'I never murdered Tilly, Bet, and that's the truth as God's my witness.'

'I never thought you did for one moment.'

'I wish she'd come forward and put an end to all this talk. I don't want my son growing up in the world with people saying his dad's a murderer.'

'Lean back and rest,' Betony said. She was worried and frightened by the colourless, leached-out look of his skin. 'Lean back in the chair and take it easy.'

'All right,' he said, and leant his head against the flat cushion that hung on tapes from the back of the chair. 'I *am* a bit tired, now that I think of it, I suppose.'

Betony lifted his booted feet and put the stool underneath them. She fetched a blanket and spread it over him, up to the chin.

'Sleep if you can. You'll be better for it. Linn and your baby are in good hands.'

'We're going to call him Robert, you know, after Bob Newers, my mate in the Army. We was going to ask if you'd be his godmother.'

'I'd be cross if you asked anyone else!'

Betony went about the kitchen; turned the napkins

airing on a string above the fire; eased the kettle out on its bracket; set the teapot on the hob to warm. The lamp on the table was burning crooked. She went and turned the wick down low. Then she took up scissors and an old newspaper and sat down with them in her lap. She began making spills, cutting and folding carefully, making hardly any noise.

'I know what you're doing,' Tom said. 'You're making spills.'

'Yes,' she said, 'I noticed the jar was almost empty.'

'That was always a favourite job of yours, even when you was a little girl. You wouldn't let nobody else make them. Nobody else done a proper job.'

He could picture her plainly at her childhood task and somehow the thought of it made him smile. Sitting back in his chair, wrapped in his blanket, he had the heat of the fire in his face, could hear the small sounds it made, and could smell the sweet smell of old mossy applewood burning on it. But slowly the world was slipping away. The picture inside his mind was fading. His blind eyes were closing of their own accord. And because he was really very tired, death came to him disguised as sleep, so that when he gave himself up to it he was still smiling.

'Michael's not here,' Mrs Andrews said. 'He motored up to London this morning and is staying the night with Major Thomas. Tomorrow he sails for South Africa.'

'How long for?' Betony asked.

'He may decide to stay for good. If he does I shall probably go out and join him there. But should he decide to return to England he would prefer not to see you again. That was the message he asked me to give you.'

'Yes. I see. In that case I think I'd better leave this with you.' Betony took the ring from her finger and placed it on the hall table. 'I came as soon as I could,' she said, 'but it seems I'm too late.'

'It wouldn't have made a scrap of difference however soon you had come. He wouldn't have seen you.'

'I'm sorry he feels so bitterly.'

'*Are* you sorry?—I very much doubt it, Betony. You never really loved Michael. I always thought that, from the very first.' Mrs Andrews was unyielding. 'You could never have done such a thing,' she said, 'if you'd really loved him.'

Armistice Day was cold and sunless. A bitter wind

blew in the churchyard yews and birches, and a few dry snowflakes fell on the people below. The war memorial, cut from a piece of Springs Hill granite, was a tall Celtic cross surmounting a rough-hewn pedestal, and stood inside the main gateway. Huntlip had given thirty-six lives. The names were cut on three sides of the stone. Some were repeated twice or three times. Hayward. Izzard. Mustoe. Wilkes.

'Thirty-six young men,' the vicar said, at the end of his address, 'whose courage and sacrifice will live forever.'

People stood very still, during the two minutes' silence, and their heads were bowed. The silence would last in many hearts. But heads were raised again during the singing of the hymn, and the frail human voices rose defiantly round the cross, strong because they sang together. The people, singing, all looked up, and the cold wind dried the tears on their faces.

Afterwards, walking home through the village, Dicky said: 'Tom's name should be on that stone by rights, along with the others.'

'Yes, perhaps so,' Betony said.

She and Dicky walked with their father. The rest of the family came behind. Jesse was staring straight ahead. He found it difficult to speak.

'No "perhaps" about it. Dicky's right. Tom gave his life for King and Country, just the same as William and Roger.'

Betony took her father's arm.

The following day, she spent three hours at Chepsworth Park, where all the invalid veterans wore sprigs of greenery in their coats, remembering their dead comrades. There were many 'helpers' there that day: every wheelchair case had been taken for an outing through the park, all the bedridden men had someone to talk to, and several ladies had banded together to put on a concert in the evening.

'Oh, we've got floods of helpers at the moment!' the superintendant said dryly to Betony. 'Armistice Day has made them remember, certainly. But it'll fall off by the end of the week and then we'll be left short-handed as always.'

'Perhaps it would help,' Betony said, 'if I came more often.'

Afterwards, on her way through Chepsworth, she stopped to look at the new memorial standing in the cathedral grounds. It was the figure of a private soldier, bareheaded save for a bandage, and he stood with his rifle in front of him, the butt on the ground, the barrel clasped between his hands, staring at the ground as though bowed down with weariness. All around the monument, the steps were strewn with laurel wreaths.

As Betony left the cathedral precincts, a column of unemployed men passed by, each with a placard on his chest and back. 'Hundreds more where we come from!' 'We take charity but what we want is work.' 'Old soldiers never die, they only fade away—from starvation!' And one man, seeing Betony coming away from the war memorial, called out to her: 'The dead are remembered all right! It's us live ones that get forgotten!'

Sipping a glass of Madeira wine in the vicarage drawing-room, Betony could easily guess why the vicar, Mr Wisdom, had summoned her there. Miss Emily Likeness, headmistress of Huntlip school for forty-three and a half years, was retiring at Christmas, reluctantly, due to a general decline in health.

'Am I correct,' the vicar asked, 'in thinking you will not be marrying Captain Andrews after all?'

'Quite correct,' Betony said.

'I am very sorry, Betony, that it has worked out so sadly for you.'

'Thank you, vicar. You're very kind.'

'I was wondering whether, in view of your changed circumstances, you'd consider taking over from Miss Likeness as headmistress of the village school. I can think of no one more suitable. Miss Likeness herself hopes you'll agree. But, of course, you needn't give

your answer tonight. You will probably wish to think
it over.'

'Yes, I will,' Betony said, 'but I think the answer
will probably be yes.'

As she was leaving, the vicar said: 'There's a
rumour in the village that Tilly Preston's been seen in
Warwick. Is it true, d'you suppose?'

'Yes. It's true. Jeremy Rye saw her there, serving in
the bar of a public house. She's been living there for
some time as the wife of the landlord.'

'Why did she never come forward, then? Surely she
must have seen the posters?'

'Jeremy Rye asked her that. She claimed she knew
nothing at all about it.'

'I never doubted that your foster-brother was innocent.'

'Neither did I,' Betony said.

Her sister Janie had been ill with 'flu. She was now
recovering, sitting up in bed, eating the grapes Betony
had brought her.

'Have you heard from Michael?'

'No, not a word.'

'Mother tells me there'll be no wedding but surely—'

'Yes. That's right. Michael's gone abroad. He doesn't
want to see me again.'

'Oh, Betony! Are you sure?'

'Don't be upset. I'm not. I feel, somehow, that it
wasn't really meant to happen.'

'But what will you *do*?' Janie asked. She could not
imagine her own life without her husband and her
three children. She could not imagine such emptiness.
'Whatever will you *do*?'

Betony smiled. She thought of the school, where she
would soon be mistress-in-charge, with over a hundred
small children in her care. She thought of the invalid
veteran soldiers needing help at Chepsworth Park, and
she thought of the grey-faced men she had seen walking the streets because they had no work to go to.

She thought, too, of Linn Mercybright and her father-
less baby.

'There's always plenty to do, Janie. It's only a question of where to begin.'